THE POET and the PAUPER

The Novels of George MacDonald
Edited for Today's Reader
by Michael Phillips

Edited Title	Original Title
The Curate of Glaston (3-in-1) includes:	
The Curate's Awakening	*Thomas Wingfold*
The Lady's Confession	*Paul Faber*
The Baron's Apprenticeship	*There and Back*
Malcolm (2-in-1) includes:	
The Fisherman's Lady	*Malcolm*
The Marquis' Secret	*The Marquis of Lossie*
The Poet and the Pauper (2-in-1) includes:	
The Baronet's Song	*Sir Gibbie*
The Shepherd's Castle	*Donal Grant*
A Scottish Collection (3-in-1) includes:	
The Maiden's Bequest	*Alec Forbes of Howglen*
The Minister's Restoration	*Salted With Fire*
The Laird's Inheritance	*Warlock O'Glenwarlock*

MacDonald Classics Edited for Young Readers
Alec Forbes and His Friend Annie

———

Discovering the Character of God by George MacDonald
Knowing the Heart of God by George MacDonald

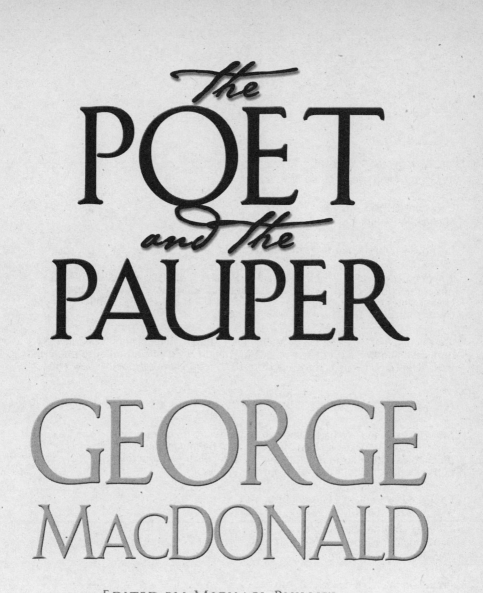

The POET and the PAUPER

GEORGE MacDONALD

EDITED BY MICHAEL PHILLIPS

BETHANYHOUSE
Minneapolis, Minnesota

Published by Bethany House Publishers
A Ministry of Bethany Fellowship International
11400 Hampshire Avenue South
Bloomington, Minnesota 55438
www.bethanyhouse.com

Printed in the United States of America

Library of Congress Cataloging-in-Publication Data
MacDonald, George, 1824–1905.
    [Baronet's song]
    The poet and the pauper / by George MacDonald ; edited by Michael Phillips.
        p. cm.
    ISBN 0-7642-2659-2 (pbk.)
    1. Highlands (Scotland)—Fiction. 2. Child witnesses—Fiction. 3. Mute persons—Fiction. 4. Friendship—Fiction. 5. Orphans—Fiction. I. Phillips, Michael R., 1946– II. MacDonald, George, 1824–1905. Shepherd's castle. III. Title: Shepherd's castle. IV. Title.
    Pr4967 .S5 2002
    823'.8—dc21
                                             2002001526

The Baronet's Song

Introduction

In 1879 one of the best-loved of all George MacDonald's Scottish novels was published, the captivating chronicle of the winsome little orphan, Sir Gibbie. An immediate success, the novel was serialized in several magazines, and within a year and a half was published in at least six different editions by various publishers in Great Britain and America.

As celebrated as MacDonald's novels were in his own time, their impact continues long after his death. In 1916 C. S. Lewis casually picked up a copy of *Phantastes* and found the entire course of his life altered. He said, "A few hours later I knew I had crossed a great frontier." Thirty years later he reflected on the worlds MacDonald had opened for him and said, ". . . when the process was complete . . . I found that I was still with Mac-Donald and that he had accompanied me all the way."

Many others through the years have similarly found MacDonald's writings to have affected them. G. K. Chesterton, for instance, referred to him as "a Scot of genius who could write fairy tales that made all experience a fairy tale."

In the Preface to her 1962 edition of *Sir Gibbie,* Elizabeth Yates comments on the book: ". . . from the moment it caught me up I was conscious of a breadth and depth and height of feeling such as I had not known for a long time. It moved me the way books did when as a child. . . . I could not put the book down until it was finished, and yet I could not bear to come to its end. Once at its last page, I felt I would have to do what I had often done as a child—turn back to the first page and begin reading all over again. I longed to tell everyone I knew to read it. . . . It would not do to tell them anything about it. This was not only a book, it was an experience." She closed by saying, "Now and then a book is read as a friend . . . and after it life is not the same . . . for it has become richer, more meaningful, more challenging. *Sir Gibbie* did this to me. *Sir Gibbie* holds within its covers to do something to all who read it."

C. S. Lewis says, "Most myths were made in prehistoric times . . . but every now and then there occurs in the modern world a genius . . . who can make such a story. MacDonald is the greatest genius of this kind I know."

He then says that MacDonald's writing gift "produces works which give us . . . as much delight and as much wisdom and strength as the works of the greatest poets. It is in some ways more akin to music than to poetry. It goes beyond the expression of things we have already felt. It arouses in us sensations we have never had before; . . . it gets under our skin, hits us at a level deeper than our thoughts or even our passions."

Both C. S. Lewis and W. H. Auden characterize MacDonald's creative power as "mythopoeic imagination." Yet while lauding him as a myth-maker, Lewis hails him as a poet and weaver of fantasies, saying, "It was in this mythopoeic art that MacDonald excelled; . . . the meaning, the suggestion, the radiance is incarnate in the whole story." Perhaps Richard Reis captured it best when he said that MacDonald "achieves a universality . . . which transcends time."

What is this peculiar quality inherent in the story of the waif with shaggy golden hair? Why has Gibbie endured in memory though the book in its original form has been out of print since early in this century? What is it that captivates readers of all ages?

Is *Sir Gibbie* myth? Is it poetry? Is it fantasy? Is it music? Or does Gibbie's magic spring from MacDonald's having simultaneously captured the essence of all four? The story tugs at us, the myth calls forth eternity in our spirits, the poetry moves us, the fantasy delights our imaginations, while all along the music makes our hearts sing.

To once again quote Lewis, "What he does best is fantasy—fantasy that hovers between the allegorical and the mythopoeic. And this, in my opinion, he does better than any man."

Several factors emerge as fundamental for an understanding of George MacDonald's writing. First, he firmly held that the deepest insights about life were not to be found in distant obscurities but in everyday relationships and ordinary contacts with the world. Therefore, his books are filled with commonplace lives. We see an agrarian world of thatched cottages with their peat fires, porridge and milk, oats and potatoes, cattle and sheep, green meadows, desolate moors, thudding wooden machinery, and wild mountains. MacDonald never forgot his humble childhood. This was the Scotland he loved, and his truths, like his people, were simple yet subtle.

In his 1914 Introduction to a new edition of *Sir Gibbie*, MacDonald's son Greville comments, "It would be hard to find any book in the English tongue that . . . more plainly displays the hidden grandeur . . . in common life than *Sir Gibbie* . . . the most direct and most beautiful of all George MacDonald's novels."

In thus conveying the soul of Scotland—its land and its people—with his descriptions of farming, shepherding and fishing, MacDonald pioneered an entire movement of realistic Scottish fiction. Many others followed him in what came to be known as the "kaleyard school" of writing.

Second, the image of childhood appears throughout his books. He loved to make up stories for his own children and read to them. On one occasion a close family friend, Lewis Carroll, asked George to read a story he had written to his own children. They loved it, and the author enlarged and published it as *Alice in Wonderland*.

MacDonald once said, "I do not write for children, but for the childlike, whether of five, or fifty, or seventy-five."

All these elements converge in the simple yet profound story of *Sir Gibbie*—the myth, the poetry, the fantasy, the love of Scotland, and the wonder of childhood.

Almost exactly a hundred years after *Sir Gibbie*'s first publication, I "met" George MacDonald, and *Sir Gibbie* was one of the first of his books

I read. Though he wrote more than fifty books in his career, no more than a scant handful were in print in the early 1970s. However, my wife and I found what we could and soon fell in love with his moving tales.

It gradually became one of my consuming passions to share the out-of-print fiction of George MacDonald with the reading public. Unfortunately, the bulk of his novels were unavailable, they were usually written in a Scotch dialect unintelligible to today's reader, and they often ran well over 500 pages.

Therefore, I undertook the redaction of MacDonald's originals, reducing them to a more manageable size and substituting contemporary English for the Doric dialect. *The Fisherman's Lady* and *The Marquis' Secret* were the first two published; this new edition of *Sir Gibbie* and its sequel follow them in the series from Bethany House.

I have edited the whole by condensing, tightening, and translating. The original *Sir Gibbie* of over 400 pages has been trimmed by about half, and I have translated into current usage such difficult-to-understand passages as:

> Gien the j'ists be strang, an' well set intil the wa's, what for sudna ye tak the horse up the stair intil yer bedrooms? It'll be a' to the guid o' the wa's, for the weicht o' the beasts 'll be upo' them to haud them doon, an' the haill hoose again' the watter . . . I'm thinkin' we'll lowse them a' else; for the byre wa's 'ill gang afore the hoose.

As young Gibbie journeys from the city, up the river Daur, to his refuge of Glashgar, so we travel with him into the world of George MacDonald, back to childhood, up the mountain, and on toward the heritage that awaits us. If, as has been suggested, the term myth is to be applied to events which have meaning beyond their literal significance, then Gibbie's pilgrimage surely qualifies. For Gibbie is symbolic of all who are engaged in life's grand adventure onward and upward into the high realms of relationship, wisdom, and love.

Michael Phillips
Eureka, California
July 1982

Contents

GLASHGAR

Grants' Cottage

The Glashb

manse

The Region of Gormgarnet

Gamekeeper's Cottage

GLASHRUACH

The Lorrie

m
e
a
d
o
w

barn house

MAINS

RIVER DAUR

Glossary

bairn—child
bossy—a seat of straw
bannock—oatmeal cake
brae—hillside
brogues—shoes
broonie—brownie, elf
burn—brook
byre—stable or barn
cantrip—trick
close—enclosed
couples—a pair of rafters that meet at the top and are tied
cowherd—one who tends cows
crofter—tenant farmer
girnel—a meal barrel
gowan—daisies
gowk—simpleton
hirsute—hairy, shaggy
laird—lord, proprietor of the land
loch—lake
manse—minister's house
Pan's pipes—a kind of wooden recorder
rick—small piles or stack of corn or grain in the field
tarn—bog, marsh
water-brose—grain cereal with liquid poured on top

1

· · · · · · · · · · · · · · · · · · ·

The City's Urchin

Come out o' the gutter, ye urchin!" cried Mrs. Croale in a harsh, half-masculine voice, standing on the curbstone of a short, narrow, dirty lane. About thirty yards from her, a child, apparently about six but in reality about eight, was down on his knees raking with both hands in the grey dirt of the street.

At the woman's cry he lifted his head, ceased his search, raised himself without getting up and looked at her. They were notable eyes out of which he looked—a deep blue and having long lashes, but more notable for their bewitching expression of confidence. Whatever was at the heart of the expression, it was something that enticed question and might want investigation. The face as well as the eyes was lovely—not very clean but chiefly remarkable from a general effect of something I can only call luminosity. The hair, which stuck out from his head in every direction, would have been of the red-gold kind had it not been sunburned into a sort of human hay. An odd creature altogether the child appeared, as from his bare knees on the curbstone he shook the gutter-drops from his dirty little hands and gazed at the woman of rebuke. It was but for a moment. The next, he was down raking in the gutter again.

The woman took a step forward; but the sound of a sharp, imperative little bell made her turn at once and reenter the shop from which she had just issued. Meantime the boy's attention seemed entirely absorbed in the gutter. Whatever passed him by, he never lifted his head but went creeping slowly on his knees along the curb still searching in the flow of the sluggish, nearly motionless current of black muck.

It was a gloomy morning toward the close of autumn. The days began and ended with a fog, but often between, a golden sunshine glorified the streets of the grey city. At this moment a ray of sunlight from between two tall houses suddenly fell upon the pavement and gutter, revealing to the boy the glistening object of his search. He made a dart upon all fours and pounced like a creature of prey upon something in the mud. He sprang to his feet and bounded with it into the sun, running and all the while rubbing it upon what he had for trousers, for which there was nothing below the knees but a few streamers. His feet as well as his knees and legs were bare and red and rough. He held up his find into the radiance of the sunlight, regarding it admiringly. It was a little earring of amethyst-colored glass. The boy was in ecstasy over his find. He rubbed the glass on his sleeve, sucked it to clear from it the last of the gutter, then held the earring once more in the sun, where, for a few blissful moments, he contemplated it in speechless wonder. He then caused it to disappear somewhere about his garments—I will not venture to say in a pocket—and ran off, his little bare feet sounding thud, thud, thud on the pavement.

Through street after street he sped, the whole built of granite—a hard, severe city; not beautiful, yet in the better parts handsome as well as massive and strong. To the boy the great city was but a house of many rooms—all for his use, his sport, his life. He did not know much of what lay within the houses; but that only added the joy of mystery.

It was in one of a third-rate sort that the urchin at length ceased his trot and drew up at the divided door of a baker's shop, opening in the middle by a latch of bright brass. But the child did not lift the latch—only raised himself on tiptoe by the help of its handle to look through the upper half of the door into the tantalizing shop. The smell that came through it could seem to the child as that of the tree of life in the Paradise of which he had never heard: scones and rolls, biscuits hard and soft, and those brown discs of delicate piecrust known as buns. But most enticing of all to the eyes of the little wanderer of the street were the penny loaves, hot smoking from the oven. The main point which made them more attractive than all the rest to him was that sometimes he did have a penny, and a penny loaf was the largest thing that could be had for a penny in the shop. So, lawless as he looked, the desires of the child were moderate, and his imagination within the bounds of reason.

Behind the counter sat the baker's wife, a stout, fresh-colored woman, simple and honest. She was knitting and dozing over her work, and never saw the forehead and eyes which gazed at her over the horizon of the door. There was no greed in those eyes—only much interest. He did not want to get in, had to wait, and while waiting enjoyed the scene before him. He knew that Mysie, the baker's daughter, was at school and would be home within half an hour. He had seen her with tear-filled eyes as she went, and learned from her the cause, and had in consequence unwittingly roused Mrs. Croale's anger. But though he was waiting for Mysie, such was the absorbing power of the spectacle before him that he never heard her approaching footsteps.

"Let me in," said Mysie with a touch of indignation at being impeded on the very threshold of her own father's shop.

The boy started and turned, but instead of moving out of the way, began searching in some mysterious receptacle hid in the recesses of his rags. A look of anxiety once appeared but the same moment vanished, and he held out in his hand the little crop of amethystine splendor. Mysie's face changed, and she clutched it eagerly.

"That's real good of you, wee Gibbie!" she cried. "Where did you find it?"

He pointed to the gutter, and drew back from the door.

"I thank you," she said heartily and, pressing down the thumbstall of the latch, went in.

"Who's that you're talking with, Mysie?" asked her mother.

"It's only wee Gibbie, Mother," answered the girl.

"What do you have to say to him?" resumed the mother; "he's hardly fit company for the likes of you who has a father and mother. You must have little to say to such a runabout laddie."

"Gibbie has a father, though they say he never had no mother," answered the child.

"A fine father!" rejoined the mother with a small scornful laugh. "Such a father, lassie, that would make truth of saying he had none! What said you to him?"

"I thanked him, 'cause I lost my earring going to school this morning and he found it for me. He was waiting for me by the door. They say he's always finding things."

"He's a good-hearted creature!" returned the mother, "—for one, that is, that's been so ill brought up."

She rose, took from the shelf a penny loaf, and went to the door.

"Here, Gibbie!" she cried as she opened it; "here's a fine piece for ye."

But no Gibbie was there. Up and down the street not a child was to be seen. The baker's wife drew back, shut the door, and resumed her knitting.

Though the sun remained hot for an hour or two in the middle of the day, in the shadows dwelt the cold breath of coming winter. To Gibbie, however, barelegged, barefooted, almost barebodied as he was, sun or shadow made small difference except as one of the musical intervals of the life that make the melody of existence. Hardy through hardship, he knew nothing better than a constant good-humored sparring with nature and circumstances for the privilege of being, enjoyed what came to him thoroughly, never mourned over what he had not and, like the animals, was at peace. When Gibbie was not looking in at a shopwindow or turning on one heel to take in all at a sweep, he was oftenest seen trotting. Seldom he walked. A gentle trot was one of his natural modes of being. And through this day he had been on the trot all the sunshine through, nevertheless, when the sun was going down there was wee Gibbie upon the trot in the chilling and darkening streets.

He had not had much to eat. He had been near having a penny loaf. Half a cookie which a stormy child had thrown away to ease his temper, a small yellow turnip the green-grocer's wife had given him, and a handful of the seaweed called "dulse" from a fishwife with a creel on her back was all he had eaten. It had been one of his meager days. But it is wonderful upon how little those rare natures capable of making the most of things will live and thrive. There is a great deal more to be gotten out of things than is generally gotten out of them, whether the thing be a chapter of the Bible or a yellow turnip. Truly Gibbie got no fat out of his food, but what he did receive was far better. What he carried was all muscle—small but hard and healthy, and knotting up like whipcord. There are all degrees of health in poverty as well as in riches, and Gibbie's health was splendid. His senses also were marvelously acute; his eyes sharp, quick, roving.

While Gibbie thus lived in the streets like a town sparrow, the human father of him would all the day be sitting in a certain dark court, as hard at work as an aching head and bloodless system would afford. The said court was off the narrowest part of a long, poverty-stricken street called the Widdiehill. In the court, against a wing of an old house, around which yet clung a musty fame of departed grandeur, rose an outside stair leading to the first floor. Under this stairway was a rickety wooden shed; in the shed sat the father of Gibbie, cobbling boots and shoes as long as, at this time of the year, the light lasted. Up that stair, and two more flights inside the house, he went to his lodging, for he slept in the garret. But when or how he got to bed, George Galbraith never knew, for by then, invariably, he was drunk. In the morning, however, he always found himself in it—generally with an aching head and always with a mingled disgust at and desire for drink. During the day, alas! the disgust departed while the desire remained, strengthening with the approach of evening. All day he worked with might and main, such might and main as he had—worked as if for his life, and all to procure the means of death.

Wee Gibbie was his only child, but about him or his well-being he gave himself almost as little trouble as Gibbie caused him. Not that he was hardhearted; if he had seen the child in want, he would, at the drunkest, have shared his whiskey with him; if he had fancied him cold, he would have put his last garment upon him. But to his whiskey-dimmed eyes the child scarcely seemed to want anything, and the thought never entered his mind that, while Gibbie always looked smiling and contented, his father did so little to make him so. He did not do well for himself, and he shamefully neglected his child. But he did well by his neighbors; he gave the best of work and made the lowest of charges. He was a man of such inborn honesty that the usurping demon of a vile thirst had not even yet, at the age of forty, been able to cast it out.

His friends addressed Galbraith as "Sir George," and he accepted the title with a certain unassumed dignity. For if it was not universally known in the city, it was known to the best lawyers in it that he was a baronet by direct derivation from the hand of King James the Sixth. The bearer of the title, however, had seen better days. George's father was a man of some standing who had given his son more than a fair education, not without some distinction. While his father was yet alive, George married the daughter of a small laird in a neighboring county. He took her home to the ancient family house in the city—the same in which he now occupied a garret and under whose outer stair he now cobbled shoes. During his father's life they lived there in peace and tolerable comfort, though in a poor enough way. His wife died, however, soon after Gibbie was born; and then George began to lose himself altogether. The next year his father died, and creditors appeared who claimed everything. Mortgaged land and houses were sold, and George was left without a penny or any means of livelihood. For heavy work he was altogether unfit; and had it not been for a bottle companion—a merry, hard-drinking shoemaker—he would have died of starvation or sunk into beggary.

The shoeman taught him his trade, and George was glad enough to work at it, both to deaden the stings of conscience and memory and to procure the means of deadening them still further.

How Gibbie had gotten thus far alive was a puzzle not a creature could have solved. It must have been by charity and ministration of more than one humble woman, but no one now claimed any particular interest in him—except Mrs. Croale, and hers was not very tender. It was a sad sight to some eyes to see him roving the streets, but an infinitely sadder sight was his father; he looked the pale picture of misery. When the poor fellow sat with his drinking companions in Mistress Croale's parlor, seldom a flash broke from the reverie in which he seemed sunk. Yet those drinking companions would have missed George Galbraith, silent as he was; for he was courteous, always ready to share what he had, and never looked beyond the present tumbler—altogether a genial, kindly, honest nature.

2

Mistress Croale's

The day went on and went out, its short autumnal brightness quenched in a chilly fog. All along the Widdiehill, the gas was alight in the low-browed dingy shops. In his shed under the stair it had been dark for some time—too dark for work, that is, and George Galbraith had lighted a candle. He never felt at liberty to quit so long as a man was recognizable in the street by daylight. But now at last, with a sigh of relief, he rose. His hand trembled with expectation as he laid from it the awl, took from between his knees the great boot on which he had been stitching a patch, lifted the yoke of his leather apron over his head and threw it aside. After one hasty glance around, he caught up a hat, which looked as if it had been brushed with grease, pulled it on his head with both hands, stepped out quickly, closed the door behind him, turned the key, left it in the lock, and made straight for Mistress Croale's. Above the door of her establishment was a small board, nearly square, upon which was painted in lead color on black the words, "Licensed to sell beer, spirits and tobacco to be drunk on the premises." There was no other sign. It was to this, his earthly paradise, that George now hastened.

George was a tall man of good figure, loosened and bowed. His face was well-favored, but not a little wronged by the beard and the dirt of the week, through which it looked haggard and white. He looked neither to the right nor left but walked on with dull gaze, noting nothing.

"He's his own worst enemy," remarked the kindly grocer's wife as he passed her door.

"Ay," responded her customer who kept a secondhand shop nearby, "ay, I daresay. But, eh! To see that poor neglected bairn o' his runnin' about the town—with little jacket left but the collar and rags for trousers! Eh, woman! It makes a mother's heart sore to see it. It would make *his* mother turn over in her grave!"

George was the first arrival at Mistress Croale's that night. He opened the door of the shop like a thief, and glided softly into the dim parlor where the candles were not yet lit. Mistress Croale was seated on a horsehair sofa in the twilight, a busy fire crackling in the grate.

"Come on in," she said hospitably as she rose.

The woman had a genuine regard for Galbraith, but in her secret mind she deplored that George should drink so inordinately and so utterly neglect his child as to let him spend his life in the streets. She comforted herself, however, with the reflection that seeing he would drink, he drank with no bad companions.

The usual company was soon assembled, the candles lit, and the toddy measured out. The conversation was for some time very dull. But the fire burned cheerfully and the kettle made many journeys between it and the table; things gradually grew more lively. Stories were told, often without any point but still with effect; reminiscences were offered and accepted with laughter; and adventures were related in which truth was no necessary element to reception. In the case of one of the company, for instance, not one of those present believed a word he said; yet as he happened to be endowed with a small stock of genuine humor, his stories were regarded with much the same favor as if they had been authentic.

But the revival scarcely reached Sir George. He said little or nothing, but between his slow gulps of toddy sat looking vacantly into his glass. It is true he smiled absently now and then when the others laughed, but that was only for manners. Doubtless he was seeing somewhere the saddest of all visions—the things that might have been. Was the chief joy his drink gave him the power once more to feel himself a gentleman? What faded ghosts of ancestral dignity the evil potion called up in the mind of Sir George—who himself hung ready to fall, the last, or all but the last, mildewed fruit of the tree of Galbraith!

In the descending frosty dark of the autumn evening, Gibbie too found himself outside Mrs. Croale's establishment. Under the window of the parlor he would stand listening for a moment, then, darting off a few yards suddenly and swiftly like a frightened bird, fall at once into his own steady trot—up the lane and down, till he reached the window again, where he would stand and listen. Whether he made this departure and return twenty or a hundred times in a night, neither he nor any other could have told. Never moth haunted lamp so persistently. Ever as he ran, up this pavement and down that, on the soft-sounding soles of his bare feet, the smile on the boy's face grew more and more sleepy; but still he smiled and still he trotted, still paused at the window and started afresh.

He was not so much to be pitied as you may think. Never in his life had he yet pitied himself. The thought of hardship or wrong had not occurred to him. It would have been difficult, if not impossible, to get the idea into his head that existence bore to him any other shape than it ought. Things were to him as they had always been. How could he question what had been from the beginning?

It was now late. The streets were empty. Neither carriage nor cart, wheelbarrow nor truck, went anymore bumping and clattering over their stones. They were well lighted with gas, but most of the bordering houses were dark. Now and then a single footfarer passed with loud, hollow-sounding boots along the pavement. A cold wind—a small, forsaken, solitary wind, moist with a thin fog—seemed, as well as wee Gibbie, to be roaming the night, for it met him at various corners and from all directions. But it had nothing to do and nowhere to go and was therefore not like Gibbie, the business of whose life was even now upon him, the mightiest hope of whose conscious being was now awake.

All he expected or ever desired to discover by listening at the window was simply whether there were yet signs of the company's breaking up; and his conclusions on that point were never mistaken. Seldom had he there heard the voice of his father. This night, however, as the time drew near when they must go and Gibbie stood once more on tiptoe with his head just on the level of the windowsill, he heard his father utter two words: "Up Daurside." They came to him through the window, in the voice he loved, plain and distinct. The words conveyed nothing to him at all, but the mere hearing of them made them memorable. For the time, however, he forgot them, for he perceived that the company was on the point of separating. From that moment he did not take his eyes off the door until he heard the first sounds of its opening. As it was hard on a midnight so cold that his feet threatened to grow indistinguishable from the slabs of pavement, he was driven, in order not to lose his toes to frostbite or to lose sight of the door, to practice the already cultivated art of running first backward, then forward, with scarcely superior speed. But it was not long before the much-expected sound of Mistress Croale's voice heralded the hour when patience would blossom into possession. Gibbie bounded up and stood still as a statue at the very door until he heard Mistress Croale's hand upon the lock; whereupon he bolted, trembling with eagerness, into the entry of a court a few houses nearer to the Widdiehill.

One after another the pitiable company issued from its paradise, and each stumbled away, too far gone for leave-taking. Most of them passed Gibbie where he stood, but he took no heed; his father was always the last—and the least capable. But often as he left her door, never did it close behind Galbraith until with her own eyes Mistress Croale had seen Gibbie dart like an imp out of the court—to take him in charge and all the weary way home hover, not very like a guardian angel in appearance but not the less one in truth, around the unstable equilibrium of his father's tall and swaying form.

And thereupon commenced a series of marvelous gymnastics on the part of wee Gibbie. Imagine a small boy with a gigantic top six times his own size, which he keeps erect on its peg not by whipping it round but by running round it himself, unfailingly applying at the very spot and at the very moment the precise measure of impact necessary to counterbalance its perpetual tendency to fall in one direction or the other. Home the big one staggered, reeled, gyrated and tumbled; round and round him went the little one, now behind, now before, now on this side, now on that, his feet never more than touching the ground but dancing about like those of a tiny prizefighter. His hands and arms acted like flying buttresses all about a universally leaning tower, propping it here, propping it there, with wonderful judgment and skill. Not once in the last year and a half, during which time wee Gibbie had been the nightly guide of Sir George's homeward steps, had the self-disabled mass fallen prostrate in the gutter, there to snore out the night.

The first real struggle of the evening commenced when they reached the foot of the outside stair over the baronet's workshop. All up the outside and the two inside stairs, his waking and sleeping were as the alternate tic-tac of a pendulum; but Gibbie stuck to his business like a man, and his resolution and perseverance were at length, as always, crowned with victory.

The house in which lords and ladies had often reposed was now filled with very humble folk who were all asleep when Gibbie and his father entered; but the noise the two made in ascending caused no great disturbance of their rest. If any of them were roused for a moment, it was but to recognize at once the cause of the tumult with the remark, "It's only wee Gibbie luggin' home Sir George," and to turn on the other side and fall asleep again.

Arriving at last at the garret door which stood wide open, Gibbie had little need of light in the nearly pitch darkness of the place, for there was positively nothing to stumble over between the door and the ancient four-post bed, which was all of his father's house that remained to Sir George. With heavy shuffling feet the drunkard lumbered laboriously bedward, and the bare posts and crazy frame groaned and creaked as he fell upon the oat chaff that lay waiting him in place of the vanished luxury of feathers. Wee Gibbie flew at the man's legs and did not rest until, one after the other, he had gotten them onto the bed. If they were not very comfortably deposited, he knew that, in his first turn, their owner would get them right.

And then came the culmination of Gibbie's day! In triumph he spread over his sleeping father his dead mother's old plaid of Gordon tartan—all the bedding they had. Without a moment's delay—no shoes even to take off—he crept under it himself and nestled close upon the bosom of his unconscious parent. A victory more! Another day ended with success. His father was safe, and all his own! The canopy of the darkness and the plaid lay over them as if they were the only two in the universe! His father, unable to leave him, was his for whole dark hours to come. It was Gibbie's paradise now! His heaven was his father's bosom, to which he clung as no infant yet ever clung to his mother's. He never thought to pity himself that the embrace was all on his side, that no answering pressure came back from the prostrate form. He never said to himself, "My father is a drunkard, but I must make the best of it; he is all I have." He clung to his one possession—only clung. This was his father—all in all to him.

The conscious bliss of the child was of short duration, for in a few minutes he was fast asleep. But for the gain of those moments, the day had been well spent.

3

• • • • • • • • • • • • • • • • • • •

Sir George

Such were the events of every night, and such they had been since Gibbie first assumed this office of guardian—a time so long in proportion to his life that it seemed to him as one of the laws of existence that fathers got drunk and Gibbies took care of them. But Saturday night was always one of special bliss for the joy to come. All Sunday his father would be his. On that happiest day of all the week, he never set his foot out of doors except to run to Mistress Croale's to fetch the dinner which she supplied from her own table and for which Sir George paid in advance on Saturday.

The streets were not attractive to the child on Sundays; there were no shops open. As to going to church, such an idea had never entered his head. He had not once for a moment imagined that anybody would like him to go to church, or that church was at all a place to which Gibbies with fathers to look after should have any desire to go. As to what church-going meant, he had not the vaguest idea; it had not even waked the glimmer of a question in his mind. All he knew was that other people went to church on Sundays. It was another of the laws of existence, the reason of which he knew no more than why his father went every night to get drunk.

There was a strange remnant of righteousness in Sir George which showed itself in his determination never to taste drink before it was dark in winter or in summer before the regular hour for ceasing work had arrived; and to this rule he kept, but with far greater difficulties, on the Sunday as well. Mistress Croale would not sell a drop of drink, not even on the sly, on the Sabbath day. George was thus driven to provide his own Sunday-night whiskey and drink it at home.

When darkness had fallen, too much ashamed to begin his drink before the child—he hated to uncork the bottle before him—Sir George sent Gibbie to Mistress Croale. She was always kind to the child and could not help feeling that no small part of what ought to be spent on him came to her; and on Sundays, therefore, partly for his sake, partly for her own, she always gave him a small glass of milk and as much dry bread as he could eat. When he returned greatly refreshed he found his father, as he knew he would, already started on the business of the evening. He had drawn the chest, the only seat in the room, to the side of the bed against which he leaned his back. A penny candle was burning in a stone black-ing bottle on the chimney piece, and on the floor beside the chest stood the bottle of whiskey, a jug of water, a stoneware mug and a wine glass.

There was no fire and no kettle. Gibbie was far from shocked; it was all in the order of things, and he went up to his father with radiant coun-tenance. Sir George put forth his hands and took him between his knees.

"Gibbie," he said solemnly, "never drink a drop of whiskey; never drink anything but water, clear water, my man."

As he said the words he stretched out his own hand to the mug, lifted it to his lips, and swallowed with a great gulp.

"Don't do it, I tell you, Gibbie," he repeated.

Gibbie shook his head with positive repudiation.

Here followed another gulp from the mug.

"Gibbie," resumed Sir George, after a brief pause, "do you know what folk'll call you when I'm dead?"

Gibbie again shook his head—with expression this time of mere igno-rance.

"They'll call you 'Sir Gibbie Galbraith,' my man," said his father, "and rightly, for it'll be no nickname, though some may laugh at you 'cause your father was a cobbler and you never had shoes on your feet. Poor fellow! But don't heed what they say, Gibbie. Remember that you're Sir Gibbie and have the honor of the family to hold up. And remember, my man, that you cannot do and drink. For it's this cursed drink that's been the ruin of all the Galbraiths as far back as I can think. My grandfather was a big, bonny man, Gibbie, but he drank up almost everything there was till there was hardly an acre left upon all Daurside to come to my father, nothing but one small house. He was a good man, my father, but his father taught him to drink while he was still young and gave him no schooling. If a kind neighbor, that knew what it was to drink, had not taught me my trade, the Lord knows what would have become of you and me, Gibbie, my man. Go to your bed now and leave me to my own thoughts, not that they're always the best of company, laddie."

Gibbie obeyed, and getting under the Gordon tartan, lay and looked out, like a weasel from its hole, at his father's back. For half an hour or so Sir George went on drinking. All at once he started to his feet and turned toward the bed, his white face distorted with agony. He paused, stretched down his hand to the floor, lifted the mug and drank a huge mouthful; then with a cough set it down and fell forward upon the bed groaning, and his voice died gradually away. Gibbie watched it all, and the awe of the unknown made his soul very still. But with his father on the bed he soon fell asleep.

Gibbie slept some time. When he woke it was pitch dark and he was not lying on his father's bosom. He felt about with his hands till he found his father's head. Then he got up and tried to rouse him and, failing, tried to get his legs onto the bed. But in that too he was sadly unsuccessful. What with the darkness and the weight of him, the result of the boy's endeavor was that Sir George half slipped, half rolled onto the floor.

Assured then of his own helplessness, wee Gibbie dragged the miserable bolster from the bed and got it under his father's head; then covered him with the plaid and, creeping under it, laid himself upon his father's bosom where he soon slept again.

He woke very cold. The room was no longer dark, for the moon was shining through the skylight. He turned to have a look at his father. The pale light shone full upon his face and it was that, Gibbie thought, which made it look so strange. He moved closer to him and stared aghast! He had never seen him look like that before, even when most drunk! He threw himself upon him in fear—he could not even have told of what. He would not wake. He was gone to see what God could do for him there, for whom nothing could be done here.

Gibbie did not know anything about death, and went on trying to wake him. At last he observed that although his mouth was wide open, the breath did not come from it. Thereupon Gibbie's heart began to fail him. But when he lifted an eyelid and saw what was under it, the house rang with the despairing shriek of the little orphan.

4

Alone in the Streets

Gibbie's agony passed and life became again life, and he ran about the streets as before. Some may think that wee Sir Gibbie—as many now called him, some knowing the truth and others in kindly mockery—would get on all the better for the loss of such a father; but it was not so. In his father he had lost his Paradise and was now a creature expelled. The streets and the people and the shops, the horses and the dogs, even the penny loaves, though he was hungry, had lost half their precious delight when his father was no longer in the accessible background, the heart of the blissful city. As to food and clothing, he did neither much better nor any worse than before; people were kind as usual, and kindness was to Gibbie the very milk of Mother Nature. Whose the hand that proffered it or what form it took, he cared no more than a stray kitten cares whether the milk set down to it be in a blue saucer or a white. But he always made the right return. The first thing a kindness deserves is acceptance, the next is transmission; Gibbie gave both without thinking much about either. For he never had taken, indeed never learned to take, a thought about what he should eat or what he should drink or wherewithal he should be clothed.

He roamed the streets, as all his life before, the whole of the day and part of the night; he took what was given him and picked up what he found. There were some who would gladly have brought him within the bounds of an ordered life; he soon drove them to despair, however, for the streets had been his nursery and nothing could keep him out of them. However Gibbie's habits might shock the ladies of the parish minister Mr. Sclater's congregation, who sought to civilize him, the boy was no more about mischief in the streets at midnight than they were in their beds. They collected enough on his behalf to board him for a year with an old woman who kept a school, and they did get him to sleep one night in her house. But in the morning she would not let him run out. Instead, she brought him into the schoolroom, her kitchen, and began to teach him to write. Gibbie failed to see the good of it. He must have space, change, adventure, air, or life was not worth the name to him. Above all, he must see friendly faces, and that of the old dame was not such. He immediately departed from her house, and it was the last she ever saw of him. Thus, after one night's brief interval of respectability, he was again a rover of the city, a flitting insect that lighted here and there and spread wings of departure the moment a fresh desire awoke.

It would be difficult to say where he slept. In summer, anywhere; in winter, where he could find warmth. Like animals better clad than he, yet like him able to endure cold, he reveled in mere heat when he could come by it. Sometimes he stood at the back of a baker's oven, for he knew all the haunts of heat about the city; sometimes he buried himself in the oat husks lying ready to feed the kiln of a meal-mill; sometimes he lay by the furnace of the steam engine of the waterworks. One man employed there, when his time was at night, always made a bed for Gibbie; he had lost his only child, and this one of nobody's was a comfort to him.

The merits the police recognized in him were mainly two—neither of small consequence in their eyes—the first, that of utter harmlessness; the second, a passion and power for rendering help, taking notable shape chiefly in two ways: The first was the peculiar faculty now rather generally known—his great gift, some said; his great luck, others called it—for finding things lost. It was no wonder the town crier had sought his acquaintance and when secured had cultivated it—neither a difficult task; for the boy, ever since he could remember, had been in the habit, as often as he saw the crier or heard his tuck of drum in the distance, of joining him and following until he had acquainted himself with all particulars concerning everything proclaimed as missing. The moment he had mastered the facts as announced, he would dart away to search and not unfrequently to return with the thing sought. The crier spoke kindly to him, as well he might, and now and then gave him a penny.

The second of the positive merits by which Gibbie found acceptance in the eyes of the police was a yet more peculiar one, growing out of his love for his father and his experience in the exercise of that love. It was, however, unintelligible to them, except on the theory commonly adopted with regard to Gibbie—namely, that he "wasna a' there." It was indeed the main cause of his being, like themselves, so much in the street at night. If the finding of things was a gift, this other peculiarity was a passion: it was to play the guardian angel to drunk folk. If such a distressed human craft hove in sight, he would instantly bear down upon and hover about him until resolved as to his real condition. If he was in such a distress as to require assistance, Gibbie never left him till he saw him safe within his own door. The police asserted that wee Sir Gibbie not only knew every drunkard in the city and where he lived, but where he generally got drunk as well.

He was least known to those to whom he rendered most assistance. Rarely had he thanks for it, never halfpence, but not unfrequently blows and abuse. For the first he cared nothing; the latter, owing to his great agility, seldom visited him with any directness. About the time the company at Mistress Croale's would be breaking up, he would on most nights be lying in wait a short distance down the Widdiehill, ready to minister to that one of his father's old comrades who might prove most in need of his assistance; and if he showed him no gratitude, Gibbie had not been trained in a school where he was taught to expect or even to wish for any.

5

•••••••••••••••••••••

Adrift

When Mistress Croale moved her establishment near the docks in the second winter after his father's death, Gibbie followed and continued to haunt it. What more than anything else attracted him to her new house was the jolly manners and openhearted kindness of most of the sailors who frequented it, with almost all of whom he was a favorite. Scarcely a night passed when he was not present at one or more of the quarrels of which the place was a hotbed. He was not shocked by the things he saw, even when he liked them least. He regarded the doings of them much as he had looked upon his father's drunkenness—as a pitiful necessity that overtook men, one from which there was no escape and which caused a great need for Gibbies. Evil language and coarse behavior alike passed over him without leaving the smallest stain upon heart or conscience, desire or will. No one could doubt it who considered the clarity of his face and eyes, in which the occasional expression of keenness and promptitude scarcely even ruffled the prevailing look of unclouded babyhood.

It is hardly necessary to remark that what kept Gibbie pure and honest was the rarely developed, ever-active love of his kind. The human face was the one attraction to him in the universe. Gibbie knew no music except the voice of man and woman; at least no other had as yet affected him.

One night in the spring he saw at Mistress Croale's for the first time an African sailor whom the rest called Sambo. Gibbie was at once taken with his big, dark, radiant eyes and his white teeth continually uncovering themselves in good-humored smiles. To Gibbie, Sambo speedily became absolutely loving and tender, and Gibbie made him full return of devotion.

One night Sambo was looking on at a game of cards in which all the rest in the room were engaged. Happening to laugh at some turn it took, one of them who was losing was offended and abused him. Others objected to his having fun without risking money and required him to join in the game. This for some reason or other he declined, and when the whole party at length insisted, Sambo positively refused. Thereupon quickly came all the many steps of the ascent—from displeasure to indignation, wrath, revenge; and then ensued a row.

Gibbie had been sitting all the time on his friend's knee, in whom, as insult followed insult, the blood kept slowly rising. At length a savage from Greenock threw a tumbler at him. Sambo, quick as a lizard, covered his face with his arm. The tumbler, falling from it, struck Gibbie on the head—not severely but hard enough to make him utter a little cry. At that sound the latent fierceness came wide awake in Sambo. Gently as a nursing mother he set Gibbie down in a corner behind him, then with one rush sent every Jack of the company sprawling on the floor, with the table and bottles and glasses atop of them. At the vision of their plight, his good humor instantly returned; he burst into a great hearty laugh and proceeded at once to lift the table from off them. That effected, he caught up Gibbie in his arms and carried him with him to bed.

In the middle of the night Gibbie half woke and, finding himself alone, sought his father's bosom; then, in the confusion between sleeping and waking, imagined his father's death come again. Presently he remembered it was in Sambo's arms he fell asleep, but where he was now he could not tell; certainly he was not in bed. Groping, he pushed a door and a glimmer of light came in. He was in a closet of the room in which Sambo slept—and something was to do about his bed. He rose softly and peeped out. There stood several men, and a struggle was going on—nearly noiseless. Gibbie was half-dazed and could not understand; but he had little anxiety about Sambo in whose prowess he had a triumphant confidence. Suddenly came the sound of a great gush, and the group parted from the bed and vanished. Gibbie darted toward it. The words, "O Lord Jesus!" came to his ears, and he heard no more; they were poor Sambo's last in this world. The light of a street lamp fell upon the bed; the blood was welling in great thick throbs out of his black throat.

For some moments Gibbie stood in ghastly terror. No sound except a low gurgle came to his ears, and the horror of the stillness overpowered him. He never could recall what came next. When he knew himself again he was in the street running like the wind, he knew not whither. It was not that he dreaded any hurt to himself; horror, not fear, was behind him.

His next recollection of himself was in the first of the morning on the

lofty chain bridge over the river Daur. Before him lay he knew not what—
only escape from what was behind. His faith in men lay in ruins. The city,
his home, was frightful to him. Quarrels and curses and blows he had
been used to, and amidst them life could be lived. If he did not consciously weave them into his theories, he consciously wrapped them up
in his confidence and was at peace. But the last thought had revealed
something unknown before. It was as if the darkness had been cloven and
through the cleft he saw into hell. A thing had been done that could not
be undone, and he thought it must be what people called murder. And
Sambo was such a good man! He was almost as good a man as Gibbie's
father, and now he would not breathe anymore! Was he gone where Gibbie's father was gone? Was it the good men that stopped breathing and
grew cold? But it was those wicked men that had deaded Sambo! And
with that his first vague perception of evil and wrong in the world began
to dawn.

Brooding thus he fell into a dreamy state in which, brokenly from here
and there, pictures of his former life grew out upon his memory. Plainer
than all the rest came the last time he stood under Mistress Croale's window waiting to help his father home. The same instant back to the ear of
his mind came his father's two words, as he had heard them through the
window—"Up Daurside."

"Up Daurside!" Here he was upon Daurside—a little way up too; he
would go farther up. He rose and went on, while the great river kept flowing the other way toward the city that had so long been his home.

Meantime, the murder came to the knowledge of the police, Mistress
Croale herself giving the information, and all in the house were arrested.
In the course of their examination, it came out that wee Sir Gibbie had
gone to bed with the murdered man and was now nowhere to be found.
Either they had murdered him too or carried him off. The news spread
and the whole city was in commotion about his fate. The city was
searched from end to end, from side to side, and from cellar to garret. Not
a trace of him was to be found—but indeed Gibbie had always been easier to find than to trace, for he had no belongings of any sort to betray
him. No one dreamed of his having fled, and search was confined to the
city. The murderers were at length discovered, tried and executed. They
protested their innocence with regard to the child and therein nothing
appeared against them beyond the fact that he was missing. The result so
far as concerned Gibbie was that the talk of the city was turned upon his
history; and from the confused mass of hearsay that reached him, Mr. Sclater set himself to discover and verify the facts. For this purpose he burrowed about in the neighborhoods Gibbie had chiefly frequented, and
was so far successful as to satisfy himself that Gibbie, if he was alive, was
Sir Gilbert Galbraith, Baronet. But his own lawyer was able to assure him
that not an inch of property remained anywhere attached to the title.
There were indeed relations of the boy's mother who were of some small
consequence in a neighboring county, also one in business in Glasgow or
its neighborhood, reported wealthy; but these had entirely disowned her

because of her marriage. All Mr. Sclater discovered besides was in a lumber room next to the garret in which Sir George died, where he found a box of papers—a glance at whose contents showed that they must at least prove a great deal of which he was already certain from other sources. A few of them had to do with the house in which they were found, still known as the Auld Hoose o' Galbraith; but most of them referred to property in land, and many were of ancient date. If the property were in the hands of descendants of the original stock, the papers would be of value in their eyes; and, in any case, it would be well to see to their safety. Mr. Sclater therefore had the chest removed to the garret of the church where it stood thereafter, little regarded, but able to answer for more than itself.

6

· · · · · · · · · · · · · · · · · · ·

Up Daurside

*G*ibbie was now without a home. He had had a whole city for his dwelling, and for the first time in his life the fatherless, motherless, brotherless, sisterless stray of the streets felt himself alone.

It was a cold, fresh morning, cloudy and changeful toward the end of April. It had rained and would rain again; it might snow. Heavy, undefined clouds hung about the east. Even to him, city-creature that he was, it was plain something was going to happen there. And happen it did presently, with a splendor that for a moment blinded Gibbie. For just at the horizon there was a long crack and the topmost arc of the rising sun shot suddenly a thousand arrows of radiance into the brain of the boy.

To no traveler could one land be so different from another as to Gibbie the country was from the town. He had seen bushes and trees before, but only over garden walls or in one or two of the churchyards. The sun seemed but to have looked up to mock him and go down again, for he had crossed the crack and was behind a thick mass of cloud; a cold, damp wind, spotted with sparkles of rain, blew fitfully from the east. Below him the gloomy river, here deep, smooth, moody, sullen, went flowing heedless to the city. Yet never once did Gibbie think of returning. He rose and wandered up the wide road along the riverbank, farther and farther from it—his only guide the words of his father, "Up Daurside"; his sole comfort the feeling of having once more to do with his beloved father so long departed. Along cultivated fields on the one side and a steep descent to the river on the other, covered here and there with trees, but mostly with rough grass and bushes and stones, he followed the king's highway. There were buttercups and plenty of daisies within his sight—primroses, too, on the slope beneath; but he did not know flowers, and his was not now the mood for discovering what they were.

The exercise revived him and he began to be hungry. But how could there be anything to eat in the desert, inhospitable succession of trees and fields and hedges, through which the road wound endlessly along like a dead street, having neither houses nor paving stone? Hunger, however, was far less enfeebling to Gibbie than to one accustomed to regular meals, and he was in no anxiety about either when or what he should eat.

The morning advanced, and by and by he began to meet a fellow creature now and then upon the road; but at sight of anyone a feeling rose in him such as he had never had toward human beings before. They seemed somehow of a different kind from those in the town, and they did not look friendly as they passed. He did not know that he presented to them a very different countenance from that which his fellow citizens had always seen him wear. He was so uncomfortable at length from the way the people he met scrutinized him that when he saw anyone coming, he would instantly turn aside and take the cover of thicket, or hedge, or stone wall, until the bearer of eyes had passed.

Up Daurside was the one vague notion he had of his calling, his destiny; and with his short, quick step, his progress was considerable. He passed house after house, farm after farm; but he went nearer none of them than the road led him. Besides, the houses were very unlike those in the city, and not at all attractive to him.

He came at length to a field sloping to the road, covered with leaves like some he had often seen in the market. They drew him; and as there was but a low and imperfect hedge between, he got over and found it was a crop of small yellow turnips. He gathered as many as he could carry and ate them as he went along. In the city he would never have dreamed of touching anything that was not given him, except it lay plainly a lost thing. But here, where everything was so different and he saw none of the signs of ownership to which he was accustomed, the idea of property did not occur to him. He came soon after to a little stream that ran into the great river. For a few moments he eyed it very doubtfully, thinking it must, like the kennels along the sides of the street, be far too dirty to drink from; but the way it sparkled and sang soon satisfied him, and he drank and was refreshed.

All day the cold spring weather continued, with more of the past winter in it than of the coming summer. The sun would shine out for a few moments with a grey, weary, old light, then retreat as if he had tried but really could not. Once came a slight snow, which melted the moment it touched the earth. The wind kept blowing cheerlessly by fits, and the world seemed growing tired of the same thing over again so often. At length the air began to grow dusk. But, happily, before it was quite dark, and while yet he could distinguish between objects, he came to the gate of a farmyard; it waked in him the hope of finding some place where he could sleep warmer than in the road, and he clambered over it. Nearest of the buildings to the gate stood an open shed. But just as he entered it, he spied at the farther outside corner a wooden structure, and through the arched door of it, he saw the floor covered with nice-looking straw. He suspected it to be a dog's kennel; and presently the chain lying beside it with a collar at the end satisfied him it was. The dog was absent and its dwelling looked altogether enticing! He crept in, got under as much of the straw as he could heap over him, and fell fast asleep.

In a few minutes, as it seemed to him, he was roused by the voice of a boy in conversation with a dog. He seemed, by the sound of the chain, to be fastening the collar on the dog's neck, and presently left. The dog, which had been on the rampage the whole afternoon, immediately turned to creep in and rest till suppertime, presenting to Gibbie the intelligent countenance of a large Newfoundland. Now Gibbie had been honored with the acquaintance of many dogs, and the friendship of most of them. Even among dogs, however, there are ungracious individuals, and Gibbie had once or twice been bitten. Hence, with the sight of the true occupant of the dwelling, it dawned upon him that the dog must be startled to find a stranger in its house and might, regarding him as an intruder rather than a guest, worry him before he had time to explain himself. He darted forward therefore to get out but had scarcely reached the door when the dog put in his nose, ready to follow with all it had. Gibbie, thereupon, began a loud barking, as much as to say, "Here I am; please do nothing without reflection." The dog started back in extreme astonishment, his ears erect and a keen look of question. What strange animal, speaking like, and yet so unlike, an orthodox dog, could have gotten into his chamber? Gibbie, amused at the dog's fright and assured by his looks that he was both a good-natured and reasonable animal, burst into a fit of merry laughter. The dog took it as a challenge to play, darted into the kennel, and began poking his nose into his visitor. Gibbie fell to patting and kissing and hugging him, glad of any companion, and they were friends at once. Both were tired, however, for both had been active that day, and few minutes of mingled wrestling and endearment, to which perhaps the narrowness of their playground gave a speedier conclusion, contented both, after which they lay side by side in peace, Gibbie with his hand on the dog's back, and the dog every now and then turning his head over his shoulder to lick Gibbie's face.

Again he was waked, this time by approaching steps, and the same moment the dog darted from under him with much rattle out of the kennel, in front of which he stood and whined expectantly. A woman was setting down something before the dog—into which he instantly plunged his nose and began gobbling. The sound stirred up all the latent hunger in Gibbie, and he leaped out, eager to have a share. A large wooden bowl was on the ground, and the half of its contents of porridge and milk was already gone. It was plain if Gibbie was to have any, he must lose no time. Had he a long nose and mouth all in one like the animal, he would have plunged them in beside the dog's. But the flatness of his mouth causing the necessity, in the case of such an attempt, of bringing the whole of his face into contact with the food, there was not room in the dish for the two to feed together. So he was driven to the sole other possible expedient, that of making a spoon of his hand. The dog neither growled nor pushed away the spoon but instantly began to gobble twice as fast as before, and presently was licking the bottom of the dish. Gibbie's hand, therefore, made but few journeys to his mouth, but what it carried him was good food—better than any he had had that day. When all was gone he crept again into the kennel; the dog followed, and soon they were both fast asleep in a tangle of arms and legs.

Gibbie woke at sunrise and went out. His host came after him and stood wagging his tail and looking wistfully up in his face. Gibbie understood him and, as the sole return he could make for his hospitality, undid his collar. Instantly the dog rushed off, cleared the gate at a bound and, scouring madly across a field, vanished from his sight; whereupon Gibbie too set out to continue his journey up Daurside.

This day was warmer; spring had come a step nearer; the dog had been a comforter to him, and the horror had begun to assuage. He began to grow aware of the things about him and to open his eyes to them. Once he saw a primrose in a little dell and left the road to look at it. Still on his right was the great river flowing down toward the home he had left—now through low meadows, now through upshouldered fields of wheat and oats, now through rocky heights covered with the graceful silver-barked birch, the mountain ash and the fir.

That second day he fared better than the first. But I must not attempt the detail of this part of his journey. It is enough that he got through it. He met with some adventures and suffered a good deal from hunger and cold. Had he not been hardy as well as fearless, he would have died. But now from this quarter, now from that, he got all that was needful for one of God's birds. Once he found in a hedge the nest of an errant and secretive hen and, recognizing the eggs as food authorized by the shopwindows and market of the city, soon qualified himself to have an opinion of their worth. Another time he came upon a girl milking a cow in a shed, and his astonishment at the marvels of the process was such that he forgot even the hunger that was rendering him faint. He had often seen cows in the city but had never suspected what they were capable of. When she caught sight of him, staring with open mouth, she was taken with such a fit of laughter that the cow, which was ill-tempered, kicked out and overturned the pail. Now, because of its troublesomeness, this cow was not milked beside the rest, and the shed where she stood was used for farm implements only. The floor of it was the earth, beaten hard and worn into hollows. When the milk settled in one of these, Gibbie saw that it was lost to the girl and found to him. Undeterred by the astounding nature of the spring from which he had just seen it flow, he threw himself down and drank like a calf. Her laughter ended, the girl was troubled; she would be scolded for her clumsiness in allowing Hawkie to kick over the pail, but the eagerness of the boy after the milk troubled her more. She told him to wait and, running to the house, returned with two large pieces of oatcake which she gave him.

Thus, one way or another, food came to Gibbie. Drink was to be had in almost any hollow. Sleep was scattered everywhere over the world. For warmth, only motion and a seasoned skin were necessary. The latter Gibbie had; the former, already a habit learned in the streets, had now become almost a passion. By this time Gibbie had gotten well up toward the roots of the hills of Gormgarnet, and the river had dwindled greatly in size. He was no longer afraid of it, but would lie for hours listening to its murmurs over the pebbly bed, and sometimes even sleep in the hollows of its banks or below the willows that overhung it. Every here and there a brown rivulet from some peat bog on a hill, brown and clear, flowed into it. Farm after farm he passed, with an occasional little village of low-thatched houses. By this time he had become greatly reconciled to the loneliness of nature, and no more was afraid in her solitary presence.

At the same time his heart had begun to ache and long after the communion of his kind. For not once since he set out (and that seemed months where it was only weeks) had he had an opportunity of doing anything for anybody—except, indeed, unfastening the dog's collar; and not to be able to help was to Gibbie like being dead.

7

••••••••••••••••••

The Barn

May had now set in, but up here among the hills she was May by courtesy only. The green crops were growing darker. The lambs were frolicking, and in sheltered places the flowers were turning the earth into a firmament. And now a mere daisy was enough to delight the heart of Gibbie. His joy in humanity so suddenly and violently checked, he had begun to see the human look in the face of the commonest flowers. The wind, of which he had scarce thought as he met it roaming the streets like himself, was now a friend of his solitude, bringing him sweet odors, alive with the souls of bees, and cooling with bliss the heat of the long walk.

One evening just as it became dark, he found himself at a rough gate through which he saw a field. There was a lovely tall hedge on each side of the gate, and he was now a sufficiently experienced traveler to conclude that he was not far from some human abode. He climbed the gate and found himself in a field of clover. It was a splendid big bed, and even had the night not been warm, he would not have hesitated to sleep in it. So down he lay in the clover and was at once unconscious.

When he woke, the moon was high in the heavens. A short distance from his couch he saw a long, low house in which there was a door, horizontally divided into two parts. Gibbie rose and walked to it and would fain have got in, to try whether the place was good for sleep, but he found both halves fast. In the lower half, however, he spied a hole, which, though not so large, reminded him of the entrance to the kennel of his dog host; but alas! it had a door too, shut from the inside. There might be some way of opening it. He felt about, and soon discovered that it was a sliding valve, which he could push to either side. It was, in fact, the cat's door, specially constructed for her convenience of entrance and exit.

The hole was a small one but tempting to the wee baronet; he might perhaps be able to squeeze himself through. He tried and succeeded, though with some difficulty. The moon was there before him, shining through a pane or two of glass over the door; and by her light on the hard, brown clay floor he was able to see about. It was a very old-fashioned barn. About a third of it was floored with wood—dark with age, almost as brown as the clay—for threshing upon with flails. At that labor two men had been busy during the most of the preceding day, and that was why, in the same end of the barn, there rose a great heap of oat straw, showing in the light of the moon like a mound of pale gold. What he saw in the other corner was still more like gold and was indeed greater than gold, for it was *life*—the heap, namely, of corn threshed from the straw. Gibbie recognized this as what he had seen given to horses. But now the temptation to sleep was overpowering and took from him all desire to examine further. He shot into the middle of the loose heap of straw, vanishing like a mole. In the heart of the golden warmth, he lay so dry and comfortable that, notwithstanding his hunger, he was presently in a faster sleep than before.

When at length Gibbie became once more aware of existence, it was through a stormy invasion of the still realm of sleep. The blows of two flails fell persistent and quick, first on the thick head of the sheaf of oats untied and cast down before them, then grew louder and more deafening as the oats flew and the chaff fluttered and the straw flattened and broke and thinned and spread—until at last they thundered in great hard blows on the wooden floor. He wormed himself softly around in the straw to look out and see.

It was well that the man with the pitchfork did not spy Gibbie's eyes peeping out from the midst of the straw; he might have taken him for some wild creature and driven the prongs into him. As it was, Gibbie did not altogether like the look of him and lay still as a stone. Then another sheaf was unbound and cast on the floor, and the blows of the flails began again. It went on thus for an hour and a half, and Gibbie dropped asleep several times. The men at length swept up the corn and tossed up the straw for the last time and went out. Gibbie crept out and began to look about him for something he could eat. The oats looked the most likely and he took a mouthful for a trial. He ground at them severely but, hungry as he was, he failed to find oats good for food. Their hard husks and dryness foiled him utterly. Looking round him he saw an open loft and, climbing on the heap in which he had slept, managed to reach it. At the farther end was a heap of hay, which he took for another kind of straw. Then he spied something he knew; a row of cheeses lay ripening on a shelf suspended from the rafters. Gibbie knew them well from the shop-windows—knew they were cheeses and good to eat, though whence and how they came he did not know, his impression being that they grew in the fields like the turnips. He pounced upon a cheese and lifted it between his two hands; it smelled good, but felt very hard. That was no matter; what else were teeth made strong and sharp for? He tried them on one of the round edges, and, nibbling actively, soon got through to the softer body of the cheese.

At length he crept softly toward the other end of the loft to see what was to be seen there. He found that the heap of hay was not in that loft at all but filled a small chamber in the stable, and when Gibbie clambered upon it, what should he see below him on the other side but a beautiful white horse. Beyond, he could see the backs of more horses, but they were very different—big and clumsy, and not white. They were all eating and this was their food on which he lay! He wished he too could eat it—and tried, but found it even less satisfactory than the oats.

A door opened beyond and a man came in and led two of the horses out, leaving the door open. Gibbie clambered down from the top of the hay into the stall beside the white horse and ran out. He was almost in the fields, had not even a fence to cross, and went straight for a neighboring hollow, where, taught by experience, he hoped to find water from a stream flowing into the great river.

8

· · · · · · · · · · · · · · · · · · · ·

Glashgar

*O*nce away from the barn, Gibbie had no thought of returning. *Up Daurside* was the sole propulsive force whose existence he recognized. But when he lifted his head from drinking at the stream and, greatly refreshed, looked up its channel, a longing seized him to know whence came the water of life which had thus restored him to bliss—how a burn first appears upon the earth. He would follow it up and see. So away he went, yielding at once to the first desire that came. He had not trotted far along the bank, however, before he saw that its course was a much longer one than he had imagined, for it turned from the mountain and led up among the roots of other hills; while here in front of him, direct from the mountain as it seemed, came down a smaller stream and tumbled noisily into this. The larger burn would lead him too far from the Daur; he would follow the smaller one. He found a wide, shallow place, crossed the larger, and went up the side of the smaller.

The stream he was now ascending ran along a claw of the mountain,

which was covered with almost a forest of pine. He trotted along the bank
of the burn, farther and farther up, until he could trot no more but had to
clamber over great stones or sink to the knees in bog. Sometimes he
walked in the water; sometimes he had to scramble up its steep sides. Its
banks were mainly of rock and heather, but now and then a small patch
of cultivation intervened. Gibbie had no thought that he was gradually
leaving the abodes of men behind; he knew no reason why in ascending
things should change. For all he knew, there might be farm after farm, up
and up forever, to the gates of heaven.

After so long wandering, Gibbie had hardly enough dress left to carry
the name. Shoes, of course, he had none. Of the shape of trousers there
remained nothing, except the division before and behind in the short petticoat to which they were reduced; and those rudimentary divisions were
lost in the multitude of rents of equal apparent significance. He had never,
so far as he knew, had a shirt upon his body; and his sole other garment
was a jacket, so much too large for him that to retain the use of his hands,
he had folded back the sleeves quite to his elbows. His head had plentiful
protection in his own natural crop. All ways his thatch of light hair
pointed, as if surcharged with electric fluid, crowning him with a wildness
which was in amusing contrast with the placidity of his countenance—a
sort of live peace abiding in that weather-beaten little face under its wild
crown of human herbage. His eyes—partly, perhaps, because there was so
little flesh upon his bones—were very large, and in repose had much of a
soft animal expression. His hands and feet were small and childishly
dainty, his whole body well-shaped and well put together—of which the
style of his dress rather quashed the evidence.

Such was Gibbie to the eye, as he rose from Daurside to the last cultivated ground on the borders of the burn and eventually came upon the
highest dwelling on the mountain. It was the abode of a cottar, and was a
dependency of the farm he had just left. The cottar was an old man of
seventy; his wife was nearly sixty. They had reared stalwart sons and
shapely daughters, now at service here and there in the valley below.

It was a very humble dwelling, built of turf upon a foundation of
stones, and roofed with turf and straw—warm, and nearly impervious to
the searching airs of the mountainside. One little window of a foot and
half square looked out on the universe. At one end stood a stack of peat,
half as big as the cottage itself. All around it were huge rocks. A few of the
commonest flowers grew about the door, but there was no garden. The
doorstep was natural stone, and a huge projecting rock behind formed
the back and a portion of one of the end walls. This latter rock had been
the attraction to the site because of a hollow in it, which now served as a
dairy. For up there with them lived the last cow of the valley—the cow that
breathed the loftiest air on all Daurside, a good cow, gifted in feeding well
upon little.

Gibbie knocked at the old, weather-beaten, well-patched door.

"Come on in, whoever ye be."

Gibbie pulled the string that came through a hole in the door; so lifting the latch, he entered.

A woman sat on a stool, her face turned over her shoulder to see who came. It was a grey face, with good, simple features and clear eyes. The plentiful hair that grew low on her forehead was half grey, mostly covered by a white cap with frills. A clean apron of blue print over a blue petticoat completed her dress. A book lay on her lap. Always when she had finished her morning's work and made her house tidy, she sat down to have her "comfort," as she called it. The moment she saw Gibbie she rose. She was rather a little woman and carried herself straight and light.

"Eh, ye poor outcast!" she said in the pitying voice of a mother. "How did ye get up here? And what do you want here? I have nothing."

Receiving no answer but one of the child's bewitching smiles, she stood for a moment regarding him, not in mere silence but with a look of dumbness. She was a mother and, more, one of God's mothers.

Now the very moment before Gibbie entered, she had been reading the words of the Lord: "Inasmuch as ye have done it unto one of the least of these, ye have done it unto me," and with her heart full of them, she had lifted her eyes and seen Gibbie. For one moment, with the quick flashing response of the childlike imagination of the Celt, she fancied she saw the Lord himself. Often had Janet pondered, as she sat alone on the great mountain while Robert was with the sheep or as she lay awake by his side at night with the wind howling about the cottage, whether the Lord might not sometimes take a lonely walk to look after such solitary sheep of His flock as they to let them know He had not lost sight of them. There stood the child, and whether he was the Lord or not, he was evidently hungry.

In the meantime, Gibbie stood motionless in the middle of the floor, smiling his innocent smile, asking for nothing, hinting at nothing, but resting his wild-calm eyes, with a sense of safety and mother-presence, upon the thoughtful face of the gazing woman. Her awe deepened. Involuntarily she bowed her head and, stepping to him, took him by the hand and led him to the stool she had left. There she made him sit while she brought forward her table, white with scrubbing. Then taking from a hole in the wall a platter of oatcakes, she set it upon the table. She next carried a wooden bowl through a whitewashed door to her dairy in the rock, and bringing it back filled, half with cream, half with milk, set that also on the table. Then she placed a chair before it and said, "Sit down and eat. If you were the Lord himself, my bonny man—and for all I know you may be—I could give you nothing better. It's all I have to offer."

Presently she came back with a look of success, carrying two eggs, which, having raked out a quantity, she buried in the hot ashes of the peats and left in front of the hearth to roast while Gibbie ate the thick oatcake, sweet and substantial, and drank such milk as the wildest imagination of a town boy could never suggest. It was indeed angels' food. Janet took a seat on a low, three-legged stool and picked up her knitting that he might feel neither that he was watched as he ate nor that she was waiting for him to finish. Every other moment she gave a glance at the stranger she had taken in; but never a word he spoke, and the sense of mystery grew upon her.

Suddenly came a great bounce and scramble; the latch jumped up, the door flew open and, after a moment's pause, in came a sheep dog— a splendid thoroughbred collie, carrying in his mouth a tiny, long-legged lamb which he dropped half dead in the woman's lap. Then, having done his duty by the lamb, he sat on his tail and stared with his two brave, trusting eyes at the little beggar that sat in the master's chair eating of the fat of the land. Oscar was a gentleman; he had never gone to school, therefore neither fancied nor had been taught that rags make an essential distinction and ought to be barked at. Gibbie was a stranger, and as a stranger Oscar gave him welcome—now and then stooping to lick the little brown feet that had wandered so far.

Like all wild creatures, Gibbie ate quickly and had finished everything set before him before the woman had finished feeding the lamb. Without a notion of the rudeness of it, his heart full of gentle gratitude, he rose and left the cottage. When Janet turned from her shepherding, there sat Oscar looking up at the empty chair.

"What's become of the laddie?" she said to the dog, who answered with a low whine, half-regretful, half-interrogative. Janet hastened to the door, but already Gibbie's nimble feet, refreshed to the tip of every toe with the food he had just swallowed, had borne him far up the hill behind the cottage, so that she could not get a glimpse of him. Thoughtfully she returned and thoughtfully removed the remnants of the meal.

When at last she had finished, put the things away and swept up the hearth, she sat down once more to read. The lamb lay at her feet with his little head projecting from the folds of her new flannel petticoat; and every time her eye fell from the book upon the lamb, she felt as if somehow the lamb was the boy that had eaten of her bread and drunk of her milk.

Not for years and years had Janet been to church. She had long been unable to walk so far; and having no book but the best, and no help to understand it but the highest, her faith was simple, strong, real, all-pervading. Day by day she pored over the great gospel until she had grown to be one of the noble ladies of the kingdom of heaven—one of those who inherit the earth and are ripening to see God. For the Master, and His mind in hers, was her teacher. She had little or no theology save what He taught her. To Janet, Jesus Christ was no object of so-called theological speculation, but a living Man who somehow or other heard her when she called to Him, and sent her the help she needed.

9

....

The Kitchen

*U*p and up the hill went Gibbie. The mountain grew steeper and more bare as he went, and he became absorbed in his climbing. All at once he discovered that he had lost the stream, where or when he could not tell. All below and around him was red granite rock.

Not once while he ascended had the idea come to him that by and by he should be able to climb no farther. For aught he knew there were oatcakes and milk and sheep and collie dogs ever higher and higher still. The sun was about two hours toward the west when Gibbie, his little legs almost as active as ever, surmounted the final slope. Running up like a child that would scale heaven, he stood on the bare round, the head of the mountain, and saw with an invading shock of amazement, and at first of disappointment, that there was no going higher; in every direction the slope was downward. He had never been on the top of anything before. He had always been in the hollows of things. Now the whole world lay beneath him. It was cold; in some of the shadows lay snow, but Gibbie felt no cold. In a glow with the climb, which at the last had been hard, his lungs filled with the heavenly air and his soul with the feeling he was above everything that was uplifted on the very crown of the earth, he stood in his rags, a fluttering scarecrow, the conqueror of height, the discoverer of immensity, the monarch of space. Nobody knew of such marvel but him! Gibbie had never even heard the word poetry, but nonetheless was he the very stuff out of which poems grow; and now all the latent poetry in him was set swaying and heaving.

He sat down on the topmost point. And slowly in the silence and the loneliness, from the unknown fountains of the eternal consciousness, the heart of the child filled. The mighty city that had been to him the universe was lost in the far indistinguishable distance; and he who had lost it had climbed upon the throne of the world. The air was still when a breath awoke—it but touched his cheek like the down of a feather—and the stillness was there again. The stillness grew great and slowly descended upon him. It deepened and deepened. It was as if a great single thought was the substance of the silence and was all over and around him, closer to him than his clothes, than his body, than his hands. In after years when Gibbie had the idea of God, when he had learned to think about Him, to desire His presence, to believe that a will of love enveloped His will, as often as the thought of God came to him, it came in the shape of the silence on the top of Glashgar.

As he sat, with his eyes on the peak he had just chosen from the rest as the loftiest of all within his sight, he saw a cloud begin to grow. The next moment a flash of blue lightning darted across the sky. The clouds swept together, and then again burst forth the lightning. He saw no flash, but an intense cloud illumination, accompanied by the deafening crack, and followed by the appalling roar and roll of the thunder. He clung to the rock with hands and feet. It was an awful delight that filled his spirit. Mount Sinai was not to him a terror. To him there was no wrath in the thunder any more than in the greeting of the dog that found him in his kennel. Gibbie sat calm, full of awe, while the storm roared and beat and flashed and ran about him. It was the very fountain of tempest. The tumult at last seized Gibbie like an intoxication; he jumped to his feet and danced and flung his arms about as if he himself were the storm. But the uproar did not last long. Almost as suddenly as it had come it was gone. The sun shone out clearly but was a long way down the west, and twilight, in her grey cloak, would soon be tracking him from the east.

Gibbie, wet and cold, began to think of the cottage where he had been so kindly received, of the friendly face of its mistress and her care of the lamb. It was not that he wanted to eat. He did not even imagine more eating, for never in his life had he eaten twice of the same charity in the same day. What he wanted was to find some dry hole in the mountain and sleep as near the cottage as he could. So he rose and set out. But he lost his way. At length he found, as he thought, the burn along whose bank he had ascended in the morning and followed it toward the valley, looking out for the friendly cottage. But the first indication of abode he saw was the wall of the grounds of the house through whose gate he had looked in the morning. He was, then, a long way from the cottage and not far from the farm; and the best thing he could do was to find again the place he had slept so well the night before. This was not very difficult even in the dusky night.

He skirted the wall, came to his first guide, found and crossed the valley stream and descended it until he thought he recognized the slope of clover down which he had run in the morning. He ran up the brae, and there were the solemn cones of the cornricks between him and the sky! A minute more and he had crept through the cathole. Happily, the heap of straw was not yet removed. Gibbie again shot into it like a mole and burrowed to the very center, there coiled himself up, and imagined himself lying in the heart of the rock on which he sat during the storm listening to the thunder winds over his head.

In spite of the cocks in the yard that made it their business to rouse sleepers to their work, he might have slept longer the next morning, for there was no threshing to wake him, had it not been for another kind of cock inside him which bore the same relation to food that the others bore to light. He peeped first, then crept out. All was still except the voices of those same prophet cocks, a moo now and then, and the occasional stamp of a great hoof in the stable. Gibbie clambered up into the loft and, turning the cheeses about until he came upon the one he had gnawed before, again attacked it and enlarged considerably the hole he had already made in it.

He heard a woman nearby and thereupon Gibbie ventured to reconnoiter a little farther. Popping in his head again, he saw that the dairy was open to the roof but the door was in a partition which did not run so high. The place from which the woman entered was ceiled, and the ceiling rested on the partition between it and the dairy; so that from a shelf level with the hole he could easily enough get on the top of the ceiling. Urged by the instinct of the homeless to understand their surroundings, this he presently effected by creeping like a cat along the top shelf.

The ceiling was that of the kitchen and was merely of boards which, being old and shrunken, had here and there a considerable crack between them. Gibbie, peeping through one after another of these cracks, soon saw several things he did not understand. Of such was a barrel churn, which he took for a barrel organ and welcomed as a sign of civilization. The woman was sweeping the room toward the hearth where the peat fire was already burning, a great pot hanging over it and covered with a wooden lid. When the water in it was hot, she poured it into a large wooden dish in which she began to wash other dishes, thus giving the observant Gibbie his first notion of housekeeping. Then she arranged the dishes on shelves and rack, except a few which she placed on the table, put more water on the fire, and disappeared in the dairy.

Thence presently she returned carrying a great jar which, having lifted a lid in the top of the churn, she emptied into it, to Gibbie's astonishment; he was not, therefore, any further astonished that no music issued when she began to turn the handle vigorously. As to what else might be expected Gibbie had not even a mistaken idea. But the butter came quickly that morning, and then he did have another astonishment, for he saw a great mass of something half-solid tumble out where he had seen liquid poured in—not that alone, for the liquid came out again too! But when at length he saw the mass, after being well washed and molded into certain shapes, he recognized it as butter, such as he had seen in shops, and had now and then tasted on the piece given him by some more-than-usually generous housekeeper. Surely he had wandered into a region of plenty! Only now when he saw the woman busy and careful, the idea of things in the country being a sort of common property began to fade from his mind and the perception to wake that they were as the things in the shops, which must not be touched without first paying money for them over a counter.

The butter-making brought to a successful close, the woman proceeded to make porridge for the men's breakfast, and with hungry eyes Gibbie watched that process next. The water in the great pot boiling like a warm volcano, she took handful after handful of meal from a great wooden dish and threw it into the pot, stirring as she threw, until the mess was presently so thick that she could no more move the spurtle in it. Scarcely had she emptied it into another great wooden bowl when Gibbie heard the heavy tramp of the men crossing the yard to consume it.

For the last few minutes, Gibbie's nostrils had been regaled with the delicious odor of the boiling meal; and now his eyes had their turn. Prostrate on the ceiling he lay and watched the splendid spoonfuls tumble out of sight into the throats of four men; all took their spoonfuls from the same dish, but each dipped his spoonful into his private cup of milk before he carried it to his mouth. A little apart sat a boy, whom the woman seemed to favor, having provided him with a plate full of porridge by himself; but the fact was, four were as many as could bicker comfortably or with any chance of fair play.

When the meal was over and he saw the little that was left with all the drops of milk from the cups tumbled into a common receptacle, to be kept, he thought, for the next meal, poor Gibbie felt very empty and forsaken. Sad at heart, he crawled away with nothing before him except a drink of water at the burn.

10

· · · · · · · · · · · · · · · · · ·

Donal Grant

It was now time he should resume his journey up Daurside, and he set out to follow the burn that he might regain the river. It led him into a fine meadow where a number of cattle were feeding. The meadow was not fenced—indeed, little more than marked off on one side from a field of growing corn by a low wall of earth, which was covered with moss and grass and flowers. The cattle were herded by a boy whom Gibbie recognized as the one he had seen as he lay spying through the crack in the ceiling. The boy was reading a book, from which every now and then he lifted his eyes to glance around and see whether any of the cows were wandering beyond their pasture of rye grass and clover. Having, then, all before him, therefore no occasion to look behind, he did not see Gibbie approaching. But as soon as he seemed thoroughly occupied, a certain black cow, with short, sharp horns and a wicked look, gradually edged nearer and nearer to the corn, and it turned suddenly and ran for it, jumping the dyke and plunging into a mad revelry of greed. The cow tore and devoured with all the haste of one that knew she was stealing.

Now Gibbie had been observant enough during his travels to learn that this was against the law and custom of the country—that it was not permitted for a cow to go into a field where there were no others; and like a shot he was after the black marauder. The same instant the herdboy, too, lifting his eyes from his book, saw her and, springing to his feet, caught up his great stick and ran also. He had more than one reason to run, for he understood only too well the dangerous temper of the cow, and saw

already made acquaintance with, and a few quarters of cakes. One of these Donal broke in two, gave Gibbie the half, replaced the other, and sat down again to the book he had been reading. Gibbie seated himself a few yards off, where in silence he ate his piece and gravely regarded Donal. His human soul had of late been starved even more than his body, and it was paradise again to be in such company. Never since his father's death had he looked on a face that drew him as Donal's. For age Donal was getting toward fifteen, and was strongly built and well-grown. A general look of honesty and an attractive expression of reposeful friendliness pervaded his whole appearance. Though conscientious in regard to his work, he was yet in danger of forgetting his duty for minutes together in his book. The chief evil that resulted from it was such an occasional inroad on the corn as had that morning taken place. He knew his master would threaten him with dismissal if he came upon him reading in the field, but he knew also his master was well aware that he did read, and that it was possible to read and yet herd well.

It was easy enough in this same meadow; on one side ran the Lorrie, on another was a stone wall, and on the third, a ditch. Only the cornfield lay virtually unprotected, and there he himself had to be the boundary. And now he sat leaning against the dyke, as if he so held a position of special defense; but he knew well enough that the dullest calf could outflank him and invade, for a few moments at the least, the forbidden pleasure ground. He had gained an ally, however, whose faculty and faithfulness he yet little knew. For Gibbie had begun to comprehend the situation. He could not understand why or how anyone should be absorbed in a book, for all he knew of books was from his one morning of dame-schooling; but he could understand that, if one's attention were so occupied, it must be a great vex to be interrupted continually. Therefore, as Donal watched his book, Gibbie for Donal's sake watched the herd and, as he did so, gently possessed himself of Donal's club. Nor had many minutes passed before Donal, raising his head to look, saw the cursed cow again in the green corn, and Gibbie manfully encountering her with the club, hitting her hard upon head and horns and deftly avoiding every rush she made at him.

"Give her it upon the nose!" Donal shouted in terror as he ran full speed to his aid, abusing Hornie in terms of fiercest vituperation.

But he need not have been so apprehensive. Gibbie heard and obeyed, and the next moment Hornie had turned tail and was fleeing back to the safety of the lawful meadow.

"Hech, creature! You must come from fighting folks!" said Donal, regarding him with fresh admiration.

Gibbie laughed; but he had been sorely put to it and big drops were coursing fast down his sweet face. Donal took the club from him and, rushing at Hornie, belabored her well, and drove her quite to the other side of the field. He then returned and resumed his book, while Gibbie again sat down nearby and watched both Donal and his charge. Surely

Gibbie had at last found his vocation on Daurside, with both man and beast for his special care!

By and by Donal raised his head once more, but this time it was to regard Gibbie. It had gradually sunk into him that the appearance and character of the boy were peculiar. He had regarded him as a little tramp whose people were not far off, and who would soon get tired of herding and rejoin his companions; but while he read, a strange feeling of the presence of the boy had been growing upon him. He seemed to feel his eyes without seeing them; and when Gibbie rose to look how the cattle were distributed, he became vaguely uneasy lest the boy should be going away. For already he had begun to feel him a humble kind of guardian angel. He had already that day enjoyed a longer spell of his book than any day since he had been herdboy at the Mains of Glashruach.

For a minute or two he sat and gazed at him. My reader must think how vastly, in all his poverty, Donal was Gibbie's superior in the social scale. He earned his own food and shelter and nearly four pounds a year besides, lived as well as he could wish, dressed warmly, was able for his work, and imagined it no hardship. Then he had a father and mother whom he went to see every Saturday and of whom he was as proud as son could be—a father who was the priest of the family, and fed sheep; a mother who was the prophetess, and kept house ever an open refuge for her children. Poor Gibbie earned nothing—never had earned more than a penny at a time in his life, and had never dreamed of having a claim to such penny. Nobody seemed to care for him, give him anything, do anything for him. Yet there he sat before Donal's eyes, full of service, of smiles, of contentment.

Donal took up his book, but laid it down again and gazed at Gibbie. Several times he tried to return to his reading, but as often resumed his contemplation of the boy. At length it struck him as something more than shyness would account for the fact that he had not yet heard a word from the lips of the child, even when running after the cows. He must watch him more closely.

By now it was his dinnertime. Again he untied his handkerchief and gave Gibbie what he judged a fair share for his bulk—namely, about a third of the whole. Philosopher as he was, however, he could not help sighing a little when he got to the end of his diminished portion. But he was better than comforted when Gibbie offered him all that yet remained to him; and the smile with which Donal refused it made Gibbie as happy as a prince would like to be. What a day it had been for Gibbie! A whole human being, and some five and twenty four-legged creatures besides to take care of!

After the dinner, Donal gravitated to his book, and Gibbie resumed the executive. Some time had passed when Donal, glancing up, saw Gibbie lying flat on his chest, staring at something in the grass. He slid himself quietly nearer and discovered it was a daisy—one by itself alone; there were not many in the field. Like a mother leaning over her child Gibbie was gazing at it. The daisy was not a cold white one, neither was it a red one; it was just a perfect daisy.

"Can you read, boy?" asked Donal.

Gibbie shook his head.

"Can't you speak, man?"

Again Gibbie shook his head.

"Can you hear?"

Gibbie burst out laughing. He knew that he heard better than other people.

"Listen to this, then," said Donal.

He took his book from the grass, and in a chant read a Danish ballad as translated by Sir Walter Scott. Gibbie's eyes grew wider and wider as he listened; it seemed as if his soul were looking out of doors and windows at once—but a puzzled soul that understood nothing of what it saw. When Donal ceased, he remained open-mouthed and motionless for a time; then, drawing himself over the grass to Donal's feet, he raised his head and peeped above his knees at the book. A moment only he gazed and drew back with a hungry sigh; he had seen nothing in the book like what Donal had been drawing from it.

"Would you like to hear it again?" asked Donal.

Gibbie's face answered with a flash and Donal read the poem again. Gibbie's delight returned greater than before, for now something like a dawn began to appear among the cloudy words. Donal read it a third time and closed the book, for it was almost the hour for driving the cattle home.

How much Gibbie even then understood of the lovely old ballad it is impossible to say. The waking up of a human soul to know itself arouses so heavy a sense of marvel and inexplicable mystery. When by slow, filmy unveilings life grew clearer to Gibbie, and he not only knew but knew that he knew, his thoughts always went back to that day in the meadow with Donal Grant as the beginning of his knowledge of beautiful things in the world of man.

Donal rose and went, driving the cattle home, and Gibbie lay where he had again thrown himself upon the grass. When he lifted his head Donal and the cows had vanished.

Donal had looked all around as he left the meadow, and seeing the boy nowhere, had concluded he had gone to his people. The impression Gibbie had made upon him faded a little during the evening. For when he reached home and had watered them, he had to tie up the animals, each in its stall, and make them comfortable for the night; next, eat his own supper; then learn a proposition of Euclid and go to bed.

11

·······················

Apprenticeship

*H*ungering minds come of peasant people as often as of any and have appeared in Scotland as many times, I fancy, as in other nations. Cheap as education then was in Scotland, the parents of Donal Grant had never dreamed of sending a son to college. It was difficult for them to save even the few quarterly shillings that paid the fees of the parish schoolmaster.

After he left school, however, and got a place as herd-keeper, he fared better; for at the Mains he found a friend and helper in Fergus Duff, his master's second son, who was then at home from college. Partly that he was delicate in health, partly that he was something of a gentleman, he took no share with his father and elder brother in the work of the farm, although he was at the Mains from the beginning of April to the end of October. He would have been much more of a man if he had thought less of being a gentleman. He had taken a liking to Donal; having found in him a strong desire after every kind of knowledge, he had sought to enliven the tedium by imparting to him of the treasures he had gathered. They were not great and could never have carried Donal far, for he himself was only a respectable student. Happily, however, Donal needed but to have the outermost shell of a thing broken for him, and that Fergus could do. By and by Donal would begin breaking shells for himself.

But perhaps the best thing Fergus did for him was to lend him books. Donal had an altogether unappeasable hunger after every form of litera-ture, and this hunger Fergus fed with the books of the house. To find him-self now in the reversed relation of superior and teacher to the little out-cast woke in Donal an altogether new and strange feeling; yet gratitude to his master had but turned itself around and had become tenderness to his pupil.

After Donal left him in the field, Gibbie lay on the grass, as happy as a child could well be. A loving hand laid on his feet or legs would have found them like ice; but where was the matter so long as he never thought of them? He could have eaten a dozen potatoes; but of what mighty con-sequence is hunger so long as it neither absorbs the thought nor causes faintness? The sun, however, was going down behind a great mountain, which cast a huge shadow, made of darkness and haunted with cold. Slid-ing across the river, over valley and field, nothing stayed its silent wave until it covered Gibbie with the blanket of the dark, under which he could not long forget that he was in a body to which cold is unfriendly. It was too cold that night to sleep in the fields when he knew where to find warmth. Like a fox into his hole, the child would creep into the corner where God had stored sleep for him; back he went to the barn, gently trotting, and wormed himself through the cathole.

The straw was gone! But he remembered the hay. And, happily, for he was tired, there stood the ladder against the loft. Up he went, nor turned aside to the cheese; but sleep was common property still. He groped his way forward through the dark loft until he found the hay, when at once he burrowed into it like a sandfish into the wet sand and slept until the stirring horses woke him.

He scrambled out on the top of the hay and looked down. The thing he would like best to do would be to look through the ceiling again and watch the woman at her work. Then, too, he would again smell the boiling porridge and the burning of the little sprinkles of meal that fell into the fire. Carefully he crept through the hole and softly round the shelf, whence he peeped once more down into the kitchen. His precautions had been so far unnecessary for, as yet, it lay unvisited, as witnessed by its disorder. Suddenly the thought came to Gibbie that here was a chance for him— here a path back to the world.

He got again upon the shelf and, with every precaution lest he should even touch a milkpan, descended by the lower shelves to the floor. There finding the door only latched, he entered the kitchen and proceeded to do everything he had seen the woman do, as nearly in her style as he could. He swept the floor and dusted the seats, the windowsill and the table with an apron he found left on a chair, then arranged everything tidily and roused the rested fire. He had just concluded that the only way to get the great pot full of water upon it would be to hang first the pot on the chain and then fill it with the water, when his sharp ears caught sounds and then heard approaching feet. He darted into the dairy, and in a few seconds had clambered upon the ceiling and was lying flat across the joists, with his eyes to the most commanding crack he had discovered. He was anxious to know how his service would be received. When Jean Mavor—she was the farmer's half sister—opened the door, she stopped short and stared; the kitchen was not as she had left it the night before!

"Hoot! I must have been walking in my sleep!" said Jean aloud. "Or maybe that good laddie Donal Grant's been giving me a helping hand. The lad's good enough to do anything."

Eagerly Gibbie now watched her motion and, bent upon learning, nothing escaped him; he would do much better next morning! At length the men came in to breakfast and he thought to enjoy the sight; but alas! it wrought so with his hunger as to make him feel sick, and he crept away out into the cornyard where he sought the henhouse. But there was no food there yet and he must not linger near; for if he were discovered they would drive him away, and he would lose Donal Grant. He had not seen him at breakfast, for indeed he seldom during the summer had a meal except supper in the house. Gibbie, therefore, as he could not eat, ran to the burn and drank. He must go to Donal. The sight of him would help him to bear his hunger.

The first indication Donal had of his proximity was the rush of Hornie past him in flight out of the corn. Gibbie was pursuing her with stones for lack of a stick. Thoroughly ashamed of himself, Donal threw his book from him and ran to meet Gibbie.

"You mustn't fling stones, creature," he said. "Haith, it's not for me to find fault though," he added, "sitting reading books like the gowk I am, and letting the beasts run wild in the corn when I'm paid to keep them out of it!"

Gibbie's response was to set off at full speed for the place where Donal had been sitting. He was back in a moment with the book, which he pressed into Donal's hand, while from the other he withdrew his club. This he brandished aloft once or twice, then starting at a steady trot, speedily circled the herd and returned to his adopted master—only to start again, however, and attack Hornie whom he drove from the corn-side of the meadow right over the other; she was already afraid of him. After watching him for a time, Donal came to the conclusion that he himself could not do more. He therefore left all to Gibbie and did not once look up for a whole hour. Everything went just as it should; and not once, all that day, did Hornie again get a mouthful of the grain. It was rather a heavy morning for Gibbie, though, who had eaten nothing, for every time he came near Donal, he saw the handkerchief bulging in the grass, which a little girl had brought and left for him. But he was a rare one both at waiting and at going without.

At last, however, Donal grew hungry himself. He laid down his book, called out to Gibbie, "Creature, it's dinnertime," and took his bundle. Gibbie drew near with sparkling eyes. There was no selfishness in his hunger, for at the worst pass he had ever reached, he would have shared what he had with another; but he looked so eager that Donal perceived he was ravenous and made haste to undo the knots of the handkerchief which Mistress Jean appeared that day to have tied with more than ordinary vigor before she intrusted the bundle to the foreman's daughter. When the last knot yielded, he gazed with astonishment at the amount and variety of provisions disclosed.

"Losh!" he explained, "the mistress must have known there were two of us."

He little thought that what she had given him beyond the usual supply was an acknowledgment of services rendered by those same hands into which he now delivered a share, on the ground of other service altogether. It is not always, even where there is no mistake as to the person who deserved it, that the reward reaches the doer so directly.

Before the day was over, Donal gave his helper more and other pay for his service. Choosing a fit time when the cattle were well together and in good position, he took from his pocket a volume of ballads and said, "Sit down, creature. I'm going to read to you."

Gibbie dropped on his crossed legs like a lark to the ground and sat motionless. Donal, after deliberate search, began to read and Gibbie to listen; and it would be hard to determine which found the more pleasure in his part. For Donal had seldom had a listener—and never one so utterly absorbed.

When the hour came for the cattle to go home, Gibbie again remained behind, waiting until all should be still at the farm. He lay on the dyke brooding over what he had heard and wondering how it was that Donal got all those strange beautiful words and sounds and stories out of the book.

12
• • • • • • • • • • • • • • • • • •

The Broonie

I must not linger over degrees and phases. Every morning Gibbie got into the kitchen in good time; and not only did he do more and more of the work, but he did it more and more to the satisfaction of Jean, until, short of the actual making of the porridge, he did everything antecedent to the men's breakfast. Without further question she attributed all the aid she received to the goodness of Donal Grant and continued to make acknowledgment of the same in both variety and quantity of victuals, whence as has been shown the real laborer received his due reward.

Until he had thoroughly mastered his work, Gibbie persisted in regarding matters from his loophole in the ceiling. Having at length learned the art of making butter, he soon arrived at some degree of perfection in it. But when at last one morning he not only churned but washed and made it up entirely to Jean's satisfaction, she did begin to wonder how a mere boy could both have such perseverance and be so clever at a woman's work. For now she entered the kitchen every morning without a question of finding the fire burning, the water boiling, the place clean and tidy, the supper dishes well washed and disposed on shelf and rack; her own part was merely to see that proper cloths were handy to so thorough a user of them. She took no one into her confidence on the matter; it was enough, she judged, that she and Donal understood each other.

And now if Gibbie had contented himself with rendering this house service in return for the shelter of the barn and its hay, he might have enjoyed both longer; but from the position of his night quarters he came gradually to understand the work of the stable also. Before long the men, who were quite ignorant of anything similar taking place in the house, began to observe, more to their wonder than satisfaction, that one or other of their horses was generally groomed before his man came to him; that often there was hay in their racks which they had not given them; and that the master's white horse every morning showed signs of having had some attention paid him that could not be accounted for. The result was much talk and speculation, suspicion and offense; for all were jealous of their rights, their duty and their dignity in relation to their horses. No man was at liberty to do a thing to or for any but his own pair. Even the brightening of the harness brass, in which Gibbie sometimes indulged, was an offense. Many were the useless traps laid for the offender, many the futile attempts to surprise him. As Gibbie never did anything except for half an hour or so while the men were sound asleep or at breakfast, he escaped discovery.

All day he was with Donal and took from him the greater part of his labor; Donal had never had such time for reading. In return Donal gave him his dinner, and Gibbie could do very well upon one meal a day. Donal paid him also in poetry. It never came into his head, seeing Gibbie never spoke, to teach him to read. Donal soon gave up attempting to learn anything from him as to his place or people or history, for to all questions in that direction, Gibbie only looked grave and shook his head. As often, on the other hand, as Donal tried to learn where Gibbie spent the night, he received for answer only one of the little fellow's merriest laughs.

Nor was larger time for reading the sole benefit Gibbie conferred upon Donal. Such was the avidity and growing intelligence with which the little, naked town savage listened to what Donal read to him that his presence added to Donal's own live soul of thought and feeling. From listening to his own lips through Gibbie's ears, he not only understood many things better but, perceiving what things must puzzle Gibbie, came sometimes to his astonishment to see that, in fact, he did not understand them himself. Thus the bond between the boy and the child grew closer—even though Donal imagined now and then that Gibbie might be a creature of some speechless race other than human.

It was not all fine weather up there among the mountains in the beginning of summer. In the first week of June even, there was sleet and snow in the wind—the tears of the vanquished Winter, as he fled across the sea from Norway or Iceland. Then would Donal's heart be sore for Gibbie, when he saw his poor rags blown about like streamers in the wind. Donal had neither greatcoat, plaid, nor umbrella wherewith to shield Gibbie's raggedness. Once in great pity he pulled off his jacket and threw it on Gibbie's shoulders. But the shout of laughter that burst from the boy as he flung the jacket from him and rushed away into the middle of the feeding herd, a shout that came from no rudeness but from the very depths of delight stirred by the loving-kindness of the act, startled Donal out of his pity into brief anger. But Gibbie dived under the belly of a favorite cow and, peering out sideways from under her while the cow went on undisturbed, showed such an innocent countenance of merriment that the pride of Donal's hurt melted away and his laughter echoed Gibbie's.

Things had gone on in this way for several weeks when one morning the men came in to breakfast all out of temper together, complaining loudly of the person unknown who would persist in interfering with their work. They were the louder that their suspicions fluttered about Fergus, who was rather overbearing with them and therefore not a favorite. He was in reality not at all a likely person to bend back or defile hands over such labor, and their pitching upon him the object of their suspicion showed how much at a loss they were. Their only ground for suspecting him was that there was no other by any imagination they could suspect. Had he been in good favor with them, they would have thought no harm of most of the things they thought he did, especially as it eased their work; but he carried himself high, they said, doing nothing but ride over the farm and pick out every fault he could find—to show how sharp he was and look as if he could do better than any of them; and they fancied he carried an evil report to his father, and that this underhand work in the stable must be part of some sly scheme for bringing them into disgrace. And now at last had come the worst thing of all: Gibbie had discovered the cornbin, and having no notion but that everything in the stable was for the delectation of the horses, had been feeding them largely with oats—a delicacy with which, in the plenty of other provisions, they were very sparingly supplied; and the consequences had begun to show themselves in the increased unruliness of the more wayward among them. Gibbie had long given up resorting to the ceiling during their breakfast and remained in utter ignorance of the storm that was brewing because of him.

The same day brought things nearly to a crisis; for the overfed Snowball, proving too much for Fergus's horsemanship, came rushing home at a fierce gallop without him, having indeed left him in a ditch by the roadside. The remark thereupon made by the men in his hearing, that it was his own fault, led him to ask questions. He came gradually to know what they attributed to him, and was indignant at the imputation of such an employment of his mornings to one who had his studies to attend to, scarcely a wise line of defense where the truth would have been more credible as well as convincing—namely, that at the time when those works could alone be effected, he lay as lost a creature as ever sleep could make of a man.

In the evening Jean sought a word with Donal and expressed her surprise that he should be able to do everybody's work about the place, warning him it would be said he did it at the expense of his own. But what could he mean, she said, by wasting the good grain to put devilry into the horses? Donal stared in utter bewilderment. He knew perfectly that to the men suspicion of him was as impossible as to one of themselves. Did he not sleep in the same chamber with them?

Then came anew the question, utterly unanswerable now—who could it be that did not only all her morning work but, with a passion for labor insatiable, part of that of the men also? With the men, she knew her nephew better than to imagine for a moment it could be he. A good enough lad, she judged him, but not good enough for that. He was too fond of his own comfort to dream of helping other people! But now, having betrayed herself to Donal, she wisely went further and secured herself by placing full confidence in him. She laid open the whole matter, confessing that she had imagined her ministering angel to be Donal himself;

now she had not even a conjecture after the person of her secret servant.

At length after a pause, her soul seemed to return into her deep-set grey eyes, and in a voice low and solemn and fraught with mystery, she said, "Donal, it's the broonie!"

Donal's mouth opened wide at the word. He had listened in his time to a multitude of strange tales and, Celtic in blood, had been inclined to believe many of them.

Jean Mavor came from a valley far in the Gormgarnet mountains, where in her youth she had heard yet stranger tales than had ever come to Donal's ears. Her brother, a hardheaded Highlander, would have laughed the notion to scorn. For the cowherd, however, as I say, the idea had no small attraction.

"Do you really think it, mem?" said Donal in wonder.

"Think what?" retorted Jean, instantly sharply jealous of being compromised.

"Do you really think there are such creatures as broonies, Mistress Jean?" said Donal.

"Who knows what there is and what there isn't?" returned Jean. She was not going to commit herself either way. Even had she imagined herself above believing such things, she would not have dared to say so. "But you hold your tongue, laddie," she went on, "and go to your work."

But either Mistress Jean's caution came too late and someone had overheard her suggestion or the idea was already abroad, for that very night it began to be reported upon the nearer farms that the Mains of Glashruach was haunted by a broonie who did all the work for both men and maids.

Quick at disappearing as Gibbie was, a little cunning on the part of Jean might soon have entrapped the broonie; but a considerable touch of fear was now added to her other motives for continuing to spend a couple of hours longer in bed than had formerly been her custom. So for yet a few days things went on much as usual; Gibbie saw no sign that his presence was suspected or that his doings were offensive.

One morning the long, thick mane of the horse Snowball was found carefully plaited up in innumerable locks. This was properly elf-work, but no fairies had been heard of on Daurside for many a long year. The broonie, on the other hand, was already in everyone's mouth—only a stray one, probably, that had wandered from some old valley away in the mountains. The rumor spread in long, slow ripples, till at last one of them struck the laird, where he sat at luncheon in the House of Glashruach.

13

•••••••••••••••••••

The Ambush

*T*homas Galbraith was by birth Thomas Durrant but had married an heiress by whom he came into possession of Glashruach and had, according to previous agreement, taken her name. When she died, he mourned her loss as well as he could, but was consoled by feeling himself now first master of both position and possession when the ladder by which he had attained them was removed. Had he been a little more sensitive still, he would have felt that the property was then his daughter's, and his only through her. But this he failed to consider.

Thoroughly respectable and a little devout, Mr. Galbraith was a good deal more of a Scotsman than a Christian. Growth was a doctrine unembodied in his creed; he turned from everything new.

To his servants and tenants he was, what he thought, just. In general expression he looked displeased but meant to look dignified. He had no turn for farming and therefore let out all his land, yet liked to interfere, and as much as possible kept a personal jurisdiction.

There was one thing, however, which if it did not throw the laird into a passion brought him nearer to the outer verge of displeasure than any other, and that was anything whatever to which he could affix the name of superstition.

He was seated with a game pie in front of him, over the top of which his daughter Ginevra was visible. The girl never sat nearer her father at meals than the whole length of the table, where she occupied her mother's place. She was a solemn-looking child of eight or nine, dressed in a brown merino frock of the plainest description. To the first glance she did not look a very interesting or attractive child; but looked at twice she was sure to draw the eyes a third time. Her father was never harsh to her, yet she looked rather frightened of him; but then he was cold, very cold. It troubled Ginevra greatly that when she asked herself whether she loved her father better than anybody else as she believed she ought, she became immediately doubtful whether she loved him at all.

She was eating porridge and milk. With spoon arrested in midpassage, she stopped suddenly and said, "Papa, what's a broonie?"

"What foolish person has been insinuating such contemptible superstition into your silly head?" he asked. "Tell me, child," he continued, "that I may put a stop to it at once."

"They say," said Ginevra, "there's a broonie at the Mains, who does all the work."

"What is the meaning of this, Joseph?" said Mr. Galbraith, turning from her to the butler with the air of rebuke, which was almost habitual to him.

"The meanin' o' what, sir?"

"I ask you, Joseph," answered the laird, "what this—this outbreak of superstition imports? You must be aware that nothing in the world could annoy me more than that Miss Galbraith should learn folly in her father's house. Pray acquaint me with the whole matter."

Joseph therewith proceeded to report what he had heard reported, which was in the main the truth, considerably exaggerated—that the work of the house was done overnight by invisible hands and the work of the stables too. In the latter, cantrips were played as well, some of the men talked of leaving the place, and Mr. Duff's own horse Snowball was nearly out of his mind with fear.

The laird clenched his teeth and for a whole minute said nothing. "It is one of the men themselves," he said at last. "Or some ill-designed neighbor," he added. "But I shall soon be at the bottom of it. Go to the Mains at once, Joseph, and ask young Fergus Duff to be so good as to stop over as soon as he conveniently can."

Fergus was pleased enough to be sent for by the laird, and soon told him all he knew from his aunt and the men, confessing that he himself had been too lazy of a morning to take any steps toward personal acquaintance with the facts. But he added that as Mr. Galbraith took an interest in the matter, he would be only too happy to carry out any suggestion he might think proper to make on the subject.

"Fergus," returned the laird, "do you imagine things inanimate can of themselves change their relations in space?"

"Certainly not, sir," answered Fergus solemnly.

"Then, Fergus, let me assure you that to discover by what agency these apparent wonders are effected, you have merely to watch. If you fail, I will myself come to your assistance."

Fergus at once undertook to watch. But he went home not quite so comfortable as he had gone; for he did not altogether, notwithstanding his unbelief in the so-called supernatural, relish the approaching situation. Belief and unbelief are not always quite plainly distinguishable from each other, and fear is not always certain which of them is his mother. He was not the less resolved, however, to sit up all night if necessary. Not even to himself did he confess that he felt frightened, for he was a youth of nearly eighteen; but he could not quite hide from himself the fact that he antici-pated no pleasure in the duty which lay before him.

For more reasons than one, Fergus judged it prudent to tell not even Auntie Jean of his intention; but waiting until the house was quiet, he stole softly from his room and repaired to the kitchen—where he sat down, took his book, and began to read. He read and read but no broonie came. His candle burned into the socket. He lighted another and read again. Still no broonie appeared and, hard and straight as was the wooden chair on which he sat, he began to doze. He began to feel very eerie as deeper and deeper grew the night around him. The night was dark—no moon and many clouds. Not a sound came from the close. The cattle, the horses, the pigs, the cocks and hens, the very cats and rats seemed asleep. There was not a rustle in the thatch, a creak in the couples. It was well, for the slightest noise would have been in great danger of scaring the household.

The hours passed slowly. Fergus dozed, read, and sat. When the grey of the dawn appeared, he said to himself he would lie down on the bench a while, he was so tired of sitting; he would not sleep. He lay down and in a moment was asleep. The light grew and grew, and the broonie came—a different broonie indeed from the one he had pictured. But as soon as he opened the door of the dairy, he was warned by the loud breathing of the sleeper and swiftly retreated. The same instant Fergus woke, stretched himself, saw it was broad daylight and, with his brain muddled by fatigue and sleep combined, crawled shivering to bed. Then in came the broonie again; and when Jean Mavor entered, there was her work done as usual.

Fergus was hours late for breakfast, and when he went into the commonroom, he found his aunt alone there.

"Well, Auntie," he said, "I think I scared your broonie!"

"Did you, man? Ay!—Then you did the work yourself to save your Auntie Jean's old bones?"

"No, no! I was too tired for that. And so would you have been yourself if you had been sitting up all night."

"Who did it, then?"

"Just yourself, I'm thinkin', Auntie."

"Never a finger of mine was laid on it, Fergus. If you scared one broonie, another came; for there's the work done, the same's ever!"

"Blast the creature!" cried Fergus.

"Whisht, whisht, laddie! He might be hearin' you this very minute."

"I beg your pardon, Auntie, but it's so very provoking!" returned Fergus, and therewith recounted the tale of his night's watch, omitting mention only of his feelings throughout the vigil.

As soon as he had had his breakfast, he went to carry his report to Glashruach.

The laird was vexed, and told him he must sleep well before night, and watch to better purpose.

The next night Fergus's terror returned in full force; but he watched thoroughly notwithstanding, and when his aunt entered she found him there, and her kitchen in a mess. He had caught no broonie, it was true, but neither had a stroke of her work been done. The floor was unswept; not a dish had been washed; it was churning-day, but the cream stood in the jar in the dairy, not the butter in the pan on the kitchen dresser. Jean could not quite see the good or the gain of it. She had begun to feel like a lady, she said to herself, and now she must tuck up her sleeves and set to work as before.

"You must add cunning to courage, my young friend," said Mr. Galbraith after another conference; and the result was that Fergus went home resolved on yet another attempt.

He felt much inclined to associate Donal with him in his watch this time, but was too desirous of proving his courage both to himself and to the world to yield to the suggestion of his fear. He went to bed with a book immediately after the noonday meal, and rose in time for supper.

There was a large wooden press in the kitchen, standing out from the wall; this with the next wall made a little recess in which there was just room for a chair; and in that recess Fergus seated himself, in the easiest chair he could get into it. He then opened wide the door of the press, and it covered him entirely.

This night would have been the dreariest of all for him, the laird having insisted that he should watch in the dark had he not speedily fallen fast asleep, and slept all night—so well that he woke at the first noise Gibbie made.

It was a broad, clear morning, but his heart beat so loud and fast with apprehension and curiosity mingled that for a few moments Fergus dared not stir, but sat listening breathless to the movement beside him, nonetheless appalling that it was so quiet. Recovering himself a little, he cautiously moved the door of the press and peeped out.

He saw nothing so frightful as he had, in spite of himself, anticipated, but was not therefore, perhaps, the less astonished. The dread broonie of his idea shrunk to a tiny, ragged urchin with a wonderful head of hair, azure eyes, and deft hands, noiselessly bustling about on bare feet. He watched him at his leisure, watched him keenly, assured that any moment he could spring upon him.

As he watched, his wonder sank. As he continued to watch, an evil cloud of anger at the presumption began to gather in his mental atmosphere and was probably the cause of some movement by which his chair gave a loud creak. Without even looking round, Gibbie darted out. Instantly Fergus was after him. Gibbie rushed from the house and across the corner of the yard, and the next Fergus saw of him was the fluttering of his rags in the wind and the flashing of his white skin in the sun as he fled across the clover field. Gibbie was a better runner for his size than Fergus, and in better training too; but alas! Fergus's legs were nearly twice as long as Gibbie's. Fergus behind him was growing more and more angry as he gained upon him but felt his breath failing him. Just at the bridge to the iron gate to Glashruach he caught him at last, and sank on the parapet exhausted. The smile with which Gibbie, too much out of breath to laugh, confessed himself vanquished would have disarmed one more hardhearted than Fergus had the fellow not lost his temper, and the answer Gibbie received to his smile was a box on the ear that bewildered him. Fergus began to ply him with questions; but no answer following, his wrath rose again, and again he boxed both his ears—without better result.

Then came the question, what was he to do with the redoubted broonie, now that he had him? He was ashamed to show himself as the captor of such a miserable culprit, but the little rascal deserved punishment, and the laird would require him at his hands. He turned upon his prisoner and told him he was an impudent rascal. Gibbie had recovered again and was able once more to smile a little. He had been guilty of burglary, said Fergus; and Gibbie smiled. He could be sent to prison for it, said Fergus; and Gibbie smiled—but this time a very grave smile. Fergus took him by the collar, which amounted to nearly a third part of the jacket, and shook him till he had half torn that third from the other two; then opened the gate and, holding him by the back of the neck, walked him up the drive, every now and then giving him a fierce shake that jarred Gibbie's teeth. Thus, over the old gravel, mossy and damp and grassy, between rowan and birch and pine and larch, looking every inch the outcast he was, did Sir Gilbert Galbraith approach the house of his ancestors for the first time.

14

. . . .

Punishment

The house he was approaching had a little the look of a prison. Of the more ancient portion, the windows were very small, and every corner had a turret with a conical cap roof. Although he had received from Fergus such convincing proof that he was regarded as a culprit, Gibbie had no dread of evil awaiting him. The highest embodiment of the law with which he had acquaintance was the police, and from not one of them in all the city had he ever had a harsh word; his conscience was as void of offense as ever it had been, and the law consequently, notwithstanding the threats of Fergus, had for him no terrors.

The laird was an early riser, and therefore regarded the mere getting up early as a virtue, altogether irrespective of how the "time thus redeemed," as he called it, was spent. This morning, as it turned out, it would have been better spent in sleep. He was talking to his gamekeeper when Fergus appeared holding the dwindled broonie by the huge collar of his tatters. A more innocent-looking malefactor surely never appeared before awful Justice! Only he was in rags, and there are others besides dogs whose judgments go by appearance. Mr. Galbraith was one of them. He smiled a grim and ugly smile.

"So this is your vaunted broonie, Mr. Duff!" he said, and stood looking down upon Gibbie.

"It's all the broonie I could lay hands on, sir," answered Fergus. "I took him in the act."

"Boy," said the laird, rolling his eyes, more unsteady than usual with indignation, in the direction of Gibbie, "what have you to say for yourself."

Gibbie had nothing to say. He smiled, looking up fearlessly in the face of the magistrate, so awful in his own esteem.

"What is your name?" asked the laird, speaking yet more sternly.

Gibbie still smiled and was silent, looking straight into his questioner's eyes. He dreaded nothing from the laird. Fergus had beaten him, but Fergus he classed with the bigger boys in the city who had occasionally treated him roughly; this was a man, and men, except they were foreign sailors or drunk, were never unkind. He had no idea of his silence causing annoyance. Everybody in the city had known he could not answer; and now when Fergus and the laird persisted in questioning him, he thought they were making kindly game of him, and smiled the more. Nor was there much about Mr. Galbraith to rouse a suspicion of the contrary; for he made a great virtue of keeping his temper when most he caused other people to lose theirs.

"I see the young vagabond is as impertinent as he is vicious," he said at last, finding that to no interrogation could he draw forth any other response than a smile. "Here, Angus," he said, turning to the gamekeeper, "take him into the coachhouse and teach him a little behavior. A touch or two of the whip will find his tongue for him."

Angus seized the little gentleman by the neck as if he had been a polecat, and at arm's length walked him unresistingly into the coachhouse. There, with one vigorous tug, he tore the jacket from his back, and his only other garment, dependent thereupon by some device known only to Gibbie, fell from him. He stood in helpless nakedness smiling still; he had never done anything shameful, therefore had no acquaintance with shame. But when the scowling keeper approached him with a heavy cart whip in his hand, he cast his eyes down at his white sides, very white between his brown arms and brown legs, and then lifted them in a mute appeal, which somehow looked as if it were for somebody else, against what he could no longer fail to perceive the man's intent. But he had no notion of what the thing threatened amounted to. He had had few hard blows in his time and never felt a whip.

"You devil's child!" cried the fellow, clenching the cruel teeth of one who loved not his brother, "I'll let you know what comes of breaking into honest people's houses and taking things that are not your own!"

A vision of the gnawed cheese, which he had never touched since the ideas of its being property awoke in him, rose before Gibbie's mental eyes, and inwardly he bowed to the punishment. But the look he had fixed on Angus was not without effect, for the man was a father, though a severe one, and was not all a brute. He turned and changed the cart whip for a gig one with a broken shaft which lay near. It was well for himself that he did so, for the other would probably have killed Gibbie. When the blow fell the child shivered all over, his face turned white, and without uttering even a moan he doubled up and dropped senseless. A swollen cincture, like a red snake, had risen all round his waist, and from one spot in it the blood was oozing. It looked as if the lash had cut him in two.

The blow had stung Gibbie's heart and it had ceased to beat. But the gamekeeper understood vagrants! The young blackguard was only shaming!

"Up with you, you devil! or I'll scar you," he said from between his teeth, lifting the whip for a second blow.

Just as the stroke fell, marking him from the nape all down the spine, a piercing shriek assailed Angus's ears, and his arm, which had mechanically raised itself for a third blow, hung arrested.

The same moment in at the coachhouse door shot Ginevra, as white as Gibbie. She darted to where he lay and there stood over him, arms rigid and hands clenched hard, shivering as he had shivered and sending from her body shriek after shriek.

"Go away, missie!" cried Angus, who had respect for this child, though he had not yet learned to respect childhood; "he's a course creature and must have a whipping."

But Ginevra was deaf to his evil charming. She stopped her cries, however, to help Gibbie up, and took one of his hands to raise him. But his arm hung limp and motionless; she let it go; it dropped like a stick and again she began to shriek. Angus laid his hand on her shoulder. She turned on him and, opening her mouth wide, screamed at him like a wild animal, with all the hatred of mingled love and fear; then she threw herself on the boy, and covered his body with her own. Angus, stooping to remove her, saw Gibbie's face, and became uncomfortable.

"He's dead! He's dead! You've killed him, Angus! You're an evil man!" she cried fiercely. "I hate you. I'll tell on you. I'll tell my papa."

"Hoot, missie!" said Angus. "It was on your own papa's orders I gave him the whip, and he well deserved it, besides. And if you don't go away and be a good young lady, I'll give him more yet."

"I'll tell God!" shrieked Ginevra with fresh energy of defensive love and wrath.

Again he sought to remove her, but she clung so, with both legs and arms, to the insensible Gibbie that he could but lift both together and had to leave her alone.

"If you dare to touch him again, Angus, I'll bite you—bite you—bite you!" she screamed in a wild crescendo.

The laird and Fergus had walked away together, perhaps neither of them quite comfortable at the orders given, but the one too self-sufficient to recall them and the other too submissive to interfere. They heard the cries, nevertheless, and had they known them for Ginevra's would have rushed to the spot; but fierce emotion had utterly changed her voice. Ginevra's shrieks brought Gibbie to himself. Faintly he opened his eyes and stared, stupid with growing pain, at the tear-blurred face beside him. In the confusion of his thoughts, he fancied the pain he felt was Ginevra's, not his, and sought to comfort her, stroking her cheek with feeble hand and putting up his mouth to kiss her. But Angus, utterly scandalized at the proceeding, and restored to energy by seeing that the boy was alive, caught her up suddenly and carried her off—struggling, writhing, and scratching like a cat.

The moment she thus disappeared, Gibbie began to apprehend that she was suffering for him, not he for her. His whole body bore testimony to frightful abuse. This was some horrible place inhabited by men such as those that killed Sambo! He must fly. But would they hurt the little girl? He thought not—she was at home. He started to spring to his feet but fell back almost powerless; then he tried more cautiously and got up wearily, for the pain and the terrible shock seemed to have taken the strength out of every limb. Once on his feet, he could scarcely stoop to pick up his remnant of trousers without again falling, and the effort made him groan with distress. He was in the act of trying in vain to stand on one foot, so as to get the other into the garment, when he fancied he heard the step of his executioner, doubtless returning to resume his torture. He dropped the rag and darted out the door, forgetting aches and stiffness and agony. All naked as he was, he fled like the wind, unseen of any eye.

He ran he knew not whither, feeling nothing but the desire first to get into some covert and then to run farther. His first rush was for the shrubbery, his next across the little park to the wood beyond. He did not feel the wind of his running on his bare skin. He did not feel the hunger that had made him so unable to bear the lash. On and on he ran. At length he came where a high wall joining some water formed a boundary. The water was a brook from the mountain, here widening and deepening into a still pool. He threw himself in and swam straight across; ever after that, swimming seemed to him as natural as walking.

Then first awoke a faint sense of safety; for on the other side he was knee deep in heather. He was on the wild hill, with miles on miles of cover! He would get right into the heather and lie with it all around and over him till the night came. Where he would go then he did not know. But it was all one, he could go anywhere. Donal must mind his cows, and the men must mind the horses, and Mistress Jean must mind her kitchen, but Sir Gibbie could go where he pleased. He would go up Daurside; but he would not go just at once; that man might be on the outlook for him.

Thus he communed with himself as he went over the knoll. On the other side he chose a tall patch of heather and crept under. How nice and warm and kind the heather felt, though it did hurt the weals dreadfully sometimes.

And now Sir Gibbie, though not much poorer than he had been, really possessed nothing separable from himself, except his hair and his nails. His sole other possession was a negative quantity—his hunger, namely, for he had not even a meal in his body; he had eaten nothing since the preceding noon. He was not nearly reduced to extremity yet though—this little heir of the world. In his body he had splendid health, in his heart a great courage, and in his soul an ever-throbbing love.

Poor Ginny was sent to bed for interfering with her father's orders; and what with the rage and horror and pity, an inexplicable feeling of hopelessness took possession of her, while her affection for her father was greatly, perhaps for this world irretrievably, injured by that morning's experience.

Fergus told his aunt what had taken place and made much game of her broonie. But the more Jean thought about the affair, the less she liked it. It was she upon whom it all came! What did it matter who or what her broonie was? What had they whipped the creature for? What harm had he done? If indeed he was a little ragged urchin, the thing was only the more inexplicable! He had taken nothing! She had never missed so much as a barley scone! The cream had always brought her the right quantity of butter! Not even a bannock, so far as she knew, was ever gone from the press, nor an egg from the bossy where they lay heaped! There was more to it than she could understand! Her nephew's mighty feat, so far from explaining anything, had only sealed up the mystery. She could not help cherishing a shadowy hope that, when things had grown quiet, he would again reveal his presence by his work, if not by his visible person. It was mortifying to think that he had gone as he came, and she had never set eyes upon him.

Donal Grant, missing his "creature" that day for the first time, heard enough when he came home to satisfy him that he had been acting the broonie in the house and the stable as well as in the field, incredible as it might well appear that such a child should have had even mere strength for what he did. Then first also, after Donal had thus lost him, he began to understand his worth, and to see how much he owed him. While he had imagined himself kind to the urchin, the urchin had been laying him under endless obligation through his gentleness and his absolute unselfishness.

15

. . . .

Refuge

It was a lovely Saturday evening on Glashgar. The few flowers about the small turf cottage scented the air in the hot western sun. The heather was not in bloom yet, and there were no trees; but there were rocks and stones and a brawling burn that half surrounded a little field of oats, one of potatoes, and a small spot with a few stocks of cabbage and kale. On the borders grew some bushes of double daisies, primroses, and carnations. These Janet tended as part of her household while her husband saw to the oats and potatoes. Robert had charge of the few sheep on the mountain which belonged to the farmer at the Mains, and for his trouble had the cottage and the land, most of which he himself had reclaimed.

They were never in any want, and never had any money except what their children brought them out of their small wages. But that was plenty for their every need; nor had they the faintest feeling that they were persons to be pitied. It was very cold up there in winter, to be sure, and they both suffered from rheumatism; but they had no debt, no fear, much love, and a large hope for what lay on the other side of death. As to the rheumatism, that was necessary, Janet said, to teach them patience, for they had no other trouble.

They were indeed growing old, but neither had begun to feel age a burden yet; and when it should prove such, they had a daughter prepared to give up service and come home to help them. Their thoughts about themselves were nearly lost in their thoughts about each other, their children, and their friends. Janet's main care was her old man, and Robert turned to Janet as the one stay of his life, next to the God in whom he trusted. While Janet prayed at home, his closet was the mountainside. All day, from the mountain and sky, from the sheep and his dog, from winter storms, spring sun and winds, summer warmth and glow, and more than all from the presence and influence of his wife, came to him somehow spiritual nourishment and vital growth. He loved life, but if he had been asked why, he might not have found a ready answer. He loved his wife—just because she was Janet.

The sun was now far down his western arc as Janet finished cleaning her cottage and gazed out toward the sunset; and as she gazed into the darkness, suddenly there emerged from it and staggered toward her—was it an angel? was it a specter? Did her old eyes deceive her? It seemed a child—reeling, and spreading out hands that groped. She covered her eyes for a moment, for it might be a vision in the sun, and looked again. It was indeed a naked child! and was she still so dazzled by the red sun as to see red where red was none?—or were those indeed blood-red streaks on his white skin? Straight now, though slow, he came toward her. It was the same child who had come and gone so strangely before! He held out his hands to her and fell on his face at her feet like one dead. Then with a horror of pitiful amazement, she saw a great cross marked in two cruel stripes on his back.

She stood half-stunned, regarding for one moment motionless the prostrate child and his wounds. The next, she lifted him in her arms and, holding him tenderly to her mother-heart, carried him into the house. There she laid him on his side in her bed, covered him gently over, and hastened to the little byre at the end of the cottage to get him some warm milk. When she returned, he had already lifted his heavy eyelids and was looking wearily about the place. She set down the milk and went to the bedside. Gibbie put up his arms, threw them around her neck, and clung to her as if she had been his mother. And from that moment she was his mother.

"What have they done to ye, my bairn?" she said, in tones of loving pity.

No reply came back—only a smile of absolute content. For what were stripes and nakedness and hunger to Gibbie now that he had a mother to love! Gibbie's necessity was to love. But here was more; here was Love offering herself to him! She raised him with one arm and held the bowl to his mouth, and he drank. When she laid him down again, he turned on his side, off his scored back, and in a moment was fast asleep. She left to make some gruel for him against his waking; and then proceeded to lay the supper for her expected children. The clean yellow-white table of soft, smooth fir needed no cloth—only horn spoons and wooden cups.

At length a hand came to the latch, and mother and daughter greeted as mother and daughter only can; then came a son, and mother and son greeted as mother and son only can. They kept on arriving singly to the number of six—two daughters and four sons, the youngest some little time after the rest. Each, as he or she came, Janet took to the bed, and showed her seventh child where he slept. Each time she showed him, she turned down the bedclothes and revealed the little smitten back. The women wept. The young men were furious, each after his fashion.

"God curse the rascal that did it!" cried one of them, clenching his teeth and quite forgetting himself in the rage of the moment.

"Laddie, take back the word," said his mother calmly. "If you don't forgive your enemies, you'll not be forgiven yourself."

The sixth of the family now entered, and his mother led him up to the bed.

"The Lord preserve us!" cried Donal Grant, "it's the creature!—And is this the way they've treated him! The quietest creature and the willingest!"

Donal began to choke.

"You know him, then, laddie?" said his mother.

"Well enough," answered Donal. "He's been with me and the cattle now, every day for weeks."

With that he hurried into the story of his acquaintance with Gibbie and the fable of the broonie. Janet desired them to say nothing about the boy in the valley but let him be forgotten by his enemies till he grew able to take care of himself. Besides, she said, their father might get into trouble with the master and the laird if it were known they had him.

Donal vowed to himself that if Fergus had had a hand in the abuse, he would never speak a civil word to him again.

He turned toward the bed and there were Gibbie's azure eyes wide open and fixed upon him.

"Eh, creature!" he cried, and darting to the bed, he took Gibbie's face between his hands and said, in a voice to which pity and sympathy gave a tone like his mother's, "What devil was it that beat you like that? I wish I had the trimmin' of him!"

Gibbie smiled.

"Has the beatin' taken the tongue from him?" asked the mother.

"No, no," answered Donal; "he's been like that ever since I've known him. I've never heard a word from the mouth of him."

"He'll be one of the deaf and dumb," said Janet.

"He's not deaf, Mother; that I know well. But dumb he must be, I'm thinkin'.—Creature," he continued, stooping over the boy, "if you hear what I'm sayin', take hold of my nose."

Thereupon, with a laugh like that of an amused infant, Gibbie raised his hand, and with thumb and forefinger gently pinched Donal's nose, at which they all burst out laughing with joy. It was as if they had found an angel's baby in the bushes and had been afraid he was an idiot but were

now relieved. Away went Janet and brought him his gruel. It was with no
small difficulty and not without a moan or two that Gibbie sat up in the
bed to take it. He took the wooden bowl and began to eat; and the look
he cast on Janet seemed to say he had never tasted such delicious food.
Indeed, he never had; and the poor cottage, where once more he was a
stranger taken in, appeared to Gibbie a place of wondrous wealth.

Janet brought out a garment of her own and aired it at the fire. It had
no lace at the neck or cuffs, no embroidery down the front. But when she
put it on him, amid the tearful laughter of the women, and had tied it
around his waist, it made a dress most becoming in their eyes, and gave
Gibbie an indescribable pleasure from its whiteness and its coolness to
his inflamed skin.

They had just finished clothing him thus when the goodman came
home, and the mother's narration had to be given afresh, with Donal's
notes explanatory and completive. As the latter reported the doings of the
imagined broonie and the commotion they had caused at the Mains and
along Daurside, Gibbie's countenance flashed with pleasure and fun; and
at last he broke into such a peal of laughter as had never, for pure merriment, been heard before so high on Glashgar. All joined involuntarily in
the laugh—even the old man who had been listening with his grey eye-
brows knit. When at last his wife showed him the child's back, he lifted
his two hands and moved them slowly up and down, as in pitiful appeal
for man against man to the Sire of the race.

They sat down to their homely meal. Simplest things will carry the
result of honest attention as plainly as more elaborate dishes. In the judgment of all her guests, the porridge was such as none could make but
mother, the milk such as none but mother's cow could yield, the cakes
such as she only could bake.

Gibbie sat in the bed like a king on his throne, gazing on his kingdom.
Gibbie could not, at that period of his history, have invented a heaven
more to his mind, and as often as one of them turned eyes toward the
bed, his face shone with merry gratitude.

It was before long almost time for the sons and daughters to go down
the hill again and leave the cottage and the blessed old parents and the
harbored child to the night, the mountain silence, and living God. The
sun had long been down; but far away in the north the faint, thin fringe
of his light garment was still visible.

"Now, lads and lassies, before we have worship, run, every one of you,"
said the mother, "and pick some heather to make a bed for the wee
man—in the nook there, at the head of ours. He'll sleep fine there, and
no harm will come near him."

She was obeyed instantly. The heather was pulled and set together
upright as it grew, only much closer, so that the tops made a dense surface.
They boxed them in below with a board or two and bound them together
above with a blanket over the top, and a white sheet over that was large
enough to be doubled and receive Gibbie between its folds. Then another
blanket was added, and the bed, a perfect one, was ready. The eldest of

the daughters took Gibbie in her arms and, tenderly careful over his hurts, lifted him from the old folks' bed and placed him in his own—one more luxurious, for heather makes a still better stratum for repose than oat chaff—and Gibbie sank into it with a sigh that was but a smile grown vocal.

Then Donal, as the youngest, got down the big Bible and laid it before his father. The old man put on his spectacles, took the book, and found the passage that fell, in continuous process, to that evening.

After the reading followed a prayer. By the time the prayer was over, Gibbie was fast asleep again. What it all meant he had not an idea; and the sound lulled him. When he woke next, from the aching of his stripes, the cottage was dark. The old people were fast asleep. A hairy thing lay by his side which, without the least fear, he examined and found to be a dog; whereupon he fell fast asleep again, if possible, happier than ever. And while the cottage was thus quiet, the brothers and sisters were still tramping along the moonlight paths of Daurside. They had all set out together, but at one point after another there had been a parting, and now they were on six different roads, each drawing nearer to the labor of the next week.

16

· · · · · · · · · · · · · · · · · · ·

A New Son

At first opportunity Donal questioned Fergus as to his share in the ill-usage of Gibbie. Fergus treated the inquiry as an impertinent interference, and mounted his high horse at once. What right had his father's herdboy to question him as to his conduct? He put it so to him and in nearly just as many words.

Thereupon answered Donal, "It's just this, you see, Fergus: You've been very good to me and I'm more obliged to you than I can say. But it would be dishonest for me to take books from you, and ask you questions I can't make out myself and then go on despisin' you in my heart for cruelty and wrong. What was the creature punished for? Tell me that. According to your aunt's account, he had taken nothing and had done nothing but good."

"Why didn't he speak up then and defend himself, and not be so confounded obstinate?" returned Fergus. "I couldn't get him to utter a single word. As for his punishment, it was by the laird's orders that Angus MacPholp took the whip to him. I had nothing to do with it." Fergus did not consider the punishment he himself had given him as worth mentioning.

"Well, I'll be a man someday, and then Angus will have to settle with me!" said Donal through his clenched teeth. "Man, Fergus! the creature's as dumb as a worm. I don't believe that he ever spoke a word in his life."

This cut Fergus to the heart, for he was far from being without generosity or pity. I fear, however, from what I know of Fergus afterward that now, instead of seeking about to make some amends, he turned the strength that should have gone in that direction to the justifying of himself to himself in what he had done. Anyhow, he was far too proud to confess to Donal that he had done wrong—too much offended at being rebuked by one he counted so immeasurably his inferior to do the right thing his rebuke set before him. What did the mighty business matter! The little rascal was nothing but a tramp; and if he didn't deserve his punishment this time, he had deserved it a hundred times without having it, and would ten thousand times again.

Ginevra was hardly the same child after the experience of that terrible morning. At no time very much at home with her father, something had now come between them, which all her struggles to love him as before were unavailing to remove. The father was too stupid, too unsympathetic, to take note of that look of fear that crossed her face if ever he addressed her suddenly.

With a cold spot in his heart where once had dwelt some genuine regard for Donal, Fergus went back to college. Donal went on herding the cattle, cudgeling Hornie, and reading what books he could lay his hands on; alas, there was no supply through Fergus anymore! The previous year, before he took his leave, he had been careful to see Donal provided with at least books for study; but this time he left him to shift for himself. He was small because he was proud, spiteful because he was conceited.

In the meantime, Gibbie slept and waked and slept again, night after night, with the loveliest days between, at the cottage on Glashgar. The morning after his arrival, the first thing he was aware of was Janet's face beaming over him with a look in her eye more like worship than benevolence. Her husband was gone, and she was about to milk the cow and was anxious lest, while she was away, Gibbie should disappear as before. But the light that rushed into his eyes was in full response to that which kindled the light in hers, and her misgiving vanished; he could not love her like that and leave her. She gave him his breakfast of porridge and milk, and went to her cow.

When she came back she found everything tidy in the cottage, the floor swept, every dish washed and set aside; and Gibbie was examining an old shoe of Robert's to see whether he could not mend it. Janet proceeded at once with joy to the construction of a garment she had been devising for him. Taking a bluewinsey petticoat of her own, drawing it in round his waist, and tying it over the chemise which was his only garment, she found as she had expected, that its hem reached his feet: she partly divided it up the middle, before and behind, and had but to back-stitch two short seams, and there was a pair of sailor-like trousers, as tidy as comfortable! Gibbie was delighted with them. Then Janet thought about a cap; but considering him a moment critically and seeing how his hair stood out like thatch eaves round his head, she betook herself instead to her New Testament.

Gibbie stood by as she read in silence, gazing with delight, for he thought it must be a book of ballads like Donal's that she was reading. But Janet found his presence and his gaze discomposing. To worship freely one must be alone or else with fellow worshipers. And reading and worshiping were often so mingled with Janet as to form but one mental consciousness. She looked up therefore from her book.

"Can you read, laddie?" she said.

Gibbie shook his head.

"Sit down then, and I'll read to you."

Gibbie obeyed more than willingly, and thus had his first lesson in the chief thing worth learning. I cannot tell how or what were the slow stages by which his mind budded and swelled until the knowledge of God burst into flower. I cannot tell the shape of the door by which the Lord entered into that house and took possession of it. I cannot even tell in what shape He appeared in Gibbie's thoughts. For Janet never suspected how utter was Gibbie's ignorance. She never dreamed that he did not know what was generally said about Jesus Christ.

So, teaching him only that which she loved, not that which she had been taught, Janet read to Gibbie of Jesus, and talked to him of Jesus, until at length his whole soul was full of the Man, of His doings, of His words, of His thoughts, of His life. Almost before he knew, he was trying to fashion his life after that of the Master.

Janet had no inclination to trouble her own head, or Gibbie's heart, with what men call the plan of salvation. It was enough to her to find that he followed her Master.

17

"Gibbie"

From that very next day after he was received into the cottage on Glashgar, Gibbie as a matter or course took upon himself any work his hand could find to do, and Janet averred to her husband that never had any of her daughters been more useful to her. At the same time, however, she insisted that Robert should take the boy out with him. She would not have him do woman's work, especially work for which she herself was perfectly able. She had not come to her years, she said, to learn idleness; and the boy would save Robert many a weary step among the hills.

"He can't speak to the dog," objected Robert, giving utterance to the first difficulty that suggested itself.

"The dog can't speak himself," returned Janet, "and the wonder is that he can understand; who knows but he may come closer to the one that's speechless like himself! Give the creature a chance, and I bet he'll make himself plain to the dog. You just try him. You tell him to tell the dog something and see what will come of it."

Robert made the experiment and it proved satisfactory. As soon as he had received Robert's orders, Gibbie claimed Oscar's attention. The dog looked up in his face, noted every glance and gesture, and, partly from sympathetic instinct, partly from observation of the state of affairs in respect of the sheep, divined with certainty what was the duty required of him, and was off like a shot.

"The two dumb creatures understand one another better than I understand either of them," said Robert to his wife when they came home.

And now indeed it was a blessed time for Gibbie. It had been pleasant down in the valley, with the cattle and Donal and foul weather sometimes; but now it was the full glow of summer; the sweet, keen air of the mountain bathed him as he ran. Gibbie was one of the meek and inherited the earth. He was of the poet-kind also and, now that he was a shepherd, saw everything with a shepherd's eyes.

It was not long before the town-bred child grew to love the heavens almost as dearly as the earth. He would gaze and gaze at the clouds as they came and went. Watching them and the wind, weighing the heat and the cold and marking many indications, some of them known perhaps only to himself, he understood the signs of the earthly times at length nearly as well as an insect or a swallow and far better than long-experienced old Robert. The mountain was Gibbie's very home; yet to see him far up on it, in the red glow of the setting sun, with his dog, as obedient as himself, hanging upon his every signal, one could have fancied him a shepherd boy come down from the plains of heaven to look after a lost lamb. Often, when the two old people were in bed and asleep, Gibbie would be out watching the moon rise.

Then there was the delight, fresh every week, of the Saturday gathering of the brothers and sisters, whom Gibbie could hardly have loved more had they been of his own immediate kin. Dearest of all was Donal, whose greeting, "Well, creature," was heavenly to Gibbie's ears. Donal would have had him go down and spend a day every now and then with him and the cattle, but Janet would not hear of it until the foolish tale of the broonie should have quite blown over.

"Eh, but I wish," she added as she said so, "I could find out something about his folk, or even where he came from or what they called him! Never a word has the creature spoken!"

"You should teach him to read, Mother," said Donal.

"How would I do that, laddie? I would have to teach him to speak first," returned Janet.

"Let him come down to me and I'll try my hand, then," said Donal.

Notwithstanding, Janet persisted in her refusal—for the present. But Donal's words set her thinking of the matter, how she might teach him to read; and at last the idea dawned upon her to substitute writing for speech.

She showed Gibbie the letters, naming each several times and going over them repeatedly. Then she gave him Donal's school slate and said, "Now, make an *A*, creature."

Gibbie did so, and well too; she found that already he knew about half the letters.

"He's no fool!" she said to herself in triumph.

The other half soon followed; and she then began to show him words. She was not very severe about the spelling, if only it was plain he knew the word.

One day, a few weeks after Gibbie had begun to read by himself, Janet became aware that he was sitting on his stool, in what had come to be called the creature's corner, more than usually absorbed in some attempt with slate and pencil. She went near and peeped over his shoulder. At the top of the slate he had written the word *give,* then the word *giving,* and below them, *gib,* then *gibing;* upon these followed *gib* again, and he was now plainly meditating something further. Suddenly he seemed to find what he wanted, for in haste, almost as if he feared it might escape him, he added a *y,* making the word *giby*—then first lifted his head and looked round, evidently seeking her. She laid her hand on his head. He jumped up with one of his most radiant smiles and, holding out the slate to her, pointed with his pencil to the word he had just completed. She did not know it for a word but sounded it, making the *g* soft. He shook his head sharply, and laid the point of his pencil upon the *g* of the *give* written above. Janet had been his teacher too long not to see what he meant, and immediately pronounced the word as he would have it. Upon this he began a wild dance, but sobering suddenly, sat down, and was instantly again absorbed in further attempt. It lasted so long that Janet resumed her previous household occupation. At length he rose, and with thoughtful, doubtful contemplation of what he had done, brought her the slate. There, under the foregone success, he had written the words, *galatians* and *breath,* and under them, *gal-breath.* She read them all, and at the last, witnessing to his success by pronouncing them to his satisfaction, he began another dance, which again he ended abruptly, to draw her attention once more to the slate. He pointed to the *giby* first, and the *galbreath* next, and she read them together. This time he did not dance but seemed waiting some result.

The idea was dawning upon Janet that he meant himself; but she was thrown off by the cognomen's correspondence with that of the laird, which suggested that the boy had been merely attempting the name of the great man of that district. With this in her mind, and doubtfully feeling her way, she essayed the tentative of setting him right in the Christian name, and said: "Thomas—Thomas Galbraith." Gibbie shook his head as before, and again resumed his seat. Presently he brought her the slate, with all the rest rubbed out, and these words standing alone—*sir giby gal-breath*. Janet read them aloud, whereupon Gibbie began dancing once more in triumph; he had, he hoped, for the first time in his life, conveyed a fact through words.

"That's what they call you, is it?" said Janet, looking motherly at him: "Sir Gibbie Galbraith?"

Gibbie nodded vehemently.

"It'll be some nickname the boys have given him," said Janet to herself, but continued to gaze at him, in questioning doubt of her own solution. She could not recall having ever heard of a Sir in the laird's family; but ghosts of things forgotten kept rising formless and thin in the sky of her memory. Had she never heard of a Sir Somebody Galbraith somewhere? And still she stared at the child, trying to grasp what she could not even see. By this time Gibbie was standing quite still, staring at her in return. He could not think what made her stare so at him.

"Who called you that?" said Janet at length, pointing to the slate.

Gibbie took the slate, dropped upon his seat and, after considerable cogitation and effort, brought her the words "Gibyse Fapher." Janet for a moment was puzzled, but when she thought of correcting the *p* with a *t,* Gibbie entirely approved.

"Who was your father, creature?" she asked.

Gibbie, after a longer pause, and more evident labor than hitherto, brought her the enigmatical word "Assotr," which, with the Sir running about in her head, quite defeated Janet.

Perceiving his failure, he jumped upon a chair and, reaching after one of Robert's Sunday shoes on the shelf, took it between his knees and began a pantomime of the making or mending of the same; it was clear to Janet he must have been familiar with the process collectively called shoemaking. And therewith she recognized the word on the slate—a sutor. She smiled to herself at the association of man and trade, and concluded that the Sir at least was a nickname. And yet whether from the presence of some rudiment of an old memory, or from something about the boy that belonged to a higher style than his present showing, her mind kept swaying in an uncertainty whose very object eluded her.

"What would you like us to call you, then, creature?" she asked, anxious to meet the child's own idea of himself.

He pointed to giby.

"Well, Gibbie," responded Janet—and at the word, now for the first time addressed by her to himself, he began dancing more wildly than ever, and ended with standing motionless on one leg; now first and at last he was fully recognized for what he was!—"Well, Gibbie, I'll call you what you think fit," said Janet. "And now go your way, Gibbie, and see that Crummie's not too far out of sight."

From that hour Gibbie had his name from the whole family—his Christian name only, however, Robert and Janet having agreed it would be wise to avoid whatever might possibly bring the boy again under the notice of the laird. The latter half of his name they laid aside for him, as parents do a dangerous or over-valuable gift to a child.

18
....

The Beast-Loon o' Glashgar

*A*lmost from the first moment of his being domiciled on Glashgar what with the good food, the fine exercise, the exquisite air, and his great happiness, Gibbie began to grow; and he took to growing so fast that his legs soon shot far out of his winsey garment. His wiry limbs grew larger without losing their firmness or elasticity; his chest, the effort in running up hill constantly alternated with the relief of running down, rapidly expanded and his lungs grew hardy as well as powerful. He became at length such in wind and muscle that he could run down a wayward sheep almost as well as Oscar. And his nerve grew also with his body and strength till his coolness and courage were splendid. Never, when the tide of his affairs ran most in the shallows, had Gibbie had much acquaintance with fears, but now he had forgotten the taste of them and would have encountered a wild highland bull alone on the mountains as readily as tie the cow Crummie up in her stall.

One afternoon, Donal, having got a half-holiday by the help of a friend and the favor of Mistress Jean, came home to see his mother, and having greeted her set out to find Gibbie. He had gone a long way, looking and calling without success, and had come in sight of a certain tiny loch that filled a hollow of the mountain. The little lake, though small in surface, was truly of unknown depth and had elements of dread about it, telling upon far less active imaginations than Donal's. While he stood gazing at it, almost afraid to go nearer, a great splash that echoed from the steep rocks surrounding it brought his heart into his mouth. Immediately followed a loud barking in which he recognized the voice of Oscar. Before he had well begun to think what it could mean, Gibbie appeared on the opposite side of the loch, high above its level, on the top of the rocks forming its basin. He began instantly a rapid descent toward the water, where the rocks were so steep and footing so precarious that Oscar wisely remained at the top and made no attempt to follow him.

Presently the dog caught sight of Donal, where he stood on a lower level, whence the water was comparatively easy of access, and starting off at full speed joined him with much demonstration of welcome. But he received little notice from Donal, whose gaze was fixed, with much wonder and more fear, on the descending Gibbie. Some twenty feet from the surface of the loch, he reached a point whence clearly in Donal's judgment there was no possibility of farther descent. But Donal was never more mistaken; for that instant Gibbie flashed from the face of the rock head foremost, like a fishing bird, into the lake. Donal gave a cry and ran to the edge of the water accompanied by Oscar, who all the time had showed no anxiety but had stood wagging his tail. When they reached the loch, there was Gibbie already but a few yards from the only possible landing place, swimming with one hand, while in the other arm he held a baby lamb, its head lying quite still on his shoulder. Then Donal first began to perceive that "the creature" was growing into an athlete.

When he landed he gave Donal a merry laugh of welcome, but without stopping flew up the hill to take the lamb to its mother. Fresh from the icy water, he ran so fast that it was all Donal could do to keep up with him.

Every time Donal came home, he would bring some book of verse with him and, leading Gibbie to some hollow, shady or sheltered as the time required, would there read to him ballads, or songs, or verse as mood or provision might suggest.

I wonder how much Gibbie was indebted to constrained silence during all these years. That he lost by it, no one will doubt; that he gained also, a few will admit. I cannot doubt it bore an important part in the fostering of the visionary thoughts and feelings and actions now growing inside him. While Donal read, rejoicing in the music of sound, Gibbie was doing something besides: He was listening with the same ears, and trying to see with the same eyes which he brought to bear upon the things Janet taught him out of the Book. Whether Donal read from a thumbed old edition, or some new tale or poem from the Edinburgh press, Gibbie was always placing what he heard by the side of what he knew, asking himself what Jesus would have done, or what He would require of a disciple.

When he sank foiled from any endeavor to understand how a man was to behave in certain circumstances, he always took refuge in doing something—and doing it better than before; leaped the more eagerly if Robert called him, spoke the more gently to Oscar, turned the sheep more careful not to scare them—as if by instinct he perceived that the only hope of understanding lies in doing. He would run to do the thing he had learned yesterday, when as yet he could find no answer to the question of today. Thus, as the weeks of solitude and thought glided by, the reality of Christ grew upon him, till in the very rocks and heather and the faces of the sheep he felt His presence everywhere. He fancied He came down every now and then to see how things were going in the lower part of His kingdom; and that when He did so, He made use of Glashgar and its rocks for His stair.

When the winter came with its frost and snow, Gibbie saved Robert much suffering. At first Robert was unwilling to let him go out alone in stormy weather; but Janet believed that the child doing the old man's work would be specially protected. He did not suffer from the cold; for, a sheep having died toward the end of the first autumn, Robert, in view of Gibbie's coming necessity, had begged of his master the skin and dressed it with the wool upon it. Of this, between the three of them, they made a coat for him, so that he roamed the hill like a savage in a garment of skin.

Before very long, it became, of course, well known about the country that Mr. Duff's crofters upon Glashgar had taken in and were bringing up a foundling—some said an innocent, some said a wild boy—who helped Robert with his sheep and Janet with her cow, but could not speak a word of either Gaelic or English. By and by strange stories came to be told of his exploits, representing him as gifted with bodily powers as much surpassing the common as his mental faculties were assumed to be under the ordinary standard. The rumor concerning him swelled as well as spread until, toward the end of his second year on Glashgar, the notion of Gibbie in the imaginations of the children of Daurside was that of an almost supernatural being who had dwelt upon, or rather who had haunted, Glashgar from time immemorial and of whom they had been hearing all their lives. Although they had never heard anything bad of him, only that he was wild, wore a hairy skin, could do more than any other boy dared attempt, was dumb, and yet sheep and dogs and cattle could understand him perfectly; and this was more than enough to envelop the idea of him in a mist of dread. When the twilight began to gather about the cottages and farmhouses for miles up and down the river, the very mention of "the beast-loon o' Glashgar" was enough to send many of the children scouring like startled hares into the house.

Gibbie little thought what clouds of foolish fancies rising from the valleys below had, by their distorting vapors, made of him an object of terror to those whom at the very first sight he would have loved and served. Among these, perhaps the most afraid of him were the children of the gamekeeper, for they lived on the very foot of the haunted hill, near the bridge and gate of Glashruach; and the laird himself happened one day to be witness of their fear. He inquired the cause, and yet again was his enlightened soul vexed by the persistency with which the shadows of superstition still hung about his lands. Had he been half as philosophical as he fancied himself, he might have seen that there was not necessarily a single film of superstition involved in the belief that a savage roamed a mountain—which was all that Mistress MacPholp, depriving the rumor of its richer coloring, ventured to impart as the cause of her children's perturbation.

But anything a hairsbreadth out of the common was a thing hated of Thomas Galbraith's soul; and whatever another believed which he did not choose to believe, he set down at once as superstition. He held therefore immediate communication with his gamekeeper on the subject. It had not occurred either to master or man that the offensive being whose doubtful existence caused the scandal was the same toward whom they had once been guilty of such brutality. The same afternoon the laird questioned his tenant of the Mains concerning his cottars, and he was assured that better or more respectable people were not in all the region of Gormgarnet.

When Robert became aware of Gibbie's gifts of other kinds than those revealed to himself by his good shepherding, he began to turn it over in his mind whether they ought not to send the boy to school that he might learn the things he was so much more than ordinarily capable of learning.

"Let him go down to the Mains and herd with Donal," said Robert to Janet. "He knows a lot more than you or me or Gibbie; and when he's learned all that Donal can show him, it'll be time to think what next."

"Well," answered Janet, "no one can say but that's sense, Robert; and though I'm loath to let the laddie go, for your sake more than my own, let him go to Donal. I hope, between the two, they won't let the cattle among the corn."

"The corn's most all cut now," replied Robert. "But he needn't go every day. He can give one day to the learning, and the next to thinking about it among the sheep. And any day you want to keep him, you can keep him; for it won't be as if he went to school."

Gibbie was delighted with the proposal.

"Only," said Robert, in final warning, "don't let them take you, Gibbie, and score your back again, my creature: and don't answer anybody when they ask what you're called, anything more than just Gibbie."

The boy laughed and nodded and, as Janet said, the boy's laugh was as good as the best man's word.

Now came a happy time for the two boys. Donal began at once to teach Gibbie arithmetic. When they had had enough of that for a day, he read Scottish history to him; and when they had done what seemed their duty by that, then came the best of the feast—whatever tales or poetry Donal had laid his hands upon.

Once they were startled by seeing the gamekeeper enter the field. The moment he saw him, Gibbie laid himself flat on the ground ready to spring to his feet and run. The man, however, did not come near them.

19

The Gamekeeper

The second winter came, and with the first frost Gibbie resumed his sheepskin coat and the brogues and leggings which he had made for himself of deerhide tanned with the hair. It pleased the two old people to see him so warmly clad. Very soon the stories about him were all stirred up afresh and new rumors added. This one and that of the children declared they had caught sight of the beast-loon, running about the rocks like a goat; and one day a boy of Angus's own, who had been a good way up the mountain, came home nearly dead with terror saying the beast-loon had chased him a long way. He did not add that he had been throwing stones at the sheep, not perceiving anyone in charge of them. So one fine morning in December, having nothing particular to attend to, Angus shouldered his double-barrelled gun and set out for a walk over Glashgar in the hope of coming upon the savage that terrified the children. He must be off; that was settled. Where Angus was in authority, the outlandish was not to be suffered. The sun shone bright, and a keen wind was blowing.

About noon he came in sight of a few sheep in a sheltered spot, where were little patches of coarse grass among the heather. On a stone a few yards above them sat Gibbie, not reading, as he would be half the time now, but busied with a set of Pan's pipes—which, under Donal's direction, he had made for himself—drawing from them experimental sounds, and feeling after the possibility of a melody. He was so much occupied that he did not see Angus approach, who now stood for a moment or two regarding him. He was hirsute as Esau, his head crowned with its own plentiful crop (even in winter he wore no cap), his body covered with the wool of the sheep, and his legs and feet with the hide of the deer, the hair as in nature, outward. The deerskin Angus knew for what it was from afar, concluding it the spoil of the only crime of which he recognized the enormity, whereas it was in truth part of a skin he himself had sold to a saddler in the next village. He boiled over with wrath and strode nearer, grinding his teeth. Gibbie looked up, knew him and starting to his feet ran to the hill. Angus, leveling his gun, shouted to him to stop, but Gibbie only ran the harder and not once looked round. Idiotic with rage, Angus fired. One of his barrels was loaded with shot, the other, with ball. Meaning to use the shot barrel, he pulled the wrong trigger and liberated the bullet. It went through the calf of Gibbie's right leg and he fell. It had, however, passed between two muscles without injuring either greatly, and had severed no artery.

The next moment Gibbie was on his feet again and running. He did not yet feel pain. Happily he was not very far from home and he made for it as fast as he could—preceded by Oscar, who, having once by accident been shot himself, had a mortal terror of guns. Maimed as Gibbie was, he could yet run a good deal faster up the hill than the rascal who followed him. But long before he reached the cottage, the pain had arrived, and the nearer he got to it the worse it grew. In spite of the anguish, however, he held on with determination; to be seized by Angus and dragged down to Glashruach would be far worse.

Robert Grant, suffering from rheumatism, was at home that day. He was seated with his pipe in his mouth and Janet was just taking the potatoes for their dinner off the fire when the door flew open, and in stumbled Gibbie and fell on the floor. The old man threw his pipe from him, and rose trembling, but Janet was before him. She dropped down on her knees beside the boy, and put her arm under his head. He was white and motionless.

"Eh, Robert!" she cried. "He's bleedin'!"

The same moment they heard quick, heavy steps approaching. At once Robert divined the truth and a great wrath banished rheumatism and age together. Like a boy he sprang to the shelf whence his yet powerful hand came back armed with a huge, rusty old broadsword that had seen service in its day. Two or three fierce tugs at the holt proved the blade immovable in the sheath, and the steps being now almost at the door, he clubbed the weapon, grasping it by the sheathed blade. Holding it with the edge downward so that the blow he meant to deal should fall from the round of the basket hilt, he heaved it aloft, the rage of a hundred ancestors welling up in his usually peaceful breast. His red eyes flashed and the few hairs that were left him stood erect on his head like the mane of a roused lion. Before Angus had his second foot over the threshold, down came the helmet-like hilt with a dull crash on his head, and he staggered against the wall.

"Take that, Angus MacPholp!" panted Robert through his clenched teeth, following the blow with another from his fist that prostrated the enemy. Again he heaved his weapon and, standing over him where he lay more than half-stunned, said in a hoarse voice, "By the great God my maker, Angus MacPholp, if you try to get up, I'll come down on you again!—Here, Oscar!—Watch him and take him by the throat if he moves a finger."

The gun dropped from Angus's hand, and Robert, keeping his eye on Angus, secured it.

"It's loaded," muttered Angus.

"Rest still, then," returned Robert, pointing the weapon at his head.

"It'll be murder," said Angus, and made a movement to lay hold of the barrel.

"Hold him down, Oscar!" cried Robert. The dog's paws were instantly on his chest and his teeth grinning within an inch of his face. "It would be but blood for blood, Angus MacPholp," he went on. "Your hour's come, my man. That child is not the first blood of man you've shed, and it's time the Scripture was fulfilled and the hand of man shed yours."

"You're not going to kill me, Rob Grant?" growled the fellow in growing fright.

"I'm going to see whether the sheriff won't be persuaded to hang you," answered the shepherd. "This must be put a stop to—Quiet! or I'll brain you, and save him the trouble!—Here, Janet, bring your pot of potatoes. I'm going to empty the gun. If he dares to move, just give him the whole boiling lot in the face; only take care and hold off the dog."

So saying he carried the weapon to the door and, in terror lest he might through wrath or the pressure of dire necessity use it against his foe, emptied its second barrel into the earth and leaned it up against the wall outside.

Janet obeyed her husband so far as to stand over Angus with the potato pot; how far she would have carried her obedience had he attempted to rise may remain a question.

When Robert returned and relieved her guard, Janet went back to Gibbie whom she had drawn toward the fire. In a minute or two more he was able to crawl to his bed in the corner, and then Janet proceeded to examine his wound.

By this time his leg was much swollen, but the wound had almost stopped bleeding, and it was plain there was no bullet in it, for there were two orifices. She washed it carefully and bound it up. Then Gibbie raised his head and looked somewhat anxiously around the room.

"You're lookin' for Angus?" said Janet; "he's yonder upon the floor. Don't be frightened; your father and Oscar have him safe enough."

"Here, Janet!" cried her husband. "If you're through with the child, I must be going."

"Hoot, Robert! You're not going to leave Gibbie and me in the house with the murderin' man!" returned Janet.

"Indeed I am, lass! Just run and bring the line that you hang the duds on while they're drying, and we'll tie the hands and feet of him."

Janet obeyed and went. Angus, who had been quiet enough for the last ten minutes, meditating and watching, began to swear furiously; but Robert paid no more heed than if he had not heard him. He stood calm and grim at his head with the clubbed sword heaved over his shoulder. When Janet came back, by her husband's directions she passed the rope repeatedly round the keeper's ankles, then several times between them, drawing the bouts tightly together. Again and again, as she tied it, did Angus meditate a sudden spring, but the determined look of Robert caused him to hesitate until it was altogether too late. When they began to bind his hands, however, he turned desperate and struck at both, cursing and raging.

"If you're not quiet, you'll taste the dog's teeth," said Robert. Angus reflected that he would have a better chance when he was left alone with Janet, and yielded. "Truth!" Robert went on as he continued his task, "I have no pity left for you, Angus MacPholp.—Now, Janet, bring a bundle of straw from the stall and lay it under his head. I must be away and get word to the sheriff. Scotland's come to a pretty end when they shoot men with guns as if they were creatures to be skinned and eaten. He may well be a keeper of game, for he's as poor a keeper of brother as old Cain himself. But," he concluded, tying the last knot hard, "we'll do what we can to keep the keeper."

So saying he put the bannock in his pocket, flung his broad blue bonnet upon his head, took his stick and, ordering Oscar to remain at home and watch the prisoner, set out for a walk of five miles as if he had never known such a thing as rheumatism. He must find another magistrate than the laird; he would not trust him where his own gamekeeper Angus MacPholp was concerned.

"Keep your eye upon him, Janet," he said, turning in the doorway. "Don't let him out of your sight before I come back with the constable. I'll be back in about three hours."

With these words he turned finally, and disappeared.

Lying thus trapped in the den of the beast-loon, the mortification of Angus at being taken and bound by an old man, a woman, and a collie dog was extreme. He went over the whole affair again and again in his mind, ever with a fresh burst of fury. It was in vain he excused himself on the ground that the attack had been so sudden and treacherous, and the precautions taken so complete. He had proved himself a fool, and the whole country would ring with mockery of him! He had sense enough, too, to know that he was in a serious as well as ludicrous predicament; he had scarcely courage enough to contemplate the possible result.

If he could but get his hands free, it would be easy to kill Oscar and disable Janet. For the idiot, he counted him nothing. He had better wait, however, until there should be no boiling liquid ready to her hand.

Janet set out the dinner, peeled some potatoes and, approaching Angus, would have fed him. In place of accepting her ministrations, he fell to abusing her with the worst language he could find. She withdrew without a word, and sat down to her own dinner; but finding the torrent of vituperation kept flowing, she rose again and, going to the door, fetched a great jug of cold water from the pail that always stood there. Coming behind her prisoner, she emptied it over his face. He gave a horrid yell, taking the douche for a boiling one.

"You don't need to cry out like that at good, cold water," said Janet. "But you'll just abstain from any more such words in my hearin', or you'll get the same every time you break out." As she spoke, she knelt and wiped his face and head with her apron.

A fresh oath rushed to Angus's lips, but the fear of a second jugful made him suppress it, and Janet sat down again to her dinner. She could scarcely eat a mouthful, however, for pity of the rascal beside her at whom she kept looking wistfully without daring again to offer him anything.

While she sat thus, she caught the swift, investigating look he cast on the cords that bound his hands, and then at the fire. She perceived at once what was passing in his mind. Rising she went quickly to the byre and returned immediately with a chain they used for tethering the cow. The end of it she slipped deftly round his neck and made it fast, putting the little bar through a link.

"Are you going to hang me, you she-devil?" he cried, making a futile attempt to grasp the chain with his bound hands.

"You'll be wanting a drop more of cold water, I'm thinkin'," said Janet. She stretched the chain to its length, and with a great stone drove the sharp iron stake at the other end of it into the clay floor.

Gibbie had fallen asleep, but he now woke and she gave him his dinner, then took her Bible. Gibbie had lain down again, and she thought he was asleep.

Angus grew more and more uncomfortable, both in body and in mind. He knew he was hated throughout the country and had hitherto rather enjoyed the knowledge; but now he judged that the popular feeling, by no means a mere prejudice, would tell against him in a trial. He knew also that the magistrate to whom Robert had betaken himself was not overly friendly with his master and certainly would not listen to any intercession from him. At length, what with pain, hunger, and fear, his pride began to yield. After an hour had passed in utter silence, he condescended to parley.

"Janet Grant," he said, "let me go, and I'll trouble you and yours no more."

"You think me some fool to listen to you?" suggested Janet.

"I'll swear any lawful oath that you want to lay on me," protested Angus, "that I'll do whatever you please to require of me."

"I don't doubt but that you would swear; but what next?" said Janet.

"What next but you'll loose my hands?" rejoined Angus.

"Don't even mention it," replied Janet; "for as you know, I'm under authority, and you yourself heard my man tell me to take every precaution not to let you go."

"Was ever a man," protested Angus, "made such a fool of by a pair of old cottars like you and Robert Grant!"

"With the help of the Lord, by means of the dog," supplemented Janet.

"Let me go, woman! I'll harm nobody. The poor idiot's not much the worse, and I'll take more care when I shoot another time."

"Wiser folks than me must see to that," said Janet.

"Hoots, woman! it was nothing but an accident."

"I don't know; but we'll have to see what Gibbie says."

"What! his word's good for nothing."

"For a penny or a thousand pounds."

"My wife will be out of her wits," pleaded Angus.

"Would you like a drink of milk?" asked Janet rising.

"I would that," he answered.

She filled her little teapot with milk, and he drank it from the spout, hoping she was on the point of giving way.

"Now," she said, when he had finished his drink, "you just make the best of it, Angus. Anyway, it's a good lesson in patience to you, and that you haven't had very often, I'm thinkin'. Robert will be here before long."

With these words she set down the teapot and went out; it was time to milk the cow.

In a little while Gibbie rose, tried to walk but failed, and getting down on his hands and knees crawled out after her. Angus caught a glimpse of his face as he crept past him, and then first recognized the boy he had lashed. Not compunction but an occasional pang of dread lest he should have been the cause of his death had served so to fix Gibbie's face in his memory that now he had a near view of him, pale with suffering and loss of blood and therefore more like his former self, Angus knew him beyond a doubt. With a great shoot of terror he concluded that the idiot had been lying there silently gloating over his revenge, waiting only till Janet should be out of sight, and was now gone after some instrument wherewith to take it. He pulled and tugged at his bonds, but only to find escape absolutely hopeless. In gathering horror, he lay motionless at last, but strained his hearing toward every sound.

The byre was just on the other side of the turf wall against which was the head of Gibbie's bed, and through the wall Gibbie had heard Janet's voice. He crawled to the end of the cottage so silently that she heard no sound of his approach. He would not go into the byre, for that might disturb her; she would have to look up to know that it was only Gibbie. He would listen at the door. He found it wide open and, peeping in, saw Crummie chewing away and Janet on her knees.

"O Lord, if you would but say what you would have done! The man's done me no ill, except he's hurt your bonnie Gibbie. It's Gibbie that has to forgive him. But my man told me not to let him up. I'm willing enough to let him go, but he's Robert's prisoner and Gibbie's enemy. He's not my prisoner nor my enemy and I don't think I have the right. And who knows but he might go shooting more folk yet 'cause I let him go."

Here her voice ceased and she fell a-moaning.

Her trouble was echoed in dim pain from Gibbie's soul. That the prophetess who knew everything should be thus abandoned to dire perplexity was a dreadful, a bewildering, fact. But now first he understood the real state of the affair in the purport of the old man's absence; also how he was himself potently concerned in the business. If the offense had been committed against Gibbie, then with Gibbie lay the power, therefore the duty, of forgiveness. Few things were easier to him than to love his enemies, and his merit in obeying the commandment was small indeed. No sooner had Janet ceased than he was on his way back to the cottage; on its floor lay one who had to be waited upon with forgiveness.

Wearied with futile struggles, Angus found himself compelled to abide his fate and was lying quite still when Gibbie reentered. The boy thought he was asleep, but on the contrary he was watching his every motion, full of dread. Gibbie went hopping upon one foot to the hole in the wall where Janet kept the only knife she had. It was not there. He glanced around but could not see it. There was no time to lose. Gibbie looked around again for a moment, as if in doubt, then darted upon the tongs and thrust them into the fire, caught up the asthmatic old bellows and began to blow the peats. Angus saw the first action, heard the second, and a hideous dismay clutched his very heart. The savage fool was about to take his revenge in pinches with the red hot tongs! Manhood held him silent until he saw him take the implement of torture from the fire, glowing not red but white hot, when he uttered such a terrific yell that Gibbie dropped the tongs but caught them up again instantly and made a great hop to Angus. If Janet had heard that yell and came in, all would be spoiled.

But the faithless keeper began to struggle so fiercely, writhing with every contortion and kicking with every inch left possible to him, that Gibbie hardly dared attempt anything for dread of burning him. With a sudden thought Gibbie sprang to the door and locked it so that Janet should not get in, and Angus, hearing the bolt, was the more convinced that his purpose was cruel so struggled and yelled all the more, with his eyes fixed on the glowing tongs now fast cooling in Gibbie's hand.

In the meantime, Janet in her perplexity had, quite forgetful of the poor cow's necessities, abandoned Crummie and wandered down the path so that she heard nothing.

Gibbie thrust the tongs again into the fire and, while blowing it, bethought him that it might give Angus confidence if he removed the chain from his neck. But to Angus the action seemed only preparatory to taking him by the throat with the horrible implement. In his agony and wild endeavor to frustrate the supposed intent, he struggled harder than ever. But now Gibbie was undoing the rope fastened round the chest. This Angus did not perceive, and when it came suddenly loose in the midst of one of his fierce, straining contortions, the result was that he threw his body right over his head and lay on his face for a moment confused. Gibbie saw his advantage. He snatched his clumsy tool out of the fire, seated himself on the corresponding part of Angus's person, and seizing with the tongs the rope between his feet held on to both in spite of his heaves and kicks. In the few moments that passed while Gibbie burned through a round of the rope, Angus imagined a considerable number of pangs; but when Gibbie rose and hopped away, he discovered that his feet were at liberty and scrambled up, his head dizzy and his body reeling. Gibbie looked up at him with a smile, and Angus did not even box his ears. Holding by the wall, Gibbie limped to the door and opened it. With a nod meant for thanks, the gamekeeper stepped out, took up his gun from where it leaned against the wall and hurried away down the hill. A moment sooner and he would have met Janet; but she had just entered the byre again to milk poor Crummie.

When she came into the cottage, she stared with astonishment to see no Angus on the floor. Gibbie, who had lain down again in such pain, made sign that he had let him go; whereupon such a look of relief came over her countenance that he was filled with fresh gladness, and was, if possible, more satisfied still with what he had done.

It was late before Robert returned—alone, weary and disappointed. The magistrate was away from home; he had waited for him as long as he dared; but at length, both because of his wife's unpleasant position and the danger to himself if he longer delayed his journey across the mountain, seeing it threatened a storm and there was no moon, he set out. That he too was relieved to find no Angus there he did not attempt to conceal. The next day he went to see him and told him that, to please Gibbie, he had consented to say nothing more about the affair. Angus could not help being sullen, but he judged it wise to behave as well as he could, kept his temper therefore, and said he was sorry he had been so hasty, but that Robert had punished him pretty well, for it would be weeks before he recovered from the blow on the head he had given him. So they parted on tolerable terms and there was no further persecution of Gibbie from that quarter.

20

•••••••••••••••••••

The Beast-Boy

*T*hat winter the old people were greater tried with rheumatism; for not only were the frosts severe but there was much rain between. Their children did all in their power to minister to their wants, and Gibbie was nurse as well as shepherd.

Gibbie still occupied his heather bed on the floor, and it was part of his business to keep up a good fire on the hearth; happily, peats were plentiful.

For weeks he had been picking out tunes on his panpipes; also, he had lately discovered that, although he could not articulate, he could produce tones, and had taught himself to imitate the pipes. Now to his delight he had found that the noises he made were recognized as song by his father and mother. From that time he was often heard crooning to himself.

Change, meantime, was in progress elsewhere, as well upon the foot as high on the side of Glashgar. Thomas Galbraith of Glashruach, Esquire, was not kept from folly by his hatred for what he called superstition; he had long fallen into what will ultimately prove the most degrading superstition of all—the worship of Mammon—and was rapidly sinking from deep to lower deep. Such was the folly of the man that he risked what he loved best in the world by investing in Welsh gold mines.

The property of Glashruach was a good one but not nearly so large as it had been, and he was anxious to restore it to its former dimensions. To increase his money that he might increase his property, he took to speculation, but had never had much success until that same year when he disposed of certain shares at a large profit—nothing troubled by the conviction that the man who bought them (in ignorance of many a fact which the laird knew) must in all probability be ruined by them. He counted this success and it gave him confidence to speculate further.

In the spring, affairs began to look rather bad for him, and in the month of May he considered himself compelled to go to London. He had a faith in his own business faculty quite as foolish as any superstition in Gormgarnet. There he fell into the hands of a certain man—a fellow who used his influence and facilities as member of Parliament in promoting bubble companies. He was close to another man, likewise of principles that love the shade; and between them they had no difficulty in making a tool of Thomas Galbraith, as chairman of a certain aggregate of iniquity.

In the course of that winter, one of Donal's sisters was engaged by the housekeeper at Glashruach to wait upon Miss Galbraith. Ginevra was still a silent, simple, unconsciously retiring and therewith dignified girl in whom childhood and womanhood had begun to interchange hues. Happy they in whom neither had a final victory! Happy also all who have such women to love! At one moment Ginevra would draw herself up with involuntary recoil from doubtful approach; the next, Ginny would burst out in a merry laugh at something in which only a child could have perceived the mirth-causing element. The people about the place loved her, but from the stillness on the general surface of her behavior, the faraway feeling she gave them, and the impossibility of divining how she was thinking except she chose to unburden herself, they were all a little afraid of her as well.

In the mind of her new maid, however, there was no strife, and the desire to be acceptable to her awoke at once and grew rapidly in her heart. She was the youngest of Janet's girls, about four years older than Donal, not clever but as sweet as honest and full of divine service. Always ready to think others better than herself, the moment she saw the still face of Ginevra, she took her for a little saint and accepted her as a queen whose will to her should be law. Ginevra, on her part, was taken with the healthy hue and honest eyes of the girl, and felt no dislike to her touching her hair nor lost her temper when she was awkward and pulled it. Before the winter was over the bond between them was strong.

One principal duty required of Nicie was to accompany her mistress every fine day to the manse, a mile and a half from Glashruach where Ginevra took instruction in the morning hours from the daughter of the parish clergyman. One morning they found, on reaching the manse, that the minister was very unwell and that in consequence Miss Machar could not attend to Ginevra; they turned, therefore, to walk home again. Now the manse, upon another root of Glashgar, was nearer than Glashruach to Nicie's home, and many a time as she came and went did she lift longing eyes to the ridge that hid it from her view. This morning Ginevra observed that every other moment Nicie was looking up the side of the mountain as if she saw something unusual upon it—occasionally, indeed, when the winding of the road turned their backs to it, stopping and turning round to gaze.

"What is the matter with you, Nicie?" she asked. "What are you looking at up there?"

"I'm wonderin' what my mother is doing," answered Nicie; "she's up there."

"Up there!" exclaimed Ginny and, turning, stared at the mountain too, expecting to perceive Nicie's mother somewhere upon the face of it.

"No, no, missie. You can't see her," said the girl; "she's not in sight. She's over beyond there. But if we were where we could see two or three sheep against the sky, we could see the house where she and my father live."

"How I should like to see your father and mother, Nicie!" exclaimed Ginevra.

"Well, I'm sure they would be right glad to see you, missie, any time you would like to go and see them."

"Why shouldn't we go now, Nicie? It's not a dangerous place, is it?"

"No, missie. Glashgar's as quiet and well-behaved a mountain as any in all the country," answered Nicie, laughing. "It's poor like my family and hasn't much to spare, but the sheep get a few nibbles upon her here and there; and my mother manages to keep a cow and get plenty of milk for her tea."

"Come then, Nicie. We have plenty of time. Nobody wants either you or me, and we shall get home before anyone misses us."

Nicie was glad enough to consent; they turned at once to the hill and began climbing. But Nicie did not know this part of it nearly so well as that which lay between Glashruach and the cottage, and after they had climbed some distance, often stopping and turning to look down on the valley below, the prospect of which, with its streams and river, kept still widening and changing as they ascended, they arrived at a place where the path grew very doubtful and she could not tell in which of two directions they ought to go.

"I'll take this way, and you take that, Nicie," said Ginevra, "and if I find there is no path my way, I will come back to yours; and if you find there is no path your way, you will come back to mine."

It was a childish proposal and one to which Nicie should not have consented, but she was little more than a child herself. Advancing a short distance in doubt, and the path reappearing quite plainly, she sat down, expecting her little mistress to return directly. No thought of anxiety crossed her mind. How should such a thought come in broad sunlight, on a mountainside, in the first of summer, and with the long day before them? There, sitting in peace, Nicie fell into a maidenly reverie, and so there Nicie sat for a long time, half dreaming in the great light without once really thinking about anything. All at once she came to herself; some latent fear had exploded in her heart. Yes! What could have become of her little mistress? She jumped to her feet and shouted, "Missie! Missie Galbraith! Ginny!" but no answer came back. The mountain was as still as at midnight. She ran to the spot where they had parted and along the other path; it was plainer than that where she had been so idly forgetting herself. She hurried on, wildly calling as she ran.

In the meantime, Ginevra, having found the path indubitable and imagining it led straight to the door of Nicie's mother's cottage and that Nicie would be after her in a moment, thinking also to have a bit of fun with her, set off dancing and running so fast that by the time Nicie came to herself, she was a good mile from her. What a delight it was to be thus alone upon the great mountain—with the earth banished so far below and the great rocky heap climbing and leading and climbing up and up toward the sky!

But the path was after all a mere sheep track and led her at length into a lonely hollow in the hillside, with a swampy peat bog at the bottom of it. She stopped. The place looked unpleasant, reminding her of how she always felt when she came unexpectedly upon Angus MacPholp. She would go no farther alone; she would wait till Nicie overtook her.

In her haste and anxiety, however, Nicie had struck into another sheep track, and was now higher up the hill; so that Ginny could see no living thing nearer than in the valley below. Never in her life before had she felt that she was alone. She had often felt lonely, but she had always known where to find the bodily presence of somebody. Now she might cry and scream the whole day and nobody answer! Her heart swelled into her throat, then sank away, leaving a wide hollow. It was so eerie! But Nicie would soon come, and then all would be well.

She sat down on a stone where she could see the path she had come a long way back. But never and never did any Nicie appear. At last she began to cry.

"O God, help me home again!" cried Ginevra, and stood up in her great loneliness to return.

The same instant she spied, seated upon a rock a little way off but close to her path, the beast-boy. There could be no mistake. He was just as she had heard him described by the children at the gamekeeper's cottage. That was his hair sticking all out from his head, though the sun in it made it look like a crown of gold or a shining mist. Those were his bare arms, and that was dreadful indeed! Bare legs and feet she was used to; but bare arms! Worst of all, making it absolutely certain he was the beast-boy, he was playing upon a curious kind of whistling thing, making dreadfully sweet music to entice her nearer that he might catch her and tear her to pieces! Was this the answer that God sent to the prayers she had offered in her sore need—the beast-boy?

Most girls would have screamed, but such was not Ginny's natural mode of meeting a difficulty. With fear she was far more likely to choke than to cry out. So she sat down again and stared at him. Perhaps he would go away when he found he could not entice her. He did not move but kept playing on his curious instrument. Perhaps by returning into the hollow she could make a circuit and so pass him lower down the hill. She rose at once and ran.

Now Gibbie had seen her long before she had seen him, but from experience was afraid of frightening her. He had therefore drawn gradually near, and sat as if unaware of her presence. Treating her as he would a bird with which he wanted to make better acquaintance, he would have her get accustomed to the look of him before he made advances. But when he saw her run in the direction of the swamp, knowing what a dangerous place it was, he was terrified; he sprang to his feet and darted off to get between her and the danger. She heard him coming like the wind at her back and, whether from bewilderment or that she did intend throwing herself into the water to escape him, instead of pursuing her former design, she made straight for the swamp. As she approached the place, there he was on the edge of a great hole half full of water as if he had been sitting there for an hour! Was he going to drown her in that hole?

She turned again and ran toward the descent of the mountain. But ere there Gibbie feared a certain precipitous spot; and besides, there was no path in that direction. So Ginevra had not run far before again she saw him right in her way. She threw herself on the ground in despair and hid her face. After thus hunting her as a cat might a mouse, or a lion a man, what could she look for but that he would pounce upon her and tear her to pieces? Fearfully expectant of the horrible grasp, she lay breathless. At length to her ears came a strange sweet voice of singing—such a sound as she had never heard before. It seemed to come from far away. The sound grew and grew, and came nearer and nearer. But although it was song, she could distinguish no vowel-melody in it, nothing but a tone-melody—a crooning, as it were, ever upon one vowel in a minor key. It came quite near at length, and yet even then had something of the far-away sound left in it. It came close, and ceased suddenly. She opened her eyes and looked up. Over her stood the beast-boy, gazing down upon her! From under a great crown of reddish gold looked out two eyes of heaven's own blue, and through the eyes looked out something that dwells behind the sky.

She lay motionless, flat on the ground, her face turned sideways upon her hands. Then a curious feeling began to wake in her of having seen him before—somewhere, ever so long ago, and that sight of him as well as this had to do with misery, with something that made a stain that would not come out. Yes—it was the very face, only larger, and still sweeter, of the little, naked child whom Angus had so cruelly lashed! That was ages ago but she had not forgotten, and never could forget either the child's back or the lovely, innocent white face that he turned round upon her. If it was indeed him, perhaps he would remember her. In any case, she was now certain he would not hurt her.

Then rose the very sun himself in Gibbie's eyes and flashed a full response of daylight—a smile that no woman, girl, or matron could mistrust. Timidly, yet trustingly, Ginevra took one hand from under her cheek and stretched it up to him. He clasped it gently. She moved, and he helped her to rise.

"I've lost Nicie," she said.

Gibbie nodded, but did not look concerned.

"Nicie is my maid," said Ginevra.

Gibbie nodded several times. He knew who Nicie was rather better than her mistress.

"I left her away back there, a long, long time ago, and she has never come to me," she said.

Gibbie gave a shrill, loud whistle that startled her. In a few seconds, from somewhere unseen, a dog came bounding to him over stones and heather. How he spoke to the dog, or what he told him to do, she had not an idea; but the next instant Oscar was rushing along the path she had come and was presently out of sight. So full of life was Gibbie, so quick and decided was his every motion, so full of expression his every glance and smile, that she had not yet begun to wonder he had not spoken; indeed, she was hardly yet aware of the fact. She knew him now for a mortal but, just as it had been with Donal and his mother, he continued to affect her as a creature of some higher world come down on a mission of goodwill to men.

Gibbie took her hand and led her toward the path she had left; she yielded without a movement of question. But he did not lead her far in that direction; he turned to the left up the mountain. It grew wilder as they ascended. But the air was so thin and invigorating, the changes so curious and interesting as now they skirted the edge of a precipitous rock, now scrambled up the steepest of paths by the help of the heather that nearly closed over it; and the reaction of relief from the terror she had suffered was so exciting that she never for a moment felt tired. Then they went down the side of a little burn—a torrent when the snow was dissolving, and even now a good stream. It was the same one, as she learned afterward, to whose song under her window she listened every night in bed. They crossed the burn and climbed the opposite bank. Then Gibbie pointed, and there was the cottage; and Nicie was coming up the path to it with Oscar bounding before her! The dog was merry, but Nicie was weeping bitterly. They were a good way off, with another larger burn between; but Gibbie whistled and Oscar came flying to him. Nicie looked up, gave a cry, and like a sheep to her lost lamb came running.

"Oh, missie!" she said, breathless, as she reached the opposite bank of the burn, and her tone had more than a touch of sorrowful reproach in it, "What made you run away?"

"There was a path, Nicie, and I thought you would come after me."

"I was a goose, missie; but I'm glad I've got you. Come along and see my mother."

"Yes, Nicie. We'll tell her all about it. You see, I haven't got a mother to tell, so I will tell yours."

Never before had Ginny spent such a happy day, drunk such milk as Crummie's, or eaten such cakes as Janet's. She saw no more of Gibbie; the moment she was safe, he and Oscar were off again to the sheep, for Robert was busy cutting peats that day and Gibbie was in sole charge. Eager to know about him, Ginevra gathered all that Janet could tell of his story, and in return told the little she had seen of it, which was the one dreadful point.

"Is he a good boy, Mistress Grant?" she asked.

"One of the best boys I ever knew," answered Janet.

Ginny gave a little sigh, and wished she were good.

"When did you see Donal?" asked Janet of Nicie.

"Not since I was here last," answered Nicie.

"I was thinkin'," returned her mother, "you should be able to see him now from the back of the big house; for he was telling me he was with the cattle in the new meadow upon the Lorrie bank."

"Oh, is he there?" said Nicie. "Maybe I can get a sight of him. He came to the kitchen door, but Mistress MacFarlane would not let him in. She would have no loons comin' about the place, she said. I said that he was my brother, and she said that was nothing to her. I told her that all my brothers were known to be good lads; but she told me to hold my tongue. I could have given her a box on the ear—I was that angry with her!"

"She'll be sorry for it some day," said Janet with a quiet smile; "and what someone's sure to be sorry for, you might as well forgive them at once."

"How do you know, Mother, that she will be sorry for it?" asked Nicie, not very willing to forgive Mistress MacFarlane.

" 'Cause the Master says we will have to pay the uttermost farthing. There's nobody to be left off. We must all do right by our neighbors."

Ginevra went home with a good many things to think about.

21

The Lorrie Meadow

It was high time, according to agricultural economics, that Donal Grant should be promoted a step in the ranks of labor. A youth like him was fit for horses and their work, and looked idle in a field with cattle. But Donal was not ambitious, at least in that direction. He was more and more in love with books and learning and the music of thought and word; and he well knew that no one doing a man's work upon a farm could have much time left for study. Therefore, with his parents' approval, he continued to fill the humbler office and receive the scantier wages belonging to it.

The day following their adventure on Glashgar, Nicie, being in the grounds with her little mistress, proposed in the afternoon that they should look whether they could see her brother down in the meadow of which her mother had spoken. Ginevra willingly agreed, and they took their way through the shrubbery to the bank of the little river—the largest tributary of the Daur from the roots of Glashgar.

"There he is!" cried Nicie.

"I see him," responded Ginny, "—with his cows all about the meadow."

Donal sat a little way from the river reading.

"He's at his book!" said Nicie.

"I wonder what book it is," said Ginny.

"That would be hard to say," answered Nicie. "Donal reads a lot of books—more, his mother says, than she doubts he can get the good out of."

"I should like to ask Donal what book he's got," said Ginny.

"I'll cry to him and you can ask," said Nicie:—"Donal!—Donal!"

Donal looked up and, seeing his sister, came running to the bank of the stream.

"Couldn't you come over, Donal?" said Nicie. "Here's Miss Galbraith who wants to ask you a question."

Donal was across in a moment, for here the water was nowhere over a foot or two in depth.

"Oh, Donal! You've wet your feet!" cried Ginevra.

Donal laughed.

"What harm will that do me, mem?"

"None, I hope," said Ginny; "but it might, you know."

"I might have been drowned," said Donal.

"Nicie," said Ginny with dignity, "your brother is laughing at me."

"No, no, mem," said Donal apologetically. "I was only so glad to see you and Nicie that I forgot my manners."

"Then," returned Ginny, quite satisfied, "would you mind telling me what book you were reading?"

"It's a book of ballads," answered Donal. "I'll read one of them to you if you like, mem."

"I should like very much," responded Ginny. "I've read all my own books till I'm tired of them, and I don't like Papa's books."

"I'll read you a little bit then and see if you like it. Here's a nice spot among the daisies."

She dropped at once on the little gowany bed, gathered her frock about her ankles, and said, "Sit down, Nicie. It's so kind of Donal to read something to us! I wonder what it's going to be."

Donal began an old ballad but then before it was finished had to rush through the burn without leave-taking, for Hornie was attempting a trespass; and the two girls, thinking it was time to go home, rose and climbed to the house at their leisure.

The next morning, not more than the gentlest hint was necessary to make Nicie remark that perhaps if they went down again to the Lorrie, Donal might come and bring the book. But when they reached the bank and looked across, they saw him occupied with Gibbie. The two had their heads close together over a slate upon which now the one, now the other, seemed to be drawing. This went on and on and they never looked up. Ginny would have gone home and come again in the afternoon, but Nicie called Donal. He sprang to his feet and came to them, followed by Gibbie. Donal crossed the burn, but Gibbie remained on the other side. When presently Donal took his book of ballads from his pocket and the little company seated themselves, Gibbie stood with his back to them and his eyes on the cattle. That morning they were not interrupted. Donal read to them for a whole hour.

After this, Ginevra went frequently with Nicie to see her mother, and learned much of the best from her. Often also they went down to the Lorrie and had an interview with Donal, which was longer or shorter as Gibbie was there or not to release him.

Ginny's life was now far happier than it had ever been. New channels of thought and feeling were opened, new questions were started, new interests awaked; so that instead of losing by Miss Machar's continued inability to teach her, she was learning far more than her former teacher could give her, learning it too with the pleasure which invariably accompanies true learning.

Though Ginevra was little more than a child, Donal felt from the first the charm of her society; and she by no means received without giving, for his mental development was greatly expedited thereby. Few weeks passed before he was her humble squire, devoted to her with all the chivalry of a youth for a girl whom he supposed as much his superior in kind as she is in worldly position. His sole advantage, in his own judgment, and that which alone procured him the privilege of her society was that he was older and therefore knew a little more.

He now first found himself capable of making verses—such as they were; and one day with his book before him he ventured to repeat, as if he read them from the book, the following. They halted a little, no doubt, in rhythm, neither were perfect, but for a beginning they had promise. Gibbie, who had thrown himself down on the other bank and lay listening, at once detected the change in the tone of his utterance, and before Donal ceased had concluded that he was not reading them but that they were his own.

> Rin, burnie! clatter;
>   To the sea win:
> Gien I was a watter,
>   Sae wad I rin.
>
> Blaw, win', caller, clean!
>   Here an' hyne awa':
> Gien I was a win',
>   Wadna I blaw!
>
> Shine, auld sun,
>   Shine strang an' fine:
> Gien I was the sun's son,
>   Herty I wad shine.

Hardly had he ended when Gibbie's pipe began from the opposite side of the water, and true to time and cadence and feeling, followed with just the one air to suit the song—from which Donal, to his comfort, understood that one at least of his audience had received his lilt. But Ginevra had not received it and, being therefore of her own mind and not of the song's, was critical.

At that very moment Hornie caused a diversion, and Gibbie understood what Donal was feeling too well to make even a pretense of going after her. I must to his praise record the fact that, instead of wreaking his mortification on the cow, Donal spared her several blows out of gratitude for the deliverance her misbehavior had wrought him. He was in no haste to return to his audience. To have his first poem thus rejected was killing. She was but a child who had so unkindly criticized it, but she was the child he wanted to please; and for a few moments life itself seemed scarcely worth having. He called himself a fool and resolved never to read another poem to a girl so long as he lived. By the time he had again walked through the burn, however, he was calm and comparatively wise and knew what to say.

"Do you hear yonder stream after you go to bed, mem?" he asked Ginevra as he climbed the bank, pointing a little lower down the stream to the mountain brook which there joined it.

"Always," she answered. "It runs right under my window."

"What kind of noise does it make?" he asked again.

"It's different at different times," she answered. "It sings and chatters in summer, and growls and cries and grumbles in winter, or after rain up in Glashgar."

"Do you think the stream's any happier in the summer, mem?"

"No, Donal; the burn has no life in it and so can't be happier one time than another."

"But when you're lying listening to the stream, did you never imagine yourself running down with it—down to the sea?"

"No, Donal; I always fancy myself going up the mountain where it comes from, and running about wild there in the wind, when all the time I know I'm safe and warm in bed. . . . Are you vexed with me, Donal?"

"No, no, mem. You're too good and pretty," answered Donal, "to be a vex to anybody."

Ginevra was silent. She could not quite understand Donal, and of this she was the more convinced when she saw the beautiful eyes of Gibbie fixed in admiration upon him.

The way Donal kept his vow never to read another poem of his own to a girl was to proceed that very night to make another for that express purpose as he lay awake in the darkness.

I doubt whether Ginevra understood this song better than the first, but she was now more careful of criticizing; and when by degrees it dawned upon Ginevra that Donal was the maker of certain of these verses he read, she grew half afraid of him and began to regard him with big eyes. He moved from a herdboy, an unintelligible person, to a poet, therefore a wonder.

22

Father and Daughter

By degrees Gibbie had come to be well known about the Mains and Glashruach. Angus's only recognition of him was a scowl in return for his smile; but, as I have said, he gave him no further annoyance, and the tales about the beast-loon were dying out from Daurside. Jean Mavor was a special friend to him; for she knew now well enough who had been her broonie and made him welcome as often as he showed himself with Donal.

In the autumn Mr. Galbraith returned to Glashruach but did not remain long. He was kinder than usual to Ginevra. Before he went he said to her that as Mr. Machar had sunk into a condition requiring his daughter's constant attention, he would find her an English governess as soon as he reached London. Meantime she must keep up her studies by herself as well as she could. Probably he forgot all about it, for the governess was not heard of at Glashruach, and things fell into their old way. There was no spiritual traffic between the father and daughter; consequently Ginevra never said anything about Donal or Gibbie or her friendship for Nicie. He had himself to blame altogether; he had made it impossible for her to talk to him. But it was well he remained in ignorance and so did not put a stop to the best education she could have at this time of her life—such as neither he nor any friend of his could have given her.

It was interrupted, however, by the arrival of the winter—a wild time in that region. To such feet as Ginevra's the cottage on Glashgar was for months almost inaccessible. More than once the Daur was frozen thick. Not a glimpse did Ginevra get all this time of Donal or of Gibbie.

At last like one of its own flowers in its own bosom, the spring began again to wake in God's thought of His world. The snow, like all other deaths, had to melt and run, leaving room for hope. Then the summer woke smiling and the two youths and the two maidens met yet again on Lorrie bank. The four were a year older, a year nearer trouble, and a year nearer getting out of it. Ginevra was more of a woman, Donal more of a poet, Nicie as nice and much the same, and Gibbie, if possible, more a foundling of the universe than ever. He was growing steadily. The mountain was a grand nursery for him and the result, both physical and spiritual, corresponded. Janet revered him as much as he revered her; the first impression he made upon her had never worn off—had only changed its color a little. More important even than a knowledge of the truth is a readiness to receive it; and Janet saw from the first that Gibbie's ignorance at its worst was but room vacant for the truth.

In the summer Mr. Galbraith reappeared unannounced at Glashruach, so changed that, startled at the sight of him, Ginevra stopped midway in her advance to greet him. The long, thin man was now haggard and worn; he looked sour and suspicious. He was annoyed that his daughter should recognize an alteration in him and, turning away, took no further notice of her presence. Ginevra knew from experience that the sight of tears would enrage him and with all her might repressed those she felt beginning to rise. She went up to him timidly and took the hand that hung by his side. He did not repel her but he left it hanging lifeless and returned with it no pressure upon her—which was much worse.

"Is anything the matter, Papa?" she asked with trembling voice.

"I am not aware that I have been in the habit of communicating with you on the subject of my affairs," he answered; "nor am I likely to begin to do so, where my return after so long an absence seems to give so little satisfaction."

"Oh, Papa! I was frightened to see you looking so ill."

"Such a remark upon my personal appearance is but a poor recognition of my labors for your benefit, I venture to think, Ginny," he said.

He was at the moment contemplating, as a necessity, the sale of every foot of the property her mother had brought him. Nothing less would serve to keep up his credit and gain time to disguise more than one failing scheme. Everything had of late been going badly. He had lost a good deal of his confidence and self-satisfaction; but he had gained no humility instead.

The servants found more change in him than Ginevra did. He found fault with everyone, so that even Joseph dared hardly open his mouth and said he must give warning. The day after his arrival he spent the morning with Angus walking over certain fields much desired, he knew, of a neighboring proprietor. Inwardly calculating the utmost he could venture to ask for them with a chance of selling, he scolded Ginevra severely on his return because she had not had lunch but had waited for him. A little reflection might have shown him she dared not take it without him. Naturally, therefore, she could not now eat because of a certain sensation in her throat. The instant he saw she was not eating, he ordered her out of the room; he would have no such airs in his family! By the end of the week such a sense of estrangement possessed Ginevra that she would turn on the stair and run up again if she heard her father's voice below.

In this evil mood he learned from someone (all his life Donal believed it was Fergus) a hint concerning the relations between his daughter and his tenant's herdboy. To describe the laird's feelings at the bare fact that such a hint was possible would be more labor than the result would repay.—What! his own flesh and blood, the heiress of Glashruach derive pleasure from the boorish talk of such a companion! It could not be true; the mere thought filled him with indignation! He was overwhelmed with a righteous disgust.

He watched and waited and more than once pretended to go away from home. At last one morning from the larch-wood, he saw the unnatural girl seated with her maid on the bank of the river, the herdboy reading to them, and on the other side the dumb idiot lying listening. Mr. Galbraith was almost beside himself. In a loud voice of bare command, he called to her to come to him. With a glance of terror at Nicie, she rose and they went up through the larches together.

I will not spend my efforts upon a reproduction of the verbal torrent of wrath with which the father assailed his shrinking, delicate, honestminded woman-child. As for Nicie, he dismissed her on the spot. She had to depart without even a good-bye from Ginevra, and went home weeping.

23

• • • • • • • • • • • • • • • • • • •

The Earthquake and the Storm

*E*ver since he became a dweller in the air of Glashgar and mindful of his first visit thereto and his grand experience on that occasion, Gibbie had been in the habit—as often as he saw reason to expect a thunderstorm—of ascending the mountain and there on the crest of the granite peak to await the arrival of the tumult.

Toward the evening of a wondrously fine day in the beginning of August, a perfect day of summer in her matronly beauty, it began to rain. All the next day the slopes and stairs of Glashgar were swept with heavy showers, driven slanting in strong gusts of wind from the northwest.

Gibbie drove his sheep to the refuge of a pen on the lower slope of a valley that ran at right angles to the wind. He then went home and, having told Robert what he had done and eaten his supper, set out in the early falling light to ascend the mountain. A great thunderstorm was at hand and was calling him. It was almost dark before he reached the top, but he knew the surface of Glashgar nearly as well as the floor of the cottage. Just as he had fought his way to the crest of the peak in the face of one of the fiercest of the blasts, a sudden rush of fire made the heavens like the smoke-filled vault of an oven, and at once the thunder followed in a succession of single, sharp explosions without any roll between. The mountain shook with the windy shocks, but the first of the thunderstorm was the worst, and it soon passed. The wind and the rain continued, and the darkness was filled with the rush of water wildly tearing down the sides of the mountain. Thus heaven and earth held communication in torrents all the night. To the ears and heart of Gibbie their noises were a mass of broken music. Every spring and autumn the floods came, and he knew them, and they were welcome to him in their seasons.

It required some care to find his way down through the darkness and the waters to the cottage, but as he was neither in fear nor in haste, he was in little danger. His hands and feet could pick out the path where his eyes were useless. When at length he reached his bed, it was not for a long time to sleep, but to lie awake and listen to the raging of the wind all about and above and below the cottage and the rushing of the streams down past it on every side.

He woke and it was morning. He rose and, dressing hastily, opened the door. What a picture of grey storm rose outspread before him! The wind fiercely invaded the cottage, thick charged with waterdrops. Stepping out he shut the door in haste lest it should blow upon the old people in bed and wake them. He could not see far on any side for the rain that fell and the mist and steam that arose, upon which the wind seemed to have no power; but wherever he did see, there water was running down. Up the mountain he went—he could hardly have told why. It was a wild, hopeless scene—as if God had turned His face away from the world and all nature was therefore drowned in tears. Gibbie stood gazing and thinking.

That moment Glashgar gave a great heave under him, then rocked and shook from side to side a little and settled down still and steady. The next instant came an explosion followed by a frightful roaring and hurling, as of mingled water and stones. On the side of the mountain beneath him he saw what through the mist looked like a cloud of smoke or dust rising to a height. He darted toward it. As he drew nearer, the cloud seemed to condense, and presently he saw plainly enough that it was a great column of water shooting up and out from the face of the hill. The mountain was cracked, and through the crack and down the hill a river was shooting a sheer cataract, raving and tearing and carrying stones and rocks with it like foam.

Suddenly Gibbie, in the midst of his astonishment and delight, noted the path of the new stream, and from his knowledge of the face of the mountain perceived that its course was direct for the cottage. Down the hill he shot after it.

The torrent had already worn for itself a channel. What earth there was it had swept clean away to the rock, and the loose stones it had thrown aside or hurled with it in its headlong course. But as Gibbie bounded along, following it with a speed almost equal to its own, he was checked in the midst of his haste by the sight, a few yards away, of another like terror—another torrent issuing from the side of the hill and rushing to swell the valley stream. Another and another he saw, with growing wonder as he ran. Two of them joined the one he was following, and he had to cross them as he could; the others he saw near and farther off. Now and then a huge boulder would go rolling, leaping, bounding down the hill before him, and just in time he escaped one that came springing after him as if it were a living thing that wanted to devour him. Nor was Glashgar the only torrent-bearing mountain of Gormgarnet that day, though the rain prevented Gibbie from seeing anything of what the rest of them were doing.

Gibbie at length forsook the bank of the new torrent to take the nearest way home. When he came near, to his amazement there stood the little house unharmed, but right next to it the garden ground was gone. He darted through the drizzle and spray, reached the door, and lifted the hatch. The same moment he heard Janet's voice in joyful greeting.

"Now, now! Come away, laddie," she said. "Who would have thought we would have had to leap the rock to get out of the water? But we're waitin' on you to go.—Come, Robert, we're off down the hill to the Mains."

She stood in the middle of the room in her best gown as if she had been going to church.

Robert rose from the edge of the bed, staff in hand, ready too. He also was in his Sunday clothes. Oscar, who could make no change of attire, wagged his tail when he saw him rise and got out of his way. The water, creeping in from all corners, threatened soon to render the place uninhabitable.

"Now, Gibbie," she said, "you go and loosen Crummie. But you'll have to lead her. She won't be able to see in such a wind as this, and there will be no plain road before her."

Gibbie shot round the corner to the byre, whence through all the roar every now and then they had heard the cavernous mooing of Crummie, piteous and low. He found a stream a foot deep running between her fore and hind legs and did not wonder that she wanted to be on the move. Speedily he loosed her and, fastening the chain-tether to her halter, led her out. She was terrified at sight of the falling water, and they had some trouble in getting her through it, but presently she was making the descent as carefully and successfully as any of them.

It was a heavy undertaking for the two old folk to walk all the way to the Mains and in such a state of the elements; but where there is no choice, we do well to make no difficulty. Janet was half-troubled that her mountain should have failed her. Robert plodded on in silence, and Gibbie was in great glee, singing after his fashion all the way, though now and then half-choked by the fierceness of the wind round some corner of rock, filled as it was with raindrops that stung like hailstones.

At length they reached the valley road. The water that ran in the bottom was the Lorrie. Three days ago it was a lively little stream. Now it had filled and far overflowed its banks to become a swift river. When they approached the bridge, however, by which they must cross the Lorrie to reach the Mains, their worst trouble lay before them. For the enemy, with whose reinforcements they had all the time been descending, showed himself ever in greater strength the farther they advanced; and here the road was flooded for a long way on both sides of the bridge. There was therefore a good deal of wading to be done. But the road was an embankment, there was little current, and in safety at last they ascended the rising ground on which the farm building stood. When they reached the yard, they sent Gibbie to find shelter for Crummie, and themselves went up to the house.

"The Lord preserve us!" cried Jean Mavor with uplifted hands when she saw them enter the kitchen.

"He'll do that, mem," returned Janet with a smile.

"But what can He do? If you're driven out of the hill, what's to become of the houses in the meadows? I'd like to know that!"

"The water's not up to your door yet," remarked Janet.

"God forbid!" retorted Jean.—"But, eh, you're wet!"

"Wet's not the word," said Robert, trying to laugh but failing from sheer exhaustion.

The farmer, hearing their voices, came into the kitchen.

"Hoot, Rob!" he said roughly as he entered, "I thought you had more sense! What's brought you here at such a time?"

"Fell necessity, sir," answered Robert.

"Necessity!" retorted the farmer. "Were you out of meal?"

"Out of dry meal, I don't doubt, by this time," replied Robert.

"Hoots! I wish we were in a like necessity—well up on the hill instead of down here upon the river-meadow. It's just clean ridiculous. You should have known better at your age, Rob. You should have thought twice, man."

"Indeed, sir," answered Robert, "there was little time to think, with the Glashgar burstin', and the water comin' in our house. You don't think Janet and me would be two such old fools as to put on our Sunday clothes to swim in if we thought to see things as we left them when we got back!"

"Haith! if the water was running into your house, man, it *was* time to leave."

The old people went to change their clothes for some Jean provided, and in the meantime she made up her fire and prepared some breakfast for them.

"And where's your dummie?" she asked, as they reentered the kitchen.

"He had poor Crummie to look after," answered Janet; "but he might have been in by this time."

"He'll be with Donal in the stall, no doubt," said Jean; "he's a little shy about comin' in without an invitation." She went to the door and called with a loud voice across the yard through the wind and the clashing torrents: "Donal, send the dummie in to his breakfast!"

"He's gone back to his sheep!" cried Donal in reply.

"Preserve us!—the creature will be lost!" exclaimed Jean.

"That's less likely than any man about the place," said Donal, half-angry with his mistress for calling his friend dummie. "Gibbie knows better what he's about than any two that thinks him a fool because he can't let out such stuff and nonsense as they can't keep in."

Jean went back to the kitchen only half reassured concerning her broonie, and far from contented with his absence. But she was glad to find that neither Janet nor Robert appeared alarmed at the news.

"I wish the creature had had some breakfast," she said.

"He had a little oatcake in his pocket," answered Janet.

"Hoots!" returned Jean.

When they had eaten their breakfast, Robert took his pipe to the barn, saying there was not much danger of fire that day; Janet washed up the dishes and sat down to her Book; and Jean went out and in, attending to many things.

24

•••••••••••••••••••

The Flood

Meantime the rain fell, the wind blew, and the water rose. Little could be done beyond feeding the animals, threshing a little corn in the barn, and twisting straw ropes for the thatch of the ricks for the coming harvest—if indeed there was a harvest, for already not a few of last year's ricks from farther up the country were floating past the Mains, down the Daur to the sea. The sight was a dreadful one to the farmers' eyes. From the Mains, to right and left as far as the bases of the hills instead of fields was water, yellow brown—here in still expanse or slow progress, there sweeping along in fierce current. The quieter parts of it were dotted with trees, divided by hedges, shaded with ears of corn; upon the swifter parts floated objects of all kinds.

Mr. Duff went wandering restlessly from one spot to another, finding nothing to do. In the gloaming, which fell the sooner that a rain blanket miles thick wrapped the earth up from the sun, he came across from the barn and, entering the kitchen, dropped weary with hopelessness on a chair.

From being nearly in the center of its own land, the farmsteading of the Mains was at a considerable distance from any other. But there were two or three cottages upon the land; and as the evening drew on, another aged pair, who lived in one only a few hundred yards from the house, made their appearance. They were soon followed by the wife of the foreman with her children, who lived farther off. Quickly the night closed in and Gibbie was not come. Robert was growing very uneasy; Janet kept comforting and reassuring him.

"There's one thing," said the old man: "Oscar's with him."

"Oscar's not with him," said Donal. "The dog came to me in the stable long after Gibbie was gone; he was lookin' for him."

Robert gave a great sigh but said nothing.

Janet did not sleep a wink that night: she had so many to pray for. Not Gibbie only, but every one of her family was in peril from the waters, all being employed along the valley of the Daur.

The dawn appeared—but the farm had vanished. Not even heads of growing corn were anywhere more to be seen. The loss would be severe, and John Duff's heart sank within him. The sheep which had been in the mown cloverfield that sloped to the burn were now all in the cornyard, and the water was there with them. If the rise did not soon cease, every rick would be afloat. There was little current, however, and not half the danger there would have been had the houses stood a few hundred yards in any direction from where they were.

"Have some breakfast, John," said his sister.

"Let them take it that hungers," he answered.

"Take it, or you'll not have the strength to be worth savin'," said Jean.

Thereupon he fell to it and ate, if not with appetite then with will that was wondrous.

The flood still grew, still the rain poured, and Gibbie did not come. Indeed, no one any longer expected him, whatever might have become of him. Except by boat the Mains was inaccessible now, they thought. Soon after breakfast, notwithstanding, a strange woman came to the door. Jean, who opened it to her knock, stood and stared speechless. It was a grey-haired woman, with a more disreputable look than her weather-flouted condition would account for.

"Grand weather for the ducks!" she said.

"Where do you come from?" returned Jean, who did not relish the freedom of her address.

"From over there," she answered.

"And how did you get here?"

"Upon my two legs."

Jean looked this way and that over the watery waste and again stared at the woman in growing bewilderment.

"Your legs must be longer than they look then, woman," said Jean, glancing at the lower part of the stranger's person.

The woman only laughed—a laugh without any laughter in it.

"Well, what do you want, now that you are here?" continued Jean with severity. "You didn't come to the Mains to tell them what kind of weather it is!"

"I came to wherever I could get," answered the woman, "and for my part, that's nothing to nobody now—though it's not as it once was—there might be more of me for the better of it. And so if you could give me a glass of whiskey   "

"You'll get no whiskey here," interrupted Jean with determination.

The woman gave a sigh and half turned away as if she would depart. But however she might have come, it was plainly impossible she could depart.

"Woman," said Jean, "know that I care nothing about you, and I don't like you, or the look of you; and if it were a fine summer night, I'd close my door in your face. But I dare not do that against my neighbor; so you can come in and sit down—my mind's spoken. You'll get what will hold the life in you, and a little bit of straw in the barn. Only you must keep quiet, for the goodman doesn't like tramps."

"Tramps here, tramps there!" exclaimed the woman, starting into high displeasure; "I would have you know I'm an honest woman, and no tramp!"

"You shouldn't look so much like one then," said Jean coolly. "But come in, and I'll say nothing so long as you behave."

The woman followed her, took the seat pointed out to her by the fire, and ate the cakes and milk handed her without a word of thanks. But she seemed to grow better tempered as she ate. On the other side of the fire sat Janet, knitting away busily with a look of ease and leisure. She said nothing but now and then cast a kindly glance out of her grey eyes at the woman.

With the first of the light, some of the men on the farm had set out to look for Gibbie, well knowing it would be a hard matter to reach Glashgar. About nine they returned, having found it impossible. One of them, caught in a current and swept into a hole, had barely escaped with his life. But they were unanimous that the dummie was better off in any cave on Glashgar than he would be in the best bedroom at the Mains if things went on as they threatened.

Robert had all the morning kept on going to the barn and back again to the kitchen, consumed with anxiety about the son of his old age. But the barn began to be flooded, and he had to limit his prayer-walk to the space between the door of the house and the chair where Janet sat— knitting busily and praying amidst the rush of the seaward torrents, the mad howling and screeching of the wind, and the lowing of the cattle.

"Is Gibbie worse off, Robert, in this water upon Glashgar, than the disciples in the boat on the Sea of Galilee when the Master didn't come to them? Take heart, man."

"You're right, Janet," answered Robert.

"Gibbie will probably be here when you least look for him," said Janet.

Neither of them caught the gleam that lighted the face of the strange woman at those last words of Janet. She looked up at her with the sharpest of glances, but the same instant compelled her countenance to resume its former expression of indifference, and under that became watchful of everything said and done.

Still the rain fell and the wind blew; the torrents came tearing down from the hills and shot madly into the rivers; the rivers ran into the valleys and deepened the lakes that filled them. On every side of the Mains, from the foot of Glashgar to Gormdhu, all was one yellow and red sea, with numberless roaring currents. It burrowed holes, opened long-deserted channels; here deposited inches of rich mold, there yards of sand and gravel; here it was carrying away fertile ground, leaving behind only bare rock or shingle where the corn had been waving; there it was scooping out the bed of a new lake. Houses were torn to pieces and their contents, as from broken boxes, sent wandering on the brown waste. Huge trees passed as if shot down an Alpine slide, cottages and bridges of stone giving way before them. Wooden mills, thatched roofs, great mill wheels went dipping and swaying and hobbling down. From the upper windows of the Mains, looking toward the chief current, they saw a drift of everything that would float—everything belonging to farms and dwellings. Chairs and tables, chests, carts, saddles, tubs of linen, beds and blankets, workbenches, harrows, girnels, planes, cheeses, churns, spinning wheels, cradles, iron pots, wheelbarrows—all these and many other things hurried past as they gazed.

The water was now in the stable and cowhouses and barn. A few minutes more and it would be creeping into the kitchen. The Daub and its tributary, the Lorrie, were about to merge their last difference on the floor of Jean's parlor. Worst of all, a rapid current had set in across the farther end of the stable, which no one had as yet observed.

Jean bustled about her work as usual and would accept no help from any of her guests in preparing dinner.

"There's one thing, Mother," said Donal, entering the kitchen covered with mud, a rabbit in one hand and a large salmon in the other, "we're not likely to starve, with salmon in the bushes and rabbits in the trees!"

Donal was being questioned by his master when the strange woman said, addressing no one in particular, "I doubt the gable of the stable will stand more than another half hour."

"It must fall then," said the farmer.

"Hoots!" said the woman, "don't talk that way, sir. You might at least give the poor beasts a chance."

"How would you do that?" said Jean. "If you cut them loose, they would but take to the water in fear and drown that much sooner."

"No, no, Jean," interposed the farmer, "they would take care of themselves to the last, and get to the driest spot possible, just as you would yourself."

"Allowing," said the stranger, "I would rather drown swimming than tied by the head. But you have a place to put them . . . What kind of floor is up the stairs there?"

"Ow, good enough floors," answered the farmer. "But it's the walls, woman, not the floor we have to be concerned about in this weather."

"If the joists be strong and well set into the walls, why shouldn't you take the horses up the stairs to your bedrooms? It'll be all to the good of the walls, for the weight of the beasts will be upon them to hold them down, and the whole house against the water. And if I were you, I would put the best of the cattle in the parlor and the kitchen here."

Mr. Duff broke into a strange laughter.

"Would you take up the carpets first, woman?" he said.

"I would," she answered; "that goes without sayin'—if there was time; but I tell you there is none; and you'll buy two or three carpets for the price of one horse."

"Haith! the woman's right," he cried, suddenly waking up to the sense of the proposal, and shot from the house.

All the women, Jean making no exception to any help now, rushed to carry the beds and blankets to the garret.

Just as Mr. Duff entered the stable from the nearer end, the opposite gable fell out with a great splash, letting in the wide level vision of turbidly raging waters, fading into the obscurity of the wind-driven rain. While he stared aghast, a great tree struck the wall like a battering ram so that the stable shook. The horses, which had been for some time moving uneasily,

were now quite scared. There was not a moment to be lost. Duff shouted
for his men; one or two came running; and in less than a minute more
those in the house heard the iron-shod feet splashing and stamping
through the water, as one after another the horses were brought across the
yard to the door of the house. Mr. Duff led by the halter his favorite Snowball, who was a good deal excited, plunging and rearing so that it was all
he could do to hold him. He had ordered the men to take the others first,
thinking he would follow more quietly. But the moment Snowball heard
the first thundering of hoofs on the stairs, he went out of his senses with
terror, broke from his master, and went plunging back to the stable. Duff
darted after him, but was only in time to see him rush from the farther
end into the swift current, where he was at once out of his depth. Instantly
caught and hurried, rolling over and over, the horse disappeared from his
master's sight.

He ran back into the house and up to the highest window. From that
he caught sight of him a long way down, swimming. Once or twice he
saw him turned heels over head. But alas! it was in the direction of the
Daur, which would soon, his master did not doubt, sweep his carcass into
the North Sea. With troubled heart he strained his sight after him as long
as he could distinguish his lessening head, but it got among some wreck
and, unable to tell anymore whether he saw it or not, he returned to his
men with his eyes full of tears.

25

• • • • • • • • • • • • • • • • • • •

Glashruach

As soon as Gibbie had found a stall for Crummie and thrown a great
dinner before her, he turned and sped back the way he had come. There
was no time to lose if he still would have the bridge to cross the Lorrie—
and his was indeed the last foot that ever touched it. Guiding himself by
well-known points, for he knew the country perhaps better than any man
born and bred in it, he made straight for Glashgar, itself hid in the rain.
Now wading, now swimming, now walking along the top of a wall, Gibbie
held stoutly on. And at length, clear of the level water and with only the
torrents to mind, he set off up the hill. It was not so hard a struggle to
cross the water, but he had still to get to the other side of several torrents
far more dangerous than any current he had been in. Again and again he
had to ascend a long distance before he found a possible place to cross,
but he reached the fold at last.

It was a little valley opening on that where lay the tarn. Swollen to a
lake, the waters of it were now at the very gate of the pen. Left where they

were, the sheep would probably be drowned; if not, they would be starved. But if he let them go, they would keep out of the water and find for themselves what food and shelter were to be had. He opened the gate, drove them out and a little way up the hill, and left them.

By this time it was about two o'clock, and Gibbie was very hungry. He had enough of the water for one day, however, and was not inclined to return to the Mains. If the cottage were still standing—and it might be— he would find plenty to eat there. He turned toward it. Great was his pleasure when, after another long struggle, he perceived that not only was the cottage there but the torrent was gone. Either the flow from the mountain had ceased or the course of the water had been diverted.

When he reached home, he swept out the water that lay on the floor, took the driest peats he could find, succeeded in lighting a large fire, and made himself some water-brose.

His hunger appeased, he sat resting in Robert's chair, gradually drying. Falling asleep, he slept for an hour or so. When he woke, he took his New Testament and began to read. He read until he came to these words: "Hereby perceive we the love of God, because he laid down his life for us, and we ought to lay down our lives for the brethren."

Gibbie said to himself, "Here am I sittin' with my fire and my soup and my Bible, and all the world below Glashgar lying in a flood! I can't lay down my life to save their souls; so I must save for them what I can—it may be but a hen or a calf."

The Bible was back in its place and Gibbie out of the door the same moment. He had not an idea what he was going to do. All he yet understood was that he must go down the hill to be where things might have to be done—and before darkness fell. He must go where there were people.

His first definitely directive thought was that his nearest neighbors were likely enough to be in trouble—"the folk at the main house." He would go straight there.

Glashruach stood on one of the roots of the Glashgar where the mountain settles down into the valley of the Daur. Immediately outside its principal gate ran the Glashburn; on the other side of the house, within the grounds, ran a smaller hill stream, already mentioned as passing close under Ginevra's window. Both these fell into the Lorrie. Between them the mountain sloped gently up for some little distance clothed with forest. On the side of the smaller burn, however, the side opposite the house, the ground rose abruptly. Straight from the mountain between the two streams Gibbie approached the house, through larches and pines, raging and roaring in the wind. Below him was a wide, swift, fiercely rushing river, where water was none before! No, he made no mistake; there was the rest of the road, the end of it next to the house! That was a great piece of it that fell frothing into the river and vanished! Bridge and gate and wall were gone utterly. The burn had swallowed them and now, foaming with madness, was roaring along a great way within the grounds and rapidly drawing nearer to the house, tearing to pieces and devouring all that defended it. Not with all he had that day seen and gone through had Gibbie until now gathered any notion of the force of the rushing water.

He darted down the hill.

Mr. Galbraith had gone again, leaving Ginevra to the care of Mistress MacFarlane, the housekeeper. At this moment, however, they were not alone, for on the other side of the fire sat Angus, not thither attracted by any friendship for the housekeeper but by the glass of whiskey which he sipped as he talked. Many a flood had Angus seen and some that had done frightful damage, but never one that had caused him anxiety; and although this was worse than any of the rest, he had not yet a notion how bad it really was.

In her room, Ginevra wandered listlessly to the window and stood there gazing out on the wild confusion—the burn roaring below, the trees opposite ready to be torn to pieces by the wind, and the valley beneath covered with stormy water. The tumult was so loud that she did not hear a gentle knock at her door. As she turned away she saw it softly open and there, to her astonishment, stood Gibbie, come, she imagined, to seek shelter because their cottage had been blown down.

"You mustn't come here, Gibbie," she said, advancing. "Go down to the kitchen, to Mistress MacFarlane. She will see to what you want."

Gibbie made eager signs to her to go with him. She concluded that he wanted her to accompany him to the kitchen and speak for him; but knowing that would only enrage her keeper with them both, she shook her head and went back to the window. The moment she looked out, she gave a cry, and stood staring. Gibbie had followed her, softly as swiftly, and looking out also saw good cause indeed for her astonishment: the channel of the raging burn was all but dry! Instantly he understood what it meant.

In his impotence to persuade, he caught the girl in his arms and rushed with her from the room. She had faith enough in him by this time not to struggle or scream. He shot down the stair with her and out of the front door. Her weight was nothing to his excited strength. The moment they issued, and she saw the Glashburn raving along through the lawn with little more than the breadth of the drive between it and the house, she saw the necessity of escape, though she did not perceive half the dire necessity for haste. Every few moments, a great gush would dash out twelve or fifteen yards over the gravel and sink again, carrying many feet of the bank with it and widening by so much the raging channel.

"Put me down, Gibbie," she said; "I will run as fast as you like."

He obeyed at once.

"Oh," she cried, "Mistress MacFarlane!—I wonder if she knows. Run and knock at the kitchen window."

Gibbie darted off, gave three loud hurried taps on the window, came flying back, took Ginevra's hand in his, drew her on till she was at her full speed, turned sharp to the left round the corner of the house, and shot down to the empty channel of the burn. As they crossed it, even to the inexperienced eyes of the girl it was plain what had caused the phenomenon. A short distance up the stream, the whole facing of its lofty right bank had slipped down into its channel. Not a tree, not a shrub, not a bed of moss was to be seen; all was bare, wet rock. Any moment the barrier might give way and the water resume its course. They made haste, therefore, to climb the opposite bank. In places it was very steep, and the soil slipped so that often it seemed on its way with them to the bottom, while the wind threatened to uproot the trees to which they clung. It was with a fierce scramble they gained the top. Then the sight was a grand one.

The arrested water swirled and beat and foamed against the landslide, then rushed to the left, through the wood, over bushes and stones, a raging river, the wind tearing off the tops of its waves, to the Glashburn, into which it plunged, swelling yet higher its huge volume. Rapidly it cut for itself a new channel. Every moment a tree fell and shot with it like a rocket. Looking up its course, they saw it come down the hillside a white streak, and burst into boiling brown and roar at their feet. The wind nearly swept them from their place; but they clung to the great stones and saw the airy torrent fill itself with branches and leaves and lumps of foam. Then first Ginevra became fully aware of the danger in which the house from which Gibbie had rescued her was standing.

"But where's Mistress MacFarlane?" she said. "Oh, Gibbie! We mustn't leave her."

He replied by pointing down to the bed of the stream; she and Angus were crossing. Ginevra was satisfied when she saw the gamekeeper with her, and they set out as fast as they could go, ascending the mountain. Gibbie was eager to have her in warmth and safety before it was dark.

It was an undertaking hard for any girl, especially such for one unaccustomed to exertion. But the excitement of battling with the storm, the joy of adventure, and the pleasure of feeling her own strength sustained her well for a long time. She never lost her courage, and Gibbie, though he could not hearten her with words, was so ready with smile and laugh, so fearless, so free from anxiety while doing everything he could think of to lessen her toil and pain, that she hardly felt in his silence any lack. It was getting dark when they reached the only spot where he judged it possible to cross the Glashburn. He carried her over and then it was all downhill to the cottage. Once inside it, Ginevra threw herself into Robert's chair and laughed, then cried, then laughed again.

Gibbie blew up the peats, made a good fire, and put on water to boil; then opened Janet's drawers and having signified to his companion to take what she could find, went to the cowhouse, threw himself on a heap of wet straw, worn out, and had enough to do to keep himself from falling asleep.

A little rested, he rose and reentered the cottage, when a merry laugh from both of them went ringing out into the storm; the little lady was dressed in Janet's workday garments and making porridge. She looked very funny. Gibbie found plenty of milk in the dairy under the rock, and they ate their supper together in gladness. Then Gibbie prepared the bed in the little closet for his guest, and she slept as if she had not slept for a week.

Gibbie woke with the first of the dawn. The rain still fell—descending in spoonfuls rather than drops; the wind kept shaping itself into long, hopeless howls, rising to shrill yells that went drifting away over the land, and then howling again. There must be more for Gibbie to do! He must go again to the foot of the mountain and see if there was anybody to help. They might even be in trouble at the Mains, who could tell!

Ginevra woke, rose, made herself as tidy as she could, and left her closet. Gibbie was not in the cottage. She blew up the fire, and finding the pot ready beside it with clean water, she set it on to boil. Gibbie did not come. The water boiled. She took it off but, being hungry, put it on again. Several times she took it off and put it on again. Gibbie never came. She made herself some porridge at last. Everything necessary was upon the table, and as she poured the gruel into the wooden dish for the purpose, she noticed a slate beside it with something written upon it. The words were, "I will cum back as soon as I cann."

She was alone, then! It was dreadful; but she was too hungry to think about it. She ate her porridge and then began to cry. It was very unkind of Gibbie to leave her, she said to herself. But, then, he was a sort of angel and doubtless had to go and help somebody else. There was a little pile of books on the table which he must have left for her. She began examining them, and soon found something to interest her so that an hour or two passed quickly. But Gibbie did not return and the day went wearily. She cried now and then, made great efforts to be patient, succeeded pretty well for a while, and cried again.

Still Gibbie did not come. Before the day was over, she had had a good lesson in praying. For here she was, one who had never yet acted on her own responsibility, alone on a bare mountainside, in the heart of a storm which seemed as if it would never cease. And not a creature knew where she was but the dumb boy, and he had left her!

The noises were terrible. Through the general roar of wind and water and rain, every now and then came a sharper sound, like a report or crack, followed by a strange thunder, it seemed. They were the noises of stones carried down by the streams, grinding against each other, and dashing stone against stone; and of rocks falling and rolling, and bounding against their fast-rooted neighbors. When it began to grow dark, her misery seemed more than she could bear; but then, happily, she grew sleepy and slept the darkness away.

With the new light came new promise and fresh hope. It no longer rained so fiercely; the wind had fallen; and the streams did not run so furious a race down the sides of the mountain. She ran to the burn, got some water to wash herself—she could not spare the clear water, of which there was some still left in Janet's pails—and put on her own clothes, which were now quite dry. Then she got herself some breakfast, and after that tried to say her prayers.

26

•••••••••••••••••••

Angus MacPholp

*G*ibbie sped down the hill through a worse rain than ever. Going down his own side of the Glashburn, the nearest path to the valley, the game-keeper's cottage was the first dwelling on his way.

It had been with great difficulty (for even Angus did not know the mountain so well as Gibbie) that the gamekeeper reached it with the housekeeper the night before. All night Angus watched, peering into the darkness, but saw nothing except three lights that burned above the water—one of them, he thought, at the Mains. The other two went out in the darkness. When the morning came, there was the Glashburn, meeting the Lorrie in his garden. But the cottage was well built and fit to stand a good siege. In a few minutes they were isolated, with the current of the Glashburn on one side and that of the Lorrie in front. When he saw the water come in at the front and back doors at once, Angus ordered his family up the stair.

As Gibbie came down the hill, he heard Mrs. MacPholp screaming in agony, and he ran at full speed toward the cottage. The gamekeeper was in the raging water trying to rescue a favorite dog. About thirty yards from the house, the current bore Angus straight into a large elder tree. He got into the middle of it and there remained, trembling. Gibbie, however, did not see him at first; plunging in, he swam round to the front of the cottage to learn what was the matter. There the wife's gesticulations directed his eyes to her drowning husband.

But what was he to do? He could swim to the tree well enough and, he thought, back again, but how was that to be made of service to Angus? If he had a line, and there must be plenty of lines in the cottage, he could send him the end of it. He caught hold of the eaves and scrambled onto the roof. But in the folly and faithlessness of her despair, the woman would not let him enter. She struck at him from the window, crying, "You'll not come in here with my husband drowning yonder! Go to him, you coward!"

Never had poor Gibbie so much missed the use of speech.

On the slope of the roof he could do little to force an entrance, there-fore threw himself off it to seek another and betook himself to the thin windows below. Through that of Angus's room he caught sight of a floating anker cask. It was the very thing! And there on the walls hung a quantity of nets and cordage! But how to get in? It was a sash-window and of course swollen with the wet, therefore not to be opened; and there was not a square in it large enough to let him through. He swam to the other side, crept softly onto the roof and over the ridge. But a broken slate betrayed him. The woman saw him, rushed to the fireplace, caught up the poker, and darted back to defend the window.

"You'll not come in here, I tell you," she screeched, "with my man stickin' in yonder tree!"

Gibbie advanced. She made a blow at him with the poker. He caught it, wrenched it from her grasp, and threw himself from the roof. The next moment they heard the poker at work, smashing the window.

"He'll be in and murder us all!" cried the mother and ran to the stair, while the children screamed with terror.

But the water was far too deep for her. She returned to the attic, barricaded the door, and went again to the window to watch her drowning husband.

Gibbie was inside in a moment and seizing the cask proceeded to attach to it a strong line. Satisfied at length, he floated out his barrel and followed with the line in his hand to aid its direction if necessary. It struck the tree. With a yell of joy Angus laid hold of it and, hauling the line taut and feeling it secure, committed himself at once to the water. He held by the barrel and swam with his legs while Gibbie, away to the side with a hold on the rope, was swimming his hardest to draw him out of the current. But a weary man was Angus when at length he reached the house. It was all he could do to get himself in at the window and crawl up the stair. At the top of it he fell benumbed on the floor.

By the time the repentant and grateful Mistress MacPholp thought of Gibbie, not a trace of him was to be seen. While they looked for him in the water and on the land, Gibbie was again in the room below carrying out a fresh thought. He emptied the cask, into which a good deal of water had got, then corked the bunghole tight, laced the cask up in a piece of net, attached the line to the net, and wound it about the cask by rolling the latter round and round. He took the cask between his hands, and pushed from the window straight into the current of the Glashburn. In a moment it had swept him to the Lorrie. By the greater rapidity of the former, he got easily across the heavier current of the latter and was presently in water comparatively still, swimming quietly toward the Mains. Not a human being was visible and but a few house roofs and tops of trees showing like low bushes. He drew near the Mains.

What was that cry from far away? Surely it must be that of a horse in danger! It brought a lusty equine response from the farm. Where could horses be with such a depth of water about the place? Then began a great lowing of cattle. But again came the cry of the horse from afar and Gibbie, this time recognizing the voice as Snowball's, forgot the rest. The cry came again and again so that he was satisfied in what direction he must look. He seemed to see white against the brown water, far away to the left. It might be Snowball on the turnpike road, which thereabout ran along the top of a high embankment. He rolled the line about the barrel and pushed vigorously for what might be the horse.

It took him a weary hour—in so many currents was he caught, one after the other, all straining to carry him far below the object he wanted to reach. When at length he scrambled on the embankment beside the poor, shivering, perishing creature, the horse gave a low neigh of delight; he did not know Gibbie, but he was a human being. He was quite cowed and submissive, and Gibbie at once set about his rescue. He tied the end of the line to the remnant of the halter on his head. Encouraged by the pressure of the halter, the horse followed, and they made for the Mains. It was a long journey, and Gibbie had not breath enough to sing to Snowball, but he made what noise he could, and they got slowly along.

27

....

The Raft

Mistress Croale was not the last who arrived at the Mains. Just after the loss of Snowball, a woman came floating into the farmyard on a raft with her four little children seated around her, holding the skirt of her gown above her head and out between her hands for a sail. She had made the raft herself by tying some bars of a paling together and crossing them with what other bits of wood she could find. Nobody knew her. She had come down the Lorrie.

The strangers were mostly in Fergus's bedroom; the horses were all in their owner's; and the cattle were in the remaining rooms. Bursts of talk among the women were followed by fits of silence. Who could tell how long the flood might last! or indeed whether the house might not be undermined before morning, or be struck by one of those big things of which so many floated by and give way with one terrible crash. Mr. Duff, while preserving a tolerable calm exterior, was nearly at his wits' end. He would stand for half an hour together with his hands in his pockets, looking motionless out of a window, murmuring now and then to himself, "This is clean ridiculous!" But when anything had to be done, he was active enough. Mistress Croale sat in a corner, very quiet and looking not a little cowed. There was altogether more water than she liked. Now and then she lifted her lurid black eyes to Janet, who stood at one of the windows, knitting away at her master's stocking and casting many a calm glance at the brown waters and the strange drift that covered them.

"If only Gibbie was here!" said Janet now and again.

"You have more than once made mention of one connected with you by the name of Gibbie," said Mistress Croale.

"Ay," answered Janet, "and what may be your interest in him?"

"Oh, nothing," returned Mistress Croale. "I knew one of that name long ago that was lost sight of."

"There's Gibbies here and Gibbies there," remarked Janet, probing her.

"But there's not many wee Sir Gibbies, or the world would not be so doomed."

Janet was arrested in her turn. Could the fierce, repellent woman be the mother of her gracious Gibbie? Could she be, and look so lost? But the loss of him had lost her perhaps. Anyhow, God was his Father, whoever was the mother of him.

"How did you come to lose your child, woman?" she asked.

But Mistress Croale was careful also, and had her reasons.

"He ran from the bloody hand," she said enigmatically.

Janet recalled how Gibbie came to her scored by the hand of cruelty.

"How did he come by the bonnie nickname?" she asked at length.

"Nickname?" retorted Mistress Croale fiercely. "His own name and title by law and right, as sure as ever there was a King James that first put his hand to makin' of baronets!—as it's often I have heard Sir George, the father of him, tell the same."

She ceased abruptly, annoyed with herself it seemed for having said so much.

"You wouldn't be the lady yourself, would you, mem?" suggested Janet in her gentlest voice.

Mistress Croale made her no answer. Perhaps she thought of the days when she alone of women did the simplest of woman's offices for Sir George.

"It's long since you lost him?" asked Janet after a pause.

"Ay," she answered, gruffly and discourteously in a tone intended to quench interrogation.

But Janet persisted.

"Would you know him again if you saw him?"

"Know him? I would know him if he had grown to be a grandfather. 'Know him,' said she! Whoever knew him as I did, child that he was, and wouldn't know him if he were dead and an angel made of him!—But well I know, it's little difference that would make!"

She rose in her excitement and, going to the other window, stood gazing vacantly out upon the rushing sea. To Janet it was plain she knew more about Gibbie than she was inclined to tell, and it gave her a momentary sting of apprehension.

"What was it about him that you knew so well?" she asked in a tone of indifference, as if speaking only through the meshes of her work.

"I'll know those who ask before I tell," she replied sullenly. But the next instant she screamed aloud, "Lord God Almighty! yon's him! yon's himself!"—and stretching out her arms, dashed a hand through a pane, letting in an eddying swirl of wind and water, while the blood streamed unheeded from her wrist.

The same moment Jean entered the room. She heard both the cry and the sound of the breaking glass.

"What set off the beggar-wife!" she exclaimed.

Mistress Croale took no heed. She stood now staring from the window still as a statue except for the panting motion of her sides. At the other window stood Janet, gazing also, with blessed face. For there, like a triton of a sea horse, came Gibbie through the water on Snowball swimming wearily.

He caught sight of Janet at the window and straightaway his countenance was radiant with smiles. Mistress Croale gave a shuddering sigh, drew back from her window, and betook herself again to her dark corner. Jean went to Janet's broonie, saving from the waters the lost and lamented Snowball. She shouted to her brother.

"John! John! here's your Snowball . . . here's your Snowball!"

John ran to her call and, beside himself with joy when he saw his favorite come swimming along, threw the window wide and began to bawl the most unnecessary directions and encouragements, as if the exploit had been brought thus far toward a happy conclusion solely through him. From all the windows Gibbie was welcomed with shouts and cheers and congratulations.

"Lord preserve us!" cried Mr. Duff, recognizing the rider at last, "it's Rob Grant's innocent! Who would have thought it!"

"Take him round the door . . . Where did you find him?—You would best get him in at the window on to the stair . . . He must be hungry.—You'll be wet, I'm thinkin'! . . . Come up the stair, and tell us all about it." A score of such conflicting shouts assailed Gibbie as he approached, and he replied to them all simply with a wide smile.

When they arrived at the door, they found a difficulty awaiting them. The water was now so high that Snowball's head rose above the lintel; and though all animals can swim, they do not all know how to dive. A tumult of suggestions immediately broke out. But Donal had already thrown himself from a window with a rope and swung to Gibbie's assistance; the two understood each other and, heeding nothing the rest were saying, held their own communications. In a minute the rope was fastened round Snowball's body and the end of it drawn between his forelegs and through the ring of his headstall. Donal swam with it to his mother on the stair with the request that as soon as she saw Snowball's head under the water, she would pull with all her might and draw him in at the door. Donal then swam back and threw his arms round Snowball's neck from below, while the same moment Gibbie cast his whole weight on it from above. The horse was over head and ears in an instant and through the door in another. With snorting nostrils and blazing eyes, his head rose in the passage, and in terror he struck out for the stair. As he scrambled heavily up from the water, his master and Robert seized him and with much petting and patting and gentling, though there was little enough difficulty in managing him now, conducted him into the bedroom to the rest of the horses. There he was welcomed by his companions and immediately began devouring the hay upon his master's bedstead. Gibbie came close behind him, was seized by Janet at the top of the stair, embraced like one come alive from the grave, and led dripping as he was into the room where the women were.

The farmer looked back from the door as he was leaving the room. Gibbie was performing a wild circular dance of which Janet was the center, throwing his limbs about like the toy the children call a Jumping Jack; this ended suddenly in a motionless ecstasy upon one leg. Having regarded for a moment the rescuer of Snowball with astonishment, John Duff turned away. It did not occur to him that it was the joy of having saved that caused Gibbie's merriment thus to overflow.

For all the excitement Mistress Croale had shown at first view of Gibbie, she sat still in her dusky corner, made no movement toward him nor did anything to attract his attention, only kept her eyes fixed upon him; and Janet in her mingled joy and pain forgot her altogether. When at length it recurred to her that she was in the room, she cast a somewhat anxious glance toward the place she had occupied all day. It was empty; and Janet was perplexed to think how she had gone unseen.

At suppertime Mistress Croale was missing altogether. Nobody could with certainty say when he had last seen her. The house was searched from top to bottom, and the conclusion arrived at was that she must have fallen from some window and been drowned—only, surely she would at least have uttered one cry! Examining certain of the windows to know whether she might not have left some sign of such an exit, the farmer discovered that the raft was gone which brought the woman and her children.

"Losh!" cried another man, "yonder will be her I saw an hour ago."

"You gowk!" said his master. "How could she go so far without going to the bottom?"

"On the raft, sir," answered the man. "I took her for a dog on a door. The wife must be a witch!"

John Duff stared at the man with his mouth open, and for half a minute all were dumb. The thing was incredible, yet hardly to be controverted. The woman was gone, the raft was gone, and something strange that might be the two together had been observed about the time when she ceased to be observed in the house.

Mr. Duff said the luck changed with the return of Snowball—his sister said, with the departure of the beggar-wife. Before dark the rain had ceased, and it became evident that the water had not risen for the last half hour. In two hours more it had sunk a quarter of an inch.

Gibbie threw himself on the floor beside his mother's chair; she covered him with her grey cloak; and he fell fast asleep. At dawn, he awoke with a start. He had dreamed that Ginevra was in trouble. He made Janet understand that he would return to guide them home as soon as the way was practicable, and set out at once to find a way.

The water fell rapidly. Almost as soon as it was morning, the people at the Mains could begin doing a little toward restoration.

In the afternoon, Gibbie reappeared at the Mains, and Robert and Janet set out at once to go home with him. It was a long journey for them—he had to take them so many rounds. They rested at several houses, and saw much misery on their way. It was night before they arrived at the cottage. They found it warm and clean and tidy; Ginevra had, like a true lady, swept the house that gave her shelter. For Ginevra it was heavenly bliss to hear their approaching footsteps; and before she left them she had thoroughly learned that the poorest place where the atmosphere is love is more homely and, by consequence, more heavenly than the most beautiful, even where law and order are elements supreme.

As to the strange woman's evident knowledge concerning Gibbie, Janet could do nothing but wait—fearing rather than hoping; but she had got so far above time and chance that nothing really troubled her, and she could wait quietly.

28

••••••••••••••••••

Mr. Sclater

*I*t may be remembered that Rev. Clement Sclater, upon Gibbie's disappearance from the city, felt great interest in his fate. From such questions as started about the boy himself, he gathered all the information at which he could arrive concerning his family and history. That done, he proceeded to attempt interesting in his unknown fortunes those relatives of Gibbie's mother whose existence and residences he had discovered. In this, however, he had met with no success.

At the house where she was born, there was now no one but a second cousin, to whom her elder brother, dying unmarried, had left the small estate of the Withrops along with the family contempt for her husband, and for her because of him. So said the cousin to Mr. Sclater. As to the orphan, he said, to speak honestly, the more entirely he disappeared, the better he would consider it. The younger brother who had taken to business was the senior partner in a large ship-building firm at Greenock.

William Fuller Withrop was a bachelor, and reputed rich. What Mr. Sclater heard of him did not arouse brilliant hopes. To leave no stone unturned, however, he wrote to Mr. Withrop. The answer he received was that the sister, concerning whose child he had applied to him, had never been anything but a trouble to the family, and it could hardly be expected of him to show any lively interest in her offspring.

Thus failing, Mr. Sclater said to himself he had done all that could be required of him.

One morning some years later, as he sat at breakfast with his wife, reading the morning paper, his eye fell upon a paragraph announcing the sudden death of a well-known William Fuller Withrop, of the eminent ship-building firm of Greenock. He had left no will but an estate of some two hundred thousand pounds.

The minister thereupon sprang from his chair and ran straight from the house to the top step of his lawyer's door.

From his lawyer he would have gone at once to Mistress Croale, but he had not an idea where she might even be heard of. For some years now she had made her living, one poor enough, by hawking small household necessities.

On her next return to the Daurfoot, as the part of the city was called where now she was most at home, she had heard the astounding and welcome news that Gibbie had fallen heir to a large property and that the reward of one hundred pounds had been proclaimed to anyone giving such information as should lead to the discovery of Sir Gilbert Galbraith, commonly known as "wee Sir Gibbie." A description of him was added, and Mistress Croale saw the necessity of haste to any hope of advantage. She had nothing to guide her beyond the fact of Sir George's habit of referring to the property on Daurside, and the assurance that with the said habit Gibbie must have been as familiar as herself.

With this initiative, as she must begin somewhere and could prosecute her business anywhere, she filled her basket and set out at once for Daurside. There, after a good deal of wandering hither and thither, she had made the desired discovery unexpectedly and marvelously, and left behind her in the valley the reputation of having been on more familiar terms with the flood and the causes of it than was possible to any but one who kept company worse than human.

29
. . . .

Mr. Galbraith

The next morning, Janet felt herself duty-bound to make inquiry concerning those interested in Miss Galbraith. She made the best of her way with Gibbie to Glashruach but found it a ruin in a wilderness. Acres of trees and shrubbery had disappeared and a hollow waste of sand and gravel was in their place. What was left of the house stood on the edge of a red, gravelly precipice of fifty feet in height. At the foot lay the stones of the kitchen wing in which had been the room whence Gibbie carried Ginevra. The newer part of the house was gone from its very roots; the ancient portion, all innovations wiped from it, stood grim, desolated, marred and defiant as of old. Not a sign of life was about the place; the very birds had fled. With difficulty they crossed the burn to the game-keeper's cottage. But they saw only a little girl who told them her father had gone to find the laird, that her mother was ill in bed, and Mistress MacFarlane on her way to her own people.

"My dear missie," said Janet, when they got home, "you must write to your father, or he'll be out of his wits about you."

Ginevra wrote therefore to the duke's and to the laird's usual address in London as well; but he was on his way from the one place to the other when Angus overtook him, and received neither letter.

Now came to the girl a few such days of delight, of freedom, of life as she had never even dreamed of. She roamed Glashgar with Gibbie, kindest and most interesting of companions. Wherever his sheep went, she went too, and to many places besides—some of them such strange, wild, terrible places as would have terrified her without him.

What a boy he was! He never hurt anything and nothing ever seemed to hurt him. And what a number of things he knew! He showed her things on the mountain, things in the sky, things in the pools and streams wherever they went. He did better than tell her about them; he made her see them, and then the things themselves told her. She was not always certain she saw just what he wanted her to see, but she always saw something that made her glad with knowledge. He had a New Testament Janet had given him which he carried in his pocket; and when she joined him, for he was always out with his sheep hours before she was up, she would generally find him seated on a stone or lying in the heather with the little book in his hand. The moment he saw her, he would spring merrily up to welcome her.

On the fourth day, the rain, which had been coming and going, finally cleared off, the sun was again glorious, and the farmers began to hope a little for the drying and ripening of some portion of their crops. Then first Ginevra asked Gibbie to take her down to Glashruach; she wanted to see the ruin they had described to her.

When she came near she neither wept nor wailed. So utterly altered was the look of everything that had she come upon it unexpectedly, she would not have recognized either place or house. They went up to a door. She seemed never to have seen it; but when they entered, she knew it as one from the hall into a passage which, with what it led to being gone, the inner had become an outer door. A quantity of sand was heaped up in the hall, and the wainscot was wet and swelled and bulging. They went into the dining room. It was a miserable sight. The thick carpet was sodden—spongy like a bed of moss after heavy rains; the leather chairs looked diseased; the color was all gone from the table; the paper hung loose from the walls.

She ascended the old stone stair which led to her father's rooms above, went into his study, and there not a hair was out of its place. She walked toward the window to look across to where once had been her own chamber. But as she approached it, there, behind the curtain, she saw her father, motionless, looking out. She turned pale and stood. Even at such a time had she known he was in the house, she would not have dared set her foot in that room. Gibbie, who had followed and entered behind her, perceived her hesitation, saw and recognized the back of the laird, knew that she was afraid of her father, and stood also waiting, he knew not for what.

Becoming aware of a presence, the laird half turned; seeing Gibbie, he imagined he had supposed the place deserted and entered in a prowling way. With stately offense the man asked what he wanted there, and waved his dismissal. Then he first saw the other, standing white-faced with eyes fixed upon him. He turned pale also, and stood staring at her. For one instant of unreasoning weakness, he imagined he saw a ghost. It was but one moment but it might have been more had not Ginevra walked slowly up to him saying in a trembling voice, as if she expected the blame of all that had happened, "I couldn't help it, Papa." He took her in his arms and kissed her. She clung to him, trembling now with pleasure as well as apprehension. But the end came sooner than she feared. For when the father rose erect from her embrace, there, to his amazement, still stood the odd-looking, outlandish intruder, smiling with the most impertinent interest!

"Go away, boy. You have nothing to do here," said the laird.

"Oh, Papa!" cried Ginevra, clasping her hands, "that's Gibbie! He saved my life. I should have drowned but for him."

The laird was both proud and stupid, therefore more than ordinarily slow to understand what he was unprepared to hear.

"I am much obliged to him," he said haughtily; "but there is no occasion for him to wait."

At this point his sluggish mind began to recall something.—Why, this was the very boy he saw in the meadow with her that morning!—He turned fiercely upon him where Gibbie lingered, either hoping for a word of adieu from Ginevra or unwilling to go while she was uncomfortable.

"Leave the house instantly," he said, "or I will knock you down."

"Oh, Papa!" moaned Ginevra wildly. "Don't speak so to Gibbie. He is a good boy. It was he that Angus whipped so cruelly—long ago. I have never been able to forget it."

Her father was confounded at her presumption. How dared she expostulate with him! She had grown a bold, bad girl! Good heavens! Evil communications!

"If he does not get out of this house directly," he cried, "I will have him whipped again! Angus!"

He shouted the name, and its echo came back in a wild tone, altogether strange to Ginevra. She seemed struggling in the meshes of an evil dream. Involuntarily she uttered a cry of terror and distress. Gibbie was at her side instantly, putting out his hand to comfort her. She was just laying hers on his arm, scarcely knowing what she did, when her father seized him and dashed him to the other side of the room. He went staggering backward, vainly trying to recover himself, and fell, his head striking against the wall. The same instant Angus entered, saw nothing of Gibbie where he lay and approached his master. Gibbie had recovered and risen. He saw now that he could be of no service to Ginevra, and that his presence only made things worse for her. But he saw also that she was unhappy about him, and that must not be. He broke into such a merry laugh—and it had need to be merry, for it had to do the work of many words of reassurance—that she could scarcely refrain from a half-hysterical response as he walked from the room. The moment he was out of the house, he began to sing; and for many minutes, as he walked up the gulf hollowed by the Glashburn, Ginevra could hear the strange, other-world voice, and knew it was meant to hold communion with her and comfort her.

"What do you know of that fellow, Angus?" demanded his master.

"He's the very devil himself, sir," muttered Angus.

"You will see that he is sent off the property at once—and for good, Angus," said the laird. "His insolence is insufferable. The scoundrel!"

On the pretext of following Gibbie, Angus was only too glad to leave the room. Then Mr. Galbraith turned upon his daughter.

"So, Ginny," he said, "that is the sort of companion you choose when left to yourself! A low, beggarly, insolent scamp! Scarcely the equal of the brutes he had the charge of!"

"They're sheep, Papa!" pleaded Ginevra, in a wail that rose almost to a scream.

"I do believe the girl is an idiot!" said her father and turned from her contemptuously.

"I think I am, Papa," she sobbed. "Don't mind me. Let me go away, and I will never trouble you anymore." She would go to the mountain, she thought, and be a shepherdess with Gibbie.

Her father took her roughly by the arm, pushed her into a closet, locked the door, went and had his luncheon and, in the afternoon, took her by coach to the principal hotel in the city, whence the next morning he sent out early to find a school where he might leave her and his responsibility with her.

When Gibbie knew himself beyond the hearing of Ginevra, his song died away and he went home sad. The gentle girl had stepped at once from the day into the dark, and he was troubled for her.

When he reached home, he found his mother in serious talk with a stranger. The tears were in her eyes and had been running down her cheeks, but she was calm and dignified as usual.

"Here he comes!" she said as he entered. "The will of the Lord be done—now and forevermore! I'm at His bidding—and so is Gibbie."

It was Mr. Sclater. The witch had sailed her raft well.

30

....

The City Again

*O*ne bright afternoon toward the close of the autumn, a company of schoolgirls, two-and-two in long file, was walking in orderly manner, a female grenadier at its head. Among the faces was one very different from the rest, a countenance almost solemn and a little sad. The other girls were looking on this side and that, eager to catch sight of anything to trouble the monotony of the daily walk; but the eyes of this one were cast down.

Suddenly came a rush, a confusion, a fluttering of the doves—whence or how none seemed to know—a gentle shriek from several of the girls, and there suddenly was an odd-looking lad who had got hold of one of the dainty, gloved hands and stood, without a word, gazing in rapturous delight.

"Go away, boy! What do you mean by such impertinence?" cried the outraged Miss Kimble, poking his chest with her parasol. Such a strange-looking creature! He could not be in his sound senses. In the meantime she had failed to observe that, after the first start, the girl stood quite still and was now looking in the lad's face, apparently forgetting to draw her hand from his. The next moment, with hasty yet dignified step, came the familiar form of their own minister, the Rev. Clement Sclater, who with reproof in his countenance, which was red with annoyance and haste, laid his hands on the lad's shoulders to draw him from the prey on which he had pounced.

"Remember, you are not on a hillside but in a respectable street," said the reverend gentleman.

The youth turned his head over his shoulder, not otherwise changing his attitude, and looking at him with some bewilderment. Then the young lady spoke.

"Gibbie and I are old friends," she said, and reaching up laid her free hand on his shoulder as if to protect him—for the vision of an old horror came rushing back on the mind of Ginevra.

Gibbie had darted from his companion's side some hundred yards off. The cap which Mr. Sclater had insisted on his wearing had fallen as he ran, and he had never missed it. His hair stood out on all sides of his head, and the sun behind him shone in it like a glory, just as when first he appeared to Ginevra in the peat-moss like an angel standing over her.

"Miss Galbraith!" said Miss Kimble, in the tone that indicates nostrils distended, "I am astonished at you! What an example to the school! I never knew you to misbehave yourself before! Take your hand from this—this—very strange-looking person's shoulder directly!"

Ginevra obeyed, but Gibbie stood as before.

"Remove your hand, boy, instantly!" cried Miss Kimble, growing more and more angry and began knocking him with her parasol, which apparently Gibbie took for a joke, for he laughed aloud.

"Pray do not alarm yourself, ma'am," said Mr. Sclater, slowly recovering his breath; he was not yet quite sure of Gibbie, or confident how best he was to be managed; "this young . . . gentleman is Sir Gilbert Galbraith, my ward. Sir Gilbert, this lady is Miss Kimble."

"Oh!" said the lady, who had ceased her battery and stood bewildered and embarrassed—the more that by this time the girls had all gathered round, staring and wondering.

Ginevra's eyes too had filled with wonder; she cast them down, and a strange smile began to play about her mouth. All at once she was in the middle of a fairy tale and had not a notion what was coming next. Her dumb shepherd boy a baronet!—and, more wonderful still, a Galbraith! She must be dreaming in the wide street! The last she had seen of him was as he was driven from the house by her father, when he had just saved her life. That was but a few weeks ago, and here he was called Sir Gilbert Galbraith! It was a delicious bit of wonder.

"Oh!" said Miss Kimble a second time, recovering herself a little, "I see! A relative, Miss Galbraith! I did not understand. That of course sets everything right—at least—even then—the open street, you know! You will understand, Mr. Sclater. I beg your pardon, Sir Gilbert. I hope I did not hurt you with my parasol!"

Gibbie laughed aloud.

"Thank you," said Miss Kimble, confused and annoyed with herself for behaving so, especially before her girls. "I should be sorry to have hurt you. Going to college, I presume, Sir Gilbert?"

Gibbie looked at Mr. Sclater.

"He is going to study with me for a while first," answered the minister.

"I am glad to hear it. He could not do better," said Miss Kimble. "Come, girls."

And with friendly farewells she moved on, her train after her.

————

Mr. Sclater had behaved judiciously and taken gentle pains to satisfy the old couple that they must part with Gibbie. One of the neighboring clergy knew Mr. Sclater well, and with him paid the old people a visit to help dismiss any lingering doubt that he was the boy's legally appointed guardian. To their own common sense, indeed, it became plain that, except some such story was true, there could be nothing to induce him to come after Gibbie or desire to take charge of the outcast. But they did not feel thoroughly satisfied until Mr. Sclater brought Fergus Duff to the cottage, to testify to him as being what he indicated. It was a sore trial, but among the griefs of losing him, no fear of his forgetting them was included. Mr. Sclater's main difficulty was with Gibbie himself. At first he laughed at the absurdity of his going away from his father and mother and the sheep. They told him he was Sir Gilbert Galbraith. He answered on his slate, as well as by signs which Janet at least understood perfectly, that he had told them so and had been so all the time, "and what difference does it make?" he added. Mr. Sclater told him he was—or would be, at least, he took care to add, when he came of age—a rich man as well as a baronet.

"Writch men," wrote Gibbie, "do as they like, and Ise stay."

Mr. Sclater told him it was only poor boys who could do as they pleased, for the law looked after boys like him so that, when it came into their hands, they might be capable of using their money properly. Almost persuaded at length that he had no choice, that he could no longer be his own master until he was twenty-one, he turned and looked at Janet, his eyes brimful of tears. She gave him a little nod. He rose and went out, climbed the crest of Glashgar, and did not return to the cottage till midnight.

In the morning appeared on his countenance signs of unusual resolve. Amid the many thoughts he had had the night before had come the question: What would he do with the money when he had it? First of all, he thought about what he could do for Janet and Robert and every one of their family. And naturally the first thing that occurred to him was to give Donal money to go to college like Fergus Duff. In that he knew he made no mistake. Had not Donal said twenty times he would not mind being a herdboy all his life if only he could go to college first? But then he began to think what a long time it was before he would be twenty-one, and what a number of things might come and go before then. Donal might by that time have a wife and children, and he could not leave them to go to college! Why should not Mr. Sclater manage somehow that Donal should go at once? Some other rich person could lend them the money, and he would pay it, with interest, when he got his. Before he went to bed he got his slate, and wrote the following: "my dear minister, If you will teak Donal too, and lett him go to the kolledg, I will go with you as seens ye like; butt if ye will not, I will runn away."

When Mr. Sclater, who had a bed at the gamekeeper's, appeared the next morning, anxious to conclude the business and get things in motion for their departure, Gibbie handed him the slate the moment he entered the cottage. While the minister read, he stood watching him.

Now Mr. Sclater was a prudent man and always looked ahead; therefore, apparently he took a long time to read Gibbie's very clear, although unscholarly, communication. Before answering it, he must settle the probability of what Mrs. Sclater would think of the proposal to take two savages into her house together, where also doubtless the presence of this Donal would greatly interfere with the process of making a gentleman of Gibbie. Unable to satisfy himself, he raised his head at length, unconsciously shaking it as he did so. That instant Gibbie was out of the house. Mr. Sclater, perceiving the blunder he had made, hurried after him, but he was already out of sight. Returning in some dismay, he handed the slate to

Janet, who with sad, resigned countenance was baking. She rubbed the oatmeal dough from her hands, took the slate and read with a smile.

"You must not take Gibbie for a young colt, Mister Sclater, and think to break him in," she said, after a thoughtful pause, "or you'll have to learn your mistake. There's not enough of himself in him for you to get a grip of him by that handle. He knows what he will have and he'll get it, as sure as it'll be right. As for Donal, Donal's my own, and I shall say nothing. Sit down, sir; you'll not see Gibbie again today."

"Is there no means of getting at him, my good woman?" said Mr. Sclater, miserable at the prospect of a day utterly wasted.

"I could give you sight of him, I daresay, but what better would you be for that? If you had all the lawyers of Edinburgh at your back, you wouldn't touch Gibbie on Glashgar."

"But you could persuade him, I am sure, Mistress Grant. You have only to call him in your own way, and he would come at once."

"What would you have me persuade him of, sir? To anything that's right, Gibbie wants no persuading; and for this that's between you, the laddies are just like brothers, and I have no right to interfere with what the one would do for the other. Things seem to me reasonable enough."

"What sort of lad is this son of yours? The boy seems much attached to him!"

"He's a laddie that's been given over to his books ever since I taught him to read myself," Janet answered. "But he'll be here tonight, I'm thinkin', to see the last of Gibbie, and you can judge for yourself."

It required but a brief examination of Donal that evening to satisfy Mr. Sclater that he was more than prepared for the university.

As to Donal's going to Mr. Sclater's house, Janet soon relieved him.

"No, no, sir," she said; "it would be to learn ways that wouldn't be fitting for a poor lad like him."

"It would be much safer for him," said Mr. Sclater.

"If I couldn't trust my Donal to his own company and the hunger for better, I would begin to doubt who made the world," said his mother; and Donal's face flushed with pleasure at her confidence. "No, he must get a garret room somewhere in the town, and there hold to his books. And you'll let Gibbie go and see him when he has time to spare. There must be many a decent woman that would be pleased to take him in."

Mr. Sclater foresaw no little trouble in his new responsibility but consoled himself that he would have more money at his command and in the end would sit, as it were, at the fountainhead of large wealth. Already, with his wife's property, he was a man of consideration; but he had a great respect for money, and much overrated its value as a means of doing even what he called good.

When Rev. Sclater and Gibbie met Miss Kimble and her "young ladies," the two had just arrived from Glashgar and were on their way from the coach office to the minister's house in Daur Street.

31

••••••••••••••••••••

Daur Street

*G*ibbie was in a dream of mingled past and future when his conductor stopped at a large and important-looking house, with a flight of granite steps up to the door. Gibbie had never been inside such a house in his life. He gave a glance around, thought it a big place, and followed Mr. Sclater up the stair with the free, mounting step of the Glashgar shepherd. Forgetful and unconscious, he walked into the drawing room with his bonnet on his head. Mrs. Sclater rose when they entered and he approached her with a smile. She shook hands with him in a doubtful kind of way.

"How do you do, Sir Gilbert?" she said. "Only ladies are allowed to wear their caps in the drawing room, you know," she added, in a tone of courteous half rebuke.

What she meant by the drawing room, Gibbie had not an idea. He looked at her head, and saw no cap; she had nothing on it but a quantity of beautiful black hair. Then suddenly he remembered his bonnet; he knew well enough bonnets had to be taken off in house or cottage. He had never done so because he had never worn a bonnet. But it was with a smile of amusement only that he now took it off.

Gibbie had not been educated in the relative grandeur of things of this world, and he regarded the things he now saw just as things, without the smallest notion of any power in them to confer superiority by being possessed. Man was the one sacred thing to Gibbie. Amidst the mere upholstery of houses and hearts, amidst the common life of the common crowd, he was what he had learned to be among the nobility and in the palace of Glashgar.

Mrs. Sclater was a well-bred woman, superior in the small duties and graces of social life. She did not much care to "play the mother to a bear cub," she said to her friends, with a good-humored laugh. "Just think," she added, "with such a childhood as the poor boy had, what a mass of vulgarity must be lying in that uncultivated brain of his! It is no small mercy, as Mr. Sclater says, that our ears at least are safe. Poor boy!" Her husband was confident that if anybody could, his wife would make a gentleman of Sir Gilbert; and he ought to know, for she had done a good deal of polishing upon him.

Mrs. Sclater's first piece of business the following morning was to take Gibbie to the most fashionable tailor in the city and have him measured for such clothes as she judged suitable for a gentleman's son. Gibbie seemed as much at home with the handsome lady as if she had been his own mother, and walked by her side with a step and air as free as the wind from Glashgar. But the new clothes felt anything but comfortable. Gibbie could endure cold or wet or hunger, he had borne pain upon occasion with complete submission; but the tight armholes of his jacket could hardly be such a decree of Providence as it was rebellion to interfere with.

Mrs. Sclater soon began to find that even in regard to social externals she could never have had a readier pupil. He watched her so closely, and with such an appreciation of the difference in things of the kind between her and her husband, that for a short period he was in danger of falling into habits of movement and manipulation too dainty for a man, a fault nonetheless objectionable in the eyes of his instructee that she, on her own part, carried the feminine a little beyond the limits of the natural. But here also she found him so readily set right that she imagined she was going to do anything with him she pleased and was not a little proud of her conquest and the power she had over the young savage.

She had yet to discover that Gibbie had his own ideas too, that it was the general noble teachableness and affection of his nature that had brought about so speedy an understanding between them in everything wherein he saw she could show him the better way, but that nowhere else would he feel bound or inclined to follow her injunctions. Much and strongly as he was drawn to her by her ladyhood and the sense she gave him of refinement, he had no feeling that she had authority over him. So neglected in his childhood, so absolutely trusted by the cottagers, who had never found in him the slightest occasion for the exercise of authority, he had not an idea of owing obedience to any but the One.

Mr. Sclater was conscientious in his treatment of him. The very day following that of their arrival, he set to work with him. He had been a tutor, was a good scholar and a sensible teacher, and he soon discovered how to make the most of Gibbie's facility in writing.

What Gibbie made of Mr. Sclater's prayers, either in congregational or family devotion, I am at some loss to imagine. Beside his memories of the direct outpouring of Janet, they must have seemed to him like the utterances of some curiously constructed automaton.

Full of the holy simplicities of the cottage, Gibbie had a good many things to meet which disappointed and perplexed him. He never came quite to understand the Sclaters.

32

•••••••••••••••••••

Donal in the City

*D*onal had not accompanied Mr. Sclater and his ward, as the minister generally styled him, to the city but continued at the Mains until another herdboy should be found to take his place. His last night he spent with his parents on Glashgar and the next morning set out to join the coach. His mother's parting words to him were, "Now, remember, you're not a straw dried on its root, but a growing stalk that must look to its grain."

It was a cold afternoon, the air half mist, half twilight, when Donal arrived at the coach office. Mr. Sclater stood waiting, welcomed him with dignity rather than kindness, hired a porter whom he told where to take the chest, said Sir Gilbert would doubtless call on him the next day, and left him with the porter.

Once in his lodgings, he approached the fire and sat down to warm himself. A few moments and he was startled by a slight noise, as of suppressed laughter. He jumped up. One of the curtains of his bed was strangely agitated. Out leaped Gibbie from behind it and threw his arms about him.

"Eh, creature! You gave me such a fright!" said Donal. "But, losh! They have made a gentleman of you already!" he added, holding him at arm's length and regarding him with wonder and admiration.

A notable change had indeed passed upon Gibbie. Mrs. Sclater had had his hair cut; his shirt was of the whitest of linen, his necktie of the richest of black silk, his clothes were of the newest cut and best possible fit, and his boots perfect. The result was altogether even to her satisfaction. In one thing only was she foiled: she could not get him to wear gloves. He had put on a pair but found them so miserably uncomfortable that, in merry wrath, he pulled them off on the way home and threw them over the Pearl Bridge. Prudently fearful of overstraining her influence, she yielded for the present and let him go without.

Mr. Sclater also had hitherto exercised prudence in his demands upon Gibbie—not that he desired anything less than unlimited authority with him but, knowing it would be hard to enforce, he sought to establish it by a gradual tightening of the rein. Gibbie had never yet refused to do anything he required of him, yet somehow Mr. Sclater could never feel that the lad was exactly obeying him. He thought it over but could not understand it and did not like it, for he was fond of authority. Gibbie in fact did whatever was required of him from his own delight in meeting the wish expressed, not from any sense of duty or of obligation to obedience. The minister had no perception of what the boy was, and had a foreboding suspicion that the time would come when they would differ.

The boys had then a jolly time of it. They made their tea, for which everything was present, and ate as boys know how: Donal enjoying the rarity of the white bread of the city; Gibbie, who had not tasted oatmeal since he came, devouring "mother's cakes." When they had done, Gibbie, who had learned much since he came, looked about the room till he found a bell rope and pulled it; whereupon the oddest-looking old woman, not a hair altered from what Gibbie remembered her, entered and, with friendly chatter, proceeded to remove the tray.

When the good woman at length left them, they uncorded Donal's chest, took out everything, put the provisions in a cupboard, arranged the few books, and then sat down by the fire for "a read" together.

The hours slipped away; it was night. And still they sat and read. It must have been after ten o'clock when they heard footsteps coming through the adjoining room. The door opened swiftly; in walked Mr. Sclater and closed it behind him. His look was angry. Gibbie had absented himself without permission, had stayed away for hours, had not returned even when the hour of worship arrived; and these were sins against the respectability of his house which no minister could pass by.

When first he entered, Gibbie rose with his usual smile of greeting, and got him a chair. But he waved aside the attention with indignant indifference and went on with his foolish reproof. Gibbie looked the minister straight in the face. His smile of welcome, which had suddenly mingled itself with bewilderment, gradually faded into one of concern, then of pity, and by degrees died away altogether, leaving in its place a look of question.

The boys remained absolutely silent. But before he had begun to draw to a close, across the blinding mists of his fog-breeding wrath, the minister began to be aware of the eyes of the dumb boy fixed upon him. They jarred him; he began to feel awkward, he hesitated, then ceased. For the moment Gibbie, unconsciously, had conquered; without knowing it he was the superior of the two, and Mr. Sclater had begun to learn that he could never exercise authority over him.

"Donal Grant," he said, "you had better go to bed at once and get fit for your work tomorrow. I will go with you to call upon the principal. Get your cap, Sir Gilbert, and come. Mrs. Sclater was already very uneasy about you when I left her."

Gibbie took from his pocket the little ivory tablets Mrs. Sclater had given him, wrote the following words, and handed them to the minister:

"Dear sir, I am going to slepe this night with Donal. The bed is bigg enuf for 2. Good night sir."

For a moment the minister's wrath seethed again, but he thought better of it.

"Then be sure you are at home by lesson time," he said. "Donal can come with you. Good night. Mind you don't keep each other awake."

Donal said, "Good night, sir," and Gibbie gave him a serious and respectful nod. He left the room, and the boys turned and looked at each other. Donal's countenance expressed an indignant sense of wrong, but Gibbie's revealed a more profound concern. He stood motionless, intent on the receding steps of the minister. The moment the sound of them ceased, he darted soundless after him to follow him home. Donal started to his feet and went as well. On and on went Mr. Sclater, and on and on went Gibbie, careful constantly not to be seen by him; and on and on went Donal careful to be seen of neither. At last the minister went up the steps of a handsome house, took a key from his pocket, and opened the door.

Gibbie turned and was quickly away and Donal was after him like a hound. But Gibbie turned a corner and was gone from his sight. Donal turned too, but Gibbie was already out of sight. Concluding that Gibbie had turned another corner ahead of him, he ran on and on, in the vanishing hope of catching sight of him; but he was soon satisfied he had lost him, and himself as well, for he had not the smallest idea how to return, even as far as the minister's house. It rendered the matter considerably worse that, having never heard the name of the street where he lodged but once—when the minister gave direction to the porter—he had utterly forgotten it.

Presently he found himself on the shore of the river. He was saying to himself whatever was he to do all night long, when round a corner a little way off came a woman. It was no use asking counsel of her, however, or anyone, he thought, so long as he did not know even the name of the street he wanted. The woman drew near. She was rather tall, erect in the back but bowed in the shoulders, with fierce black eyes which were all that he could see of her face, for she had a little tartan shawl over her head. But those eyes were enough. They were just passing each other under a lamp when she looked hard at him and stopped.

"Man," she said, "I have set eye upon your face before!"

"If that be the case," answered Donal, "you've set your eye upon it again."

"Where do you come from?" she asked.

"That's what I would like to ask myself," he replied. "But, woman," he went on, "I fancy I have set an eye upon your eye before—but I can't well say your face. Where do you come from?"

"Know you a place they call Daurside?" she rejoined.

"Daurside's a long place," answered Donal; "and this must be about the tail end of it, I'm thinkin'."

"You're not far wrong there," she returned. "You have a quick tongue in your head for a lad from Daurside."

"I never heard tongues were cut any shorter there," said Donal; "but I didn't mean any offense."

"There's none taken," answered the woman. "Know ye a place they call the Mains of Glashruach?"

As she spoke she let go her shawl and it opened from her face like two curtains.

"Lord! it's the witch-wife!" cried Donal, retreating a pace in his astonishment.

The woman burst into a great laugh—a hard, unmusical, but not unmirthful laugh.

"Ay!" she said. "Was that how the folk would have it about me?"

"It wasn't much wonder, after you waded through water yards deep, and then went down the flood on a raft."

"Well, it was the maddest thing!" she returned, with another laugh which stopped abruptly. "I wouldn't do the like of that again to save my life. But the Almighty carried me through. And how's wee Sir Gibbie?— but we're just at the door of my small room—come in . . . I don't know your name. Come quiet up the stairs and tell me about it."

"Well, I would like to rest for a bit, for I have lost myself, and I am tired," answered Donal. "I just left the Mains yesterday."

"Come in and welcome; and when you're rested, and I'm rid of my basket, I'll send you on your way home."

Donal was too tired and too glad to be once more in the company of a human being to pursue further explanation at present. He followed her, as quietly as he could, up the dark stair. When she struck a light, he saw a little garret room—better than decently furnished, it seemed to the youth from the hills, though his mother would have thought it far from tidy. The moment the woman got a candle lighted, she seated herself and began to relate her adventures in quest of Gibbie. Someday she would tell him, she said, the whole story of her voyage on the raft, which would make him laugh. Then she told him a great deal about Gibbie and his father.

"And now," remarked Donal, "he'll be thinkin' about it all over again as he runs about the town this very minute lookin' for me!"

"Don't trouble yourself about him," said the woman. "He knows the town as well as any of the rats knows the drains. But where do you put up?" she added, "It's time decent folks were going to their beds."

Donal explained that he knew neither the name of the street nor of the people where he was lodging.

"Tell me something about the house or the folk or what they're like, and it may be that I'll know them," she said.

But scarcely had he begun his description of the house when she cried, "Hoot, man! It's at Lucky Murkinson's you are, in the Widdiehill. Come with me, and I'll take you home in a jiffy."

So saying, she rose, took the candle, showed him down the stair, and he followed.

It was past midnight and the moon was down, but the streetlamps were not yet extinguished and they walked along without anything to interrupt their conversation.

Before they reached the Widdiehill, Donal, with the open heart of the poet, was full of friendliness to her and rejoiced in the mischance that had led him to make her acquaintance.

"You know, of course," he happened to say, "that Gibbie's with Master Sclater?"

"Well enough," she answered. "I have seen him too; but he's grown into a grand gentleman now, and I wouldn't like to be affronted laying claim to the acquaintance—welcome as he once was to my house!"

"You little know Gibbie," he said, "if you think that way of him! Go to the minister's door and ask for him! He'll be down the stair like a shot.—But, indeed, maybe he's come back and is in my room now! Will you come up the stair and see?"

"No, I won't do that," said Mistress Croale.

She pointed out the door to him but herself stood on the other side of the way till she saw it opened by Mistress Murkinson in her nightcap and heard her make jubilee over his return.

Gibbie had come home and gone out again to look for him, she said.

"Well," remarked Donal, "there would be small good in my going to look for him. It would be but the sheep going to look for the shepherd."

"You're right there," said his landlady. "A lost child should sit down and sit still."

"Well, you go to your bed, mem," returned Donal. "Let me see how your door works, and I'll let him in when he comes."

Gibbie came within an hour and all was well. They made their communication, of which Donal's was far the more interesting, had their laugh over the affair, and went to bed.

33

The Sinner

*T*he minister's anger went on smoldering all night, and in the morning he rose with his temper very feverish. During breakfast he was gloomy but would confess to no inward annoyance. What added to his unrest was that although he felt insulted, he did not know what precisely the nature of the insult was.

Gibbie made his appearance at ten o'clock, and went straight to the study, where at the hour the minister was always waiting him. He entered with a smile. The minister said, "Good morning," but gruffly, and without raising his eyes. Gibbie seated himself in his usual place, arranged his book and slate and was ready to commence when the minister, having now summoned resolution, lifted his head, fixed his eyes on him and said sternly, "Sir Gilbert, what was your meaning in following me after refusing to accompany me?"

Gibbie's face flushed. He had no idea he'd been seen. But he took his slate, found his pencil, wrote, and handed the slate to the minister. There stood these words: "I thout you was drunk."

His eyes flaming, his cheeks white with passion, Mr. Sclater started to his feet, and with the flat of the slate came down a great blow on the top of Gibbie's head. Happily, the latter was the harder of the two, and the former broke, flying mostly out of the frame. It took Gibbie terribly by surprise. Half-stunned, he started to his feet, and for one moment the wild beast which was in him, as it is in everybody, rushed to the front of its cage. It would have gone ill then with the minister had not as sudden a change followed; the flame of Gibbie's wrath went out, and a smile of compassion overspread his countenance. Bur Mr. Sclater saw no compassionate brother before him, for when Gibbie rose he drew back to better his position. When he stepped back, he stumbled and fell. Gibbie darted forward and began to help him up like a child.

Having regained his legs, the minister stood for a moment, confused and half-blinded. The first thing he saw was a drop of blood stealing down Gibbie's forehead. He was shocked at what he had done. In truth he had been frightfully provoked, but it was not for a clergyman so to avenge an insult, and as mere chastisement it was brutal. What would Mrs. Sclater say to it? The rascal was sure to make his complaint to her!

And there too was Gibbie's friend, the herdlad, in the drawing room with her!

"Go wash your face," he said, "and come back again directly."

Gibbie put his hand to his face and, feeling something wet, looked, and burst into a merry laugh.

"I am sorry I have hurt you," said the minister, not a little relieved at the sound; "but how dare you write such a—such an insolence? A clergyman never gets drunk."

Gibbie picked up the frame which the minister had dropped in his fall. A piece of the slate was still sticking in one side, and he wrote upon it: "I will kno better the next time. I thout it was alwais whiskey that made people like that. I beg your pardon, sir."

He handed him the fragment, ran to his own room, returned presently looking all right. When Mr. Sclater would have attended to his wound, he would not let him even look at it, laughing at the idea. Still further relieved to find there was nothing to attract observation to the injury, and yet more ashamed of himself, the minister made haste to the refuge of their work.

From that time, after luncheon, which followed immediately upon lessons, Gibbie went and came as he pleased. Mrs. Sclater begged he would never be out after ten o'clock without having let them know that he meant to stay out all night with his friend. Not once did he neglect this request, and they soon came to have perfect confidence not only in any individual promise he might make, but in his general punctuality. Mrs. Sclater never came to know anything of his wounded head.

Mr. Sclater had not been long teaching Gibbie before he began to desire to make a scholar of him. Partly from being compelled to spend some labor at it, the boy was gradually developing an unusual facility in written expression. All he cared about was to say what he meant, and avoid saying something else; to know when he had not said what he meant, and to set the words right.

His guardian lost no time in having his organs of speech examined by a surgeon in high repute, a professor of the university; but Dr. Skinner's opinion put an end to question and hope together. Gibbie was not in the least disappointed. He had got on very well as yet without speech. It was not like sight or hearing. The only voice he could not hear was his own, and that was just the one he had neither occasion nor desire to hear. As to his friends, those who had known him the longest minded his dumbness the least. But the moment the defect was understood to be irreparable, Mrs. Sclater very wisely proceeded to learn finger speech; and as she learned it, she taught it to Gibbie.

As to his manners, which had been and continued to be her chief care, she never could get them to take on the case-hardening needful for what she counted the final polish. They always retained a certain simplicity which she called childishness. It came in fact of childlikeness, but the lady was not child enough to distinguish the difference. In after years, however, Gibbie's manner was almost universally felt to be charming.

One night on their way home from an evening party, the minister and his wife had a small difference, probably about something of as little real consequence to them as the knowledge of it is to us; but by the time they reached home, they had gotten to the very summit of politeness with each other. Gibbie was in the drawing room, as it happened, waiting their return. At the first sound of their voices, he knew before a syllable reached him that something was wrong. When they entered, they were too much engrossed in difference to heed his presence and went on disputing—with the utmost external propriety but with a sense of injury in every tone. A discreet, socially wise boy would have left the room, but how could Gibbie abandon his friends? He ran to the side table. With a vague presentiment of what was coming, Mrs. Sclater, feeling rather than seeing him move across the room like a shadow, sat in dread expectation. And presently her fear arrived, in the shape of a large New Testament and a face of keen discomfort. He held out the book to her, pointing with a finger to the words: "Have salt in yourselves, and have peace one with another." What Gibbie made of salt, I do not know; but the rest of the sentence he understood.

The lady's cheeks had been red before, but now they were redder. She rose, cast an angry look at the dumb prophet, a look which seemed to say, "How dare you suggest such a thing?" and left the room.

"What have you got there?" asked the minister, turning sharply upon him. Gibbie showed him the passage.

"What have you got to do with it?" he retorted, throwing the book on the table. "Go to bed."

————

Mistress Croale grew more and more desirous of looking upon the object of her recent windfall and summoned resolution at last. She went to the market a little better dressed than usual and when business there was over and she had shut up her little box of a shop, she walked to Daur Street to the minister's house.

They were in the middle of their soup when the maid informed her master that a woman was at the door wanting to see Sir Gilbert.

Gibbie looked up, put down his spoon, and was rising to go when the minister, laying a hand on his arm, pressed him gently back to his chair, and Gibbie yielded, waiting.

"What sort of a woman?" he asked the girl.

"A decent-looking, working-like body," she answered. "I couldn't see her very well, it's so foggy tonight around the door."

"Tell her we're at dinner; she may call again in an hour or tomorrow morning.—I wonder who she is," he added, turning, he thought, to Gibbie.

But Gibbie was gone. He had passed behind his chair, and all Mr. Sclater saw of him was his back as he followed the girl from the room. In his eagerness he left the door open, and they saw him dart to the visitor, shake hands with her in evident delight, and begin pulling her toward the room.

Now Mistress Croale, though nowise inclined to quail before the minister, would not willingly have intruded herself upon him, especially while he sat at dinner with his rather formidable lady. But she fancied that Gibbie was taking her where they might have a quiet talk together, and remained thus mistaken until she stood on the threshold. Looking up, she started, stopped, made a bow to the minister and another to the minister's lady, and stood doubtful, if not a little abashed.

"Oh . . . it's you, Mistress Croale," said Mr. Sclater, rising, "—I will speak to you in the hall."

Mrs. Croale's face flushed and she drew back a step. But Gibbie still held her and, with a look to Mr. Sclater that should have sent straight to his heart the fact that she was dear to his soul, kept drawing her into the room; he wanted her to take his chair at the table. How friendly the warm air felt! How consoling the crimson walls with the soft flicker of the great fire upon them! How delicious the odor of the cockie-leekie! She could give up whiskey a good deal more easily, she thought, if she had the comforts of a minister to fall back upon! And this was the same minister who had once told her that her soul was as precious to him as that of any other in his parish—and then driven her from respectable Jink Lane to the disreputable Daurfoot! It all passed through her mind in a flash, while yet Gibbie pulled and she resisted.

"Gilbert, come here," called Mrs. Sclater.

He went to her side.

"Really, Gilbert, you must not," she said, rather loud for a whisper. "If you are to be a gentleman, and an inmate of my house, you must behave like other people. I cannot have a woman like that sitting at my table. Do you know what sort of a person she is?"

Gibbie's face shone up. He raised his hands. He was already able to talk a little.

"Is she a sinner?" he asked on his fingers.

Mrs. Sclater nodded.

Gibbie wheeled round and sprang back to the hall, whither the minister had ejected Mistress Croale and was now talking to her with an air of confidential condescension, willing to wipe out any feeling of injury she might perhaps be inclined to cherish at not being made more welcome. To the minister's consternation, Gibbie threw his arms round her neck and gave her a great hug.

"Sir Gilbert!" he exclaimed, the more angry that he knew Gibbie was in the right, "leave Mistress Croale alone, and go back to your dinner immediately . . . Jane, open the door."

Jane opened the door, Gibbie let her go, and Mrs. Croale went. But on the threshold she turned to the minister: "Well, sir," she said, with a certain sad injury not unmingled with dignity, "you have stepped over my doorstep many times, and with sorer words in your mouth than I used to pay you back. And I never told you to go. So first you turn me out of my own house and now you turn me out of yours; and what's left for you but to turn me out of the house of the Lord? And, indeed, sir, you need never wonder if the likes of me doesn't care about coming to hear the preached gospel—we would fain see a practiced one!"

"You shall have a plate of soup, and welcome, Mistress Croale!" said the minister, "—Jane, take Mistress Croale to the kitchen with you, and—"

"The devil's tail in your soup!" cried Mistress Croale, drawing herself up suddenly. "When did I turn into a beggar? Was it your soup or your grace I sought for, sir? The Lord judge between me and you! There's first that will be last, and last that will be first. But the one's not me, and the other's not you, sir."

With this she turned and walked down the steps, holding her head high.

"Really, Sir Gilbert," said the minister, going back into the dining room—but no Gibbie was there! Nobody but his wife, sitting in solitary discomposure at the head of the dinner table. The same instant, he heard a clatter of feet down the steps and turned quickly into the hall again, where Jane was in the act of shutting the door.

"Sir Gilbert's run out after the woman, sir!" she said.

"Hoot!" grunted the minister, greatly displeased, and went back to his wife.

"Take Sir Gilbert's plate away," said Mrs. Sclater to the servant.

"That's his New Testament again!" she went on, when the girl had left the room.

"My dear! my dear! take care," said her husband. He had not much notion of obedience to God, but he had some idea of respect to religion.

"Really, Mr. Sclater," his wife continued, "I had no idea what I was undertaking. But you gave me no choice. The creature is incorrigible. But of course he must prefer the society of women like that. They are the sort he was accustomed to when he received his first impressions, and how could it be otherwise? You knew how he had been brought up, and what you had to expect!"

"Brought up!" cried the minister. "You should have seen him about the streets!"

Nothing further was said until the second course was on the table. Then the lady spoke again.

"You really must teach him the absurdity of attempting to fit every point of his behavior to—to—words which were of course quite suitable to the time when they were spoken, but which it is impossible to take literally nowadays. Why! You saw him throw his arms around the horrid creature's neck!—Well, he had just asked me if she was a sinner. I made no doubt she was. With the word, off goes my gentleman to embrace her!"

Here they laughed together.

Dinner over, they went to a missionary meeting, where the one stood and made a speech and the other sat and listened, while Gibbie was having tea with Mistress Croale.

From that day Gibbie's mind was much exercised as to what he could do for Mistress Croale, and now first he began to wish he had his money. As fast as he learned the finger alphabet, he had taught it to Donal and, as already they had a good many symbols in use between them—so many indeed that Donal would often instead of speaking make use of signs— they had now the means of communication almost as free as if they had had between them two tongues instead of one. It was easy therefore for Gibbie to impart to Donal his anxiety concerning her, and his strong desire to help her. And doing so, he lamented in a gentle way his present inability. This communication Donal judged it wise to impart in his turn to Mistress Croale.

"You see, mem," he said in conclusion, "he's some way or another gotten it into his head that you're just a bit over free with the bottle. I don't know. You'll be the best judge of that yourself!"

Mistress Croale was silent for a whole minute. From the moment when Gibbie forsook his dinner to go with her, the woman's heart had begun to grow to the boy, and her old memories fed the new crop of affection.

"Well," she replied at length, "—I may not be so ill as he thinks me, for he had his poor father before his eyes; but the child's mostly in the right, and we must look to it and see what can be done. For eh! I would be loath to disappoint the bonnie lad! My bonnie wee Sir Gibbie—I can't help calling him wee Sir Gibbie. All the town called him that, although he'll be a big man someday. And as for his title, I was always one to give honor where honor is due, and never once, as well as I knew him, did I call his honest father anything but Sir George, even though he was just a hard-working cobbler, and on Saturdays was pleased to have a wash in my bedroom and put on a clean shirt of my dead husband's—rest his soul!— and spend the evening in my place."

34

The Girls

*I*t had come to be the custom that Gibbie should go to Donal's every Friday afternoon about four o'clock and remain with him till the same time on Saturday, which was a holiday with both. One Friday, just after he was gone, the temptation seized Mrs. Sclater to follow him and pay the lads an unexpected visit to see what they were about.

It was a bright, cold afternoon; and in fur tippet and muff, amidst the snow that lay everywhere, she set out. As she was passing a certain baker's shop through a neighboring street approaching the Widdiehill, something made her stop and look in through the glass. There she saw Gibbie seated on the counter, legs dangling, eating a penny loaf. A very pretty girl, with whose company Gibbie was evidently much pleased, stood behind the counter. At the moment she was laughing merrily and talking gaily to Gibbie. Clearly they were on the best of terms and the boy's bright countenance, laughter and eager motions were making full response to the girl's words.

Mrs. Sclater, gazing through the glass, found a large justification for displeasure. She opened the door sharply and stepped in. Gibbie jumped from his seat on the counter and, with a smile of playful roguery, offered it to her. A vivid blush overspread Mysie's fair countenance.

"I thought you had gone to see Donal," said Mrs. Sclater in the tone of one deceived, and took no notice of the girl.

Gibbie gave her to understand that Donal would arrive presently, and they were then going to the pier that Donal might learn what the sea was like in a nor'-easter.

"But why did you make your appointment here?" asked the lady.

"Because Mysie and I are old friends," answered the boy on his fingers.

Then first Mrs. Sclater turned to the girl. Having gotten over her first indignation, she spoke gently and with a frankness natural to her.

"Sir Gilbert tells me you are old friends," she said.

Thereupon Mysie told her the story of the earring, which had introduced their present conversation, and added several other little recollections, in one of which she was drawn into a description, half pathetic, half humorous, of the forlorn appearance of wee Gibbie as he ran about in his truncated trousers. Mrs. Sclater was more annoyed, however, than interested, for in view of the young baronet's future she would have had all such things forgotten.

Hardly anybody was ever in less danger of falling in love than Gibbie.

And the thing would not have been worth recording but for the new direction it caused Mrs. Sclater's thoughts; measures, she judged, must be taken.

Recalling what her husband had told her of the odd meeting between the boy and a young lady at Miss Kimble's school, some relation, she wondered whether she might turn the acquaintance to account. There was no reason why she should not ask Miss Kimble to come and spend the evening, and bring two or three of the elder girls with her. A little familiarity with the looks, manners, and dress of refined girls of his own age would be the best antidote to his taste for low society, from that of baker's daughters downward.

Mr. Galbraith had not taken Miss Kimble into his confidence with respect to his reasons for so hurriedly placing his daughter under her care. Hence, when Mrs. Sclater's invitation arrived, the schoolmistress was aware of no reason why Miss Galbraith should not be one of the girls to go with her, especially as there was her cousin, Sir Gilbert, whom she herself would like to meet again in the hope of removing the bad impression which she feared she must have made upon him.

One day, then, at luncheon, Mrs. Sclater told Gibbie that some ladies were coming to tea, and they were going to have supper instead of dinner. He must put on his best clothes, she said. He did as she desired, was duly inspected, approved on the whole, and finished off by a few deft fingers at his necktie and a gentle push or two against his hair thatch, and was seated in the drawing room with Mrs. Sclater when the ladies arrived. Ginevra and he shook hands, she with the sweetest of rose flushes, he with the radiance of delighted surprise. But a moment after, when Mrs. Sclater and her guests had seated themselves, Gibbie, their only gentleman, for Mr. Sclater had not yet made his appearance, vanished from the room. Tea was not brought until some time after when Mr. Sclater came home, and then Mrs. Sclater sent Jane to find Sir Gilbert; but she returned to say he was not in the house. The lady's heart sank; her project had miscarried!

The case was, however, very much otherwise. The moment Gibbie ended his greetings, he had darted off to tell Donal; it was not his custom to enjoy anything shareable alone.

The news that Ginevra was at that moment seated in Mrs. Sclater's house raised such a commotion in Donal's atmosphere that his heart beat like the trample of a trotting horse. He never thought of inquiring whether Gibbie had been commissioned by Mrs. Sclater to invite him, or reflected that his studies were not half over for the night. Gibbie simply told him by two signs that he must put on his Sunday clothes.

Donal's preparations took a long time, and before they reached the house, tea was over and gone. They had had some music; and Mrs. Sclater was now talking kindly to two of the schoolgirls who, seated erect on the sofa, were looking upon her elegance with awe and envy. Ginevra was looking at the pictures of an annual. Mr. Sclater was making Miss Kimble agreeable to herself.

The door opened. Donal entered and walked across the room to Ginevra. Mrs. Sclater rose; Mr. Sclater threw himself back and stared—the latter astounded at the presumption of the youths, the former uneasy at the possible results of their ignorance. To the astonishment of the company, Ginevra rose, respect and modesty in every feature, as the youth, clownish rather than awkward, approached her. Almost timidly she held out her hand to him. He took it in his horny palm, shook it hither and thither sideways until Ginevra took charge of it herself again. Gibbie danced about behind him, all but standing on one leg but for Mrs. Sclater's sake restraining himself. Ginevra sat down and Donal, feeling very clumsy, looked about for a chair; then first espying Mrs. Sclater, he went up to her with the same clamping stride, but without embarrassment, and spoke, holding out his hand.

"How are you tonight, mem! I didn't see your pretty face when I came in. A grand house, like this—and I'm sure, mem, it couldn't be too grand for yourself, but it's perplexin' to plain folk like me that's used to more room, and less in it."

Donal was thinking of the meadow on the Lorrie bank.

"You will soon get accustomed to our town ways, Mr. Grant. I am glad to see you have friends here," she added.

"Only one, mem. Gibbie and me—"

"Excuse me, Mr. Grant, but would you oblige me—of course with me it is of no consequence, but just for habit's sake—would you oblige me by calling Gilbert by his own name, Sir Gilbert, please. I wish him to get used to it."

"As you will, mem. Well, as I was saying, Sir Gibbie—Sir Gilbert, that is, mem—an' myself, we have known Miss Galbraith for a long time, being of the laird's own folk, as I may say."

"Will you take a seat beside her, then," said Mrs. Sclater and, rising, placed a chair for him near Ginevra, wondering how any Scotch laird, the father of such a little lady as she, could have allowed her such an acquaintance.

To most of the company Donal must have looked very queer. Gibbie, indeed, was the only one who saw the real Donal. To the school ladies, mistress and pupils, he was simply a clodhopper and from their report became a treasure of poverty-stricken amusement to the school. Often did Ginevra's cheek burn with indignation at the small insolences of her fellow pupils.

"I thank you, mem," said Donal, as he took the chair; and fell into some rather long, and to some unintelligible, Scotch storytelling.

Gibbie, behind Donal's chair, was delighted, but the rest of the company, understanding his words yet not comprehending a single sentence he uttered, began to wonder whether he was out of his mind and were perplexed to see Ginevra listening with such respect.

Ginevra said little in reply. She had not much to say. In her world the streams were still, not vocal. But Donal meant to hold a little communication with her which none of them, except indeed Gibbie—he did not mind Gibbie—should understand.

"Well, well, Donal!" broke in the pompous voice of Mr. Sclater, who, unknown to the poet, had been standing behind him almost the whole time, "you have given the ladies quite enough of your romancing. That sort of thing may do very well around the fire in the farm kitchen, but it's not the sort of thing for a drawing room. Besides, the ladies don't understand your word of mouth; they don't understand such broad Scotch. Come with me, and I'll show you something."

He thought Donal was boring his guests, and at the same time was preventing Gibbie from having the pleasure in their society for which they had been invited.

Donal rose, replying, "Do you think so, sir? Didn't you understand me, mem?" he added, turning to Ginevra.

"Every word, Donal," she answered.

Donal followed his host, contented.

Gibbie took Donal's place and began to teach Ginevra the finger alphabet. The other girls found him far more amusing than Donal. And he had such a romantic history! And was a baronet!

In a few minutes Ginevra knew the letters, and presently she and Gibbie were having a little continuous talk together, a thing they had never had before. It was so slow, however, as to be rather tiring. It was mainly about Donal. But Mrs. Sclater opened the piano and made a diversion. She played something brilliant and then sang an Italian song. Then she asked Miss Kimble to play something, who declined but said that Miss Galbraith should sing—"That little Scotch song you sing now and then, my dear," she added.

Ginevra rose timidly but without hesitation and, going to the piano, sang a simple old Scottish air for which had been written five verses. Before she ended, the minister, the late herdboy and the baronet were grouped crescent-wise behind the music stool.

Three of them knew that the verses were Donal's. If the poet went home feeling more like a fellow in a blue coat and fustian trousers or a winged genius of the tomb, I leave my reader to judge. Anyhow, he felt he had had enough for one evening and was able to encounter his work again. Perhaps also, when supper was announced, he reflected that his reception had hardly been such as to justify him in partaking of their food, and that his mother's hospitality to Mr. Sclater had not been in expectation of return. As they went down the stair, he came last and alone behind the two whispering schoolgirls; and when they passed on into the dining room, he left the house and ran home to the furniture shop and his books.

35

••••••••••••••••••

Growing

*I*n obedience to the suggestion of his wife, Mr. Sclater did what he could to show Sir Gilbert how mistaken he was in imagining he could fit his actions to the words of our Lord.

But in talking thus to Gibbie, the minister but rippled the air. He was too familiar with truth. The unseen Lord and His reported words were to Gibbie realities. He had never *resolved* to keep the words of the Lord; he just kept them. The effect of it all upon Gibbie was to send him to his room to his prayers, more eager than ever to keep the commandments of Him who had said, "If ye love me. . . ." Comforted then and strengthened, he came down to go to Donal.

It will be plain from what I have told that Donal's imagination was full of Ginevra, and his was not an economy whose imagination could enjoy itself without calling the heart to share. Gibbie and he seldom talked about Ginevra. She was generally understood between them.

Mrs. Sclater showed herself sincere, after her kind, to Donal as well as to Gibbie. She told Gibbie that he must talk to Donal about his dress and his speech. That he was a lad of no common gifts was plain, she said, but were he ever so "talented" he could do little in the world, certainly would never raise himself, so long as he dressed and spoke ridiculously. The wisest and best of men would be utterly disregarded, she said, if he did not look and speak like other people. Gibbie thought with himself this could hardly hold, for there was John the Baptist; he answered her, however, that Donal could speak very good English if he chose. As to his dress, Donal was poor, Gibbie said, and could not give up wearing any clothes so long as there was any wear in them. "If you had seen me once!" he added, with a merry laugh to finish for his fingers.

Mrs. Sclater spoke to her husband, who said to Gibbie that if he chose to provide Donal with suitable garments, he would advance him the money.

Gibbie would thereupon have dragged Donal at once to the tailor; but Donal was obstinate. "No, no," he said; "I'll wear the clothes out. You can tell Mrs. Sclater that by the time I have anything to say to the world, it won't be my clothes that will make folks listen; and if she considers the ones that I have now too much a disgrace for her, she must just not invite me, and I'll not come; for I can't presently help them."

"What will you do when you are a minister?" asked Gibbie on his fingers.

"Me a minister?" echoed Donal. "Me a minister!" he repeated. "Losh, man! If I can save my own soul, it will be all I'm fit for. No, no; if I can be a schoolmaster and help children to be good, as my mother taught me, and have some time to read, and a few shillings to buy books, I'll be a happy man!"

"But wouldn't you like to have a wife, Donal, and children, like your father and mother?" spelled Gibbie.

"No, no; no wife for me, Gibbie!" answered the philosopher. "Who would have a poor schoolmaster or a shepherd?—except it was maybe some lass like my sister Nicie that wouldn't know Euclid from her stockings or Burns from a milldam."

When they met on Friday evening, they would rove the streets, Gibbie taking Donal to the places he knew so well in his childhood and enjoying it the more that he could now tell him so much better what he remembered. The only place he did not take him to was Jink Lane to the house that had been Mistress Croale's. He did take him to the court in the Widdiehill and showed him the Auld Hoose o' Galbraith and the place under the stair where his father had worked. The shed was now gone; the neighbors had by degrees carried it away for firewood. The house was occupied still as then by a number of poor people, and the door was never locked, day or night, anymore than when Gibbie used to bring his father home. He took Donal to the garret where they had slept—one could hardly say lived—and where his father had died. The door stood open and the place was just as they had left it.

"If I was you, Sir Gilbert," said Donal, who now and then remembered Mrs. Sclater's request to use Gibbie's title, "I would have Mr. Sclater keep a sharp lookout for the first chance of buyin' back this house. It would be a great pity if it should get much worse before you get it. Eh! Such tales as this house could tell!"

"How am I to do that, Donal? Mr. Sclater would not mind me. The money's not mine yet, you know," said Gibbie.

"The money is yours, Gibbie," answered Donal; "it's yours just as the kingdom of heaven is yours. It's only that you can't just lay your hands upon it yet. The sooner you let Mr. Sclater know that you know what you're about, the better. And, believe me, when he comes to understand that you want that house, he'll not be a day going to somebody or another about it."

Donal was right, for within a month the house was bought and certain necessary repairs commenced.

Mrs. Sclater continued to invite young ladies to the house for Gibbie's sake, and when she gave a party, she took care there should be young people at it; but Gibbie, although kind and polite to all, did not much enjoy these gatherings. The little pocket money Mr. Sclater allowed him was chiefly spent at the shop of a certain secondhand bookseller, nearly opposite Donal's room. These volumes were considered by Gibbie to be Donal's, and by Donal, Gibbie's. Every Saturday, as before, Gibbie went to see his father and mother. Janet kept fresh and lively, although age told on her, she said, more rapidly since Gibbie went away.

Six weeks of every summer between Donal's sessions, while the minister and his wife took their holiday, Gibbie spent with Robert and Janet. It was a blessed time for them all. He led then just the life of the former days with Robert and Oscar and the sheep, and Janet and her cow and the New Testament—only he had a good many more things to think about now, and more ways of thinking about them. With his own hands he built a little porch to the cottage door, with close sides and a second door to keep the wind out. Donal and he had carried up the timber and the mortar. But although he tried hard to make Janet say what more he could do for her, he could not bring her to reveal any desire that belonged to this world—except, indeed, for two or three trifles for her husband's warmth and convenience.

They almost always called him Sir Gibbie, and he never objected or seemed either annoyed or amused at it. He took it just as the name that was his, the same way as his hair or his hands were his; he had been called wee Sir Gibbie for so long.

The minister kept Gibbie hard at work, and by the time Donal's last winter came, Gibbie was ready for college also. Mr. Sclater consented to Gibbie's lodging with Donal. He would have insisted on them taking rooms in some part of the town more suitable to the young baronet's position, but by this time Gibbie seldom found difficulty in having his way with his guardian.

One day early in the session, as the youths were approaching the gate of Miss Kimble's school, a thin, careworn man in shabby clothes came out and walked along, eventually meeting them. It was the laird. They lifted their caps, but in return he only stared or, rather, tried to stare, for his eyes seemed able to fix themselves on nothing. He was now at length a thoroughly ruined man and had come to the city to end his days in a cottage he had purchased for his daughter. Mr. Sclater, who was unwearily on the watch over the material interests of his ward, had already, through his lawyer and without permitting his name to appear, purchased the whole of the Glashruach property. For the present, however, he kept Sir Gilbert in ignorance of the fact.

36

●●●●●●●●●●●●●●●●●●●

Fergus Duff

In every way the Laird had sunk to the bottom of manhood. It was very sad to Ginevra to see him thus shrunk and withered. Nothing interested him; he never looked at the paper, never cared to hear a word of news. It was a comfort that now in his misery she was able, if not to forget those painful thoughts about him, at least to dismiss them in the hope that as already such a change had passed upon him, further and better change might follow.

She was still the same small brown bird as of old. She had the sweetest, rarest smile—not frequent and flashing like Gibbie's, but stealing up from below, like the shadowy reflection of a greater light. Her atmosphere was an embodied stillness; she made a quiet wherever she entered. She was not beautiful, but she was lovely; and her presence at once made a place such as one would desire to be in. The most pleasant of her thoughts were of necessity those with which the two youths were associated. How dreary but for them would the retrospect of her life have been! Several times every winter they had met at the minister's, and every summer she had again and again seen Gibbie with Mrs. Sclater; once or twice she had had a walk with them, and every time Gibbie had something of Donal's to give her.

Twice Gibbie had gone to see her at the school, but the second time she asked him not to come again as Miss Kimble did not like it. He gave a big stare of wonder; but followed the stare with a swift smile, for he saw she was troubled; he asked no questions, waiting for the understanding of all things. But now, when or where was she ever to see them? Gibbie was no longer at the minister's and she dared not ask Donal to call; her father would be indignant. And for her father's sake she would not ask Gibbie; it might give him pain. Also, the thought that he would of a certainty behave so differently to him now that he was well-dressed and mannered like a gentleman was almost unendurable to her.

Mr. and Mrs. Sclater had called upon Ginevra and her father the moment they were settled in the cottage; but Mr. Galbraith would see nobody. When the gate bell rang, he always looked out and, if a visitor appeared, withdrew to his bedroom.

One brilliant Saturday morning, the second in the session, the ground was hard with an early frost; Mrs. Sclater rang the said bell. Mr. Galbraith, peeping from the window, saw a lady's bonnet. She walked in, followed by Gibbie, and asked Ginevra to go with them for a walk. She went and asked her father.

"Why do you ask me?" returned her father. "My wishes are nothing to anyone now; to you they never were anything."

"I will stay at home if you wish, Papa—with pleasure," she replied, as cheerfully as she could after such a reproach.

"By no means. If you do I shall go and dine at the Red Hart," he answered.

It made her miserable for a while, of course, but she had gotten so used to his way of breaking a gift as he handed it that she answered only with a sigh. In haste she put on her little brown-ribboned bonnet, took the moth-eaten muff that had been her mother's, and joined Mrs. Sclater and Gibbie, beaming with troubled pleasure. Life in her was strong, and their society soon enabled her to forget not her father's sadness but his treatment of her.

At the end of the street, they found Donal waiting them—without greatcoat or muffler, the picture of such health as suffices to its own warmth. Away they walked together westward, then turned southward. Mrs. Sclater and Gibbie led, and Ginevra followed with Donal. And they had not walked far before something of the delight of old times on Glashruach began to revive in the bosom of the sober girl. In vain she reminded herself that her father sat miserable at home, but the sun and the bright air like wine in her veins were too much for her. Donal had soon made her cheerful, and now and then she answered his talk with even a little flash of merriment.

They crossed the bridge, hung high over the Dour, by which on that black morning Gibbie had fled. And there, for the first time, with his three friends about him, he told on his fingers the dire deed of the night and heard from Mrs. Sclater that the murderers had been hanged. Ginevra grew white and faint as she read his fingers and gestures, but it was more at the thought of what the child had come through than from the horror of the narrative. They then turned eastward to the sea and came to the top of the rock border of the coast, with its cliffs rent into gullies—eerie places to look down into, ending in caverns into which the waves rushed with bellow and boom. Although so nigh the city, this was always a solitary place; yet rounding a rock they came upon a young man, who hurried a book into his pocket and would have gone by the other side; but, perceiving himself recognized, he came to meet them, and saluted Mrs. Sclater, who presented him to Ginevra as Rev. Mr. Duff.

"I have not had the pleasure of seeing you since you were quite a little girl, Miss Galbraith," said Fergus.

Ginevra said coldly she did not remember him. The youths greeted him in careless student fashion. They had met now and then about the college; and little, meaningless talk followed.

He was to preach the next day—and for several Sundays following—at a certain large church in the city, at the time without a minister. And when they came upon him he was studying his sermon—not the truths of the Book but his manuscript, studying it in the sense in which actors use the word, learning it by heart.

Fergus never forgot that he was a clergyman, always carrying himself according to his idea of the calling; therefore when the interchange of commonplaces flagged, he began to look for some remark to make sufficiently tinged with his profession to be suitable.

"I was watching these waves when you found me; they seem to be such a picture of the vanity of human endeavor! But just as little as those waves would mind me if I told them they were wasting their labor on these rocks will men mind me when I tell them tomorrow of the emptiness of their ambitions."

"Hoots, Fergus!" said Donal. "Why should you, in that case, go on preaching, setting them such a poor example?"

Fergus gave him a high-lidded glance, vouchsafing no replying. He just stared. What did his father's herdboy mean by talking such to him? Although now about to take his degree of Master of Arts, Donal was still to Fergus the cleaner-out of his father's stalls, an upstart whose former position was his real one—toward him at least, who knew him. And did the fellow challenge him to a discussion? Or did he presume on the familiarity of their boyhood and wish to sport his acquaintance with the popular preacher? On either supposition, this fellow was impertinent!

A good deal of discussion followed, most of it to Fergus's discomfort.

"I hope, ladies, your wits are not quite swept away in this flood of Highland logic," he said at length.

"You have a poor opinion of the stability of our brains, Mr. Duff," said Mrs. Sclater.

"I was only judging by myself," he replied, a little put out. "I can't say I understood our friends here. But this is Saturday, and tomorrow is my workday, you know, ladies," he said. "If you would oblige me with your address, Miss Galbraith, I should do myself the honor of calling on Mr. Galbraith."

Ginevra told him where they lived, but added she was afraid he must not expect to see her father, for he had been out of health lately and would see nobody.

"At all events I shall give myself the chance," he rejoined and, bidding the ladies good-bye and nodding to the youths, turned and walked away.

On Monday Fergus went to pay his visit to Mr. Galbraith. As Ginevra had said, her father did not appear; but Fergus was far from disappointed. He had taken it into his head that Miss Galbraith sided with him when that ill-bred fellow made his ungrateful attack upon him, and was much pleased to have a talk with her. Ginevra thought it would not be right to cherish against him the memory of the one sin of his youth in her eyes, but she could not like him. She was heartily tired of him before he went. When he was gone, she found as she sat with her father that she could not recall a word he had said. As to what had made the fellow stay so long, she was therefore positively unable to give her father an answer; the consequence of which was that the next time he called, Mr. Galbraith, much to her relief, stood the brunt of his approach and received him.

The ice thus broken, his ingratiating manners and the full-blown respect he showed Mr. Galbraith so won upon him that when he took his leave, he gave him a cordial invitation to repeat his visit. He did so, in the evening this time and, remembering a predilection of the laird's, begged for a game of backgammon. The result of his policy was that for many weeks that followed, every Monday evening at least, he spent with the laird. Ginevra was grateful to him for his attention to her father and his efforts to draw him out of his gloom, so she came gradually to let a little light of favor shine upon him. And if the heart of Fergus Duff was drawn to her, that is not to be counted to him a fault—neither that, his heart thus drawn, he should wish to marry her. He could easily have gotten a rich wife, but he was more greedy of distinction than money; and to marry the daughter of a man to whom he had been accustomed in childhood to look up to as the greatest in the known world was in his eyes like a patent of nobility and would be a ratification of his fitness to mingle with the choice of the land.

37

. . . .

The Quarry

*I*t was a cold night in March, cloudy and blowing. Donal and Gibbie were at the North Church to hear Fergus preach in the pulpit that had now become his own. The people had been gathering since long before the hour, and the youths could find only standing room near the door.

There was, however, no mistaking either Ginevra's bonnet or the long neck of her father. They sat a good way in front, about the middle of the great church. At the sight of them, Gibbie's face brightened and Donal's turned pale as death. For only the last week he heard of the frequent visits of the young preacher to the cottage and the favor in which he was held by both father and daughter. Donal's state of mind since had not been, with all his philosophy to rectify and support it, an enviable one. That he could not for a moment regard himself as a fit husband for the lady-lass, or dream of revealing himself or her to the insult which his offer as a son-in-law would bring on them both from the laird, was not a reflection to render the thought of such a bag of wind as Fergus Duff marrying her one whit the less horrible.

Had the laird been in the same social position as before, Donal would have had no fear of his accepting Fergus; but misfortune alters many relations. Fergus's father was a man of considerable property, Fergus himself almost a man of influence and already in possession of a comfortable

income. It was possible to imagine that the impoverished Thomas Galbraith, Esq., late of Glashruach, might contrive to swallow what annoyance there could not but in any case be in wedding his daughter to the
son of John Duff, formerly his own tenant of the Mains.

The young men were among the first out and, going round to another
door by which they judged Ginevra and her father must issue, there stood
waiting. Fergus soon was standing beside them but seemed not to see
them, and they were nowise inclined to attract his attention. At last out
came Ginevra—like a daisy among the mown grass!—with her father. She
saw Donal, glanced from him to Gibbie, cast down her sweet eyes, and
made no sign. Fergus had already advanced and addressed the laird.

"Ah, Mr. Duff!" said Mr. Galbraith. "Excuse me, but would you oblige
me by giving your arm to my daughter? I see a friend waiting to speak to
me. I shall overtake you in a moment."

Fergus murmured his pleasure, and Ginevra and he moved away
together. The youths for a moment watched the father. He dawdled—evidently wanting to speak to no one. They then followed the two, walking
some yards behind them. Every other moment Fergus would bend his
head toward Ginevra; once or twice they saw the little bonnet turn
upward in response or question. When the youths reached the street
where the cottage stood, they turned the corner after them and walked
quickly up to them where they stood at the gate waiting for it to be
opened.

"Such a grand night!" said Donal, after the usual greetings. "Sir Gibbie
and me's been having a walk in the moonlight. The moon's so bright you'd
think she had light enough to keep the clouds off her, wouldn't you, mem?
But no! they'll be upon her, I'm afraid, soon enough. See the clouds there
among the moon? . . . Well, good night, mem. Good night, Fergus."

Therewith Donal walked on, doubtless for the moment a little relieved.
But before they had walked far, he broke down altogether. "Gibbie," he
said, "the rascal's going to marry the lady-lass! And it drives me mad to
think it. If I could but have a chance to speak to her—once—just once!
Lord! what'll come of all the gowans upon the Mains, and the heather
upon Glashgar!"

Gibbie's face had grown white in the moonglow and his lips trembled.
He put his arm through Donal's and clung to him, and in silence they
went home. When they reached Donal's room, Donal entered and shut
the door behind him, leaving Gibbie outside. He stood for a moment like
one dazed, then suddenly coming to himself, turned, left the house, and
ran straight to Daur Street.

When the minister's door was opened to him, he went to the dining
room, knowing Mr. and Mrs. Sclater would then be at supper. Happily for
his intent, the minister was at the moment having his tumbler of toddy
after the labors of the day. His wife, therefore, when she saw Gibbie, rose
and, meeting him, took him with her to her own little sitting room where
they had a long talk. The result appeared the next night in a note from

Mrs. Sclater to Gibbie, asking him and Donal to spend the evening of Tuesday with her.

The next night Donal, trembling, accompanied Gibbie. The hospitable crimson room, with its round table set out for a Scottish tea and its fire blazing hugely, received them. And there sat Ginevra by the fire with her pretty feet on a footstool before it! (In those days ladies wore open shoes, and showed dainty stockings.) Her face looked rosy from the firelight. She received them, as always with the same simple sincerity that had been hers on the bank of the Lorrie burn. But Gibbie read some trouble in her eyes, for his soul was all touch and, like a delicate spiritual seismograph, responded at once to the least tremble of a neighboring soul.

When tea was over, Gibbie went to the window and peeped out. Returning presently he spelled with fingers and signed with hands to Ginevra that it was a glorious night; would she not come for a walk? Ginevra looked to Mrs. Sclater.

"Gibbie wants me to go for a walk," she said.

"Certainly, my dear—if you are well enough to go with him," replied her friend.

"I am always well," answered Ginevra.

"I can't go with you," said Mrs. Sclater, "for I expect my husband any moment; but what occasion is there, with two such knights to protect you?"

Perceiving Gibbie's design, Donal cast him a grateful glance while Ginevra rose hastily and ran to put on her outer garments. Plainly to Donal, she was pleased to go.

When they stood on the pavement, there was the moon, the very cream of light, ladying it in a blue heaven. The steps of the youths rang on the pavement, and Donal's voice seemed to him too loud. He spoke low, and Ginevra answered him softly. They walked close together and Gibbie flitted to and fro, now on this side, now on that, now in front of them, now behind.

"How did you like the sermon last evening, mem?" asked Donal.

"Papa thought it a grand sermon," answered Ginevra.

"And yourself?" persisted Donal.

"Papa tells me I am no judge," she replied.

"That's as much as to say you didn't like it as well as he did!" returned Donal, in a tone expressing some relief.

"Mr. Duff is very good to my father, Donal," she rejoined, "and I don't like to say anything against his sermon; but all the time I could not help thinking whether your mother would like this and that. For, you know, any good there is in me I have got from her and from Gibbie—and from you, Donal."

The youth's heart beat with a pleasure that rose to physical pain.

Donal remaining silent, Ginevra presently returned him his own question.

"How did you like the sermon, Donal?"

"Do you want me to say, mem?" he asked.

"I do, Donal," she answered.

"Well, I would just say, in general, I can't think much of a sermon that might make someone think more of a preacher than Him that he comes to preach about. I mean that I don't see how anybody was to love God or his neighbor a jot more for hearing that sermon on Sunday night."

"That's just what I was feeling," she replied. "I am sorry for Mr. Duff if he has taken to preaching where he does not understand."

They had left the city behind them and were walking on a wide-open road, with a great sky above it. On its borders were small, fenced fields and a house here and there with a garden. But this night the earth was nothing; what was in them and over them was all. Donal felt that with this wonder by his side, to be doomed to go on walking to all eternity would be a blissful fate were the landscape turned to a brickfield and the sky to persistent grey.

"Would you take my arm, mem?" he said at length, summoning courage. "I just find myself like a horse with a rein broken, going through the air this way."

Before he had finished the sentence, Ginevra had accepted the offer. It was the first time. His arm trembled. He thought it was her hand.

"You're not cold, are you, mem?" he said.

"Not in the least," she answered.

A moment more and Donal broke out singing:

My thoughts are like fireflies, pulsing in moonlight;
     My heart is a silver cup, full of red wine;
My soul a pale gleaming horizon, whence soon light
     Will flood the gold earth with a torrent divine.

"What was that, Donal?" cried Ginevra.

"Oh, nothing," answered Donal. "It was only my heart laughing."

"Say the words," said Ginevra.

"I can't—I don't know them now," replied Donal.

"Oh, Donal! Are those lovely words gone—altogether—forever? Shall I not hear them again?"

"I'll try to remember them when I go home," he said. "I can't think of them now. I can think of nothing but one thing."

"And what is that, Donal?"

"Yourself," answered Donal.

Ginevra's hand lifted just a half of its weight from Donal's arm, like a bird that had thought of flying, then settled again.

"It is very pleasant to be together once more as in the old time, Donal—though there are no daisies and green fields.—But what place is that?"

Instinctively, almost unconsciously, she wanted to turn the conversation. The place she pointed to was an opening immediately on the roadside, through a high bank—narrow and dark, with one side half-lighted by the moon. She had often passed it, walking with her schoolfellows, but had never thought of asking what it was. In the shining dusk it looked strange and a little dreadful.

"It's the quarry, mem," answered Donal; "don't you know that? That's where most of the whole town came from. It's an eerie kind of place to look at in this light. I'm surprised you never saw it."

"I have seen the opening there but never took much notice of it before," said Ginevra.

"Come and I'll let you see it," said Donal. "You wouldn't be afraid to come and see what the moon makes of it, would you, mem?"

"No, Donal. I would not be frightened to go anywhere with you. But—"

"Eh, mem! it makes me right proud to hear you say that. Come, then."

So saying, he turned aside and led her into the narrow passage, cut through granite. Gibbie, thinking they had gone to have but a peep and return, stood in the road looking at the clouds and the moon and crooning to himself. By and by, when he found they did not return, he followed them.

When they reached the end of the cutting, Ginevra started at the sight of the vast gulf, the moon showing the one wall a ghastly grey, and from the other throwing a shadow half across the bottom. But a winding road went down into it, and Donal led her on. The side of the quarry was on one hand, and on the other she could see only into the gulf, and she was afraid to take her hand from his arm.

"Oh, Donal!" she said at length, almost in a whisper, "this is like a dream I once had, of going down and down a long, roundabout road, inside the earth."

Presently Donal again began to sing.

"Are you sure there are no holes—full of water—down there?" she faltered.

"Ay, there's one or two," replied Donal, "but we'll keep out of them."

Ginevra shuddered but was determined to show no fear. They stepped at last on the level below, covered with granite chips and stones and great blocks. There shone the moon on the corner of a pool, the rest of which crept away in the blackness under an overhanging mass. She caught his arm with both hands. He told her to look up. Steep granite rock was above them all around—on one side dark, on the other, mottled with the moon and the thousand shadows of its own roughness. Over the gulf hung vaulted the dark blue, cloud-blotted sky, whence the moon seemed to look straight down upon her, asking what they were about.

Suddenly Donal caught her hand. She looked in his face. It was not the moon that could make it so white.

"Ginevra!" he said with trembling voice.

"Yes, Donal," she answered.

"You're not angry with me for calling you by your name? I never did it before."

"I always call you Donal," she answered.

"That's natural. You're a grand lady, and I'm nothing but a herd-laddie."

"You're a great poet, Donal, and that's much more than being a lady or a gentleman."

"Ay, maybe," answered Donal listlessly, "but a poor lad like me dares not lift an eye to a grand lady like you, mem. My time is nearly over at the college, and I see nothing for it but to go home and hire myself out. I'll be better working with my hands than with my head when I have no hope left of seeing your face again. Eh, mem, but you are pretty! But you don't know yourself how pretty you are . . . what a subversion you make in my heart and my head."

Still she looked him in the eyes, like one bewildered, unable to withdraw her eyes from his. Her face too had grown white.

"Tell me to hold my tongue, mem, and I'll hold it," he said.

Her lips moved, but no sound came.

"I well know," he went on, "you can never look on me as anything more than a kind of human bird that you would keep in a cage and listen to when he sang. And whether you grant me my prayer or not, you will never see me again. The only difference will be that I'll either hang my head or hold it up for the rest of my days. I would fain know that I wasn't despised."

"What is it, Donal?" said Ginevra, half inaudibly and with effort; she could scarcely speak for a fluttering in her throat.

"I beseech you upon my knees," he went on, as if she had not spoken, "at the favor of your sweet soul, to lay upon me—as upon the lips of the soul that sang you the songs you liked so well to hear when you were but a lassie—one solitary kiss. I swear by the Truth I'll think of it but as you think, and no man or woman or child, not even Gibbie himself, shall know—"

The last word broke the spell upon Ginevra.

"But, Donal," she said, as quietly as when years ago they talked by the Lorrieside, "would it be right?—a secret with you I could not tell to anyone?—not even if afterward—"

Donal's face grew so ghastly with despair that absolute terror seized her; she turned from him and fled, calling, "Gibbie! Gibbie!"

He was not many yards off, approaching the mound as she came from behind it. He ran to meet her. She darted to him like a dove pursued by a hawk, threw herself into his arms, laid her head on his shoulder, and wept. Gibbie held her fast, and with all the ways in his poor power sought to comfort her. She raised her face at length. It was all wet with tears which glistened in the moonlight. Hurriedly Gibbie asked on his fingers:

"Was Donal not good to you?"

"He's beautiful," she sobbed; "but I couldn't, you know, Gibbie, I couldn't . . . I don't care a straw about position and all that—who would with a poet?—But I couldn't, you know, Gibbie. I couldn't let him think I might have married him—in any case; could I now, Gibbie?"

She laid her head again on his shoulder and sobbed. Gibbie did not well understand her. Donal, where he had thrown himself on a heap of granite chips, heard and understood, felt and knew and resolved all in one. The moon shone, and the clouds went flitting about, and still the two, Ginevra and Gibbie, stood motionless—Gibbie with the tears in his eye, and Ginevra weeping as if her heart would break. And behind the granite blocks lay Donal.

Again Ginevra raised her head.

"Gibbie, you must go and look after poor Donal," she said.

Gibbie went, but Donal was nowhere to be seen. To escape the two he loved so well, he had crept away softly into one of the many recesses of the place. Again and again Gibbie made the noise with which he was accustomed to call him, but Donal gave back no answer; and they understood that wherever he was he wanted to be left to himself. They climbed again the winding way out of the gulf and left him the heart of its desolation.

"Take me home, Gibbie," said Ginevra, when they reached the high road.

As they went, not a word more passed between them. Ginevra was as dumb as Gibbie, and Gibbie was sadder than he had ever been in his life—not only for Donal's sake, but because, in his inexperienced heart, he feared that Ginevra would not listen to Donal because she could not, because she had already promised herself to Fergus Duff. With all his love to his kind, he could not think it well that Fergus should be made happy at such a price. He left her at her own door and went home, hoping to find Donal there before him.

He was not there. Hour after hour passed, and he did not appear. At eleven o'clock, Gibbie set out to look for him, but with little hope of finding him. He went all the way back to the quarry. Gibbie went home again, and sat up all night, keeping the kettle boiling, ready to make tea for him the moment he should come in. But even in the morning Donal did not appear.

He might hear of him at the college, he thought, and went at the usual hour. Sure enough, as he entered the quadrangle, there was Donal going in at the door leading to the moral philosophy classroom. For hours, neglecting his own classes, Gibbie watched about the court, but Donal never showed himself. Gibbie concluded he had gone home by Crown Street, and himself returned, almost sure of now finding him in his room—although probably with the door locked. The room was empty and no one had seen him.

Donal's final examination, upon which alone his degree now depended, came on the next day. Gibbie watched at the certain corner and, unseen, saw him pass—with a face pale but strong, eyes that seemed not to have slept. After that he did not see him once till the last day of the session arrived. Then in the public room he saw him go up to receive his degree. As they came from the public room, Gibbie lay in wait for him once more, but again in vain.

When he reached his lodging, he found a note from Donal waiting him in which he bade him good-bye, said he was gone home, and asked him to pack up his things for him.

A sense of loneliness, such as in all his forsaken times he had never felt, overshadowed Gibbie. It troubled him a little that he must now return to Mr. Sclater. But it would not be for long.

Mr. Sclater had thought of making a movement toward gaining an extension of his tutelage beyond the ordinary legal period, on the ground of unfitness in his ward for the management of his property. But Gibbie's character and scholarship had deterred him from the attempt. In the month of May, therefore, when, according to the registry of his birth in the parish book, he would be of age, he would also be his own master so far as other mortals were concerned.

Gibbie was in no haste to return to Daur Street. He packed Donal's things, with all the books they had bought together, and committed the chest to the landlady. He then told her he would rather not give up his room yet, but would like to keep it on for a while, and come and go as he pleased.

He told her he would sleep there that night, and she got him his dinner as usual; after which, putting a Greek book in his pocket, he went out, thinking to go to the end of the pier and sit there awhile.

The next day Gibbie went back to his guardians. At his request Mrs. Sclater asked Ginevra to spend the following evening with them; he wanted to tell her about Donal. She accepted the invitation. But in a village near the foot of Glashgar, Donal had that morning done what was destined to prevent her from keeping her engagement; he posted a letter to her. He had recalled the verses he sang to her as they walked that evening, and now sent them—complete in a very different tone. Not a word accompanied them.

My thoughts are like fireflies pulsing in moonlight;
 My heart like a silver cup full of red wine;
My soul a pale gleaming horizon, whence soon light
 Will flood the gold earth with a torrent divine.

My thoughts are like worms in a starless gloamin';
 My heart like a sponge that's fillit wi' gall;
My sowl like a bodiless ghaist sent roamin',
 To bide i' the mirk till the great trumpet call.

But peace by upo' ye, as deep as ye're lo'esome!
 Brak na an hoor o' yer fair-dreamy sleep,
To think o' the lad wi' a weicht in his bosom,
 'At ance sent a cry till ye oat o' the deep.

Some sharp rocky heicht, to catch a far mornin'
 Ayont a' the nichts o' this warld, he'll clim',
For nane shall say, Luik! he sank doon at her scornin',
 Wha rase by the han' she hield frank oot to him.

The letter was handed, with one or two more, to Mr. Galbraith at the breakfast table. He did not receive many letters now and could afford time to one that was for his daughter. He laid it with the rest by his side and after breakfast took it to his room and read it. He could no more understand it than Fergus could the Epistle of the Romans. But he had begun to be afraid of his daughter. He laid the letter aside, said nothing and waited, inwardly angry. After a while he began to flatter himself with the hope that perhaps it was but a sort of impertinent valentine, the writer of which was unknown to Ginevra. From the moment of its arrival, however, he kept a stricter watch upon her and that night prevented her from going to Mrs. Sclater's.

38

. . . .

Of Age

There was no rejoicing upon Gibbie's attainment of his twenty-first year. His guardian, believing he alone had acquainted himself with the date and desiring in his wisdom to avoid giving him a feeling of importance, made no allusion to the fact, as would have been most natural, when they met at breakfast on the morning of the day. But, urged thereto by Donal, Gibbie had learned the date for himself and finding nothing was said, fingered to Mrs. Sclater, "This is my birthday."

"I wish you many happy returns," she answered. "How old are you today?"

"Twenty-one," he answered—by holding up all his fingers twice and then a forefinger.

She looked struck and glanced at her husband who, thereupon in his turn, gave utterance to the usual formula of goodwill and said no more. Seeing he was about to leave the table, Gibbie claimed his attention, spelling on his fingers very slowly (for Mr. Sclater was not adept at following this mode of communication).

"If you please, sir, I want to be put in possession of my property as soon as possible."

"All in good time, Sir Gilbert," answered the minister, with a superior smile, for he clung with hard reluctance to the last vestige of his power.

"But what is good time?" spelled Gibbie with a smile, which nonetheless that it was of genuine friendliness indicated there might be difference of opinion on the point.

"Oh! We shall see," returned the minister coolly. "These are not things to be done in a hurry," he added, as if he had been guardian to twenty wards before. "We'll see in a few days what Mr. Torrie proposes."

"But I want my money at once," insisted Gibbie. "I have been waiting for it, and now it is time; why should I wait still?"

"To learn patience, if for no other reason, Sir Gilbert," answered the minister with a hard laugh, meant to be jocular. "But indeed such affairs cannot be managed in a moment. You will have plenty of time to make a good use of your money, if you should have to wait another year or two."

So saying he pushed back his plate and cup and rose from the table.

"When will you see Mr. Torrie?" asked Gibbie, rising too and working his telegraph with greater rapidity than before.

"By and by," answered Mr. Sclater and walked toward the door. But Gibbie got between him and it.

"Will you go with me to Mr. Torrie today?" he asked.

The minister shook his head. Gibbie withdrew, seeming a little disappointed. Mr. Sclater left the room.

"You don't understand business, Gilbert," said Mrs. Sclater.

Gibbie smiled, got paper and pen and, sitting down at the table, wrote as follows:

"Dear Mr. Sclater: As you have never failed in your part, how can you wish me to fail in mine? I am now the one accountable for this money, which surely has been idle long enough, and if I leave it still unused, I shall be doing wrong, and there are things I have to do with it which ought to be set about immediately. I am sorry to seem impertinent, but if by twelve o'clock you have not gone with me to Mr. Torrie, I will go to Messrs. Hope & Waver, who will tell me what I ought to do next, in order to be put in possession. It makes me unhappy to write like this but I am not a child any longer, and having a man's work to do, I cannot consent to be treated as a child. I will do as I say. I am, dear Mr. Sclater, your affectionate ward, Gilbert Galbraith."

He took the letter to the study and, having given it to Mr. Sclater, withdrew. The minister might have known by this time with what sort of a youth he had to deal! He came down instantly, put the best face on it he could, said that if Sir Gilbert was so eager to take up the burden, he was ready enough to cast it off, and they would go at once to Mr. Torrie.

With the lawyer, Gibbie insisted on understanding everything, and that all should be legally arranged as speedily as possible. Mr. Torrie saw that if he did not make things plain or gave the least cause for doubt, the youth would most likely apply elsewhere for advice. Therefore he took trouble to set the various points, both as to the property and the proceedings necessary, before him in the cleanest manner.

"Thank you," said Gibbie, through Mr. Sclater. "Please remember I am more accountable for this money than you, and am compelled to understand!" Janet's repeated exhortations on the necessity of sending for the serpent to take care of the dove had not been lost upon him.

The lawyer being then quite ready to make him an advance of money, they went with him to the bank where Gibbie wrote his name and received a checkbook. As they left the bank, he asked the minister whether he would allow him to keep his place in his house till the next session and was almost startled at finding how his manner to him was changed. He assured Sir Gilbert, with a deference and respect both painful and amusing, that he hoped he would always regard his house as one home, however many besides he might now choose to have.

So now at last Gibbie was free to set about realizing a long-cherished scheme.

The repairs upon the Auld Hoose o' Galbraith were now nearly finished. In consequence of them, some of the tenants had had to leave, and Gibbie now gave them all notice to quit at their earliest convenience, taking care, however, to see them provided with fresh quarters, for several of the houses in the neighborhood had been bought for him at the same time with the old mansion. As soon as it was empty, he set more men to work, and not a little of the old stateliness began to reappear. He next proceeded to furnish certain of the rooms. By the time he had finished, his usual day for going home had arrived. While Janet lived, the cottage on Glashgar was home. Just as he was leaving, the minister told him that Glashruach was his. Mrs. Sclater was present and read in his eyes what induced her instantly to make the remark: "How could that man deprive his daughter of the property he had to take her mother's name to get!"

"He had misfortunes," indicated Gibbie, "and could not help it, I suppose."

"Yes, indeed!" she returned, "—misfortunes so great that they amounted to little less than swindling. I wonder how many he has brought to grief besides himself! If he had Glashruach once more, he would begin it all over again."

"Then I'll give it to Ginevra," said Gibbie.

"And let her father coax her out of it, and do another world of mischief with it!" she rejoined.

Gibbie was silent. Mrs. Sclater was right! To give is not always to bless. He must think of some other way.

He would liked to have seen Ginevra before he left but had no chance. He had gone to the North Church every Sunday for a long time now for the sake of seeing his lost friend. Had he not lost her when she turned from Donal to Fergus? Did she not forsake him too when she forsook his Donal? His heart would rise into his throat at the thought, but only for a moment. Now and then he had from her a sweet smile, but no sign that he might go and see her. Whether he was to see Donal when he reached Daurside, he could not tell; he had heard nothing of him since he went. His mother never wrote letters.

Notwithstanding his new power, it was hardly with his usual elation that he took his seat on the coach. But his reception was the same as ever. At his mother's persuasion, Donal, he found, instead of betaking himself again to bodily labors as he had purposed, had gone in search of some situation as a tutor.

"He'll be the better for it in the end," she said with a smile of the deepest sympathy, "though, being my own, I can't help being sorry for him. But the Lord was in the earthquake, and the fire, and the wind that blew the rocks, though the prophet couldn't see him. Donal will come out of this with more room in his heart and more light in his spirit."

Gibbie took his slate and wrote, "If money could do anything for him, I have plenty now."

"I know your heart, my child," replied Janet; "but no; the poor fellow must wrestle out of the thicket as best he can—sore scratched, no doubt. Eh! It's a fearful and wonderful thing that drawing of heart to heart, and then a great snap and a start back, and there's miles between them! The Lord alone knows the bottom of it."

Gibbie told her that Glashruach was his. Then first the extent of his wealth seemed to strike his old mother.

"Eh! You'll be the laird, will you, then? To think of this house and all being wee Gibbie's! Well, it beats all. The ways of the Lord are to be thought upon! He made David a king, and Gibbie He's made the laird! Blest be His name."

"They tell me the mountain is mine," Gibbie wrote. "Your husband shall be laird of Glashgar if he likes."

"No, no," said Janet, with a loving look. "He's too old for that. What better would Robert be to be laird? We pay no rent as it is, and he has as many sheep to love as he can well know one from the other. I know nothing that he lacks but Gibbie to go with him about the hill. A neighbor's laddie comes and goes, to help him, but, eh, says Robert, he's no Gibbie!—But if Glashruach be your own, my bonnie man, you must go down there this very night, and give a look to the burn; for the last time I was there, I thought it was creeping in underneath the bank fearfully like for what's left of the old house, and the sooner it's looked after the better. Eh, Sir Gibbie, but you should marry the bonnie lady, and take her back to her own house."

Gibbie gave a great sigh to think of the girl that loved the hill and the heather and the burns shut up in the city, and every Sunday going to the great church. To him Glashgar was full of God; the North Church or Mr. Sclater's church—well, he had tried hard, but had not succeeded in discovering temple signs about either.

The next day he sent to the city for an architect; and within a week masons and quarrymen were at work, some on the hill, blasting blue boulders and red granite, others roughly shaping the stones, and others laying the foundation of a huge facing and buttressing wall, which was to slope up from the bed of the Glashburn fifty feet to the foot of the castle, there to culminate in a narrow terrace with a parapet. Others again were clearing away what of the ruins stuck to the old house in order to leave it, as much as might be, in its original form. There was no space left for rebuilding, neither was there any between the two burns for adding afresh. The channel of the second remained dry, the landslip continuing to choke it, while the stream fell into the Glashburn. But Gibbie would not consent that the burn Ginevra had loved should sing no more as she had heard it sing. Her chamber was gone and could not be restored, but another chamber should be built for her, beneath whose window it should again rain; when she was married to Fergus, and her father could not touch it, the place should be hers.

More masons were gathered and foundations blasted in the steep rock that formed the other bank of the burn. The main point in the building was to be a room for Ginevra. He planned it himself—with a windowed turret projecting from the wall, making a recess in the room overhanging the stream. The turret he carried a story higher than the wall, and in the wall placed a stair leading to its top, whence over the roof might be seen great Glashgar and its streams coming down from heaven and singing as they came. Then from the middle of the first stair in the old house—the wall a yard and a half thick having been cut through—a solid stone bridge with a pointed arch was to lead across the burn to a like landing in the new house—a closed passage, with an oriel window on each side, looking up and down the stream, and a steep roof. And while these works were going on below, two masons high on the mountain were adding to the cottage a warm bedroom for Janet and Robert.

The architect was an honest man and kept Gibbie's secret, so that, although Gibbie was constantly about the place, nothing disturbed the general belief that Glashruach had been bought and was being made habitable by a certain magnate of the county adjoining.

39

The Auld Hoose o' Galbraith

One cold afternoon in the end of October, when Mistress Croale was shutting up her shop in the market, Gibbie came walking up the long gallery with the light hill step which he never lost. Startling her with a hand on her shoulder, he made signs that she must come with him. She made haste to lock her door, and they walked side by side to the Widdiehill.

They turned into the close of the Auld Hoose o' Galbraith, and Gibbie led her up the dark stair. At the top, on a wide hall-like landing, he opened a door. She drew back with amazement. But his smile reassured her and she stepped in.

It was a grand room, rich and somber in color, old-fashioned in its somewhat stately furniture. A glorious fire was blazing and candles were burning. The table was covered with a white cloth and laid for two. Gibbie shut the door, placed a chair for Mistress Croale by the fire, seated himself, took out his tablet, wrote, "Will you be my housekeeper? I will give you 100 pounds a year," and handed it to her.

"Lord, Sir Gibbie!" she cried, jumping to her feet, "have you lost your wits? How would an old wife like me look in such a place—and in such duds as this? It would make Satan laugh, and that he does but seldom."

Gibbie rose and, taking her by the hand, led her to the door of an adjoining room. It was a bedroom as grand as the room they had left, and if Mistress Croale was surprised before, she was astonished now. A fire was burning here too, candles were alight on the dressing table, a hot bath stood ready, and on the bed lay a dress of rich black satin, with linen and everything to collars, cuffs, mittens, cap and shoes. All these things Gibbie had bought himself, using the knowledge he had gathered in shopping with Mrs. Sclater and the advice of her dressmaker, whom he had taken into his confidence and who had entered heartily into his plan. He made signs to Mistress Croale that everything there was at her service, and left her.

Like one in a dream she yielded to the rush of events, not too much bewildered to dress with care, and neither too old nor too wicked nor too ugly to find pleasure in it. She might have been a born lady just restored to the habits of her youth, to judge by her delight over the ivory brushes and tortoise-shell comb and great mirror. In an hour or so she made her appearance—I can hardly say reappeared, but wiping the tears from her eyes like a too-blessed child. Gibbie was so satisfied with her appearance that, come of age as he was and vagrant no more, he first danced around her several times with a candle in his hand—much to the danger but nowise to the detriment of her finery—then set it down and executed his old lavolta of delight, which, as always, he finished by standing on one leg.

They then sat down to a nice nondescript meal, also of Gibbie's own providing.

When it was ended, he went to a bureau and brought thence a paper plainly written to this effect: "I agree to do whatever Sir Gilbert Galbraith may require of me, so long as it shall not be against my conscience; and consent that, if I taste whiskey once, he shall send me away immediately, without further reason given."

He handed it to Mistress Croale. She read and instantly looked about for pen and ink; she dreaded seeming for a moment to hesitate. He brought them to her, she signed, and they shook hands.

He then conducted her all over the house—first to the rooms prepared for his study and bedroom, and next to the room in the garret which he had left just as it was when his father died in it. Then, on the floor between, he showed her a number of bedrooms, all newly repaired and freshly painted, including double windows, the inside ones filled with frosted glass. These rooms, he gave her to understand, he wished her to furnish. Going back to the sitting room, he proceeded to explain his plans, telling her he had furnished the house that he might not any longer be himself a stranger as to have no place to take a stranger to. Then he got a Bible which was in the room and showed her those words in the book of Exodus, ". . . also, thou shalt not oppress a stranger; for ye know the heart of a stranger, seeing ye were strangers in the land of Egypt." While she thought again of her wanderings through the country and nights in the open air, he made her understand that whomsoever he should at any time bring home, she was to treat as his guest. She might get a servant to wait upon herself, he said, but she herself must help him to wait upon his guests.

She expressed hearty acquiescence but would not hear of a servant; the more work, the better for her, she said. She would tomorrow arrange for giving up her shop and disposing of her stock and the furniture in her garret. Next he insisted that she should never utter a word as to the use he intended making of his house; if the thing came out, it would ruin his plans. And thereupon he took her to the ground floor and showed her a door in communication with a poor little house behind, by which he intended to introduce and dismiss his guests, that they should not know where they had spent the night. Then he made her read to him the hundred and seventh Psalm, after which he left her, saying he would come to the house as soon as the session began, which would be in a week; until then he should be at Mr. Sclater's.

Left alone in the great house—like one with whom the most beneficent of fairies had been busy—the first thing Mistress Croale did was to go and have a good look at herself from head to foot. She was satisfied with everything she saw there except her complexion, and that she resolved should improve. She was almost painfully happy. Out there was the Widdiehill, dark and dismal and cold, through which she had come, sad and shivering and haunted with miserable thoughts, into warmth and splendor and luxury and bliss! Wee Sir Gibbie had made a lady of her! If only poor Sir George were alive to see it!

40

The Laird and the Preacher

Since he came to town, Gibbie had seen Ginevra but once—that was in the North Church. She looked so sad and white that his heart was very heavy for her. Could it be that she repented? She must have turned down Donal to please her father! If she would marry Donal, Gibbie would give her Glashruach. She should have Glashruach all the same whatever she did, only it might influence her father. He paced up and down before the cottage once for a whole night, but no good came of that. He paced before it from dusk to bedtime again and again in the hope of speaking to Ginevra, but he never saw even her shadow on the white blind. He went up to the door once, but in the dread of displeasing her lost his courage and paced the street the whole morning instead, but saw no one come out.

Fergus had gradually become essential to the small remaining happiness of which the laird was capable. He had gained his favor chiefly through the respect and kindly attention he showed him. The young preacher knew little of the laird's career, and looked upon him as an unfortunate man, toward whom loyalty now required even a greater show of respect than while he owned his father's farm.

Fergus at length summoned courage to ask him if he might pay his addresses to Miss Galbraith. The old man started, cast on him a withering look, murmured "The heiress of Glashruach!" then remembered, threw himself back in his chair, and closed his eyes. The father reflected that if he accepted him, he might leave the miserable cottage and go to the manse; it would be of consequence to have a clergyman for a son-in-law. Slowly he raised himself in his chair.

"You have my permission, Mr. Duff."

The young preacher hastened to find Ginevra but only to meet a refusal, gentle and sorrowful. He pleaded for permission to repeat his request after an interval, but she distinctly refused. Disappointed and annoyed he was, but he sought and fancied he found reasons for her decision which were not unfavorable to himself, and continued to visit her father as before, saying to him he had not quite succeeded in drawing from her a favorable answer but hoped to prevail. He nowise acted the despairing lover, but made grander sermons than ever and, as he came to feel at home in his pulpit, delivered them with growing force. But delay wrought desire in the laird; and at length one evening, having by cross-questioning satisfied himself that Fergus made no progress, he rose and, going to his desk, handed him Donal's verses. Fergus read them and remarked he had read better, but the first stanza had a slight flavor of Shelley.

"What I want to know is," said Mr. Galbraith, "whether they do not suggest a reason for your want of success with Ginny. Do you know the writing?"

"I cannot say I do. But I think it is very likely that of Donal Grant; he sets up for the Burns of Daurside."

"Insolent scoundrel!" cried the laird.

"But, my dear sir," said Fergus, "if I am to understand these lines—if you will excuse me for venturing to say so—what I read in them is that whoever the writer may be, the lady, whoever she may be, had refused him."

"You cannot believe that the wretch had the impudence to make my daughter—the heiress of—at least—What! make my daughter an offer! She would at once have acquainted me with the fact, that he might receive suitable chastisement. Let me look at the stuff again."

"It is quite possible," said Fergus, "it may be only a poem some friend has copied for her from a newspaper."

While he spoke, the laird was reading the lines and persuading himself he understood them. With sudden resolve, the paper held torchlike in front of him, he strode into the next room where Ginevra sat.

"Do you tell me," he said fiercely, "that you have so far forgotten all dignity and propriety as to give a dirty cowboy the encouragement to make you an offer of marriage? The very notion sets my blood boiling."

Ginevra had turned white; but looking him straight in the face, she answered, "If that is a letter for me, you know I have not read it."

"There! See for yourself."

She took the verses from his hand and read them. Even with her father standing there watching her like an inquisitor, she could not help the tears coming into her eyes as she read.

"There is no such thing here, Papa," she said. "They are only verses bidding me good-bye."

"And what right has any such fellow to bid my daughter goodbye? Explain that to me, if you please."

"Why should I make both him and you uncomfortable, Papa—when there was not going to be anything more of it?"

"Why, then, do you go hankering after him still, and refusing Mr. Duff? It is true he is not exactly a gentleman by birth, but he is such by education, by manners, by position, by influence."

"Papa, I have already told Mr. Duff, as plainly as I could without being rude, that I would never let him talk to me so. What lady would refuse Donal Grant and listen to him!"

"You are a bold, insolent hussy!" cried her father in a rage, and left the room to rejoin Fergus.

They both sat silent for a while—then the preacher spoke.

"Other communications may have reached her from the same quarter," he said.

"That is impossible," rejoined the laird.

"I don't know that," insisted Fergus. "There is a foolish—a half-silly companion of his about town. They call him Sir Gibbie Galbraith."

"Ginny knows no such person."

"Indeed she does, I have seen them together."

"Oh! You mean the lad the minister adopted! The urchin he took off the streets!—Sir Gibbie Galbraith!" he repeated sneeringly, but as one reflecting, "—I do vaguely recall a slanderous rumor in which a certain female connection of the family was hinted at.—Yes! That's where the nickname comes from. And you think she keeps up a communication with the clown through him?"

"I don't say that, sir. I merely think it possible she may see this Gibbie occasionally; and I know he worships the cowboy."

For a while thereafter Ginevra tried hard to convince her father that his notion of her conduct, or Gibbie's or Donal's was mistaken. He would listen to nothing she said, continually insisting that the only amends for her past was to marry according to his wishes; to give up poetry and cowboys and dumb rascals, and settle down as a respectable matron. Then Ginevra became absolutely silent. He stormed at her for her sullenness, but she persisted in her silence, sorely distressed to find how dead her heart seemed to be growing under his treatment of her.

41

•••••••••••••••••••

Differences

Gibbie found everything at the Auld Hoose in complete order for his reception. Mistress Croale had been very diligent and promised well for a housekeeper—looked well, too, in her black satin and lace. She had a good meal ready for him with every adjunct in proper style.

Everything went comfortably. Gibbie was so well in mathematics, thanks to Mr. Sclater, that he did all requisite for honorable studentship; but having no desire to distinguish himself, he had plenty of time for more important duty. Now that he was by himself, as if old habit had returned in the shape of new passion, he roamed the streets every night. His custom was this: after dinner, which he had when he came from college about half past four, he lay down and slept till half past six; then he had tea and after that studied till ten o'clock, where he took his Greek Testament. At eleven he went out for an hour longer—during which time Mistress Croale was in readiness to receive any guest he might bring home.

Some nights he would not meet a single wanderer; occasionally he would meet two or three in the same night. When he found one, he would stand regarding him until he spoke. If the man was drunk he would leave him; such were not those for whom he could now do most. If he was sober he made him signs of invitation. If he would not go with him, he left him but kept him in view and tried him again. If still he would not, he gave him a piece of bread and left him. If the stranger called to him, he stopped and by circuitous ways brought him to the little house at the back. It was purposely quite dark. If the man was too apprehensive to enter, he left him; if he followed, he led him to Mistress Croale. If anything suggested the possibility of helping further, a possibility turning entirely on the person's self, the attempt was set on foot; but in general, after a good breakfast, Gibbie led him through a dark passage into the darkened house, and dismissed him from the door by which he had entered. He never gave money and never sought such guests except in the winter. Indeed, he was never in the city in the summer. It was a tolerable beginning, and during the time not a word reached him indicating knowledge of his proceedings, although within a week or two a rumor was rife in the lower parts of the city of a mysterious being who went about doing this and that for poor folk.

Mr. and Mrs. Sclater could not fail to be much annoyed when they found he was occupying the Auld Hoose with "that horrible woman" for a housekeeper; they knew, however, that expostulation with one possessed by such a headstrong sense of duty was utterly useless.

Fergus had now established himself in the manse of the North Church, and thither he invited Mr. and Miss Galbraith to dine with him on a certain evening. Her father's absolute desire compelled Ginevra's assent; she could not, while with him, rebel absolutely. Fergus did his best to make the evening a pleasant one and had special satisfaction in showing the laird that he could provide both a good dinner and a good bottle of port. Two of his congregation, a young lawyer and his wife, were the only other guests. The laird found the lawyer an agreeable companion, chiefly from his readiness to listen to his old law stories, and Fergus laid himself out to please the two ladies. Secure of the admiration of one, he hoped it might help to draw the favor of the other.

It grew late. The dinner had been at a fashionable hour; they had stayed an unfashionable time. It was nearly twelve o'clock when guests and host left the house in company. The lawyer and his wife went one way, and Fergus went the other with the laird and Ginevra.

Hearing the pitiful wailing of the child and the cough of a woman as they went along a street bridge, they peeped over the parapet and saw upon the stair leading to the lower street a woman with a child asleep in her lap, trying to eat a piece of bread and coughing as if in the last stage of consumption. On the next step below sat a man hushing in his bosom the baby whose cry they had heard. They stood for a moment, the minister pondering whether his profession required of him action, and Ginevra's gaze fixed on the head and shoulders of the foreshortened figure of the man, who vainly as patiently sought to soothe the child by gently rocking it to and fro. But when he began a strange humming song to it, which brought all Glashgar before her eyes, Ginevra knew beyond a doubt that it was Gibbie.

At the sound the child ceased to wail, and presently the woman with difficulty rose, laying a hand for help on Gibbie's shoulder. Then Gibbie rose also, cradling the infant on his left arm and making signs to the mother to place the child on his right. She did so and, turning, went feebly up the stair. Gibbie followed with the two children, one lying on his arm, the other with his head on Gibbie's shoulder, both wretched and pining with grey cheeks and dark hollows under their eyes. From the top of the stair they went slowly up the street, the poor woman coughing and Gibbie crooning to the baby, who cried no more but now and then moaned. Then Fergus said to the laird:

"Did you see that young man, sir? That is the so-called Sir Gilbert Galbraith we were talking of the other night. They say he has come into a good property, but you may judge for yourself whether he seems fit to manage it!"

Ginevra withdrew her hand from his arm.

"Good God, Ginny!" exclaimed the laird, "you do not mean to tell me you have ever spoken to a young man like that?"

"I know him very well, Papa," replied Ginevra collectedly.

"You are incomprehensible, Ginny! If you know him, why do I not know him? Why have you concealed from me your acquaintance with this—this—person?"

"Because I thought it might be painful to you, Papa," she answered, looking in his face.

"Painful to me! Why should it be painful to me—except indeed that it breaks my heart as often as I see your invincible fondness for low company?"

"Do you desire me to tell you, Papa, why I thought it might be painful to you to make that young man's acquaintance?"

"I do distinctly. I command you."

"Then I will: that young man, Sir Gilbert Galbraith—"

"Nonsense, girl! There is no such Galbraith. It is the merest of scoffs."

Ginevra did not care to argue with him this point. In truth she knew little more about it than he.

"Many years ago," she recommenced, "when I was a child—excuse me, Mr. Duff, but it is quite time I told my father what has been weighing upon my mind for so many years."

"Sir Gilbert!" muttered her father contemptuously.

"One day," again she began, "Mr. Fergus Duff brought a ragged little boy to Glashruach—the most innocent and loving of creatures, who had committed no crime but that of doing good in secret. I saw Mr. Duff box his ears on the bridge; and you, Papa, gave him over to that wretch, Angus MacPholp, to whip him—so at least Angus told me, after he had whipped him till he dropped senseless. I can hardly keep from screaming now when I think of it."

"All this, Ginny, is nothing less than cursed folly. Do you mean to tell me you have all these years been cherishing resentment against your own father for the sake of a little thieving rascal, whom it was a good deed to frighten from the error of his ways? I have no doubt Angus gave him merely what he deserved."

"You must remember, Miss Galbraith, we did not know he was dumb," said Fergus, humbly.

"If you had had any heart," said Ginevra, "you would have seen in his face that he was a perfectly angelic child. He ran to the mountain without a rag to cover his bleeding body, and would have died of cold and hunger had not the Grants, the parents of your father's herdboy, Mr. Duff, taken him to their hearts and been father and mother to him."—Ginevra's mouth was opened at last.—"After that," she went on, "Angus shot him like a wild beast when he was quietly herding Robert Grant's sheep. In return Sir Gilbert saved his life in the flood. And just before the house of Glashruach fell—the part in which my room was—he caught me up, because he could not speak, and carried me out of it; and when I told you that he had saved my life, you ordered him out of the house, and when he was afraid to leave me alone with you, you dashed him against the wall and sent for Angus to whip him again. But I should have liked to see Angus try it then!"

"I do remember an insolent fellow taking advantage of the ruinous state the house was in, to make his way into the study," said the laird.

"And now," Ginevra continued, "Mr. Duff makes question of his wits because he finds him carrying a poor woman's children, going to get them a bed somewhere! If Mr. Duff had run about the streets when he was a child, like Sir Gilbert, he might not perhaps think it so strange he should care about a houseless woman!"

Ginevra burst into tears.

"Abominably disagreeable!" muttered the laird. "Hold your tongue, Ginny, you will wake the street. All you say may or may not be quite true; I do not say you are telling lies, or even exaggerating; but I see nothing in it to prove the lad a fit companion for a young lady. Very much to the contrary. I suppose he told you he was your injured, neglected, ill-used cousin? He may be your cousin; you may have any number of such cousins, if half the low tales concerning your mother's family be true."

Ginevra did not answer him—did not speak another word. When Fergus left them at their own door, she neither shook hands with him nor bade him good night.

"Ginny," said her father the moment he was gone, "if I hear of your once speaking again to that low vagabond—and now I think of it," he cried, interrupting himself with a sudden recollection "—there was a cobbler fellow in the town here they used to call Sir Somebody Galbraith!—that must be his father! Whether the Sir was title or nickname, I neither know nor care. A title without money is as bad as a saintship without grace. But this I tell you, that if I hear of your speaking one word, good or bad, to the fellow again, I will turn you out of the house."

To Ginevra's accumulated misery, she carried with her to her room a feeling of contempt for her father, with which she lay struggling in vain half the night.

42

• • • • • • • • • • • • • • • • • •

Ginevra

*A*lthough Gibbie had taken no notice of the laird's party, he had recognized each of the three as he came up the stair and in Ginevra's face read an appeal of deliverance. It seemed to say, "You help everybody but me! Why do you not come and help me too? Am I to have no pity because I am neither hungry nor cold?" He did not, however, lie awake thinking what he should do; long before the poor woman and her children were in bed, he had made up his mind.

As soon as he came home the next day and had hastily eaten his dinner, acting upon his vague knowledge of law business lately acquired, he bought a stamped paper, wrote upon it, and put it in his pocket. Then he took a card and wrote on it, "Sir Gilbert Galbraith, Baronet of Glashruach," and put that in his pocket also. Thus provided he walked deliberately along Pearl Street out into the suburb and, turning to the right, rang the bell at the garden gate of the laird's cottage. When the maid came, he gave her his card and followed her into the house. She carried it into the room where, dinner over, the laird and the preacher were sitting with a bottle of the same port between them which had pleased the laird at the manse. Giving time to read the card and no more, Gibbie entered the room; he would not risk a refusal to see him.

It was a small room with a round table. The laird sat sideways to the door; the preacher sat between the table and the fire.

"What the devil does this mean?" cried the laird.

His big tumbling eyes had required more time than Gibbie had allowed. When with this exclamation he lifted them from the card, they fell upon the object of his imprecation standing in the middle of the room between him and the open door. The preacher, snug behind the table, scarcely endeavored to conceal the smile with which he took no notice of Sir Gilbert. The laird rose in the perturbation of mingled anger and unpreparedness.

"Ah!" he said, but it was only a sound, not a word, "to what—may I ask . . . have I—I have not the honor of your acquaintance, Mr. . . . Mr.—" Here he looked again at the card he held, fumbled for and opened a double eyeglass, then with deliberation examined the name upon it, thus gaining time and gathering his force for more. "Mr. . . . ah, I see! Galbraith, you say.—To what, Mr., Mr. . . ."—another look at the card—"Galbraith, do I owe the honor of this unexpected . . . and . . . and—I must say—unlooked-for visit—and business, I presume, it must be that brings you, seeing I have not the honor of the slightest acquaintance with you?"

He dropped his eyeglass with a clatter against his waistcoat, threw the card into his finger-glass, raised his pale eyes, and stared at Sir Gilbert with all the fixedness they were capable of; he had already drunk a good deal of wine. Gibbie answered by drawing from the breastpocket of his coat the paper he had written and presented it like a petition. Mr. Galbraith sneered and would not have touched it had not his eye caught the stamp, which from old habit at once drew his hand. From similar habit, or perhaps to get it nearer the light, he sat down. Gibbie stood, and Fergus stared at him with insolent composure. The laird read, but not aloud: "I, Gilbert Galbraith, Baronet, hereby promise and undertake to transfer to Miss Galbraith, only daughter of Thomas Galbraith, Esq., on the day when she shall be married to Donal Grant, Master of Arts, the whole of the title deeds of the house and lands of Glashruach, to have and to hold as hers, with absolute power to dispose of the same as she may see fit. Gilbert Galbraith, Old House of Galbraith, Widdiehill, March," etc., etc.

The laird stretched his neck like a turkeycock and gobbled inarticulately, threw the paper to Fergus and, turning on his chair, glowered at Gibbie. Then suddenly starting to his feet, he cried, "What do you mean, you rascal, by daring to insult me in my own house? Damn your insolent foolery!"

"A trick! A most palpable trick! And an exceedingly silly one!" pronounced Fergus, who had now read the paper. "Quite as foolish as unjustifiable! Everybody knows Glashruach is the property of Major Culsalmon!"—Here the laird sought the relief of another oath or two. "Make haste before worse comes of it. You have been made a fool of."

When Fergus began to speak, the laird turned and, while he spoke, stared at him with lackluster yet gleaming eyes. Poor Gibbie stood shaking his head, smiling, and making eager signs with hands and arms; but in the laird's condition of both heart and brain, he might well forget that Gibbie was dumb.

"Why don't you speak, you fool?" he cried. "Get out and don't stand making faces there. Be off with you."

Gibbie pointed to the paper, which lay before Fergus, and placed a hand first on his lips, then on his heart.

The laird swore at him, choking with rage. "Go away, or, by God! I will break your head!"

Fergus at this rose and came round the table to get between them. But the laird caught up a pair of nutcrackers and threw it at Gibbie. It struck him on the forehead and the blood spurted from the wound. He staggered backward. Fergus seized the laird's arm and sought to pacify him.

Her father's loud tones had reached Ginevra in her room. She ran down and that instant entered; Gibbie all but fell into her arms. The moment's support she gave him and the look of loving terror she cast in his face restored him, and he was again firm on his feet, pressing her handkerchief to his forehead. Fergus, leaving the laird, advanced with the intention of getting him safe from the house. Ginevra stepped between them. Her father's rage thereupon broke loose. He seized hold of her with violence and dragged her from the room. Fergus laid hands upon Gibbie more gently, and would have half forced, half persuaded him to go. A cry came from Ginevra; refusing to be sent to her room before Gibbie was in safety, her father struck her.

Gibbie would have darted to help her. Fergus tried to hold him fast but knew nothing of Gibbie's strength, and the next moment he found himself on his back upon the table, amidst the crash of wineglasses and china. Having locked the door, Gibbie sprang to the laird who was trying to drag his daughter, now hardly resisting, up the first steps of the stair. He took him round the waist from behind, swept him to the other room, and there locked him up also. He then returned to Ginevra where she lay motionless on the stair, lifted her in his arms, and carried her out of the house. He did not stop until, having reached the farther end of the street, he turned the corner of it into another equally quiet.

Under a dull, smoky oil lamp Gibbie stopped. He knew by the tightening of her arms that Ginevra was coming to herself.

"Let me down," she said feebly.

He did so but kept his arm round her. She gave a deep sigh, and gazed bewildered. When she saw him, she smiled.

"With you, Gibbie!" she murmured. "—But they will be after us!"

"They shall not touch you," signified Gibbie.

"What was it all about?" she asked.

Gibbie spelled on his fingers. "Because I offered to give you Glash-ruach if your father would let you marry Donal."

"Gibbie! How could you?" she cried almost in a scream; pushing away his arm, she turned from him and tried to run; but after two steps, she tottered to the lamppost and leaned against it.

"Then come with me and be my sister, Ginevra, and I will take care of you," spelled Gibbie. "I can do nothing to take care of you while I can't get near you."

"Oh, Gibbie! Nobody does like that," returned Ginevra, "—else I should be so glad to!"

"There is no other way then that I know. You won't marry anybody, you see."

"Won't I, Gibbie? What makes you think that?"

"Because of course you would never refuse Donal and marry anybody else; that is not possible."

"Oh! don't tease me, Gibbie."

"Ginevra, you don't mean you would?"

In the dull light, and with the imperfect means of Gibbie for the embodiment of his thoughts, Ginevra misunderstood him.

"Yes, Gibbie," she said, "I would. I thought it was understood between us ever since that day you found me on Glashgar. In my thoughts I have been yours all the time."

She turned her face to the lamppost. But Gibbie made her look.

"You do not mean," he spelled very hurriedly, "that you would marry *me?—Me?* I never dreamed of such a thing!"

"You didn't mean it then!" said Ginevra with a cry—bitter but feeble with despair and ending in a stifled shriek. "What have I been saying then! I thought I belonged to you! I thought you meant to take me all the time!" She burst into an agony of sobbing. "I have been alone all the time and did not know it!"

She sank on the pavement at the foot of the lamppost, weeping sorely and shaken with her sobs. Gibbie was in sad perplexity. Heaven had opened before his gaze; its colors filled his eyes; its sounds filled his ears and heart and brain. But the portress was busy crying and would not open the door. Neither could he get at her to comfort her—her eyes being wanted to cry with, his poor signs were of no use. Gibbie held one of her hands and stroked it. Then he pulled off his coat and laid it softly upon her. She grew a little quieter.

"Take me home, Gibbie," she said in a gentle voice.

Gibbie put his arms around her and helped her to her feet. She looked at him and saw a face glorious with bliss. Never, not even on Glashgar in the skincoat of the beast-boy had she seen him so. And in his eyes was that which triumphed, not over dumbness but over speech. It brought the rose-fire rushing into her wan cheeks; she hid her face on his bosom; and under the dingy, red flame of the lamp in the stony street, they held each other, as blessed as if they had been under an orange tree haunted with fireflies. For they knew each the heart of the other.

How long they stood thus, neither of them knew. The lady would not have spoken if she could, and the youth could not if he would. But the lady shivered; and because she shivered, she would have the youth take his coat. He mocked at cold. He made her put her arms in the sleeves, and buttoned it around her; both laughed to see how wide it was. Then he took her by the hand and led her away, obedient as when first he found her and her heart upon Glashgar. Like two children, holding each other fast, they hurried along, in dread pursuit. He brought her to Daur Street and gave her to Mrs. Sclater's arms. Ginevra told her everything, except that her father had struck her, and Gibbie begged her to keep his wife for him till they could be married. Mrs. Sclater behaved like a mother to them, sent Gibbie away and Ginevra to a hot bath and to bed.

Gibbie went home as if Pearl Street had been the stairs of Glashgar and the Auld Hoose a mansion in the heavens. Love had been gathering and ever storing itself in his heart so many years for this brown dove! Now at last the rock was smitten and its treasure rushed forth. Gibbie's was love simple, unselfish, undemanding—not merely asking for no return but asking for no recognition, requiring not even that its existence should be known. He was a rare one, who did not make the common desire, namely to be loved, for love itself.

Some would count worthless the love of a man who loved everybody. There would be no distinction in being loved by such a man!—and distinction, as a guarantee of their own great worth is what such seek. There are women who desire to be the sole object of a man's affection, and are all their lives devoured by unlawful jealousies. A love that had never gone forth upon human being but themselves would be to them the treasure to sell all that they might buy. And the man who brought such a love might in truth be all-absorbed therein himself. The poorest of creatures may well be absorbed in the poorest of loves. The man who loves most will love best. The man who thoroughly loves God and his neighbor is the only man who will love a woman ideally—who can love her with the love God thought of between them when He made man male and female.

Because Gibbie's love was toward everything human, he was able to love Ginevra as Donal was not yet grown able to love her. His love to Ginevra stood like a growing thicket of aromatic shrubs, until her confession set the fire of heaven to it. He had never imagined, never hoped, never desired she should love him like that. She had refused his friend, the strong, the noble, the beautiful, Donal the poet; and it never could but from her own lips have found way to his belief that she had turned her regard upon wee Sir Gibbie, a nobody, who to himself was a mere burning heart running about in tattered garments. Immeasurably the greater therefore was his delight. The sum of happiness in the city, if gathered that night into one wave, could not have reached halfway to the crest of the mighty billow tossing itself heavenward as it rushed along the ocean of Gibbie's spirit.

43

• • • • • • • • • • • • • • • • • • •

Preparations

*H*aving reflected that Ginevra was underage and they must be careful, the next morning, the first thing after breakfast, Mr. Sclater resumed with considerable satisfaction his office of guardian. Holding no previous consultation with Gibbie, he walked to the cottage and sought an interview with Mr. Galbraith.

"I have to inform you, Mr. Galbraith," he began, "that Miss Galbraith—"

"Oh!" said the laird, "I beg your pardon; I was not aware it was my daughter you wished to see."

He rose and rang the bell. Mr. Sclater, annoyed at his manner, held his peace.

"Tell your mistress," said the laird to the maid, "that the Rev. Mr. Sclater wishes to see her."

The girl returned with a scared face and the news that her mistress was not in her room. The laird's loose mouth dropped looser.

"Miss Galbraith did us the honor to sleep at our house last night," said Mr. Sclater deliberately.

"The devil!" cried the laird, relieved. "Why!—What!—Are you aware of what you are saying, sir?"

"Perfectly; and of what I saw too. A blow looks bad on a lady's face."

"Good heavens! The little hussy dared to say I struck her?"

"She did not say so; but no one could fail to see someone had. If you do not know who did it, I do."

"Send her home instantly, or I will come and fetch her!" cried the laird.

"Come and dine with us if you want to see her. For the present she remains where she is. You want her to marry Fergus Duff; she prefers my ward, Gilbert Galbraith, and I shall do my best for them."

"She is underage," said the laird.

"That fault will rectify itself as fast in my house as in yours," returned the minister. "If you invite the publicity of a legal action, I will employ counsel and wait the result."

"Mr. Sclater," said the laird at length, "I am shocked, unspeakably shocked, at my daughter's conduct. To leave the shelter of her father's roof in the middle of the night and—"

"About seven o'clock in the evening," interjected Mr. Sclater.

"—and take refuge with strangers!" continued the laird.

"By no means strangers, Mr. Galbraith!" said the minister. "You drive your daughter from your house and are shocked to find she has taken refuge with friends!"

"She is an unnatural child. She knows well enough what I think of her, and what reason she has given me so to think."

"When a man happens to be alone in any opinion," remarked the minister, "even if the opinion should be of his own daughter, the probabilities are he is wrong. Everyone but yourself has the deepest regard for Miss Galbraith."

"She has always cultivated strangely objectional friendships," said the laird.

"For my own part," said the minister, as if heedless of the laird's last remark, "I do not know a lady I should prefer for a wife to my ward."

The minister's plain speaking was not without effect upon the laird. It made him uncomfortable. He sat silent a while. Then, gathering all the pomp and stiffness at his command, he announced, "Oblige me by informing my daughter," he said, "that I request her, for the sake of avoiding scandal, to return to her father's house until she is of age."

"And in the meantime you undertake—"

"I undertake nothing!" shouted the laird in his feeble yet harsh voice.

"Then I refuse to carry your message. I will be no bearer of that from which, as soon as delivered, I should dissuade."

"Allow me to ask, are you a minister of the gospel and stir up a child against her own father?"

"I am not here to bandy words with you, Mr. Galbraith. It is nothing to me what you think of me. If you will engage not to urge your choice upon Miss Galbraith, I think it probable she will at once return to you. If not—"

"I will not force her inclinations," said the laird. "She knows my wish, and she ought to know the duty of a daughter."

"I will tell her what you say," answered the minister, and took his departure.

When Gibbie heard, he was not at all satisfied with Mr. Sclater's interference to such result. He wished to marry Ginevra at once in order to take her from under the tyranny of her father. But he was readily convinced it would be better, now things were understood, that she should go back to him and try once more to gain him. The same day she did go back.

Ginevra soon found that her father had not yielded the idea of having his own way with her, but her spirits and courage were now so good that she was able not only to endure with less suffering but to carry herself quite differently.

At the end of the month Gibbie went home to Glashgar as usual, telling Ginevra he must be present to superintend what was going on at Glashruach to get the house ready for her. But he said nothing of what he was building there. By the beginning of the winter, they had gotten the buttress wall finished, also the shell of the new house roofed in. Since the first day the weather had permitted, the masons were at work again. The bridge was built, the wall of the old house broken through, the turret carried aloft. All the hollow where the little burn had carried away pinewood and shrubbery, gravel drive and lawn, had been planted mostly with fir trees; and a weir of strong masonry, a little way below the house, kept the water back, so that it rose and spread and formed a still pool just under the house. If Ginevra pleased, Gibbie meant to raise the weir and have quite a little lake in the hollow. A new approach had been contrived and was nearly finished before Gibbie returned to college.

44

The Wedding

In the meantime, Fergus by degrees lost heart and hope so far as concerned Ginevra and at length told the laird that, much as he valued his society and was indebted for his kindness, he must deny himself the pleasure of visiting anymore at the cottage. The laird blustered against his daughter and expostulated with the preacher. But Fergus had at last learned his lesson and was no longer to be blinded. Besides, there had lately come to his church a certain shopkeeper, retired rich, with one daughter; and as his hope of the dignity of being married to Ginevra faded, he had come to feel the enticement of Miss Lapraik's money and good looks. Within three months, he married Miss Lapraik, and lived respectably ever after. He took to writing hymns, became popular afresh through his poetry, and exercised a double influence for the ultimate humiliation of Christianity.

As soon as Gibbie returned, Ginevra let him know things were going badly with her father. They met, consulted, and agreed that the best thing was to be married at once. They made their preparations, confident that, if asked, he would refuse his permission, and proceeded, for his sake, as if they had had it.

One morning as he sat at breakfast, Mr. Galbraith received from Mr. Torrie, whom he knew as the agent in the purchase of Glashruach and whom he supposed to have bought it for Major Culsalmon, a letter, more than respectful, stating that matters had come to light regarding the property which rendered his presence on the spot indispensable for their solution, especially as there might be papers of consequence in some drawer or cabinet of those he had left locked behind him. The present owner, therefore, through Mr. Torrie, begged most respectfully that Mr. Galbraith would sacrifice two days of his valuable time and visit Glashruach. The result, he did not doubt, would be to the advantage of both parties. If Mr. Galbraith would kindly signify to Mr. Torrie his assent, a carriage with postilions, in order that he might make the journey in all possible comfort, should be at his house the next morning at ten o'clock, if that hour would be convenient.

For weeks the laird had been an unmitigated bore to himself, and the invitation laid hold upon him by the most projecting handle of his being, namely, his self-importance. He wrote at once to signify his gracious assent; and in the evening told his daughter he was going to Glashruach on business and had arranged for Miss Kimble to come and stay with her till his return.

At nine o'clock the schoolmistress came to breakfast, and at ten a traveling carriage with four horses drew up at the door looking nearly as big as the cottage. With monstrous stateliness and a fur coat on his arm, the laird descended to his garden gate and got into the carriage, which instantly dashed away for the western road, restoring Mr. Galbraith to the full consciousness of his inherent grandeur. If he was not exactly laird of Glashruach again, he was something quite as important. His carriage was just out of the street when a second, also with four horses, drew up at the garden gate, to the astonishment of Miss Kimble. Out of it stepped Mr. and Mrs. Sclater, then a young gentleman whom she thought very graceful until she discovered it was that low-lived Sir Gilbert, and Mr. Torrie the lawyer! They came trooping into the little drawing room, shook hands with them both, and sat down, Sir Gilbert beside Ginevra—but nobody spoke.

What could it mean! A morning call? It was too early. And four horses to a morning call! A pastoral visitation? Four horses and a lawyer to a pastoral visitation! A business call? It must after all be a pastoral visitation, for there was the minister commencing a religious service!—during which, however, it suddenly revealed itself to the horrified spinster that she was part and parcel of a clandestine wedding! An anxious father had placed her in charge of his daughter, and this was how she was fulfilling her trust! There was Ginevra being married in a brown dress! And to that horrid lad, who called himself a baronet and hobnobbed with a low market woman!

But alas! Just as she was recovering her presence of mind, Mr. Sclater pronounced them husband and wife! She gave a shriek, at which the company, bride and bridegroom included, broke into "a loud smile." The ceremony over, Ginevra glided from the room and returned almost immediately in her little brown bonnet. Sir Gilbert caught up his hat and Ginevra held out her hand to Miss Kimble. Then at length the abashed and aggrieved lady found words of her own.

"Ginevra!" she cried, and burst into tears.

Ginevra kissed her and said: "Never mind, dear Miss Kimble. You could not help it. The whole thing was arranged. We are going after my father, and we have the best of horses."

Mr. Torrie laughed outright.

"A new kind of runaway marriage!" he cried. "The happy couple pursuing the obstinate parent with four horses! Ha! ha! ha!"

"But after the ceremony!" said Mr. Sclater.

Here a servant ran down the steps with a carpetbag and opened the gate for her mistress. Lady Galbraith got into the carriage; Sir Gilbert followed. There was kissing and tears at the door. Mrs. Sclater drew back; the postilions spurred their horses; off went the second carriage faster than the first. And the minister's party walked quietly away, leaving Miss Kimble to declaim to the maid of all work, who cried so that she did not hear a word.

Between the second stage and the third, Gibbie and Ginevra came in sight of their father's carriage. Having arranged that the two carriages should not change horses at the same places, they easily passed unseen by him. He was thinking of nothing so little as their proximity as he sat in state before the door of a village inn.

Just as Mr. Galbraith was beginning to hope the major had contrived a new approach to the place, the carriage took an unexpected turn. He found presently they were climbing, by a zigzag road, the height over the Lorrie burn; but the place was no longer his, and to avoid a sense of humiliation, he avoided taking interest in the change.

A young woman—it was Donal's eldest sister, but he knew nothing of her—opened the door to him and showed him up the stair to his own study. There a great fire was burning; but, beyond that, everything, even to the trifles on his writing table, was just as when last he left the house. His chair stood in its usual position by the fire, and wine and biscuits were on a little table near.

"Very considerate!" he said to himself. "I trust the major does not mean to keep me waiting, though. Deuced hard to have to leave a place like this!"

Weary with his journey, he fell into a doze, dreamed of his dead wife, woke suddenly and heard the door of the room open. There was Major Culsalmon entering with outstretched hand! and there was a lady—his wife, doubtless! But how young the major was! He had imagined him a man in middle age at least!—Bless his soul! Was he never to get rid of this impostor fellow! It was not the major! It was the rascal calling himself Sir Gilbert Galbraith!—the half-witted wretch his fool of a daughter insisted on marrying! And—bless his soul again! There was the minx, Ginny! Looking as if the place was her own! The silly tears in her eyes too! It was all too absurd! He had just been dreaming of his dead wife, and clearly that was it! He was not awake yet!

He tried hard to wake, but the dream mastered him.

"Ginny!" he said as the two stood for a moment regarding him a little doubtfully, but with smiles of welcome, "what is the meaning of this? I did not know Major Culsalmon had invited you! And what is this person doing here?"

"Papa," replied Ginevra, with a curious smile, half merry, half tearful, "this person is my husband, Sir Gilbert Galbraith of Glashruach; and you are at home in your own study again."

"Will you never have done masquerading, Ginny?" he returned.

"Inform Major Culsalmon that I request to see him immediately."

He turned toward the fire and took up a newspaper. They thought it better to leave him. As he sat, the truth by degrees grew plain to him. But not one other word on the matter did the man utter to the day of his death. When dinner was announced, he walked straight from the dining room door to his former place at the foot of the table. But Robina Grant was equal to the occasion. She caught up the dish before him and set it at the side. There Gibbie seated himself; and, after a moment's hesitation, Ginevra placed herself opposite her husband.

The next day Gibbie provided him with something to do. He had the chest of papers found in the Auld Hoose o' Galbraith carried into Mr. Galbraith's study, and the man found both employment and interest for weeks in deciphering and arranging them. Among many others concerning the property, its tenures and boundaries, appeared some papers which, associated and compared, threw considerable doubt on the way in which portions of it had changed hands. The laird was keen of scent as any nose-hound after dishonesty in other people. In the course of a fortnight he found himself so much at home in his old quarters, and so much interested in those papers and his books, that when Sir Gilbert informed him Ginevra and he were going back to the city, he pronounced it decidedly the better plan, seeing he was there himself to look after affairs.

For the rest of the winter, therefore, Mr. Galbraith played the grand seigneur as before among the tenants of Glashruach.

45

· · · · · · · · · · · · · · · · · · · ·

The Burn

The moment they were settled in the Auld Hoose, Gibbie resumed the habits of the former winter. What a change it was to Ginevra—from imprisonment to ministration!

Every winter for many years, Sir Gilbert and Lady Galbraith occupied the Auld Hoose; which by degrees came at length to be known as the refuge of all that were in honest distress. The next year they built a house in a sheltered spot on Glashgar, and thither from the city they brought many invalids to spend the summer months under the care of Janet and her daughter Robina, whereby not a few were restored. The first summer, Nicie returned to Glashruach to wait on Lady Galbraith, was more her friend than her servant, and when she married, was settled on the estate.

For some time Ginevra was fully occupied in getting her house in order and furnishing the new part of it. When that was done, Sir Gilbert gave an entertainment to his tenants. The laird preferred a trip to the city, "on business," to the humiliation of being present as other than the greatest; though perhaps he would have minded it less had he ever himself given a dinner to his tenants.

Jean Mavor was beside herself with joy to see her broonie now lord of the land and to be seated beside him in respect and friendship. But her brother said it was "clean ridic'lous"; and not to the last would he consent to regard the new laird as other than half-witted, insisting that everything was done by his wife, and that the talk on his fingers was a mere pretense.

When the main part of the dinner was over, Sir Gilbert and his lady stood at the head of the table and, he speaking by signs and she interpreting, made a little speech together. In the course of it, Sir Gibbie took the occasion to apologize for having once disturbed the peace of the countryside by acting the supposed part of a broonie. In relating his adventures of the time, he accompanied his wife's text with such graphic illustration of gesture that his audience laughed at the merry tale till the tears ran down their cheeks. Then with a few allusions to his strange childhood, he thanked the God who led him through thorny ways into the very arms of Robert and Janet Grant, from whom—and not from the fortune he had since inherited—came all his peace.

"He desires me to tell you," said Lady Galbraith, "that he was a stranger, and you folk of Daurside took him in. And if ever he can do a kindness to you or yours, he will. He desires me also to say that you ought not to be left ignorant that you have a poet of your own, born and bred among you—Donal Grant, the son of Robert and Janet, the friend of Sir Gilbert's heart, and one of the noblest of men. And he begs you to allow me to read you a poem he had from him this very morning—probably just written. It is called 'The Laverock.' I will read it as well as I can. If any of you do not like poetry, he says—I mean Sir Gilbert says—you can go to the kitchen and light your pipes, and he will send your wine there to you."

She ceased. Not one stirred, and she read the verses.

After the reading of the poem, Sir Gilbert and Lady Galbraith withdrew and went toward the new part of the house, where they had their rooms. On the bridge, over which Ginevra scarcely ever passed without stopping to look both up and down the channel in the rock, she lingered as usual, gazing from its windows. Below, the burn opened out on the great valley of the Daur; above was the landslip, and beyond it the stream rushing down the mountain. Gibbie pointed up to it. She gazed a while, and gave a great sigh.

"Let us see it from my room, Gibbie," said Ginevra.

They went up, and from the turret window looked down upon the water. They gazed until, like the live germ of the gathered twilight, it was scarce to be distinguished but by abstract motion.

"It's my ain burnie," said Ginevra, "an' it's ain auld sang, I'll warran' it hasna forgotten a note o' 't! Eh, Gibbie, ye gie me a' thing!"

"Gien I was burnie, wadna I rin!" sang Gibbie, and Ginevra heard the words, though Gibbie could utter only the air he had found for them so long ago. She threw herself into his arms and, hiding her face on his shoulder, clung silent to her silent husband. Over her lovely bowed head, he gazed into the cool spring night, sparkling with stars and shadowy with mountains. His eyes climbed the stairs of Glashgar to the lonely peak dwelling among the lights of God; and if upon their way up the rocks they met no visible sentinels of heaven, he needed neither; ascending stairs nor descending angels, for a better than the angels was with them.

The
Shepherd's
Castle

Introduction

There have been critics through the years who have made the claim that George MacDonald was not a novelist of the highest merit. Being no literary expert, I can't say; they may be right. Certainly much in his writing defies hasty reading and therefore inhibits public response. His novels are long; decoding the frequently used dialect can be troublesome; and sentences of 100 and 150 words are common, sometimes running in excess of 200.

I am undaunted by these objections in my enthusiasm for MacDonald's work because I cannot segregate my understanding of the novelist from the man. I am not so much concerned with stylistic difficulties or theological intricacies as I am with the far more significant issues: What does this man, the sum total of everything he was, have to offer me as a person? How can he cause me not only to enjoy life through his books, but how can he widen my horizons, broaden my perspective? How can he help me grow?

At this point George MacDonald becomes a writer of the highest caliber. Because he was a *man* of the highest caliber—a man whose marriage and family was solid (he and his wife Louisa had eleven children); whose personal and private virtues were impeccable; whose integrity was unquestioned; and who was loved, admired, and even revered by all who knew him. So much was his loss felt upon his death that articles and even books were written with the sole purpose of extolling his life and character.

What made the man so unusual, so respected, and his books so loved—both in his lifetime and more than a hundred years after their publication?

It can be reduced, I think, to the simple prescription which guided the course of MacDonald's entire life: the love of truth. It was the search for wisdom—clear-headed, compassionate, biblically based, and intellectually sound—which inspired and unified every word MacDonald wrote. His books thus contain power on a more profound level than can be appreciated from mere words, and those who compare and critique and seek to understand them on the surface level alone will always be left dissatisfied.

It is against the backdrop of MacDonald's life (1824–1905) that we find most clearly illuminated his relentless pursuit of reality and his compulsion to share his findings. It was not an easy life but one marked with poverty, diseased lungs, and other forms of poor health, hardship, and ceaseless labor to support his family. But perhaps most noteworthy in his biography was an event which occurred in 1853 when he was 29, newly married, and still full of youthful vision and idealism.

He had felt God's call to a vocation in the ministry, had studied successfully toward that end, and in 1850 had become the pastor of a chapel in Arundel, Scotland. His warm, imaginative, human, and progressive ideas, however, were found to be unorthodox, according to the rigid standards of the religious establishment of the day; and by 1852 he was in trouble with the deacons of the church and they charged him with heresy. They tried various subtle means to get rid of him and his family, most painful of which was the lowering of his salary to a mere $250-$400 annually. But they had misjudged him; he simply responded that the family must try to live on less. And try they did, with the help of a few sympathetic parishioners. But by 1853 the situation had become intolerable, both financially and in the open knowledge that his preaching was unacceptable to the deacons. He was forced to resign.

For a time MacDonald held to his dream of preaching. But he was completely unwilling to compromise either his views or his ministry to accommodate church leaders. Branded as "questionable" from his experience at Arundel, no opportunities presented themselves.

Being denied a pulpit after hearing God's call on him forced George MacDonald to look for another medium through which to circulate his essentially spiritual message. He turned to lecturing, tutoring, fill-in preaching, and writing as a matter of necessity—to put bread on his family's table. But he never forgot his brief stay in Arundel and the narrow-mindedness which had so rigidly rejected him. The severity of that memory drove him all his life long both to present an alternative view of God's character from what he perceived existed in the minds of most church leaders and to live a life consistent with his beliefs.

Therefore, though he embarked on a career as a novelist, the spiritual truths he longed to convey remained his ultimate priority. Commercially successful as many were, his stories offered a forum to declare his image of God; artistic craftsmanship remained a secondary concern. Something greater than wealth or public acclaim drove him into print. If the organized Church would not have him, the truth, notwithstanding, had to be told. By the time—some ten years later—that MacDonald's reputation and fame as a writer and spiritual sage had asserted themselves, he could again have hoped for a pulpit, even a fashionable one. But he was so against compromise in any form and was at the same time all but certain that accepting a ministerial post would inevitably lead exactly to that point, that he stopped considering the possibility. By then his writing was earning a steady yet meager living, and he stuck with it.

MacDonald's clash with the deacons had not been his first encounter with intolerant religiosity. His grandmother had been a ruthlessly strict Calvinist, and throughout his life he continued to bump headlong into the shortsightedness which in large measure characterized the theology of the nineteenth-century Church. The circumstances of his life, therefore, were among the most important factors which shaped his thought and work. Had he not recoiled from the stringent Calvinism of his upbringing and been removed from a position of ministry, he might never have been forced to pose questions others were afraid to consider—might never have been moved to present his less-harsh view of God's mercy, justice, and love.

His stories are compelling in themselves. But, clearly, much more than plot is contained within their pages. This is not to say he wrote with specific symbolism or allegory always in mind. More than once he commented that such was not the case. He loved creating enjoyable stories to delight his readers. Yet his attitude toward truth and the resultant wisdom were so deeply ingrained in the depths of his being that his spiritual perspectives could not help but overflow onto the printed page.

Donal Grant was first published in 1883 as a sequel to his extremely popular *Sir Gibbie* (the modern version of which—entitled *The Baronet's Song*—is published in the Bethany House Publishers series). In less than two years *Donal Grant* had been released in six different editions. It was MacDonald's longest novel, just a few short of 800 pages. And in many ways it could be said to be his most pastoral in the sense that he used it to reflect a great deal on spiritual matters not necessarily germaine to the story line itself. It is my sincere hope that with some of the verbosity pruned away in this edited edition, *The Shepherd's Castle*, MacDonald's truth-loving heart will shine through.

Mike Phillips
Eureka, California

Contents

Glossary

bairn—child

bartizan—a small overhang from a wall for lookout

bracken—coarse ferns

brawly—splendidly

close—an enclosed place

corbel steps—hollow or niches left in walls for decorating, figures, or statues

coronach—melody, tune

collop—small slice of meat

kirk-session—church service

mews—sheds for animals, stables

pastern-joint—the joint in a horse's leg next to the foot

skene dhu—large knife

ostler—hostler, person who has the care of horses at an inn

parapet—a low protective wall or railing at the edge of a platform or walkway

wynd—alley

GALLERY

SITTING ROOM

DINING ROOM

ARCTURA'S BEDROOM

INTERIOR OF THE CASTLE

HIDDEN CHAMBER

Closet

O
DO

H I D D E

Sheds

Donal's Room

Spiral Staircase

NORTH TOWER

ROOM EARL'S APARTMENT

To Other Parts
Of the Castle

SECOND
FLOOR

EARL'S
OFFICE

Closet
Under
Stairs

Built-up
Wall

FIRST
FLOOR

Passageway Behind Chapel

Balcony

A R E A S

Passageway Floor

CHAPEL

Stone

ROUND FLOOR
MAIN HALL

CRYPT

The CASTLE GRAHAM

1
•••••••••••••••••••••

Foot Faring

$\mathcal{I}$t was a lovely morning in the first of summer. Donal Grant was descending a path on a hillside to the valley below—a sheep track of which he knew every winding better than anyone. But he had never gone down the hill with the feeling he had today, so he was not about to go up it again. He was on his way to pastures very new and to him, at this moment, not very inviting. Though his recent past contained the memory of pain, his heart was too full to remain troubled for long—nor was his a heart to harbor care.

A great, billowy waste of mountains lay beyond him, amongst which played the shadows at their games of hide-and-seek. Behind Donal lay a world of dreams into which he dared not turn and look, yet from which he could scarcely avert his eyes.

He was nearing the foot of the hill when he stumbled and almost fell, reminding him of the unpleasant knowledge that the sole of one of his shoes was all but off. Never had he left home for college that his father had not made personal inspection of his shoes to see that they were fit for the journey, but on this departure they had been forgotten. He sat down and took off the failing equipment. It was too far gone to do anything temporary with it. The only thing was to take off the other shoe and go barefoot. He tied the two together with a piece of string, made them fast to his deerskin knapsack, and resumed his walk. The misfortune did not trouble him much. To have shoes is a good thing; to be able to walk without them is better. But it had been long since Donal had walked barefoot, and he found his feet, like his shoe, weaker in the sole than was pleasant.

At every stream he came to he bathed his feet. He had no certain goal, though he knew his direction and was in no haste. He had confidence in God and in his own powers as the gift of God, and knew that wherever he went he need not be hungry long, even should the little money in his pocket be spent. It is better to trust in work than in money; God never buys anything, and is forever at work. Donal was now descending the heights of youth to walk along the king's highroad of manhood. He had lost his past—that of a shepherd and a student—but not so as to be ashamed. His future was now before him.

He had set out before the sun was up, for he did not wish to be met by friends or acquaintances. Avoiding the well-known farmhouses and occasional villages, he took his way up the river. He was making his way toward the eastern coast, in the certain hope of finding work of one kind or another. He could have been well content to pass his life as a shepherd, like his father, but for two things: he knew what it would be well for others to know; and he had a hunger after the society of books. A man must be able to do without whatever is denied him, but when his heart is hungry for an honest thing, he may use honest endeavor to obtain it. Donal desired to be useful and to live for his generation, also to be with his books. To be where there was a good library would have suited him better than buying books, for he knew of the strong inclination to accumulate and hoard. But who would have thought, meeting the youth as he walked the road with shoeless feet, that he sought the harbor of a great library in some old house, so as to day after day feast on the thoughts of men who had gone before him!

As he walked, the scents the wind brought him from the field and gardens and moor seemed sweeter than before, for they were seeking to comfort him. The wind hovered about him as if it would fain have something to do in the matter; the river rippled and shone as if it knew something worth knowing as yet unrevealed. The delight of creation is verily in secrets, but in secrets as truths on the way. And as he made his way, already something of the old mysterious loveliness—which had temporarily vanished from his awareness—of the face of the visible world had returned to it, with the dawning promise of a new creation, ready to receive the new that God had waiting for him. He would look the new life in the face and be what it should please God to make him.

He was now walking southward but would soon, when the mountains were well behind him, turn toward the east. He carried a small pouch, filled chiefly with oatcake and hard skim-milk cheese. About two o'clock he sat down on a stone and proceeded to make a meal. A brook from the hills ran near, and for that reason he had chosen the spot, his fare being dry. He seldom took any other drink than water.

He drew from his pocket a small, thick volume he had brought as the companion of his journey, and read as he ate. His seat was on the last slope of a grassy hill, where many-hued stones rose out of the grass. A few yards beneath was a country road, and on the other side of the road a small stream in which the brook that ran swiftly past, almost within reach of his hand, eagerly lost itself. Perfuming the air on the farther bank of the stream grew many bushes of meadow sweet, or queen-of-the-meadow as it is called in Scotland; and beyond lay a lovely stretch of nearly level pasture. Farther eastward all was a plain, full of farms. Behind him rose the hill, shutting out his past; before him lay the plain, open to his eyes and feet. God had walled up his past and was disclosing his future.

When he had eaten his dinner, its dryness forgotten in the condiment his book supplied, he rose. Taking his bonnet from his head, he filled the cap from the stream and drank heartily, then emptied it, shook the last drops from it, and put it again on his head.

"Ho, young man!" cried a voice.

Donal looked up and saw a man in the garb of a clergyman regarding him from the road.

"Good day to you, sir," said Donal, "I had no idea there was living creature near me."

"Which way are you going?" asked the minister, adding, "You're a scholar, I see," with a glance toward the book he had left open on his stone.

"Not so much as I would like to be," answered Donal.

"A modest youth, I perceive!" returned the clergyman.

"That depends on what you mean by scholar."

"Oh," answered the minister, in a bantering humor willing to draw the lad out, "the learned man modestly calls himself a scholar."

"Then there was no modesty in saying I was not so much a scholar as I should like to be; every scholar would say the same."

"A very good answer! You'll be a learned man someday."

Donal picked up his pouch and book and came down the road. He would rather have forded the river and gone to inquire his way at the nearest farmhouse, but he thought it polite to walk a little way with the clergyman.

"How far are you going?" asked the minister at length.

"As far as I can," replied Donal.

"Where do you mean to pass the night?"

"In some barn, perhaps, or on some hillside."

"I am sorry to hear you can do no better."

"You don't think, sir, what a decent bed costs; and barns and hillsides are generally clean. Many's the time I've slept out of doors. It's a strange notion some people have, that it's more respectable to sleep under man's roof than God's."

"To have no settled abode . . ." said the clergyman, and paused.

"Like Abraham?" suggested Donal with a smile. "I once fell asleep on the top of Glashgar; when I woke the sun was looking over the edge of the horizon. I rose and gazed about me as if I were but that moment created. If God had called me, I should hardly have been astonished."

"Or frightened?" asked the minister.

"No, sir; why should a man fear the presence of his Savior?"

"You said God," answered the minister.

"God is my Savior. Into his presence it is my desire to come."

"Under shelter of the atonement," supplemented the minister.

"If you mean by that, sir," said Donal, "anything to come between my God and me, I'll have none of it. I'll have nothing hide me from him who made me. I wouldn't hide a thought from him. The worse it is, the more he needs to see it."

"What book is that you're reading?" asked the minister sharply. "It's not your Bible, I'll be bound! You never got such notions from it." He was perturbed at the presumptuous youth.

"It's Shelley," answered Donal.

The minister had never read a word of Shelley but had a very decided opinion of him. He gave a loud, rude whistle.

"So! that's where you go for your theology! I was puzzled to understand you, but now all is plain! Young man, you are on the brink of perdition. That book will poison your very vitals!"

"Indeed, sir, it will never go deep enough for that. But it came near touching them as I sat eating my bread and cheese."

"He's an infidel!" said the minister fiercely.

"A kind of one," returned Donal, "but not of the worst sort. It's the people who call themselves believers that drive the like of poor Shelley to the mouth of the pit."

"He hated the truth," said the minister.

"He was always seeking after it," said Donal, "though, to be sure, he didn't get to the end of the search. Just listen to this, sir, and see whether it be very far from Christian."

Donal opened his little volume and sought his passage and read it. Ending, the reader turned to the listener. But the listener had understood little of the meaning and less of the spirit.

"What do you think of that, sir?" asked Donal.

"Sheer nonsense!" answered the minister. "Passivity seems the gist of the author's intent, but where would Scotland be now but for resistance?"

"There's more than one way of resisting, though," returned Donal. "Enduring evil was the Lord's way. I don't know about Scotland, but I fancy there would be more Christians in the world and of a better stamp if that had been the mode of resistance always adopted by those who called themselves such. Anyhow, it was his way."

"Shelley's, you mean?"

"I mean Christ's. In spirit Shelley was far nearer the truth than those who made him despise the very name of Christianity without knowing what it really was. But God will give every man fair play."

"Young man!" said the minister, with an assumption of great solemnity and no less authority, "I am bound to warn you that you are in a state of rebellion against God, and he will not be mocked. Good morning!"

Donal sat down on the roadside and took again his shabby little volume. When the clergyman was long out of sight he rose and went on, and soon came to a bridge by which he crossed the river. Then he went on through the cultivated plain, his spirits never flagging. He was a pilgrim on his way to his divine fate.

2

•••••••••••••••••••••

In Lodgings

The night began to descend. Donal wearily looked about for a place of repose. But there was a long twilight before him and it was warm. For some time the road had been ascending; and by and by he found himself on a bare moor, among heather not yet in bloom, and a forest of bracken. Donal walked along the high table till rest looked blissful. Then he turned aside from the rough track into the heather and bracken. When he came to a little dry hollow with a yet thicker growth of heather, its tops close almost as those of his bed at his father's cottage, he sought no further. Taking his knife, he cut a quantity of heather and ferns and heaped it on the top of the thickest bush; then creeping in between the cut and the growing, he cleared the former from his face that he might see the worlds over him, and putting his knapsack under his head, fell fast asleep.

He woke with a clear mind and peaceful soul and set out to continue his journey. By midday the blue line of the far ocean rose on the horizon before him.

It was evening when he drew near the place toward which he had directed his steps—a little country town, not far from a famous seat of learning. Here he planned to make inquiry before going farther. His own parish minister knew the minister of Auchars and had given Donal a letter of introduction. The country around had a number of dwellings of distinction, and at one or another of these he hoped might be children in need of a tutor.

The sun was setting over the hills behind him as he entered the little town. At first it looked to be but a village, for on the outskirts were chiefly thatched cottages, with here and there a slated house of one story and an attic. But presently began to appear houses of larger size. All at once he found himself in a street, partly of quaint gables with corbel steps. The heart of the town was a yet narrower street, with several short closes and wynds opening out of it—all of which had ancient-looking houses. There were many shops, but their windows were those of dwellings, as the upper parts of their buildings mostly were. The streets were unevenly paved with round, water-worn stones.

The setting sun sent his shadow before him, and he looked on this side and that for the hostelry whither he had sent his chest before leaving home. Before long he caught sight of the sign he was in search of. It swung in front of an old-fashioned, dingy building with much of the old-world look that pervaded the town. The last red rays of the sun were upon it, lighting up a sorely faded coat of arms. A man stood in the doorway, hands in his trouser pockets, and looked with contemptuous scrutiny at the barefooted lad approaching him.

"A fine day, landlord," said Donal.

"Ay," answered the man without changing posture, looking Donal up and down, then resting his eyes on the bare feet and upturned trousers.

"This'll be the Morven Arms, I'm thinking?" said Donal.

"It doesn't take much to think that," returned the innkeeper, "with the sign hanging right there."

"Ay," rejoined Donal, glancing up, "but it's not everyone that has the privilege of knowing the heraldry like yourself. I saw the coat of arms with the two red horses upon it. But I'm not from around here and didn't know it the Morven crest for certain."

The innkeeper—one John Glumm by name—said nothing. He merely gave an offended sneer and turned toward the house.

"I was thinking to put up with you tonight if you could accommodate me at a reasonable rate," said Donal.

"I don't know," replied Glumm with his back to him, hesitating between unwillingness to lose a penny and resentment at Donal's supposed ridicule. "What would you call reasonable?"

"I wouldn't grudge sixpence for my bed; a shilling I would."

"Well, ninepence then—for you don't seem overcome with money."

"No," answered Donal, "I'm not that. Whatever my burden, that's not it. I have a chest coming by the carrier direct to the Morven Arms. It'll be here in time, no doubt."

"We'll see it when it comes," remarked the landlord, implying the chest was easier invented than believed in.

"The worst of it is," continued Donal, "I can't well show myself around without shoes. I have a pair in my chest, and another on my back—but none for my feet."

"There's cobblers enough around," said the innkeeper.

"Well, I'll see about that. I would like a word with the minister. Could you direct me to the manse?"

"He's not home. But it's of small consequence; he doesn't care about tramps, honest man that he is. He won't waste much time on the likes of you."

Donal gave a laugh. "I'm thinking you wouldn't waste much on a tramp either!" he said.

"I would not," answered Glumm. "It's the job of the honest to discourage the lawless."

"You wouldn't hang the poor creatures, would you?" asked Donal.

"I would see a lot more of them hanged."

"For not having a roof over their heads? That's mighty hard! What if you was one day to be in need yourself?"

"We'll wait till that day comes. But what are you standing there for? Are you coming in or not?"

"It's been a rather cold welcome," said Donal. "I'll just take a look about before I make up my mind. A tramp, you know, doesn't need to stand on ceremony!"

He turned away and walked farther along the street.

He had not gone far before he came to a low-arched gateway in the middle of a poor-looking house. Within it sat a little bowed man, cobbling diligently at a boot—the very man Donal needed!

"It's a bonny night," greeted Donal.

"You may well say so," replied the cobbler without looking up, for a critical stitch occupied him at the moment.

Donal stood for a moment regarding the man and his work. In a minute the cobbler lifted a little wizened face and a pair of twinkling eyes to those of the student, revealing a soul as original as his own.

"You'll be wanting a job in my line, I'm thinking," he said with a kindly nod toward Donal's shoeless feet.

"There's small doubt of that," returned Donal. "I had hardly begun—but was too far from home to go back—when the sole of my shoe came off and I had to walk with none but my own. But I brought them on with me hoping to find one of your profession who would help me."

He took the shoes from his back and, untying the string that bound them, presented the ailing one to the cobbler.

"That's what we would call death!" remarked the cobbler, slowly turning the invalidated shoe.

"Ay, death it is," answered Donal; "it's a sad divorce between soul and body."

The cobbler was submitting the shoes, first the sickly, now the sound one, to a thorough scrutiny.

"You don't think them worth mendin', no doubt," remarked Donal with a touch of anxiety in his tone.

"I never thought that where the leather would hold together," replied the cobbler. "But I confess I'm uncertain how to charge for my work. It's not merely the consideration of the time it'll take me to mend a pair, but what the wearer's likely to get out of them. I can't take more than the job'll be worth to the wearer. And yet the worse the shoe, the more time they take to make them worth anything again."

Donal was charmed with his new acquaintance. "Surely," he said, "you must be paid in proportion to your labor."

"In that case I would often have to say to a poor body that hadn't another pair in the world that their one pair of shoes wasn't worth mending."

"But how can you make a living otherwise?"

"Hoots, the Master of the trade sees to my wages!"

"And who may that be?" asked Donal, well foreseeing the answer.

"He was never cobbler himself, but he was once a carpenter and now he's lifted up to be head of all the trades; and there's one thing he can't stand, and that's overcharging."

He stopped. But Donal held his peace, waiting; and he went on.

"To them that makes little, for reasons of being kind to their neighbor, he gives the better wages when they go home. To them that makes all they can, he says, 'You helped yourself; help away, you have your reward.'

"But about these shoes of yours, I don't well know. They're well enough worth doing the best I can for, but tomorrow's Sunday and what do you have to put on?"

"Nothing—till my chest comes. I'm not that particular about going to church. But if I did want to go, I wouldn't fancy the Lord affronted with me for the bare feet he himself made."

The cobbler caught up the worst shoe and began upon it at once. "You'll have your shoe, sir," he said, "but I won't finish till tomorrow. I'll bring it to you; where will you be?"

"That's what I would like to ask you about," answered Donal. "I had thought about putting up at the Morven Arms, but there's something I don't like about the landlord. Do you know any decent, clean place where they would give me a room to myself, and not ask more than I'd be able to pay them?"

"We have a little room ourselves," said the cobbler, "at the service of any decent wayfaring man that can stand the smell of the leather-work and put up with us and our ways. For payment you can pay what you think it's worth. We're not very particular."

"I take your offer with thankfulness," answered Donal.

"Well, let's go in by that door there and you can meet my wife. Doory—she's some hard o' hearing!—Doory! Here's a believing lad—but I'm thinking he must be a gentleman—who came needing a shoe repaired. Can we give him a night's lodging?"

"Well enough," said Doory. "He's welcome to what we have."

Turning, she led the way into the house, while her husband returned to his workshop to continue with the troubled shoe.

Following the old woman, Donal soon found himself in an enchanting room with white walls, brown-hued but clean-swept wooden floor on which shone a keen-eyed little fire from a low grate. Two easy chairs stood on each side of the fire. A kettle was singing on the hob. The white deal table was set for tea—with a fat brown teapot, and cups of a gorgeous pattern in bronze.

"I'll let you see what accommodation we have," said Doory, "and if it suits you, you'll be welcome."

She opened a farther door to one side of the fireplace, disclosing a neat little parlor. The floor was sanded and so much the cleaner than if it had been carpeted. A small mahogany table, black with age, stood in the middle. On a side table covered with a cloth of faded green lay a large family Bible; behind it were a few books and a tea caddy. In the side of the wall opposite the window was a box bed. To the eyes of the shepherd-born lad, it looked the most desirable shelter he had ever seen.

He turned to his hostess and said, "I'm afraid it's too good for me. What could you let me have it for by the week? I would like to stay with you, but where and when I may get work I can't tell, so I mustn't take it for more than a week."

"Make yourself at ease till tomorrow's over," said the old woman. "On Monday the three of us'll talk about it."

Well content and with hearty thanks, Donal committed his present fate into the hands of the humble pair; and after much washing and brushing and all that was possible to him in the way of dressing, he reappeared in the kitchen. There tea was ready, with the cobbler seated in the window, a book in his hand.

"Come to the table, Andrew," said the old woman, "if you can part with that book of yours, and let your soul give way to your bodily needs."

Andrew rose and walked toward the table. "Would you allow me to ask your name?" he said to Donal.

"My name's Donal Grant," replied Donal as they sat down.

The cobbler said a little prayer, and then they began to eat—first of oatcake, baked by the old woman, then of loaf-bread, as they called it.

Andrew Comin, before offering him house room, would never have asked anyone what he was. But he would have thought it an equal lapse in breeding not to show interest in the history as well as the person of a guest.

After a little more talk, the cobbler said, "And what is it you do, sir, in the Lord's world? But if anything gives you reason to prefer waiting till you know Doory and me a bit better, count my ill-mannered question not even asked."

By this time Donal knew he had got hold of a pair of originals, and it was a joy to his heart. "There's nothing," answered Donal, "that I wouldn't want to tell you about myself."

"Tell us what you will, and keep what you will," said the cobbler.

"I was brought up a herd-laddie," proceeded Donal, "but then a friend—you may have heard his name, Sir Gilbert Galbraith—made the beginning of a scholar out of me. And now I have my degree from the old university of Inverdaur."

"I thought as much!" cried Mistress Comin. "I was sure you must have come from the college seeing as how your feet weren't so well furnished as your head."

"I have a pair of shoes in my chest though—when that comes," said Donal, laughing.

A good deal of warm conversation followed and thus the evening wore away. The talk nourished the very soul of Donal, who never loved wisdom so much as when she appeared in peasant garb.

"I wonder," said Doory at length, "why young Eppie's not putting in her appearance? I was sure she'd be here tonight. She hasn't been near us in a week."

The cobbler turned to Donal to explain. "Young Eppie's a grandchild, sir—the only one we have. She's a well-behaved lass, though taken up with things of this world more than her grannie and me would wish. She's in a place not far from here—not an easy one to give satisfaction in. But she's not doing that bad."

The words were hardly spoken when a light foot was heard coming up the stair. The door of the room opened and a nice-looking girl of about eighteen came in.

"Well, young Eppie, how's it with you?" asked the old man.

"Brawly, thank you, Grandfather," she answered. "How's it with yourself?"

"Oh, well, cobblet!" he replied.

"How's things going up at the castle?" asked the grandmother.

"Oh, just as usual—only the housekeeper's been ill, and that puts more on the rest of us."

"And how's my lord, lass?"

"Oh, much the same—up the stairs and down the stairs for most of the night, and nearly invisible all day."

The girl cast a shy glance now and then at Donal. Bethinking himself that they might have matters to talk about, he rose and, turning to his hostess, said: "With your leave, goodwife, I'll go to my bed. I've traveled a matter of thirty miles today on my bare feet."

"Eh, sir!" she exclaimed, "I ought to have considered that! Come, young Eppie, we must get the gentleman's bed made up for him."

With a toss of her pretty head, Eppie followed her grandmother to the next room, casting a glance behind her that seemed to ask what she meant calling a lad without shoes or socks a gentleman. Not the less readily or actively, however, did she assist her grandmother in preparing the tired wayfarer's couch. In a few minutes they returned and told him the room was quite ready for him.

He heard them talking for a while after the door was closed, but the girl soon took her leave. He was falling asleep in the luxury of conscious repose when the sound of the cobbler's hammer for a moment roused him, and he knew the old man was again at work on his behalf. A moment more and he was fast asleep.

3

First Days in Auchars

The next day Donal again had shoes to wear, for the cobbler had worked on them more the previous night and early on Sunday morning. Donal willingly agreed, once asked, to go to church with the cobbler and his wife. They left the town and were soon walking in meadows through which ran a clear river, shining and speedy in the morning sun. Beyond lay a level plain stretching toward the sea, divided into numberless fields and dotted with farmhouses and hamlets. On the side where they walked, the ground rose in places into small hills, many of them wooded. Half a

mile away was one of conical shape, on whose top towered a castle. Old
and gray and sullen, it lifted itself from the foliage about it like a great
rock from a summer sea, and stood out against the clear blue sky of the
June morning. The hill was covered with wood, mostly rather young, but
at the bottom were some ancient firs and beeches. At the top, round the
base of the castle, the trees were chiefly delicate birches with moonlight
skin, and feathery larches not thriving over well.

"What do they call yon castle?" questioned Donal. "It must be a place
of some importance."

"They mostly just call it the castle," answered the cobbler. "It's old
name is Graham's Grip. It's the Lord Morven's place and they call it Castle
Graham; the family name's Graham, you know. That's where young Eppie's
in service. And that reminds me, sir, you haven't told me what kind of
place you're looking for yourself. It's not that a poor man like me could
help, but it's good to let folks know what you're after. A word goes asking
long after it's out of sight—and the answer sometimes comes from far
away. The Lord sometimes brings things about in the most unlikely fashion."

"I'm ready for anything I'm fit to do," said Donal, "but I have had what's
called a good education—though I've learned more from my own needs
than from my books. So I would rather till the human than the earthly soil,
taking more interest in the schoolmaster's crops than the farmer's."

"Would you object to one pupil by himself—or maybe two?"

"No, surely—if I thought myself fit."

"Eppie mentioned last night that there was word about the castle of a
tutor for the youngest. Do you have any means of approaching the place?"

"Not till the minister comes home," answered Donal. "I have a letter to
him."

"He'll be back by the middle of the week, I hear them say."

"Can you tell me anything about the people at the castle?" asked
Donal.

"I could," answered Andrew, "but some things is better found out than
told beforehand. Every place has its own shape and most things has to
have some adjusting to make them fit."

The church stood a little way out of the town, in a churchyard; overgrown with grass, which the wind blew like a field of corn. Many of the
stones were out of sight in it. The church, a relic of old Catholic days, rose
out of it like one that had taken to growing and so got the better of his ills.
They walked into the musty, dingy, brown-atmosphered house. The cobbler led the way to a humble place behind a pillar. The service was not
so dreary as usual; the sermon had some thought in it, and Donal's heart
was drawn to the man speaking in the minister's stead.

The next day, after breakfast, Donal said to his host: "Now, I must pay
you for my shoe."

"No, no," returned the cobbler, "there's just one prejudice I have left
concerning the Sabbath day. I can't bring myself to take money for any
work done on it. You'll do as much for me someday."

"I see it would be useless to argue," said Donal. "There's nothing left me but to thank you. There is the lodging and the board, though—I must know about that before we go further."

"They're none of my business," replied Andrew. "I leave that to the goodwife. She's a capital manager and won't overcharge you."

Donal could not but yield, and presently went out for a stroll.

He wandered along the bank of the river till he came to the foot of the hill on which stood the castle. Seeing a gate, he approached it and, finding it open, went in. A slow ascending drive went through the trees round and round the hill. He followed it a little way. An aromatic air now blew and now paused as he went. When he had gone a few yards out of sight of the gate, he threw himself down among the trees and fell into a reverie.

As his thoughts were coming and going in his brain, Donal heard a slight sound somewhere near him—the lightest of sounds indeed, the turning of the leaf of a book. He raised his head and looked but could see no one. At last, up through the tree trunks on the slope of the hill, he caught sight of the shine of something white; it was the hand that held an open book. He took it for the hand of a lady. The trunk of a large tree hid the reclining form.

He rose quietly, but not quietly enough to steal away. From behind the tree a young man, rather tall and slender, rose and came toward him.

"I presume you are unaware that these grounds are not open to the public?" he said with a touch of haughtiness.

"I beg your pardon, sir," said Donal. "I found the gate open and the shade of the trees was enticing."

"It is of no consequence," returned the youth; "only my father is apt to be annoyed if he sees anyone."

He was interrupted by a cry from farther up the hill.

"Oh, there you are, Percy!"

"And there you are, Davie!" returned the youth kindly.

A boy of about ten came toward them rapidly, jumping stumps and darting between bushes.

"Take care, Davie!" cried the other; "you may slip on a root and fall."

"Oh, I know better than that. But you are busy."

"Not in the least. Come along."

Donal lingered; the youth had not finished his sentence.

"I went to Arkie," said the boy, "but she couldn't help me. I can't make sense out of this."

He had an old folio under one arm, with a finger of the other hand in its leaves.

"It is a curious taste for a child," said the youth, turning to Donal, in whom he had recognized the peasant-scholar; "this little brother of mine reads all the dull old romances he can lay his hands on."

"Perhaps," suggested Donal, "they are the only fictions within his reach. Could you not turn him loose on Sir Walter Scott?"

"A good suggestion!" he answered, casting a keen glance at Donal.

"Will you let me look at the passage?" said Donal to the boy, holding out his hand.

The boy opened the book and gave it to him. On the top of the page Donal read: *The Countess of Pembroke's Arcadia*. He had read of the book but had never seen it.

"That's a grand book!" he said.

"Horribly dreary," remarked the elder brother.

The younger reached up and laid his finger on the page next to him.

"There, sir," he said; "that is the place—do tell me what it means."

"I will try," answered Donal; "I may not be able."

He began to read at the top of the page.

"That's not the place, sir," said the boy. "It is there."

"I must know something of what goes before it first," returned Donal.

"Oh, yes, sir; I see," he answered and stood silent.

He was a fair-haired boy, with ruddy cheeks and a healthy look—evidently sweet tempered.

Donal presently saw both what the sentence meant and the cause of its difficulty. He explained the thing to him.

"Thank you! Thank you! Now I shall get on!" he cried and ran up the hill.

"You seem to understand boys," said the brother.

"I have always had a sort of ambition to understand ignorance."

"Understand ignorance?"

"You know, what queer shapes the shadows of the plainest things take. I never seem to understand anything till I understand its shadow."

The youth glanced keenly at Donal.

"I wish I had had a tutor like you," he said.

"Why?" asked Donal,

"I should have done better. Where do you live?"

Donal told him he was lodging with Andrew Comin, the cobbler. A silence followed.

"Good morning!" said the youth.

"Good morning, sir," returned Donal, and went away.

On Wednesday evening Donal went to the Morven Arms to inquire for a third time if his box had come. The landlord said that if a great heavy tool chest was the thing he expected, it had come.

"Donal Grant would be the name upon it," said Donal.

"Indeed, I didn't look," said the landlord. "It's in the backyard."

As Donal went through the house to the yard, he heard something of the talk going on in a room where a few of the townsfolk were drinking, and heard the name of the earl mentioned.

One of the persons there assembled was a stranger who had been receiving from the others various pieces of information concerning the town and its neighborhood.

"I knew the old man well," a wrinkled, gray-haired man was saying. "A very different man from this present earl. He'd sit down with any poor body like myself and have a drink and share news and never think anything of it. But this man, haith! Who ever saw him share a word with anyone!"

"I never heard how he came to the title. They say he was but some distant cousin," remarked a stout farmer-looking man.

"Hoots! He was the last earl's brother, with right to the title, but none to the property. That he's only taking care of till his niece comes of age. He was always about the place before his brother died, and they were friends as well as brothers. They say that the Lady Arctura—have you ever heard such a heathenish name for a lass!—is bound to marry the young lord. There's a heap of gossip about the place and the people and their strange ways. They tell me none can be said to know the earl but his own man. For myself, I never came into their counsel—not even to the buying or selling of a lamb."

"Well," said another, "we know from Scripture that the sins of the fathers is visited upon the children to the third and fourth generation—and who can tell?"

"Who can tell," rejoined another, who had a judicial look about him in spite of an unshaven beard and a certain general disregard to appearances, "who can tell but the sins of our fathers may be lying upon some of ourselves at this very moment?"

By this time Donal was well past the open room and, though he would liked to have joined into the discussion, proceeded to locate his trunk. Borrowing a wheelbarrow, he trundled the chest home and, unpacking it downstairs, carried his books and clothes to his room.

The next day he put on his best coat and went to call on the minister. Shown into the study, he saw seated there the man he had met on his first day's journey, the same who had parted from him in such displeasure. He presented his letter.

Mr. Carmichael gave him a keen glance, but uttered no word until he had read it.

"Well, young man," he said looking up at him with concentrated severity, "what would you have me to do?"

"Give me the chance, if you please, of any employment in the scholastic line you may happen to hear of, sir; that's all," answered Donal.

"Ah," said the clergyman, "but that *all* is a very great deal! What if I see myself set in charge over young minds and hearts and bound to guard them from such influences as you would exercise over them? For I know you better already than this good man whose friendship with your parents gives him a kind interest in you. You little thought how you were undermining your prospects last Friday when you spoke as you did to a stranger on the road. My old friend would scarcely wish me to welcome to my parish a person whom if he had known him better he would have been glad to get rid of from his own. You may go to the kitchen and have some dinner—I have no desire to render evil for evil—but I will not bid you Godspeed."

"I thank you," answered Donal, "but I shall get my dinner from a more willing hand than yours. Good morning, sir!"

On the doorstep he met a youth he had known by sight at the university, who had the reputation of being one of the worst behaved there; he must be the minister's son.

A little ruffled and not a little disappointed, Donal walked away. Almost unconsciously he took the road to the castle, and coming to the gate, leaned on the top bar and stood thinking.

Suddenly down through the trees came Davie bounding, pushing his hands through between the bars, and shook hands with him.

"I have been looking for you all day!" he said.

"Why?" asked Donal.

"Forgue sent you a message."

"I have had no message."

"Eppie took it this morning."

"Ah, that explains it! I have not been home since breakfast."

"It was to say that my father would like to see you."

"I will go and get the letter and then I shall know what to do."

"Why do you live there? The cobbler is such a dirty little man. Your clothes will smell of leather."

"His hands do get dirty," said Donal, "but from honest labor. And if you could see his heart—that is as clean as it can be!"

"Have you seen it?" said the boy, looking up at Donal unsure whether he was making game of him or meaning something very serious.

"I have had a glimpse or two of it. I never saw a cleaner soul. You know, my dear boy, there's a cleanness much deeper than the skin."

"Can you ride?" inquired Davie.

"Yes, a little."

"Who taught you?"

"An old mare I was fond of."

"Ah, you are making a game of me!" said Davie.

"I never make game of anyone," replied Donal. "But now I must go and find the letter."

"I would go with you," said the boy, "but my father won't let me beyond the grounds. I don't know why."

Donal hastened home and found himself eagerly expected, for the letter young Eppie had brought was from the earl. It informed Donal that it would give his lordship pleasure to see him, if he would favor him with a call.

In a few minutes he was again on the road to the castle.

4

·····················

In the Castle

$\mathcal{N}$ot a person did he meet on his way from the gate up through the wood. He ascended the hill with its dark firs up to its crown of silvery birches, above which rose the gray mass of the fortress. He saw now the back, then the front, as the slowly circling road brought him ever closer. Turret and tower, pinnacle and battlement appeared and disappeared as he climbed. Not until at last he stood on the top and from an open space beheld it all could he tell what it was really like. It was grand, but looked a gloomy place to live.

He stood on a broad grassy platform from which rose a graveled terrace, and from the terrace the castle. He ran his eye along the front seeking a door, but saw none. Ascending the terrace by a broad flight of steps, he approached a deep recess in the front, where two portions of the house of differing dates nearly met. Inside this recess he found a rather small door, flush with the wall, thickly studded and plated with iron, surmounted by the Morven horses carved in gray stone, and surrounded with several moldings. Looking for some means of announcing his presence, he saw a handle at the end of a rod of iron, and pulled, but heard nothing: the sound of the bell was smothered in a wilderness of stone walls. By and by, however, appeared an old servant.

"The earl wants to see me," said Donal.

"What name?" said the man.

"Donal Grant; but his lordship will be nothing the wiser, I suspect; I don't think he knows my name. Tell him—the young man he sent for to Andrew Comin's."

The man left him and Donal began to look about. The place where he stood was a mere entry, a cell enclosed in huge walls of nothing but bare stone. It was a full ten minutes before the man returned and requested him to follow him.

Crossing through several rooms, they entered a large octagonal space, its doors of dark shining oak with carved stone lintels and door-posts, and its walls adorned with arms and armor almost to the domed ceiling. Into it descending like a gently alighting bird came the end of a great turnpike stair, of slow sweep and enormous diameter. Like the revolving center of a huge shell, it went up out of sight, with promise of endless convolutions beyond. It was of ancient stone, but not worn as would have been a narrow stair, and onto this stairway went the man, followed by Donal.

With the stair yet ascending above them as if it would never stop, the man paused upon a step no broader than the rest and, opening a door in the round of the wall, said, "Mr. Grant, my lord," and stood aside for Donal to enter.

He found himself in the presence of a tall but bowed man, with a large-featured white face, thin and worn and a deep-sunken eye that gleamed with an unhealthy life. His hair was thin, but plentiful enough to cover his head, and was only streaked with gray. His hands were long and thin and white; his feet, if not large, were at least in large shoes, looking the larger that they came out from narrow trousers of the check called in Scotland shepherd-tartan. He wore also a coat of light blue cloth, which must have been many years old, so high was its collar of velvet and so much too wide was it for him now. A black silk neckerchief was tied carefully about his throat, and a waistcoat completed his costume. On his long little finger shone a stone which Donal took for a diamond. He motioned Donal to a seat, and turned to his writing, with a rudeness more like that of a successful contractor than a nobleman. But it gave Donal the unintended advantage of becoming a little acquainted both with his lordship and with his surroundings.

The room in which he sat was comfortably furnished, though not large; it was wainscoted, with a good many things on the walls—two or three riding whips, a fishing rod, a pair or two of spurs, a sword with gilded hilt, a strange-looking dagger like a flame of fire, one or two old engravings, and what looked like a plan of the estate. The one window looked to the south, and the summer sun was streaming in. The earl seemed about sixty or sixty-five years of age, and looked as if he had rarely or never smiled. Donal tried to imagine what the advent of a smile would do for his face, but failed in the attempt.

After a time the earl raised himself, pushed his writing from him, turned toward Donal, and said with courtesy, "Excuse me, Mr. Grant; I wished to talk to you with the ease of duty done."

More polite the earl's address could not have been, but there seemed nevertheless something between him and Donal that was not to be passed—nothing positive, but a gulf of the negative.

"I have plenty of time at your lordship's service," replied Donal.

"You have probably guessed already why I sent for you?"

"I have hoped, my lord; but guesses and hopes require confirmation or dissolution."

The earl seemed pleased with his answer. There was something of old-world breeding about the lad that commended him to the man of the older world. Such breeding is nothing rare among Celt-born peasants.

"My boys told me they had met a young man in the grounds—"

"For which I beg your lordship's pardon," said Donal. "I did not know the place was forbidden."

"Do not mention it. I hope you will soon be familiar with the place. I am glad of the mistake. They told me you had a book of poetry in your hand, also that you explained to the little fellow something that puzzled him. I surmised you might be a student in want of a situation. I had been looking out for a young man to take charge of the boy, and I thought it possible you might serve my purpose. Lord Forgue has just come home from St. Cross's and will soon leave for Oxford. Over him, of course, you would have no direct authority, but you could not fail to influence him. He never went to school, but had tutors till he went to college. Do you honestly think yourself one to be trusted with such a charge? I do not doubt you can give such an account of yourself as will show you fit for it?"

Donal had not a glimmer of false modesty, and answered immediately, "I do honestly believe I am, my lord."

"Tell me something of your history—where were you born? and what were your parents?"

Thereupon Donal told all he thought it of any consequence to the earl to know about him.

His lordship did not once interrupt him with question or remark, but heard him in silence.

When he had ended, he said, "Well . . . I like all you tell me. Those who have not had too many advantages are the more likely to enter into the difficulties of others and give them the help they require. You have, of course, some testimonials to show?"

"I have some from the professors, my lord, and one from the minister of the parish, who knew me all the time I was a farm servant before I went to college."

"Show me what you have," said his lordship, more and more pleased with him.

Donal took the papers from the homely pocketbook his mother had made for him and handed them to the earl. His lordship read them with some attention, folding each as he finished with it, and returning it to him without remark, saying only with the last, "Quite satisfactory."

"But," said Donal, "there is one thing I should be more at ease if I told your lordship. The minister of this parish would tell you I was an atheist, or something very like it—an altogether unsafe person to trust with the care of man, woman, or child. But he knows nothing of me."

"On what grounds, then, would he say so?" asked the earl—without showing the least discomposure. "I thought you were a stranger to this place."

Donal told him how they had met, and what had passed between them, and how the minister had behaved when he presented his introduction. The earl heard him gravely, made no comment, was silent for a moment, and then said, "Should Mr. Carmichael address me on the subject, which I do not think likely, he will find me by that time too much prejudiced in your favor to be readily influenced against you. But I can easily imagine his mistaking your freedom of speech. You seem to me scarcely prudent enough for your own interests. Why say all you think? You seem afraid of nothing."

"That's true, my lord."

The earl was silent; his gray face seemed to grow grayer, but it might be only that the sun just then went under a cloud and was suddenly folded in its shadow.

After a moment he spoke again. "I am quite satisfied with you, so far as I know you, Mr. Grant. And as I should not like to employ you in direct opposition to Mr. Carmichael, the best way will be to arrange matters at once before he can hear anything of the affair; then I can tell him I am bound to give you a trial. What salary do you want?"

Donal replied he would prefer leaving the salary to his lordship's judgment, if upon trial he found his work worth paying.

"I am not a wealthy man," said his lordship, "and would prefer some understanding on the matter."

"Try me, then, for three months—I can't show how I do in less than that. Give me my board and lodging, the use of your library, and at the end of the time a ten-pound note to send home. After that we shall both see."

The earl smiled and agreed. Donal departed to prepare for taking up his abode at the castle the next day, and with much satisfaction and a full heart walked to his lodging. He had before him the prospect of pleasant work, plenty of time and books to help pursue the studies he most loved, an abode full of interest and beauty, and something to send home to his parents.

In the evening Donal settled his account with the cobbler's wife. But he found her demand so much less than he expected that he had to expostulate. She was firm, however, and assured him she had gained, not lost. As he was putting up his things, she said, "Leave a book or two so that when you come back to visit, the place will look like home to you. We'll call the room yours. Come as often as you can. It does my Andrew's heart good to have a talk with someone that knows something of what the Master would be at."

The next morning a cart came from the castle to fetch his box; and after breakfast he set out for his new abode.

Once more he took the path by the riverside. The morning was glorious. The sun and the river and the birds were jubilant, and the wind gave life to everything. There were dull wooden sounds of machinery near, no discord with the sweetness of the hour, speaking only of activity, not labor. These bleaching meadows went a long way by the riverside, and from them seemed to rise the wooded base of the castle. Donal's bosom swelled with delight.

He was soon climbing to the castle, where he was again admitted by the old butler.

"Mr. Grant," he said, "I'll show you at once how you can go and come at liberty"; and therewith led him through doors and along passages to a postern opening on a little walled garden at the east end of the castle. "That," he said, "you will find convenient. It is, you observe, at the foot of the northwest tower, and the stair in that tower leads to your room, so that you can come and go as you please. I will show it to you."

He led the way up a stair so narrow it might almost have gone inside the newel of the great turnpike staircase. Up and up they went, until Donal began to wonder; and still they went up and passed door after door.

"You're young, sir," said the butler, "and sound of wind and limb or I would not have put you here. You will think nothing of running up and down."

"I never was up one so high before," said Donal. "The stair up the college tower is nothing to it!"

"Oh, you'll soon learn to shoot up and down it like a bird. I used to do so almost without knowing it when I was page boy to the old lord. I got into the way of keeping a shoulder foremost, and screwing up and down as if I was a blob of air rather than a lanky lad. How this old age does play the fool with us!"

They reached the top. The stair indeed went a little farther, for it seemed to go on through the roof; apparently the tower had been meant to go higher yet. But at the place they had reached was a door; the man opened it, and Donal found himself in a small room, nearly round, a portion of the circle taken off by the stair. On the opposite side was a window projecting from the wall, whence he could look in three different directions. The wide country lay at his feet. He saw the winding road by which he had ascended, the gate by which he had entered, the meadow with its white stripes through which he had come, and the river flowing down the vale. He followed it with his eyes: lo, there was the sea, shining in the sun like a diamond shield!

The walls were bare even of plaster; Donal could have counted the stones in them, but they were dry as a bone.

"I see, sir," the butler said, "you are wondering how to keep warm here in the winter. See here, you can shut this door over the window. See how thick and strong it is; and there is your grate. And for wood and peats and coal, there is plenty to be had below. It is a labor to carry them up, but if I was you, I would set to it nights, when nobody was about and I had nothing else to do, and carry till I had a good stock laid in."

"But," said Donal, "I should fill up my room so that I could not move about in it."

"Ah, you don't know," said the old man, "what a space you have here, all to yourself! Come this way."

Two or three steps more up the stair, just one turn, and they came to another door. It opened into a wide space, and from it, still following, Donal stepped on a ledge without any parapet that ran round the front part of the tower, passing above the window of his room. It was well he had a tolerably steady brain, for he had to wonder why the height should affect him more than that of a much higher rock up on Glashgar. But doubtless he would soon get used to it, for the old man had stepped out upon the ledge without the smallest hesitation! Round the tower he followed him. Nearly opposite the door on the other side, a few steps rose to a watchtower—a sort of ornate sentry-box in stone, where one might sit and regard the whole country before him. Avoiding this, another step or two led them to the roof of the castle, consisting of great stone slabs. A

broad passage ran between the rise of the roof and a battlemented parapet; here was no danger of falling. Advancing a little way they arrived at a
flat roof, to which they descended by a few steps. Several rough wooden
sheds, with nothing in them, clung together at one side.

"Here is stowage enough!" announced the old man.

"Doubtless!" answered Donal, the idea of his aerie growing more and
more agreeable the longer he contemplated it. "But would there be no
objection to my using it for such a purpose?"

"What objection could there be?" returned the butler. "I do not believe
a single person but myself knows there is such a place."

"And shall I be allowed to lay in what stock I please?"

"Everything is under my care, and I allow you," said the butler, with no
little importance. "Of course you will not waste—I am dead against waste,
but as to necessaries, keep your mind easy, sir."

Donal never thought to ask why he was placed so apart from the rest
of the family, but that he should have such entire command of his own
leisure and privacy as this isolation yielded him was a consequence
exceedingly satisfactory. The butler left him with the information that dinner would be ready for him in the schoolroom at seven o'clock, and
Donal proceeded at once to settle himself in his new quarters.

5

· · · · · · · · · · · · · · · · · ·

A Mystery

$\mathscr{R}$eturning to his circular room and finding some shelves in a recess of
the wall, Donal arranged his books upon them, laid his few clothes in the
chest of drawers, put on his lighter pair of shoes and a clean shirt, got out
his writing material, and sat down. Though his open window was so high,
the warm pure air came in full of the aromatic odors rising in the hot
sunshine from the young pine trees far below, while from a lark above
descended news of heaven's gate. The scent came up and the song came
down all the time he was writing to his mother—a long letter. When he
had closed and addressed it, he fell into a reverie. He was glad he was to
have his meals by himself; he would be able to read all the time. But how
was he to find the schoolroom? Surely someone would fetch him. They
would remember that he did not know his way about.

It was yet an hour to dinnertime when, finding himself drowsy, he
threw himself on his bed and presently fell fast asleep. The night
descended while he slept, and when he came to himself, its silences were
deep around him. But it was not fully dark; though there was no moon,
the twilight was long and clear. He could read by it the face of his watch,

and found it was twelve o'clock! No one had missed him, or taken pains to find him, and now he was very hungry! But he had been hungrier before and survived it. What did it matter? Then he remembered that in his pouch were still some remnants of oatcake. Never before had he fallen so suddenly and so fast asleep except after a hard day's labor. He was not particularly tired, having done little for many days. It must be something in the high air of the place, perhaps in the new sense of ease.

He took his pouch and, stepping out on the bartizan, crept with careful steps round to the watchtower. There he seated himself in the stone chair and ate his dry morsels in the starry presences with profound satisfaction. His sleep had refreshed him and he was wide awake.

All at once came to his ear, through the night, a strange something. Whence it came or what it was, he could not even conjecture. Was it a moan of the river from below? Was it a lost music tone that had wandered from afar and grown faint? Was it one of those mysterious sounds he had read of, born in the air itself, and not yet explained of science? Or was it a stifled human moaning? He could not tell; he must wait and listen.

Presently came a long protracted tone, as if the sound of some muffled musical instrument. Truly night was the time for strange things!

Again the sound—hardly to be called sound. It was like that which the organ gives out too deep to affect the hearing, only this seemed rather too high to be heard—for he could not be sure his ear heard it at all; it seemed only his soul that heard it. He would steal softly down the stone stair. Might he somewhere, in or out of the house, find its source? Some creature might be in trouble and need help!

He crept back along the bartizan. The stair was dark as the very heart of night. He groped his way down, arrived at the bottom, and felt about but could not find the door to the outer air which the butler had shown him; it was wall wherever his hands fell. Then he could not find again the stair he had left and could not tell in which direction it lay.

He had gotten into a long windowless passage connecting two wings of the house, and in this he was feeling his way, fearful of falling down some stair or trap. He came at last to a door—low-browed like almost all in the house. Opening it—was it the faintest gleam of light he saw? And was that again the sound he had followed, fainter and farther off than before—a downy wind-wafted plume from the skirt of some stray harmony?

At such a time of the night surely it was strange! It must come from one who could not sleep, and was solacing himself with sweet sounds. If so it was, he had no right to search further. But how was he to return? He dared hardly move, lest he should be found wandering over the house in the dead of night like a thief, or one searching after its secrets. He would have to sit down and wait for the morning; its earliest light would perhaps enable him to find his way back to his quarters.

Feeling about him a little, his foot struck against the step of a stair. Examining it with his hands, he believed it the same as he had ascended in the morning. Even in a great castle, could there be two such royal stairs? He sat down upon it, and leaning his head on his hands, composed himself to a patient waiting for the light.

After perhaps an hour, he sprang suddenly to his feet. That was no musical tone which made the darkness shudder around him! It was a human groan—a groan as of one in dire pain, the pain of a soul's agony. The next instant Donal was feeling his way up—cautiously, as if each succeeding step he might come against the man who had groaned. Tales of haunted houses rushed into his memory.

Up and up he felt his way, all about him as still as darkness and night could make it. A ghostly cold crept through his skin and there was a pulling at the muscles of his chest. As he felt his way along the wall, sweeping its great endless circle round and round in spiral ascent, all at once his hand seemed to go through it. He stopped. It was the door of the room into which he had been shown to meet the earl. It stood wide open. A faint glimmer came through the window from the star-filled sky. He stepped just within the doorway. Was that not another glimmer on the floor—from the back of the room through a door he did not remember having seen yesterday? There again was the groan, and close at hand! He approached the second door. It was in the same wall as that by which he had entered, but close to the other side of the room. It must open under the curve of the great staircase. What room could be there? He found when he went through it that there was but room to turn right round to a second door in the same plane, immediately on the other side of the wall which stood at right angles to both and which separated them from each other. This door was open. A lamp, nearly spent, hung from the small room which might be an office or study. It had the look of an antechamber, but that it could not be, for there was but one door.

In the dim light he saw a vague form leaning up against one of the walls as if listening to something through it. As he gazed it grew plainer to him, and he saw a face, its eyes staring wide, which yet seemed not to see him. It was the face of the earl. Donal felt as if in the presence of the disembodied. The figure turned its pale face to the wall, put the palms of his hands against it, and moved them up and down, this way and that, then looked at them, and began to rub them against each other.

Donal came to himself. He concluded it was a case of sleep-walking. He had read that it was dangerous to wake the sleeper, but that he seldom came to mischief when left alone. He was about to slip away as he had come when the faint sound of a far-off chord crept through the silence. The earl again laid his ear to the wall. But there was only silence. He went through the same dumb show as before, then turned as if to leave the place.

Donal turned also and hurriedly felt his way to the stair. Then first he was in danger of terror; for in stealing through the darkness from one who could find his way without his eyes, he seemed pursued by a creature not of this world. On the stair he went down a step or two, then lingered, and heard the earl come on it also. He crept close to the newel on the inside turn, leaving the great width of the stair free, but the steps of the earl went upward. Donal descended, sat down again at the bottom of the stair, and began again to wait. No sound came to him through the rest of the night. The slow hours rolled away, and the slow light drew nearer. Now and then he was on the point of falling into a doze but would suddenly start wide awake, listening through a silence that seemed to fill the whole universe and deepen around the castle.

At length he was aware that the darkness had, unobserved of him, grown weaker—that the approach of the light was at hand. He sought the long passage by which he had come, and felt his way to the other end; it would be safer to wait there if he could get no farther. But somehow he came to the foot of his own stair and sped up as if it were the ladder of heaven. He threw himself on his bed, fell fast asleep, and did not waken till the sun was high.

6

●●●●●●●●●●●●●●●●●●●

Becoming Acquainted

Old Simmons, the butler, awakened him.

"I was afraid something was the matter, sir, when they told me you did not come down to dinner last night, and that you had not appeared for breakfast this morning."

"If I had been awake," said Donal, "I should not have known where to find my breakfast. You forget that the knowledge of an old castle is not an intuition."

"How long will you take to dress?" he asked.

"Ten minutes," answered Donal.

"Then I will come again in ten minutes; or, if you are willing to save an old man's bones, I will be at the bottom of the stair in ten minutes to take charge of you. I would have looked after you better yesterday, but his lordship was taken very poorly last night, and I had to be in attendance upon him till after midnight."

When he reached it, Donal thought it impossible he should ever by himself have found his way to the schoolroom. With all he could do to remember the turnings, he found the endeavor at last hopeless, and for the time gave it up. Through passages of many various widths and lengths, as it seemed to him, through doors apparently in all directions, upstairs and down they went, and at last came to a long low room, barely furnished, with an immediate access to the open air. The windows looked upon a small grassy court with a wall round it and a sun-dial in the center of it, while a door opened immediately on a paved court in the center of the castle. At one end of the long room a table was laid for him, with ten times as many things as he could desire to eat, although the comparative abstinence of the previous day had prepared him for a good breakfast. The butler himself, a good-natured old fellow with a nose somewhat too red to be preferred for ordinary wear by one in his responsible position, waited upon him.

"I hope the earl is all right again this morning," Donal said.

"Well, I can't say he is quite himself. He's but a delicate man, is the earl, and has been so long as I have known him, which is now a good many years. He was long with the army in India, and the sun, they say, gave him a stroke, and ever since he has bad headaches during which he don't let no one near him, not even his own sons, or his niece as is devoted to him. But in between he's pretty well, and nothing displeases him more than to have any inquiry made after his health or how he may have slept the night! But he's a good master, and I hope to end my days with him. I'm not one as likes to see new faces an' new places every year. One good place is enough for me. Take some of this gamepie, sir, you'll find it good."

Donal made haste with his breakfast, and to Simmons' astonishment had ended when he thought him just well begun.

"Where should I likely come upon the young gentleman?" Donal asked.

"Master David is wild to see you, sir. When I've cleared away, you have only to ring this bell out of that window, and he'll be with you as fast as he can lay his feet to the ground. For Lord Forgue, he'll come to you, I daresay, when he's in the humor. He's the earl that is to be, you know, sir, though he's not to have the property. Castle and all belongs to my lady Arctura. It's all arranged, as everybody knows. They say the brothers agreed about that years ago. She's a little older, but that don't matter where there's a title on the one side, and the property belonging to it on the other, and cousinship already between them."

For an old servant, Donal thought him very communicative concerning family affairs; but then doubtless he told no more than, as he said, everybody knew. But what a name to give a girl—Arctura. Surely it was a strange house he had gotten into!

As soon as Simmons had cleared the table, Donal rang the handbell from the window. A shout mingled with the last tones of it, then the running of swift feet over the stones of the court, and Davie burst into the room.

"Oh, sir!" he cried, "I am so glad . . . It is so good of you to come!"

"Well, Davie," returned Donal, "everybody has got to do something to carry the world on a bit. I have got to work, and my work now is to help make a man of you. But I can't do much unless you help me. Only, mind, if I seem not to be making a good job of you, I shan't stay many hours after the discovery. So if you want to keep me, you must mind what I say."

"But it will be so long before I am a man," mourned Davie.

"Not so long, perhaps. It depends greatly on yourself. The boy that is longest in becoming a man is the boy that thinks himself a man before he is like one."

"Oh, come then, let us do something to make a man of me!" urged Davie.

"Come along," assented Donal. "What shall we do first?"

"Oh, I don't know. You must tell me, sir."

"Tell me, Davie, what you would like best to do—I mean, if you might do what you pleased."

Davie thought for a little while, then said: "I should like to write a book."

"What kind of a book?"

"Oh, a beautiful story, of course!"

"Isn't it just as well to read such a book? Why should you want to write one?"

"Oh, because then I should have it go just as I wanted it! I am always—almost always—disappointed with the thing that comes next. But if I were to write it myself, then I couldn't get tired of it, you know, because it would be just as I wanted it, and not as somebody else wanted it."

"Well," said Donal, after thinking for a moment, "suppose you begin to write a book."

"That would be such fun. So much better than learning verbs and nouns!"

"But the verbs and the nouns are just the things that go to make a story—with not a few adjectives and adverbs, and a host of conjunctions—and, if it be a very moving story, then a good many interjections . . . and all these you've got to put together so they make good sense, or it will never be a story that you will like to read, and I shall like to read, and your brother and cousin will like to read—and perhaps your father too!"

"Oh no, sir. Papa wouldn't read a story. Arkie told me he wouldn't. She doesn't either. But Percy reads lots—only he won't let me read the ones he reads."

"Well," said Donal, "perhaps you had better not begin the story till I see whether you know enough about those verbs and nouns to do it decently well. Show me your school books."

"There they all are—on that shelf. I haven't opened one of them since Percy came home and laughed at them all. Then Arkie—that's Lady Arctura, our cousin, you know—said Percy might teach me himself; and he wouldn't; and she wouldn't; and I've had such a jolly time of it ever since—doing nothing but reading books out of the library! Have you seen the library, Mr. Grant?"

"No; I've hardly seen anything yet. Suppose we begin by your showing me about the place."

During the first day and the next, Donal did not even come in sight of any other of the family. But on the third day, after their short early school—for he seldom let Davie work till he was tired—going with him through the stable-yard, they came upon Lord Forgue as he mounted his horse—a nervous, fiery, thin-skinned thoroughbred. The moment his master was on him, he began to back and rear. Forgue gave him a cut with his whip. He went wild, plunging and dancing and kicking. The young lord was a horseman in the sense of having a good seat; but he knew little about horses—they were to him creatures to be compelled, not friends. As he was raising his arm for a second useless and cruel blow, Donal darted to the horse's head.

"You mustn't do that, my lord!" he said. "You'll drive him mad."

But the worst part of Forgue's nature was uppermost; in his rage all the vices of his family rushed to the top. He looked down on Donal with a fury checked only by contempt.

"Keep away," he spat, "or it will be the worse for you. What do you know about horses?"

"Enough to know that you are not being fair to him. I will not let you strike the poor animal."

"Hold your tongue and stand away, or by—"

"You won't frighten me, sir," interrupted Donal.

Forgue brought down his whip with a great stinging blow upon Donal's shoulder and back. The fierce blood of the highland Celt rushed to his brain, and had not the man in him held firm there might have been miserable work. But though he clenched his teeth, he ruled his tongue and held his hands.

"My lord," he said after one instant's thunderous silence, "there's that in me that would think as little of throttlin' you as you do of ill-usin' your poor beast. But I'm not going to drop his quarrel and take up my own. That would be cowardly." Here he patted the creature's neck and, recovering his composure, went on, "I tell you, my lord, the curb-chain is too tight. The animal is suffering as you cannot imagine."

"Let him go," cried Forgue, "or I will make you!"

He raised his whip again, the more enraged that the groom stood looking on with his mouth open.

"I tell your lordship," said Donal, "it is my turn to strike. And if you hit the animal again before that chain is slackened, I will pitch you out of the saddle!"

For answer Forgue struck the horse over the head. The same moment he was on the ground. Donal had taken him by the leg and thrown him off. Forgue was not horseman enough to keep his hold of the reins, and Donal led the horse a little way off, leaving Forgue to get up in safety. The poor animal was pouring with sweat, shivering and trembling, yet throwing his head back every moment. Donal could scarcely undo the chain; it was twisted—his lordship had fastened it himself—and sharp edges pressed his jaw at the least touch of the rein. He had not yet rehooked it when Forgue was upon him with a second blow of the whip.

The horse was frightened afresh at the sound, and it was all Donal could do to hold him, but he succeeded at length in calming him. When he looked about him, Forgue was gone. He led the horse into the stable, put him in his stall, and proceeded to unsaddle him. It was then he first was aware of the presence of Davie. The boy was stamping—with fierce eyes and white face—choking with silent rage.

"Davie, my child," said Donal, and Davie recovered his power of speech.

"I'll go and tell my father!" he shouted and made for the stable door.

"Which of us are you going to tell on?" asked Donal with a smile.

"Percy, of course!" he replied, almost with a scream. "You are a good man, Mr. Grant, and he is a bad fellow. My father will give it to him well. To dare strike you—"

"No, you won't, my boy. Listen to me. Some people think it's a disgrace to be struck. I think it's a disgrace to strike. I have a right over your brother by that blow, and I mean to keep it—for his good. You didn't think I was afraid of him?"

"No, anybody could see you weren't a bit afraid. I would have struck him again, even if he had killed me for it!"

"I don't doubt you would. But when you understand, you will not be so ready to strike. I could have killed your brother more easily than to have held off his horse. You don't know how strong I am, or what a blow of my fist would be to a delicate fellow like that. I hope his fall has not hurt him."

"I hope it has—a little, I mean, only a little," said the boy, looking in the face of his tutor. "But tell me why you did not strike him. It would be good for him to be well beaten."

"It will, I hope, be better for him to be well forgiven; he will be ashamed of himself the sooner, I think. But why I did not strike him was that I am not my own master."

"But my father, I am sure, would not have been angry with you. He would have said you had a right to do it."

"Perhaps; but the earl is not the master I speak of."

"Oh?"

"God says I must not return evil for evil, a blow for a blow. I don't mind what people say about it; he would not have me disgrace myself. He never threatened those that struck him."

"But he wasn't a man, you know."

"Not a man! What was he then?"

"He was God, you know."

"And isn't God a man—and ever so much more than a man?"

The boy made no answer, and Donal went on, "Do you think God would have his child do anything disgraceful? What God wants of us is to be downright honest, and do what he tells us without fear."

Davie was silent. Donal said no more, and they went for their walk.

———

Away from Davie, Donal spent his time in his tower chamber or out of doors. All the grounds were open to him except a walled garden on the southeastern slope, looking toward the sea, which the earl kept for himself, though he rarely walked in it. On the side of the hill away from the town was a large park reaching down to the river and stretching a long way up its bank—with fine trees and beautiful views to the sea in one direction and to the mountains in the other. Here Donal would often wander, now with a book, now with Davie. The boy's presence was rarely an interruption to his thoughts when he wanted to think. On the river was a boat, and though at first he was awkward in the use of the oars, he was soon able to enjoy thoroughly a row up or down the stream, especially in the twilight.

The next day he was alone with his book under a beech tree on a steep slope to the river. Reading aloud, he did not hear the approach of his lordship.

"Mr. Grant," he said, "if you will say you are sorry you threw me from my horse, I will say I am sorry I struck you."

"I am very sorry," said Donal, rising, "that it was necessary to throw you from your horse; and perhaps your lordship may remember that you struck me before I did so."

"That has nothing to do with it. I simply propose a compromise . . . if you will do the one, I will do the other."

"What I think I ought to do, my lord, I do without bargaining. I am not sorry I threw you from your horse, and to say so would be to lie."

Forgue's anger began to rise once more, but he controlled himself. He was evidently at strife with himself: he knew he was wrong but could not bring himself to say so. It is one of the poorest of human weaknesses that a man would be ashamed of saying he has done wrong instead of so ashamed of having done wrong that he cannot rest till he has said so. For the shame cleaves fast until the confession removes it.

He walked away a step or two and stood with his back to Donal, poking the point of his stick into the grass. All at once he turned and said, "I will apologize if you will tell me one thing. Why did you not return either of my blows yesterday?"

"Because to do so would have been to disobey the instructions I am under."

"I only wanted to know it was not cowardice; I could not make an apology to a coward."

"If I were a coward, you would owe me an apology all the same, and he is a poor creature who will not pay his debts. But I hope it will not be necessary I should ever have to convince you I have no fear of you."

Forgue gave a little laugh. A moment's pause followed, then he held out his hand, in a half-hesitating, rather sheepish way.

"My lord," returned Donal, "I bear you no ill will and I would gladly shake your hand. But not in a halfhearted way—and no other way is possible while you are still uncertain whether I am a coward or not."

Saying not another word, Forgue turned and walked away, offended anew.

————

The housekeeper at the castle was a good woman, and very kind to Donal, feeling perhaps that he fell the more to her care that he was by birth of her own class; for it was said in the castle, "The tutor makes no pretense of being a gentleman." Sometimes when his dinner was served, Mrs. Brooks herself would appear to insure proper attention to him, and would sit down and talk to him while he ate, ready to rise and serve him if necessary. Their early days had had something in common, though she came from the southern highlands of green hills and more sheep. She gave him some rather needful information about the family; and he soon perceived that there would have been less peace in the house but for her gentle temper and good sense.

Lady Arctura was the daughter of the last Lord Morven, who left her sole heir to the property; Forgue and his brother Davie were the sons of the present earl. The present lord was the brother of the last, and had lived with him for some years before he succeeded to the title. He was a man of peculiar habits; nobody ever seemed to take to him and, since his wife's death, his health had been precarious. Though a strange man, he was a just if not generous master. His brother had left him guardian to Lady Arctura, and he had lived in the castle as before. His wife was a very lovely but delicate woman, and late in her life had been confined to her room. Since her death a great change had passed upon her husband. Certainly his behavior was sometimes hard to understand.

7

....

Prejudiced by Opinion

It was now almost three weeks since Donal had become a resident of the castle, and he had scarcely set eyes on the lady of the house. Once he had seen her back, and more than once he had caught a glimpse of her profile; but he had never really seen her face, and they had never spoken to each other.

One afternoon he was sauntering along a neglected walk, under the overhanging boughs of an avenue of beeches. He never went out without a book, though he often came back without having even glanced at it. This time it was a copy of the Apocrypha, which he had never seen till he found it in the library. In his usual unhurried fashion, he had begun to read. Taken with the beauty of the passage, he sat down on an old stone roller, whose carriage had rotted away and vanished years ago, and read aloud.

He had just finished a passage and stopped to think when, lifting his eyes, he saw Lady Arctura standing before him with a strange listening look. She was but a few paces from him, and seemed to have been arrested by what she heard as she was about to pass him. She looked as if there were a spell upon her. Her face was white, and her lips white and a little parted. Donal had but a glance of her, for his eyes, obeying a true instinct of good breeding, returned again at once to his book, and he sat silent and motionless, not saying a word. For one instant, his ears told him, she stood quite still; then he heard the soft sound of her dress as with all but noiseless foot she stole back and sought another way home.

She was rather tall, fair-skinned but dark-haired, like her cousin Forgue. Her figure was eminently graceful; Donal saw this when he looked up at the sound of her retreating steps. He did not speculate much of the cause of her strange behavior; he only thought she need not have run away as if he were something dangerous.

Though never yet had a word passed between her and anyone on the subject, Lady Arctura knew, as somehow everyone both in the castle and the town believed, that the desire of the earl was that she should marry his son, and so the property and the title be again joined. To this neither she nor Lord Forgue had made any objection; though indeed how could either, if ever so much inclined, seeing the notion had never yet been mentioned to either? And from any sign on either side, no one could have told whether it would be acceptable to either. They lived like brother and sister, apparently without much in common, and still less of misunderstanding. There might have been more likelihood of their taking a fancy to each other if they had seen a little less of each other than they did, though indeed they were but little together, and never alone.

Very few visitors came to the castle, and then only to call some of the gentry of the neighborhood, and occasionally one of the Perthshire branches of the family. Lord Morven very seldom saw anyone, his excuse being his health, which was constantly poor and often caused him suffering. Simmons, the butler, was also his chief personal attendant, and when he was worst, no one else saw him.

Lady Arctura was on terms of intimacy with Sophie Carmichael, the minister's daughter. Her father had poured out his dissatisfaction with the character of Donal, and his indignation at his conduct. The more unjustifiably her father spoke against him, the more bitterly did Miss Carmichael regard him, for she was a loyal daughter and looked up to her father as the wisest and best man in the parish. Wherefore she very naturally repeated his words to Lady Arctura. She in her turn repeated them to her uncle; but he would not pay much heed to what she said. The thing was done. He had seen and talked with Donal, and liked him. The young man himself had told him of the clergyman's disapprobation. Lady Arctura did not refer again to the matter. But she remained somewhat painfully doubtful about Donal and could not satisfy herself as to what she was to conclude from his reading the Apocrypha. Doubtless the fact was not to be interpreted to his advantage, for he was reading what was not the Bible when he might have been reading the Bible itself; and, besides, the Apocrypha was sham Bible and therefore must be rather wicked.

Miss Carmichael was the only so-called friend that Lady Arctura had. Miss Carmichael was a woman about twenty-six—a woman in all her wants like—alas!—too many Scottish girls, long before she was out of her teens. Self-sufficient, assured, with hardly shyness enough for modesty, a human flower cut and dried, an unpleasant specimen and by no means valuable from its scarcity. From her childhood she had had the ordering of all Lady Arctura's opinions; whatever Sophie Carmichael said, Lady Arctura never thought of questioning.

Lady Arctura was in herself a gentle creature who shrank from either giving or receiving a rough touch; but she had an inherited pride, by herself quite unrecognized as such, which made her capable both of hurting and of being hurt. Next to what she had been taught to consider the true doctrines of religion, she respected her own family, which in truth had no other claim to respect than that its little good and much evil had been done before the eyes of a large part of many generations. Hence she was born to think herself distinguished, and to imagine a claim for the acknowledgment of distinction upon all except those of greatly higher rank than her own. Yet she had a real instinct, not only for what was good in morals, but for what was good in literature as well. The keen conscience of the girl had made her very early turn herself toward the quarter where the sun ought to rise. Unhappily, she had not gone direct to the heavenly well—the very word of the Master himself. How could she? From very childhood her mind had been filled with traditional utterances concerning the divine character and the divine plans—the merest inventions of men far more desirous of understanding what they were required to understand than of doing what they were required to do.

The very sweetness of their nature forbids such to doubt the fitness of the claims of others. She had had a governess of the so-called orthodox type, a large proportion of whose teaching was of the worst kind of heresy, for it was lies against him who is light, and in whom is no darkness; her doctrines were so many smoked glasses held up between the mind of her pupil and the glory of the living God—such as she would have seen for herself in time had she gone to the only knowable truth concerning God, the face of Jesus Christ. Had she set herself to understand him, she would have neither believed these things nor taught them to her little pupil. Nor had she yet met with anyone to help her to cast aside the doctrines of men. Arctura's friend did nothing to lead her, nor could she have succeeded had she attempted it.

8

••••••••••••••••••••

Lessons

*A*ll this time, Donal never had seen the earl but once or twice at a distance. Lord Morven had never revealed any interest in, not to say anxiety, as to how Davie was getting on. Lady Arctura, on the other hand, had been full of a more serious anxiety concerning him. Heavily prejudiced against the tutor by what she had heard from her friend, she naturally dreaded his poisoning the mind of her cousin.

There was a small recess in the schoolroom, and in this Donal was one day sitting with a book while Davie was busy writing; it was past school hours, but the weather did not invite them out of doors and Donal had given Davie a poem to copy. Lady Arctura came into the room—as she had never done before since Donal came—and thinking he was alone, began to talk to the boy, supposing he was kept in for some fault. She spoke in a low tone, and Donal, busy with his book, did not for some time even realize that she was present; neither, when he did begin to hear her, did he suspect she fancied they were alone. But by degrees her voice grew louder, and presently these words reached him:

"You know, Davie dear, every sinner deserves God's wrath and curse, both in this life and that which is to come; and if it hadn't been that Jesus Christ gave himself to bear the punishment for us, God would send us all to the place of misery! It is only for Jesus' sake, not ours, that he pardons us."

She had not ceased when Donal rose in the wrath of love, and came out into the light like an avenging angel.

"Lady Arctura!" he said, "I dare not sit still and hear such false impressions given concerning God."

Lady Arctura started in dire dismay, but in virtue of her breed and her pride recovered herself almost immediately, and called anger to her aid. What right had he to address her? She had not spoken to him; he ought to have been silent. And he dared assert his atheistic heresies to her very face!

She drew herself up and said, "Mr. Grant, you forget yourself!"

"I'm very willing to do that, my lady," said Donal, "but I cannot forget the honor of my God. If you were a heathen woman, I might consider whether the hour was come for enlightening you further; but to hear one who has had the Bible in her hands from her childhood tell an impressionable young child that the God who made him does not really care about him without answering a word would be cowardly!"

"What do you know about these things? What gives you a right to speak?" questioned Lady Arctura.

"First," answered Donal, "I had a Christian mother who taught me to love nothing but the truth; and next, I have studied the Bible from my childhood; and best of all to give me a right to speak, I have tried to do what the Master tells me. And I set to my seal that God is true, and there is no unfairness or human theology in him. I love him with my whole heart, my lady."

Arctura tried to say she too loved him so, but her conscience interfered, and she could not.

"I don't say you don't love him," Donal went on, "but how you can and believe such things of him, I don't understand."

Before he finished the sentence Lady Arctura had turned and swept from the room, trembling from head to foot. She could not have told why she trembled. But she was no sooner out of the room than she called Davie to come to her. Davie looked up into Donal's face, mutely asking whether he should obey her.

"Go to her," said Donal. "I do not interfere between you and your cousin—only between her and her false notion of Jesus Christ's Father."

In less than a minute Davie came back, his eyes full of tears.

"Arkie says she is going to tell Papa you are not fit to be my tutor. Is it true, Mr. Grant, that you are a dangerous man? I never thought it—though I have wondered you should carry such a big knife."

Donal laughed.

"It was my grandfather's skene dhu," he said. "I mend my pens with it. But it is strange, Davie, that when anybody knows something other people don't know, they are so often angry with him, and think he wants to make them bad, when he wants to help them to be good."

"But cousin Arkie is good, Mr. Grant!"

"I am sure she is. But she does not know so much about God, as I do, or she would never say such things of him; we must talk about him more after this."

"No, no, please, Mr. Grant! We won't say a word about him, for Arkie says except you promise never to speak of God to me, she will tell Papa, and he will send you away."

"Davie," said Donal with solemnity, "I would not give you such a promise for the gift of this grand castle and all that is in it; no, I wouldn't to save your life and that of everybody here. But I'll tell you what," said Donal, with a sudden happy thought, "I will promise not to speak about God at any other time if she will promise to sit by when I do—say, once a week. Perhaps we shall do what he tells us all the better that we don't talk so much about him."

"Oh, thank you, Mr. Grant! I will tell her," cried Davie, jumping up greatly relieved. "Oh, thank you, Mr. Grant," he repeated. "I could not bear you to go away. And you won't say any naughty things, will you? For Arkie reads her Bible every day."

"So do I, Davie."

"Do you?" returned Davie. "I'll tell her that too, and then she will see she must have been mistaken."

Davie hurried to his cousin with Donal's suggestion. It threw her into no small perplexity—first from doubt as to the propriety of the thing proposed, next because of the awkwardness of it; then from a little fear, lest his specious tongue should lead herself into the bypaths of doubt, and to the castle of Giant Despair—at which indeed it was a gracious wonder she had not arrived before. What if she should be persuaded of things she could not honestly disbelieve, but which yet it was impossible to believe and be saved?

And what would Sophie say? Lady Arctura would have sped to her friend for counsel before giving any answer to the audacious proposal, but the young woman was just then away from home for a fortnight, and she must resolve on something before then.

Lady Arctura would not say no; but she did not say yes. And after waiting for a week without receiving any answer to his proposition, Donal said to Davie, "We shall have a lesson in the New Testament tomorrow; you had better mention it to your cousin."

The next morning Donal asked him if he had mentioned it. The boy said he had.

"What did she say, Davie?"

"She said nothing, only looked strange."

When the hour of noon was past and Lady Arctura had not appeared, Donal said, "Davie, we'll have our New Testament lesson out of doors; that is the best place for it."

"That is the best place," responded Davie, jumping up. "But you're not taking your book, Mr. Grant."

"Never mind; I will give you a lesson or two without book first. I have got it in my heart."

But just as they were leaving the room, there was Lady Arctura with Miss Carmichael approaching it.

"I understood," said Arctura, with the more haughtiness that she desired to show her position unshaken, "that you . . ."

Here she hesitated, and Miss Carmichael took up the word.

"— that you consented to our presence that we might form our own judgment on the nature of the religious instruction you give your pupil."

"I invited Lady Arctura to be present when I taught my pupil," said Donal.

"Then are you not going to give him a lesson?" said Arctura.

"As your ladyship made me no reply, and school hours were over, I concluded you were not coming."

"And you would not give the lesson without her ladyship?" said Miss Carmichael.

"Excuse me," returned Donal, "we were going to have it out of doors."

"But you had agreed not to give him any so-called religious instruction but in the presence of Lady Arctura."

"By no means. I only offered to give it in her presence if she chose.

There was no question of the lesson being given."

Miss Carmichael looked at Lady Arctura as if to say, "Is he speaking the truth?" Donal knew Miss Carmichael by sight, but had never spoken to her, and had indeed never before seen her face distinctly. The handsome, hard-featured woman was dressed according to that wave of the tide of fashion that had reached Auchars. It was an ugly fashion, but so far as taste was free to operate, that of Miss Carmichael showed itself good. She was said to be engaged to a professor of theology, and I think it very probable, but I do not believe she had ever in her life been in love with anybody but herself. She was a good theologian—so good that when she was near, you could not get within sight of God for her theology and herself together.

Donal did not at all relish her interference. He could not at first see how to meet the difficulty. Without saying what he would do, he put his hand on Davie's shoulder and walked toward the lawn and the ladies followed. He tried to forget their presence and be conscious only of that of his pupil and the Master of them both.

"Davie," he said, "how do you fancy the first lesson in the New Testament ought to begin?"

"At the beginning," answered Davie, who had by this time learned to answer a question directly.

"Well, there was one who said, 'I am the beginning and the end, the first and the last'; and who can there be to begin about but him? All the New Testament is about him. A great many years ago there appeared in the world men who said that a certain man had been their companion for some time and had just left them; that he was killed by cruel men, and buried by his friends; but, as he had told them before, he would lay in the grave only three days, and rise from it on the third; and after a good while, during which they saw him several times, went up into the sky, and disappeared. . . . It isn't a very likely story, is it?"

"No," replied Davie.

Here the two friends behind exchanged looks of horror. Neither spoke, but each leaned eagerly forward, fascinated in the expectation of yet worse to follow.

"But, Davie," Donal went on, "however unlikely it must have seemed to those who heard it, when you come to know the kind of man of whom they told it, you will see nothing could be more suitable than just what they said. And, Davie, I believe every word of it.

"For, Davie," continued his tutor, "the man said he was the Son of God, come down from his Father to see his brothers, his children, his Father's sheep, and take back home with him to his Father anyone who would go."

"Excuse me," here interrupted Miss Carmichael, with a knowing smile, "what he said was, that if any man believed in him, he should be saved."

"Run along, Davie," said Donal, "I will give you more of what he said in the next lesson."

Donal lifted his hat and would have gone toward the river. But Miss Carmichael, stepping forward, said: "Mr. Grant, I cannot let you go till you answer me one question: do you believe in the atonement?"

"I do," answered Donal.

"Favor me, then, with your views upon it," she said.

"Are you troubled in your mind on the subject?" asked Donal.

"Not in the least, thank God," she replied, with a slight curl of her lip.

"Then I see no occasion for giving you my views. Nothing is more distasteful to me than talking about holy things in a mere analytical fashion."

"But I insist."

Donal smiled.

"Of what consequence can my opinions be to you, ma'am? or why should you compel a confession of my faith?"

"As the friend of this family and the daughter of the clergyman of this parish, I have a right to know what your opinions are—not certainly for your own sake, but because you have a most important charge committed to you: a child for whose soul you will have to account."

"For that and all things else I am accountable only to one."

"To Lord Morven?"

"No."

"You are accountable to him for what you teach his child."

"I am not."

"What! he will turn you away at a moment's notice if he learns what cannot fail to displease him."

"Of course he can. I shall be quite ready to go—as ready as he to send me. If I were accountable to him, that should never be."

"I do not understand you."

"If I were accountable to him for what I teach, I should of course teach only what he pleased. But do you suppose I would take any situation on such a condition? God forbid!"

"It is nothing to me, or his lordship either, I presume, what you would or would not do."

"Then I can see no reason why you should detain me longer. Lady Arctura, I did not offer to give my lesson in the presence of any other than yourself. I will not do so again. You will be welcome, for you have a right to know what I am teaching him. If you bring another except it be my Lord Morven, I will take Davie to my own room."

With these words he left them and took no notice of a far from flattering remark of Miss Carmichael, uttered loud enough for him to hear as he went.

Lady Arctura was sorely bewildered. She could not but feel that her friend had not shown the better advantage, and that the behavior of Donal had been dignified. But surely he was very wrong ... what he said to Davie sounded so very different from what she heard in church, as well as from her helper, Miss Carmichael. It was a pity she had heard so little; he would have gone on if only Sophie had had patience and held her tongue. Perhaps he might have spoken better things if she had not interfered.

"I have heard,enough!" said Miss Carmichael. "I will speak to my father at once."

The next day Donal received from her a note to the following effect:

> Sir: In consequence of what I felt bound to report to my father of the conversation we had yesterday, he desires that you will call upon him at your earliest convenience. He is generally at home from three to five.
> Yours truly,
> Sophie Agnes Carmichael

To this Donal immediately replied:

> Madam: Notwithstanding the introduction I brought him from another clergyman, your father declined my acquaintance, passing me afterward as one unknown to him. From this fact, and from the nature of the report which your behavior to me yesterday enables me to suppose you must have carried to him, I can hardly mistake his object in wishing to see me. I will attend the call of no man to defend my opinions, and your father's I have heard almost every Sunday since I came to the castle. I have been from childhood familiar with them.
> Yours truly,
> Donal Grant

Not another word did he hear from either of them.

But Miss Carmichael impressed upon the mind of her friend that she ought to do what she could to protect her little cousin from the awful and all but inevitable consequences of his false teaching. If she was present when the tutor mistaught him, he might perhaps be prevented from speaking such wicked things as he otherwise would. Lady Arctura might even have some influence, if she would but take courage to reason with the man and show him where he was wrong. Upon the next occasion, therefore, she appeared in the schoolroom at the hour appointed, and with a cold bow, took the chair Donal placed for her.

"Now, Davie," said Donal, "what was it I told you last time?"

Davie, who had never thought about it since, for the lesson had been broken off before Donal could bring it to its natural fruit, thought back, and said:

"That Jesus Christ rose from the dead."

"What did he die for? Do you know?"

Here Davie had a good answer, though a cut and dried one: "To take away our sins," he said.

"What are sins, Davie?"

"Bad things, sir."

"Yes; the bad things we think, and the bad things we feel, and the bad things we do. Have you any sins, Davie?"

"Yes, I am very wicked."

"How do you know that?"

"Arkie told me."

"What is being wicked?"

"Doing bad things."

"What bad things do you do?"

"I don't know, sir."

"Then you don't know you are wicked; you only know that Arkie told you so."

Lady Arctura drew herself up, indignant at his familiar use of her name; but Donal was too intent to perceive the offense he had given.

"I will tell you," Donal went on, "something you did wicked today." Davie grew rosy red. "I saw you pull the little pup's ears till he screamed out. Was that a thing that Jesus would have done when he was a little boy?"

"No, sir."

"Why?"

"Because it would have been wrong."

"I suspect, rather, it was because he would have loved the little pup. He didn't have to think about its being wrong. He loves every kind of living thing; and he wants to take away your sin because he loves you— not merely to make you not cruel to the little pup, but to make you love every living creature. Ah, Davie, you cannot do without Jesus, and neither can I. I should be the most contemptible creature, knowing him as I do, not to love him with all the heart I shall have one day when he has done making me!"

"Is God making you yet, Mr. Grant? I thought you were a grown-up man."

"Well, I don't think he will make me any taller," smiled Donal; "but what is inside me, the thing I love you with, and the thing I think about God with, the thing I read the Bible with—that thing God keeps on making bigger and bigger. I do not know where it will stop, but I know where it will not stop. That thing is me, and God will keep on making it bigger to all eternity, though he has not even got me into right shape yet."

"Why is he so long about it?"

"I don't think he is long about it; I know he could do it quicker if I were as good as by this time I ought to have been. . . . The lesson's done, Davie," said Donal as he rose and went, leaving the boy with his cousin.

The tears were rolling down Arctura's face without her being aware of it; for she was saying to herself, "He is a well-meaning man, but dreadfully mistaken; the Bible says believe, not obey!" The poor girl, though she read her Bible regularly, was so blinded by the dust and ashes of her teaching that she knew very little of what was actually in it. Obedience is the road to all things. It is the only way to grow able to trust him. Love and faith and obedience are sides of the same prism.

Regularly after that, Lady Arctura came to the lesson—always intending to object as soon as the lesson was over. But always before the end came, Donal had said something that went so to her heart that she could say nothing. As if she too had been a pupil, as indeed she was far more than either knew, she would rise when Davie rose, and go away with him. But then she would go alone into the garden, or to her own room, where sometimes she would find herself wishing the things Donal said were true.

9

•••••••••••••••••••••

Two Plots

$\mathcal{D}$onal made more and more of a companion of Davie, and such was the relationship between them that he would sometimes have him in his room even when he was writing. And when he thought it time to begin to lay in his fuel supply for the winter, to whom but Davie need he apply to help him?

"Up in this tower, Davie," he said, "it would be impossible for me to work without a good fire, when the nights are long and the darkness like solid cold. Mr. Simmons says I may have as much coal and wood as I like; will you help me carry it up?"

Davie sprang to his feet as if he would begin that very minute.

"I shall never be able to learn my lessons if I am cold," said Donal, who found he could not now bear a low temperature as well as when he was always in the open air.

"Do you learn lessons, Mr. Grant?"

"Yes, indeed, I do," replied Donal. "For I have found that one great help to the understanding of the best things is the brooding over the words of them as a hen broods over her eggs."

They began to carry up the fuel together, Donal taking the coals and Davie the wood. But Donal got weary of the time it took, and set out to find a quicker way. With this in view, next Saturday afternoon he walked to a small fishing village, the nearest on the coast, about three miles off. There he succeeded in hiring a spare boat-spar, with a block and a quantity of rope, which he carried home, not without some labor. The spar he ran out through a notch of the battlement over the parapet of the roof, near the sheds the butler had shown him, and having stayed it well back to one of the chimneys, put his rope through the block at the peak of it and lowered it with a hook at the end. A moment of Davie's help below, and a bucket filled with coals was on its way up. They spent thus an hour of a good many of the cool evenings of autumn, and Davie enjoyed it immensely; and when at length he saw the heap on the roof, he was greatly impressed with how much could be done by a little at a time. Then Donal told him that if he worked well through the week, every Saturday evening he should spend an hour with him in his room, when they would do something together.

After his first visit to the village, Donal went again and again, for he had made the acquaintance of some of the people and liked them. Amongst them, however, was one who had seemed rather to keep aloof from him as he had tried to draw him into conversation. But one day as he was walking home again, this man overtook him and, saying he was going in his direction, thus tacitly offered his company. He lounged along by the side of Donal with his hands in his pockets, as if he did not care to walk, yet got over the ground as fast as Donal, who with yet some remnant of the peasant's stride covered the road as if he meant walking. But after their greetings a great silence fell between them, which lasted till the journey was halfway over. Then the fisherman spoke.

"There's a lass at your hoose, sir," he said, "they ca' Eppie Comin."

"There is," answered Donal.

"Do you know the lass, sir—to speak to her, I mean?"

"Surely," replied Donal. "I know her grandfather and grandmother well."

"Decent fowk they are!" said the lad.

"They are that!" responded Donal. "As good people as I know."

"Would you like to do them a good turn?" asked the fisherman.

"Indeed I would."

"Well it's just this, sir. I have strong doubts whether it's going well with the lass at the castle."

As he spoke he turned away his head, and spoke in such a low, muffled voice that Donal could but just make out what he said.

"You must be a little plainer if you would have me do anything," returned Donal.

"I'll be plain enough with you, sir," said the man. "You should know that I've had a fancy for the lass for a long time. Her and me's been courting now for two years and were getting along fine till this last spring, when all at once she turned highty-tighty like. And not once could I get her to say what it was that had changed. I couldn't think what had come over her. But at last I discovered—and I won't say how—that she was holding company with another, and who but the young lord of the castle yonder. She's taken up with him, they tell me, and can think of nothing but him, and I'm afraid for the lassie."

"Why afraid?" asked Donal.

"Even though after all this there could never be anything more between us, still, it's for her I'm worried, not my own sake. He doesn't mean fair by her. He's telling her things, but I believe he has no intention of marrying her."

"The charge is a serious one," said Donal. "Why are you telling me this?"

"Because I look to you to get me word of the man."

"That you may wring his neck? You should not have told me so much. If you were to wring his neck, I should be part in the murder."

"Would you have me let the lassie get hurt without doing anything?" asked the fisherman.

"By no means. I would do something myself, now I know of it, whoever the girl was. And it happens she is the granddaughter of my best friends."

"Sir, you won't fail me?"

"I tell you, I will try to help somehow. But I will not do as you ask me. You might spoil everything. I'll turn the thing over in my mind. I promise you I will do something—what, I cannot yet say. You had better go home, and I will come to you tomorrow."

They walked on again in gloomy silence for some minutes. Suddenly the fisherman held out his hand to Donal, grasped his with a convulsive energy, turned, and without another word went back.

Donal had to think. What could he do? What ought he to attempt? From what he had seen of the young lord, he could not believe he intended any wrong to the girl; he might be selfishly amusing himself and was hardly one to reflect that the least idle familiarity with her was wrong. The thing, if there was the least truth in it, must be put a stop to at once. But it might be all a fancy of the justly jealous lover, to whom the girl had not of late been behaving as she ought. True or not, there was danger to the girl either way. The readiest and simplest thing, of course—go to the youth himself, tell him what he had heard, and ask him if there was any ground for it. Whether there was or not, would it not be better to find the girl another place? In any case, distance must be put between them. He would tell her grandparents as soon as possible; but he feared they had no very great influence with her.

Donal was still in meditation when he reached home, and still undecided as to what he should do. He was crossing a small court when he saw the housekeeper making signs to him from the window of her room. He turned and went to her. It was of Eppie she wanted to speak to him.

"It's a queer thing," she began, "for an old woman like me"—she was not much over forty—"to come to a young gentleman like yourself with such a talk. But I might as well tell you the whole story."

Here Mrs. Brooks paused for a time. She was a florid, plump, good-looking woman, with thick auburn hair—one of those women who is in soul as well as body always to the discomfiture of wrong and the healing of strifes. Left a young widow, she had refused many offers, for she thought she had done all that was required of her in the way of marriage. The moment she sat down, smoothing her apron on her lap, and looked one in the face with clear blue eyes, he must have been either a suspicious or an unfortunate man who would not trust her. She would put her hands to anything to show a young servant how a thing ought to be done, or to relieve anyone from cook to housemaid who was ill or had a holiday. Donal had taken to her, as like do to like. He did not now hurry her, but waited.

"I was out in the yard to look after my hens about dusk last night and I saw the door to the barn left open. As I crept closer, what should I hear but quiet laughing and whispering. Well, I stood there and listened—but eh, sir, give a peek out the door there and see if there's anyone there listening; I wouldn't trust that gowk Eppie a hair! She's as sly as a snake.—Nobody there? Well, close the door and I'll go on with my tale. I stood and listened, as I said, but I couldn't make out a thing 'cause they were both talking their quietest. So I crept inside slowly to see if I could see anything, for that was the next closest road to the truth in the matter.

"Now there was a great heap of straw in one corner and there sat the two of them. Well when he saw me, up sprang my lord as if he had been caught stealing—as maybe he was, maybe he wasn't; I couldn't tell. Eppie would have hidden where she was or crept out behind my back, but I was by then able to see clearly enough even in the darkness and I said, 'No, no, my lass! Don't go out that way.' 'Oh, Mrs. Brooks,' said my lord, too civil, 'don't be too hard on her.' And I said, 'My lord, you ought to know better.' And then to them both I said, 'Now go your ways—but not together. Go up to your own room, Eppie,' I said, 'and if I don't see you there when I come in, it's straight to your grandmother I'll go this very night.'

"Eppie, she went, and my lord just stood there glaring at me. I turned on him and said, 'I won't ask what you mean, my lord, but you know well enough what it looks like, and I would never have expected it from you!' He began to stammer and begged me to believe there was no mischief between the two of them and that he wouldn't harm the lassie to save his life, and in a way I couldn't in my heart but pity them both—they were such children, doubtless drawn together without thought of evil but each by the other's pretty face, naturally enough. So as he beseeched me, I foolishly promised not to tell his father if he on his side would promise to have nothing more to do with Eppie. And that he did. But I still don't think the thing can be left this way, for if ill was to come of it, then where would we be?"

"I will speak to him," said Donal, "and see what humor he is in. That may help to clear up what we ought to do. It's always best to do nothing but the best."

After a question or two more, Donal went to go to his room. But he had not reached the top of the stair when he realized he must speak to Lord Forgue at once. He turned and went down again, straight to the room where the brothers generally sat together.

When he reached the room, only Davie was there, poring over a worn folio. Donal asked him if he knew where his brother was. He answered that he went out a little while before, and would not let him go with him. Donal hurried down to Mrs. Brooks.

"Do you know where Eppie is?" he asked.

"Is she not in the house? . . . I will go and see."

She returned in no small perturbation.

Donal at once made up his mind to look for her at the cobbler's.

The night was pretty dark, but the moon would be up by and by. He walked rapidly to the town, but saw no one on the way. When he reached the cobbler's house, he found him working as usual. The couple was wondering a little that young Eppie had not made her appearance. Donal was very uneasy, not knowing where to seek her, yet restless to protect her, when he heard a light, hurried foot on the stair. "Here she comes at last!" said her grandmother, and she entered with the look of one who had been running. She said she could not get away so easily now.

Said Donal to himself, "If you have begun to lie, things are going very ill with you!" but he did not say that he had left the house after her.

After sitting a few minutes, she rose suddenly, saying she must go, for she was wanted at home. Donal rose also and said, as the night was dark, and the moon not yet up, it would be as well if they went together. At this her face flushed, and she began to murmur an objection. She had to go into the town first, to get something she wanted. Donal said he was in no hurry and would go with her. She cast an inquiring, almost suspicious look upon her grandparents, but made no further objection, and they went out together.

They walked to a shop and went in together. Eppie bought one or two little things of the sort men call finery, because they do not wear such themselves, and then looked timidly at Donal—either to indicate that she was ready to go, or to inquire what mood he was in toward her—perhaps whether there was any chance of her being able to get rid of him. Leaving the shop, they walked back the way they had come, little thinking, either of them, that their every step was dogged. Kennedy the fisherman, although firm in his promise not to go near the castle, could not remain quietly at home but, knowing it was Eppie's day for visiting her folk, had gone to the town, and was lingering about in the hope of seeing her. He was not naturally suspicious: justifiable jealousy had rendered him such. And when he saw the two together, he began to ask whether Donal's anxiety to keep him from encountering Lord Forgue might not be due to other grounds from those given or implied. So he followed, careful they should not see him, lest so he should shut the door of knowledge against himself.

When they came to the baker's shop, Eppie, in a voice that in vain sought to be steady, asked Donal if he would be so good as wait for her in the street a moment while she went in to speak to Lucy Leper, the baker's daughter. Donal made no difficulty, and she went in, leaving the door open as she found it.

A pleasant smell of bread came from inside, and did what it could to entertain Donal as he waited in the deserted street. While he stood no one entered or came out.

"Eppie's holding a long talk with Lucy Leper!" he said to himself, but waited without impatience a long time longer. He began at length to fear she must have been taken ill, or have found something wrong in the house that required her help. When more than half an hour was gone, he thought it time to go into the shop to make inquiry.

No one inside had seen anything of Eppie. Donal saw he had been tricked and turned with apology to go.

When he opened the door, there came through the house from behind a blast of cold wind, which enabled him at once to understand: there must be an open outer door in that direction. Seeing no one, the girl had slipped through the house and out again by the back door, leaving her troublesome squire to cool himself with vain expectancy in the street.

Donal made haste to the road home.

But she had tried the trick once too often, for on a similar occasion she had served her fisherman in like fashion. Still following them, and seeing her go into the baker's, Kennedy conjectured at once her purpose and, hurrying to the other exit, saw her come out the court and again followed her.

As Donal hastened homeward, the moon rose. It was a lovely night. Absorbed in the beauty of it, he trudged on. Suddenly he stopped. Was it sounds of lamentation he heard on the road before him? He could see no one. At the next turn, however, and in the loneliest part of the way, was lying something dark, like the form of a man. He ran to it. A pale, death-like face looked up. . . . It was that of Lord Forgue—and without breath or motion! There was a cut in his head, from which the pool had flowed. Donal examined him anxiously. The wound had stopped bleeding. What was he to do? There was but one thing. He drew the helpless form to the side of the road and, leaning it up against the earth-dyke, sat down on the road before it, and so managed to get it upon his back and rise with it. If he could but get him home unseen, much scandal might be avoided. He got on very well with him on the level road, but, strong as he was, he did not find it an easy task, so laden, to climb the steep approach to the castle, and had little breath left when he reached it.

He carried him straight to the housekeeper's room. It was not yet more than half past ten o'clock; and though the servants were mostly in bed, Mrs. Brooks was still moving about. He laid his burden on her sofa, and hastened to find her.

Like a sensible woman, she kept her horror and dismay to herself, and expressed them only in haste to help. She got some brandy, and they managed to make him swallow a little, and then he began to recover. They bathed his wound, and did for it what they could, then carried him to his own room, and got him to bed. Donal sat down beside him, and stayed there. He was restless all the night, but toward morning fell into a sound sleep, and was still asleep when the housekeeper came to relieve his attendant.

Then first Donal heard of Eppie. As soon as Mrs. Brooks left him with his patient, she went to Eppie's room and found her in bed, pretending to be asleep, and had left her undisturbed, thinking she would come easier at the truth if she took her unprepared to lie. It came out afterwards that she was not so heartless as she seemed. She found Lord Forgue waiting her upon the road, as she had expected. A few minutes after, Kennedy came up to them. Forgue told her to run home at once and not to say a word; he would soon settle matters with the fellow. She went off like a hare, and till she was out of sight, the two men stood looking at each other. Kennedy was a powerful man, and Forgue but a stripling; the latter trusted, however, to his skill, and did not fear his adversary. What passed between them Donal never heard. Forgue did not even know who his antagonist was.

The next day he seemed in no danger, and his attendants agreed that nothing should yet be said about the matter. It was given out that his lordship would be confined to his room for a few days, but nothing was said in explanation.

The next day, in the afternoon, Donal went to see if he could fall in with Kennedy, loitered a while about the village, and made several inquiries after him; but no one had seen him.

His lordship recovered as rapidly as could have been expected. Davie was sorely troubled that he was not allowed to go and see him, but Donal did not wish it yet, for he would have been full of question and remark and speculation.

10

•••••••••••••••••••

An Altercation

At length one evening, Donal knocked at the door of Forgue's room and went in. He was seated in an easy chair before a blazing fire, looking very comfortable, and showing in his habitually pale face no sign of a disturbed conscience.

"My lord," said Donal, "you will hardly be surprised to find I have something to talk to you about."

His lordship made him no answer—only looked silent in his face. Donal went on.

"I want to speak to you about Eppie Comin."

Forgue's face flamed up.

"Mr. Grant," he said, "I should have thought it hardly necessary to remind you that, although I have availed myself of your superiority in some branches of study, I am not your pupil, and you have no authority over me."

"The reminder is perfectly unnecessary, my lord," answered Donal. "I am not your tutor, but I am the friend of Andrew Comin and his wife, and therefore, so far as may be, of Eppie."

His lordship drew himself up yet more erect in his chair, and there was now a sneer on his face. But Donal did not wait for him to speak.

"Don't imagine, my lord," he continued, "that I am presuming on the fact I had the good fortune to come up in time to take you on my back and carry you home; that I should have done for your lordship's stable-boy had I found him in similar plight. But just as I interfered for you then, I am bound to interfere for Eppie now. Not that she is in worse danger than you, for the danger of doing a mean and wicked action is a far worse danger than that of suffering it, whatever be the consequences."

"You insolent . . ." the young man swore, leaping to his feet. "What right have you to speak so to me? Do you think because you are going to be a parson, you may make a congregation of me, whether I please or not?"

"I have not the slightest intention of being a parson," returned Donal quietly, "but I do hope to be an honest man—which your lordship is in great danger of ceasing to be."

"Get out of my room!" cried Forgue, swearing again.

Donal took a seat opposite him.

"Then, by heaven! if you do not . . . I . . . I will!" shouted Forgue.

He rose and was moving toward the door; but before he reached it, Donal was standing with his back against it. He locked it and took out the key. Glaring at him, the youth could not speak for fury. He turned and caught up a chair. To think of a clodhopper interfering between him and any girl! He must be in love with her himself! Forgue rushed at Donal with the chair. One twist of Donal's ploughman hand wrenched it from him. He threw it over the youth's head upon the bed, and stood motionless and silent, waiting till the first of his lordship's rage should subside. In a few minutes he saw his eye begin to quail. Forgue went back to his chair.

"Now, my lord," said Donal, following his example and sitting down, "will you hear me?"

"I'll be damned if I do!" he answered, flaring up again at the first sound of Donal's voice.

"I'm afraid you'll be damned if you don't," returned Donal. "I am come to warn your lordship. Do you not know the course you are pursuing is a dishonorable one?"

"I ought to know what I am about better than you."

"Perhaps so; but I doubt it. I should scorn to behave to a woman as you are doing now."

"What do you imagine I am doing now?"

"There is no imagination in this—that you are behaving to a young woman as no man ought except he meant to marry her if she would have him."

"How do you know I do not mean to marry her?"

"Do you mean to marry her?"

"What right have you to ask?"

"For my own sake if for no other; I live under the same roof with you both."

"I never told her I would marry her."

"I never supposed you had."

"Well, what then?"

"I repeat, such attentions as yours must naturally be supposed by any innocent girl to mean marriage."

"What if she is not such an innocent girl as you would have her?"

"My lord, you are a scoundrel."

"A scoundrel!"

"I used the word, my lord."

For a moment it seemed as if the youth would break out into a fresh fury; but a moment and he laughed instead—not a nice laugh.

"Come now," he said. "There is nothing between me and the girl—nothing whatever, I give you my word, except an innocent flirtation. Ask herself."

"My lord," said Donal, "I believe what you mean me to understand; it is just what I supposed. I thought nothing worse of it myself."

"Then why the devil do you kick up such an infernal shindy about it?"

"For these reasons, my lord—"

"Oh, come! don't be long-winded."

"You must hear me."

"Go on; I'm submissive."

"I will suppose she does not imagine you mean anything you would call serious with her."

"She can't."

"Why not?"

"She's not a fool, and she can't imagine me such a blazing idiot!"

"But may she not suppose you love her?"

He tried to laugh.

"You have never told her so?—never said or done anything to make her think so?"

"Oh, well! she may say so to herself—after a sort of fashion."

"Is she likely to call it love of such sort herself? Would she speak to you again if she heard you talking so of the love you give her?"

"You know as well as I do the word has many meanings."

"And which is she likely to take—that which is confessedly false and worth nothing?"

"She may drop it when she pleases."

"Doubtless. But in the meantime, will she not take your words of love for far more than they are worth?"

"She says she knows I will soon forget her."

"She might say to herself all the contemptuous things you have now said of your relation to her, but would that keep her from being so in love with you as to cause her misery? You don't know what the consequences may be of her loving you with a love awakened by yours but infinitely stronger."

"Oh, women don't die nowadays for love," said his lordship, feeling a little flattered.

"It would be well if some of them did! for they never get over it. But she may live to hate the thought of the man that led her to think he loved her, and so taught her to believe in nobody."

"She has her share in the amusement, and I take my share, by Jove, in the danger! She's a very pretty, sweet, clever, engaging girl," said Forgue with a flare.

"What you say only shows the more danger to her. You must have behaved to her so much the more like a genuine lover. For your so-called danger, my lord, I cannot say I have much sympathy. Any suffering you may have will hardly persuade you to the only honorable escape."

"By Jove," cried Forgue, "you don't dream of getting me to marry the girl! That's coming on rather strong with your friendship for the cobbler!"

"No, my lord; if things are as you have said, I have no such desire. I will let your father know when circumstances drive me so far as that. What I do want is to put a stop to the whole affair. To make overtures of love to a girl in any such fashion is a mean thing, and it has already brought on you some of the chastisement it deserves."

His lordship started to his feet in a fresh access of rage. "You dare tell me to my face that I had a thrashing!"

"Most assuredly, my lord. The fact stands just so."

"I gave him as good as he gave me."

"That is nothing to the point—though from the state I found you in, I can hardly believe it. Pardon me, I do not mean you behaved like what you call a coward, or took your punishment without defending yourself."

Lord Forgue was almost crying with rage. "I have not—not done with him yet!" he stammered. "Tell me who the rascal is, and if I don't make of him what he made of me, may—"

"Stop, stop, my lord. All that is entirely useless. I will not tell you who the man is. However little I may approve of his way of settling differences, and I speak with some authority; having received blows from you without returning them, I so strongly feel he gave you no more than you deserved that I will take no step whatever to have the man punished for it."

"We shall see! You make yourself art and part with him!"

Donal held his peace.

"You will not tell me the villain's name?"

"No."

"Then I will find it out and kill him."

"That he may do first. He threatened to kill you. I will do what I can to prevent it. Shall I inform the police? Would you have the whole affair come out?"

"I will kill him," repeated Forgue through his clenched teeth. "Leave the room."

"When you have given me your word that you will not speak again to Eppie Comin."

"I will not give you any such word." His lordship said this more from perversity than intent, for he had begun to wish himself clear of the affair—only how was he to give in to this unbearable clown!

"Then she will be sent away. I will give you till tomorrow to think of it," said Donal, and opened the door.

"Oh, go along with your preaching!" said Forgue testily, and Donal went.

In the meantime Eppie had soundly been taken to task by Mrs. Brooks and told that if once she spoke a word to Lord Forgue, that very day she should have her dismissal. Then she assured Donal that she would not let the foolish girl out of her sight, whereupon Donal thought it better to give Lord Forgue another day to make up his mind.

On the second morning Forgue came to the schoolroom just as lessons were over, and said frankly: "I've made a fool of myself, Mr. Grant.

Make what excuse for me you can. I am sorry for my thoughtless behavior. Believe me, I meant no harm. I have quite made up my mind there shall be nothing more between us."

"You'll not speak to her again?"

"It might be difficult . . . but I will do my best—except where it might be awkward."

Donal was not quite satisfied, but thought it best to leave it so. Forgue seemed entirely in earnest.

For a time Donal remained in doubt whether he should mention the thing to Eppie's grandparents. But after reflection, realized he owed it to them on the basis of their friendship.

That same night he went to see them.

As Donal was returning home later in the dark of a clouded moonlight, just as he reached the place where he had found Lord Forgue, he saw the figure of a man apparently waiting for someone. He put himself a little on his guard and went on. It was Kennedy. When he knew Donal, he came up to him in a hesitating way, revealing, as it seemed to Donal, some shame even in the way his legs moved, though his walk was still the fisherman's slouch.

"Kennedy," said Donal, for the other seemed to wait for him to speak first, "you may thank God you are not now hiding from the police."

Kennedy was silent.

"Well," said Donal, "it may be some comfort to you to know that, for the present at least, and I hope for altogether, the thing is put a stop to. The housekeeper at the castle knows about it, and we will both do our best. Her grandparents know too. She and Lord Forgue have both promised there shall be no more of it. And I do believe, Kennedy, there has been nothing more than great silliness on either side. I hope, whatever turns up, you will not forget yourself again."

Kennedy promised to govern himself, and they parted friends.

11

•••••••••••••••••••

The Legend

*T*he days went on and Donal saw next to nothing of the earl. Thrice he had met him on his way to or from the walled garden in which he took what little exercise he ever did take; on one of those occasions his lordship had spoken to him very courteously, on another had scarcely noticed him, and on the third passed him without the smallest recognition. Donal, who with equal mind took everything as it came, did not trouble himself about the matter.

Lord Forgue's ardor after mathematics and Greek, such as it had been, was now so much abated that he no longer sought the superior scholarship of Donal. Of Lady Arctura Donal saw as little as ever, and of Miss Carmichael, happily, nothing at all. But it pained him to see Lady Arctura, as often as he chanced to pass her about the place, looking so far from peaceful.

The autumn passed, and the winter was at hand. Davie was looking forward to skating, and in particular to the pleasure he was going to have in teaching Mr. Grant, who had never done any.

Donal continued to visit the Comins often and found continued comfort and help in their friendship, while the letters he received from home, especially those from his friend, Sir Gibbie, who not unfrequently wrote for Donal's father and mother, were a great nourishment to him.

As the cold and the nighttime grew, the water level rose in the well of Donal's soul, and the poetry began to flow. Up in his aerie he led a keener life, breathed the breath of a more genuine existence than the rest of the house. No doubt the old cobbler, seated over a mouldy shoe, breathed a yet higher air than Donal weaving his verse or reading grand old Greek in his tower; but Donal was on the same path—that of his divine destiny.

One afternoon when the last of the leaves had fallen, Donal, seated before a great fire of coal and logs, turned to his table and began to write. While he was writing the wind had risen. It was now blowing a gale. He rose to light his lamp and looked out of the window. He heard the wind and saw the clouds sweeping before it. A strange feeling came over him in his reverie, and he was suddenly all ears to listen. Again . . . yes! it was the same sound which had sent him that first night wandering through the house in fruitless quest. It came in two or three fitful chords that melted into each other. He went to the door, opened it and listened. A cold wind came rushing up the stair. He heard nothing. He stepped out on the stair, shut his door, and listened. It came again—a strange unearthly sound. If ever disembodied sound went wandering in the wind, just such a sound must it be. Almost immediately it ceased—then once more came again, but apparently from far off, dying away on the distant waves of the billowy air out of whose wandering bosom it seemed to issue. It was as the wailing of a summer wind, caught and swept along in a tempest from the frozen north.

The moment he ceased to expect it anymore, he began to think whether it must not have come from the house after all. He stole down the stair. What he would do he did not know. He could not go following an airy nothing all over the house, a great part of which he as yet knew nothing. And there were whole suites of rooms into which, except the earl and Lady Arctura were to leave home for a while, he could not hope to enter.

Later that evening, when he had returned to his room after tea and was sitting again at work, now reading and meditating, he became aware of another sound—one most unusual to his ears, that of the steps of someone coming up the stair—heavy steps, not such as of one accustomed to running up and down on ordinary service. He waited, listening. The steps came nearer and nearer and stopped at his door. A hand fumbled about it and found the latch, lifted it and entered. To Donal's surprise, and something to his dismay, it was the earl. The dismay was from his appearance. He was deadly pale, and his eyes more like those of a corpse than of a man moving about among his living fellows. Donal started to his feet. The earl turned his head toward him; but in his look there was no atom of recognition, not as much as amounted to an acknowledgment of his presence. He turned away immediately, went to the window, and there stood much as Donal had stood a little while before, looking out, but with the attitude of one listening rather than one trying to see. There was indeed nothing now but the blackness to be seen—nor anything to be heard but the roaring of the wind. The time to Donal seemed long; it was but about five minutes. As he stood looking at the earl, once more came a musical cry out of the darkness. Immediately came from the earl what seemed a response—a soft, low murmur, by degrees becoming audible, in the tone of a man meditating aloud. From his words he seemed to be still hearing the sounds aerial, though they came no more to the ears of Donal.

"Hark the notes! Clear as a flute! Full and downy as a violin! They are colors! They are flowers! They are alive! I can see them as they grow, as they blow! Those are primroses! Those are pimpernels!"

Then he turned, and with a somewhat quickened step, left the room, hastily shutting the door behind him, as if to keep back the creature of his vision.

Strong-hearted and strong-brained, Donal had yet stood absorbed as if he too were out of the body. He paused a moment helpless, then pulled himself together and tried to think. His first impulse was to follow; a man in such a condition, whatever was the condition, was surely not one to be left to go whither he would among the heights and depths of the castle, where he might break his neck any moment. Interference no doubt was dangerous, but he would follow him at least a little way. He heard the steps going down the stair before him, and made haste after him. But before the earl could have reached the bottom of the stair, the sound of his descending steps ceased; and Donal knew he must have left it by one of the doors opening on other floors. He returned to his room.

Donal would gladly have told his friend the cobbler all about the strange occurrence, but he did not feel sure it would be right to carry from it a report of the house where he held a position of trust. He resolved, therefore, to seek an opportunity to speak with Mrs. Brooks, if not actually to reveal to her all that had taken place—at least to see if anything could be drawn from her by planting several judicious suggestions in her ear. He had now been at the castle long enough, he thought, to have a right to know some of what the domestics said of the old palace, even if the stories thus gained were not always accurate history. He was sure they must have also heard the strange music and was curious to know their conclusions on the matter.

One evening, therefore, he visited her in the kitchen, engaged her in conversation and asked about the castle.

"There are tales about it, you know, Mr. Grant."

"I'd like to hear, if you have the time," said Donal.

"Whether it belongs to this castle by right I cannot tell, but as I have heard it attributed to another, I daresay it is widespread and you have heard it before. It is this: During the earldom of a certain recklessly wicked man, who not only oppressed his poor neighbors but actually went so far as to break the Sabbath and behave as wickedly on that as on any other day of the week, a company was seated late on Saturday night, playing cards, and drinking, and talking. And all the time Sunday was drawing nearer and nearer, and nobody heeded. At length one of them, seeing the hands of the clock at a quarter to twelve, made the remark that it was time to stop. He did not mention the sacred day, but all knew what he meant. Thereupon the earl laughed, and told him that if he was afraid of the kirk-session, he might go and another would take his hand. But the man sat still, and said no more till the clock gave the warning to the hour. Then he spoke again, and said it was almost the Sabbath day, and they ought not to go on playing. As he said it his mouth was pulled up on one side. But the earl struck his fist on the table, and swore a great oath that if any man rose he would run him through.

" 'What care I for the Sabbath!' he said. 'I gave you your chance to go,' he added, turning to the man who had spoken—he was dressed in black like a minister—'and you would not take it; now you shall sit where you are.' He glared fiercely at the man, and the man returned his gaze with an equally fiery stare. And now the company first began to discover what perhaps through the fumes of the whiskey and the smoke of the pine-torches they had not observed before, that none of them knew the man; not one of them had ever seen him before. And they looked at him and could not turn their eyes from him, and a cold terror began to creep through their vitals. But the stranger kept his fierce, scornful look fixed on the earl, and spoke: 'And I have given you your chance,' he said, 'and you would not take it; now you shall sit still where you are, and no Sabbath shall you ever see.' That moment the clock began to strike, and the man's mouth came straight again. But when the hammer had struck six times, it struck no more, and the clock stopped. 'This day twelvemonth,' said the man, 'you shall see me again, and once the same time every year till your time is up—and I hope you will enjoy your game!' The earl would have sprung to his feet, but could not, and the man was nowhere to be seen. He had vanished, taking with him both door and windows of the room— not as Samson carried off the gates of Gaza, however, for he left not the least sign of where they had been. And from that day to this no one has been able to find the room; and there the wicked earl and his companions to this day sit playing with the same pack of cards and waiting their doom. Some have said that on that same day of the year—only, unfortunately, testimony differs as to the day—shouts of drunken laughter may be heard issuing from somewhere in the castle; but as to whence they come, none can ever agree as to the direction even from which they come. . . . That is the story."

"And a very good one too!" approved Donal. "I wonder what the ground of it is? Small enough foundation is wanted for such. It must have had its beginning as well as every true story."

Donal thought it prudent not to tell her what had happened to him just yet, and after a few more minutes of pleasant talk, thanked her for the story, bade her good-night, and retired to his room.

12
. . . .

Dinner With the Earl

The winter came at last in good earnest—first black frost, then white snow, then sleet and wind and rain; then it went back to snow again, which fell steady and calm and lay thick. Next came hard frosts that brought Davie plenty of skating and the delight of teaching his master. Donal had many falls but was soon, partly in virtue of those same falls, a very decent skater. Davie claimed all the merit of the successful training; and when his master did anything particularly well, Davie would immediately remark with pride that it was he who had taught him to skate.

But Donal was not all the day with Davie, and lately had begun to feel a little anxious about the time the boy spent away from him—partly with his brother, partly with the people about the stable, and partly with his father. Concerning his time with his father, Donal, after what he had seen and heard, was more than concerned about the latter but felt it a very delicate thing to ask Davie any questions on the subject. At length, however, Davie himself began to open up on the matter.

"Mr. Grant," said he one day, "I wish you could hear the grand fairy stories Papa tells!"

"I wish I might," answered Donal.

"I will ask him to let you come and hear. I have told him that you make fairy tales, too; only he has another way of doing it, quite; and I must confess," added Davie, "that I do not follow him so easily as you. Sometimes he talks about Mama, I think, but so strangely that I cannot be sure whether it is not a part of the fairy tale—and sometimes the stories are so terrible that I beg him to stop."

"And does he stop?"

"Well . . . no—I don't think he ever does. When a story is once begun, I suppose it ought to be finished. . . ."

Donal did not reply, but could not help thinking there were stories it was better to cut short the telling of as soon as begun.

So the matter rested for the time, and nothing more was heard of it. But about a week after, Donal one morning received through the butler an invitation to dine with the earl. He concluded that this was due to Davie, and expected to find him with his father. He put on his best clothes and followed the butler up the grand staircase. All the great rooms of the castle were on the first floor, but he passed the entrance to them, following his guide up and up, winding and winding, to the second floor, where the earl had his own apartment. Here he was shown into a comparatively small room, richly furnished after a somberly ornate fashion, but the drapery and coverings much faded and worn even to considerable shabbiness. It had been for a century or so in use as the private sitting room of the lady of the castle, and was now used, perhaps in memory of his wife, by the master of the house. Here he received his sons, and now Donal. The room in which Donal first saw him was a story-and-a-half lower; there he received those who came to him on such business as he was compelled to pay or seem to pay attention to.

There was no one in the room when Donal entered, but in about ten minutes a door opened at the farther end, and Lord Morven entered from his bedroom. Donal rose. The earl shook hands with him with some faint show of kindness. Almost the same moment the butler entered from a third door and said that dinner waited. The earl turned and led the way, and Donal followed. The room they entered was again a rather small one, more like a breakfast than dinner room. The meal was laid on a little round table for two. Simmons alone was waiting. While they ate and drank, which his lordship did sparingly, not a word was spoken. Donal would have found it embarrassing had he not been prepared for any amount, almost any kind, of the peculiar. Beyond the silence there was nothing else that was strange, except that his lordship took no notice whatever of his guest, leaving all the attention to the care of the butler. He looked very white and worn—Donal thought a good deal worse than when he saw him first. His cheeks were more sunken, his hair more gray, and his eyes more weary, with a consuming fire in them—he no longer had much fuel but was burning only the remnants. He stooped over his plate as if to hide the operation of eating and drank his wine with a trembling hand. Every motion seemed to Donal to indicate an apparent indifference to both food and drink; it was easy from the way in which his lordship sat for Donal to make such observation. At length the more solid part of the meal was removed, and he was left alone with the strange man, fruit upon the table, and two wine decanters, from one of which the earl helped himself, and passed it to Donal, saying as he did so, "You are very good to my little Davie, Mr. Grant. He is full of your kindness to him. There is nobody like you!"

"A little goes a long way with Davie, my lord."

Donal murmured something to the effect that the highest duty must be the pleasantest action; and that Davie, of all the boys he had had to teach, was by far the easiest to get on because his moral nature was the most teachable.

"You greatly gratify me, Mr. Grant," said the earl. "I have long wished to find such a man as I see you are for my boy. I wish I had found you when Forgue was preparing for college—but you could not then have been prepared for such a charge."

"True, my lord; I was at that time at college myself in the winter, and the rest of the year helping my father with his sheep, or working on his master's farm."

"Yes, yes, I remember, you told me something of your history before. You Scotch peasants are a wonderful people!"

"I am not aware of anything wonderful in us, my lord. But you may rest assured as to Davie, that what I think good I will do for him as long as your lordship gives me the privilege of being with him."

"I wish that might be the measure of his privilege," said his lordship. "But you cannot be a tutor always. You must be soon entering on some more important sphere of labor. Doubtless you are in training for the church?"

"My lord, I have no such goal in my eye."

"What!" cried his lordship; "you cannot intend to give your life to teaching—though it may be a right noble calling. You would then of course be a schoolmaster? I have one such position almost in my gift."

"My lord," returned Donal, "I never trouble about my future. I have got on very well as yet without doing so, and I have no intention of lading the mule of the Present with the camel load of the Future. I will take what comes—what is sent me, that is."

"If I were a rich man, Mr. Grant," the earl continued, "which it may sound strange to you to hear me say I am not, but which is nevertheless true; for as everyone about here knows, not an acre of the property belongs to me or goes with the title. Davie, dear boy, will have nothing but a thousand or two. Lord Forgue, will, however, be well provided for by the marriage I have in view for him."

"I hope there will be some love in it," remarked Donal uneasily.

"I had no intention," returned his lordship, with cold politeness, "of troubling you concerning Lord Forgue. You are of course interested only in your pupil Davie."

"I beg your pardon, my lord," said Donal; and his lordship immediately resumed his former condescendingly friendly, half-sleepy tone of conversation.

"Yes, Davie, poor boy—he is my anxiety! What to do with him, I have not yet succeeded in determining. If the Church of Scotland were Episcopal now, we might put him into that; he would be an honor to it. But alas! where there are positively no dignities, it would not be fair to one of his birth and social position to tie him down to a few shabby hundreds a year and the associations he would necessarily be thrown into—however honorable the thing in itself!" he added, with a bow to Donal, apparently unable to get it out of his head that he was a clergyman in prospect at least and purpose.

"Davie is not quite a man yet," said Donal, "and by the time he begins to think of a profession, he will, I trust, be a good deal fitter to make a choice than he is now. The boy has a great deal of common sense. If your lordship will pardon me, I cannot help thinking there is no need for your lordship to trouble yourself about him—at least not before some liking or preference begins to show itself."

"Ah, it is very well for one in your position to speak in that way, Mr. Grant. Men like you are free to choose; you may make your bread as you please. But men in our position are greatly limited in their choice; the paths open to them are few. They are compelled to follow in certain tracks. You are free, I say; we are not. Tradition oppresses us. I could well wish I had been born in your humbler but in truth less contracted sphere. Certain careers are hardly open to you, to be sure, but the vision of your life in the open air, following your sheep, and dreaming all things beautiful and grand in the world beyond you—none of which is to be found on a nearer view—is entrancing. That is the life to make a poet ... Take another glass of wine, Mr. Grant," said his lordship, filling his own from the other decanter.

Donal half-mechanically filled a glass from the decanter which his host pushed toward him.

"I should like you," resumed his lordship, after a short pause, "to keep your eyes open to the fact that Davie must do something for himself, and let me know by and by what you think him fit for."

"I will with pleasure, my lord. Tastes may not be infallible guides to what is good for us, but they may conduct us to the knowledge of what we are fit for—whether that be fit for us remaining still a question."

"Extremely well said!" returned the earl.

"Shall I try how he takes to trigonometry—for land survey and measuring? There is a good deal to do in that way now. Gentlemen are now beginning to take charge of the lands of their higher relatives. There is Mr. Graeme, your own factor, my lord—a relative, I understand."

"A distant one," answered his lordship with marked coolness, "hardly to be counted. Kinship is an awkward thing. The man who has would be the poorest in the clan if he gave to every needy relation that turned up."

"In the Lowlands, my lord, you don't count kin as we do in the Highlands. My heart warms of itself to the word kinsman."

"You have not found kinship as I have. To tell you the truth," he went on, "at one period of my history I gave and gave till I was tired of giving; it was just as unsatisfactory as possession. Ingratitude was the sole return. At one time I had large possessions—larger than I like to think of now. If I had the tenth part of what I have given away, I should not now be uneasy concerning Davie's future."

"There is no fear of Davie, my lord, so long as he is brought up with the idea that he must work for his bread."

His lordship made no answer, and Donal saw that his look was far away from the present. A moment more, and he rose and began to pace the room. An indescribable something that suggested an invisible cloud seemed to hover about his forehead and eyes, which if not fixed on very vacancy itself, appeared to have gotten somewhere in the neighborhood of it. At length he opened the door by which he had entered, and as he did so he went on with something he had begun to say to Donal—of which, although Donal heard every word and seemed on the point of understanding something, he had not yet caught any sense when his lordship disappeared. But as he went on talking, and kept up the tone of one conversing with his neighbor, Donal thought it his part to follow him, and found himself in his lordship's bedroom. But out of this his lordship had already gone, through an opposite door. And Donal, still following, was presently where he had never been before, in an old picture gallery of which he had heard Davie speak, but which the earl kept private. It was a long, narrow place, hardly in width more than a corridor, and to Donal nowhere appearing to afford distance enough for seeing any picture properly; But he could ill judge, for the sole light in the place came from the fires and candles in the rooms whose doors they had left open behind them, and just a faint glimmer from the vapor-buried moon, sufficing to show the outline of window after window, and revealing something of the great length of the gallery. By the time Donal caught sight of the earl, he was some distance down, holding straight on into the long dusk, and still talking.

"This is my favorite promenade," he said, as if brought a little to himself by the sound of Donal's overtaking steps. "After dinner, always, Mr. Grant, wet weather or dry, still or stormy, I walk here. What do I care for the weather! It will be time when I am old to consult the barometer!"

Donal wondered a little—there seemed no great hardihood in the worst of weathers to go pacing a picture gallery, where the worst storm that ever blew could reach one only with little threads through the chinks of windows and doors—which were doubled. "Yes," his lordship went on, "I taught myself hardship in my boyhood, and I now reap the fruits of it in the prime of life. . . . Come here! I will show you a prospect unequalled."

He stopped in front of a large picture and began to talk as if an expatiation upon the points of a real landscape outspread before him. His remarks belonged to something magnificent; but whether they were applicable to the picture Donal could not tell; there was light enough only to return a faint gleam from its gilded frame.

A sudden change came over Donal, absorbing him so in its results that for itself he never thought even of trying to account. Something seemed to give way in his head. He heard and knew the voice of his host, but seemed also in some inexplicable way to see the things which had their being only in the brain of the earl. Whether he went in very deed out with him into the night, he did not know—he felt as if he had gone, but thought he had not—but when he woke the next morning in his own bed at the top of the tower, to which he had some memory of climbing, he was as weary as if he had been walking all night through.

13

· · · · · · · · · · · · · · · · · · · ·

Bewildered

*H*is first thought was of a long and delightful journey he had made on horseback in the company of the earl, through scenes of entrancing interest and variety; but the present result was a strange sense of weariness, almost of misery. What had befallen him to account for this? Was the thing a fact or a fancy? If a fancy, how was he so weary? If a fact, how could it have been? Had he indeed been the earl's companion through such a long night as it seemed? He was confused, bewildered and haunted with a kind of shadowy misery. Nothing like it had he ever experienced before. At last he bethought himself that as he had been so little accustomed to wine, he must have inadvertently taken more than his head could stand. Yet he remembered leaving his glass unemptied to follow the earl, and certainly it was some time after that before the "something" came on that made of him a man beside himself. Could it really have been drunkenness? Had it been slowly coming on without his knowing it? He could hardly believe it. Whatever it was, it had left him unhappy, almost ashamed. What would the earl think of him? He must have come to the conclusion that such a man was unfit any longer to take charge of his son. For his own part, he did not feel that he was to blame, but rather that an accident had befallen him.

His hour for rising in winter being six, he got up and found to his dismay that it was almost ten o'clock. He dressed in haste and went down, wondering that Davie had not come to find him.

In the schoolroom he found Davie waiting. The boy sprang up and darted to meet him.

"I hope you are better, Mr. Grant," he said. "I am so glad you are able to come down!"

"I am quite well," answered Donal. "I can't think what made me sleep so long! Why didn't you come and wake me, Davie, my boy?"

"Because Simmons told me you were not well, and I must not disturb you if you were late in coming down to breakfast."

"I hardly deserve any breakfast," rejoined Donal; "but if you will stand by me, and read while I take my coffee, we shall save a little time so."

"Yes, sir. But your coffee must be quite cold. I will ring."

"No, no; I must not waste any more time. A man who cannot drink cold coffee ought to come down while it is hot."

"Forgue won't drink cold coffee," said Davie; "I don't see why you should."

"Because I prefer to do with the coffee as I please—not to have hot coffee for my master. I won't have it mean anything to me what humor the coffee may be in. I will be Donal Grant, whether the coffee be cold or hot. There is a bit of practical philosophy for you, Davie!"

Their conversation lasted while Donal ate his breakfast, with the little fellow standing beside him.

But, naturally, as soon as lessons were over, he fell again to thinking what could have befallen him the night before. The earl must have taken notice of it, for surely Simmons had not given Davie those injunctions of himself—except indeed Lord Morven had exposed his condition even to him. At what point did the aberration, whatever was its nature, begin? If the earl had spoken to Simmons, then kindness seemed to have been intended him; but it might have been merely care over the boy himself that his feelings toward his tutor should not receive a shock.

He resolved to request an interview with the earl and make his apologies, explaining the mishap as the result of ignorance arising from inexperience in the matter of strong drink. As soon as his morning's work with Davie was over, he sought Simmons and found him in the pantry rubbing up the forks and spoons.

"Ah! Mr. Grant," he said, before Donal could speak, "I was just coming to you with a message from his lordship. He wants to see you."

"And I came to you," replied Donal, "to say I wanted to see his lordship."

"That's well fitted, then, sir," returned Simmons. "I will go and see. His lordship is not up nor likely to be for some hours yet; he is in one of his low fits this morning. He told me you were not quite yourself last night."

As he said this his red nose seemed to examine Donal's face with a kindly, but not altogether sympathetic, scrutiny.

"The fact is, Simmons," answered Donal, "not being used to wine, I drank more of his lordship's than was good for me."

"His lordship's wine—" murmured Simmons, and there checked himself. "—How much of it did you drink, sir, if I may ask such a question?"

"I had one glass during dinner, and nearly two glasses after."

"Pooh! pooh, sir! That would never hurt a strong man like you!"

So saying, while he washed his hands and took off his white apron, Simmons departed on his errand to his lordship's room, while Donal went to the foot of the grand staircase and there waited. As he stood, he heard a light step above him and, involuntarily glancing up, saw the light shape of Lady Arctura just appearing round the last visible curve of the spiral stair, coming down rather slowly and very softly, as if her feet were thinking. She seemed to check herself for an infinitesimal moment, then immediately moved on again as he stood aside with bended head to let her pass. If she acknowledged his salutation it was with the slightest return, but she lifted her eyes to his face as she passed him with a look that seemed to him to have in it a strange wistful trouble—not very marked, yet notable. She passed on and vanished, leaving that look a lingering presence in Donal's thought. What was it . . . Had he really seen it, or had he only imagined it?

Simmons kept Donal waiting a good while. He had found his lordship getting up, and had had to stay to help him dress. At length he came, excusing himself that his lordship's temper at such times was not of the evenest and required a gentle hand. His lordship would see him and could Mr. Grant find the way himself, for his old bones ached with running up and down those endless stone steps? Donal answered he knew the way and sprang up the stair. But his mind was more occupied with the coming interview than with his recollection of the way, which caused him to take a wrong turn after leaving the stair. The consequence was that he presently found himself in the picture gallery. A strange feeling of pain, as if of the presence of a condition he did not wish to encourage, awoke in him at the discovery. Having entered it, as he judged, at the farther end, he walked along, thus taking the readiest way to his lordship's apartment. Either he would find him in his bedroom or could pass through that to his sitting room. As he passed he glanced at the pictures on the walls. So far as he knew he had never been in the place except in the dark, to recognize some of them as forming parts of the stuff of a dream in which he had been wandering through the night. Here was something to be meditated upon—but for the present postponed. His lordship was waiting for him.

Arrived, as he thought, at the door of the earl's bedroom, a sweet voice, which he knew at once as Lady Arctura's, called to him to enter. It was not the earl's chamber, but a lovely though rather dark and gloomy little room, in which sat the lady writing at a carved table of black oak. Even in that moment Donal could not help feeling how much better it would have been for the thought-oppressed girl to have a room where the sunshine had free entrance and play. A fire blazed cheerfully in the old-fashioned grate, but there was only one low lattice window, and that to the west. She looked up.

"I beg your pardon, my lady," he said; "my lord wished to see me, but I find I have lost my way, and taken your door for that of his room."

"I will show you the way," said Lady Arctura gently.

As they turned, Donal saw that here the gallery, instead of ending, took a sharp turn and he was still at some distance from the earl's bedroom. Lady Arctura, however, did not take him farther along the gallery, but through a door into a winding, narrow passage by which she brought him within sight of the door of his lordship's sitting room. She pointed it out to him and turned away. He knocked once more, and the voice of the earl told him to enter.

His lordship was in his dressing gown, stretched on a couch of faded satin of a gold color, against which his pale yellow face looked cadaverous.

"Good morning, Mr. Grant!" he said. "I'm glad to see you better."

"I thank you, my lord," returned Donal. "You were kind enough to wish to see me. I have to make an apology. I cannot understand how it was except that I have been so little accustomed to strong drink of any sort that—"

"There is not the smallest occasion to say a word," interrupted his lordship. "Believe me, you did not once forget yourself, or cease to behave like a gentleman."

"Your lordship is very kind. Still I cannot help being sorry. I shall take good care in the future."

"It might be as well," conceded the earl, "to set yourself a limit—necessarily in your case a narrow one. Some constitutions are so immediately responsive."

"Sometimes, apparently, when it is too late!" rejoined Donal. "But I must not annoy your lordship with any further expression of my regret!"

"Will you dine with me again tonight?" said the earl. "I am lonely now and may well be glad of such a companion. I am not by nature unsociable—much the contrary indeed. You may wonder that I do not admit my own family more freely; but they are young and foolish; and my wretched health causes me to shrink from the loud voices and abrupt motions of mere lads."

"But Lady Arctura!" thought Donal. Aloud, he said, "Your lordship will find me but a poor substitute, I fear, for the society you would prefer. But what I am is at your lordship's service."

As he spoke Donal could not help turning his mind with a moment's longing and regret to his nest in the tower and the company of his books and his thoughts; these were to him far preferable to any of the social elements offered him as yet by his host.

"Then come this evening and dine with me."

Donal promised.

In the evening he went as before, conducted by the butler, and was formally announced. With the earl, to his surprise, he found Lady Arctura. The earl made Donal give her his arm, and himself followed.

It was to Donal a very different dinner from that of the evening before. Whether the presence of his niece made the earl rouse himself to be agreeable, or he had grown better since the morning and his spirits had risen, certainly he was not like the same man. He talked in a rather ponderously playful way, told two or three good stories, described with vivacity some of the adventures of his youth, spoke of several great men he had met, and in short was all that could be desired of a host. Donal took no wine during dinner, and the earl as before took very little, Lady Arctura none. She listened respectfully to her uncle's talk and was attentive when Donal spoke; he thought she looked even sympathetic once or twice. When the last of the dinner was removed and the wine placed on the table, his lordship looked to Donal's eyes as if he expected his niece to go; but she kept her place. He asked her which wine she would take, but she declined any. He filled his glass, and passed the decanter to Donal. He too filled his glass, and drank slowly.

Talk revived, but Donal could not help fancying that the eyes of the lady now and then sought his with a sort of question in them—almost as if she feared something might be going to happen to him. He attributed it to her having heard that he had taken too much the night before and felt the situation rather unpleasant. He must, however, brave it out. When he refused a second glass, which the earl by no means pressed upon him, he thought he saw her look relieved.

In the course of the talk they came upon sheep, and Donal was telling them some of his experiences with them and their dogs, himself greatly interested in the subject. Then all at once, just as before, something seemed to burst in his head, and immediately, although he knew that he was sitting at the table with the earl and Lady Arctura, he could not be certain that he was not at the same time upon the side of a lonely hill. Closed in a magic night of high summer, his woolly and hairy friends lying all about him, a light glimmered faintly on the heather a little way off, which he knew for the flame that comes from the feet of the angels when they touch ever so lightly the solid earth. He seemed to be reading the thoughts of his sheep as he had never been able to do before, yet all the time he went on talking and knew that he was talking to the earl and the lady.

At length he found everything about him changed and he was all but certain that he was no longer in their company, but alone and outside the house—walking, indeed, swiftly through the park, in a fierce wind from the northeast; battling with it, he seemed to be ruling it like a fiery horse. Presently came a hoarse, terrible music, the thunderous beat of the waves on the low shore. He felt it through his feet, as one feels without hearing the low tones of an organ for which the building is too small to allow the natural vibration. It was drawing him to the sea—whether in the body or out of the body he could not have told. His feet were now wading through the wave-beaten sand. Through the darkness he could see the white fierceness of the hurrying waves as they rushed to the shore. He rushed into the water and the breaking wave drenched him from head to foot. A moment's bewilderment, and he came to himself sitting on the sand in a cold wind, and wet to the skin, upon the border of a fierce stormy sea. He dragged himself up and set out for home; and by the time he reached the castle he had gotten quite warm. His own door at the foot of the tower was open, he crept up to bed, and was soon fast asleep.

14

••••••••••••••••••••

Lady Arctura

*T*he next day, he was not so late as previously, and before he had finished his breakfast had made up his mind that he must beware of the earl. He was satisfied that such could not be the consequence of one glass of wine. If the earl asked, he would again go to dinner with him, but would take no wine.

School was just over when Simmons came to him from his lordship, to inquire after him, and ask him to dine with him again that evening. Donal immediately consented.

This time Lady Arctura was not there. After, as during dinner, Donal declined to drink. His lordship cast on him a very keen and searching glance, but it was only a glance, and took no further notice of his refusal. After that, however, the conversation which had not been brilliant from the first, sank and sank; and after a cup of coffee, his lordship remarking that he was not feeling so well as usual, begged Donal to excuse him and proceeded to retire. Donal rose and, expressing a hope that his lordship would have a good night and feel better in the morning, left the room.

The passage outside was lighted only by a rather dim lamp, and in the distance Donal saw what he could but distinguish as the form of a woman standing by the door which opened upon the great staircase. He supposed it at first to be one of the maids; but the servants were so few compared with the size of the castle that one was seldom to be met on any of the stairs or in any of the passages and, besides, the form was standing as if waiting for someone. Drawing near, he saw it was Lady Arctura and would have passed her with a bow. But before he could lay his hand on the lock, hers was there to prevent him. He then saw that she was agitated and that she stopped him thus because her voice had at the moment failed her. The next, however, she recovered it, and with it her self-possession.

"Mr. Grant," she said in a low voice, "I wish to speak to you—if you will allow me."

"I am at your service, my lady," answered Donal.

"But we cannot here . . . My uncle—"

"Shall we go into the picture gallery?" suggested Donal; "there is moonlight there."

"No; that is still too near my uncle. His hearing is sometimes preternaturally keen; and besides, as you know, he often walks there after his eve-

ning meal. But—excuse me, Mr. Grant—you will understand me presently—are you . . . are you quite—"

"You mean, my lady, am I quite myself this evening?" said Donal, wishing to help her with the embarrassing question and speaking in the tone
she had taken. "I have drunk no wine tonight."

With that she opened the door and descended the stairs, he following;
but as soon as the curve of the staircase hid the door she stopped, and
turning to him said, "I would not have you mistake me, Mr. Grant. I should
be ashamed to speak to you if—"

"Indeed I am very sorry," said Donal, "though hardly so much to blame
as I fear you think me."

"There . . . you mistake me at once. You suppose I think you took too
much wine last night. That would be absurd. I saw what you took well
enough. But we must not talk here. Come."

She turned again and went down the stair, leading the way straight to
the housekeeper's room. There they found her darning a stocking.

"Mrs. Brooks," said Lady Arctura, "I want to have a little talk with Mr.
Grant, and I did not know where to take him. There is no fire in the
library; may we sit here?"

"By all means! pray sit down, my lady. Why, child! you look as cold as
if you had been out on the roof . . . There, sit close to the fire . . . you are
trembling!"

Lady Arctura obeyed like the child Mrs. Brooks called her, and sat
down in the chair given to her.

"I've got something to see to in the still-room," said Mrs. Brooks. "You
sit there and have your talk. Sit down, Mr. Grant. I'm glad to see you and
my lady come to word of mouth at last. I began to think you never would!"

Had Donal been in the way of looking at his fellow for the sake of
interpreting his words, he would now have seen a shadow sweep over
Lady Arctura's face, followed by a flush, and would have attributed it to
displeasure at the words of the housekeeper. But he sat looking into the
fire, with an occasional upward glance, waiting for what was to come, and
saw neither shadow nor flush. Lady Arctura also sat for some time gazing
into the fire, and seemed in no haste to begin.

"You are so good to Davie!" she said at length, and stopped.

"No better than I have to be," returned Donal. "Not to be good to Davie
would be to be a wretch."

"It is only fair to confess that he is much more manageable since you
came. Only that is no good if the change does not come from a good
source."

"Grapes do not come from thorns, my lady. That would be to allow in
evil a power of working good." To this she did not reply.

"He minds everything I say to him now," she resumed presently. "What
is it that makes him so good?—I wish I had such a tutor."

She stopped again. She had spoken out of the simplicity of her
thought, but the words looked as if they ought not to have been said.

"What can have passed in her?" thought Donal. "She is so different. Her very voice is changed."

"But that is not what I wanted to speak to you about, Mr. Grant," she resumed, "though I did want you to know I was aware of the improvement in Davie. I want to say something about my uncle."

Here followed another pause—embarrassing to the reticent lady, not at all to Donal.

"You may have noticed," she said at length, "that, though we live together, and he is the head of the house as my guardian, there is not much communication between us."

"I have gathered as much. I cannot tell Davie not to talk to me."

"Of course not. Lord Morven is a very strange man. I cannot pretend to understand him, and I do not want either to judge him or to set him out to the judgment of another. I can only speak of a certain fact concerning yourself which I do not feel at liberty to keep from you."

Once more a pause followed.

"Has nothing occurred to you?" she said at length, abruptly. "Have you not suspected him of trying experiments upon you?"

"I have had an undefined ghost of a suspicion that pointed in that direction," answered Donal. "I suppose he is a dabbler in physiology and he has a notion in his head he wants to verify. Tell me what you please about it."

"I should never have known anything about it, though—my room being near his—I should have been the more perplexed about some things had he not, I do most entirely believe, made a similar experiment with me a year ago."

"Is it possible?"

"It may be all a fancy—I don't mean about what he did, of that I am sure—but I do sometimes fancy I have never been so well since. It was a great shock to me when I came to myself—you see, I am trusting you, Mr. Grant. You will remember I dared not have done so had I not believed you would be at least as discreet as myself in the matter. I believe the chief cause of the state of his health is that for years he has been in the habit of taking some horrible drug for the sake of its mental effects. You know there are people who do so. What the drug is, I don't know, and I would rather not know. It seems to me just as bad as taking too much wine. He prides himself on his temperance in that respect. But he says nothing of the other thing."

"And he dared give it to you—whatever it was?" said Donal with indignation.

"I am sure he gave me something. For once that I dined with him—but I cannot describe to you the strange effect what he gave me had upon me. I think he wanted to watch the effect of it on one who knew nothing of what she had taken. For my part I found it very different. I would not go through such agonies again for the world!"

She ceased. Donal saw that she was struggling with a painful memory. He hastened to speak.

"Thank you heartily, my lady, for your warning. It was because of such a suspicion that this evening I did not even taste the wine. If I have not taken any of the drug in something else, I am safe from the insanity—I can call it nothing less—that has possessed me the last two nights."

"Was it very dreadful?" asked Lady Arctura.

"On the contrary, it gave me a feeling of innate faculty such as I could never have conceived of."

"Oh, Mr. Grant, do take care! Do not be tempted to take it again. I don't know what it might not have led me to do if I had found it pleasant; for I am sorely tried with painful thoughts. I feel sometimes I would do almost anything to get rid of them."

"If it was as bad as that," said Donal, "the shield of God's presence must have been over you."

"How glad I should be to think so! But we have no right to think so till we believe in Christ . . . and . . . it is a terrible thing to say—I don't know that I believe."

"Whoever taught you that will have to answer for teaching a terrible lie," said Donal.

"I know he makes his sun to shine and his rain to fall upon the good and the bad, but that is only of this world's things."

"Are you able to worship a God who will give you all the little things he does not care much about, but will not give you help to do the things he wants you to do, but which you do not know how to do?"

"But there are things he cannot do till we believe."

"That is very true. But that does not say that God does not do all that can be done for even the worst of men to help them believe. He finds it very hard to teach us, but he is never tired of trying. Anyone who is willing to be taught of God will be taught, and thoroughly taught by him."

"I am afraid I am doing wrong in listening to you, Mr. Grant. I do wish what you say might be true, but are you not in danger—you will pardon me for saying it—of presumption? How could all the good people be wrong?"

"Because the greater part of the teachers among them have always set themselves more to explain God than to obey him. The gospel is given not to redeem our understandings, but our hearts; that done, and only then, our understandings will be free. If the things be true which I have heard from Sunday to Sunday in church since I came here, then the Lord brought us no salvation at all, but only a change of shape to our miseries. It has not redeemed you, Lady Arctura, and never will. Nothing but Christ himself for your very own teacher and friend and brother, not all the doctrines about him, even if every one of them were true, can save you."

"But how should men know that such is not the true God?"

"If a man desires God, he cannot help knowing enough of him to be capable of learning more. His idea of him cannot be all wrong. But that does not make him fit to teach others all about him—only to go on to learn for himself."

"But you must allow that God hates and punishes sin—and that is a terrible thing."

"It would be ten times more terrible if he did not hate and punish it. Do you think Jesus came to deliver us from the punishment of our sins? He would not have moved a step for that. The terrible thing is to be bad, and all punishment is to help to deliver us from it, nor will it cease till we have given up being bad. God will have us good."

Lady Arctura sat motionless, divided between the reverence she felt for distorted and false forms of truth taught her from her earliest years, and her desire after a God whose very being is the bliss of his creatures. Some time passed in silence, and then she rose. She held out her hand to him with a kind of irresolute motion, then suddenly smiled and said, "I wish I might ask you something. I know it is a rude question, but if you could see all, you would answer me, and let the offense go."

"I will answer you anything you choose to ask."

"That makes it even more difficult, but I will ask it. Davie says you write poems—you gave him one of yours, I believe. He showed it to me. Did you *really* write that poem—compose it, I mean, yourself?"

Donal looked at her. Her face grew very red.

"I hope you will forgive me," she said. "I hope I have not offended you very much."

"Nobody ought to be offended at being asked such a question, or being asked for proof. I am not offended—and, yes, I did write the poem. And—if you will do me the favor to wait here a few moments till I come back—I will show you the proof. I shall not be long, but it is some small distance from here to the top of the north tower."

"Davie told me it was there they had put you; do you like it? Do you not find it terribly cold?"

Donal assured her he could not have had a place more to his liking, and left her to go fetch his proofs. Before she could well think he had reached the foot of his stair, he was back with a bundle of papers in his hand, which he laid before her on the table.

"There," he said, "if you will go over these, you will see—hardly the poem as you may have read it, but the process of its growth. First you will find it blocked out rather roughly. Then clean at first, but afterwards scored and scored. Above you will see the words I chose instead of the first, and afterwards again rejected, till at last I reached those I let stand."

"I shall find it most interesting," said Lady Arctura. "I never saw anything of the kind before, and had no idea how verses were made. Do all verses take as much labor as is evident here?"

"Some take much more, some none at all. The labor is in getting the husks of expression cleared off the thought so that it may show for what it is."

At this point Mrs. Brooks, thinking the young people had had time enough for their conference, returned and the three sat a while and had a little talk. Then Lady Arctura kissed the housekeeper and bade her good-night; and Donal presently retired to his aerial chamber, with quite another idea of the lady of the house than he had gathered from the little he had seen of her before.

From that time, Donal and she met much oftener about the place; and now they never passed without a mutual smile and greeting.

In two days she brought his papers back to the schoolroom, and told him she had read every erasure and correction and could no longer have a doubt, even had she not now perfect confidence in him, that the man who had written those papers must be the maker of the verses.

15

••••••••••••••••••

Intervention

*L*ord Forgue had been on a visit to Edinburgh for some time, and doubtless there been made much of, and had returned with a considerable development of haughtiness. He kept so much to himself that even Davie lamented to his tutor that Forgue was not half so jolly as he used to be. But from his very love of loyalty and right, Donal was forced before long to take the part of the disrupting foreign element.

For more than a week Eppie had not been to see her grandparents; and as that same week something had prevented Donal also from paying them his usual visit, the old people had naturally become uneasy. Hence, one frosty twilight when the last of the sun lay cold in the west, Andrew Comin appeared in the kitchen asking to see Mrs. Brooks. He was kindly received by the servants, among whom Eppie was not present; and Mrs. Brooks, who had a genuine respect for the cobbler, soon came to greet him. She told him she knew no reason why Eppie had failed in visiting them: she would send for her and she could explain herself. In the meantime she sent to tell Donal as well that Andrew Comin was in the kitchen.

Donal would much rather have had his friend up to his room; but he dreaded giving the old man such a climb, therefore rose at once and ran down to him.

"Come out, Andrew," said Donal, as he shook hands with him, "if you're not tired. It's a fine night, and we can talk well in the gloamin'."

Going out by the kitchen door, they went first into the stableyard. Thence they arrived at the mews, now rather neglected. Here a door in the wall opened on a path between the trees. It was one of the pleasantest walks in the immediate proximity of the castle.

When they had gone the length of the little avenue and were within less than two trees of the door of the fruit garden, it opened and was immediately and hurriedly shut again—not, however, before Donal had seen the form of Eppie. He called her name and ran to the door, followed by Andrew; the same suspicion had struck both of them at once. Donal seized the latch and would have opened the door, but someone within held it against him; and he heard the noise of an attempt to push the rusty bolt into the staple. He set his strength to it and forced it open, warding a blow from his head as he entered. Lord Forgue was on the other side of the door, and a little way off stood Eppie, trembling. Forgue stood in a fury mingled with dismay, for he knew to what he exposed himself.

Donal turned away from him and said to the girl, "Eppie, here's your grandfather come to see after you."

The cobbler, however, went up to Lord Forgue.

"You're a young man, my lord," he began, "and may regard it as folly in an old man to interfere between you and your will; but I warn you, my lord, that except you cease to carry yourself toward my granddaughter in a manner you would not wish represented to his lordship, your father, he shall be informed of the affair. Eppie, you come home with me."

"I will not," said Eppie, her voice trembling with passion, though which passion it was hard to say. "I am a free woman. I make my own living, and I will not be treated like a child!"

"I will speak to Mrs. Brooks," said the old man with quiet dignity and self-restraint.

"And make her turn me away!" said Eppie.

She seemed quite changed—bold and determined—and was probably relieved that she had no more to play a false part. His lordship stood on one side and said nothing.

"But don't you think for a moment, Grandfather," continued Eppie, "that whatever she does, I will go home with you! I will go into lodgings. I have saved a little money, and as I can never get another place if you behave so as to take away my character, I will leave the country altogether."

Here his lordship, having apparently made up his mind, advanced and with strained composure said, "I confess, Mr. Comin, things do look against us. It is awkward that you should have found us together, but you know"—and here he attempted a laugh—"we are told not to judge by appearances!"

"We may have no choice but to act by them, though, my lord," said Andrew. "At the moment I should indeed be sorry to judge either of you by them. Eppie must come home with me, or she will find it the more displeasant—perhaps for both of you."

"Oh, if you threaten us," said his lordship contemptuously, "then of course we are very frightened; but you had better beware, for thereby you will only make it the more difficult—perhaps impossible, who can tell—for me to do your granddaughter the justice I have always intended."

"What your lordship's notion o' justice may be, I will not trouble you to explain," said the old man. "All I desire is that, whatever may have passed between you, she will come with me."

"Let us leave the matter to Mrs. Brooks," said Forgue. "I shall soon satisfy her that there is no occasion for any hurry. Believe me, you will only bring trouble on the innocent."

"Then it cannot be on you, my lord, for in this thing you have not behaved as a gentleman ought," said the cobbler.

"You dare tell me so to my face!" cried Forgue, striding up to the little old man.

"Yes, for I would say it behind your back," replied the cobbler. "Didn't your lordship promise there should be an end to this whole miserable affair?"

"Not to you," replied his lordship.

"To me you did," said Donal, who had hitherto only waited in silence.

"Do hold your tongue, Grant, and don't make things worse. To you I can easily explain it. Believe me, a fellow may break his word to the ear and yet keep it to the sense."

"The only thing that could make that true would be that you had married or were about to marry her."

Eppie would here have spoken; but she gave only a little cry, for Forgue put his hand over her mouth.

"You hold your tongue," he said; "you will only complicate matters! Mr. Grant, I shall be happy to explain it to you. You have nothing whatever to do with what may be going on in the house; you have but to do your part of the work. You can scarcely have forgotten that you are my brother's tutor, not mine! To interfere with what I do is nothing but a piece of idiotic impertinence!"

"The impertinence I intend to be guilty of is to get an audience with your father."

"You will not, if I give you such explanation as will satisfy you that I have done the girl no harm, and that I mean honestly by her?" said Forgue in a somewhat conciliatory tone.

"In any case," returned Donal, "you having once promised and then broken your promise, I shall without fail tell your father all I know."

"And ruin her and perhaps me too for life?"

"The truth will ruin only what it ought."

Forgue sprang upon him and struck him a heavy blow between the eyes. He had been having lessons in boxing while in Edinburgh and now had confidence in himself. It was a well-planted blow, and Donal was altogether unprepared for it. He staggered back against the wall and for a moment or two could not see, while all he knew was that there was something or other he had to attend to. He did not see that his lordship, excusing himself doubtless on the ground of necessity and that there was a girl in the case, would have struck him again. But the old man saw it and, throwing himself between, received the blow. He fell at Donal's feet.

As Donal came to himself, he heard a groan from the ground. He looked down, saw Andrew, and understood.

"Dear old man," he mourned, "did he dare strike you too?"

"He didn't mean it," returned Andrew feebly. "Are you getting over it? . . . He gave you a terrible one!"

"I shall be all right in a minute," answered Donal, wiping the blood out of his eyes. "I've a good hard head, thank God. But what has become of them?"

"You didn't think he was waiting to see us get better," said the cobbler. "I wonder whether they've gone into the house?"

They were now on their feet, looking at each other through the star-light, bewildered, and uncertain what step to take next.

They were walking toward the house. After what had happened, Andrew said he could not go in; he would walk gently home, and perhaps Donal would overtake him.

It was an hour and a half before Andrew got home, for it turned out one of his ribs was broken and Donal had not overtaken him. Having washed the blood from his face, Donal sought Simmons.

"His lordship can't see you now, I am sure, sir," answered the butler, "for Lord Forgue is with him."

Donal turned away and went up the stairs to his lordship's apartment. As he passed the door of the earl's bedroom opening on the corridor, he heard voices in debate and found no one in the sitting room. It was no time for ceremony: he knocked at the door of the bedroom. The voices within were too loud; he knocked again, and received an angry summons to enter. He did so, closed the door behind him and stood near it in sight of his lordship, waiting what should follow.

Lord Morven was sitting up in bed, his face so pale and distorted that Donal could hardly recognize his likeness. At the foot of it stood Lord Forgue, his handsome, shallow face flushed with anger, his right arm straight down by his side and the hand of it clenched hard. He turned when Donal entered. A fiercer flush overspread his face, but almost immediately rage seemed to yield to contempt, for a look of determined insult changed it and he turned away. Possibly even the appearance of Donal was a relief to being alone with his father.

"Mr. Grant," stammered his lordship, speaking with pain, "you are just in time to hear a father curse his son—for curse him I will if he does not presently change his tone."

"A father's curse shall not make me play a dishonorable part!" said Forgue, looking, however, anything but honorable.

"Mr. Grant," resumed the father, "I have found you to be a man of sense and refinement. If you had been tutor to this degenerate boy, the worst trouble of my life would never have come upon me!"

Forgue's lip curled but he did not speak, and his lordship went on, "Here is this fellow come to tell me to my face that he intends the ruin and disgrace of the family by a low marriage!"

"It would not be the first time it was so disgraced!" said the son—"if fresh peasant-blood be a disgrace to it."

"The hussy is not even a wholesome peasant girl!" cried the father. "Who do you think she is, Mr. Grant?"

"I do not require to guess, my lord," replied Donal. "I came to you now to inform your lordship of what I had myself seen as connecting Lord Forgue with one of the household."

"She must leave the house this instant!"

"Then I too leave it, my lord!" announced Forgue.

"With what funds, may I presume to ask? Have you been assuming a right to your pleasure with my purse as well?"

His lordship glanced anxiously toward his bureau. The look of indignant scorn on Forgue's face was followed by what might have been the pain of remembered dependence. But instead of answering his father's taunt, he turned his attack upon Donal.

"Your lordship certainly does not flatter me with confidence," he said, "but it is not the less my part to warn you against this man. It is months since first he knew of what was going on between us; he comes to tell you now because I was this evening compelled to chastise him for rude interference."

"And it is no doubt to the necessity for forestalling his disclosure that I owe the present ingenious confession!" said Lord Morven. "But explain, Mr. Grant."

"My lord," said Donal calmly, "I was some time ago made aware that something was going on between them and was, I confess, more alarmed for the girl than for him—the more that she is the child of friends to whom I am much beholden. But on the promise of both that the thing should be at an end, I concluded it better not to trouble your lordship with the affair. I may have made a mistake in this, but I sought to do the best. When, however, this night I saw that I had been hoodwinked and that things were going on as before, it became imperative on my position in your lordship's house that I should make you acquainted with the fact."

"The young blackguard! You had the testimony of your own eyes?" said his lordship, casting a fierce glance at his son.

"Allow me to remark," said Forgue, "that I deceived no one. What I promised was that that affair should not go on. It did not; the thing from that moment assumed an altogether serious aspect. Witness my presence in your bedchamber, my lord, to tell you I have given my word to marry the girl."

"I tell you, Forgue, if you marry her I will disown you."

Forgue smiled an impertinent smile and held his peace: the threat had for him no terror worth defending himself from.

"I shall be the better able," continued his lordship, "to provide suitably for Davie; he is something like a son! But hear me, Forgue: you ought to be well enough aware that if I left you all I had, it would be but beggary for one handicapped with an ancient title. You may think my anger with you very amusing, but it comes solely of anxiety on your account. Nothing but a suitable marriage can save you from the life of a moneyless noble. Even could you ignore your position, you have no profession, no trade, even, in these trade-loving days, to fall back upon. Except you marry as I please, you will have nothing but the contempt of a title without one farthing to sustain it."

Forgue was silent. But rage was growing more fierce within him. At length he spoke and his words compelled Donal to a measure of respect for him, though all the time he could not help doubting the genuineness of the ring of his words.

"My lord," Forgue said, "I have given my word to the girl"—he never once uttered her name to his father in Donal's hearing—"that I will marry her; would you have me disgrace the family by breaking my word?"

"Tut! tut! There are words and there are words! No one dreams of obligation in the rash promises of a lover. Still less are they binding where the man is not his own master. You are not your own master; you are under bonds to your country."

While they talked, Donal, waiting his turn, stood by quietly. To hear his lordship utter such things was as abominable in his ears as any foul talk of hell. The moment his lordship ceased, he turned to Forgue, and said: "My lord, you have removed my harder thoughts of you. You have broken your word in an infinitely nobler way than I believed you capable of."

Lord Morven stared dumbfounded.

"Your comments are out of place, Mr. Grant," said Forgue, with something of recovered dignity. "The matter is between my father and myself. If you wanted to beg my pardon, you might have found a more fitting opportunity."

Donal held his peace. He had felt bound to show his sympathy with his enemy wherein he was right. More than that was not at the moment called for.

The earl was perplexed. His one poor ally had apparently gone over to the enemy. He took a glass with some colorless liquid in it from the table by his bedside and drank its contents; then, after a moment's silence as if of exhaustion and suffering, said to Donal, "Mr. Grant, I desire a word with you. Leave the room, Forgue."

The moment he was out of the room and had closed the door behind him, the earl said, "Just look through that little hole in the panel, Mr. Grant, and tell me whether the fire is burning in the next room."

"It is blazing," said Donal.

"Had there been a head between, you would not have seen the fire. I am glad he yielded, for otherwise I should have had to ask you to put him out, and I hate rows. I presume you would have been able?"

"I think so," said Donal.

"And you would have done it?"

"I would have tried."

"Thank you. But you seemed a moment ago ready to take his part against me!"

"On the girl's part—yes; for his own sake, too, as an honest man."

"Come now, Mr. Grant; I understand your prejudices. But a moment's reflection will satisfy you that a capable man like yourself can make his living anyhow; while to one born to bear the burden of a title, and without the means of supporting it, marriage with such a girl would mean ten times the sacrifice."

"I do not dispute a word of what you have said, my lord," answered Donal, "but my feeling is that the moment a man speaks words of love to a woman, that moment rank and privilege vanish from between them."

The earl gave a small, sharp smile.

"You would make a good attorney, Mr. Grant; but if you had known half as much of the world as I have, you would modify your feeling at least if not your opinion. Mark this: The marriage shall not take place—by Jove! Do you imagine I could for one moment talk of it with such coolness were there the smallest actual danger of its occurrence? If I did not know that it could not, shall not take place? The boy is a fool, and I will let him know he is a fool! One word from me, and the rascal is paralyzed. Will you do so much for me as tell him what I have just said? The marriage shall not take place, I repeat. Sick man as I am, I am not yet reduced to lying in bed and receiving announcements of the good pleasure of my sons."

He took up a small bottle, poured a little from it into a glass, added water, and drank it, then resumed, "Now for the girl; who knows about the affair in the house?"

"So far as I am aware, no one knows of what has just come to light, except her grandfather who was with me when we came upon them in the fruit garden. If Lord Forgue tells no one, no one is likely to hear of it."

"Then let no further notice be taken of it. Tell no one—not even Mrs. Brooks. Let the young fools do as they please."

"I cannot consent to that, my lord."

"Why? What the devil have you to do with it?"

"I am bound by my friendship with the old man—"

"Pooh! pooh! Don't talk rubbish. What is it to any old man? Let them go their own way. I was foolish myself to take the matter so seriously. It will all come right. If no opposition be offered, the affair will soon settle itself. By Jove, I'm sorry you interfered. It would have been much better left alone."

"My lord," said Donal, "I can listen to nothing more in this vein."

"Very well. All I ask is—give me your promise not to interfere."

"I will not."

"Thank you."

"My lord, you mistake. I meant you to understand that I would give you no such pledge. What I can do, I do not know; but if I can do anything to save that girl from disgrace, I will do it."

"Disgrace! You seem to think nothing of the only disgrace worth the name—that of an ancient and noble family."

"The honor of that family, my lord, will be best preserved in the person of the girl."

"Curse you! Do you take me for your pupil? Do you think to preach to me? You must do as I tell you in my house, or you will soon see the outside of it! Come, I will tell you what: marry the girl yourself—they say she is deuced pretty—and I will give you—I will give you five hundred pounds for your wedding journey. Only take her away!—Poor Davie! I am sorry."

"Is it your lordship's wish I should give Lord Forgue your lordship's message before I go?"

"Go? Where?—Ah, on your wedding journey. Ha, ha!—No, it will hardly be necessary then."

"I did not mean that, my lord."

"Where then? To tell the stupid cobbler to come and fetch the slut? I will see to that. Ring the bell there."

"I am sorry to refuse anything your lordship desires of me, but I will not ring the bell."

"You won't?"

"No, my lord."

"Then, get out! Be off to your lessons. I can do very well without you. Mind you, don't let your insolent face come across my path. You are good enough for Davie, but you won't do for me."

"If I remain in your house, my lord, it will be as much for Eppie's as for Davie's sake."

"Get out of my sight!" was his lordship's reply, and Donal went.

He had hardly closed the door behind him when he heard the bell ring violently; and before he reached the bottom of the stair, he met the butler panting up as fast as his short legs and red nose would permit him to answer it. He would have stopped to question Donal, but Donal hastened past him to his own room and there sat down to think what he ought to do.

16

••••••••••••••••••••

Andrew Comin

*H*ad Donal Grant's own dignity in the eyes of others been with him a matter of importance, he would have left the castle the moment he had gotten his things together; but he thought much more of Davie and much more of poor Eppie. What was to be done for her? There was little good to be expected from such a marriage, but was it likely the marriage would ever take place? Was he at liberty to favor it any more than to oppose it? He was in the castle in the pay of the lord of it—not as the friend of the cobbler or his granddaughter. First of all, he must see Andrew Comin again—the rather that he was anxious about him after the rough treatment he had received. He hastened therefore to the town.

He found the old woman in great distress; not merely was she sorely troubled concerning the child, but she had her husband's condition also to make her unhappy; for the poor man was suffering great pain, so much that the moment Donal saw him he went without a word to fetch medical aid. The doctor said there was a rib broken, got him to bed, bound him up and sent him some medicine. All done that could be done, Donal sat down to watch beside him. Andrew lay very still, with closed eyes and a white face.

The old woman too was very calm, only every now and then she would lift her hands and shake her head and look as if the universe were going to pieces, because her old man lay there broken by the hand of the ungodly. When he coughed and the pain was keenest, every pang seemed to go through her body to her heart. Love is as lovely in the old as in the young.

Donal could not leave her to the labor of watching the night long. He wrote to Mrs. Brooks, telling her he would not be home that night but would be back to breakfast in the morning; and, having found a messenger at the inn, Donal made his arrangements to watch through the night.

It glided quietly over. Andrew slept a good deal and seemed to be having pleasant visions. He did not wake till the day began to dawn, when he asked for something to drink. Seeing Donal and perceiving that he had been by his bedside all the night, he thanked him with a smile and a little nod.

When Donal reached the castle, he found his breakfast waiting him and Mrs. Brooks also waiting to help him to it and let him know something that had taken place which also concerned his friends. Eppie, she said, had this morning not come down at the proper time, and when she sent after her, still did not come. Then she went up herself and found her in a strange mood. She would explain nothing, only declared herself determined to leave the castle that very day, and she was now packing her things to go; nor did Mrs. Brooks see any good in trying to prevent her. Work was worthless when the heart was out of it.

Donal agreed with her and said if only she would go home, there was enough for her to do there; for her grandfather was in bed with a broken rib and very feverish. Old people's bones were brittle and not easy to mend. There would be plenty to do before they got him round again.

Mrs. Brooks agreed it would be the best thing for her to go home where she would be looked after by those who had a better right and a smaller house. The girl would never do at the castle, it was clear. Donal asked her if she could see that she went home. Mrs. Brooks said she would take her home herself, adding, "The lass is not a bad one. She wants some o' the Lord's own discipline, I'm thinkin'."

Managed by the housekeeper, Eppie readily yielded; she was even readier to go home to help her grandmother nurse her grandfather than Mrs. Brooks had expected. With all her faults, she was an affectionate girl and was concerned to hear of the state of her grandfather—the more that, if she did not know, she must have suspected something of how he had met with his accident.

Mrs. Brooks got ready a heavy basket of good things for Eppie to carry home to her grandmother and, I suspect, made it the heavier for the sake of punishing Eppie a little.

She was kindly received and without a word of reproach by her grand-mother. The invalid smiled to her when she came near his bedside, and the poor girl turned away to conceal the tears she could not repress. She loved her grandparents and she loved the young lord, and she could not get the two loves to dwell peaceably in her mind together—a common difficulty with our weak, easily divided emotions. Tearfully but diligently, Eppie set about the duties laid upon her. She was very gloomy and wept not a little but was nevertheless diligent; doubtless she found some refuge from anxious thought in the service she rendered. What she saw as probable prospect for her future, I cannot say; but for the present she was parted from her lover, in whose faithfulness her utmost confidence at one moment was dashed by huge uncertainty the next. The faith of feeling will always be a thing of moods, whether its object be God or man.

17

....

Gradual Changes

$\mathcal{U}$p at the castle things fell into their old routine. Nothing had been arranged between Lord Forgue and Eppie, and his lordship seemed content that things should be as they were. Mrs. Brooks let him know that Eppie had gone home; he made neither remark nor further inquiry, and, indeed, manifested no interest in the matter. It was well his father should not see it necessary to push things farther. Forgue had told him his mind, and so relieved himself; but he did not want to be turned out of the castle. Without means, what was he to do? He had pledged himself to nothing; but the marriage could not be today or tomorrow. And in the meantime, he could, while she was at home, see her perhaps even more easily than at the castle. As to the old fellow, he was sorry he had hurt him, but he could not help it; if he would get in the way, how could he? But he had to get rid of the tutor! Things would have been much worse if he himself had not got first to his father! He would now wait a bit, and see what would turn up. For the tutor-fellow, he must not quarrel with him downright. No good would come of that. He only knew, or imagined, that he was in love with the girl; what was to come of it was all in the clouds. He said to himself he was willing to work for his wife if he only knew how. And, alas, it would take years before he would be able to earn even a woman's wages. In the meantime he loafed about as much as he dared, haunting the house where she was in hope of falling in with her, but not once presuming to enter it even in the dark; but for many days Eppie never went out of doors except into the garden at the back, and he never even saw her.

Though she had never spoken of it to anyone, Arctura had more than a suspicion that something was going on between her cousin and the pretty maid; and after Eppie had left the house, more than one—Davie amongst them, though he did not associate the two things—observed that Arctura was more cheerful than before. But there was no increase of relationship between her and Forgue. The earl had been wise enough to say nothing openly to either of them, for he knew the thing would have a better chance on its own inherent merits of youth and good looks and advantages on both sides. As yet, however, they had shown no sign of drawing to each other.

About this time, her friend, Miss Carmichael, returned from a rather lengthened visit. But now, after the kind of atonement that had taken place between Arctura and Donal, it was with some anxiety she looked forward to seeing her friend.

Donal and she had never had any further talk, much as she would have liked it, upon things poetic. She had been reading *Paradise Lost*, and would have liked much to talk to Donal about the poem but had not the courage.

Of course, when her friend came to see her, Miss Carmichael at once perceived a difference in Arctura's manner, which set her thinking. Miss Carmichael was not one to do or say anything without thinking about it first. There was something different in Arctura's carriage. Miss Carmichael saw that if she was to keep her influence over the weak-minded girl, as she counted her—all for her good of course!—she must take care to steer clear of any insignificant prejudices. So now she was the more careful—said nothing, or next to nothing, but watched her keenly and not the less slyly that she looked her so straight in the face every time she spoke.

They went for a little walk in the grounds; and so it was ordered that on their return they met Donal setting out on an excursion with Davie. Arctura and Donal passed with a bow and a friendly smile; Davie stopped and spoke to them, then bounded after his friend.

"Have you been attending Davie's scripture lesson regularly?" asked Miss Carmichael.

"No; I have only been once since you left," replied Arctura, glad—she could not quite have told why—to be able to give the negative answer.

"What, my dear! Have you been leaving your lamb to the will of the wolf?"

"I begin to doubt if he is a wolf."

"Ah, so well draped in his sheepskin? I am afraid he thinks to devour sheep and shepherd too," said Miss Carmichael with a searching glance at her friend—a glance intended to look what it was.

"Don't you think," suggested Lady Arctura, "when you are not able to say anything, it is better not to be present? Then your silence cannot look like agreement."

"But you could always protest simply by saying it was all wrong and you did not agree with him."

"But what if you were not sure that you did not agree with him?"

"I thought as much," said Miss Carmichael to herself.

Thus, long after Miss Carmichael had taken a coldly sorrowful farewell of her, Arctura went round and round the old millhorse track of her self-questioning.

From that day Arctura's search took a new departure. It is strange how often one may hear a thing, yet never have really heard it. The heart can hear only what it is capable of; but alas for him who will not hear what he is capable of hearing!

His failure to get word or even sight of Eppie, together with some possible uneasiness at the condition in which the grandfather continued, combined to make Lord Forgue accept the invitation—which his father had taken pains to have sent him—to spend three weeks or a month with a distant relative in the north of England. He would rather be out of the way till, however the thing might turn, it should blow over. He would gladly have sent a message to Eppie, but there was no one he could trust with it; Davie was too much under the influence of his tutor. So he went away without word, and Eppie soon began to imagine he had deserted her forever. For a time her tears flowed freely, but she soon began to feel something of relief in having the question decided, for she could not herself see how they were ever to be married. She would have been content to love him always, she said to herself, were there no prospect of marriage or even were there no marriage in question; but would he remain true to her? She did not think she could expect it; so with many tears she thought she gave him up. He had loved her, and that was a grand thing!

There was much that was good and something that was wise in the girl, notwithstanding her folly in allowing such a lover to become intimate with her. Eppie attended to her duties, took her full share in all that had to be done, and reaped much commendation, which hardly served to make her happy, from her grandmother, willing to read in her the best. And so the dull days went by for her.

18

· · · · · · · · · · · · · · · · · · ·

The Ghost Music

One stormy night in the month of March, when a bitter east wind was blowing, Donal, seated at the plain deal-table which he had gotten Mrs. Brooks to find for him, was drawing upon it a diagram in the hope of finding a simplification of some geometrical difficulty for Davie. A sudden sense of cold made him cast a glance at his fire. He had been aware that it was sinking but had forgotten it. It was now very low, and he must go at once upon the roof to fetch from his store both wood and coal. In certain directions of the wind this was a rather ticklish task, but he had taken the precaution of putting up here and there a handful of rope. He closed the door behind him to keep in what warmth he might and, ascending the stairs to another door a few feet higher, stepped out on the flat that ran along the thickness of the wall. With the roof on one side and a small parapet on the other, he stood for a moment to look around him. It was a moonlit night, so far as the clouds would permit the light of the moon to issue. The roaring of the sea came like a low rolling mist across the flats. As he stood, the wind seemed suddenly to change and take a touch of south in its blowing. The same instant came to his ear a loud wail of the ghost music haunting the house. There was in it the cry of a discord, mingling with a wild rolling change of harmonies. It came again and again and more continuously than he had ever heard it before. Now there was indeed some chance of following the sound, he thought. As a gazehound with his eyes and sleuthhound with his nose, he stood ready to start hunting with his listening ear. And now he came almost to the conclusion that the seeming approach and recession of the sounds was occasioned only by changes in their strength, not by any alteration of the position of their source. Had Donal ever in his life heard an Aeolian harp, he would have thought of it now.

"Surely it must be something on the roof," he said; and throwing down the pail he had brought for his fuel and forgetting the dying fire in his room, he got down on his hands and knees, first to escape the wind in his ears, and next to diminish its hold on his person. He crept away over roof after roof like a cat, stopping every moment a new gush of the sound came to determine what direction it was from and then starting once more in the chase of it. Upon a great gathering of roofs like those of the castle, erected at various times on various levels and with all kinds of architectural accommodations of one part to another, sound would be constantly deflected, and there would be as many difficulties in tracing a sound as inside the house. Sometimes he had to stop altogether where he was unable to get a peep at his course beyond. At one such moment, when it became all but quite dark, he had to stop in a half-crouching position upon a high-pitched roof of great slabs, his fingers clutched around edges of the stones and his mountaineering habits standing him in good stead, but protected a little from the full force of the blast by a huge stack of chimneys that rose to windward of him.

While he clung thus and waited, once more, louder than he had yet heard—it seemed in his very ear—arose the musical ghost cry. The moon came out as at the call to see, but there was nothing for Donal to see— nothing to suggest a possible origin of the sound. As if disappointed, the moon instantly withdrew, the darkness again fell, and the wind rushed upon him stronger than ever. With that came the keen slanting rain, attacking him as with fierce intent of protecting the secret, and plainly there was little chance of success that night. He must put off the hunt till daylight. If there was any material factor in the sound, he would be better able to discover it in the daylight. By the great chimney stack he could identify the spot where he had been nearest to it. There remained for the present but the task, perhaps a difficult one, of finding his way back to his tower.

And difficult it was—considerably more difficult than he had anticipated. He had not an idea in which direction the tower lay—had not even an idea left of the track, if track it could be called, by which he had come. One thing only was clear—it was somewhere other than where he was. He left the place, therefore, and like any other honest pilgrim who knows he must go somewhere else, he began his wanderings. But on his backward way he seemed to be far more obstructed than on his way thither. Again and again he could get no farther in the direction he was trying; again and again he had to turn and try another way. It was half an hour at least before he came to a spot which he knew. He caught at length the outline of one of the sheds in which lay his stores, and from that his way was plain. He caught up his pail, filled it hurriedly with coal and wood, and hastened to his nest as fast as rather stiffened joints would carry him, though with little hope indeed of finding his fire still in life and capable of recovery.

But when he stepped from the roof onto the stair and had gone down a few steps, a strange sight indeed was there waiting him. Below him on the stair, just outside his door, with a small, dim wax taper in hand, stood the form of a woman. Plainly to be seen from the position of her hand and her head, she had just knocked and was listening for an answer. So intent was she and still so loud was the wind among the roofs that she did not hear Donal's step above her. For the first moment he was afraid to speak, lest he should startle her, whoever it was, with a voice from an unexpected quarter; but presently the figure knocked again, and then he felt he must speak; his voice would startle less than his approach from behind her. He made, however, a pardonable attempt at ventriloquy, saying with a voice intended to sound farther away than it was, "Come in." The hand sought a handle, searched and found the latch and opened the door. As she did so, the light fell on her face, and Donal saw it was Lady Arctura. Then he spoke.

"I will be with you immediately, my lady," he said and, descending, entered the room after her—a less than pleasant object to behold after his crawling excursion in wind and rain on the roof.

She started a little at hearing the voice behind her and, turning, gazed on him with a slight shadow of dismay.

Donal was more like a sweep returning from his work than a tutor in a lord's castle, and he bore in his hand a pailful of coals. Catching at once the meaning of her look, he made haste to explain, though in truth he had more cause to be surprised at her presence than she at his appearance.

"I have been out on the roof for the last hour and a half," he said.

"What were you doing there, if I may ask?" she said, with a strange mingling of expressions on her countenance, "and in such a night?"

"I heard the music, my lady—the ghost music, you know, that they say haunts the castle, and—"

"I heard it too," she said, almost under her breath and with a look almost of terror. "I have often heard it before, but I think never so loud as tonight. Have you any idea about it, Mr. Grant?"

"None whatever, except that I am now nearly sure the source of it is somewhere about the roof."

"I should be very glad if you could clear up the mystery."

"I have some hope of doing so. But you are not frightened, my lady?" he asked, seeing her catch hold of the back of a chair, as if ready to sink. "Do sit down," he continued, placing a seat for her; "I will get you some water."

"No, no; I shall be all right in a moment," she answered. "Your stair has taken my breath away, and then my uncle is in such a strange condition. That is why I came to you."

"You need hardly be much disturbed by that, for you must have often seen him so before."

"Yes—but never as tonight."

"I have already seen him more than once in the strangest condition for a man in his senses."

"But is he in his senses?"

"At times not, I suppose."

"Would you come with me?"

"Anywhere."

"Come, then," she said and, leaving the room, led the way by the light of her candle down the stair. About halfway, she stopped at a door and, turning, said with a smile like that of a child—and perhaps the first untroubled look Donal had yet seen upon her face—"How delightful it is to be free from fear! I am not the least afraid, now you are with me."

"That makes me very glad," said Donal. "By the way, do you think the music has anything to do with your uncle's condition?"

"I do not know; I have sometimes thought it had. But it is difficult to be sure about anything."

She turned again hastily and, entering a part of the castle with which Donal had no acquaintance, led him, after many bewildering turns, on to the great staircase down which she continued her course. Donal began to wonder what time of the night it could be, the house was all so still; nobody seemed awake in it. But there were, as I have said, comparatively so few servants for the size of it that the same might have been almost at any hour. She went very fast and lightly down the stair, and for a moment Donal almost lost sight of her in the great curve. Presently, however, he overtook her and, laying his hand on her arm, said in a half whisper, "Pardon me, my lady, but tell me first what you want me to do, that I may be prepared."

"Nothing, nothing. Only come and see. He will not see you."

Without another word Donal again followed her. She led him to the room on the stair where first he had seen the earl. There was no light in it. Across the near end of it she led him, as he had himself gone once before, through a door, round the edge of its back wall under the ascending spiral of the stair, and into the little chamber behind, which seemed a cut-off and forgotten corner. As he entered it, he heard for one moment the murmuring of a voice, he thought, but immediately it was gone and the deepest silence filled the world. One step within the door Arctura stood still, turned her head toward Donal, and held high the taper. But she looked only at Donal, and not in the direction she wanted him to look. The feeble light fell on the form of the earl. A small box stood against the foot of the wall opposite the door. His back to them, he stood on it, hands stretched above his head, without shifting or moving a muscle or uttering a sound. What could it mean? Donal gazed in a blank dismay. Not a minute passed, but he thought it a long and painful time, when the murmuring came again. Donal listened as to a voice from another world:

"And we indeed justly; for we receive the due reward of our deeds; but this man hath done nothing amiss!"

Silence again fell, but the form did not move, and still the two stood regarding him.

From far away came the sound of the ghost music. The head against the wall began to move as if waking from sleep. The hands sank along the wall, and fell by his sides. The earl gave a deep sigh, and stood leaning his forehead against the wall. Donal touched Lady Arctura and said with his eyes, "Had we not better go? He will presently look round."

She signaled assent, and they turned softly and left the room, Lady Arctura still leading.

She went straight to the library. Its dark oak cases and old bindings were hardly able to reflect a ray of the poor taper she carried, but the fire was not yet quite out. She set down the light, turned toward Donal, and looked at him in silence.

"What does it all mean?" he asked in a hoarse whisper.

"God knows," she returned solemnly, but with less emotion than Donal would have expected.

"Are we safe?" he asked. "How can you tell he will not come here?"

"I do not think he will. I have seen him in many parts of the house, but never here."

As she spoke the door swung noiselessly open, and the earl entered. His face was ghastly pale; his eyes were wide open, and he came straight toward them. But he did not see them; or, if he did, he saw them but as phantoms of the dream in which he was walking. He drew a chair to the embers of the fire—to his fancy, I believe, a great and comfortable blaze— sat for a moment or two looking into them, then rose and going to a distant part of the room took down a book from a shelf. Returning with it to the fire, he drew toward him Arctura's tiny taper, opened the book and began to read in an audible murmur.

With a mutual glance, the two stole out of the room and left the dreamer to his dreams.

"Do you think," said Donal, "I ought to tell Simmons? He must know more about his master than anyone else."

"It would be better. You know where to find him?"

"I do not."

"I will show you a bell that rings in his room. He will think his lordship has rung it and will look for him till he finds him."

They went and rang the bell and soon heard the steps of the faithful servant seeking his master. Then they bade each other good-night, and parted.

19
••••••••••••••••••

Meeting of the Three

In the morning Donal heard from Simmons that the earl was very ill—indeed, could not raise his head.

"The way he do moan and cry," said Simmons, "you would think surely either he was out of his mind, or had something heavy upon it. But all the years I have known him, every now and then he has been like that, then back to his old self again, little the worse for it."

Toward the close of morning school, just as Donal was beginning to give Davie his "lesson in religion," as Davie called it, Lady Arctura entered the schoolroom and sat down beside Davie. And Donal, in what he said to Davie, had therefore a special regard to the lady.

"What would you think of me, Davie," he asked, "if I were very angry with you because you did not know something I had never taught you?"

Davie only laughed. It was to him an impossible supposition.

"You wouldn't do that, sir! I know you wouldn't," he said after a moment.

"Why should I not?"

"It isn't your way, sir."

"One question more: what is faith?"

"To go at once and do the thing he tells us."

"If you don't, then you haven't faith in him?"

"No; certainly not."

"But might not that be his fault?"

"Yes—if he was not good; if I could not trust him; if he said I was to do one kind of thing and did another himself, then of course I could not have faith in him."

"Now tell me, Davie, what is the biggest faith of all—the faith to put in the one only thoroughly good person."

"You mean God, Mr. Grant?"

"Whom else could I mean?"

"You might mean Jesus."

"They are all one there; for they mean always the same thing, do always the same thing, always agree.

"Now tell me, Davie, what is the faith to put in him?"

"Oh, it is everything!" answered Davie.

"But what first?" asked Donal.

"First it is to do what he tells us."

"Yes, Davie; if ever we get hungry to see God, we must look at his picture."

"Where is that, sir?"

"Ah, Davie ... don't you know that besides being himself, and just because he is himself, Jesus is the living picture of God?"

"I know, we have to go and read about him in the book."

"But may I ask you a question, Mr. Grant?" said Arctura.

"I only hope I may be able to answer it," returned Donal.

"When we read about Jesus, we have to draw for ourselves the likeness of Jesus from words."

"I understand you quite," answered Donal. "Some go to other men to draw it for them; and some go to others to tell them what they are to draw for themselves—thus getting all their blunders in addition to those they must make for themselves. But the nearest likeness you can see of him is the one drawn by yourself from thinking about him while you do what he tells you. No other is of any vital use to you. And just here comes in the great promise he made. He had promised to come himself into our hearts, to give us his spirit, the very presence of his soul to our souls, talking in language that cannot be uttered because it is too great and strong and fine for any words of ours. So will he be much nearer to us than even his personal presence to us would be; and so we shall see him and be able to draw for ourselves the likeness of God. But first of all, and before everything else, mind, Davie, obedience!"

"Yes, Mr. Grant; I know," said Davie.

"Then off with you to the games God has given you."

"I'm going to fly my kite, Mr. Grant."

"Do. God likes to see you fly your kite. Don't forget it is all in his March wind it flies. It could not go up a foot but for that."

Davie went, but Arctura did not follow him.

"You have heard that my uncle is very poorly today?" she said.

"I have. Poor man!" said Donal.

"He is in a very peculiar condition."

"Of body and mind both, I should think. He greatly perplexes me."

"You would be quite as much perplexed even if you had known him so long as I have. Never since my father's death, which seems a century ago, have I felt safe; and never in my uncle's presence at ease. I seem not to get any nearer to him as the weeks go past! And do you know, Mr. Grant, it seems to me that the cause of all discomfort and strife is never that we are too near others, but that we are not near enough."

"I understand you," he said, "and entirely agree with you."

"I never feel that my uncle cares a straw for me except as one of the family and the possessor of its chief property. He might have liked me better, perhaps, if I had been dependent on him, instead of he in a measure on me. It sounds very horrid, but one gets compelled to look some things in the face."

"How long will he be your guardian?" asked Donal.

"He is no longer my guardian legally. The time set by my father's will was over last month. I am twenty-three and my own mistress. But of course my father's brother is welcome to live in my house as long as he pleases. It is much better for me, too, to have the head of the house to protect me. I only wish he were a little more like other people. But this is not what I wanted to talk to you of . . . Tell me about the ghost music; we had not time to talk about it last night."

"I got pretty near, at least so it seemed, to the place it came from. The wind blew so, and it was so dark that I could do nothing more then."

"But you will try again on the first opportunity?"

"I will not wait for one."

"But I shall be rather sorry, to tell the truth, if you find out it has indeed a natural cause."

"For that matter, my lady, how can there be any other than a natural cause? God and nature are at one, a unity. You may have remarked that the music is heard only in stormy nights, or at least nights when a good deal of wind is blowing?"

"I have heard it in the daytime."

"But on a windy day?"

"When you mention it, I think so. I am at least certain I never heard it on a still summer night."

"Do you think it comes in all storms?"

"I think not. But what of that?"

"That perhaps it has something to do not merely with the wind, but with the direction of the wind."

"I cannot say you enlighten me much!"

"Might not that account for its uncertainty? The instrument might be a fixed and accessible one, yet the opportunity of investigation rare. Experiment is not permitted us; we cannot make the wind blow when we will, neither can we vary the direction of the wind."

"Then how can you do anything till such another wind comes and sets the music going?"

"Last night I got so near the place whence the sounds seemed to come that I think now the eye may supplement the ear and come upon the music bird silent on her nest."

"What if you find nothing?"

"Something there may be for all that. I may even find the wrong thing, and yet the right thing be there. If the wind falls, as I think it will by the time school is over in the afternoon, I will go again and see what I can find. One thing I noticed last night, that the sound came first at a sudden change of the wind—toward the southeast, I think—a less-than-usual quarter for it to come from. It was blowing in a wild way about the house last night."

Lady Arctura's eyes opened wide.

"I think," she said, "the wind has something to do with my uncle's worst fits. When the wind blows so angrily, those words always come to me—'The prince of the power of the air, the spirit that works in the children of disobedience.' "

"Would you like to join the search, my lady?"

"You don't mean to go on the roof? Should I be able?"

"I would not have you go in the night, with the wind blowing," said Donal with a laugh, "but you can at least look out and see and judge for yourself. I could make it quite easy for you. When I tell you I mean to take Davie with me, you may think I do not count it very dangerous."

"But will it be safe enough for Davie?"

"I can venture more with Davie than with another because he obeys in a moment."

"I will promise to obey, too, if you will take me," said Arctura.

"Then be at the schoolroom at four o'clock, my lady. But we will not go except the wind be fallen."

"All right!" agreed Arctura, who, as soon as she heard that Davie would be of the party, was as ready to go as Davie himself.

When Davie heard what his tutor proposed for him, he was filled with the restlessness of anticipated delight. Often while helping Donal to get up his stock of fuel, he had gazed at the roof with longing eyes; but Donal had never let him go upon it, reserving the pleasure for the time when he could have thorough confidence in him. It was to Davie the prospect of a grand adventure.

The hour came, and with the very stroke of the clock Lady Arctura was at the schoolroom door. A moment and lessons were over; and the three set out for the north tower, to climb the spiral stair, as Davie now always called it.

But what a change had passed upon Lady Arctura! She was cheerful, merry—with Davie almost gay. She tripped lightly along with Davie, Donal following. Davie told her he had no idea what a jolly girl she was.

"I did not know you were like this," he remarked. "A body would think you had been at school with Mr. Grant. Oh, you don't know how much happier it is to have somebody you must mind."

Donal heard this last remark, and spoke: "If having me, Davie, doesn't help you to do just as well and be as happy without as with me, it will be all in vain."

"Mr. Grant! How can I be so happy without you as with you? It is not reasonable to expect it—is it now?"

"Perhaps I should not have said 'happy,' " answered Donal, who never refused to be put right. "What I mean is, as able to go on and order your ways all right. What I want most of all to teach you," he added, "is to leave the door on the latch for someone—you know whom I mean—to come in."

This he said for the sake of the less-declared pupil.

"Race me up the stair, Arkie," said Davie when they came to the foot of the spiral.

"Very well," assented his cousin.

"Which side will you have—the broad or the narrow?"

"The broad."

"Well, then—one, two, three, and away we go!"

Davie mounted like a clever goat, his hand and arm thrown about the newel, and slipping easily round it. Arctura's ascent was easier but slower, and she found her garments in her way. She gave it up and waited for Donal, who was ascending leisurely. Davie, thinking he heard her footsteps behind him, flew up shrieking with the sweet terror of imagined pursuit.

"What a sweet boy he is!" said Arctura when Donal overtook her.

"Yes," answered Donal; "one cannot help fancying such a child might run straight into the kingdom of heaven. Yet I suppose he must have his temptations and trials before he will be fit for it. It is out of the storm alone that the true peace comes."

"Then I may hope that what I have got to go through will not be lost, but will serve some good in me?"

There had never been any allusion to her trouble between them, but Donal took it as understood and answered, "Doubtless. Every pain and every fear, yes, every doubt is a cry after God. What mother refuses to go to her child because he is only crying, not calling her name?"

"Oh, if I could but think that! It would be so delightful—I mean to be able to think that about God. For, don't you think, if it be all right with God—I mean, if God be such a God that we can love him with all our heart and all our strength of loving, then all is well? Is it not so, Mr. Grant?"

"Indeed it is!"—*And you are not far from the kingdom of heaven*, he was on the point of saying but did not, because she was in it already— only unable yet to verify the things around her, like the man who had but halfway received his sight.

When they reached the top, he took them past his door and higher up the stair to another, opening on the roof, upon which they at once stepped out. Donal told Davie to keep close to Lady Arctura and follow him. He led them first to his stores of fuel, his "ammunition," he said, for fighting the winter. Then he showed them where he was when he first heard the music the night before, how he had thrown down his bucket to follow it, and how when he came back he had to feel for it in the dark. Then he began to lead them, as nearly as he could, the way he had then gone, but with some detours for their sakes. One steep-sloping roof they had to cross, but it had a little stair of its own up the middle of it and down the other side. They came at last, however, to a part over which, seeing it in the daylight, he was not quite sure about taking them. Stopping to bethink himself, they all turned and looked behind. The sun was approaching the sea and shone so bright over the flat, wet country that they could not tell where the sea began and the land ended. But as they looked, a great cloud came over the sun, and the land lay low and desolate between. The spring was gone, and the winter was there. A gust of wind, full of keen, dashing hail, drove sharp in their faces.

"Ah, that settles the question!" said Donal. "We must not go any farther just at present. The music bird must wait. We will call upon her another day. It is funny, isn't it, Davie, to go a bird's-nesting after music on the roof of the house!"

"Hark!" said Arctura; "I think I heard it! The music bird wants us to find her nest! I really don't think we ought to go back for a little blast of wind and a few pellets of hail. What do you think, Davie?"

"Oh, for me, I don't think I would turn for ever so big a storm," said Davie, "but you know, Arkie, it's not you or me; it's Mr. Grant that's the captain of this expedition, and we must do as he bids us."

"Oh, surely, Davie! I never meant to dispute that. Only Mr. Grant is not a tyrant and will let a lady say what she thinks."

"Oh, yes, he likes me to say what I think; he says we can't get at each other otherwise. And, do you know, he obeys me sometimes!"

Arctura glanced a keen look of question at the boy.

"It is quite true," said Davie. "Last winter, for days together, not all day, you know, I had to obey him most of the time; but at certain times I was as sure of Mr. Grant doing as I told him as he is now of me doing as he tells me."

"What are those times?" asked Arctura.

"It was when I was teaching him to skate," answered Davie with a kind of triumph. "He said I knew better than he did there, and therefore he would obey me."

"Oh, yes, I would believe it—perfectly well," said Arctura.

Here Donal suddenly threw an arm round each of them, for he stood between them, and pulled them down to a sitting position. The same instant a fierce blast burst upon the roof. Donal had seen the squall whitening the sea, and looking nearer home saw the tops of the trees all streaming toward the castle. The storm fell upon them with fury. But seated they were in no danger, for they were almost under the lee of a parapet.

"Hark!" said Arctura again, "there it is!"

They all heard the wailing cry of the ghost music. But while the blast continued they dared not continue their hunt after it. Still they heard it. It kept on in fits and gusts of sound till the squall ceased, as suddenly almost as it had risen. Then the sky was again clear, and the sun shone out as a March sun can between the blundering blasts and the swan-shot of the flying hail.

"When the storm is upon us," said Donal as they rose from their crouching position, "it seems as if there never could be any sunshine more; but our hopelessness does not keep back the sun when his hour to shine is come."

"I understand," said Arctura. "When one is miserable, misery seems the law of being. There is some thought which it seems nothing can ever set right; but all at once it is gone—broken up and gone like that hail cloud."

"Do you know why things so often come right?" said Donal.

"I think I know what you are thinking, but I do not want to answer," said Arctura.

"Why do things come right so often, Davie, do you think?" repeated Donal.

"Is it," returned Davie, "because they were made right to begin with?"

"There is much in that, Davie; but there is a better reason than that. It is because things are all alive, and the life at the heart of them, that which keeps them going, is the great, beautiful God. So the sun forever returns after the clouds."

"You speak always like one who has suffered," said Arctura, with a kind look up at him.

"Who has not that lives at all?"

"That is how you are able to help others."

"Am I able to help others? I am very glad to hear it. My ambition would be to help other people."

"You make it sound as if you have no ambition?"

"Where your work is laid out for you, there is no room for ambition. You have got your work to do. But give me your hand, my lady; put your other hand on my shoulder. You stop there, Davie, and don't move till I come to you. Now, my lady, a little jump! That's it! Now you are safe. You were not afraid, were you?"

"Not in the least—with you to help me. But did you come here in the dark?"

"Yes; but there is sometimes an advantage in the dark; you do not see how dangerous the way is. We sometimes take the darkness about us for the source of all our difficulties, but that may be a great mistake. Christian would hardly have dared go through the valley of the shadow of death had he not had the shield of darkness about him."

"Can the darkness be a shield? Is not the dark the evil thing?"

"Yes, the dark of distrust and unwillingness, not the dark of mere human ignorance. Where we do not see we are protected. And what can our self-protection do for us by day any more than by night? The things that are really dangerous to us are those that affect the life of the image of the living God." Donal had stopped in the earnestness of his talk, but now turned to go on. "There is my mark!" he said, "that chimney stack! I was close by it when I heard the music very near me indeed; but then all at once it grew so dark with clouds deepening over the moon that I could do nothing more. We shall do better now in the daylight, and three of us together!"

"What a huge block of chimney!" exclaimed Arctura.

"Is it not!" returned Donal. "It indicates the greatness of the building below us, of which we can see so little. It is like the volcanoes of the world, telling us how much fire is necessary to keep the old earth warm."

"I thought it was the sun that kept the earth warm," said Davie.

"So it is, but not the sun alone. The earth is like the human heart. The great glowing fire is God in the heart of the earth, and the great sun is God in the sky, keeping it warm on the other side. Your gladness and pleasure, your trouble when you do wrong, your love for all about you, that is God inside you; and all the beautiful things and lovable people, all the lessons you get, and whatever comes to you, is God outside of you—But now," said Donal. "I must go round and have a peep at the other side of the chimneys."

He disappeared, and Arctura and Davie stood waiting his return. They looked each in the other's face with delight, as if in the conscious sharing of the great adventure. Beyond their feet lay the wide country and the great sea; over them the sky with the sun in it going down toward the sea; under their feet the mighty old pile that was their house; and under that the earth with its molten heart of fire. But Davie's look was in reality one of triumph in his tutor.

"I am his pupil, too, Davie," she said, "though I do not think Mr. Grant knows it."

"How can that be," answered Davie, "when you are afraid of him? I am not a bit afraid of him!"

"How do you know that I am afraid of him?" she asked.

"Oh, anybody could see that!"

Since she turned the talk on Donal, Arctura had not cared to look the boy in the face. She was afraid she had spoken foolishly, and Davie might repeat her words. She did not quite wish to hasten any further intimacy; things seemed going in that direction fast enough. Her eyes, avoiding Davie's countenance, kept reconnoitering the stack of chimneys.

"Aren't you glad to have such a castle to call your own—to do what you like with, Arkie? You could pull it all to pieces if you liked!"

"Would it be less mine," said Arctura, "if I were not at liberty to pull it to pieces? And would it be mine when I had pulled it to pieces, Davie?"

Donal had come round the other side of the stack and heard what she said.

"What makes a thing your own, do you think, Davie?" she went on.

"To be able to do with it what you like," replied Davie.

"Whether it be good or bad?"

"Yes, I think so," answered Davie, doubtfully.

"There I think you are quite wrong," she rejoined. "The moment you begin to use a thing wrong, that moment you make it less yours. I can't quite explain it, but that is how it looks to me."

She ceased and after a moment Donal took up the question.

"Lady Arctura is quite right, Davie," he said.

"The nature, that is the use of a thing, is the way by which it can be possessed. The right to use to the true purpose and the power to do so is what makes a thing ours. Suppose you had a very beautiful picture, but from some defect in your sight you could never see that picture as it really was, while a servant in the house not only saw it as it was meant to be seen but had such an intense delight in gazing at it that even in his dreams it came to him and made him think of many things he would not have thought of but for knowing it. . . . Which of you, you or the servant in your house, would have the more real possession of that picture? You could sell it away from yourself, and never know anything about it; but you could not by all the power of a tyrant take away that picture from your servant."

"Ah, now I understand," said Davie, with a look at Lady Arctura which seemed to say, "You see how Mr. Grant can make me understand?"

"I wonder," said Lady Arctura, "what that curious opening in the side of the chimney stack means? It can't be meant for the smoke to come out."

"No," said Donal; "there is not a mark of smoke about it. Besides, if it had been meant for that, it would hardly have been put halfway from the top. I can't make it out. A hole like that in any chimney would surely interfere with the draught. The mouth of that chimney seems to be up among the rest of them. I must get a ladder and see whether it be truly a chimney."

"If you were to put me up on your shoulders," said Davie, "I should be able to see into the hole."

"Come then; up you go!" said Donal.

And up went Davie, standing on his tutor's shoulders, and peeped into the slit which ran horizontally across.

"It looks very like a chimney," he said, turning his head and thrusting it in sideways, "It goes right down to somewhere," he said. "But there is something across it a little way down—to prevent the jack-daws from getting in, I suppose."

"What is it?" asked Donal.

"Something like a grating," answered Davie. "No . . . not a grating exactly. It is what you might call a grating, but it seems made of wires all running one way. I don't think it would keep a strong bird out if he wanted to get in."

Aha! said Donal to himself, *I suspect there is something here.* . . . "What if those wires were tuned! Did you ever see an Aeolian harp, my lady?" he asked. "I never did myself."

"Yes," answered Lady Arctura, "once when I was a little girl. And now you suggest it, I think the sounds we hear are not unlike those of an Aeolian harp! The strings are all about the same length—I remember that—only differently tuned. But I do not understand the principle of it at all. Somehow they all play together and make the strangest, wildest harmonies, when the wind blows across them in a particular way."

"I fancy we have found the nest of our music bird," said Donal. "The wires Davie speaks of may be the strings of an Aeolian harp. I wonder if there is any possibility of a draught across them! I must get up and see. I will go and get a ladder."

"But how could there be an Aeolian harp up here?"

"*Something* is here," answered Donal, "which needs accounting for; it may be an Aeolian harp."

"But in a chimney . . . the soot would spoil the strings!"

"Then perhaps it is not a chimney: is there any sign of soot about, Davie?"

"No, sir; there is nothing but pretty, clean stone and lime."

"You see, my lady, we do not even know that this is a chimney."

"What else could it be, standing with the rest?"

"At least it has never served the uses of a chimney, so far as we can see. It may have been built for one. If it had ever been used for one, the marks of smoke would remain had it been in disuse ever so long. But now we will go, and tomorrow I will come up with a ladder."

"Will you not get it now?" urged Arctura. "I should so like to be there when it was found out."

"As you please, my lady. I will go at once and get a ladder. There is one not far from the bottom of the tower."

"If you do not mind the trouble; I should so like to see the end of the thing."

"I will come and help you carry it," said Davie.

"You mustn't leave your cousin alone. Besides, I am not sure I can get it up the stair. I am afraid it is too long. Anyhow you could not very well help me. If I find I cannot get it up that way, we will rig up our old tackle and fetch it up as we did the fuel."

He went, and the cousins sat down to wait his return. It was a cold evening, but Arctura was well wrapped up and Davie was hardy. They sat at the foot of the chimneys and began to talk.

"Are you very fond of my brother?" asked Davie.

"Why do you ask me that?"

"Because they say you and he are going to be married someday, and yet you don't seem to care to be much together."

"It is all nonsense," replied Arctura, reddening. "I wish people would not talk such foolishness."

"Well, I do think he is not so fond of you as of Eppie."

"Hush! hush! you must not talk of such things."

"But I've seen him kiss Eppie, and I never saw him kiss you."

"No, indeed!"

"But is it right of Forgue, if he is going to marry you, to kiss Eppie?—that's what I want to know!"

"But he is not going to marry me."

"He would if you told him you wished it. Papa wishes it very much."

"How do you know that?"

"From many things I have heard him say. Once he said, 'Afterwards, when the house is our own,' and I asked him what he meant by it, and he said, 'When Forgue marries your pretty cousin, then the castle will be Forgue's. That will be how it ought to be, you know; for property and title ought never to be parted.'"

The hot blood rose to Arctura's temples; was she a thing to be flung in as a makeweight to property?

"You would not like to have to give away your castle, would you, Arkie?" he went on.

"Not to anyone I did not love."

"If I were you, I would not marry anyone, but keep my castle to myself. I don't see why Forgue or anyone else should have your castle."

"Then you think I should make my castle my husband?"

"He would be a good, big husband anyhow, and a strong one, and one that would defend you from your enemies and not talk when you wanted to be quiet."

"That is all very true; but one might for all that get a little weary of such a stupid husband, however big and strong he might be."

"But he would never be a cruel husband. I have heard Papa say a great deal about some cruel husbands; it seemed sometimes as if he meant himself; but that could not be, because Papa could never have been a cruel husband."

Arctura made no reply. All but vanished memories of things she had heard when a child, hints and signs here and there that all was not right between her uncle and aunt, vaguely returned. Could it be that now at last he was repenting of harshness to his wife, and the thought of it was preying upon him and driving him to a refuge of lies? But in the presence of the boy she could not think thus about his father, and was relieved by the return of Donal.

He had found it rather a difficult job to get the ladder round the sharp curves of the stair; but now at last they saw him with it upon his shoulder coming over a distant part of the roof.

"Now we shall see!" he exclaimed as he set it down, leaned it up against the chimney, and stood panting.

"You have tired yourself out," said Lady Arctura.

"Well, where's the harm in that, my lady? A man was meant to get tired a good many times before he lies down for the last time," rejoined Donal lightly.

Davie said, "Mr. Grant, was a woman meant to marry a man she does not love?"

"No, certainly, Davie."

"Mr. Grant," said Arctura hurriedly, in dread of what Davie might say next, "what do you take to be the chief duty of one belonging to an ancient family and inheriting a large property? Ought a woman to get rid of it, or attend to its duties herself?"

Donal thought a little.

"The property called mine belongs to my family rather than to me," she went on, "and if there had been a son it would have gone to him. Should I not be doing better for the family by giving it up to the next heir, and letting him manage it?"

"It seems to me," said Donal, "the fact that you would not have suc-ceeded had there been a son points to another fact, that there has been another disposer of events concerned in the matter.

"God, of course, is over all, and overrules all things to his ends.

"And if he has been pleased to let the property come to you, he expects you to perform the duties of it."

"But might it not be one's duty to get rid of property in order that those to come after might not be burdened with its temptations and responsibilities?"

"Not, at least, by merely shifting the difficulties from your own family to that of another. Besides, it would be to take the appointment of things into your own hands instead of obeying the orders given you. Nothing that is against God's way can be true; and therefore I say the value of property consists only in its being means to work his will. There is no success in the universe but in his will being done."

Arctura was silent. Knowing that here she must think, and would think, Donal went no further for the time; a house must have its foundations well settled before they are built upon. He turned to his ladder, set it up carefully, mounted and peered into the opening. At the length of his arm he could reach the wires Davie had described. They were taut and free of rust—were therefore not iron or steel. He saw also that a little down the shaft light came in from the opposite side—there was an opening there too. Next he saw that each following string—for strings he already counted them, each horizontal—was placed a little lower than that before it, so that their succession was inclined to the other side and downwards—apparently in a plane between the two openings that a draught might pass along them in one plane, and that their own plane. This must surely be the instrument whence the music flowed! He descended.

"Do you know, my lady," he asked Arctura, "how the Aeolian harp is placed in relation to the wind that wakes it?"

"The only one I have seen," she answered, "was made to fit into a window, in which the lower sash was opened just wide enough to let it in, so that the wind entering must pass across the strings."

Then Donal was satisfied—he was at least all but certain.

"Of course," he said to Arctura, after describing to her the whole arrangement, "we cannot be absolutely certain until we have been here present with the music and have experimented by covering and uncovering the opening. For that we must wait the next southeast wind."

"I should so much like to be here," she said, "when it comes!"

"If it be neither dark, nor in the middle of the night," said Donal, "nothing will be easier." So they descended and parted.

20

·····················

Kennedy and Forgue

*B*ut Donal did not feel that even after such experimentation would he have exhausted the discovery. That the source of the music was an Aeolian harp in a chimney that had never been used might be enough for the other dwellers in the castle, but Donal wanted to know as well to what room it was a chimney. For the thought had struck him—could the music have anything to do with the main legend that hung vaporous about the ancient house? Perhaps he might not so immediately have sought a possible connection but that the talk concerning the unknown room in the castle had gone on spreading. At the same time were heard increasing hints as to a ghost being even now seen at times about the castle. As to this, Donal had concluded that one or two of the domestics might have had a glimpse of the earl in his restless night walks about the house and had either imagined a ghost or had chosen to use the memory of their own fright to produce like effect upon yielded listeners. Various were the conjectures as to what ghost it might be. Donal, by nature strongly urged toward the roots of things, could not fail to let his mind cherish a desire to discover whether any or how much truth was at the root of it—for a root, great or small, there must be to everything. But he had no right to go prying about the place or do anything which, if known, might be disagreeable. He must take an opportunity of first suggesting the idea to Lady Arctura. By the way she took it he would be guided. For the present he must wait.

His spare hours were now much occupied with his friend Andrew Comin. The good man had so far recovered as to think himself able to work again; but he soon found there was very little he could do. His strength was gone, and the exertion necessary for the lightest labor caused him pain. His face had grown very white and thin, and he had made up his mind that he was not to get better but was to go home through a lingering illness. He was ready to go and ready to linger, as God pleased.

The time was now drawing nigh for the return of Lord Forgue, but Eppie had learned only of his absence and nothing concerning his return. But almost as if she foresaw it, there was a restless light in her eyes.

When Stephen Kennedy heard that Eppie had gone back to her grandparents, a faint hope revived in him; he knew nothing of the late encounter between the lovers and her friends. He but knew that she was looking sad, as if she had lost her lover, and it seemed to him as if now she might at least admit him to be of some service to her. Separation had created more and more gentle thoughts of her in his heart; he was ready to forgive everything if only she would let him love her again. He haunted the house in the hope of getting a peep of her. When she began to go again into the town, he saw her repeatedly, following her for the sake of being near her but taking care she should not see him; and he succeeded in escaping her notice.

At length, however, one night a month after her return, he summoned the courage to accost her. Eppie had gone into the baker's whose daughter was her friend; Kennedy had seen her go in, and stood in the shadow, waiting for her to come out. He was all but determined to speak to her that night if he could. She remained within a good while. At length she appeared. By this time, however, Kennedy's courage had nearly evaporated, and when he saw her coming he stepped under an archway, let her pass, and followed again. All at once resolve again awoke in him. She started when he stepped in front of her and gave a little cry.

"Don't be afraid of me, Eppie," said Kennedy. "I wouldn't hurt a hair of your head."

"Go away," said Eppie. "You've no right to come around me."

"None but the right of loving you better than ever," said Kennedy, "if only you'd let me show it."

The words softened her. She began to cry.

"If anything I could do would take the grief from you, Eppie," said Kennedy, "you've only to ask. I won't ask you to marry me; I know you wouldn't care about that. But if I could be a friend or help you out of your troubles, I'm ready to lay in the dirt for you."

For sole answer, Eppie went on crying. She was far from happy. She had nearly, she thought, persuaded herself that all was over between her and Lord Forgue, and she felt almost as if she could but for shame have allowed Kennedy to comfort her as an old friend. But everything in her mind was so confused and everything around her so miserable that there was nothing to be done but cry. And as she continued crying, Kennedy, in the simplicity of his heart and the desire to comfort her, came quietly but with throbbing heart up to her; putting his arm around her, he said again: "Don't be afraid, Eppie. I'm too sore-hearted to hurt you. I don't want to presume, but are you in need of anything? I heard about your grandfather's troubles too. If it's turning scarce with you or your folk, anything I have my mother and I will share with you."

"Thank you, Stephen," said Eppie, touched with his goodness, "but there's no necessity. We have plenty."

"If the young lord had wronged you in any way—"

She turned on him with a quickness that was almost fierce.

"I want nothing from you, Stephen Kennedy," she said; "My lord's nothing to you—and not much yet to me," she added with sudden reaction and an outburst of self-pity, and she fell again sobbing.

With the timidity of a strong man before a girl he loves and whose displeasure he fears, Kennedy tried to comfort her, seeking to wipe her eyes with her apron, as if that would stop her tears. While he was thus engaged, another man, turning a corner quickly, came nearly upon them. He started back, then came nearer as if to satisfy himself who they were. It was Lord Forgue.

"Eppie!" he cried, in a tone in which indignation blended with surprise.

Eppie uttered a little shriek and ran to him, but he pushed her away.

"My lord," said Kennedy, "the lass wants none of your help—or mine. But I swear by God that if you do her any wrong, I'll not rest night or day till I've made you repent it."

"Go to the devil!" retorted Forgue. "What have you to do with her? Speak out and you may take her. I am hardly prepared to go halves with you."

Again Eppie would have clung to him, but again he pushed her away.

"Oh, my lord!" and she could go no further for weeping. This touched him.

"How is it I find you here with this man?" he asked. "I don't want to be unfair, but this is rather too much."

"My lord," said Kennedy.

"Hold your tongue and let her speak for herself."

"I didn't meet him, my lord. I never asked him to come near me," sobbed Eppie. "You see what you've done!" she went on, turning in anger on Kennedy, "nothing but grief you have brought upon me. What business is it of yours!"

Kennedy turned without a word and went. Eppie with a fresh burst of tears turned to go also. But she had satisfied Forgue that there was nothing between them, and taking his turn he was soon more successful than Kennedy in consoling her.

He had while absent been able enough to get on without her; but no sooner was he home than in the weary lack of anything else to interest him, the feelings began to revive. Satisfied that the interview had not been of her seeking, neither was to her satisfaction, he felt the tide of old tenderness come streaming back over the ghastly sands of jealousy. And before they parted he had made with her an appointment to meet the next night in a more suitable spot.

Before Eppie reentered the house, she did her best to remove all traces of the varied emotions she had undergone; but she could not help the shining of her eyes, for the lamp of joy relighted in her bosom shone through them. Donal was seated by her grandfather reading to him. I believe those last days of sickness and weakness were among the most blessed of his life. Donal looked up when Eppie entered, and the same moment knew her secret. "She has seen Forgue!" he said to himself.

When Lord Morven heard of his son's return he sent for Donal, received him in a friendly way, gave him to understand that however he might fail to fall in with his views, he depended thoroughly on whatever he said or undertook, and made to him the request that he would keep him informed of anything he might be able to discover with regard to his son's proceedings. "I am told the girl has gone back to her relations," he concluded.

Donal replied that he could not consent to watch Lord Forgue, which would be neither more nor less than to take the position of a spy.

"I will however warn him," he concluded, "that I may see it right to let his father know what he is about. I fancy, however, he knows that pretty well already."

"Pooh! that would be only to give him warning—to teach him the necessity for the more cunning!" said the earl.

"I can do nothing underhanded," replied Donal. "I will help no man to keep an unrighteous secret, but neither will I secretly disclose it."

Meeting Forgue a few days after, his lordship would have passed him without recognition, but Donal stopped him and said: "I believe, my lord, you have seen Eppie since your return."

"What the deuce is that to you?"

"I wish your lordship to understand that whatever comes to my knowledge concerning your proceedings in regard to her, I consider myself at perfect liberty to report to your father if I see fit; he has a right to know of them."

"Thank you! The warning was quite unnecessary. Still, it is an advantage few informers would have given me, and I thank you, for so far I am indebted to you. It does nothing, however, to redeem you from the shame of such a profession!"

"When your lordship has proved himself an honorable gentleman, it will be possible for me to take some interest in what you may think of my proceedings."

"As much as to say you do not think me an honorable man!" said Forgue with a sneer.

"Only at present that I continue in doubt of you. Time will show what is in you."

"Oh, hang your preaching!" Forgue answered, speaking as he went without turning his head.

21

••••••••••••••••••••

Miss Carmichael

Things went on for a while with nothing new occurring. Donal seldom met Lady Arctura, and when he did, received from her no encouragement to address her. But he could not help thinking the troubled look had begun to reappear on her face. And now she was more than ever in the company of Miss Carmichael. Donal had good cause to fear that the pharisaism of her would-be directress was coming down upon her, not like rain on the mown grass but like snow on the spring flowers. The impossibility of piercing the lovers of tradition in any vital part is a sore trial to the old Adam still unslain in lovers of the Truth. At the same time, no discipline is more potent in giving patience opportunity for working her perfect work.

Donal prayed for Lady Arctura and waited. The hour was not yet ripe.

One bright autumn day, Donal was walking along through the avenue of beech trees, his book in his hand, now and then reading a little and now and then looking up to the half-bared branches, now and then, like Davie, sweeping a cloud of the fallen leaves before him. He was in this childish act when, looking up, he saw the two ladies approaching a few yards in front. But he did not see the peculiar look Miss Carmichael threw her companion. "Behold your prophet!" it said. He would have passed, but Miss Carmichael stopped with a smile which was bright because it showed her good teeth, but was not pleasant because it showed nothing else.

"Glorying over the fallen, Mr. Grant?" she said.

Donal, in his turn, smiled.

"That is scarcely Mr. Grant's way," said Arctura, "—so far at least as I have known him!"

"Poor children!" said Miss Carmichael, affecting a sympathy with the fallen leaves.

"Pardon me," said Donal, "if I grudge them your pity; it seems to me misplaced. There is nothing more of children in those leaves than there is in the hair that falls on the barber's floor."

"I don't think it very gracious to pull a lady up so sharply," returned Miss Carmichael. "I spoke poetically."

"There is no poetry in what is not true," rejoined Donal. "Those are not the children of the tree. Those beechnuts among the fallen leaves—they are the children of the tree."

"Lost like the leaves!" sighed Miss Carmichael, willing to shift her ground.

"Why do you say they are lost?"

"But you must allow that some things are lost!" said Miss Carmichael.

"Yes, surely!" answered Donal. "Why else should he have to come and look for them till he find them?"

This was hardly such an answer as the theologian had expected, and she was not immediately ready with her rejoinder.

"But some of them are lost after all!" she finally murmured.

"Doubtless," replied Donal. "Some of his sheep run away again. But he goes after them again."

"Does he always?"

"Yes."

"I do not believe it."

"Then you do not believe that God is infinite?"

"Yes, I do."

"How can you? Is he not the Lord God merciful and gracious?"

"I am glad you know that."

"But if his mercy and his graciousness are not infinite, then he is not infinite."

"There are other attributes in which he is infinite."

"But he is not infinite in them all if he is not infinite in those which are the most beautiful, the most divine."

"I do not care for human argument. I go by the Word of God."

"Let me hear, then."

"There is the doctrine of adoption," she said; "does not that teach us that God chooses to make some his children and not others?"

"God's mercy is infinite; and the doctrine of adoption is one of the falsest of all the doctrines invented by the so-called Church, and it is used by yet less loving teachers to oppress the souls of God's true children."

"You may think as you please, Mr. Grant, but while Paul teaches the doctrine, I will hold it. He may perhaps know a little better than you."

"Paul teaches no such doctrine. He teaches just what I have been saying. The Word applies it to the raising of one who is a son to the true position of a son."

"It seems to me presumptuous of you to determine what the apostle meant."

"Why, Miss Carmichael, do you think the gospel comes to us as to a set of fools? I am bound by the command of the Master to understand the things he says. He commands me to see their rectitude, because, they being true, I have to be able to see them true. Any use of a single word Paul says to oppress a human heart with the feeling that it is not the child of God comes of the devil. To fulfill the very necessities of our being, we must be his children in brain and heart, in body and soul and spirit, in obedience and hope. Then only is our creation fulfilled—then only shall we be what we were made for."

He ceased. Miss Carmichael was astonished and intellectually cowed, but her heart was nowise touched. She had never had that longing after closest relation with God.

"I do hope what you say is true, Mr. Grant!" sighed Arctura.

"Oh, yes, hope . . . we all hope!" said Miss Carmichael. "But it is the Word we have to do with, not hope."

"I have given you the true Word," said Donal and here lifted his bonnet to pass on.

When he was gone, the ladies resumed their walk in silence.

At length Miss Carmichael spoke: "Well, I must say, of all the conceited young men I have had the misfortune to meet, your Mr. Grant is the first in self-assurance and forwardness."

"Are you sure, Sophie," rejoined Arctura, "that it is self-assurance and not conviction of the truth of what he had to say, that gives him the courage to speak as he does?"

"How can it be when it is not true?—when it goes against all that has for ages been taught and believed?"

"What if God should now be sending fresh light into the minds of his people?"

"The old is good enough for me."

"But it may not be good enough for God. What if Mr. Grant should be his messenger to us?"

"A likely thing, indeed! A mere student from the North, raw from college!"

"No matter! I can't help hoping he may be right after all. Was not that the way they spoke in the old time, when they said, 'Can any good thing come out of Galilee?' "

"Ah, I see the influence has gone further with you than I had feared! You are infected not merely with his doctrine but with his frightful irreverence. To dare the comparison of that poor creature with Jesus Christ!"

"If he were a messenger of Jesus Christ," said Arctura quietly, "—I neither say he is or he is not—but the reception you now give him would be precisely what he would expect, for the Lord said the disciple should be as his Master!"

The words entered and stung. Miss Carmichael stopped short, her face in a flame, but her words were cold and hard.

"I am sorry," she said, "our friendship should come to so abrupt a conclusion, Lady Arctura; but it is time it should end when you can speak so to me, who have for so many years done my best to help you! If that is the first result of your new gospel—well! Remember who said, 'If an angel from heaven preach any other gospel to you than I have preached, let him be accursed!' "

She turned back to go again down the avenue.

"Oh, Sophia! do not leave me so!" cried Lady Arctura.

But Sophie was already yards away, her skirt making a small whirlwind that went following her among the withered leaves. Arctura burst into tears and sat down at the root of one of the great beeches. Miss Carmichael never looked behind her but went straight home.

Donal was walking quietly back, trying with but partial success to dismiss the thought of what had occurred, when a little fluffy fringe of one of poor Lady Arctura's sobs reached his ear. He looked up and saw her sitting like one rejected, weeping. He could not pass and leave her thus. But he approached her slowly, that she might have time to get over the worst of her passion. She heard his steps in the withered leaves, glanced up, saw who it was, buried her face for one moment in her hands, then sought her handkerchief, raised her head and rose with a feeble attempt at a smile.

"Mr. Grant," she said, coming toward him, "St. Paul said that should an angel from heaven preach any other gospel than his, he was accursed. 'Let him be accursed,' he said. Even an *angel from heaven*, you see, Mr. Grant! It is terrible!"

"It is terrible, and I say amen to it with all my heart," replied Donal. "But the gospel you have received is not the gospel of Paul, but one substituted for it—by no angel from heaven, but by men who in order to get

them into their own intellectual pockets melted down the gold of the kingdom and recast it in the moulds of legal thought. But they meant well,
seeking to justify the ways of God to men; therefore the curse of the apostle does not fall, I think, upon them."

"Oh, I do hope what you say is true!" said Arctura.

"You can find nothing but what the Lord teaches you. If you find what
I tell you untrue, it will be in not being enough—in not being grand and
free and bounteous enough. Only you must leave human teachers altogether, and give yourself to him to be taught."

"I will try to do as you tell me," said Arctura.

"If there is anything that troubles you," said Donal, "I shall be most
glad to try and help; but it is better there should not be much talk."

With these words he left her. Arctura followed slowly to the house and
went straight to her own room, her mind filling as she went.

Donal was glad indeed to think that now at length an open door stood
before the poor girl. After this, for a good many days, they did not so
much as see each other.

22

• • • • • • • • • • • • • • • • • • •

Morven House

The health of the earl was as usual fluctuating. It depended much on
the nature of his special indulgences. There was hardly any sort of nar-
cotic with which he did not at least experiment, if not indulge. In so doing
he made no pretense even to himself of the furtherance of knowledge; he
knew that he wanted solely to find how this or that, modified or combined, would affect him. He believed neither like saint nor devil: he
believed and did not obey; he believed and did not yet tremble.

According to the character and degree of his indulgence, I say, the one
day he was better, the other worse. But however the different things might
vary in their operations upon him, to one end at least they all tended, and
that was the destruction of whatever remained to him of a moral nature.

Moved all his life by rebellion against what he called the convention-
alities of society, he had committed great wrongs—whether also what are
called crimes, I cannot tell; no repentance had followed, whatever
remorse the consequences of them may have occasioned. Even the possibility of remorse was gradually disappearing from his nature.

One morning before the earl was up, he sent for Donal and requested
him to give Davie a half-holiday, in order for Donal to do something for
him instead.

"You know, or perhaps you don't know," he said, "that I have a house in the town—the only house, indeed, now belonging to the title. It is a strange and not very attractive house; you must have noticed it—on the main street, a little before you come to the Morven Arms."

"I believe I know the house, my lord," answered Donal, "with strong iron stanchions to the lower windows, and—"

"Yes, that is the house; I see you know it. It is there I want you to go for me; you don't mind it, do you?"

"Not in the least," answered Donal.

"I want you to search a certain bureau there for some papers."

"You would like me to go at once?"

"Yes."

"Very well, my lord," said Donal.

"By the way," said the earl, as if he had but just thought of the thing, "have you no news to give me about Forgue's affair?"

"No, my lord," answered Donal. "Whether they meet now I do not know, but I am afraid."

"Oh, I daresay," rejoined his lordship, "like many another, the whim is wearing off! But I don't trust him much."

"He gave you no promise, if you remember, my lord."

"I remember very well; why the deuce should I not remember? I am not in the way of forgetting things! No, by Jove! nor forgiving them either! Where there is anything to forgive there is no fear of my forgetting! I remember that I may not forgive."

He followed this inhuman utterance with a laugh, as if he would have it pass for a joke, but there was no ring in the laugh.

He then gave Donal detailed instructions as to where the bureau stood, how he was to open it with a curious key he made him find in one of the drawers in the room, how also he was to open the more secret part of the bureau in which the papers lay.

"Forget!" he echoed, returning to his last utterance; "I have not been in that house for twenty years! You can judge whether I forget! No!" he added with an oath, "If I found myself forgetting I should think it time to look out; but there is no sign of that yet, thank God! There! Take the keys and be off with you! Simmons will give you the key to the house. You had better take the one for the door in the alley; it is easier to open."

Donal left and went at once to Simmons, asking for the key of the side door, which opened in the close. The butler went to fetch it but returned saying he could not lay his hands upon it; but there was the key to the front door, which, however, he was afraid might prove rather stiff to turn. Donal, taking what he could get and oiling it well, set out for Morven House. But on his way he turned aside into the humble dwelling in which he had spent so many hours.

Andrew seemed so much worse that he thought he must be sinking. So, too, apparently thought Andrew, for the moment he saw Donal he requested they might be left alone for a few minutes.

"It's over for this world, my friend. It's coming—the hour of darkness. But the thing that's true when the light shines is just as true in the dark.

God'll give me the grace to lie still. But I have just one favor to beg you, not for my sake, but for hers. If you have warning, will you be with me when I go? It may be a comfort to me—I don't know. But I do know it'll be a great comfort to Doory. She won't find herself so lonesome, losing sight of her old man, if his heart's friend is beside him when he goes."

"Please God, I'll be at your command," said Donal.

"Now, ask Doory to come, for I don't want to see any less of her than I can. It may be years before I get sight of her loving face again."

Donal obeyed, called Doory, and took his leave.

Opposite Morven House was a building which had at one time been the stables to it but was now part of a brewery, and a high wall shut it off from the street. It was now dinnertime with the humble people of the town, and there was not a soul visible in the street; so Donal put the key in the lock of the front door, opened it, and entered without a soul having seen him, so far as he knew. So far successful, for he desired to rouse no idle curiosity, he moved almost on tiptoe as he entered the deserted place. He was in a lofty hall, rising high above the first story. The dust lay thick on a large marble table in it—but what was that?—a streak all across it, brushed sharply through the middle of the dust. It was strange! But he could not pause to speculate now. He must do his work first, and he proceeded therefore to find the room to which the earl had directed him. He hastened, but softly, to the bureau, and applied its key. Following carefully the directions given him, for the lock had more than one quip and wanton wile about it, he succeeded in opening it. His instructions had been so complete that he had no difficulty in finding the secret place, nor the packet which was concealed in it.

But just as he laid his hands upon it, he was suddenly aware of a swift passage past the door of the room and apparently up the next stair. There was nothing he could distinguish as footsteps, or even as the rustle of a dress, only a ghost-like motion that could not be described. He darted to the door, which he had only by instinct shut behind him, and opened it swiftly and noiselessly. Nothing was to be seen! But it need be no ghost. The stairs were covered with thick carpet, and a light foot might have passed and gone up without any sound at all. It was but the wind of the troubled air that had told the tale.

He turned and closed the bureau, leaving the packet where it lay. If there was anyone in the house, who could tell what might follow? It was in truth the merest ghost of a sound he had heard; but he would go after it. Someone might be using the earl's house for his own purposes. He must find out.

Going softly up, he paused at the top and looked around him. An iron clenched door stood nearly opposite the head of the stair; and at the farther end of the long passage a door stood a little way open. From that direction came the sound of a little movement and then of low voices—one surely that of a woman. Then it flashed upon Donal that this might be the place of Eppie's rendezvous with Forgue. Afraid of being discovered before he had gathered his wits, he stepped softly across the passage to the door opposite, opened it, not however without some noise, and stepped in, standing for a moment in dread of having thus given an alarm.

There came a cry along the passage, and the door at the end opened. A hurried step came along, passed Donal, and went down the stair.

"If I am right, now is my time," said Donal to himself, "Eppie is left alone."

He issued from his retreat and went along the passage. The door at the end of it was half open, and Eppie stood in the gap. Whether she had seen him come out of the room, I do not know; but she stood gazing with widespread eyes of terror, as if looking on the approach of a ghost. As he came nearer the blue eyes opened wider and seemed to fix in their orbits. Just as her name was on his lips, Eppie dropped with a moan on the floor. Donal caught her up and hurried down the stairway. He had but reached the first floor when he heard the sound of swift ascending steps, and the next moment was face-to-face with Forgue. The latter started back and for a moment stood staring. But mounting rage restored him to his self-possession. His first thought had been, like that of Ahab, "Hast thou found me, O mine enemy?" But his first words were: "Put her down, you scoundrel!"

"She can't stand," replied Donal quietly.

"You've killed her, you confounded, sneaking spy!"

"Then I should have been more kind than you!"

"What are you going to do with her?"

"Take her home to her dying grandfather."

"You've hurt her, you devil! I know you have!"

"She is only frightened. She is coming to herself already. I feel her coming awake."

"You feel her!" cried Forgue with a great oath; "I will make you feel me presently. Put her down, I say!" He hissed the words from between his teeth, for he dared not speak aloud for fear of rousing the neighborhood.

Eppie began to writhe and struggle in Donal's arms. Forgue laid hold of her, and Donal was compelled to put her down. She threw herself into the arms of her lover and was on the point of fainting away again for joy at her deliverance.

"Go out of the house, you spy!" said Forgue.

"I am here by your father's desire," said Donal.

"As a spy," insisted Forgue.

"Not to my knowledge," returned Donal. "He sent me to look for some papers."

"You lie!" said Forgue; "I see it in your face."

"So long as I speak the truth," said Donal, "it matters little to me that you should think me a liar. But, my lord, I request that you will give Eppie to me that I may take her home."

"A likely thing!" said Forgue, holding Eppie to him and looking with contempt at Donal.

"Then I tell you, on the word of a man whom neither you nor the world shall find a liar, that I will rouse the town and have a crowd about the house in five minutes."

"You are the devil, I do believe, come from hell for my ruin!" cried Forgue. "There! Take her. Only mind it is you and not I to blame that I do not marry her! I would have done my part. Leave us alone, and I'll marry her; take her from me in this sneaking fashion, and I make no promises!"

"Oh, but you will, dearest?" said Eppie in a beseeching, frightened tone.

Forgue pushed her from him. She burst into tears. He took her in his arms and began soothing her like a child, assuring her he meant nothing by what he had said.

"You are my own little wife," he went on; "you know you are, whatever your enemies may drive us to. Nothing can part us now. Go with him for the present. The time will come when the truth shall be known, and we will laugh at them all. If it were not for your sake and the scandal of the thing, I should send the villain to the bottom of the stair in double-quick time. But it is better to be patient."

Sobbing bitterly, Eppie went with Donal down the stair, leaving Forgue shaking with impotent rage behind him. When they got into the street Donal turned to lock the door. Eppie seized the opportunity, darted from him, and ran down the alley to the side door. But it was locked, and she could not get in. Then came a sudden thought to Donal. He was with her in a moment.

"You go home alone, Eppie," he said. "It will be just as well you should not go in with me. I am going to see Lord Forgue out of this!"

"Oh, you won't hurt him!" pleaded Eppie.

"I will not if I can help it; but he may put it out of my power to spare him. I don't want to hurt him; there is no revenge in me. You go home. It will be better for him as well as for you."

She went slowly away, weeping, but trying to keep what appearance of calm she might. As soon as she was round the corner, Donal hurried into the house by the front door; hastening to the side door, he took the key from the lock. Then returning to the hall, he summoned Forgue.

"My lord," he said at the bottom of the stair, loud enough to be heard through the empty house, "I have got both the keys; the side door is locked, and I am about to lock the front door. I do not want to shut you in. Pray come down before I go." Forgue came leaping down the stair and threw himself upon Donal. A fierce struggle commenced for the posses- sion of the key which Donal held in his hand. The sudden assault stag- gered Donal, and he fell on the floor with Forgue above him, who imme- diately laid hold of the key and tried to wrest it from him. But Donal was much the stronger of the two and had soon thrown his lordship off him. For a moment Donal was a little tempted to give him a good thrashing, but the thought of Eppie helped him to restrain himself. Donal would not let him up, but contented himself with holding him down till he yielded. For a while Forgue kept kicking and striking out in all directions but at last lay still.

"Will you promise to walk out quietly if I let you up?" asked Donal, still holding him down. "If you will not, I will drag you out into the street by the legs."

"I will," said Forgue; getting up, he walked out and away without another word.

Donal locked the door and, forgetting all about the papers, went back to Andrew's. There was Eppie busy in the outer room. She kept her back to him, and he took care not to address her. With a word or two to the grandmother—a hint to keep the girl in the house as much as possible and a reminder that she might have no other to send for him if her husband should want him—he took his leave and went home, revolving all the way one question after another as to what he ought to do. Should he tell the father how the son was carrying himself, or should he not? Had the father been a man of rectitude, or even so far such as to dread the doing more than the suffering of evil, Donal would not have hesitated a moment. But knowing the earl did not care one pin what became of Eppie so long as his son was prevented from marrying her, Donal did not feel bound by the mere fact that he was tutor to the younger son, without the smallest responsibility for the other, to carry the evil report of the elder. The father might have a right to know, but had he a right to know from him?

23

························

A Wrathful Admission

Scarcely had he entered the castle, where his return had been watched for, when Simmons came with the message that his lordship wanted to see him. That was the first Donal remembered that he had not brought the papers! Had he not been sent for, he would have gone back at once to fetch them. As it was, he must see the earl first.

He found him in a worse condition than usual. His last drug mixture had not agreed with him or he had taken too much, and the reaction was correspondent. Anyhow, he was in a vile temper. Donal told him at once he had been to the house and had found the papers, but had not brought them—had, in fact, forgotten them.

"A pretty fellow you are!" cried the earl. "What, you have left those papers lying about where any rascal may find them and play the deuce with the history of my house!"

Donal tried to assure him that they were perfectly safe, under the same locks and keys as before. But the earl, having mistaken something he said and having had it explained, broke out upon him afresh, as one always going about the bush and never coming to the point.

"How the devil was it you locked them up again and did not bring them with you?" he asked.

Then Donal told him he had heard a noise in the house. He told as much of the story, in fact, as his lordship permitted; for straightway he fell out upon him again for meddling with things which did not belong to him. What had he to do with his son's pleasures? Things of the sort were much better taken no notice of, especially within the household. At the castle the linen had to be washed out elsewhere, but it was not done in the great court!

Donal took advantage of a pause to ask whether he might not go back directly and bring the papers. He would run all the way, he said.

"No, you bungler," answered the earl. "Give me the keys—all the keys—house keys and all. I will never trust such a fool again with anything."

At this juncture, just as Donal had laid the keys on his lordship's table—he was still in bed—Simmons appeared, saying that Lord Forgue desired to know if his father would see him.

"Oh, yes! send him up," cried the earl in a fury. "Let me have all the devils at once. I may as well swallow all the blasted sulphur at once!"

There is no logic to be looked for where a man is talking out of a deeper discomfort than the matter in hand. His lordship's rages had to do with abysses of misery no man knew but himself.

"You go into the next room, Grant," he ordered when Simmons was gone, "and wait there till I call you."

Donal retired, sat down, took a book from the table and tried to read. He heard the door open and close again, and then the sounds of their two voices. By degrees they grew louder, and at length the earl roared out, but so wildly and incoherently that Donal caught only a word here and there.

"I'll be cursed soul and body but I'll put a stop to this! Why, you son of a snake, I have but to speak the word, and you are—well, what?—Yes, but I'll hold my tongue for the present. By Jove! I have held it too long already, though—letting you grow up the most damnably ungrateful dog that ever snuffed carrion, while I was periling my soul for you, you rascal!"

"What have you to give me, my lord, but the title!" said Forgue coolly. "Thank heaven, *that* you cannot take from me, however good your will may be. My country will see to that."

"You and your country!" he cursed. "You have no more right to the title than the beggarly kitchen maid you have consorted with. If you but knew yourself, you would crow in another fashion."

Up to this last sentence Donal had heard only a word here and there and had set all he did hear down to his lordship's fierce, scolding folly of rage; but now it was time he should speak. He opened the door.

"I must warn your lordship," he said, "that if you speak so loudly, I shall hear every word you say."

"Hear and be cursed! That fellow there—you see him standing there—

the mushroom that he is! Good God! How I loved his mother! And this is the way he serves me! But there was a Providence in the whole affair! It has all come out right! Small occasion had I to be breaking my heart and conscience over it ever since she left me! Hang the rascal! He's no more Forgue than you are, Grant, and never will be a Morven if he live a hundred years! He's not one whit better than any urchin in the street. His mother was the loveliest woman ever breathed! . . . and loved me—ah! It is something after all to have been loved so—and by such a woman! A woman, by Jove! ready and willing and happy to give up—give up everything for me! *Everything*, do you hear, you confounded rascal? I was never married to her! Do you hear, Mr. Grant? I take you to witness my words: She, that fellow's mother, and I were never married—not by any law, Scotch or French or Dutch, what you will!" Cursing again, he shouted, "He may go about his business when he pleases. Oh, yes! Pray do! Go and marry your scullion when you please! You are your own master—very much indeed your own master—free as the wind that blows to go where you will and do what you please! I wash my hands of you. It is nothing, and a good deal less than nothing to me! I tell you once for all, the moment I know for certain that you are married to that girl, that very moment I publish to the world—that is, I acquaint certain gossips with the fact I have just told you, and the next Lord Morven will have to be hunted for like a truffle!"

He burst into a fiendish fit of laughter and fell back on his pillow, dark with rage and the unutterable fury that made of his whole being a moral volcano. The two men had been standing as if struck dumb, Donal truly sorry for him upon whom this phial of devilish wrath had been emptied, and the other white and trembling with dismay. An abject creature he looked, crushed by his cruel parent. When his father ceased, unable from the reaction of his rage to go on, Forgue still stood speechless and as if all power to move or speak were gone from him. A moment and he turned whiter still, uttered a groan, and wavered. Donal caught and supported him to a chair, where he leaned back with the perspiration streaming down his face.

Donal thought what a pity it was that one capable of such emotion in a matter concerning his worldly position should be apparently so indifferent to what alone can in reality affect a man—the right or wrong of his actions. The father, too, seemed now to have lost the power of motion, and lay with his eyes closed, breathing heavily. But presently he made what Donal took for a sign to ring the bell. He did so, and Simmons came. The moment he entered and saw the state his master was in, he hastened to a cupboard in the room, took thence a bottle, poured from it a teaspoonful of something colorless and gave it to him in water. It brought his lordship to himself. He sat up again, and in a voice hoarse and terrible as if it came from the tomb, said, "Think, Lord Forgue, of what I have told you. While you do as I would have you, all is safe. But take your way without me, and I will take mine without you. You can go."

Donal went at once, leaving Forgue where he had placed him, apparently still unable to move.

And what was Donal to do or think now? Perplexities accumulated upon him. Happily there was time to think and pray. Alas for the children upon whom the sins of the fathers are visited by those guilty or capable of like sins themselves! What was he to do? He would rather have had nothing to do with the matter; but if he had to do with it, he must act. In the meantime, however, he could have no assurance that the earl was speaking the truth—that he was not merely making the statement and using the threat that he might have his way with his son! True or not, what a double-eyed villain was the father!

24

· · · · · · · · · · · · · · · · · · ·

The Passing of the Cobbler

*O*ne thing only was clear to Donal, that for the present he had literally nothing to do with the affair. There was now no immediate question concerning the succession. Before that arose Forgue might be dead; before that, his father might have betrayed the secret of his birth; and, more than all, the longer Donal thought about the affair the greater was his doubt whether the father had spoken the truth. Certainly the man who could to his son say such a thing of his mother must be capable of the wickedness the supposition assumed. But the thing remaining uncertain; he was assuredly not presently called upon to act in the matter. He could not, however, fail to be interested in seeing how Forgue would carry himself; his behavior now would go far to settle his character for life. If he were indeed as honorable as he would like to be thought, he would explain all to Eppie and set himself to find some way of earning his and her bread. But the youth himself did not seem to doubt the truth of what had fallen in rage from his father's lips; to judge by his appearance, in the few and brief glances Donal had of him during the next week or so, the iron had sunk into his soul. He looked more wretched than Donal could have believed it possible for man to be.

Forgue's mother had been the truest of wives to his father, though Donal could by no means feel sure that his father had been the same to her! But what kind of a father was this, thought Donal, who would thus defile his son's conscience?

Andrew Comin stayed yet a week—slowly, gently fading out into life. Donal was with them when he went, but there was little done or said. He crept into the open air in his sleep, to wake from the dreams of life and the dreams of sleep both at once, and to see them all mingling together behind him.

Doory was perfectly calm. When Andrew gave his last sigh, she sighed too and said, "I won't be long, Andrew!" and said no more. Eppie wept bitterly. Some of her sorrow was that she had not done as he would have had her, and more came from the thought of how little he had reproached her.

Donal went every day to see them till the funeral was over—at which it was surprising to see so many of the townsfolk. Most of them had regarded the cobbler as a poor, talkative enthusiast with far more tongue than brains. Because they were so far behind and beneath him, they saw him very small. ·

For some time Donal's savings continued to support the old woman and her granddaughter. But before long she got so much to do in the way of knitting stockings and other small things, and was set to so many light jobs by kindly people who respected her more than her husband because she was more ordinary. Miss Carmichael had offered to do what she could to get Eppie a place, if she answered certain questions to her satisfaction. How she met her catechising, I do not know; anyhow, she so far satisfied her interrogator that Miss Carmichael set herself in earnest to find for her a place in Edinburgh. Eppie wept bitterly at the thought of leaving, but she knew there was no help for it; rumor had been cruel and not all untrue, and in that neighborhood there was no place for her such as she would take. And all the time she waited, not once did Lord Forgue, so far as she knew, try to see her.

A place was found for her, one in which she would be well looked after, Miss Carmichael said, easily persuading the old grandmother. With many tears, and without one sight of her lover, Eppie went away. Then things with Donal returned into the old grooves at the castle, only the happy knowledge of his friend the cobbler hammering and stitching down below was gone. It did not matter; the craftsman was a nobleman now— because such had he always been.

Forgue kept mooning about, doing nothing and recognizing nowhere any prospect of help save in utter defeat. He was to be seen oftener than before on horseback, now riding furiously over everything, as if driven by the very wind, now dawdling along with the reins on the neck of his weary animal. Thus Donal once met him in a narrow lane. The moment Forgue saw him, he pulled up his horse's head, spurred him hard, and flew past Donal as if he did not see him but looking as if he would have had the lane yet narrower—Donal shoved himself half into the hedge and escaped with a little mud.

25

•••••••••••••••••••

One Mystery Solved

*O*ne morning, as Donal sat in the schoolroom with Davie, there came a knock to the door, and Lady Arctura entered.

"The wind is blowing from the southeast," she remarked.

"Listen then, my lady, whether you can hear anything," said Donal. "I fancy it is a very precise wind that is required to enter properly."

"I will listen," she answered, and went away.

The day passed and he heard nothing more. He was at work in his room in a warm, evening twilight, when Davie came running to his door and said that Arkie was coming up after him. He rose and stood at the top of the stair to receive her. She had heard the music, she said, very soft. Would he not go on the roof?

"Where were you, my lady," asked Donal, "when you heard it? I have heard nothing up here."

"In my own little parlor," she answered. "It was very faint, but I could not mistake it."

They went at once upon the roof. The wind was soft and low, an excellent thing in winds. They made their way quickly over the roof. They knew the paths of it better now, and they had plenty of light, although the moon, rising large and round, gave them little of hers yet. The three were presently at the foot of the great chimney stack, which grew like a tree out of the roof, its roots going down to the very roots of the house itself. There they sat down and waited and listened.

"I am almost sorry to have made this discovery," said Donal.

"Why?" asked Lady Arctura. "Should not the truth be found, whatever it may be?"

"Most certainly," answered Donal. "And if this be the truth, as I fully expect it will prove, then it is well it should be found to be the truth. What I meant was that I could have wished—I should have liked better that it had been something we could *not* explain."

They listened, and there came a low, prolonged wail.

Donal had left the ladder on the roof in readiness from their last visit; he set it up in haste, climbed to the gap, and with a great sheet of brown paper which he had had ready in his room, stood leaning against the chimney, on the northern side of the cleft, waiting for the next outcry of the prisoned chords while Arctura stood at the bottom of the ladder looking up. For some time there was no further sound, and he was getting a little tired of his position, when suddenly came a louder blast, and he heard the music quite distinctly in the shaft beside him. It swelled and grew. He spread his sheet of paper over the opening; the wind blew it flat against the chimney; the sound immediately ceased. He removed it, the wind still blowing, and again came the sound quite plainly. The wind grew stronger and they were able to use the simple experiment until there was no shadow of a doubt left in either of their minds that they had discovered the source of the music. By certain dispositions of the paper they were even able to modify it.

At length Donal descended, and addressing Davie, said, "Davie, I wish you not to say a word about this to anyone until Lady Arctura or I give you leave. You have a secret with us now, and with no other person. You know the castle belongs to Lady Arctura, and she has a right to ask you not to say this to anyone without her permission. I have a reason, my lady, for wishing this," he added, turning to Arctura. "I will immediately tell you why I wish it, but I do not want Davie to know yet. You can at once withdraw your prohibition, you know, if you should not think my reason a good one."

"Davie," said Arctura, "I too have faith in Mr. Grant; and I beg you will do as he says."

"Oh, surely, Cousin Arkie!" said Davie; "I would have minded without being told so very solemnly."

"Very well, then, Davie," said Donal, "you run down and wait for me in my room. I want to have a little talk with Lady Arctura. Mind you go exactly the way we came."

Davie went and Donal, turning to Arctura, said, "You know the story of the hidden room in the castle, my lady?"

"Surely you do not believe in that!" she answered.

"I think there may be such a place, though I need not therefore accept any of the stories I have heard about it."

"But, surely, if there were such a place it would have been found long ago."

"They might have said that on the first reports of the discovery of America!" returned Donal. "Would you like to know the truth about this as well as about the music?"

"I should indeed. But would not you be sorry to lose another mystery?"

"On the contrary, there is only the rumor of a mystery now; we do not know that there really is one. We do not quite believe the report. We are not indeed at liberty, in the name of good sense, quite to believe it now. But perhaps we may find that there is really a mystery—but I would not for a moment annoy you. I do not even wish to press it."

Lady Arctura smiled very sweetly.

"I have not the slightest objection," she said. "If I seemed for a moment to hesitate, it was only that I wondered what my uncle would say. I should not like to vex him."

"Certainly not; but do you not think he would be pleased?"

"I will speak to him," she said, "and find out. He hates what he calls superstition, and I fancy has more curiosity than delight in legendary things; he will be willing enough, I think. I should not wonder if he joined you in the search."

But Donal thought with himself that if the earl were so inclined, it was strange he had never undertaken the thing. Something in Donal said that the earl would not like the proposal.

They were now slowly making their way to the stair.

"But just tell me, Mr. Grant, how you would set about it," said Arctura.

"If the question were merely whether or not there were such a room, I would—"

"But how could you tell that there was one except you found it?"

"By finding that there was some space not accounted for."

"I do not see how."

"Would you mind coming to my room? It will be a lesson for Davie, too. I will show you in a few minutes."

She assented. They joined Davie, and Donal gave them a lesson in cubic measure and contents. He showed them how to tell exactly how much space must be inside any given boundaries; if they could not find so much, then some of it was hidden somehow. If they measured all the walls of the castle, allowing of course for the thickness of those walls, and then, measuring all the rooms and open places within those walls, allowing also for the dividing walls, found the space they gave fell short of what they had to expect, they must conclude either that they had measured or calculated wrong, or that there was a space in the castle to which they had no access.

"But," continued Donal, "if the thing was to discover the room itself, I would set about it in a different way. I should not care about all that previous measuring; I should begin to go all over the castle, and get it right in my head, fitting everything inside the castle into the shape of it in my brain. Then if I came to a part I thought suspicious, I should examine that more closely, take exact measurements both of the angles and sides of the different rooms, passages, etc., and so find whether they enclosed more than I could see. I need not trouble you with the exact process as there will probably be no occasion to use it."

"Oh, yes, there may be," returned Lady Arctura. "I think my uncle will be quite willing."

With that she turned to the door and they went down together. When they reached the hall Davie ran away to get his kite and go out.

"But you have not told me why you would not have the music spoken of," said Arctura, stopping and turning to Donal.

"Only because, if we went to make any further researches, the talk about the one would make them notice the other; and the more quietly it can be done the better. If we resolve to do nothing, we may at once unfold our discovery."

"We will be quiet in the meantime," agreed Arctura.

That night the earl had another of his wandering fits, also that night the wind blew strong from the southeast. Whether that had anything to do with the way in which he heard his niece's proposal the next day is not certain but the instant he understood what she wished, his countenance grew black as thunder.

"What!" he cried. "You would go pulling the grand old hulk to pieces for the sake of a foolish tale about the devil and a rascally set of card players! By my soul! I'll be cursed if you do—not while I'm above ground, at least! That's what comes of giving such a place into the hands of a woman! It's sacrilege! By heavens, I'll throw my brother's will into chancery rather!"

He went on raging so that he compelled her to imagine there was more in it than seemed; and while she could not help trembling at the wildness of the temper she had roused, she repented of the courtesy she had shown him; after all, she had a perfect right to make what investigations she pleased. If her father had left her the property, doubtless he had good reasons for doing so. And those reasons might have lain in the character of the man before her!

"I beg your pardon, my love," he said in sudden realization of his last insult, "but he was my brother, and has been dead and gone for so many years! 'Tis no great treason to remark upon the wisdom of a dead man— dead and all but forgotten! Doubtless he was your father—"

"He *is* my father!" said Arctura sternly and coldly.

"Ah; well, as you please!"

"I wish you good-night, my lord," said Arctura, and came away very angry.

In the morning she found that while she was no longer in wrath against him, any sense of his having authority over her had all but vanished. It was not his suggestion concerning her father's will that had offended her but the way he spoke of her father. He might do as he pleased about the will! She would do as she pleased about the house. If her father knew him as she knew him, and wisely feared his brother's son would be like him, certainly he had done well to leave the property to her! But what was she to say to Mr. Grant about the present matter? She thought and thought, and concluded to say nothing but encourage him to make some of the calculations he had proposed. This she did, and for some days nothing more was said. But she was haunted with that interview with her uncle, and began to be burdened with vague uneasiness as to the existence of some dreadful secret about the house.

26

The Dream

*O*ne evening, as Donal was walking in the park, Davie, who was now advanced to doing a little work without his master's immediate supervision, came running to him to say that Arkie was in the schoolroom and wanted to see him.

He hastened to her.

"I want a word with you without Davie," she said, and Donal sent the boy away.

"I have debated with myself all day whether I should tell you," she began, with a trembling voice, "but I think I shall not be so much afraid to go to bed tonight if I tell you what I dreamt last night."

Her face was very pale, and there was a quiver about her mouth.

"Do you think it is very silly to mind one's dream?" she added.

"Silly or not," answered Donal, "it is pretty plain you have had one that must be paid some attention to."

"This one has taken such a hold of me," said Arctura, trying to smile, "that I cannot rest till I have told it, and there is no one I could tell it to but yourself. Anyone else would laugh at me—at least I know Sophie would. I fell asleep as usual, no more inclined to dream than usual, except that I had for some days been troubled with the feeling that there was something not right about the house. In my dream I found myself in the midst of a most miserable place. It was like deserted brick-fields—that had never been of any use. Heaps of bricks were all about, but they were all broken, or only half burnt. For miles and miles they stretched around me. I walked and walked to get out of it. Not a soul was in sight, nor sign of human habitation.

"All at once I saw before me a church. It was old, but showed its age only in being tumbled down and dirty. I feared it but had to go in. It looked as if nobody had crossed its threshold for a hundred years. The pews remained, but they were mouldering away; the soundingboard had half fallen on the pulpit and rested its edge on the book board; and the great galleries had tumbled in parts into the body of the church, and others hung sloping from the walls. When I had gone in a little way, I saw that the center of the door had fallen in, and there was a great, descending, soft-looking slope of earth, mixed and strewn with bits of broken and decayed wood from the pews that had fallen in when the ground gave way—or it might be from the coffins of the dead, underneath which the gulf had opened. I stood gazing down in horror. It went down and down—

I could not see how far. I stood fascinated with the unknown depth, and the feeling of its possible contents, when suddenly I perceived that something was moving in the darkness—something dead. It came nearer, and I saw it was slowly climbing the slope—a figure as of one dead and stiff, laboring up the steep incline. I would have shrieked, but I could neither cry nor move.

"When the figure was about three yards below me, at last it raised its head. It was my uncle—but as if he had been dead for a week, and all dressed for the grave. He raised his hand and beckoned me—and I knew in my soul that down there I must go, without question. I *had* to go; and I never once thought of resisting. Immediately my heart became like lead, and I began the descent. My feet sank in the mould of the ancient dead as I went; it was soft as if thousands of graveyard moles were forever burrowing in it; down and down I went, sinking and sliding with the moving heap of black earth. Then I began to see the sides and ends of coffins in the earth that made the walls of the gulf; these coffins came closer and closer together and, at length, scarcely left me room to get through without touching them. But I sought courage in the thought that these had been long dead, and must by this time be at rest—though my uncle was not—and would not stretch out mouldy hands to lay hold of me. At last I saw he had got to the very bottom of the descent, where it was not possible to go any farther, and I stood and waited.

"Then I was able to speak and I said to my uncle, 'Where are you taking me?' but he gave me no answer. I saw now that he was heaving and pulling at a coffin that seemed to bar up the way in front. I began to think I was dead and condemned to be there. But just as my uncle got the coffin out of the way, I saw a bright silver handle on it with the Morven crest. And the same instant the lid of it rose and one rose out of it; it was my father, and he looked alive and bright, and my uncle looked beside him like a corpse.

" 'What do you want here with my child?' he said; and my uncle seemed to cower before him. 'This is no place for her,' he continued and took my hand in his, 'Come with me, my child.' And I followed him—oh, so gladly! And my fear was all gone, and so was my uncle. My father was leading me up where we had come down, but just as we were stepping up, as I thought, into the horrible old church, where do you think I found myself—in my own room! I looked around me, and no one was near me, and I was very sorry my father was gone, but glad to be in my own room. Then I woke, but not in my bed—I was standing in the middle of the floor, just where my dream had left me! That was the most terrible thing about it. I cannot get rid of the thought that I went somewhere wandering about. I have been haunted the whole day with the terror of it. It keeps coming back and back."

"Did your uncle make you take anything?" asked Donal.

"I do not see how he could; but that would have explained it."

"You should change your room, and get Mrs. Brooks to sleep near you."

"That is just what I should like, but I am ashamed to ask her."

"Tell her you had a dreadful dream, and would like to change your room for a while."

"I will. I feel almost as if I had been poisoned."

Gladly would Donal have offered to sleep, like one of his own old collies, on the doormat to make her feel more safe; but that would not do. Mrs. Brooks was the only one to help her. Arctura had her bed moved to another part of the castle altogether, and Mrs. Brooks slept in the dressing room.

For Donal, the dream roused strange thoughts in him. He would gladly have asked to occupy her room for a while, but he feared that would keep Lady Arctura's imagination active, which already seemed overwrought.

He had begun to make some observations toward verifying the existence of the hidden room. But he made them in the quietest way, attracting no attention, and had already satisfied himself it could not be in this part of the castle. It might be in the foundations, amongst the dungeons and cellars, and built up; but legend pointed elsewhere. If he could have had anyone, even Davie, to help him, he would have set himself at once to find out what was to be found concerning the musical chimney; but that he could not easily do alone, for he could not go poking here and there into every room and examining its chimney without attracting attention. And as to his measurements, such was the total irregularity of a building that had grown through centuries to fit the varying needs and changing tastes of the generations that he found it harder to satisfy himself than he had thought.

27

Another Mystery Begun

The autumn brought terrible storms. Many fishing boats came to grief. Of some, the crews lost everything; of others, the loss of their lives delivered them from the smaller losses. There were many bereaved families in the village, and Donal went about amongst them, doing what he could and seeking help for them where his own ability would not reach their necessity. Lady Arctura needed no persuasion to go with him on many of his visits, and this interchange with humanity in its simpler forms was of the greatest service in her renewed efforts to lay hold upon the skirt of the Father of men. She did not yet know that to love our neighbor is to be religious; and the man who does so will soon find that he cannot do without that higher part of religion, which is the love of God, without which the rest will sooner or later die away. She found the path to God the easier that she was now walking it in company with her fellows. We do not understand the next page of God's lesson book; we see only the one before us. Nor shall we be allowed to turn the leaf until we have learned its lesson.

One day after the fishing boats had gone out, there came on a terrible storm. Most of them made for the harbor again—such as it was—and succeeded in gaining its shelter. But one boat failed. How much its failure was owing to Lord Forgue and Eppie cannot be said; but I'm sure a fisherman whose heart has been broken will not battle against the forces of nature with the same will and determination as one whose love is waiting for him. In any case, Stephen Kennedy's boat drifted in to shore bottom upward. His body came ashore close to the spot where Donal, half asleep, half awake, dragged the net out of the wave. There was sorrow afresh throughout the village. Kennedy was a favorite; and his mother was left with no son to come sauntering in with his long slouch in the gloamin'. What Forgue thought, I do not know—nothing at all, probably, as to any share of his in the catastrophe. But I believe it made him care a little less about marrying the girl, now that he had no rival ready to take her. Soon after, Forgue left the castle, and if his father knew where he was, he was the only one who did. He did not even say goodbye to Arctura. His father had been pressing his desire that he would begin to show some interest in the owner of the castle; Forgue professed himself unequal to it at present; but he said that if he were away for a while it would be easier when he returned.

The storms were over, and the hedges and hidden roots had begun to dream of spring. One afternoon Arctura, after Davie was gone, with whom she had been at work in the schoolroom over some geometry, told Donal her dream had come again.

"I cannot bear it," she said. "This time I came out not into my own room, but onto the great stair, I thought; and I came up the stair to the room I am in now, and got into bed. And the dreadful thing is that Mrs. Brooks tells me she saw me standing in the middle of the floor."

"Do you imagine you had been out of the room?" asked Donal in some dismay.

"I do not know; I cannot tell. If I were to find that I had been, it would drive me out of my senses, I think. I keep on thinking about the lost room; and I am almost sure it has something to do with that! When the thought comes to me I try to send it away, but it keeps coming."

"Would it not be better to find the place, and have done with it?" inquired Donal.

"If you think we could," she answered, "without attracting any attention."

"If you will help me, I think we can," he answered. "That there is such a place I am greatly inclined to believe."

"I will help you all I can."

"Then first, we will make a small experiment with the shaft of the music chimney. It has never been used for smoke, at least since those chords were put there; might it not be the chimney to the very room? I will get a weight and a strong cord. The wires will be a plague, but I think we can manage to pass them. Then we shall see how far the weight goes down and shall know on what floor it stops. That will be something gained, limiting so far the plane of inquiry. It may not be satisfactory, you know; there may be a turn in it to prevent the weight from going to the bottom; but it is worth trying."

Lady Arctura seemed already relieved and brightened by the proposal.

"When shall we set about it?" she asked almost eagerly.

"At once, if you like," said Donal.

She went to get a shawl that she might go on the roof with him. They agreed it would still be better not to tell Davie. There should be no danger of their design drifting into public knowledge.

Donal found a suitable cord in the gardener's toolhouse, also a seven-pound weight. But would that pass the wires? He laid it aside, remembering an old eight-day clock on a back stair, which was never going. He hastened to it, and got out its heavier weight, which he felt almost sure might get through the chords. These he carried to his own stair, at the foot of which he found Lady Arctura waiting for him.

There was that in being thus associated with the lovely girl, and in knowing that she trusted him implicitly, looking to him for help and even protection, that stirred to its depths Donal's deeply devoted nature.

His thoughts were on her as he followed Arctura up the stair, she carrying the weight and the cord, he the ladder, which was not easy to get round the screw of the stair. Arctura trembled with excitement as she ascended, and grew frightened as often as she found she had outstripped him. Then she would wait till she saw the end of it come poking round, when she would start again toward the top.

Her dreams had disquieted her, and she feared at times they might be sent as a warning. But the moment she found herself in the healthy, open air of Donal's company, her doubts seemed to vanish. Was he not much more childlike, much more straightforward? Nothing but the truth could be of the smallest final consequence. Thus meditated Arctura as she climbed the stair, and her hope and courage grew.

By the time she reached the top she was radiant, not merely with the exertion of climbing, burdened down as she was; she was joyous in the prospect of a quiet hour with one whose presence and words gave her strength, who made the world look less mournful.

They stepped out upon the roof into the gorgeous afterglow of an autumn sunset.

They stood for a moment in deep enjoyment, then simultaneously turned to each other.

"My lady," said Donal, "with such a sky as that out there, it hardly seems as if there could be room for such a thing as our search tonight. The search into hollow places, hidden of man's hands, does not seem to go with it at all!"

"But there may be nothing, you know, Mr. Grant!" said Arctura, a little troubled about her ancient house.

"True; but if we do find such a room, you may be sure it has had to do with terrible wrong, though what that may have been we may never find out. I doubt if we shall even discover any traces of it. I hope, in any case, you will keep up a good courage."

"I shall not be afraid while you are with me," she answered. "It is the terrible dreaming that makes me weak. In the morning I tremble as if I had been in the hands of some evil power in the night."

Donal turned his eyes upon her. How thin she looked in the last of the sunlight! A pang went through him at the thought that one day he might be alone with Davie in the castle, untended by the consciousness that a living loveliness was somewhere flitting about its gloomy walls. But now he would banish the thought!

They turned from the sunset and made their way to the chimney stack. There once more Donal set up his ladder and, having tied the clock weight to the end of his cord, dropped it in. With a little management he got it through the wires. Then it went down and down, gently lowered, till the cord was all out, and still it would go.

"Do run and get some more," said Arctura in some excitement.

"You do not mind being left alone?" asked Donal.

"Not if you will not be long," she answered.

"I will run," he said. And run he did, for she had scarcely begun to feel the loneliness when he returned, panting.

Taking the end she had been holding, he tied on the fresh cord he had brought and again lowered away. Just as he was beginning to fear that after all he had not brought enough, the weight stopped.

"If only we had eyes in that weight," said Arctura, "like those the snails have at the end of their horns!"

"We might have greased the weight," remarked Donal, "as they do the sea lead to know what kind of thing is at the bottom! It would be something to see whether it brought up ashes. I will move it up and down a little and if it will not go any farther, then I will mark the string and draw it up."

He did so.

"Now we must mark on it the height of the chimney above the parapet wall," said Donal; "and I will lower the weight into the little court until this last knot comes to the wall; then we shall know how far down the height of the house it went inside.—Ah, I thought so!" he went on, looking over, "Only to the first floor, or thereabouts—No, I think it is lower! But you see, my lady, the place with which the chimney, if chimney it be, communicates is somewhere about the middle of the house, and it may be on the first floor. We can't judge very well here. Can you imagine what place it might be?"

"I cannot," answered Lady Arctura; "but I will go to every room tomorrow—or this evening, perhaps."

"Then I will draw the weight back up and let it down the chimney again as far as it will go; I will leave it there for you to see, if you can, somewhere below. If you find it, then we must leave the chimney and try another plan."

It was done, and they descended together. Donal went back to the schoolroom, not expecting to see Lady Arctura before the next day. But in half an hour she came to him, saying she had been into every room on the floor and its adjoining levels, but had failed to see the weight in any chimney.

"The probability, then, is that somewhere thereabouts," said Donal, "lies the secret; but we cannot be sure, for the weight may never have reached the bottom of the shaft but be resting at some angle in its course. Now, let us think what we shall do next."

As he spoke he placed a chair for her by the fire. Davie was not there, and they had the room to themselves.

28

· · · · · · · · · · · · · · · · · · · ·

Clues

They were hardly seated when Simmons appeared, saying he had been looking everywhere for her ladyship, for his lordship was taken as he had never seen him before. He had fainted right away in the halfway room, as they called that on the stair.

"We will go at once, Simmons. Hurry and get what things you think likely; you know him much better than I do."

Lady Arctura and Donal hastened to the room indicated, and there saw the earl stretched motionless and pale on a couch. But for a twitching in a muscle of the face they might have concluded him dead. When Simmons came they tried to get something down his throat, but without success; he could not swallow. Lady Arctura thought it would be better to get him to his room, and the two men carried him up the stair.

He had not been laid long on his bed before he began to come to himself; and then Lady Arctura thought it better to leave him with Simmons. She told him to come to the library when he could and let them know how he was. In about an hour he came and told them his master was better.

"Do you know any cause for the attack?" asked her ladyship.

"No, my lady—only this," answered the butler, "that while I was there with him, giving him my monthly accounts—I wonder he takes the trouble to ask for them! He pays so little attention to the particulars!—I was standing by my lord doing nothing, while he was pretending to look at my bills, when all at once there came a curious noise in the wall. I'm sure I can't think what it was—an inward rumbling it was, that seemed to go up and down the wall like a scraping or scratching, and then stopped altogether. It sounded nothing very dreadful to me, only perhaps if it had been in the middle of the night, I mightn't have liked it. But his lordship started, turned quite pale and gasped; and then he cried out and laid his hand on his heart. I made haste to do what I could for him, but it wasn't altogether like one of his ordinary attacks, and I got frightened and came for you. He's such a ticklish subject, you see, my lady! I get quite alarmed sometimes to be left alone with him. It's his heart, you see, my lady; and you know, my lady—I should be sorry to frighten you—but you know, Mr. Grant, with that complaint a gentleman may go off at any moment, without warning. I must go back to him now, my lady, if you please."

When Simmons was gone, Arctura turned and looked at Donal.

"We must be careful," he said.

"We must," she answered.

"Thereabouts is one of the few places in the house where you can hear the music."

"But why should my lord be so frightened?"

"He is not like other people, you know. He leads such a second life because of the things he takes that I believe he does not know with any certainty whether some things actually happen to him or not. But I must go."

"One word," said Donal; "where did you used to hear the music? It seems to me, when I think of it, that though all in the house have heard it, you and your uncle have heard it oftener than anyone else."

"I hear it in my own room, the one I moved from. I don't think my uncle does in his; but you know where we found him that night; in his strange fit he often goes there. But we can talk more tomorrow. Goodnight."

"I will remain here for the rest of the evening," said Donal, "in case Simmons might want me to help with his lordship."

It was well into the night, and Donal still sat reading in the library, when Mrs. Brooks came to him. "He's better now," she said. "He's taken one or another of those horrid drugs he's always puttering with—trying, no doubt, to find the secret of living forever. But if I was him I would give up the ghost at once."

"What makes you say that, Mrs. Brooks?" asked Donal.

"Because I've heard from them that knew that when the fit was upon him he was terrible cruel to the bonnie wife he'd married somewhere abroad and brought home with him—to a coldhearted country, I have no doubt she thought it, poor thing."

"But how could he have been cruel to her in the house with his brother? Certainly *he* would never have connived at the ill-treatment of any woman under his roof, even if his brother was the wretch to be guilty of it."

"How do you know what the previous earl was like?"

"I only know," said Donal, "that such a sensitive daughter could hardly have been born from any but a man who would at least behave with tolerable decency to a woman."

"Well, you're right," said Mrs. Brooks. "They say he was a tender man. But he was far from healthy and was by himself a lot, nearly as much as the present earl. And the lady was that proud and devoted to the man that never a word of what went on reached his brother. His cruelty came—my old auntie said—from some kind of madness that there's no name for yet. Cries in the night and white cheeks and red eyes in the morning tell their tale. Anyway, she died who might have lived if it weren't for him, and her child died before her; and wrongs to children and women stick long to the walls of the universe. Some said she came after him again after she was gone. I don't know, but I've seen and heard about his house . . . but I'll hold my tongue, I know nothing. All I say is that he was no good man to the poor woman; for when it comes to that, we're all women together. She didn't die here, I understand."

29
• • • • • • • • • • • • • • • • • • •

Arctura's Room

The next day, when he saw Lady Arctura, Donal said to her, "It seems to me, my lady, that if your uncle heard the noise of our plummet inside the wall, the place can hardly be on the floor you searched; for that room, you know, is on the stair before you come to the first floor. Still, sound does travel so through a wall! We must take ourselves to measurement, and that is not easy to do thoroughly without being seen.

"There was another thing, however, that came into my head last night. You tell me you hear the music in your room. I should like, if you would let me, to have a look about it; something might suggest itself. Is it the room I saw you in when once I opened the door by mistake?"

"Not that," answered Arctura, "but the bedroom opening from it—the one I have left for the present. You can examine it when you please. Will you come now?"

"Is there any danger of the earl's suspecting what we are after?"

"Not the least. The room is not far from his but is not in the same block of the building, and there are thick walls between. Besides, he is too ill to be up."

She led the way, and Donal followed up the main staircase to the second floor and into the small, curious, old-fashioned room, evidently one of the oldest in the castle. Inside, it was very charming with the oddest nooks and corners, recesses and projections. Donal cast round his eyes; turning to Lady Arctura he said, "I feel," his eyes straying about the room as if in search of a suggestion, "as if I were here searching into a human nature. A house looks always to me so like a mind—full of strange, inexplicable shapes at first sight, which gradually arrange, disentangle and explain themselves as you go on to know them. In all houses there are places we know nothing about yet, just as in our own selves."

"It is a very old house," said Arctura; "so many hands have been employed in the building through so many generations."

"That is true; but where the house continues in the same family, the builders have transmitted their nature as well as their house to those who come after them."

"Then you think," said Arctura, almost with a shudder, "that I cannot but inherit from my ancestors a nature like the house they have left me? That the house is therefore a fit outside to my inner nature—as the shell fits the snail?"

"Yes, probably so, but with an infinite power to modify the relation. I do not forget that everyone is born nearer to God than to any ancestor, and that it rests with everyone to cultivate either the godlikeness in him, or his ancestral nature—to choose whether he will be of God, or those that have gone before him in the way of the world."

"That seems to me very strange doctrine," murmured Arctura in some uncertainty.

"It is, however, unavoidably true that we inherit from our ancestors tendencies to both vices and virtues. That which was a vice indulged in by my great-great-grandfather possibly may be in me a tendency to the same or a similar vice."

"Oh, how horrible!" cried Arctura.

"We need God not the more, but we know the better *how much* we need him," said Donal. "In you they are not vices—only possibilities which cannot become vices until they are obeyed. It rests with the man to destroy in himself even the *possibility* of them by opening the door to him who knocks. Then, again, there are all kinds of counteracting and redeeming influences in opposite directions. Perhaps, wherein the said ancestor was most wicked, his wife, from whom is the descent as much as from him, was especially lovely. The ancestor may, for instance, have been cruel, and the ancestress tender as the hen that gathers her chickens under her wing. The danger, in an otherwise even nature, is of being caught in some sudden gust of unsuspected passionate impulse and carried away of the one tendency before the other has time to assert and the will to rouse itself."

"You comfort me a little."

"And then you must remember," continued Donal, "that nothing in its immediate root is evil; that sometimes it is from the best human roots that the worst things spring, just because the conscience and the will have not been brought to bear upon them. But this is not the room in which you have heard the music!"

"No, it is through here."

Lady Arctura opened the door of her bedroom. Donal glanced round it. It was as old-fashioned as the other.

"What is behind that press there—that wardrobe, I think you call it?" asked Donal.

"Only a shallow recess," answered Lady Arctura. "I had the wardrobe put there but was disappointed to find it too high to get into it—that is all; there is no mystery there!"

Had the wardrobe stood right into the recess, possibly Donal would not have thought anything about it; but having caught sight of the opening past the side of it, he was attracted by it and fancied he should like to examine it. It was in the same wall in which was the fireplace, but it did not seem formed by the projection of the chimney into the room. It did not go to the ceiling.

"Would you mind if I moved the press a little aside?" he asked.

"Do what you like," she answered.

Donal moved it with ease—it was a rather small, moveable cabinet. The opening behind it was small and rather deep for its size. The walls were wainscotted all around to the height of four feet or so, but the recess was not. There were signs of hinges and a bolt at the front edges of it, which seemed to show that it had once been a cupboard or wardrobe with a door that probably corresponded with the wainscotting, only there were no signs of shelves in it. It seemed as old as the wall, and the plaster as hard as the stone itself. But he still was not satisfied. Taking a big knife from his pocket, he began tapping it all round. The moment he struck the right-hand side of it, he started. There was something peculiar about the sound it gave. The wall was smoother than the rest too, though quite as hard.

"You do not mind if I make a little dust here?" he asked.

"Do anything you please," answered Lady Arctura again.

"Then could you find me something to put down on the floor, that the housemaid may see nothing to attract her attention?"

Arctura brought him a towel and he spread it on the floor. The point of his knife would not go through the plaster. It was not plaster, he thought, but stone whitewashed—one smooth stone or slab, for he could find nothing like a joint. Searching with his knife near the edge of the recess, however, he found its outer limit a few inches from the edge, and began to clear it. It gave him a line straight from the bottom to the top of the recess where it turned in at right angles.

"There does seem, my lady," said Donal, "to be some kind of opening here which has been closed up, though of course it may turn out of no interest to us; shall I go on and see what it really is?"

"By all means," she answered, turning pale.

Donal looked at her a little anxiously. She understood his look.

"You must not mind my feeling a little silly," she said. "I am not silly enough to give way to it."

Donal smiled a satisfied smile and went on again with his knife; eventually he had cleared the whole outline of a slab of stone, or it might be slate, that filled nearly all the side of the recess. It was scarcely sunk in the wall, and had but a thin coating of plaster over it. Clearing the plaster, then, from the outside edge of the recess, he came upon a piece of iron fixed in it, which might have been part of some former fastening. He showed it to his companion.

"Go on! go on!" she only said.

"I fear I must get a better tool or two," answered Donal. "How will you like to be left?"

"I can bear it. But do not be long. A few minutes may be enough to evaporate my courage."

Donal hurried down to get a hammer and chisel and a pail to put the broken plaster in. Lady Arctura stood and waited, and the silence closed in upon her.

She began to feel eerie. After a moment she started to her feet with a smothered cry; a knock sounded on the door of the sitting room, between which and the bedroom where she was the door stood open. She darted to it and flung it closed, then to the wardrobe/press—it was very light, and with one push she had it almost in its place again. Then she opened the door between the two rooms, thinking she would wait for a second knock before she answered, that it might seem she had not heard the first. But as she opened the one door, the other slowly, softly opened also a little way, and the face she would least have chosen to see looked in. At that moment she would rather have had a visit from behind the press! It was her uncle. His face was cadaverous and his eyes dull, but with a kind of glitter in them and his bearing like that of a housebreaker. In terror lest he should come into the room and discover what they had been about, and in terror lest Donal should the next moment appear in the passage, and aware that even at that early hour of the day her uncle was not quite himself, with sudden intuitive impulse she cried out hurriedly almost the moment she saw him.

"Uncle! Uncle! what is that behind you?"

She thought afterwards it was a cruel thing to do, but she did it, as I have said, by swift, unreflecting instinct.

He turned like one struck on the back, imagined something doubtless of which Arctura knew nothing, cowered to two-thirds of his height and crept swiftly away. Though herself trembling from head to foot, Arctura was seized with such a pity that she followed him till she saw him into his room. But she dared not go farther—she could not have said why. She stood a moment in the passage and presently thought she heard his bell ring. This caused another undesirable risk; Simmons might meet the returning Donal! But she was the next moment relieved by seeing Donal appear round the corner in the passage, carrying the implements he had gone to procure. She signed to him to make haste, and he was hardly inside her room when she saw Simmons coming along on his way to his master's room. She drew the door to her, as if she had just come out, and said to Simmons, "Knock at my door as you come back, and tell me how he is. I heard his bell ring."

"I will, my lady," answered Simmons and went on. Then Arctura told

Donal to go on with his work but stop it the moment she made a noise with the handle of the door. She then assumed a place outside till Simmons should reappear. For full ten minutes she stood waiting; it seemed an hour. Though she heard Donal at work within and knew Simmons must soon reappear, though the room behind her was her own and known to her from childhood, the long, empty passage in front of her, as familiar to her as any in the house, appeared almost frightful. At last she heard her uncle's door and then steps, and the butler came.

"I can't make him out, my lady," he said. "It is nothing very bad, I think, this time; but, my lady, he gets worse and worse—always taking more and more of them horrid drugs. It's no use trying to hide it; he'll drop off sudden one o' these days. It's not one nor two, nor half a dozen sorts he keeps mixing! The end must come, and what it'll be, who can tell! It's better you should be prepared for it when it do come, my lady! I've just been a-giving him some under the skin—with a little sharp-pointed thing. You know, my lady, he says it's the only way to take some medicines. He's just a slave to his medicines, my lady!"

30

The Hidden Chambers

*A*rctura returned to Donal and told him what had happened. He had found the plaster hard but had already knocked it all away, disclosing a slab much like one of the great stones covering some of the roofs. Nor was it long now before he succeeded in prying it out. The same instant a sense of dank chill assailed them both, accompanied by a humid smell as from a long-closed cellar. The room grew cold and colder as they stood and looked, now at each other, now at the opening in the wall, where they could see nothing but darkness. Donal was anxious to see how she would take it. In truth he had enough to do to hide for her sake all expression of the awe he felt creeping over him; he must treat the thing as lightly as he could!

"We are not very far from something, my lady!" he said. "It makes one think of what he said who carried the light everywhere—that there is nothing covered that shall not be revealed, neither hid that shall not be known. Shall we leave it and put in the stone again?"

"I can bear anything," said Arctura, with a shiver, "except an unknown, terrible something."

"But what can you do when we have found it all out?"

"I can let the daylight in upon it."

Donal was glad to see her color return as she spoke, and a look of determination come in her eyes.

"You will not be afraid, then, to go down with me?" he said. "Or will you not rather wait till I explore a little, and come and let you know what I have found?"

"That would be cowardly. I will share with you. I shall be afraid of nothing . . . not much—not too much, I mean—with you with me."

Fancying from his lack of immediate reply that Donal was hesitating to take her she said, "See! I am going to light a candle and ask you to come down with me—if down it be, for who knows yet if it be not up?"

She lighted the candle.

"We had better lock the door, don't you think, my lady?" said Donal. "If anyone were to come, it might be awkward."

"So it would be to have the door locked," answered Arctura. "And we should have to lock both doors!—I mean the one into the passage, too, and that would make it look very strange if I were wanted. We had better replace the wardrobe as nearly as we can—pull it after us when we are behind it."

"You are right, my lady. But I will first stow these things—may I put them here?"

"Anywhere out of sight."

"Now, can you take some matches with you?"

"Yes, to be sure."

"I will let you carry the candle. I must have my hands free. You will let the light shine as much past me as you can, that I see as well as I may where I am going. But I shall depend most on what my hands and feet tell me."

Their preparations made, Donal took the light and looked in at the opening. It went into the outside wall of the house and turned immediately to the left. He gave back the candle to Arctura and went in. Arctura followed close behind, holding the light the best she could. There was a stair in the thickness of the wall, going down steep and straight. It was not wide enough to let two go down abreast.

"Put your hand on my shoulder, my lady," said Donal. "That will keep us together; and if I fall, you must stand till I get up again."

She did as he said, and they began their descent. The steps were narrow and high, therefore the stair was steep, but there was no turning. They had gone down about thirty steps when they came to a level passage, turning again at right angles to the left. It was twice the width of the stair; the sides of it, like those of the stair, were unplastered, of roughly dressed stones. It led them straight to a strong door which opened toward them but which they could not move. It was locked, and in the rusty lock, through the keyhole, they could see the key in it. But to the right was another door, smaller, which stood open. They went through and by a short passage entered an open space. Here on one side seemed no wall, and they stood for a moment afraid to move lest they should stumble into darkness. But by sending the light in this direction and that, and feeling about with hands and feet, they soon came to an idea of the kind of place in which they were. It seemed a sort of little gallery with arches on one side, opening into a larger place, the character of which they could only conjecture, so vaguely could they see into it. Almost all they could determine was that it went below and rose above where they stood. Behind them was a plain wall such as they had already passed on both sides of them.

They had been talking in suppressed, awe-filled whispers, and were now in silence, endeavoring to send their sight through the darkness when Donal said, "My lady, listen."

Yes, from above their heads came the soft, faint sounds of the aerial music. It had such a strange effect!—like news of the still airy night and the keen stars. It restored Arctura's courage greatly.

"That must be just as the songs of angels sounded, with news of high heaven, to the people of old times!" she said.

But Donal's mind was in a less poetic mood. He was occupied with the material side of things at the moment.

"We cannot be far," he said, "from the place where our plummet came down! But let us try on a little farther."

At the other end of the little gallery, they came again to a door on to a stair, turning again to the right, and again they went down. Arctura kept up bravely. The air was not so bad as they might have feared, though it was very cold and damp. This time they went down only about seven feet or so, and came to a door to the right. To Donal's hand it revealed itself as much decayed; and when he raised an ancient rusted latch and pushed it, it swung open against the wall, dropping from one hinge as it moved. Two steps more they descended, and stood on a floor, apparently of stone.

Donal thought at first they must be in one of the dungeons of the place which had been built over; but recalling how far they had come down, he saw it could not be so.

A halo of damp clung to the weak light of their candle, and it was some moments before they even began to take in the things around them so as to perceive what sort of a place they were in. Something about the floor caught Donal's eye; and looking down in the circle of the light, he saw, thickly covered with dust as it was, that it was of marble, in squares of black and white. Then there came to him a stream of white from the wall, and he saw it was a tablet of marble; and at the other end was something that looked like an altar, or perhaps a tomb.

"We are in the old chapel of the castle, I do believe!" he said—but he added instantly with an involuntary change of voice and a shudder through his whole being, "What is that?"

Arctura turned; her hand sought his, and clasped it convulsively, nor did she make other answer. They stood close to something on which their glance had not yet rested; for Arctura had been holding the candle so that the light had been between them and it. Before they could be conscious of even an idea of what it might be, they both felt the muscles of neck and face drawn. They gazed, perception cleared itself, and slowly they not only saw but understood what the thing was. They saw and knew, with strangest dream-like incongruity and unfitness, that the thing they stood beside was a bedstead—dark, with carved posts and wooden tester, low but richly carved. Even their one poor candle sufficed to show it suffi- ciently—a carved bedstead in the middle of the floor of what was plainly a chapel!

There was no speculating for them, however; they could only see, not think. Donal took the candle from Arctura and moved it about. From under the tester hung large fragments of some heavy stuff that had once served for curtains. They did not dare touch it. It looked as if it had scarcely as much cohesion as the dust on a cobweb. It was dust indeed, hanging together only in virtue of the lightness to which its decay had reduced it. On the bedstead lay a dark mass that looked like bedclothes and bedding turned to dust, or almost to dust, for they could see some- thing like embroidery. Yet in one or two places—oh so terrible in its dis- mal ash-like decay, dark almost like burnt paper or half-burnt rags, flaky and horrid. But, heavens! What was that shape in the middle of the heap? And what was that on the black pillow? And what was that thick line stretched toward one of the posts at the head? They stared in silence. Arctura pressed close to Donal. Involuntarily, almost, his arm went round her to protect her from what threatened indeed to overwhelm even him- self—an unearthly horror.

Plain to the eyes of both, though neither spoke to say so, the form in the middle of the bed before them was that of a human body, which had slowly crumbled where it lay. Bedding, blankets and quilts, sheets and pil- lows; and the line of a long arm that came out from under the clothes and pointed away toward the right-hand bedpost. But what was that which came down from the bedpost to meet the arm of dust?

"Dear God in heaven!" Donal whispered through stiff lips. There was a ring round the post, and from it came a chain; and there was another ring on the pillow, through which—yes, actually through it, though it was dust—the line of dust passed. The thing was clear—so far clear, at least, that here was a deathbed—indeed, perhaps a murderbed, certainly a bier, for still upon it lay the body that had died on it—had lain, as it seemed, for hundreds of years, nor ever been moved for kindly burial. The place had been closed up and so left! A bed in a chapel, and one dead thereon! Had the woman—for Donal imagined he could see even then in the form of the dust that it was the body of a woman—been carried thither for the sake of dying in a holy place, the victim of a terrible revenge? Had she been left to die perhaps in hunger or in disease?

Before the two horrified onlookers left the place, another conjecture had occurred to both of them which neither spoke: Neglected or tended, who could tell? But there she had died, and so been buried!

Donal felt Arctura trembling on his arm, either from the cold or the gathering terror of the place in the presence of ancient, unburied death. He drew her closer and, turning, would have borne her from it. But she said, whispering in his ear almost, as if the dust might hear and be disturbed, "I am not afraid—not very. Do not let us go till we have seen—till we have discovered everything possible to know about this."

They moved from the bed and went to the other end of the chapel, almost clinging to each other as they went. They noted three narrow, lancet windows, with what seemed stained glass in them, and a stone wall outside them. The tablet carved with an inscription they did not stop and read.

They came to a marble-topped altar table which had also been covered with a piece of embroidery. There on the remains of the cloth lay something that more than suggested the human shape—small, so small though—plainly the dust of a very small child. The sight was full of suggestion as sad as it was fearful. Neither of them spoke. The awful silence of the place seemed to settle down around them. Donal cast his eyes around once more. As near as he could judge, the place might be fifteen feet wide and five and twenty long, but it was hard to tell with so little light. He was anxious now to get Lady Arctura out of it. There would be plenty of time to examine further. He drew her away and she yielded.

When they reached the narrow stair, he made her go first. As they passed the door on the other side of the little gallery, Donal thought that here was the direction of further investigation; but he would say nothing of it until Lady Arctura should be a little accustomed to the thought of the strange and terrible things they had already discovered. So slowly, the lady still in front, they ascended to the room they had left. Donal replaced the slab and propped it in its position, so that there should be as little draught as possible to betray the gap; having replaced the press, he put a screw through the bottom of it from the inside into the floor, so as to fix it in its place, lest anyone should move it.

The difficulty now was how to part, after such an experience together, and spend the rest of the day separated! There was all the long afternoon and the evening to be accounted for!

"What a happy thing," said Donal, "that you had already changed to another bedroom!"

"It is well indeed!" she answered quietly.

Looking in her face now once more, for he had then just risen from fixing the press, he saw that she looked very white, as was not surprising.

"Do sit down for a minute, my lady," he said. "I would run and send Mrs. Brooks to you, but I do not like to leave you."

"No, no; we will go down together!"

The air of the place and its terrible contents had begun to show their effects. But with a strong effort she seemed now to banish their oppression and rose to go down. But Donal felt she must continue with him as much as possible for the rest of the day.

"Would you not like, my lady," he ventured to say, "to come to the schoolroom this afternoon, and do something while I give Davie his lessons?"

"Yes," she answered at once.

"But how am I to carry away this pail of plaster without being seen?" he inquired briskly to help her fasten her attention on something else. "That is the next thing."

"I will show you the way to your own stair," she replied, "without going down the great staircase—the way we came once, you may remember. Then you can take it to the top of the house till it is dark. I know you don't mind what you do. But I do not feel comfortable about my uncle's visit. I hope he does not already suspect something! If he were to come in now, however, I think he would guess everything correctly. I wonder if he knows where the chapel is—and all about the stair here!"

"It is impossible to say. I think he is a man to enjoy having and keeping a secret. But tell me now, my lady," Donal went on, "don't the things we were discussing previously about the likeness of house to man find general corroboration in our discovery? Here is the chapel of the house, the place they used to pray to God when, perhaps, they did not do so anywhere else in the whole building; and it is lost, forgotten, filled with dust and damp—and the mouldering dead lying there before the Lord, waiting to be made alive again—waiting to praise him!"

"I will clean out the temple!" announced Arctura. "I will pull down that wall and the light shall come in again through those windows and astonish the place with its presence. And all the house will be glad, because there will no more be a dead chapel at the heart of it, but a living temple with God himself in it—there always and forever!"

She had spoken in great excitement, her eyes shining in her pale face; she ceased and burst into tears. Donal turned away and proceeded to fill the pail with the broken plaster, and by the time he had done it she had recovered her usual calm. They went as far as the turret stair together and there parted till after luncheon, Donal going up and Arctura going down.

31

A Confidential Talk

As the clock in the schoolroom was striking the hour for lessons, Arctura entered. As if she had been a pupil from the first, she sat down at the table with Davie, who thought it delightful to have cousin Arkie for a fellow pupil.

After school, Davie went to his rabbits.

"Mrs. Brooks invites us to take supper with her," said Lady Arctura. "I asked her to ask us. So if you do not mind, Mr. Grant, you had better make a good tea, and we shall not have dinner today. You see, I want to shorten the hours of the night as much as I can, and not go to bed till I am quite sleepy. You don't mind, do you?"

"I am very glad, and you are very wise, my lady," responded Donal. "I quite approve of the plan and shall be delighted to spend as much of the night in Mrs. Brooks' parlor as you please."

"Don't you think we had better tell her all about it?"

"As you judge fit, my lady. The secret is in no sense mine; it is only yours, and the sooner it ceases to be a secret the better for all of us, I venture to think."

"I have only one reason for a delay," she returned. "I need hardly tell you what it is!"

"You would avoid any risk of annoying your uncle, I presume."

"Yes; I cannot quite tell how he might take it, but I know he would not like it. It is perhaps natural that a man like him should think of himself as having the first and real authority in the house, but there are many reasons why I should not give way to that."

"There are indeed!" assented Donal.

"Still, I should be sorry to offend him more than I cannot help. If he were a man like my father, I should never dream of going against his liking in anything; I should, in fact, leave everything to him as long as he pleased to take interest in what was going on. But, you know, being the man he is, that would be absurd. I must not—I dare not—let him manage affairs for me much longer."

"You will not, I hope, do anything without the advice—I should say, the presence of a lawyer," suggested Donal; "I mean, in conference with your uncle?"

"Do you say so?"

"I do indeed. I think it would be very undesirable. I fear I have less confidence in your uncle than you have!"

"Well, poor man! We must not begin comparing our opinions about him; he is my father's brother, after all, and I shall be glad if I get through without offending him."

At nine o'clock they were in the housekeeper's room, a low-ceiled but rather large room, lined almost all round with oak presses, which were Mrs. Brooks' delight, for she had more than usual nowadays of the old-fashioned housekeeper about her. She welcomed them as if she had been in her own house, and made an excellent hostess, presiding over a Scotch supper of minced collops and mashed potatoes, and she gave them some splendid coffee, on the making of which she prided herself. Upon the coffee waited scones of the true sort, just such as Donal's mother would occasionally make for the greatest kind of treat they ever had. He thought it the nicest meal he had had since leaving home. And this night, the conversation took such a turn that, to Arctura's delight, he was led to talk about his father and mother and the surroundings of his childhood.

He told her all about the life he had led; how at one time he kept cattle in the fields; at another, sheep on the mountains; he told how he had come to be sent to college, and then came all the story about Sir Gilbert

Galbraith. The night wore on, and Arctura was enchanted. For himself Donal found it a greater pleasure than he had dared hope to call back the history which already seemed so far behind him. Nor was the discovery a pain, as he certainly would have found it had it come of his ceasing to care for Lady Galbraith; she was the dearest of sisters, whom he would rather now have for a sister than for a wife. It was far the better thing that she should be Gibbie's wife and Donal's sister. When they got to heaven, she would give him the kiss she had refused him down in the granite quarry!

All at once a sound of knocking fell on his ear. He started. There was something in it that affected him strangely. Neither of his companions took any notice of it. Yet it was now past one o'clock. It was like a knocking three or four times with the knuckles of the hand against the other side of the wall of the room.

"What can that be?" he said, listening for more.

"Have you never heard that before, Mr. Grant?" said the housekeeper. "I've grown so used to it my ears hardly take notice."

"What is it?" asked Donal.

"Ay, what is it? Tell me that if you can," she returned. "It comes, I believe, every night. But I couldn't take an oath upon it, I've so entirely ceased to pay attention to it. There's queer things about many an old house, Mr. Grant, that'll take the day of judgment to explain. But they come no nearer than the other side of the wall, so far as I know."

"Well, I won't ask you for any more tonight, but we must now tell you something!" said Lady Arctura. "Only you must tell nobody, just yet; there are reasons . . . Mr. Grant has found the lost room!"

For a few moments Mrs. Brooks said nothing. She neither paled nor looked incredulous; her face was simply fixed and still, as if she were thinking of something to put alongside of what was now told her.

"Then there *was* such a place," she said at last. "Many was the time I thought about looking for it, just to please myself, but the right time never came. It's small wonder, then, that we should hear raps and sounds about the house."

"You will think differently when we tell you what we found in it," said Arctura. "That was why I asked you to let us come to supper with you; I was afraid to go to bed for thinking about it."

"You've been into it, my lady!—And what did you see?" asked Mrs. Brooks with growing eyes.

"It is the old chapel of the house. I have heard there is mention made of it in some of the old papers in the iron chest. No one, I suppose, ever dreamed that the room they told such stories of could be the chapel! Yet what should we find there but a bed . . . and in the bed not the skeleton but the dust of a woman! And on the altar lay another dust—that of a child!"

"The Lord be about us! and between us and harm!" cried the housekeeper, her well-seasoned composure giving way at last. "You saw that with your own eyes, my lady?—Mr. Grant! How could you let her ladyship see such things! I thought you would have had more sense!"

"My lady has more sense than you seem to think, Mrs. Brooks!" returned Donal, laughing a little. "I had no right to go without her ladyship if she wanted to accompany me."

"That's very true; but, eh, my bonnie bairn, such sights is not for you!"

"I ought to know what is in my own house!" said Arctura with a little involuntary shudder. "But I shall feel more comfortable now you know too. Mr. Grant would like to have your advice as to what we ought to do with the—the remains. You'll come and see the place, Mrs. Brooks?"

"Yes, surely; when you please, my lady—but not tonight, you do not mean tonight?"

"No, certainly! Not tonight. I wonder if any of the noises we hear in this house are made by ghosts wanting to let you know their bodies are not buried yet!"

"I wouldn't wonder!" answered Mrs. Brooks thoughtfully.

"What would you have us do with the dust?" asked Donal.

"I would have you bury it as soon as possible."

"That is certainly the natural thing! The human body is not in any case to be treated as less than sacred," said Donal.

"I'll turn the thing over in my mind, sir. I wouldn't willingly have a heap of clash in the countryside about it," said Mrs. Brooks.

So the thing was left for the meantime. Donal accompanied the two to the door of their chamber and then betook himself to the high places of the castle, where more than once, in what remained of the night, he awoke fancying he heard the sounds of the ghost music sounding its coronach over the strange bier down below.

32

A Strange Burial

There are men of inactive natures who cannot even enjoy seeing activity around them; but such was not Lord Morven by nature. He indeed had led in his youthful years what might be called a stormy life. But the day that his passions began to yield, his self-indulgence began to take the form of laziness.

He more and more seldom went out of the house or left his rooms. At times he would read a great deal, and then again for days would not open a book but seemed absorbed in meditation.

A mind thoroughly diseased will even seek to atone for wrong by fresh wrong. He was ready now to do anything to restore his sons to the position of which he had deprived them through the wrong he had done his wife. So far I will go in the mention of his wickedness toward her as to state that, upon frequent occasions, he had in the moral madness of the self-adoration which had possessed him, inflicted hideous bodily pains and sores and humiliations upon her—to see, as he said to himself, how much she would bear for his sake. And now, through all his denials to himself of a life beyond, the conviction would occasionally overwhelm him that he would one day meet her again; then it would at least be something to tell her what for her sake he had done for her children. The real had departed from him, and in its place a false appearance of the real had been submitted.

The next night, as if by a common understanding, the three met again in the housekeeper's room, where she had supper waiting them as before. As by common consent, the business of the meeting was postponed until supper was over. Arctura happening to mention the music that was said always to announce the death of the head of a neighboring house, Donal remarked that this tradition might have been what suggested to someone to make the Aeolian harp, by which the sounds that had so often puzzled the inhabitants of the castle were now apparently explained.

"But now, Mistress Brooks," said Donal, "have you made up your mind what you would have us do with the dust in the chapel?"

"I've been thinking," answered Mrs. Brooks, "that, seeing it's a pretty starry night, the best way would be, this very night, when the house is asleep, to lift and lay it down—the three of us."

"Tonight, you say, Mrs. Brooks?"

"The sooner the better, don't you think?"

Arctura only looked at Donal.

"Surely," he answered.

"I'll get a fine old sheet," said the housekeeper, "and into it we'll lay the remains, and roll them up, and carry them to their home."

"But," said Donal, "don't you think it would be better for you and me to get all done in the chapel first, so that Lady Arctura need not go down there again? She could join us when we have got all ready."

"She wouldn't like to be left here alone. I don't suppose there can be anything so very fearsome after so many years are over."

"There is nothing fearsome at all," said Arctura.

"Then there's no reason why she shouldn't go with us—she need not touch anything."

Mrs. Brooks went to one of her presses and brought out a sheet. Then they went up to Lady Arctura's room and thence descended to the chapel. Only one word was uttered as they went; halfway down the narrow descent Mistress Brooks murmured, "Eh, sirs!" and no more.

They each carried a light, and now its first visitors could see better what it was like. A stately little place it was, and when the windows were once again opened, as Arctura resolved they should soon be, it would be beautiful. But now they must get to the task they had set themselves.

The whole of the bedding, as they soon found, had first rotted and then turned to all but dust. The bed joints seemed to hold together more from habit than strength. The three stood by the side of this bier of sleep, looking on it for some moments in silence. No wonder their hearts felt strange, or that when at length they spoke, it was in little above a whisper. Donal alone meditated the practical part, for it was Mrs. Brooks' introduction to the scene of ancient death.

At last he spoke. "How are we to get all this dust into the sheet, Mrs. Brooks?" he said.

"All this dust? No, no," returned the housekeeper; "we have only to do with our own kind! Look here, Mr. Grant; I have respect for the dead; I have no difficulty about handling anything belonging to them. Lay the sheet handy, and I'll lay in the dust handful by handful. If it hadn't been that he took it again, the Lord's own body would have come to something like this!"

Donal looked at Arctura, and Arctura smiled.

Donal laid the sheet on the floor, and began to lift and lay in it the dry dust, first from the altar, then from the bed, with here and there a little bit of bone. Mrs. Brooks helped, but would have prevented Arctura. The girl was not pleased, however, and insisted on having her share in the burying of her own people, whom God knew and she would know one day. For of all fancies, the fancy that we go into the other world like a set of spiritual moles burrowing in the dark of a new and altogether unknown existence, not as children with a history and an endless line of living ancestors, is of the most foolish. She would yet talk to those whose dust she was now reverently lifting in her hands. Then Donal knotted the sheet together, and they rested from their work, and began to look around them a little. Arctura and the housekeeper went peering about in the half-darkness, finding here and there signal remnants of the occupancy of the place; Donal looked for indications of former means of communication with the outer world. That could not be the only way to the chapel by which they had come, neither could that be the only other by the door they had passed as they came down, for it communicated on the inside with such a narrow approach.

Outside the immediate door by which they had entered the chapel there was a passage running parallel with the wall under the windows; it turned at right angles, behind the wall against which the altar stood. Then first it struck him that the altar was in the wrong position—in the west end, namely; it had probably been moved for some reason when the bed was placed there; as it now stood it could not be seen from the little gallery except by leaning over and looking straight down. Under the gallery was the angled continuation of the passage, and there in the wall he saw signs that required further examination. "There must have been an entrance there once," he said to himself.

In the meantime the two women had made a somewhat appalling discovery. Between the foot of the bed and the altar was a little table, on which were two drinking vessels, apparently of pewter, and the mouldered remains of a pack of cards. Surely these had something to do with the legends that had survived the disappearance of the place!

But it was time to finish what they had begun. Donal took up the parcel of dust. Arctura led the way, as knowing it better than Mrs. Brooks, and Donal brought up the rear with his bundle. They went softly across the castle, now up, now down, now turning a corner in one direction, now another in the opposite, and at last arrived at the door opening upon what was now called, by more than one in the castle, Mr. Grant's stair. By that they descended; and, without danger of disturbing the house, though not without some fear of possibly meeting the earl in one of his midnight wanderings, they reached the open air. They took their way down the terraces and across the park to the place of ancient burial.

They reached the ruin in the hollow where it stood in a clump of trees. Inside its walls they removed a number of stones, and Donal dug a grave, not very deep—that was hardly necessary for such tenants. Then they laid the knotted sheet, covered it up with earth, and laid again the stones upon the spot. It lay very near to kindred, probably ancestral dust, for the ruin was ancient. Then they returned as they went, and that funeral walk was not likely ever to be forgotten.

33

· · · · · · · · · · · · · · · · · · ·

Discoveries!

Whatever Lady Arctura might decide concerning the restoration of the chapel to the light of day, Donal thought it would not be amiss for him, without mentioning it to her, to find out what he could about the relation of the place to the rest of the house. So that being Saturday, he resolved to go down alone that afternoon, telling no one, and explore. First of all he would try to open the door on a level with the little gallery.

As soon as he was free, therefore, he got the tools he judged likely to be necessary, and went down. The door was of strong, sound oak, with ornate iron hinges going all across it. He was on the better side for opening it, that is the inside; but though the ends of the hinges and their bearing pins in the wall were exposed, he soon saw that the door was so well within the frame that it was useless to think of heaving the former off the latter. The lock and its bolt were likewise exposed to his examination; they were huge, and the key was on the other side and in the lock, so that he could not have picked it had he been more of a locksmith than he was. The nails that fastened it to the door were so hard fixed that he was compelled to give up the idea of removing it; they were probably riveted through a plate of iron on the other side.

But there was the socket into which the bolt shot—merely an iron staple. He might either force this out with a lever if he could find one strong enough and could manage to apply it, or, which was the more hopeful way, he might file it through. He would try the latter. When he had roughly removed the scales of rust with which it was caked, he found its thickness considerably less than it seemed, and set himself to the task of filing it through, first on the top and then on the bottom. It was slow but a sure process and would be in less danger of being heard than any more violent one.

The work was very slow—the impression he made on the hard iron with the worn file was only enough to prevent him from throwing it aside as useless. He went on at it for a long time, until at last weariness overtook him.

He did not go back that night, but went instead to the town to buy a new and more suitable file.

It was Monday night before Donal again went down into the hidden parts of the castle. Arctura had come to the schoolroom but seemed unable to do her work; and Donal would not tell her what he was doing, for fear of making her think of things it was better should drift farther away in the past of her memory. But he was certain she would never be quite herself until the daylight entered the chapel and all the hidden places of the house were open to the air of God's world.

With his new file he made better progress than before and soon had finished cutting through the top of the staple. Trying it then with a poker he had brought down for a lever, he broke the bottom part across and there was nothing to hold the bolt. With a little creaking noise of rusty hinges, the door slowly opened to his steady pull on the lock.

He threw the light of his candle into the space unclosed. There was nothing, it appeared, but a close screen or wall of plank. When he gave it a push, however, it yielded; it was close-fitting and without any fastening. It disclosed a small closet or wardrobe, on the opposite side of which was another door. This he could not at once open. Plainly, however, it was secured with merely a small common lock, such as is on any cupboard, and it cost him little trouble to force it. The door opened outwards. He looked in and saw a little room, of about nine feet by seven. There was in it nothing but an old-fashioned secretary or bureau—not so old, it struck him, as that he had seen in the Morven House in the town, and a seat like a low music stool before it.

How did it first get into the little place? He looked all round. The walls were continuous; there was not another door! Above the bureau was a little window—or it seemed a window but was so overgrown with dirt that he could not certainly tell whether it was more than the blind show of an eye with a wall behind it. The bureau might get through the oak door behind, but it could not, he thought, have reached that through any of the passages he had come through; and if there had been any wider approach in that direction, surely it had been built up long before this piece of furniture was made. If his observations and reasoning were correct, it followed that there must, and that not so very long ago, have been another entrance to the place in which he stood. There might be something in the bureau to reveal how it had come there, or show how long it had been left there.

He turned to look at the way he himself had entered. It was through a common-looking wardrobe that filled up the end of the little room, which there narrowed to about five feet. When the door in the back of it was shut, it looked merely the back of the closet.

He turned again to the bureau. There was a strange feeling at his heart. He never thought whether or not he had a right to look into it. He felt himself all the time acting merely in the service of Lady Arctura. Besides, why should he imagine anybody's secret there? Nobody alive could know of this chamber. The bureau stood open and on it lay writing paper, some of it on large sheets all stained with dust and age and blot. A pen lay with them, and beside was a glass ink bottle of the commonest type in which the ink had dried into flakes. He took up one of the sheets with a great stain on it. The bottle must have been overturned . . . But was it ink? No; it could not be! It stood up too thick on the paper. With a gruesome shiver, Donal wetted his finger and tried the surface of it; a little came off and looked of a faint suspicious reddish brown. He held the faded lines close to the candle and tried to decipher them. He sat down on the stool and read thus—his reading broken by the spot which had for the present obliterated a part of the writing. There was no date:

"My husband for such I will—blot—are in the sight of God—blot—men why are ye so cruel what—blot—deserve these terrors—blot—in thought have I—blot—hard upon me to think of another."

Here the writing came below the blot and went on unbroken. "My little one is gone, and I am left lonely, oh! so lonely. I cannot but think that if you had loved me as you once did, I should yet be clasping my little one to my bosom and you would have a daughter to comfort you after I am gone. I cannot long survive this—ah! there my hand has burst out bleeding again; but do not think I mind it; I know it was only an accident. You never meant to do it, though you teased me by refusing to say so—besides, it is nothing. You might draw every drop of blood from my body and I would not care, if only you would not make my heart bleed so—oh, it is gone all over my paper, and you will think I have done it to let you see how it bleeds. But I cannot write it all over again—it is too great a labor and too painful to write. But I dare not think where my baby is; for if I should be doomed never to see her because of the love I have borne for you, and if I am cast out from God because I loved you more than him, I shall never—"

Here the writing stopped abruptly; the bleeding of the hand had probably brought it to a close, and it had never been folded up and never sent. Donal looked for a date; there was none upon the sheet he had read. He held it up to the light and saw a paper mark; and close by lay another sheet with merely a date in the same handwriting, as if the writer had been about to commence another in lieu, perhaps, of the one spoiled. He laid the papers thoughtfully down.

He took a packet of papers from a pigeonhole of the desk, and undid the string around them; they were but bills, but they had plenty of dates! From comparison of the dates and handwriting, he had not a doubt left that the letter he had partly read was written by the late wife of the present earl—wife as she had been considered.

What was he to do now? He had thought he was looking into matters much older—things over which the permission of Lady Arctura, by right, extended. But now he knew differently. Still, the things he had discovered were only such as she had a right to know; though whether he was to tell her at once, he would not yet make up his mind. He put the papers back, took up his candle, and with a feeling of helpless dismay withdrew to his own chamber. When he reached the door of it, yielding to a sudden impulse, he turned away, went farther up the stair and out upon the roof.

It was a frosty night, with all the stars brilliant overhead. He looked up and said, "Oh, God of men! Your house is filled with light; in you there is no darkness. Be my life; fill my heart with your light that I may never hunger or thirst after anything but your will; that I may walk in the light, and that from me light, and not darkness, may go forth."

34

· · · · · · · · · · · · · · · · · · · ·

Further Search

When are you going down again to the chapel, Mr. Grant?" asked Lady Arctura the next day after school. She was better and had come again to lessons.

"I want to go this evening—by myself, if you don't mind, my lady," he answered. "I want to find out all I can; but I can't help thinking it would be better for you not to go down again till you are ready to order everything cleared away. If I were you, I would just have it done and say nothing till it was finished."

So again at night Donal went down—this time chiefly intent on learning whether there was any other way open out of it and on verifying its position in the castle, of which he had now a pretty good idea. He went first to the end of the passage parallel with the length of the chapel; turning round the west end of it, he there examined the signs he had before observed. Yes! Those must be the outer ends of two of the steps of the great staircase, coming through and resting on the wall. That end of the chapel, then, was close to the great spiral stair. Plainly too a door had been there built up in the process of constructing the stair. The chapel had not been entered from that level at least since the building of the great stair. Before that, there had probably been an outside stair to this door, in an open court.

Finding no other suggested direction for inquiry, Donal was on his way out and already near the top of the stair in the wall, thinking that in the morning he would take fresh observations outside, when up from behind came a blast of air which blew out his candle. He shivered—not with the cold of it but from a feeling of its unknown origin. It seemed to indicate some opening to the outer air which he had not discovered. He lit his candle, turned and again descended, carefully guarding the flame with one hand.

But might not the wind have been a draught down the shaft in which were stretched the music chords? No, for in that case they would have loosed some light-winged messenger with it. It must come from lower than that, indicating some gap he had failed to find. If it would but come again when he was below! He crossed the little gallery, descended, and went into the chapel; it lay as still as a tomb; but because it was a tomb no more, he felt as if it were deserted—as if some life had gone out of it. He looked all round it, searching closely the walls where he could reach and staring as high as the light would show, but could perceive no sign of possible entrance for the messenger blast. But just as he was leaving it the wind came again—plainly along the little passage he had left but a few minutes ago. It kept blowing when he turned into it, and now he thought it came upwards. As he stooped to examine the lower parts of the passage, his light was again blown out. Having once more relighted his candle, he searched along the floor and the adjacent parts of the walls, and presently found, close to the floor in the inner wall—that is, the wall of the chapel itself—an opening that seemed to go downwards through it. But if that was its direction, why had he not seen it inside the chapel? He then recalled that, although from the landing place of the stair there was a step down into the chapel, there were three or four down to the passage. He concluded therefore that this opening went down under the floor of the chapel, probably into a crypt, where not unlikely lay yet more dust of the dead; if there was here a way into that, he might be nearer a way out. The opening showed only a mere narrow slit, but there might be more of it under the floor.

Among the slabs with which the chapel was paved was one that went all the length of the slit. He would try to raise this one. That would want a crowbar. He would get one at once. Having got so far, he could not rest till he knew more! It must be very late. Would the people in the castle be in bed yet? He could not tell; he had left his watch in his room. It might be midnight, and here he was, burrowing like a mole about the roots of the old house.

He crept up again and out by his own turret stair to the toolhouse, which he found locked. But lying near was a half-worn shovel, which he thought might do; he would have a try with it. He went once more into the entrails of the house, and down to the place of its darkness. There, endeavoring to insert the sharp edge of the worn shovel in the gap between the stone he wanted to raise and the one next it, he succeeded even more readily than he had dared hope. He soon lifted it, disclosing the slope of a small opening down into a place below. How deep the place might be, and whether it would be possible to get out of it again, he must try to discover before venturing down. There could be small risk of setting such a place on fire; he took a piece of paper from his pocket and, lighting it, threw it in. It fell and lay burning on something that looked like a small, flat gravestone. The descent was little more than about seven feet, into what looked like a cellar. He hesitated no longer, got into the opening, slid down the slope, and dropped—with no further hurt than grazing his nose on the wall as he descended.

Donal looked about him. There was the flat stone that looked like a gravestone, but there was not even an inscription upon it. It lay in a vaulted place, unpaved, with a floor of hard-beaten earth. Searching about the walls, he soon caught sight of what looked like the top of an arch rising from the floor in one of them, as near as he could judge, just under the built-up door in the passage above. There was room enough to creep through. He crept, and found himself under the first round of the great spiral stair. On the floor of the small, enclosed space, at the bottom of its well, was a dustpan and a housemaid's brush—and there was the tiny door through which they were shoved after their morning's use upon the stair! Through that he crept next: he was in the great hall of the house, from which the stair ascended.

Afraid of being by any chance discovered, he put out his light and proceeded up the stair in the dark. He had gone but a few steps when he heard the sound of descending feet. He listened and listened; they turned into the room on the stair. As he crept past it, he heard sounds which satisfied him that the earl was in the little closet behind it. Everything now came together in his mind. He hurried up to Lady Arctura's sitting room and thence descended, for the third time that night, to the old oak door. Entering the little chamber and hastening to the farther end, he laid his ear against the wall.

Plainly enough he heard sounds—such sounds as he had before heard from the mouth of the dream-walking (rather than sleep-walking) earl. He was moaning and calling in a low voice of entreaty after someone whose name never grew audible to the listener on the other side of the wall.

"Ah!" thought Donal, "who would find it hard to believe in roaming and haunting ghosts, who had once seen this poor man going about the house like Lady Macbeth, possessed by the seven demons of his own evil and cruel deeds and without hope of relief in heaven—only in the grave, nor much in that! How easily I could punish him now with a lightning blast of hellish terror!" It was but a thought; it did not even amount to a temptation, for Donal knew he had no right. Vengeance belongs to the Lord, who alone knows what use to make of it.

He heard the lean hands of the earl, at the ends of his long arms, go sweeping slowly over the wall. He had seen the thing, else he would not have recognized the sounds; and he heard him muttering still, but much too low for him to distinguish the words. By this time Donal was so convinced that he had to do with a dangerous and unprincipled man that he would have had little scruple in listening if he could have heard every word, and letting what knowledge of him come that might come.

It is only Righteousness that has a right to secrecy and does not want it. Evil has no right to secrecy, alone intensely desires it, and rages at being foiled of it.

But Donal could not remain there longer; he felt sick of the whole thing, and turned away at length hastily. But forgetting the one seat, and carrying his light too much in front of him to see it, he came against and knocked it over, not without noise. A loud cry from the other side of the wall told the dismay he had caused. It was followed by a stillness, and then a moaning.

As soon as he was out, and had replaced the obstructions to the entrance, he went to find Simmons, and sent him to look after his master.

Hearing nothing afterwards of the affair, he did not doubt that the victim of his awkwardness put the whole thing down, if indeed he knew anything of it the next day, to the mingling of imagination with fact in the manner he was so accustomed to, disabling him from distinguishing between the one and the other or indeed caring to do so.

35

· · · · · · · · · · · · · · · · · ·

Explaining the Lost Room

*T*ender over Lady Arctura, Donal made up his mind to ask a few questions of the housekeeper before disclosing further what he had found. In the evening, therefore, he sought her room while Arctura and Davie, much together now, were reading in the library.

"Did you ever hear anything about that little room behind the earl's business room on the stair, Mistress Brooks?" he asked.

"I can't say I ever did," she answered. "My old auntie did mention something to me once about some place—wait a moment—I have a willing memory; maybe it'll come back to me. It was something about building up and taking down, and something he was going to do but never did. Just give me time, I'll remember it."

Donal waited and said not a word; he would not hurry her.

"I remember this much," she said at length, "that they used to be together in that room. And I remember too that there was something about building up one wall and pulling down another—it's coming back to me."

She paused again a while, and then said: "All I can recollect, Mr. Grant, is that after her death, he built up something not far from that room—

there was something about making the room bigger. But how that could be by building something up, I can't think. Yet I feel sure that was what he did."

"I think I have a glimmer of light on the thing," said Donal. "Would you mind coming to the place? To see it might help us."

"Certainly I will. But let's make sure his lordship's quiet for the night before we go."

"That will be as well," said Donal. "But I hope you will say nothing further to my lady just yet."

"It might be worse for her not to be told. Besides she might be displeased to think we were doing things of ourselves in her house. She has the pride of her family, Mr. Grant, though she never shows it to you or me."

"For tonight let us think over it, and if you are of the same mind tomorrow, we will tell her. I am not willing to do anything rashly."

To this proposal Mrs. Brooks agreed, and as soon as the household was quiet, they went together to the room on the stair, where Donal stood for some time looking about him to no purpose.

"What's that on the wall?" he said at last, pointing to the back wall of the room—that, namely, on the other side of which was the little room haunted by both mind and body of the earl.

Two arches, drawn in chalk, as it seemed, had attracted his gaze. Surely light out of the darkness was drawing nigh!

As near as Donal could judge, the one arch was drawn opposite where he believed the hidden chamber was; the other right against the earl's closet, as it had come to be called in the house, for all knew his lordship had some strange attraction to it—most of them thinking he there said his prayers. It looked just as if they had been marked out for the piercing of the wall with such arches in order to throw the two little rooms on the other side as recesses into the larger. But if that was the earl's intent, why first build a wall—that doubtless to which Mrs. Brooks referred, doubtless also that across the middle of what had evidently been one room before.

"That!" returned Mrs. Brooks.

"Yes, those two arches, drawn on the wall."

The housekeeper looked at them thoughtfully.

"Now there," she said slowly, "I can't help but think—yes, I'm sure that's the very thing my aunt told me about. Those are the places you see marked there, where he was going to take the wall down to make the room larger. But, then, where could be the wall she said something about his building?"

"Look," said Donal; "I will measure the distance from the door there on this side of the wall to the other side of this first arch. . . . Now come into the little room behind. Look here! This same measurement takes us right up to the end of the room! So, you see, if we were to open that second arch, it would be into something behind this wall."

"Then this must be the very wall he built up."

"What could he have had it built up for if he was going to open the other wall?" said Donal. "I must think it all over! It was after his wife's death?"

"Yes, I believe so, for I remember something about it besides!"

"Could it have been for the sake of shutting out or hiding anything?" suggested Donal.

"It might have been to get rid of something he couldn't bear to look at anymore," she replied. "And I do remember a certain thing—curious! But what then about the opening of it afterwards?"

"Only, you see, he has never done it!" said Donal. "The thing takes a shape to me something in this way: That he wanted to build something out of sight—but in order to prevent speculation, he professed the intention of casting the whole into one room, then built the wall on the pretense either that it was necessary to support something when the other was broken through, or that two recesses with arches would look better. So pretending, he got the thing done, and then put off and off opening the arches, on one pretext or another, till the thing should be forgotten altogether—as you see it is already, almost entirely. And now I must tell you," Donal went on, "that I have been behind that wall, and have heard the earl moaning and crying on this!"

"God bless me," cried the good woman. "I'm not easily frightened, but that's fearsome."

"You would not care then to come to that side of the wall with me?"

"No, no, not tonight. Come to my room and have a drop of toddy, or if you won't have that I'll make you a cup of coffee; and then I'll tell you the story—for it's coming back to me now—that what made my aunt tell me about the building up of that wall. Indeed, I've now hardly a doubt left that the thing was just as you say."

Donal making no objection, they went together to her room. But when they reached it, Donal entering first started back at the sight of Lady Arctura sitting by the fire as if waiting for them. "My lady!" cried the housekeeper, "I thought I left you sound asleep!"

"So I was, I daresay," answered Arctura; "but I woke again, and finding you had not come up, I thought I would go down to you. I was certain you and Mr. Grant would be somewhere together! Have you been discovering anything more?"

Mrs. Brooks cast a glance at Donal which, notwithstanding what she said before, he could not but take as a warning not to say anything about the earl. So he left it to her to tell as much or as little as she pleased.

"We've been prowling about the house, my lady, but not down yonder. I think you and me would better leave that to Mr. Grant."

"It would be better for a time, I think, my lady," agreed Donal. "When you are quite ready to have everything set to rights and have a resurrection of the old chapel, then you can go and see everything. For my part I would rather not talk more about it just at present," he added.

"As you please, Mr. Grant," replied Lady Arctura. "We will say nothing more till I have made up my mind, as you say. I don't want to vex my uncle, and I find the question a difficult one. Shall we not go to bed now, Mistress Brooks?"

All through this time, the sense of help and safety and protection in the presence of the young tutor was growing in the mind of Arctura. It was nothing to her that he was the son of a very humble pair; that he had been a shepherd and a cowherd, and farm laborer. And now nearly all she knew about him was that he was a tower of strength. She questioned herself in no way about the matter. Falling in love was a thing that did not suggest itself to her. If she were now in what others would consider danger, it was of a more serious thing altogether; for the lower is in its very nature transient, while the higher is forever.

The next day again she did not appear, and Mrs. Brooks said she had persuaded the girl to keep to her bed for a day or two. There was nothing really the matter with her, she said herself, but she was so tired she did not care to lift her head from the pillow. She had slept very well and was not troubled about anything. She had asked Mrs. Brooks to beg Mr. Grant to let Davie come and read to her; and to choose something for him to read which would be good for him as well as for her. Donal did as she requested and did not see Davie again till the next morning.

"Oh, Mr. Grant," he cried, "you never saw anything so pretty as Arkie in bed! She is so white and so sweet, and she speaks with a voice so gentle and low! And then she was so kind to me for going to read to her! She looks as if she had just said her prayers, and God told her she should have everything she wanted."

Donal wondered a little. What Davie said must indicate that she was finding the rest she sought. But why was she so white? Surely she was not going to die! And with that there shot a pang to his heart, and he felt that if she were to go out of the castle, it would be hard to stay in it, even for the sake of Davie. He did not either for a moment imagine himself fallen in love; he had loved once, and his heart had not yet done aching at the memory of bygone pain! But he could not hide from himself that the friendship of Lady Arctura, and the help she sought of him and he was able to give her, had added a fresh and strong interest to his life. And now to have helped this lovely young creature, whose life seemed wrapped in an ever-closer-clasping shroud of perplexity, was a thing for him to be glad of.

At the end of a week she was better and able to see him. She had the bed in which the housekeeper slept moved into her own room, and made the dressing room, which also was large, a sitting room for herself. It was sunny and pleasant; just the place, Donal thought, he would have chosen for her. She greatly needed the sun—as who does not? The bedroom too, which the housekeeper had persuaded her to choose when she left her own, was one of the largest in the house—old-fashioned like all the rest, but as cheerful as stateliness would permit, with gorgeous hangings and great pictures.

The next day she told him she had a beautiful night, full of the loveliest dreams—one of which was that a sweet child came out of a grassy hillock by the wayside, called her mamma, and said she was so much obliged to her for taking her off the cold stone and making her a butterfly; and with that the little child spread out gorgeous and great butterfly wings and soared away up to the white cloud that hung over her. There she sat looking down on her and laughing merrily.

36

. . . .

Breaking Down the Wall

The morning after the last meeting in the housekeeper's parlor, as Donal sat in the schoolroom with Davie, he became aware that for a time indefinite he had been hearing the noise of blows of some laborious sort that seemed to come from a great distance, but which, when he grew attentive to it, seemed to come from somewhere in the castle itself.

"Davie," he said, "go and see if you can find out what's happening."

The recollection of what had occurred the night before had not only made him a little anxious but unwilling to be found asking questions or showing the smallest curiosity himself.

Davie came back in no small excitement.

"Oh, Mr. Grant, what do you think!" he cried. "I do believe my father is going to look for the lost room! They are breaking down a wall in the little room—behind Papa's business room!—on the stair, you know!" he added, fancying from Donal's silence that he could not quite succeed in identifying the place he described. But Donal's silence had a very different cause; he was dismayed to think what might be the consequences if Davie was right. If the earl knew the hidden part of the castle before, which was scarcely to be doubted, for he was not the man to have left undiscovered the oak door at the back of the press, then he would know that things there had been meddled with! He started to his feet.

"You may go and see them at work, Davie," he said. "We won't have any more lessons this morning. Was your papa with the workmen?"

"I did not see him. Simmons told me he had sent for the masons this morning to come at once, and when they came, sent him to tell them to take that wall down. He would be with them before they got through it. Thank you, Mr. Grant! It is such fun making a hole in a wall into somewhere you don't know where. It may be a place you know quite well, or a place you never saw before!" In his excitement, Davie's words tumbled out in a rather haphazard fashion. He quickly ran off.

The moment he vanished, Donal sped to the bottom of his own stair where he kept some tools and other things, made choice of some of them, went up and then down along the wall to the oak door. There was no time to get a new staple to it, but he remembered that he had seen another in the same post, a little lower down. If he could get that out and drive it in close beside the remains of the other, so as to receive the bolt of the lock and mask the broken parts he could not remove, that would be the main thing effected, and the rest would be comparatively easy! All the way he heard the masons pounding at the wall; it must surely have been built with cement and be of considerable thickness.

He reached the place and, passing through two of the doors, opened the last a little way and peeped. They had not yet got through the wall, for no light was visible! He made haste to restore everything as nearly as possible to the position in which he saw them when he first entered—which was not difficult, seeing there were but two articles of furniture in the chamber, and a few papers on the cover of the bureau. And as he lingered the huge blows were falling, like those of a ram on the wall of a besieged city of which he was the whole garrison. They were close by him on the other side, shaking the whole place. The plaster was falling in his sight, but no ray came through. He stepped into the press and drew the door after him. With his last glance behind he saw a stone fall from the middle of the wall into the room, and a faint gleam of light enter.

He hurried away. The demolition would go on much faster now that they had pierced the wall. Attacking the spare staple, therefore, with a strong lever, he succeeded in drawing it from the post and then drove it in beside the other, so as to take its place and the bolt. His noises were hidden in those of the workmen, for he took care to time his blows to theirs.

When he found that it would bear a good push, he let it alone. Having taken care to leave no sign of his work or his passing presence that could be helped, he turned away and ran down to the chapel. There he must see what could be done to prevent any notice that the dust of the dead had been disturbed! He gathered from the floor behind the altar all the dust he could sweep up, and laid it as nearly as he could in the form of the little heap they had removed; then on the bed he restored, with the dust of the bedding, a little of the outline as it had struck him when he first saw it. This done, he closed the door as it had been when he pushed it off its broken hinge, and would have ascended; but Donal bethought him that the slab lay lifted from its place in the floor of the passage and might betray the knowledge he so much desired to conceal. It took him but a moment to replace it, and sweep the loose earth into the crypt. Then he went up the stair, out of breath with eagerness rather than haste.

As he passed the oak door he laid his ear to it; someone was in the room. The sounds of battering had ceased, but the lid of the bureau slipped from some hand and fell with a loud bang. The wall could not be half down yet; the earl must have got into the place as soon as it was practicable! Donal hastened away. The earl might come through any moment; and though Donal had a better right to be there than he, Donal would not have liked at all to be found there by him.

The moment he was out, he put the slab in the opening and secured it there with a strut between it and the opposite side of the recess, so that it could not be pushed out from the inside. Then, as there was no time to fill up the possible crevices around it, he made haste to close the shutters and draw the curtains of the room, that no light might pass. It was possible that the earl, even though he knew of the other way into the chapel, had never discovered this; but if he had, or if he found the stair in the wall now for the first time and, coming up, saw no light and found the stone immovable, he would, Donal hoped, be satisfied that it had never been displaced. He then went to Lady Arctura's room. She was there.

"I have a great deal to tell you," he said hurriedly. "I have been keeping several things from you, meaning to tell you another time, and at this moment I cannot. I dread, too, lest the earl should find me with you!"

"Why should you mind that?" said Arctura, with just the slightest reddening of her pale cheek.

"Because he is suspicious about the lost room, and I must make haste to close up the entrance to it."

"You surely would not shut him in, if he be there?"

"No; there is no possibility of that. He has this morning had another way broken into it—at least I am all but sure. Please take care not to let him see that you know anything about it. Davie thinks he is set on finding the lost room: I think he knows all about it. You can ask him what he has been doing, on the ground of what Davie says."

"I understand; I hope I shall be able to steer clear of anything like a story, for if I stumble into one, then I must tell everything! But I will be careful."

"I have so much to tell you! Come to Mrs. Brooks' room tonight, my lady, if you want to hear."

In the afternoon he was in the schoolroom as usual. Davie was full of the news of the curious little place his father had discovered by knocking down the wall; but, he said, if that was the lost room, he did not think it was worth making such a fuss about. It was nothing at all but a kind of big closet, with just an old desk-sort of thing in it. Davie little imagined that what there was in that closet, in that bureau, was capable of affecting his history.

Arctura thought it better not to go near the place; but, anxious as she was, knowing nothing of the other entrance or where it was except that, having seen the oak door, she thought it might be through there, she yet kept quiet till dinnertime. Her uncle had invited her that day to dine with him, intending probably to make the more or less explanatory testament which presently her questions drew from him. She did not think it would do to show an indifference she did not feel about what had been going on.

"What were you doing this morning, Uncle?" she asked. "There was such a noise of thumping and knocking in the castle! It seemed where I sat as if it shook its very foundations. Davie said you must be determined, he thought, to find out the lost room; is it really that, Uncle?"

"Nothing of the kind, my love," he answered. "You will see what it is as soon as they have cleared away the stones and mortar. I do hope they will not spoil the great stair carrying it down; there is no other way of getting rid of it. I suppose you came up the back stair?"

"I did; it is the nearer way from the room I am in for the present. But tell me, then, what you are doing."

"Simply this, my dear; before my wife, your aunt, died, we had made a plan together for throwing that closet behind my room on the stair into it, in the shape of recess. In preparation for that I had a wall built across the middle of the closet, to make two recesses of it, and also to act as a buttress to make up for weakening the wall of the room by opening two such large archways in it, lest that should affect the house above it. Then your aunt died, and I hadn't the heart to do anything more with it. So one half of the little room behind remained cut off altogether. But I had built up in it an old bureau containing papers of some consequence; you see, it was not convenient to remove it. It was heavy and was intended to remain in the same position after the walls were opened. So I left it, thinking it was only for a short time. Now I want some of those papers, and the wall has had to come down again."

"But, Uncle, what a pity!" said Arctura. "Why not open the arches? The recesses would have been so nice in that room!"

"I am very sorry I did not think of asking what you would like done about it, my child; but I never thought of your taking any interest in the matter. No doubt the idea was a good one: but my wife being gone, with whom only I had talked over the thing, I lost all my interest in it. You will observe, I was only restoring what I myself disarranged—not meddling with anything you had done or anything that belonged to the condition of the castle before. But we can easily build it up again and open the arches now."

"No, no, Uncle! if you do not care about it, neither do I. But now you have the masons here, why should we not go on, and make a little search for the lost room?"

"As to that, my dear, we might pull down the whole castle to find it and be none the wiser. Why, the building up of that half of the little closet sort of place I have just had disclosed again may have given rise to the whole story!"

"Surely, Uncle, the legend is much older than that!"

"It may be; but you cannot be sure. Once it was going, it would immediately begin to cry back to a more remote age for its origin. You cannot prove that anyone ever spoke of it before the date of the building of that foolish wall."

"No, I cannot certainly! But, surely, there are some who remember hearing the story long before that!"

"It may be; but nothing is so treacherous as a memory in the face of a general belief. And I would advise you, if you care to live in peace, and for my sake if not for your own, to hold your tongue about it. We should immediately have the place besieged with antiquarians and ghost hunters."

The next morning Arctura went to see the alteration and found the whole of the rubbish already cleared away. She opened the door, and there was the little room nearly twice its former size, and the two bureaus standing side by side with each other. Donal had seen the place some hours before her, and had found the one he had left open shut and locked; he knew there were reasons. She peeped into the cupboard at the end of the room, but had no suspicion there was a door in the back of it.

That morning she made up her mind that she would go no farther at present in the affair of the chapel; she could not, except she were prepared to break with her uncle. She would consult her man of business the first time she saw him; but the thing could wait, and she would not send for him.

When she saw Donal in the evening she told him her resolve, and he could not say she was wrong. There was no necessity for opposing her uncle in such a matter—there might soon come things in which she *must* oppose him. Donal told her how he had gotten into the closet from behind, and the story of what happened the night before and had led, he supposed, to the opening of the place. He did not tell her of the unsent letter he had found, any more than of the words her uncle had dropped in his wrath concerning the social position of his son. The time might come when Donal would find it imperative to do so, but in the meantime he shrank from making the relation in which Arctura stood to her uncle more uncomfortable than it already was. In the meantime they must leave the chapel alone and no more set foot in it till such time as Lady Arctura was prepared to take her own way with it.

Donal had the suspicion, and it grew upon him, not only that the earl had known of the chapel and its conditions for a long time, but that it was not safe for such a man to have such a secret—to know more of the inward facts and relations of the house than the rest who lived in it. This was not in reality the case, however; the earl might imagine he was the sole possessor of the ancient secret, but there were three more in the house who knew it as well as he—one of them, perhaps better.

37

· · · · · · · · · · · · · · · · · ·

Lord Forgue Again

*T*hings again went on very quietly for a time. Lady Arctura grew better, continued her studies, and made excellent progress.

By and by came the breath of a change over the contented course of things at the castle. After the absence of months, Lord Forgue reappeared—cheerful, manly, on the best terms with his father, and willing to be on still better terms with his cousin. He had left the place a mooning youth; he came back, so far as the first glance could read him, an agreeable man of the world—better in carriage, better in manners, better in temper. The young man was full of remark not devoid of anecdote and personal observation both of nature and human nature; attentive to both his father and his cousin, but not too attentive; jolly with Davie, distant with Donal, yet polite to him.

Gradually, with undefined gradations, he began to show himself not indifferent to the charms of his fair cousin—and indeed make some revelation of wonder that he had not felt them long before. He saw and professed concern that her health was not quite such as it had been; sought her in her room when she did not appear at lunch or dinner; took an interest in the books she was reading, and even in her studies with Donal which she carried on just as before; and, in a word, behaved like a good brother-cousin who would not be sorry to be something more.

And now, strange to say, the earl began to appear occasionally at the family table, and, apparently in consequence of this, Donal was requested rather than invited to take his meals with them. His presence made it easier for Lord Forgue to show himself the gentleman and man of the world he now set up for; and indeed he brought manners to the front. Yet there was sometimes condescension in the politeness he showed Donal. He was gracious, dignified, attentive, amusing, accurate, ready—everything but true.

He had been in Edinburgh a part of the time, away in England another part, and had many things to tell of the people he had seen and the sport he had taken a share in. He had developed and cultivated a vein of gentlemanly satire, showing himself keen to perceive and analyze the peculiarities of others. Questioned concerning them, however, from a wider, human point of view, he was unable to give any genuine account of them. Donal saw more and more clearly that the man was a gulf filled with a thin mist that prevented one from seeing to the bottom of it. He showed himself more and more submissive to the judgment of Arctura, and seemed to welcome that of his father, to whom he was now as respectful as such a father could wish a son to be.

Two years before this time, Lady Arctura had been in the way of riding a good deal; but after an accident to a favorite horse, for which in part she blamed herself, she had never cared to ride again. For a time she constantly declined to ride with Forgue. In vain he offered his own horse, assuring her that Davie's pony was quite able to carry him; she would not accept his offer. But at last one day, mostly from fear of doing injury to a bettering nature, she consented and so enjoyed the ride—felt indeed so much the better for it that she did not so positively as before decline to allow her cousin to get for her a horse fit to carry her; and Forgue, taking the remainder for granted, was fortunate enough, with the help of the factor, Mr. Graeme, to find a beautiful creature, just the sort of animal to please her. Almost at the sight of him she confirmed the purchase.

This put Forgue in great spirits and much contentment with himself.

For he did not doubt that, having thus gained unlimited opportunity of having her alone with him, he would soon withdraw her entirely from the absurd influence which, to his dismay, he discovered that Donal had in his absence gained over her. He ought not to have been such a fool, he said to himself, as to leave the poor child to the temptations naturally arising in such a dreary solitude! First of all he would take her education in hand himself, and give his full energy to what was lacking in it. She should speedily learn, to begin with, the contrast between the attentions of a gentleman and those of a clodhopper!

He had himself in England improved his riding as well as his manners, and now knew at least how a gentleman, if not how a man, ought to behave to the beast that carried him, so that there was not much of the old danger of offending Arctura by his treatment of him. More than all, having ridden a good deal with the ladies of the house where he had been visiting, he was now able to give Arctura a good many hints, the value of which she could not fail to discover in the improvement of her seat, her hand, her courage. And he knew there was no readier way to the confidence and gratitude of his cousin than that of showing her a more excellent way in anything about which she cared. He knew himself able likewise to praise her style with an honesty that was not feigned and therefore had force.

But if he thought that by teaching her to ride he could make her forget the man who had been teaching her to live, he was mistaken in the woman he set himself to captivate. Invigorated by the bright, frosty air, the life of the animal under her, and the exultation of rapid motion, she by and by appeared more in health, more merry and full of life than perhaps ever before. He put it all down to his success as a man upon the heart of a woman.

Flying across a field in the very wildness of pleasure, her hair streaming behind her and her pale face glowing, she would now and then take such a jump as Forgue would declare he dared not face in cold blood. He began to wonder that he could have been such a fool as to neglect her.

But Forgue was afraid of Arctura. The more he admired her, the more determined he grew; and the more satisfied he became with what he counted improvement in himself, the more confident he became . . . so long as the world was kept in the dark as to one thing, it might know what it would of all besides! If but once he had the position of rightful owner of the property, who was there that even knowing would care to dispute his right to the title? Besides, he was by no means certain that his father had not merely uttered a threat. Surely if it were a fact, he would, even in rage diabolic, have kept it to himself.

Impetuous, and accustomed to what he counted success, he did not continue his attentions to his cousin very long without beginning to make more indubitable advances. But all the time Arctura, knowing in a vague way how he had been carrying himself before he went, never imagined that he would approach her on any ground but that of cousinship and a childhood of shared sports.

She had not been made acquainted with what had passed concerning him and Eppie; but she had seen something herself of what was going on and when Eppie was dismissed had requested an explanation, as she had a right to do, from her housekeeper, contenting herself at the same time with rather undefined replies. She had seen too that Donal was far from pleased with the young lord, and she knew well enough that Forgue had been behaving badly. No small part indeed of her kindness to him now arose from the fact that he was or had been in disgrace; she was sorry for him. Without speculating on what had been wrong or what ought in consequence to have confronted the wrong, she presumed everything was over that ought to be over, but had never dreamed he was now daring approach her in the way of courtship.

By and by she began to perceive that she had been allowing him too much freedom except she was prepared to hear something that would demand answer. So the next day, much to his surprise, she declined to go out riding with him.

It was stranger that they had not had a ride together for a fortnight, the weather having been unfavorable; now when a day came more than ordinarily lovely because of the season into which it broke like a smile, she would not go with him! He quickly became annoyed and then alarmed, fearing some adverse influence. They were sitting in the breakfast room, a small room next to the library, into which Donal had just gone.

"Why will you not ride with me, Arctura?" said Forgue reproachfully. "Are you not well?"

"I am quite well," she answered.

"It is such a lovely day," he pleaded.

"But I am not in the mood. There are other things in the world besides riding. Ever since you got Larkie for me, I have been wasting my time riding too much. I have been learning next to nothing."

"Oh, bother learning! What have you to do with learning! I'm sure I've had enough of it, and wish it had been less. Your health is the first thing."

"I do not think so. It would be better to learn some things even with the loss of health. Besides, a certain amount of learning is as good for the health as horse exercise."

"What learning is it you are so fond of? Perhaps I could help you with it."

"Thank you, Forgue," she answered, laughing a little. "But I have a very good master already; Davie and I are reading Greek and mathematics with Mr. Grant."

Forgue's face flushed.

"I ought to know quite as much of both as he does!" he said.

"Ought, perhaps! But you do not, because you never studied much."

"I know enough to teach you."

"Yes, but I know enough not to let you try!"

"Why?"

"Because you can't teach."

"How do you know that?"

"Because you do not love either Greek or mathematics, and no one who does not love can teach."

"That is some schoolmaster nonsense! If I don't love Greek enough to teach it, I love you enough to teach you," said Forgue. "Why then deprive me of your company to learn it?"

"You are my riding master," said Arctura; "Mr. Grant is my master in Greek and mathematics."

Forgue just managed to strangle in time an imprecation upon Donal. He tried to laugh, but there was not a laugh inside him.

"Then you won't ride today?" he said.

"I won't," replied Arctura.

"I cannot see what should induce you to let that fellow have the honor of teaching you!" said Forgue after a pause. "He is a dull, pedantic, ill-bred man!"

"He is my friend," said Arctura, raising her head and looking her cousin in the eyes, as much as to say, "Do not let me hear that again."

"I assure you, you are quite mistaken in him," he said.

"I do not ask your opinion of him," returned Arctura coldly. "I merely acquaint you with the fact that he is my friend."

Here's the devil and all to pay! thought Forgue. *Who would have imagined such a spirit in the girl!* But he saw he must not go further.

"I beg your pardon," he said. "I did not mean to make myself disagreeable. You see him with different eyes from mine."

"And with better opportunity of judging!"

"He has never interfered with you as he has with me," said Forgue foolishly, for his anger was rising.

"But indeed he has!"

"He has! confound his impertinence! How?"

"He won't let me study as much as I want —Now tell me how he has interfered with you."

Forgue would rather not enter into explanations.

"We won't quarrel about such a trifle," he said, attempting a tone of gaiety, which immediately grew serious. "We who have so long been so much to each other—" But there he stopped.

"I do not—I am not willing to think I know what you mean," said Arctura. "I thought, after what had passed—I would rather not allude to such things—but—"

In her turn she ceased, remembering that he had really said nothing.

"I see he has been talking against me!"

"He never did to me. But I have myself seen enough, I am ashamed to say, to prevent me from ever supposing it possible you would—"

Here she found it necessary to stop again.

"If you mean," he said, plucking up his fast-failing courage, "that unfortunate piece of boyish folly—you know I was but a youth!"

"How many months ago?" said Arctura; but Forgue saw no need for precision.

"I assure you," he said, "on the word of a gentleman, there is nothing between us now. It is all over; and more than that, I am heartily ashamed of it."

A pause of a few seconds followed: it seemed to both like as many minutes.

Forgue broke it, for it was unbearable.

"Then you will come out with me today?"

But now she knew her danger yet better than before. At once and decidedly she declined.

"No," she said; "I will not."

"Well," he returned, with simulated coolness, "this is, I must say, rather cavalier treatment!—to throw a man over who has loved you so long, for the sake of a Greek lesson!"

"How long, pray, have you loved me?" said Arctura, growing angry at his untruthfulness. "Ever since you got tired of poor Eppie? I was very willing to help you to pass a pleasant time in the country; but as you seem to think I have been encouraging you, I am sorry it is no longer possible. I am a little particular as to the sort of man I should like to marry, and you are not up to the mark, Lord Forgue!"

"And Mr. Grant is?"

"He has neither asked me nor rendered it impossible I should listen to him."

"You punish me pretty sharply, my lady, for a slip of which I told you I was ashamed!" said Forgue. "It was the merest—"

"I do not want to hear anything about it," said Arctura sternly. "If you have set your heart on the property, which I do not doubt you think ought to go with the title, you were unfortunate in imagining me one who did not care for the proprieties of life! You had better go and have your gallop; you may have my horse if you prefer him to your own."

She would not have spoken as she did had he not roused her indignation by his contempt of Donal. She felt honesty required her to make common cause with one to whom she owed so much.

Forgue turned on his heel and left the room. Arctura took up her books and walked to the schoolroom, passing Forgue on her way. He had been lingering to see whether she would in reality go to the schoolroom. Surely she had been but attempting to pique him! It was hard to believe she did not wish to go with him—preferred a Greek lesson from the clown Grant to a ride with Lord Forgue!

When he saw her pass toward the schoolroom with her books in her hand, he did not know what to think. For the present, however, he would show no offense and in sign of taking the thing coolly, he would ride her horse.

But, alas, the poor animal had to suffer for the fellow's ill humor! The least motion of Larkie that displeased him—and he was ready for nothing but displeasure, as one doing and imagining himself to suffer wrong—put him in a rage. Disregarding all he had learned, he treated the horse so foolishly and so tyrannically that he brought him home quite lame. To his additional annoyance, he knew that he had thus himself put an end, for some time at least, to any feeblest hope of riding with Lady Arctura. Instead, however, of going and telling her what he had done, he put Larkie in the stable and sent for the farrier.

A week passed and then another, and he said nothing more about riding. But that week a furious jealousy mastered him. For a time he scorned to give place to it because of the insult it was to himself to allow it true, but gradually it grew active in him. This country bumpkin, this cowherd, this man of spelling books and grammars, was poisoning his cousin's mind against him! Of course, he said to himself, he did not imagine for a moment that she would disgrace herself by falling in love with a fellow just escaped from the plough-tail. If only he had not been so silly as to fall in love with a vulgar little thing that had not an idea in her head, and got at last to be so unpleasant.

That wretched schoolmaster—he must point out to his father the necessity of getting rid of the fellow! He had a fancy that he was doing well with Davie, but what revolutionary notions he would put into him! He was certain to unfit him for taking his place in the real world. And if it came to that, why not send the two away together somewhere till things were settled? If he were dismissed without good reason shown, it would make matters worse.

He did mention the matter to his father, but the earl thought it would be better to win over Donal to his side. He counselled his son that there were Grants of good family, and that besides the pride of every Highlander was such as to brook no assumption of superiority. He would but make of him an implacable enemy if he did or said anything to hurt him. Forgue did not argue with his father; he had given that up. For the present he would just let things slide, and stand by and watch.

38

· · · · · · · · · · · · · · · · · · ·

An Accident and a Holiday

*O*ne step Forgue took: He began to draw to himself the good graces of Lady Arctura's former friend, Miss Carmichael. He did not know how little she could serve him when he called upon her father. After that they had a good deal of communication with each other. The lady, without being consciously insincere, flattered the gentleman, and so speedily gained his esteem and confidence. Careful not to say a word against his cousin, she made him feel more and more that the chief danger to him lay in the influence of Donal. She fanned thus the flame of his jealousy of the man whom he now thought he had disliked from the first.

But, after all, what could he do? If only Davie would fall ill, and have to be taken for change of air! But Davie was always in splendid health and spirits.

By and by Forgue began to confide in Miss Carmichael with regard to Arctura. Now that he saw himself in danger of being thwarted, he fancied himself more in love with her than he actually was. And as he had got more familiar with the idea of his false birth, although even to himself he did not choose to confess he believed it, he made less and less of it.

When he hinted to his father his genuine fear that he was not destined to succeed with Arctura, the earl laughed at the foolish doubt; but in certain of his moods, the earl contemplated the thing as an awful possibility. It was not that he loved his sons much, though he loved Davie more than Forgue; but the only way in which those who recognize that they are on the road to the grave can fancy themselves holding on to the things of this life is through their children. Then, too, he loved in a troubled, self-reproachful way the memory of their mother, and through her cared for his children more than he knew. As to the relation in which they stood to society, he did not care for that, so long as it remained undiscovered. He rather enjoyed the idea of stealing a march on society, and seeing from the other world the sons he had left at such a disadvantage behind him, and arrogating the place which the fools of society would never have granted them.

And now Arctura avoided her cousin as much as she could. They met at meals, and as nearly as she could she behaved as if nothing unpleasant had happened between them and things were on the same footing as before he went away. But the sense that he was watching her often prevented her from going out when otherwise she would.

One day when he had pretended to be gone for some hours, he met her walking in the park.

"You are very cruel to me, Arctura," he said, with a look of dejection.

"Cruel?" returned Arctura coldly. "I am not cruel. I would not willingly hurt anyone."

"You hurt me very much, not to let me have the least morsel of your society!"

"You see me every day at breakfast—at least when you are down in time, and every day at lunch and dinner when you choose to be present!"

"How can I bear to sit at the table near you when you treat me with such coldness."

"You compel me to do so, when you sit staring at me as if you would eat me, and look angry at every civil word I speak to another. If you are content to be my cousin, things will go smoothly enough; but if you are still set on what cannot be—once for all, it is of no use. I could never love you in that way! You care for none of the things I live for. You may think me hard, but it is much better we should understand each other. If you think, because my father left me the property, you have a claim upon me, it is a claim I will never acknowledge. I would ten thousand times rather you had the property and I were in my grave. You will easily find someone in every way better fitted for you."

"I will do anything, learn anything you please!" said Forgue, with difficulty restraining his anger.

"I know very well what such submission is worth," said Arctura. "I should be everything till we were married, and then nothing."

She would not have spoken in just such a tone had she not been that day more than usually annoyed with his behavior to Donal, and at the same time particularly pleased with the calm, unconsciously dignified way in which Donal took it, casting it from him as the rock throws aside the sea wave, as if it did not concern him.

———

It was a lovely day in spring.

"Please, Mr. Grant," said Davie, "may I have a holiday today?"

Donal looked up at him with a little wonder; the boy had never before made such a request.

"Certainly, Davie, you may," he answered at once; "but I should like to know what you want it for."

"I will soon tell you that, sir," answered Davie. "Arkie wants very much to have a ride today. She says Larkie—I gave him that name, to rhyme with Arkie—she says Larkie has not been out for a long time, and she does not want to go out with Forgue. I suppose he has been rude to her; and so she asked me if I would go with her on my pony."

"You will take good care of her, Davie?"

"Oh, yes! I will take care of her; and she will take care of me: that's the way, isn't it? You need not be anxious about us, Mr. Grant. Arkie is a splendid rider, and she is pluckier than she used to be!"

Donal did, however, feel a little anxious. He repressed the feeling as unfaithful, but still it returned. He could hardly go with them; there was no horse for him, and if he went on foot he feared to spoil their ride. Besides, he had no desire to fan Forgue's jealousy. So he went to his room, got a book, and strolled into the park.

Forgue was not about the stable. Larkie, though much better, was not yet cured of his lameness and had not been much exercised. Arctura did not even know that he had been lame, or that he was now rather wild, and a pastern-joint not equal to his spirit. The boy, who alone was about the stable, either did not understand or was afraid to speak, so that she rode him in a danger of which she knew nothing. The consequence was that, jumping the merest little ditch in a field not far outside the park, they had a fall, and Larkie got up and limped home; but his mistress lay where she fell. Davie, wild with fright, galloped home for help. From the height of the park Donal saw him tearing along, and knew that something must be amiss. He ran straight for the direction in which he came, saw him, climbed the wall, found his track through the field and, following it, came where Arctura lay.

The moment he saw her, his presence of mind returned. There was a little clear water in the ditch; he wet his handkerchief and bathed her face. She came to herself and smiled when she saw who was by her, and tried to rise, but fell back.

"I believe I am hurt," she said. "I think Larkie must have fallen."

Donal tried to raise her, that he might carry her home, but she moaned so that he saw she was too much hurt. Davie was gone for help; it would be better to wait. He pulled off his coat and laid it over her; then, sitting down, he raised her partly from the damp ground against his knees and his arms. Then she seemed easier and smiled, but did not open her eyes.

They had not long to wait. Several persons came running—among them Lord Forgue. He cast a look of hatred at Donal, and fell beside his cousin on his knees, taking her hand in his. Donal, of course, did not move, and finding Forgue persistent in seeking to attract her attention to himself, saw it was for him to give orders.

"My lady is much hurt," he said to the servants; "one of you go off at once for the doctor; the others bring a hand-barrow—I've seen one about the place—with the mattress of a sofa on it, and make haste."

While waiting, he had been going over in his mind what ought to be done.

"What have you to do with giving orders!" demanded Forgue.

"Do as Mr. Grant tells you," said Lady Arctura, without opening her eyes.

The men at once departed, running. Forgue rose from his knees and, with one look at Donal, walked slowly to a little distance and stood gnawing his lip. There was silence for a time.

"My lord," said Donal, "please run to the house and fetch a little brandy for her ladyship; I fear she has fainted."

It was cutting to be sent about by the fellow, but what could Forgue do but obey. He started at once and with tolerable speed. Then Arctura opened her eyes and smiled at Donal.

"Are you suffering much, my lady?" he asked, greatly moved.

"A good deal," she answered. "But I don't mind it. Thank you for not leaving me. I have no more than I can bear. It is bad when I try to move."

"They will not be long, now," he returned.

At last he saw them coming with the extemporized litter, and behind them Mrs. Brooks, pale but quiet and ready, carrying the brandy, and with her Lord Forgue and one of the maids.

As soon as she came up, she stooped and spoke in a low voice to Donal, inquiring where the injury was, and Donal told her he feared it was her spine but did not know. Then Mrs. Brooks put her hands under her, the maid took her feet and Donal, gently rising, raised her body. They laid her on the litter; except a moan or two, and sometimes a look of pain that quickly passed, she gave no sign of suffering. Once or twice she opened her eyes and looked up at Donal as he carried her, for he kept his place at her head; then, as if satisfied, she closed them again. Before they reached the house the doctor met them, for they had to walk slowly so as not to shake her.

Forgue came behind in a devilish humor. He knew that his ill usage of Larkie and then his neither saying nor allowing anything to be said about it must have been the cause of the accident, for he knew the horse was not fit to be ridden. "Served her right!" he caught himself saying once, and was ashamed. Self is the most cursed friend a man can have.

She was carried to her room, and the doctor examined her, but could not say much. There were no bones broken, he said, but she must keep very quiet. She gave a faint smile at the word and a pitiful glance at Donal, whom the doctor had requested to remain when he turned the rest, all but Mrs. Brooks, out of the room. He ordered the windows to be darkened; she must, if possible, sleep.

As Donal was following the doctor from the chamber, Lady Arctura signed to Mrs. Brooks that she wanted to speak to him. He came. She was weak now, and he had to bend over her to hear.

"You will come and see me, Mr. Grant?"

"I will indeed, my lady."

"Every day?"

"Yes, most certainly," he replied, with a glance at Mrs. Brooks.

She smiled, and so dismissed him. He went with his heart full.

A little way from the door of the room stood Forgue, evidently watching for him to come out. He had sent the doctor to his father. Donal passed him with a bend of the head, which Forgue did not return, but followed him to the schoolroom.

"It is time this farce was over, Grant!" he said.

"Farce! My lord," repeated Donal indignantly.

"These attentions of yours to my lady, I mean."

"I have paid her no more attention than I would your lordship had you required it," answered Donal sternly.

"I don't doubt you would rather have me where her ladyship is now; that would be convenient enough. But I say again, it is time this were put a stop to, and stopped it shall be. Ever since you came you have been at work on the mind of that inexperienced girl with your humbug of religion—for what ends of your own, I do not care to inquire; and now you have half killed her by persuading her to go out with you instead of me. The brute was lame and not fit to ride, and you ought to have seen it!"

"I had nothing to do with her going, my lord. She asked Davie to go with her, and he had a holiday for the purpose."

"All very fine, but—"

"My lord, I have told you the truth because it was the truth, not to justify myself. . . . But tell me one thing, my lord: If my lady's horse was lame, how was it she did not know it, and you did?"

Forgue was taken aback by the question and thought Donal knew more than he did.

"It is time the place was clear of you!" he said.

"I am your father's servant, not yours," answered Donal.

Forgue turned on his heel, and went to his father. He told him he had no longer any doubt that Donal was prejudicing the mind of Lady Arctura against him. Not until it came out in the course of the conversation that followed did he give the earl to know of the accident she had had.

He professed himself greatly shocked, but got up with something almost like alacrity from the sofa on which he had been lying, and went down to inquire after her. He would have compelled Mrs. Brooks to admit him had she been one atom less firm than she was, and Arctura would have been waked from a sleep invaluable to hear his condolements on her accident. But he had to return to his room without gaining anything.

If she were to go, the property would be his—that is, if she died without leaving a will. He sent for his son and cautioned him over and over, insisting even with vehemence that he should do nothing to offend either her or any friend of hers, but should keep a fair behavior to all, and wait what might come. Who could tell? It might prove a more serious thing than as yet it seemed!

Forgue tried to feel shocked at his father's cool speculation; but he could not help allowing to himself that if she was determined not to receive him as her husband, the next best thing in the exigency of affairs would certainly be that she should leave a world for whose uses she was ill fitted, and go where she would be happier, leaving certain others to occupy the things she had no further need of and which all the time were more really theirs than hers. True, she was a pleasant thing to look upon, and if she had loved him, he would have preferred the property with her; but if it was to be his the other way, there was this advantage, that he would be left free to choose. When one consents to evil, his progress in it may be of appalling rapidity!

In the meantime the poor girl lay suffering—feverish and restless. When the night came, Mrs. Brooks would let no one sit up with her but herself. The earl would have had her send for a "suitable nurse." A friend of his in London would find one for her, but Mrs. Brooks would not hear of it. And before the night was over she had more ground than she had expected to congratulate herself that it had been impossible for her to yield. For in her wanderings it was plain that the heart of her young mistress was more occupied with the tutor than her senses with the pain she was suffering. She spoke in her delirium, constantly desiring his presence.

In the middle of the night she grew so unquiet that the housekeeper, calling the maid she had put in a room near to watch while she was gone for a few minutes, ran like a bird to Donal's room and asked him to come down. Donal had but partially undressed, thinking his help might be wanted, and was down almost as soon as she.

Donal went to the bedside. She was moaning and starting, sometimes opening her eyes, but distinguishing nothing. He laid his hand on hers. She gave a sigh, as of one relieved, a smile flickered over her face, and she lay still for some time without showing any further sign of suffering. Donal sat down beside her and watched. The moment he saw her begin to be restless or appear distressed, he laid his hand upon hers, with the same result: She was immediately quiet, and slept as if she knew herself safe. When he saw her about to wake, he withdrew, having previously arranged it with her nurse that he would remain in the corridor till she called him again.

And so things went on, for nights not a few. He slept instead of working by himself when his duties with Davie were over, and at night, wrapped in his plaid, lay down in the corridor, ready the moment he was called. For even after Arctura began to get better, her nights were still troubled. The strange discoveries made in the castle haunted her sleep with their own dream variations, and her nights would have been far from suitably refreshing and her recovery much retarded had not Donal been near to make her feel that she was not abandoned to the terrors she had yet to pass through. For her restoration it was chiefly rest she needed; but she had received a severe physical shock, and it was to the doctor doubtful if she would ever be strong again.

One night the earl, wandering about the house in the anomolous and diseased condition of neither ghost nor genuine mortal, came suddenly in the corridor upon what he took for a huge animal lying in wait to devour whoever might pass that way. He was not terrified, for he was accustomed to such things, and thought at first it did not belong to this world, but one of those to which drugs are the porters. He approached to see what it was, and stood staring down upon the somewhat undefined mass. Slowly it rose to its feet and confronted him, if confronting could be understood where both head and face remained so undefined. Donal took care to keep his plaid over and around his head so that the earl should not identify him. If the man took him for a robber, he would run. But he had hope in the probable condition of the earl—who in fact turned from him and walked away.

His lordship had his suspicions, however, and concluded that his son was right, that Donal was madly in love with his foolish niece, and she, being ill, could rest nowhere but with the devotion of a savage outside her door. If he did not take suitable precautions one way or another, the rascal might be too much for the gentleman. At his last interview with him, he had begun not only to hate but to fear the country lad. And now he made up his mind that it was very nearly time to be rid of him. Only it must be done cautiously—managed with the appearance of a thoroughly good understanding, so that neither he nor the lady should suspect.

The earl set himself to think how best the thing could be effected. It would be well to have him out of the house before she was able to see him again. And if in the meantime she should die, all would be well, and there would be no cause for uneasiness as to what might have come to pass.

Arctura continued slowly to recover. It was some weeks after the accident, and she had not yet left her room, but she had been getting up on the sofa for a good many days, and the doctor was more sanguine about her final recovery. And now there was a talk of her going into the library. Donal had seen her many times, but the earl had never suspected. With a woman of sense like Mrs. Brooks about, Lord Morven had been kept out of her room the entire time. But the moment he heard the library spoken of, he saw that he must delay no longer. Besides, he had by this time contrived a very neat little plan.

He sent for Donal. He had been thinking, he said, that he would want a holiday this summer; he had not seen his parents since he came to the castle. He had himself been thinking it very desirable that Davie should see a little of the true world—something of another kind of life from that to which as yet he had been accustomed. He would take it as a great kindness if Donal, who had always seemed to have a regard to the real education of his pupil, would take Davie home with him when he went, and let him see and understand the ways of life among the humbler classes of the nation—so that if ever he came to sit in Parliament, which he hoped was not absurd in the case of a boy like Davie, he might know the very heart of the people for whom he would have to legislate.

Donal listened and agreed as far as he could with the remarks of his lordship. In himself he had not the least faith now, he wondered what sort of a fool the earl thought him, to imagine that after all that had passed between them he should yet place any confidence in what he said. But he listened. What the earl really had in his mind, he could not even surmise; but to take Davie with him to his father and mother was a delightful idea.

It was easy now for his father and mother to take the boy as well as himself into the house as guests, their worldly condition having been and continuing to be so much bettered by the kindness of their friend, Sir Gibbie. There might be some other reason behind the earl's request, he reflected, which it would be well for him to know; but he would sooner discover that by a free consent than by hanging back; and anything bad it could hardly be. He shrank from leaving Lady Arctura while she was still so far from well, but she was getting better much faster now, and for a fortnight there had been no necessity for his presence to soothe her while she slept. Neither did she yet know, so far at least as Donal or Mrs. Brooks were aware, that he had ever been near her in the night.

It was, as things stood between him and Lord Forgue, well on that ground also, he thought, that he should be away for a while. It would give a chance in that foolish soul for things to settle themselves down, a time for common sense to assume the reins where no yet better coachman was at all likely for some time to mount the box. He had of course heard nothing of the strained relations between him and Lady Arctura, or he might have been a little more anxious.

When Davie heard the proposal, he went wild with joy. Actually to see the mountains, and the sheep, and the collies, of which Donal had told him such wonderful things! To be out all night, perhaps, with Donal and the dogs and the stars and the winds! Perhaps it would come on a storm and he would lie in Donal's plaid under some great rock, and hear the wind roaring around them but not able to get at them. And the sheep would come and huddle close up to them, and keep them so warm with their wooly sides and he would stroke their heads and love them.

The proposal was eagerly accepted by both. They packed their knapsacks, got their boxes ready for the carrier, and one lovely morning late in spring, just as summer was showing her womanly face through the smiles and tears of spring, they set out together.

It was with no small dismay that Arctura heard of the proposal. She said nothing, however, and it was only when Donal came to take his leave of her that she broke down a little. She spoke with great composure at first, and but for her face Donal would not have known she was in the least uneasy. He spoke to the look.

"We shall often wish, Davie and I, that you were with us," he said.

"Why?" was all she could trust herself to rejoin.

"Because we shall often feel very happy, and then we shall wish you had the same happiness," he answered.

She burst into tears.

"Don't think me very silly," she said. "I know God is with me; and as soon as you are gone I will go to him to comfort me. But I cannot help feeling as if I were being left like a lamb among wolves. I could not give any reason for it; I only feel as if some danger were close upon me.—Dear Mrs. Brooks, I know I have you with me, and I would trust you with anything. Indeed, if I hadn't you," she added, laughing through her tears, "I should be ready to run away with Mr. Grant and Davie!"

"If I had known you felt like that," said Donal, "I would not have gone. And yet I do not see how I could have avoided it, being Davie's tutor and bound to do as his father wishes. And in three weeks or a month we shall be back."

"That is a long time!" said Arctura, ready to weep again.

Arctura speedily recovered her composure and with the gentlest smile bade Donal goodbye.

"Write to me," said Donal, "if anything comes to you that you think I can help you in. And be sure I will make haste to you the moment you let me know you want me."

"Thank you, Mr. Grant; I know you mean every word you say. If I need you, I will not hesitate to send for you—only if you come, it will be as my friend, and not—"

"It will be as your servant, and not as Lord Morven's," supplied Donal. "I quite understand. Goodbye. God will take care of you; do not be afraid."

He turned and went; he could no longer bear the look of her eyes.

The day was a glorious one, and Davie, full of spirits, could not understand why Donal seemed so unlike himself.

"Poor Arkie would scold you, Mr. Grant!" he said.

He avoided the town and walked a good distance round to get onto the road beyond it, his head bent as if he were pondering a pain.

After a few days of easy walking they climbed the last hill, crossed the threshold of Robert Grant's cottage, and were both clasped in the embrace of Janet.

Then followed delights which more than equalled the expectations of

Davie. He had never had an imagination of such liberty as he now enjoyed. He delighted most in the twilight on the hillside, with the sheep growing dusky around him.

And now Donal's youth began to seem far behind him. How much of this happy change was owing to his interest in Lady Arctura enabling his mind to recover its own healthy tone, he did not inquire.

Sir Gibbie and Lady Galbraith listened almost open-mouthed to his tale of the discovery of the lost chapel, holding the dust of the dead and, perhaps, sometimes their wandering ghosts. They assured him that if he would only bring Lady Arctura to them, they would take care of her. Had she not better give up the weary property, they said, and come and live with them, and be as free as a lark? But Donal said that if God had given her a property and no other calling, he certainly would not have her forsake her post, but wait for him to relieve her. She must administer her own kingdom before she could have an abundant entrance into his. Only he wished he were near to help her, for now she would be less strong than before; and they allowed he was right.

39

• • • • • • • • • • • • • • • • • • •

A Sinister Plot

*H*e had been at home about ten days, during which not a word had come to Davie or himself from the castle. He was beginning to grow not anxious but hungry for news of Lady Arctura, when from a sound sleep he started suddenly awake one midnight to find his mother by his bedside; she had roused him with difficulty.

"Laddie," she said, "I'm thinking you're wanted."

"Where am I wanted, Mother?" he asked, rubbing his eyes but with anxiety already throbbing at his heart.

"At the castle," she replied.

"How do you know that?" he asked.

"I would have a hard time telling you," she answered. "You may call it what name you like, but if I was you, Donal, I would be off before the day breaks to find out what they're doing with that poor lady."

By this time Donal was out of bed and hurrying on his clothes. He had the profoundest faith in whatever his mother said. Was this a second sight she had had? She might have had a dream, or some impression so deep that she could not but yield to it. One thing only was plain, there was no time to be lost in asking questions. It was enough to him that his mother said, "Go," and that it was for the sake of Lady Arctura that she wanted him to go. How quickest could he go? There were horses at Sir Gibbie's; it would save much time if he took one. Putting a crust of bread in his pocket, he set out running. There was a little moonlight, enough for one who knew every foot of the way, and in half an hour of swift descent he was at the stable door of Glashruach.

By this time he knew all the ways of the place, and finding himself unable to rouse anyone, speedily gained an entrance and opened the door; he found Sir Gibbie's favorite mare, and without a moment's hesitation saddled, bridled, led her out and mounted her. His mother would go down as soon as it was light, and let them know if he should have found it necessary to rob the stable.

And now that he was safe in the saddle, with four legs under him and time to think, he began to turn over in his mind what he must do. But he soon saw that he could plan nothing until he knew what was the matter of which he had dreadful forebodings. Was it not possible that a man in the mental and moral condition of the earl would risk anything and everything, unrestrained by law or conscience, to secure the property for his son, and through him for the family? The earl might—might poison her, smother her, kill her somehow! And then rushed into his mind what the housekeeper had told him about the earl's cruelty to his wife.

He would have blamed himself bitterly for having gone away had he not been sure that he was not following his own will in the matter. But now he would be restrained by no considerations of delicacy toward the earl or anyone; whatever his hand found to do, he would do, regardless of how it might look. If he could not readily get a word with Lady Arctura, he would at once seek the help of the law, tell what he knew, and get a warrant of search. He dared not think what he dreaded. Doubtless the way to help her would be unfolded to him as he went on. And so he rode on, taking good care of his horse, lest much haste should make the less speed. But the animal was strong and in good condition, and by the time he had seen the sun rise, climb the heavens, and go halfway down their western slope, having stopped three times to refresh her, he found himself nearing the place of his desire.

The sun went down and the stars came out, and the long twilight began. But before he had got a mile farther he became suddenly aware that the sky had clouded over, the stars had vanished, and the rain was at hand. The day had been sultry, and the relief had arrived.

When he reached the town, he rode into the yard of the Morven Arms, and having there found a sleepy ostler, gave up his horse; he would be better without her at the castle. He was just setting out to walk to the castle when the landlord appeared—who, happily, had by this time learned to pay proper respect to the tutor at the castle.

"We didn't expect to see you, sir, not at this time," he said.

"Why not?" returned Donal, scenting information.

"We thought you were away for the summer, seeing you took the young gentleman with you and the earl himself was not far behind following you."

"Where is he gone?" asked Donal.

"Oh, don't you know, sir? Haven't you heard?"

"Not a word."

"That's strange, sir. There's a clearance at the castle. Everyone's leaving. First went my Lord Forgue, and then my lord himself and my lady, his niece, and then the housekeeper Mrs. Brooks went, for her mother was dying, they say. I'm thinking there must be a wedding at hand. There was some word of fixing up the old house in the town here, 'cause Lord Forgue didn't want to be in the castle any longer. It's strange you haven't heard, sir," he went on, for Donal stood absorbed in the hearing. "Surely some letter must've miscarried." Donal felt as if the sure and firm-set earth were giving way under his feet.

"I will run up to the castle, and hear all about it from some of the people," he said. "Look after my horse, will you?"

"But I'm telling you, sir, you'll find nobody there," said the man. "They've all gone. To the best of my knowledge, there's not a soul about the place—except maybe deaf Betty Lobban who couldn't hear the angel at the sound of the last trumpet."

"Then you think there is no use in going up?" he said.

"Not the smallest," answered the innkeeper.

"Get me some supper then. I will take a look at my horse, and be in by and by."

He went and saw that the horse was being ministered to, and then set off for the castle as fast as his legs would carry him. There was foul play somewhere beyond a doubt—where or what sort he could not tell, but first he must make sure that the man's report was correct. If it was, he would go straight to the constable.

He mounted the hill, and drew near the castle. A terrible gloom fell upon him; there was not a light in the sullen pile. He went to the main entrance and rang the great bell as loud as he could ring it, but there was no answer to the summons, which echoed horribly as if the house were actually empty. He rang again, and again came the horrible yelling echo, but no more answer than if it had been a mausoleum. Although he had been told enough to know what to expect, his heart sank within him. Once more he rang and waited; but there was neither sound nor hearing. The place grew so terrible to him as he stood there that, had he found the door was wide open, he would almost have hesitated to enter.

But something urged him from within: His mother had sent him here. Surely she was only the agent of another. And here was his first chance of learning whither they had gone. There might be a letter or some message for him. Anyhow, he knew that he had to go into that house. There was false play. He kept repeating to himself. But what was it? And where was it to be met and defeated? As to getting into the house, there was no difficulty, and he made no delay. He had in his pocket the key to his own stair, which he generally carried; and if he had not had it, he would yet soon have got in, for he knew all the ins and outs of the place better than anyone else about it. As it was, however, he had to climb over two walls before he got to the door of the north tower. Happily he had left it locked when he went away, else probably they would have secured it otherwise. He went softly and with a strange feeling of dread up the stair to his room.

He must settle in his mind what he was to do first, or rather what he was to do at all. He would not go roaming about the house at the risk of coming unexpectedly upon the deaf old woman and terrifying her out of her senses; that would not be the way to get any information out of her. If there were no false play, he went on thinking as he walked wearily up the stair, surely at least Mrs. Brooks would have written to let him know they were going. If only he could learn where she was. He grew more and more weary as he ascended, and when he reached the top, he staggered into his own room and fell on the bed in the dark.

But he could not rest; the air of the place was stifling. The storm had ceased for a while, but the atmosphere was yet full of thunder and terribloppressive. He got up ready to faint and opened the window. A little breath of air came in and revived him; then came a little wind, and in it the moan of what they used to call the ghost music. It woke many reminiscences. There again was the lightning. The thunder broke with a great roar that bellowed among the roof and chimneys. The storm would do him good. He went out on the roof and mechanically took his way toward the stack of chimneys in which was the Aeolian harp. At the base he sat down and stared into the darkness. The lightning came, and he saw the sea lie watching like a perfect peace to take up drifting souls, and the land bordering it like a waste of dread. Then came the thunder so loud that it not only deafened but seemed to blind him, so that his brain turned into a lump of clay—and then a lull.

And in the lull seemed to come a voice calling . . . calling, from a great distance; was it possible? Was he the fool of weariness and excitement, or did he actually hear his own name? What could it be but the voice of Lady Arctura, calling to him from the spirit world? They had killed her, but she had not forgotten him. She was calling to remind him that they would meet by and by in the land of liberty. His heart swelled in his bosom. Came another roar of thunder, and when that ceased, there was the voice again: "Mr. Grant! Mr. Grant! come; come!" and he thought he heard also but could not be sure, "You promised!" A wail of the ghost music followed close, and that seemed to come from behind him, not from the chimney. Working apparently by contraries it woke in him a thought which surely would have waked sooner but for the state he was in.

"God in heaven!" he whispered. Could she be down there in the chapel? He sprang to his feet. With superhuman energy he gave a spring and caught hold of the edge of the cleft, drew himself up till his mouth was on a level with it, and called aloud, "Lady Arctura!" There came no answer.

"I am stupid as death!" he said to himself, "I have let her call me in vain!"

"I am coming!" he cried, and filled with sudden life and joy, dropped on the roof and sped down the stair to the door that opened on the second floor. He knew the way so well that he needed but a little guidance from his hands, and would not strike a light, to reach Lady Arctura's forsaken chamber. He hurried to the spot where the wardrobe had stood, prepared with one shove to send it out of his way. There was nothing there! His heart sank within him. Was he in a terrible dream? He had made a mistake! He had trusted too much to his knowledge of the house, and had deceived himself as to where he was! Clearly he was not in the right room! He must at last strike a light, for he had no longer a notion where he was. Happily he had several with him.

Alas! he was where he had intended to be! It was her room! There was the wardrobe a yard or so away from its usual position; but where it had stood there was no recess! Fresh plaster gave clear sign of where it had been, and that was all. It was no dream, but an awful succession of facts!

He did not lose a moment contemplating the change. It would take him perhaps hours to break through, though the mortar was not yet hard. Instinctively clutching his skene dhu, he darted to the stair. It must have been the voice of Arctura he had heard! She was walled up in the chapel! Down the great stair with the swift, strong, noiseless foot of the Highlander he sped, to the door of the earl's business room, through which alone was the closet behind it and the oak door to be reached. It was locked!

There was one way left! Down to the foot of the stair he shot. Good heavens! If that way also should have been known to the earl! His heart beat so that he could hardly breathe. He crept through the little door underneath the stair, and made a great noise with the pan and brush left lying there, but was now past fear of being heard. The low arch behind, through which he had crept, was not built up! In a moment he was in the crypt of the chapel.

"There was but one difficulty left; could he get up into the opening through the wall from the passage above? Or in it, could he, on the steep slope of the same, find purchase for his feet so as to lift the slab he had there replaced? He sprang at the slope, but there was no hold, and as often as he tried he slipped down again immediately. He tried and tried again till he was worn out and almost in despair. She might be dying, and he was close to her and could not reach her! He stood still for a moment to think. Then came to his mind the word, "He that believeth shall not make haste"; and he thought within himself—as he could not at that moment have thought, had he not thought of it many a time before—that God cannot well help men when their minds are in such a tumult that they will not hear what he is saying to them. With the fear that his friend might be at the point of death within a few feet of him, and for want of him, Donal had yet the strength and wisdom to be quiet and to listen!

And as he stood there in the dark, the vision of the place came before him as when first he saw it, when he threw in the lighted envelope, and in the vision was the stone like a gravestone on which it fell and burned. He started at once from his quiescence, dropped on his hands and knees, and crawled until he found it. Then out came his knife, and he dug away the earth at one end until he could get both hands under it, when he heaved it from the floor, and shifting it along, got it under the opening in the wall.

40

· ·

The Mind of the Earl

*M*oral madness, cruelty and, I am old-fashioned enough to think, demoniacal temptation working on a mind that had ceased almost to distinguish between the real and the unreal had culminated in a hideous plot, in which it would be hard to say whether folly, crime, or cunning predominated. The earl had made up his mind that if the daughter of his brother should continue to refuse to carry out what he asserted and probably believed to have been the wish of her father, to marry her cousin, she should, provided there were another world to go to, go there before him, and leave her property to the son for whom he had resolved to make up to his mother for the wrong he had done her. At the same time he hoped a little fright would serve, and she would consent to marry Forgue to escape the fate she should soon see hanging over her; in prospect of which probability he took care that Forgue should not bear a blame, sending him out of the way to London.

The moment Donal was gone, the earl began, therefore, to make himself charming, as he had well known how in his youth; and soon he had reason to be satisfied that interest could yet rouse something in him of the old gift of pleasing. The earl prevailed upon Arctura to accompany him to London also—merely for a month or so, he said, while Davie was gone. He would take her here and take her there, and introduce her to the best society in the capital. She did not expect much from the undertaking; but the prospect of again seeing London, where she had not been since she was a little girl with her father, had its attractions for her imagination, and she consented—not, however, without writing to Donal to communicate the fact. The letter—it is hardly needful to ask how—never reached him.

Nobody nowadays, the earl said, ever saw anything of his own country. She should, for he would take her by the road he used to travel himself when he was a young man. He sent Simmons before him and contrived that almost as soon as he and the lady were gone, Mrs. Brooks should receive a letter from the clergyman of the parish in a remote part of Caithness where her mother, now a very old woman, lived, saying that she was at the point of death and could not die in peace until she had seen her daughter. The whole thing was the work of a madman—excellently contrived. Mrs. Brooks had at once obeyed the summons and gone. He knew that she would leave someone in the house, but he knew also who that was likely to be—namely, old deaf Betty Lobban; this was an advantage for his plot.

After the first night on the road, he turned across country and a little toward home; after the next night, he drove back. As it was by a different road, Arctura suspected nothing. When they had come to within a few hours of the castle, they stopped at a little inn for tea, and there he managed to give her a dose of one of those drugs he had with him. At the next place he represented her as his daughter with whom, because of sudden illness, he was anxious to reach home however late. He gave an imaginary name to the place and kept on the lost post-boy, who knew nothing of the country. He, knowing it well from old time, gave directions that completely bewildered the boy, and set them down at their own castle door supposing it to be an altogether different part of the country. It was a kind of thing quite after the earl's own heart, for he delighted in making a fool of a fellow mortal. Last of all, he sent him away so as altogether to avoid the town, where alone, so far as the outlook of the earl went, it was of importance that nothing should be known of his return.

How he could effect what followed, I hardly know. But he had the remains of great strength and, when under certain influences which he knew how to manage, was for the time almost as strong as he had ever been; he contrived to get the lady up to his room on the stair and through the oak door.

He had previously made preparations in the chapel with his own hands. All was in beautiful readiness; the prospect of what he was going to do woke no unpleasing recollection of former cruel delights and made him, for the moment, feel almost young again. So far, the plan he had drawn up he had carried out perfectly.

When Arctura woke from her unnatural sleep, she did not at first even trouble herself to think where she was. But as she came to herself, she tried to localize herself. The last place she could recall was the little inn where they had their tea. She must have been taken ill, she thought, and was now in a room of the same. It was quite dark, and she wished they had left a light by her. She seemed to lie comfortably enough; but she had a suspicion that it was but a very poor place, not overly clean, and was glad to find that she lay in her clothes.

Thus thinking, she turned on her side; something pulled her—something on her wrist. She did not remember that she had been wearing a bracelet, but she must have one on and it had gotten tangled in the coverlet somehow. She tried to unclasp it but could find no way, neither from the shape of the thing could she remember which of her bracelets it was. And there was something attached to it. It felt like a chain—a thick chain! It was very odd! What could it mean? She did not yet trouble herself, however, but lay quietly, coming to fuller consciousness.

Then she became aware of what had been pressing on her unready recognition—namely, a strange air, rather than odor, in the room. It was by no means definite; yet she thought she had smelt it before, and not very long ago. Suddenly it flashed upon her that it was the smell of the lost chapel! But that was at home in the castle, and she had left that two days before! She would have started up. The dews of agonized horror began to roll down her face. She was pulled hard by the wrist. She was lying where that heap of dust had lain! She was manacled with the same chain in which that woman had died hundreds of years ago! In one moment her being so recoiled from the horror that she seemed on the edge of madness.

All her senses now fully awake, she was engulfed by the memory of her feelings when first she came down into the place. A vivid picture of exactly what the darkness was hiding from her caused the tide of terror to further rise and soon threaten to become altogether monstrous.

It began to thunder, first with a low, distant, muttering roll, then with a loud and near bellowing. Some people are strangely terrified at thunder, but Arctura had never been; and now it comforted her as with the assurance that God was near. And as she lay and listened to the great organ of the heavens, to her spirit it seemed to grow articulate; God seemed to be calling to her and saying, "Here I am, my child! Do not be afraid." Then she reasoned with herself that the worst that could happen to her was to lie there till she died of hunger, and that could not be so very bad.

Then mingled with the thunder came a wail of ghost music. She started with a strange feeling that she had heard it a hundred times while lying there in the dark alone, and only now for the first time was waking up to the fact. She herself was the lady they had shut up there to die, and she had lain there for ages, every now and then hearing that sound of the angels singing. Her mind was beginning to wander. She reasoned with herself and dismissed the fancy, but it came and came again, mingled with the memories of the times she had spent on the roof with Donal.

By and by she fell asleep, and woke before the presence of a terror which seemed to have been growing in her sleep. She sat up and stared before her into the dark. It came nearer and nearer. It was but a fancy, and she knew it. She cried aloud. It came nearer still; but the instant it was about to seize her came a sudden change. Her fear was gone and in its place a sense of absolute safety; there was nothing in all the universe to be afraid of. It was a night of June, and roses . . . roses everywhere. What was it? Had God sent her mother to think her full of roses? Why her mother, when God himself is the heart of every rose that ever bloomed? She would have sung aloud for joy, but no voice came from her; she could not utter a sound. Then came the thought of Donal surging into her heart. If she were to die down here, then one day he would come and find her. Then Donal's voice seemed strangely mingled with music and thunder— a voice from far away, and she did not know whether it was her fancy or she really heard him. But it filled her so with delight that she tried to answer him, but her voice died away in her throat.

41

• • • • • • • • • • • • • • • • • • • •

Deliverance

*P*ressing with all his might against the sides of the sloping windowsill, if window that opening into the crypt could be called, Donal did at last push up the slab so far as to get a hold with one hand on the next to it and so save himself from slipping down again—as up to that moment he had been constantly doing. But the weight of it was now resting on his fingers. He kept still for a few minutes to gather strength; then slowly he turned himself on his side and gradually got the other hand also through the crack. Then hauling himself up with all his force, careless of what might happen to his head, with the top of it he raised the stone so as to get head and neck through. And now if it did not strangle him before he got farther, the thing was done. He gave one more Herculian lift of his body—for he had at once to lift his own weight and that of the stone— and like a man rising from the dead rose from the crypt into the passage.

But the door of the chapel was closed.

"My lady!" he cried, "don't be afraid. I am going to drive the door open. You must not mind the noise! It is only Donal Grant!"

"Only Donal Grant!" She heard the words! They woke her from her swoon of joy. "Only Donal Grant!" What less of an only could there be in the world for her! Was he not the messenger of he who raises the dead! "Only Donal Grant!"

She tried to speak but not a word would come. Donal, fearing lest, after all, he had arrived too late, drew back a pace and sent such a shoulder against the door that it flew to the wall and fell with a great crash on the floor. The same moment Donal was in the chapel.

"Where are you, my lady?" he said, but still she could not speak.

He began feeling about.

"She can never be on the terrible bed!" he murmured to himself.

She heard him, and fear lest he should turn away and think she was not there after all gave her voice.

"I don't mind it now you are there!" she whispered.

"Thank God," he cried, "I have found you at last!" and then, worn out, he sank on his knees, with his head on the bed, and fell to sobbing like a little child.

She put out her hand through the darkness to lay it on his head, but she could not reach him. He heard the rattle of the chain and understood.

"Chained too, my dove!" he said, involuntarily in Gaelic. But he wept no more; again he thanked God and took courage. New life seemed to rush through every vein, and he rose to his feet conscious of strength like a giant.

"Can you strike a light, Donal, and let me see you?" asked Lady Arctura. It was the first time she had said his name directly to him; it had been often on her lips that night.

He did as she requested and for a moment they looked at each other. She was not so changed as he had feared to find her. Terrible as had been her trial, it had not lasted very long and had been succeeded by a heavenly joy. She was paler than usual, yet there was a rosy flush over her beautiful face; her arm was stretched toward him, clasped by the rusty ring, just as they had together imagined the arm of the dead lady, before time had turned it to dust, had tightened the chain that held it to the bedpost. She was in her traveling dress, just as her uncle had brought her back.

"How pale and tired you look," she said.

"I am a little tired," he confessed. "I have come straight from home. My mother sent me to you. She said I must come, but she did not tell me why I was to come."

"It was God sent you, Donal," she returned—and then she told him what she knew of her story.

"But," said Donal, "how could the villain have got the ring on your wrist?"

He looked closer, and saw that her hand was swollen and the skin abraided.

"He has forced it on!" he exclaimed. "How it must hurt!"

"It does hurt," she replied, "but I did not notice it before. It was such a little thing beside the misery and terror of finding myself alone in the place whose horrors had so often haunted me."

Donal took the little hand in his. It was much swollen. But where the ring was now on the wrist it lay loose.

"Do you suppose he meant to leave me here to die?" Arctura wondered.

"It is impossible to tell," returned Donal. "It is hard to believe anything so bad even of one who could do as he has done. But in truth I suspect we have had to do with more of a madman than anyone knew. We must leave nothing in his power anymore. I will strike another light and see whether there is anything about the place to show whether he plotted this or it was a sudden idea that came to him."

He did so. The bed had been smoothed a little, apparently, and a traveling rug spread over the dust; that was all the preparation made. Whether it had been done beforehand or only when he brought her to it could not be determined. There was no other change they could see in the place. Whether he meant her to lie there as she was to die, or only to frighten her into compliance with his wishes, neither of them could tell. Donal told her then how it was that he had come.

"Now will you take me away?" she said.

"I must first get rid of the chain," answered Donal. "That may be a little difficult; but it is only a matter of patience."

"You will not leave me?"

"Only to get what tools I may want."

"But after that?" she said.

"Not until you wish me to," he answered.

There came a great burst of thunder. It was the last of the storm, and when it had bellowed and shuddered and gone and come rolling up again, at last it died away in the great distance with a low, continuous rumbling as if it would never cease.

Out of the tense heart of the silence came a slow step, seemingly far off, but approaching.

"It is the earl!" whispered Arctura.

"He will find the door open!" said Donal and darted to set it up.

"Never mind," said Arctura. "His imagination will account for it at once. It does for everything where he has no suspicion. He will think it was the thunder. I wonder if he has a light!" she added hurriedly. "If he has, you must get behind the altar." The step came nearer. Evidently he was coming through the dark and had no light.

"Do not speak a word," instructed Donal; "let him think you are asleep. I will stand so that if he comes near the bed he shall come against me. He shall not touch you!"

"Arctura!" said a deep voice. It was the earl. She made no answer.

"Dead of fright, I daresay!" muttered the voice. "I will strike a light and see. I hope she will not prove as obstinate as her mother—I mean her aunt!" Donal stood intently watching for the light. After some fumbling came a sputter and a gleam, but the match failed. Donal marked the spot and the distance; before he could try another, Donal made a swift blow as near as he could judge through the space. It struck his arm and knocked the box from his hand.

"Ha!" the earl cried out, and there was terror in the cry, "she strikes me through the dark!"

Donal prepared for a struggle but kept very still. He must run no shadow of a risk that could be avoided so long as Arctura was not out of the earl's power. She was not yet even free from the chain! Arctura kept as still as he. But the earl turned and went away.

"I will bring a light!" he muttered. The moment Donal heard the door close above, he said to Arctura: "Now, my lady, you heard him say he would bring a light; I dare not leave you alone with him, but somehow I think it better I should not encounter him yet. Do you mind being left a few minutes while I fetch some tools to set you free?"

"No, certainly," she answered.

"I will be back before him," he answered.

"Be careful you do not meet him," warned Arctura.

Now that the slab was raised, there was no difficulty in Donal's way either in going or returning. He sped away, and in a time that seemed short even to the prisoner, he was back. There was no time to file through ring or chain. He attacked the staple in the bedpost and drew it. Then he wound the chain round her arm and fastened it there.

He had by this time made up his mind what would be best to do with her. He had been at first inclined to carry her out of the house altogether. The factor and his sister were away, but there was Andrew Comin's Doory. It would, however, be yielding their enemy an advantage to leave him in possession of the house, he thought. Awkward things might result from it, and tongues of inventive ignorance and stupidity would wag wildly. He would take her to her own room, and there watch her as he would a child, leaving no chance for anyone to come near her.

"There! You are free, my lady," he said. "Now come."

He took her hands, and she raised herself wearily.

"The air is so close!" she said.

"We shall soon be in better," answered Donal.

"Shall we go out on the roof?" she said, like one talking in her sleep.

"I will take you to your own room," assured Donal. "But I will not leave you," he added quickly, seeing a look of anxiety cloud her face, "at least so long as your uncle is in the house. I do wonder what he has done with Mistress Brooks."

"Take me where you will," said Arctura.

There was no way for them to get out but through the crypt. Donal got down first, and she followed without hesitation. Then there was only the little closet under the stair to creep through, and they were in the hall of the castle.

As they went up the stair, Donal had an idea.

"He can't have got back yet!" he said. "We will take away the key from the oak door; he will only think he has taken and mislaid it and thus not discover so soon that you are gone. I wonder what he will do when he does not find it? Will he leave you to die there, or get help to get you out?"

He did as he said, locked the oak door and brought away the key. They then went together to the room she had last occupied on the first floor. The door was a little ajar, and there was a light in it. They went softly up and peeped in. There was the earl turning over the contents of Arctura's writing desk.

"He will find nothing," she murmured, "either to serve him or hurt me!"

"We will go to your old room," said Donal. "You will not mind it now, I know. The recess itself is built up with bricks and mortar; he cannot come near you from that way!"

As soon as they reached the two rooms, Donal secured all the doors, then lit a fire. He left her while he went to look for something to eat, having first agreed upon a certain knock, without which she was to open to no one.

While she was yet changing the garments in which she had lain on the terrible bed, she heard the earl pass and the door of his own room close. Apparently he had made up his mind to let her spend the night without another visit, for he himself had received a terrible fright in the place. A little longer and she heard Donal's gentle signal at her door. He had brought some biscuits and a little wine in the bottom of a decanter from the housekeeper's room; there was literally nothing in the larder, he reported.

They sat down and ate together. Donal told her his adventures, and she repeated hers, so far as she knew them—also about Forgue's suit and her refusal to listen to him, as perhaps explaining the earl's design. They agreed that the first thing to be done was to write to the factor to come home at once and bring his sister with him. Then Donal set to with his file to free her from her bracelet. It was not an easy job. There was the constant danger of hurting her, especially as her hand was so swollen; and, besides, the rust filled and blunted his file. It took a long time.

"There!" he said at last. "And now, my lady, you must take some rest. Lock both your doors. I will sleep here; this sofa will do well. Ah, the key of this door is gone! So much the better. I will draw the sofa across it, so that even if he should come wandering here in the night, he may find a small obstruction."

In the night Donal heard the earl's door open, and he quickly followed him. He went to the oak door and tried in vain to open it.

"She has taken it!" Donal heard him say in a trembling voice.

All night long the earl roamed the house, a spirit grievously tormented; then in the gray of the morning, having probably almost persuaded himself that the whole affair was but a trick of his imagination, he went back to his room and to bed, taking yet an extra dose of his medicine as he lay down.

In the morning Donal left the house, having first had a word with Arctura through the door. Hastening to the inn, he paid his bill, bought some things for their breakfast and, mounting his horse, rode back up to the castle and rang the bell—then, no notice being taken, he went and put up his horse and let himself into the house. He began to sing and, so singing, came up the stair and along the corridor where the earl lay.

This waked him, and brought him to the door in a rage. But the moment he saw Donal his countenance fell; his usual coolness seemed to give way.

"What the devil are you doing here?" he demanded.

"They told me in the town that you were in England, my lord!—Please tell me, where is my lady?"

"I wrote to you," said the earl, "that we were gone to London, and that you need be in no haste to return. I trust you have not brought Davie with you."

"I have not, my lord."

"Then pray make what haste back to him you can. I cannot have him left alone with bumpkins! But you may stay there with him as long as you find it convenient—till I send for you. He can study there as well as here. I will pay what board you think proper—for both of you. Now, go! I am home but for a few hours on business and off again by the afternoon coach!"

"I do not go, my lord, until I have seen my mistress."

"Your mistress! Who, pray, is your mistress? I thought I was your master, if it comes to that."

"I am no longer in your service, my lord. If there is any penalty for lack of due warning, I am ready to render good reason."

"Then what in the name of God have you done with my son?"

"In good time, my lord, when you have told me where my mistress is! I return to this house as Lady Arctura's servant, not your lordship's; and I desire to know where I shall find her."

"Go to London, then."

"What address, please—that I may write to her and receive her orders here?"

"You leave this house instantly," said the earl, unable, however, to conceal some anxiety, if not dread; "I will not have you here in my absence—and her ladyship's too!"

"My lord, I am not ignorant of how things stand with regard to the house; it belongs to my mistress, and from her alone I will receive orders. Here I remain till I have her command to go."

"Very well, then! By all means remain."

"I ask you again for her address, my lord."

"Find it for yourself. Because you will not obey my orders, am I therefore to obey yours?"

His lordship turned on his heel and flung his door shut.

"It will be my turn presently," Donal muttered.

Donal went to Lady Arctura, told her what he had done, and produced his provisions. Together they prepared their breakfast. By and by the earl came from his room, and they partly heard, partly saw him go here and there all over the house, and then turn again to his own apartment. He seemed neither to have eaten nor drunk all the time he was in the castle.

About an hour before the starting of the afternoon coach, they saw him leave the house. He went down the hill toward the town, not once looking back. They turned and looked at each other. A profound pity for the wretched old man was the feeling at that moment, I believe, in the minds of each. Then followed one of intense relief and liberty.

"Perhaps you would like to get rid of me now, my lady," said Donal; "but I don't see how I well can leave you. I should be miserable to think of you here in the house by yourself; would you have me go and fetch Miss Carmichael?"

"No, certainly," answered Arctura. "I cannot, after what has passed, apply to her the moment I am in trouble."

"I am glad you think so; it would be to lose the advantage of your uncle not knowing what had become of you."

"I should certainly like to see what he will do next. Just think, Mr. Grant, if I were to die now, the property would pass into the hands of my uncle, and then into those of Forgue!"

"You can make a will, as your father did," answered Donal.

Arctura stood thoughtfully for a moment.

"I am so ashamed of myself, Mr. Grant!" she said. "If Forgue had sooner sought me, when I did not know anything against him and when life was so terribly dreary, I cannot say that I might not have been persuaded to! But tell me, is he such a bad man as I have sometimes feared? You don't think he had any knowledge of this design of his father?"

"I cannot think so. I will not believe he would have allowed you to die in the chapel, which I suppose his father must now intend—but—but—I should like to know what has become of poor Eppie!"

It was not long before he learned.

42

. . . .

New Life in the Castle

That same afternoon, to the great delight of both, Mrs. Brooks returned half wild with anxiety. From the moment when she discovered herself fooled, she had been dreading all manner of terrible things, yet none so terrible as her mistress had to tell her. There seemed likely to be no end to her objurgations and exclamations, when at length she held Lady Arctura safe in her arms.

"Now I can leave you in peace, my lady," said Donal.

"Now you can stay where you are and be thankful," retorted Mrs. Brooks. "Who knows what the mad earl—for mad I'll uphold him to be—who knows what he might do next? Indeed, Mister Grant, I cannot let you out of the house."

"I was only thinking of going down to Mistress Comin's," said Donal.

"Well, you can go; but mind you're home in good time."

"I will do exactly as my lady pleases."

"Then come," said Arctura.

Donal went, and the first person he saw when he entered the house was Eppie. She turned instantly away, and left the room; he could not help seeing why.

Presently the old woman came and welcomed him with her usual cordiality, but not her usual cheerfulness. Since her husband's death, he had scarcely noted any change in her manner till now; she looked weary of the world.

She sat down, smoothed her apron on her knees, gave him one glance in the face, then looked down at her hands and had nothing to say.

"I can tell what must be ailing you, Doory," said Donal, "with the child in a woman's worst way. But listen to me. The lass is not lost yet. She's misguided. But if it makes her hold closer to the rest of God's flock, she'll find out it wasn't for the lack of his care or mercy that this happened to her. And it isn't as if she's been caught stealing. She's wronged her poor self, and no one else. But we must love her the more."

"Eh, but you speak like my Andrew!" cried the poor woman, wiping her eyes with her apron. "I'll do what I can for her, but there's no hiding of it."

"She must bear her burden, poor lass. The Lord'll do as he likes about it . . . I suppose there's no doubt who's the father?"

"None. The Lord forbid that it's possible . . . but it's the young lord."

Two days after, Mr. Graeme, the factor, and his sister returned. They lived on the estate in a modest house, from which they managed the business affairs of the earl, collecting rents and handling tenant complaints. At Lady Arctura's request, they moved into the castle for a time. Then followed a solemn conference in which, however anxious she was to say nothing against her uncle, Lady Arctura told both that of late she had become convinced that her uncle was no longer capable of attending to her affairs; that they had had a difference and he was gone for the present. She desired of them as a personal favor that they would not allude to her being at the castle; she had gone away with her uncle and was supposed to be with him, but had returned, and her uncle did not know that she was at home. She did not wish him to know. She desired for the present to remain hidden. Mr. Graeme would in the meantime prepare for a thorough understanding of matters as between her and her uncle.

In the course of the investigations that thereupon followed, it became clear that a good deal of the moneys of the estate received by his lordship were in no way by them to be accounted for; and then Lady Arctura directed that further proceedings should be stayed until the earl should be present to explain, but that no more money was to be handed over to him. Her name, however, must not be mentioned.

For some time Mr. Graeme heard nothing of him; but by and by came directions as to where and how money was to be forwarded. Forgue wrote but his father signed. Mr. Graeme replied, excusing himself as he could, but sent nothing. They wrote again. Again he excused himself. The earl threatened. Mr. Graeme took no heed. Months passed thus, but neither of the two appeared to enforce their demands. Forgue could not without his father; and his father had reasons for staying away. At length the factor wrote that he would pay no money but to Lady Arctura herself. The earl himself wrote in reply, asking if he had been asleep all this time that he did not know she had died in London and been six weeks in her grave. Again the factor did not reply.

Life was going on very quietly in the castle. Davie had long been at home, lessons were to the hour as before, and Lady Arctura took a full share in them. Only Donal was a little anxious at some signs in her which he could not help taking for those of failing health.

All about the castle was bustling labor—masons and carpenters busy from morning to night. For the very next day after Mr. Graeme's return, Lady Arctura began at once to admit the light of day upon the secret of centuries. The wall that masked the chapel windows was pulled down; the windows, which had in them hardly a crack, were thoroughly cleaned;

the passage under them, which had once been a sort of arcade, was opened to the great stair where Donal had seen the ends of the steps coming through. The way was cleared to the oak door by taking away the masking press; and after Lady Arctura had had a small, sweet-toned organ built in the little gallery, she had the stair from her own room opened again and fitted with a door, that she might go down when she pleased, as she did often, to play on the organ—above which still at times, in winds from southeast, the Aeolian harp dreamed out the music of the spheres.

The terrible bed had been of course removed. In taking it to pieces for the purpose, the joints crumbled to dust and the rest of it was burned; but the story of its finding was written by Donal and placed among the records of the family.

The alterations that naturally took place in restoring the chapel to the castle admitted much more light and air into it, adding beauty and health-fulness and, without destroying anything valuable in the antiquity of the building, rendered it a much better place to live.

But it soon became evident to others as well as Donal that the things Lady Arctura had to pass through had exercised a very damaging influ-ence on her health. For some time she seemed to be pining, but nothing was plainly amiss with her. She seemed always happy, but her strength at times would suddenly desert her, and she would sink with a little laugh on the nearest support. No one, however, feared anything very soon or very definite.

When twelve months had come and gone, the earl one day stood before the castle, half doubting whether it was his own; he wanted to come to a proper understanding with his factor and to see Davie, whom, hearing Donal had resumed his relation with him, he had willingly left in his care. He had driven up to the point where the road turned off to the stables, and thence walked. The great door was standing open; he entered and walked up.

What odd change was this on the stair—a door that had not been there before? At least he had never seen it. Who could have dared make such a change in his house? The thing was bewildering, but he was accus-tomed to being bewildered.

He opened the door—a new handsome one of oak—and entered an arcade with arches to the open air; he might have seen it as he approached the house, but he had not looked up. At the end of it was the door of the chapel. He started back in dismay; the lost chapel with all its horrible secrets wide open to the eye of day! He went in. It was clear and clean—no hideous bed, no darkness, no dust, and the air trembling with the delight of the organ breath, which went rushing and rippling through it in all directions. He said to himself he had never had just such a pecu-liar experience. He had often doubted whether things were or were not the projections of his own brain; knew that sometimes he could not tell. But never before had he had the real appearance and the unreal of fact brought so immediately face-to-face with each other.

Everything was just as clear to his eyes as if he were in the prime of youth and health, and yet he was positively, absolutely certain there could be no reality in what he so indubitably saw. At the same time, he was by no means certain that the things which seemed last in his experience to have taken place there had really taken place at all. He had managed to get in doubt about this the moment he failed to find the key. When he would ask himself what had become of his niece, he would to himself reply that doubtless she was all right. She did not want to marry Forgue, the rascal—and quite right, too, if she had known him as he did!—and so had slipped out of the way somewhere. She had never cared about the property so long as he was the guardian of the lady and the next heir to it. She had come of age, it was true, but he had not rendered his accounts or yielded his stewardship. If she had died anywhere, the property was his. She never could have had the heart to leave it to anyone but him. She had always been very friendly with him, and he had loved her like his own flesh and blood.

But at other times he did not doubt that he had starved her to death in the chapel and was tormented as with all the furies of hell. In his night visions he would see her lying, wasting away, hear her moaning and crying in vain for help; the hardest heart is yet at the mercy of a roused imagination. He would see her body in the various stages of decay as the weeks passed. When would the process be over, that he might go back to the place? Pretending to have just found the lost room, he could carry away the bodies together and have them honorably buried. Should he pretend that it had lain there for centuries like the others, or insist that it must be she who had so unaccountably disappeared? She had got shut up there and had not been able to get out again. If he could but find an old spring lock to put on the door. But people were so plagued sharp nowadays. They found out everything—and he positively could not afford to have everything found out. No; God himself, if there were such an indefinite entity anywhere, must not be allowed to know everything.

He stood staring. And as he stood, a change began to grow in him; perhaps, after all, what he saw, might actually be. If so, then the whole thing it had displaced must have been a fancy—a something he had seen only in his dreams and visions. God in heaven, if it could but be proven that he had never done anything such as he had thought belonged to this place—then all the other wicked things he was guilty of, or of which he had at least always supposed himself guilty, and which had been so heavy upon him all his life that it never seemed of the smallest use to try to repent of them, might be forgiven him.

If only he had never murdered anybody! After all, there might be a God then, and he might if he tried be able to thank him. But for what? That he was not going to be damned for the thing he had never done? A thing he had only had the unspeakable misfortune to dream he had done? And God never to have interfered to prevent him from having the horrible fancy that he had done it? What was the good of having a God that would not do that much for you, but would leave his creatures to make the most horrible fools of themselves? Bah! There was life in the old dog yet! If only he could know that he had fancied the whole thing.

The music ceased, and the silence was a shock to him. Again he began to stare about him. He looked up, and there in the gallery, but seeming to his misty sight in the dim chapel to come out of the wall, was the pale face of the girl he did not know whether he had or had not murdered. He took her for one of his visions. She looked sweetly at him. She had come to forgive his sins; for Arctura, who had never thought with bitterness of her uncle's cruelty, had always thought of him pitifully, had often longed for the opportunity of letting him know that she had him in her heart still. Therefore looking down and seeing him there, she regarded him with an expression which spoke to the spark of good still left in him. Was it then true? Was there no sin of murder on his soul? Had he waked from a horrid dream and was she there to assure him that he might yet look with hope to the world to come? He stretched out his arms toward her. She turned away, and he thought she had vanished. But it was only to fly down the stair. The next moment she was in the chapel and had taken the old man in her arms. He had not heard her and was still gazing at the spot she had left. The contact of the material so startled him, causing such a revulsion, that he uttered a loud cry, shoved her from him, and stood looking at her in worse perplexity than ever. Knowledge and fact seemed face-to-face opposed to each other.

"Don't be frightened, Uncle," said Arctura, "I am not dead. You left me to die; but, see, the place of death has become a place of praise; the sepulchre was always only the resurrection house! Here I am—alive!"

The earl stood motionless. His eyes were fixed upon her. His lips moved tremulously once or twice, but no word came. How much he took in of what she was saying, who can tell? At last he turned from her, glanced round the place, and said, "This is a great improvement!"

Arctura could say nothing more. She turned and walked out and up the great stair, her uncle following her.

Not once looking behind her, she went to her room, rang the bell, sent for Donal, and told him what had passed.

"I will go to him," said Donal; and Arctura said nothing more, leaving the whole matter in his hands.

43

· · · · · · · · · · · · · · · · · · · ·

Hard Words

The earl was in his own room, which was much as he had left it; Donal found him lying on the couch.

"My lord," he said, "you must be aware that there are reasons why you should not present yourself here—in your niece's house."

The earl started from the sofa in one of his ready rages; whatever his visions might be, his rages were real enough. With all the names of contempt and hatred he could heap upon him, he ordered Donal out of the room and out of the house. Donal stood and answered nothing till the rush of his wrath had somewhat abated. Then he spoke.

"My lord," he said, "there is nothing I would not do to serve your lordship. I would go on my knees to you to make you sorry. But I have now to tell you, with as little offense as may be, that if you do not walk quietly out of the house, you must be expelled like any other intruder!"

"Intruder, you dog!"

"Intruder, my lord—the worst that could show himself here! The man who would murder his hostess, his brother's child—I do not mince matters, my lord—is surely the worst of intruders."

"Good heavens!" cried the earl, changing his tone with an attempted laugh, "has the poor, hysterical girl succeeded in filling a man of common sense like you with her childish, ridiculous fancies? I never moved a finger to injure her since the day I took her first in my arms when she was two hours old."

"You must excuse me for preferring my lady's testimony to yours, my lord," said Donal.

The earl caught up the poker and made a blow at Donal's head, which he avoided. The blow fell on the marble chimney piece and broke it. Donal wrenched the poker from him while his arm was yet jarred by the impact.

"My lord," he said, "if you do not know that what you have just said is not true, it is because you have made yourself unable to distinguish between fact and imagination. I myself unchained her from the bed in the chapel—where you had left her to die. You were yet in the house when I did so. I locked the door, that you could not enter again. I have the key now."

"You dirty rascal! If it had not been for you, then, I should have gone again presently and saved her life, and made her come to terms!"

"But as you had lost the key, and feared to expose yourself, rather than that you went away and left her to perish. And you wanted to compel her to marry your son, on the ground that the title and the property ought to go together, when with my own ears I heard your lordship tell him that he had no right to any title!"

"What a man may say in a rage goes for nothing," said the earl, but rather sulkily than fiercely.

"Not so with what a wife writes in sorrow!" said Donal. "I have heard the truth from your late wife as well as from your own mouth," said Donal, loosely using the term "wife."

"The testimony of the dead will hardly be taken at second hand in any law court," rejoined the earl.

"If after your lordship's death the man who is now called Forgue should dare to assume the title of Morven, I will publish the fact and court inquiry. As to the title, I care nothing, but he shall succeed to no property if I can prevent it; he is too unworthy. Then let him, if he can, produce the proofs of your marriage. And now, my lord, I must again beg you to leave the house, else I must make you."

His lordship glanced around the room as if looking for another weapon. Donal took him by the arm.

"There is no room for more ceremony," he said. "I shall be sorry to be rough with your lordship, but you will compel me. Please remember I am the younger and the stronger man."

As he spoke he let the earl feel the ploughman's grasp on his arm. The earl saw it was useless to struggle. He threw himself again on the couch.

"I will not leave the house; I am come home to die!" he cried, almost with a shriek. "I am dying, I tell you! I cannot leave the house! Besides, I have no money. Forgue has got it all."

"There is a large sum due the estate unaccounted for!" said Donal.

"It is lost—all lost, I tell you. I have nowhere to go, and I am dying!"

Donal's heart smote him. He stood back a little from him and gave himself time.

"You would wish, then, to retire, my lord, I suppose?" he said, after his pause.

"The sooner to be rid of you!" was the earl's answer.

"I fear, my lord, if you will stay here, you are not so soon to get rid of me! Have you brought Simmons with you, may I ask?"

"No, blast him! He is like the rest of you; he has left me."

"I will help you to bed, my lord."

"Go about your business! I will get myself to bed."

"I will not leave you till I see you in bed," said Donal with decision, and rang the bell.

When the servant came, he desired that Mrs. Brooks would come to him. She came instantly. Before his lordship had time even to look at her from where he lay on the couch, Donal asked her to be so good as get his lordship's bed ready. He would help her. She looked at him but said nothing. Donal returned her gaze with one she read and correctly, as meaning,

"I know what I am doing, Mistress Brooks. My lady must not turn him out. I will take care he does no mischief."

"What are you two whispering at there?" cried the earl—there had not been the ghost of a whisper! "Here am I at the point of death, and you will not let me go to bed!"

"Your room will be ready in five minutes, my lord," said Mrs. Brooks, and the two set to work in earnest.

When it was ready, "Now, my lord," said Donal, returning to the sitting room, "will you come?"

"When you are gone. I will have none of your cursed help!"

"My lord, I am not going to leave you."

With much grumbling and a very ill grace, his lordship submitted and Donal got him to bed.

"Now put that cabinet by me on the table," he ordered.

It was that in which he kept his drugs, and was just as he had left it.

Donal opened the window, took up the cabinet, and threw it out bodily.

With a bellow like that of a bull, the earl sprang out of bed just as the crash reached their ears from below. He ran at Donal as if he would have sent him after the cabinet. Donal caught him and held him fast.

"My lord," he said, "I will nurse you, serve you, do anything for you, but for the devil I'll not move hand or foot. Not one drop of that hellish stuff shall pass your lips while I can help it."

"But I shall die of the horrors!" shrieked the earl, struggling to get to the window, as if he could yet do something to save his precious extracts, tinctures, and compounds.

"We will send for a doctor," said Donal. "A very clever young fellow has come to the town since you left; perhaps he will be able to help you. I mean to do what I can to make your life of some value to yourself."

"None of that rubbish!" he cursed. "My life is of no end of value to me as it is. Besides, it's too late. If I were young now, with a constitution like yours and the world before me, there might be some good in a paring or two of self-denial."

"I have no desire to keep you alive, my lord; I only wish to let you get some of the good of this world before you pass on to the next."

He rang the bell again.

"You're a friendly fellow," grunted his lordship, and went back to his bed to meditate how to gain his desires.

Mrs. Brooks came.

"Will you send down to Mr. Avory, the new surgeon," said Donal, "and ask him, in my name, to be so good as to come up to the castle?" The earl lay with closed eyes, a terrible expression of pain and of something like fear every now and then passing over his face.

He declared he would see no doctor but his old attendant Dowster; yet all the time he was longing for the young man to appear and do what he could to save him from the dreaded jaws of death.

The doctor came and was shown into the sitting room, where Donal went to him, leaving the door open that the earl might hear what passed between them. He told him he had sent for him without his lordship's consent, but that he believed he would not refuse to see him; that he had been long in the habit of using narcotics and stimulants—in the wildest fashion, he suspected—though perhaps he knew more about them in some ways then anybody else; that he, Donal, had sent for Mr. Avory trusting he would give his help to the entire disuse of them, for the earl was killing himself, body and soul, with them.

"To give them up entirely will cost him considerable suffering," cautioned Mr. Avory.

"I know that, and he knows it too, and does not want to give them up; but it is absolutely necessary he should be delivered from the habit."

"If I am to undertake the case, I must act according to my own judgment," said the doctor.

"It is I who have sent for you," persisted Donal, "and we must have an understanding. You must promise two things, or take your fee and go."

"I may as well hear what they are."

"One is that you will at least make his final deliverance from the habit your object; the other, that you leave nothing in his own hands as to any medicine you give him."

"I agree to both heartily; but all will depend on his nurse."

"I will nurse him myself."

After a question or two, the doctor went to his patient. The earl gave one glance at him, recognized in the young man a look of determination, felt unable to dispute him, and submitted.

While the doctor sat with the earl, Donal went to Lady Arctura, and told her what had passed. She approved of what he had done, and thanked him for understanding her so well.

44

Rehabilitation

A dreary time followed. More than once or twice the patient lay awake half the night, howling in misery and accusing Donal of the most heartless cruelty. "I was never so cruel to those I treated worst! You sit there gloating over my sufferings! 'Now,' you say to yourself, 'he is in hell! What a splendid twinge he had from that red-hot pair of tongs!—There, he's got to drink that hair-soup!' Give me that cabinet, will you?" he cursed.

And so on, and on and on.

"How do you think you will be able to do without it," returned Donal, on one such occasion, "when you find yourself in the other world?"

"I'm not there yet! Besides, when I am, it will be under new, quite new conditions so, my dear boy, just go to my portmanteau—you know where it is, and get me—"

"I will get you nothing of that sort."

"You want to kill me!"

"What should you be kept alive for? To eat opium? I have other work than that. I would not move a finger to keep you alive with such a life. But I wouldn't mind dying to make you able to go on without it."

"Oh, spare me your preaching!"

But the power of the evil habit did abate a little, and though every now and then it seemed to return as strong as ever, it was plain the suffering did not continue so great. As to moral improvement, it was impossible to say anything with confidence.

By and by the gentle ministrations of his niece did seem to touch the earl a little. Once he sat looking at her for some time, then said: "I hope I did not hurt you much."

"When?" she asked.

"Then," he answered.

"Oh, no, you did not hurt me."

"Another time I was very cruel to your aunt; do you think she will forgive me?"

"Yes, I do."

"Then you must have forgiven me?"

"Of course I have."

"Then you think God will forgive me?"

"I do, if you ask him. But you must leave off, you know, dear Uncle, and try to be good."

"Well, you are a fine comforter! But one might after all refuse to be good. I feel pretty sure I should, so he had better let me alone as I am!"

"But God can do more than that to compel us to be good—a great deal more than that! Indeed, dear Uncle, we must repent."

He said no more; and Donal, having heard a little of the conversation, thought it time to relieve Arctura.

———

"I suppose you mean to marry that dreadful rascal of a tutor!" said the earl suddenly to Arctura one day when she was seated with a piece of work by his bedside, and he had lain silent some time.

She started up in dread, thinking Donal might have heard, but was relieved to see him fast asleep on the couch in the next room.

"He would not thank you for the suggestion, I fear," she said, attempting a laugh. "He is far above me!"

"Is there no chance for Forgue then?"

"Not the smallest. I would rather I had died where you left me than—"

"Don't, if you love me, refer to that again!" he cried. "I was not myself."

"I will not mention it again," she said.

But these talks were on one or two of his best times; at others, he would be sullen, cantankerous, abusive to all who came near him. But as he grew less able to help himself, those about him grew more compassionate, and treated him like a spoiled but really sick child.

One night Donal, hearing him restless, got up from the chair where he watched by him most nights and saw that he was staring, but could not possibly be seeing with the bodily eyes, whose peculiar condition showed that they regarded nothing material. The earl gave a great sigh and his jaw fell. For a moment he seemed to Donal to be dead; but presently he came to himself, like one waking from a troubled sleep. He had left a terrible dream behind him, which was yet pulling at the skirts of his consciousness.

"I've seen her," he said. "She's waiting for me, she says, to take me; but I could not make out where she said she was going to take me. She did not look very angry, but then she never did look very angry, even when I was worst to her. Grant, you'll be marrying someday, I suppose, but don't lose sight of Davie. Make a man of him, I tell you, and his mother will thank you. She was a good woman, his mother, though I did what I could to spoil her! I never succeeded there; and that was how she kept her hold of me to the very last. If I had succeeded in spoiling her, there would then have been a genuine heir to the earldom of Morven! As it is there is nothing to be done. Only if I had not been such a fool and let it out, who would have been the worse? The man is no worse himself!"

"He is no better since he knew it," said Donal.

"He's a heartless, unnatural rascal, I know," said his father. "He has made a stupid fool of me. His mother must see it is not my fault. I would have set things right if I could, but it was too late; and then, you tell me, she has a hand in letting the truth out herself—leaving her letters about! That's some comfort! She won't be hard on me. If only there was a chance of God being half as good to me as my poor wife. I will call her my wife in spite of all the priests in the stupid universe. She was my wife, and she deserved to be my wife; and if I had her now, I would marry her, just because I know she would be foolish enough to like it, though I would not do it all the time she was alive, let her beg ever so. Where was the use, you know, of giving in, when I kept her in hand so easily that way?

"That was it . . . it was not that I wanted to do her any wrong. But the man should keep the lead. You mustn't play out your last trump and not keep the lead. If I had known my poor wife was going to die, I would have done whatever she wanted. We had merry times together too. It was those cursed drugs that let the soul out of me for the devil to take its place. But I should like, just for once, to verify the old sensation—to know how I used to feel. Look here now, Grant; if there were any way of persuading God to give me a fresh lease on life, why shouldn't you ask him? I would make you any promise you please—give you any security you wanted that I would hereafter live a godly, righteous, and sober life."

"But," said Donal, "suppose God read your heart and saw that you would go on as bad as ever, if he gave you another moment?"

"He might give me a chance! I count it very hard he should expect a poor fellow like me to be as good as he is!"

"A poor fellow made in the image of God, though!"

"A very poor image, then!" said the earl with a sneer. "If that was all he could do that way, why did he not make us in some other body's image? It might have been more to the purpose!"

Donal thought with himself for a moment.

"Did you ever know a good woman, my lord?" he asked.

"Know a good woman! There was my own mother; she was rather hard on my father, now and then, I thought; but she was a good woman."

"Your mother was good, and you are worse; whose fault is that?" Donal asked.

"Oh, my own, no doubt! I'm not ashamed to own up to it!"

"Would to God you were ashamed," said Donal; "for you shame your mother in being worse than she was. But it is no use talking. God has not made you miserable enough yet."

"I am more miserable than you or anyone can think."

"Why don't you cry out to him to deliver you?"

"I would, I tell you, if it weren't that I would put off seeing my wife as long as I can."

"Don't you want to see her?"

"Not just yet; I should like to be a little better first. I doubt if she would be willing to touch me just at present with that white, small, firm hand of hers she used to catch hold of me with when I hurt her. By Jove, if she had been a man, she would have made her mark in the world! She had a will and a way with her. If it hadn't been that she loved me—me, do you hear, you dog!—me that there's nobody left in the world now to care a worm-eaten nut about! It makes me as proud as Lucifer to think of it! She had a conscience. She would often just smile—fit to make a mule sad! I was too proud to be sad. And then when her baby was dying, and she wanted me to take her for a minute, while she got her something, and I wouldn't. She laid down the baby, and got it herself, and when she came again, the child, absurd little thing, was—was gone—dead. I mean gone *dead*, never to cry anymore, and lay there like a lump of white clay. She looked at me, and never in this world smiled again—nor cried either—all I could do to make her do either!"

The wretched man burst into tears. The man himself may not even know why he weeps and his tears may yet indicate the turn on the road. The earl was as far from a good man as man well could be; there were millions of spiritual miles between him and the image of God; he had wept, it was hard to say at what—plainly not at his own cruelty, not at his wife's suffering, not in pity for the little child whose mother had asked her father to take her, but whose father had refused, so that the little soul went away with no human embrace at the parting. No human being, least of all himself, could have told why he wept; but there was in those tears some contact of his human soul with the great human soul of God. Surely God saw this. He who will not let us out until we have paid the uttermost farthing, rejoices over the offer of the first golden grain in payment. Easy to please is he—hard indeed to satisfy.

45

....

Confessions

Suddenly the strength of Lady Arctura seemed to give way. She had a sharp attack of hemorrhage, and from that hour began to sink. But it was spring, with the summer at hand, and they hoped she would soon recover sufficiently to be removed to a fitter climate; she did not herself think so. Donal's heart was at times sorer than he had thought it ever could be again.

One day as he sat in her room, having been reading a little to her—sat looking at her, and not knowing how sad the expression of his countenance was, she looked up at him, smiled, and said, "You think I am unhappy. You could not look at me like that if you did not think so. But I am not; I am only tired. Oh, Donal, if it hadn't been for you, God would have been to me now far off as before."

"No—no, if God had not sent me," returned Donal, "he would have sent somebody else."

"I am very glad he sent you, though! I should never have loved any other so much!"

Donal's eyes filled with tears. He knew she loved him; he loved her; all was so natural that it could not be otherwise. He never presumed to dream that the great, lovely lady would once think of him as he had thought of Ginevra. He was her servant, willing and loving as any angel.

"You're not vexed with your pupil, are you?" she resumed, again looking up in his face, this time with a rosy flush over her own.

"Why?" said Donal, wondering.

"For speaking so to my schoolmaster?"

"Angry because you love me!"

"No, of course!" she said. "You knew that must be. How could I but love you—better than anyone else in all the world. You have given me life. I could not have spoken to you like this, though, if I had not known that I was dying."

The word shot a sting as a fire through Donal's heart.

"You are always a child, Donal," she went on. "I tell you, I love you, Donal. Don't look like that," she continued; "you must not forget what you have been teaching me all this time—that the will of our God is all in all. You have taught me that, and I love you—love you next to God with a true heart."

Donal was crying; he could not speak.

"I have nothing to be ashamed of in speaking to you. Would you mind marrying me before I go? I want to be able to say in heaven, when I have to speak about you, 'My husband taught me this,' 'My husband used to say that to me!' I should like to say to Jesus, 'Thank you, my Lord, for the husband you made, and taught, and sent to me, that I might be his child and his sister and his wife all in one!' "

She was sitting on a low chair, with the sunlight across her lap, and the firelight on her face. Donal knelt down gently, and laid his hands in the sunlight on her lap. She laid both her hands on his.

"I have something to tell you," he said; "and then you must speak again."

"Tell me," said Arctura.

"When I came here," said Donal, "I thought my heart was so nearly broken that it could not love anymore. I loved you from the very first. When I saw you troubled, I longed to take you up in my arms; but never once, my lady, did I think of your caring for my love. I do not think I could ever have had the presumption to imagine such a thing. For ever since the misery of her refusing to kiss me just once for a goodbye . . . I felt far too clownish and ugly for any lady to look at; I knew plenty about sheep and dogs, but nothing about ladies, except how worthy of God's making they looked. I knew about hillsides and skies, but not about drawing rooms—and I thought love was over for me."

He stopped. Her hands lay upon his, and did not move to leave them, only fluttered a little as she said, "Is she still—is she—alive?"

"Oh, yes, my lady."

"Then don't you think she may change her mind?"

Donal laughed—an odd laugh, but it did Arctura good to hear it.

"No danger of that, my lady! She has got the best husband in the world—a much better than . . . than I should have been."

"That can't be!"

"Why, my lady, he's Sir Gibbie! She's Lady Galbraith! I would never have wished her mine if I had known that she loved Gibbie. I love her next to him; and you would love her if you knew her!"

"Then . . . then—"

"What, my lady?"

"Won't you say something to me?"

"What should I say? What God pleases is settled for me—fast as the roots of the universe, and lovely as its blossoms."

Arctura burst into tears.

"Then you cannot love me! You do not care for me!"

Donal began to understand. Now he understood that she had spoken and was listening in vain for the echo that ought to have followed; she thought herself unloved, for the signs of love had not appeared. He rose, took her up in his arms like the child to whom he had been likening her, and with her head on his shoulder and his face bent down on hers, went walking about the room with her, patting and soothing her and holding her close to his heart.

"I love you," he said, "and love you to all eternity! I have love enough to live upon now if you should die this night. It is more than my heart will hold!"

Arctura's arms, which were round Donal's neck, at length signed a gentle prayer for release; when he set her gently down in her chair again, her face was more beautiful than he had ever seen it before, and whatever it may have indicated of her physical condition, the rose that bloomed there was the rose of a deeper health than any she had yet known.

"When shall we be married?" said Donal.

"Soon, soon," answered Arctura; "I am going very fast!"

"When you please, my love," said Donal.

She laid her head on his bosom.

"We need not make haste," she said. "We are as good as married now. We both know that each loves the other. How I shall wait for you in heaven! You will be mine, you know—a little bit mine—won't you?—even if you should marry some beautiful lady when I am gone. I shall love her when she comes."

"Arctura," said Donal, "you do not know me yet!" and she never ventured another word of that kind to him.

46

....

The Ceremony

The next day she called Mr. Graeme and sent him to fetch the family lawyer from Edinburgh. Alone with him she gave instructions concerning her will. I fancy from what dropped from the man of business afterwards that she had to behave to him with what he counted imperiousness. He would have expostulated with the lady on the way she chose to leave her money.

"Sir!" she said.

"You have a cousin who inherits the title?" he suggested.

"Mr. Fortune," she returned, "I am not unacquainted with my own family. Perhaps I know a little more of it than you do. I have not much time to spare, and I did not send for you to consult you, but to ask you to draw up my will according to my wishes. If it goes against your conscience to do as I wish, say so, and I will send for another."

Mr. Fortune said not a word more, but took his instructions, rose, and was about to go.

"When will you bring me the will to sign?" she asked.

"In the course of a week or two, my lady."

"If it is not in my hands by the day after tomorrow, I will send for a gentleman from the town to draw it up."

"You shall have it, my lady," assured Mr. Fortune. And she did have it, and the will was signed and witnessed, no one knowing a word of the contents except two.

After this she grew very weak. Donal said no word about the marriage. She should do just as she pleased. He was now nearly all day by her bedside, reading to her when she was able to listen, talking to her, or sitting silent when she was not.

Mrs. Brooks now gave herself entirely to the nursing of her ladyship, and Arctura told her the relation in which she and Donal stood to each other. It cost the good woman many tears, for she thought such a love one of the saddest things in the world.

The earl about this time was a little better, though there was no prospect of even a temporary recovery. He had grown much gentler, and something of sadness had partially displaced the sullenness of his bearing. He showed concern at his niece's illness, and as she was now again in the sunny room on the lower floor, he had himself carried down every other day to see her for a few minutes and learn how she was getting on. She received him always with the greatest gentleness. Her last words to him he would often repeat to himself.

"If there is anything I can do for you—when we meet again, dear Uncle, be sure I shall be ready."

"Tell my wife," had come to his lips, but no further. He postponed the message, and did not see her again in this world.

It was a morning in the month of May when Donal, who was lying on the couch in the neighboring room, heard Mrs. Brooks call him: "My lady wants you, sir," she said.

He started up, and went to her.

"Send for the minister," she whispered—"not Mr. Carmichael; he does not know you! Send for Mr. Graeme too; he and Mrs. Brooks will be witnesses. I must call you husband once before I die!"

"I hope you will many a time after!" he returned.

With some careful questioning on the part of the minister, to satisfy himself that she knew what she said and desired to be called wife before she went, he did as he was requested and wrote a certificate of the fact, which was duly signed and witnessed by the three.

The bridegroom gave his bride one gentle kiss, and withdrew with the clergyman to the next room.

"This is a strange proceeding!" remarked the minister.

"Not so strange perhaps as it looks, sir!" said Donal.

"On the brink of the other world!"

"The other world and its brink too are his who ordained marriage!"

"I have heard of you," returned the clergyman, "as one of those who do not hesitate for their own ends to misuse scripture!" The man had a painful doubt that he had been drawn into some plot.

"Sir!" said Donal sternly, "If you thought there was any impropriety in the ceremony you have now performed, why did you perform it? I beg you will reserve the remarks you ought to have made before."

The man was not a little astonished at the tone assumed by Donal; but he saw at once that the less said the better.

Donal had next a brief interview with Mr. Graeme. The factor did not know for what he had been summoned and was in a condition of some bewilderment. He little suspected, however, how the thing bore on his own future, and readily gave Donal a pledge of silence for the present concerning the ceremony. He regarded it as the mere whim of a dying girl, which, for the sake of the family, had better be ignored and forgotten. How it might affect the property he could only conjecture. There was the will for one thing! But if the marriage was proved, the will, made before it, was of no avail.

I will not pain my readers by lingering over the quiet, gently sad time that followed. Donal was to Arctura, as she said, like father, brother, husband, all in one.

"I think," said Donal, sitting that same night by her bed, "when my mother dies, she will go at once to somewhere near you; for there never was a more godlike woman than she. I will, if I may, send you a message by her. But it can only tell you what you will know—that I love you and am waiting to come to you."

"I shall not be far from you, dear, I think—sometimes," she said, speaking very low, and with difficulty. "If you dream anything nice about me, think I am thinking about you."

After that she fell into a deep sleep, and slept for some hours. Then she sat up suddenly, and Donal went behind her and supported her. She looked a little wild, shuddered, murmured something which neither he nor Mistress Brooks could understand, and threw herself back into her husband's arms. From troubled suffering her face changed to an expression of loveliest contentment, and she was gone.

47

· · · · · · · · · · · · · · · · · ·

The Will

*W*hen her will was read, it was found that she had left everything to Donal, except some legacies and an annuity to Mrs. Brooks.

When Mr. Graeme rose to go, congratulating Donal as he did so, politely, but without any special cordiality, Donal said to him: "If you're walking toward home, I will walk with you. I have something to talk to you about."

"I shall be happy," said Mr. Graeme. He was feeling it not a little hard that the heir presumptive to the title should have to tend the family property in the service of a peasant.

"Lord Morven cannot live long," said Donal. "Perhaps it is not to be wished that he should."

Mr. Graeme made no answer. Donal resumed, "I think I ought to let you know at once that you are the successor to the title."

"I am at loss to know on what you found such a statement."

"No one knows it but myself. Lord Morven knows that his son has no right to succeed, but I do not think he knows that you have. I am prepared, if not to prove, at least to convince you that he and the lady who passed for his wife were never married."

Mr. Graeme was for a moment silent. Then he laughed a little laugh. "The head of the family has to bow to the peasant proprietor of its land!"

"I hope you do not believe that I contrived my marriage for the sake of the property?"

"Excuse me, Mr. Grant, but the girl was dying, and you knew it!"

"I do not understand you."

"What did you marry her for then?"

"To call her my wife."

"What was the good of that?"

"Does it need explanation? Well—let it pass! It is enough that we both wished it because we loved each other."

"It will be difficult to convince the world that such was your sole motive."

"Having no respect whatever for the judgment of the world, I shall be satisfied if I convince you. The world need never hear of the thing. Would you, Mr. Graeme, have had me, loving her as I do and she loving me as she does, refuse to marry her because the world, or indeed not a few honest men like yourself, would say I could have had regard only to the property? . . . but what I wanted to have a talk with you about," resumed Donal, "was this: the fact is simply I do not want this property. I thank God for Lady Arctura—her wealth I do not desire." He never spoke of his wife in the past.

"But may it not be your duty to keep it, Mr. Grant?—Pardon me for suggesting duty to one who knows so much more about that than I do."

"I have reflected, and do not think God wants me to keep it."

"But there are duties to people involved," he said. "My sister and I have had many talks as to what we would do if the land were ours."

"And yours it shall be," said Donal, "if you will take it—as I should if I had not other work to do—as a trust for the good of all whom the land supports."

Donal thought the teacher's a higher calling than the landowner's. "For," he continued, "it is better to help make good men than happy tenants. These in their turn will be good landlords. . . . Besides," he added, "I know how to do the one, and I do not know how to do the other. There would always be a prejudice against me because of my birth; and people would regard any changes I might make as the result of my lowly upbringing and foolish fancy for reform."

Mr. Graeme nodded, but said nothing.

"But," Donal went on, "if you will accept my offer, I hope you will not think me interfering if I talk with you from time to time concerning the principles of things that come up. One thing I would always have to satisfy myself about was that truth and justice were being done. I have no doubts about you, but I want to know how relations stand between those under your charge. Men have such absurd notions about possession, always trying to call their own things it is impossible, by their very nature, ever to possess."

Mr. Graeme nodded his assent.

"As heir to the title and as head of the family, and all the prestige that gives, you have it in your power to do more than any other with the property; and I will gladly give it over to you altogether. I would not have my attention taken from my own calling."

"Your thoughts are most generous, Mr. Grant."

"It is not generous at all. My dear Graeme, you do not know how little of a temptation such things are to me."

After further talk, their interview ended with Donal's thinking still better of him than before, and being satisfied that the man was honest and well equipped to take up the charge Donal felt bound to place in his hand.

The earl was sinking fast. After his niece's death, no one would do for him but Donal; nobody could please him but Donal. His mind as well as his body was much weaker.

"Who will have the property now?" he asked one day. "I have heard that my factor has a pretty near chance, but I never inquired. You see, if my son was not to have it, I did not care much who did."

"Mr. Graeme will have it," said Donal. "Title and property will both be his."

"And my poor Davie?" said the earl with a look of pitiful question in the eyes that gazed up into Donal's face.

"I will see to him," said Donal. "When you and I meet, my lord—by and by, I shall not be ashamed before you."

His words satisfied the earl. He sent for Davie and told him he was always to do as Mr. Grant wished, that he left him in his charge, and that he must behave to him like a son.

In the evening Donal went out into the old garden. There all the feelings came over him again which first led to his writing the poem that had done so much for him. He went up and down the grassy paths for a while, until joined by Miss Graeme.

"I couldn't help thinking," she said as she came up to him, "that I saw Lady Arctura walking by your side. But I beg your pardon . . . how could I be so heartless?"

"Her name from you will always be pleasant to me," returned Donal. "I was thinking of her. She will be with me wherever I walk or rest; so I shall never be sad. God is with me, and I do not weep because I cannot see him. I simply wait."

Miss Graeme was in tears.

Soon Mr. Graeme joined them.

"I do not think the earl will last many days," Donal said to him. "Don't you think it would be advisable at once upon his death to take possession of the house in town? It is the only property that goes with the title now. Then of course you would at once make your abode in the castle, for if Forgue disputed the one, he would dispute the other as well. When the old man is gone, you will find in his papers proofs innumerable that his son has no claim. I will, if you like, have a deed of gift drawn up, but I would rather you seemed to come in by natural succession. And then I have one more favor to ask of you . . . the house in town is of no great use to you. Would you let me have the use of it? I should like to live there and have a school. Davie will help me—for a while at least. We will not try hard to get pupils, but when we do get one we will try to make a man of him—"

Here Mr. Graeme interrupted.

"You will never make a living that way!" he said.

"Ah," said Donal, "you have not an idea on how little I can live!"

————

The next day the earl died.

Donal wrote to let his son know he was dead. The next day Forgue came; he would know how things were. He met the new earl in the hall.

"Mr. Graeme," he said—

"Lord Morven," corrected Mr. Graeme. The young fellow uttered a great oath, turned on his heel, and left them to bury his father without him. He had scarcely been a father; why should his son be a son?

The funeral over, the new Lord Morven squeezed Donal's hand—they understood each other. The new earl seldom did anything of importance after that without consulting Donal, and Donal had the more influence both with landlord and with tenants that he had no financial stake in the property.

The same week he left the castle and went into old Morven House. The people said Mr. Grant had played his cards well.

Davie, to whom no calamity could be overwhelming so long as he had Mr. Grant, went with him gladly, content to live with him till he should go to college.

They went to the house together, accompanied by Mrs. Brooks. With the full approbation of Miss Graeme, she had been persuaded to keep house for him. Together they unlocked the door. The house, Mrs. Brooks said, was in an awful state. There was not much for the mason to do, but plenty for the carpenter; it had had nothing done to it for generations. The best thing would be to go away for a while, and stay away till she told them it was ready for them.

Nothing could have suited Donal better. He went home again to his hills, taking Davie with him. When they returned to Auchars, Sir Gibbie and his wife came with them and stayed for some weeks.

Lord Morven and Miss Graeme had done their best to make the house what Donal would like. But in the castle they kept for him the rooms that Lady Arctura had called her own, and there he gathered together all the little personal possessions of his wife. To these rooms he went on holidays and always on Sunday evening.

It was some time before Donal had any pupils, and he never had many, being regarded as a man most peculiar, whose ideas and education were extremely odd. It was granted, however, that if a boy stayed, or rather if Donal Grant allowed him to stay long enough, he was sure to turn him into a gentleman. That which was deeper than the gentleman, which was the life of him, people seldom saw or would have valued if they had seen. Most parents would like their children to have a chance of escaping eternal misery; but as to becoming sons and daughters of God, that is hardly worth their while!

So Donal lives—the few wise souls in the neighborhood know—as the heart of the place, the man to go to with any question, difficulty, or trouble. Most of his early friends are gone, but he yet wears the same solemn look accompanied by the same hovering smile. It seems to say to those who can read it, "I know in whom I believe . . . and all is well."